Jack London Six Pack

Jack London Six Pack

By

Jack London

Enhanced Media
2016

White Fang by Jack London. First published in 1906.

Hoboes That Pass in the Night by Jack London. From *The Road* by Jack London. First published in 1907.

The Call of the Wild by Jack London. First published in 1903.

Love of Life by Jack London. First published in *Love of Life and Other Stories* in 1903.

A Day's Lodging by Jack London. First published in *Love of Life and Other Stories* in 1903.

John Barleycorn by Jack London. First published in 1913.

Enhanced Media Publishing
Los Angeles, CA.

First Printing: 2016.

ISBN-13: 978-1534907812

ISBN-10: 1534907815

Contents

"I would rather be a superb meteor, every atom of me in magnificent glow, than a sleepy and permanent planet."

-    Jack London.

The Call of the Wild

Chapter I. Into the Primitive

"Old longings nomadic leap,
Chafing at custom's chain;
Again from its brumal sleep,
Wakens the ferine strain."

Buck did not read the newspapers, or he would have known that trouble was brewing, not alone for himself, but for every tide-water dog, strong of muscle and with warm, long hair, from Puget Sound to San Diego. Because men, groping in the Arctic darkness, had found a yellow metal, and because steamship and transportation companies were booming the find, thousands of men were rushing into the Northland. These men wanted dogs, and the dogs they wanted were heavy dogs, with strong muscles by which to toil, and furry coats to protect them from the frost.

Buck lived at a big house in the sun-kissed Santa Clara Valley. Judge Miller's place, it was called. It stood back from the road, half hidden among the trees, through which glimpses could be caught of the wide cool veranda that ran around its four sides. The house was approached by gravelled driveways which wound about through wide-spreading lawns and under the interlacing boughs of tall poplars. At the rear things were on even a more spacious scale than at the front. There were great stables, where a dozen grooms and boys held forth, rows of vine-clad servants' cottages, an endless and orderly array of outhouses, long grape arbors, green pastures, orchards, and berry patches. Then there was the pumping plant for the artesian well, and the big cement tank where Judge Miller's boys took their morning plunge and kept cool in the hot afternoon.

And over this great demesne Buck ruled. Here he was born, and here he had lived the four years of his life. It was true, there were other dogs, There could not but be other dogs on so vast a place, but they did not count. They came and went, resided in the populous kennels, or lived obscurely in the recesses of the house after the fashion of Toots, the Japanese pug, or Ysabel, the Mexican hairless,—strange creatures that rarely put nose out of doors or set foot to ground. On the other hand, there were the fox terriers, a score of them at least, who yelped fearful promises at Toots and Ysabel looking out of the windows at them and protected by a legion of housemaids armed with brooms and mops.

But Buck was neither house-dog nor kennel-dog. The whole realm was his. He plunged into the swimming tank or went hunting with the Judge's sons; he escorted Mollie and Alice, the Judge's daughters, on long twilight or early morning rambles;

on wintry nights he lay at the Judge's feet before the roaring library fire; he carried the Judge's grandsons on his back, or rolled them in the grass, and guarded their footsteps through wild adventures down to the fountain in the stable yard, and even beyond, where the paddocks were, and the berry patches. Among the terriers he stalked imperiously, and Toots and Ysabel he utterly ignored, for he was king,— king over all creeping, crawling, flying things of Judge Miller's place, humans included.

His father, Elmo, a huge St. Bernard, had been the Judge's inseparable companion, and Buck bid fair to follow in the way of his father. He was not so large,—he weighed only one hundred and forty pounds,—for his mother, Shep, had been a Scotch shepherd dog. Nevertheless, one hundred and forty pounds, to which was added the dignity that comes of good living and universal respect, enabled him to carry himself in right royal fashion. During the four years since his puppyhood he had lived the life of a sated aristocrat; he had a fine pride in himself, was even a trifle egotistical, as country gentlemen sometimes become because of their insular situation. But he had saved himself by not becoming a mere pampered house-dog. Hunting and kindred outdoor delights had kept down the fat and hardened his muscles; and to him, as to the cold-tubbing races, the love of water had been a tonic and a health preserver.

And this was the manner of dog Buck was in the fall of 1897, when the Klondike strike dragged men from all the world into the frozen North. But Buck did not read the newspapers, and he did not know that Manuel, one of the gardener's helpers, was an undesirable acquaintance. Manuel had one besetting sin. He loved to play Chinese lottery. Also, in his gambling, he had one besetting weakness—faith in a system; and this made his damnation certain. For to play a system requires money, while the wages of a gardener's helper do not lap over the needs of a wife and numerous progeny.

The Judge was at a meeting of the Raisin Growers' Association, and the boys were busy organizing an athletic club, on the memorable night of Manuel's treachery. No one saw him and Buck go off through the orchard on what Buck imagined was merely a stroll. And with the exception of a solitary man, no one saw them arrive at the little flag station known as College Park. This man talked with Manuel, and money chinked between them.

"You might wrap up the goods before you deliver 'm," the stranger said gruffly, and Manuel doubled a piece of stout rope around Buck's neck under the collar.

"Twist it, an' you'll choke 'm plentee," said Manuel, and the stranger grunted a ready affirmative.

Buck had accepted the rope with quiet dignity. To be sure, it was an unwonted performance: but he had learned to trust in men he knew, and to give them credit for a wisdom that outreached his own. But when the ends of the rope were placed in the stranger's hands, he growled menacingly. He had merely intimated his displeasure, in his pride believing that to intimate was to command. But to his surprise the rope tightened around his neck, shutting off his breath. In quick rage he sprang at the man, who met him halfway, grappled him close by the throat, and with a deft twist threw him over on his back. Then the rope tightened mercilessly, while Buck strug-

gled in a fury, his tongue lolling out of his mouth and his great chest panting futilely. Never in all his life had he been so vilely treated, and never in all his life had he
been so angry. But his strength ebbed, his eyes glazed, and he knew nothing when
the train was flagged and the two men threw him into the baggage car.

The next he knew, he was dimly aware that his tongue was hurting and that he
was being jolted along in some kind of a conveyance. The hoarse shriek of a loco-
motive whistling a crossing told him where he was. He had travelled too often with
the Judge not to know the sensation of riding in a baggage car. He opened his eyes,
and into them came the unbridled anger of a kidnapped king. The man sprang for
his throat, but Buck was too quick for him. His jaws closed on the hand, nor did
they relax till his senses were choked out of him once more.

"Yep, has fits," the man said, hiding his mangled hand from the baggage man,
who had been attracted by the sounds of struggle. "I'm takin' 'm up for the boss to
'Frisco. A crack dog-doctor there thinks that he can cure 'm."

Concerning that night's ride, the man spoke most eloquently for himself, in a little shed back of a saloon on the San Francisco water front.

"All I get is fifty for it," he grumbled; "an' I wouldn't do it over for a thousand,
cold cash."

His hand was wrapped in a bloody handkerchief, and the right trouser leg was
ripped from knee to ankle.

"How much did the other mug get?" the saloon-keeper demanded.

"A hundred," was the reply. "Wouldn't take a sou less, so help me."

"That makes a hundred and fifty," the saloon-keeper calculated; "and he's worth
it, or I'm a squarehead."

The kidnapper undid the bloody wrappings and looked at his lacerated hand. "If
I don't get the hydrophoby—"

"It'll be because you was born to hang," laughed the saloon-keeper. "Here, lend
me a hand before you pull your freight," he added.

Dazed, suffering intolerable pain from throat and tongue, with the life half throt-
tled out of him, Buck attempted to face his tormentors. But he was thrown down
and choked repeatedly, till they succeeded in filing the heavy brass collar from off
his neck. Then the rope was removed, and he was flung into a cagelike crate.

There he lay for the remainder of the weary night, nursing his wrath and wounded pride. He could not understand what it all meant. What did they want with him,
these strange men? Why were they keeping him pent up in this narrow crate? He did
not know why, but he felt oppressed by the vague sense of impending calamity.
Several times during the night he sprang to his feet when the shed door rattled open,
expecting to see the Judge, or the boys at least. But each time it was the bulging
face of the saloon-keeper that peered in at him by the sickly light of a tallow candle.
And each time the joyful bark that trembled in Buck's throat was twisted into a savage growl.

But the saloon-keeper let him alone, and in the morning four men entered and
picked up the crate. More tormentors, Buck decided, for they were evil-looking
creatures, ragged and unkempt; and he stormed and raged at them through the bars.
They only laughed and poked sticks at him, which he promptly assailed with his

teeth till he realized that that was what they wanted. Whereupon he lay down sullenly and allowed the crate to be lifted into a wagon. Then he, and the crate in which he was imprisoned, began a passage through many hands. Clerks in the express office took charge of him; he was carted about in another wagon; a truck carried him, with an assortment of boxes and parcels, upon a ferry steamer; he was trucked off the steamer into a great railway depot, and finally he was deposited in an express car.

For two days and nights this express car was dragged along at the tail of shrieking locomotives; and for two days and nights Buck neither ate nor drank. In his anger he had met the first advances of the express messengers with growls, and they had retaliated by teasing him. When he flung himself against the bars, quivering and frothing, they laughed at him and taunted him. They growled and barked like detestable dogs, mewed, and flapped their arms and crowed. It was all very silly, he knew; but therefore the more outrage to his dignity, and his anger waxed and waxed. He did not mind the hunger so much, but the lack of water caused him severe suffering and fanned his wrath to fever-pitch. For that matter, high-strung and finely sensitive, the ill treatment had flung him into a fever, which was fed by the inflammation of his parched and swollen throat and tongue.

He was glad for one thing: the rope was off his neck. That had given them an unfair advantage; but now that it was off, he would show them. They would never get another rope around his neck. Upon that he was resolved. For two days and nights he neither ate nor drank, and during those two days and nights of torment, he accumulated a fund of wrath that boded ill for whoever first fell foul of him. His eyes turned blood-shot, and he was metamorphosed into a raging fiend. So changed was he that the Judge himself would not have recognized him; and the express messengers breathed with relief when they bundled him off the train at Seattle.

Four men gingerly carried the crate from the wagon into a small, high-walled back yard. A stout man, with a red sweater that sagged generously at the neck, came out and signed the book for the driver. That was the man, Buck divined, the next tormentor, and he hurled himself savagely against the bars. The man smiled grimly, and brought a hatchet and a club.

"You ain't going to take him out now?" the driver asked.

"Sure," the man replied, driving the hatchet into the crate for a pry.

There was an instantaneous scattering of the four men who had carried it in, and from safe perches on top the wall they prepared to watch the performance.

Buck rushed at the splintering wood, sinking his teeth into it, surging and wrestling with it. Wherever the hatchet fell on the outside, he was there on the inside, snarling and growling, as furiously anxious to get out as the man in the red sweater was calmly intent on getting him out.

"Now, you red-eyed devil," he said, when he had made an opening sufficient for the passage of Buck's body. At the same time he dropped the hatchet and shifted the club to his right hand.

And Buck was truly a red-eyed devil, as he drew himself together for the spring, hair bristling, mouth foaming, a mad glitter in his blood-shot eyes. Straight at the man he launched his one hundred and forty pounds of fury, surcharged with the pent passion of two days and nights. In midair, just as his jaws were about to close on the man, he received a shock that checked his body and brought his teeth together with an agonizing clip. He whirled over, fetching the ground on his back and side. He had never been struck by a club in his life, and did not understand. With a snarl that was part bark and more scream he was again on his feet and launched into the air. And again the shock came and he was brought crushingly to the ground. This time he was aware that it was the club, but his madness knew no caution. A dozen times he charged, and as often the club broke the charge and smashed him down.

After a particularly fierce blow, he crawled to his feet, too dazed to rush. He staggered limply about, the blood flowing from nose and mouth and ears, his beautiful coat sprayed and flecked with bloody slaver. Then the man advanced and deliberately dealt him a frightful blow on the nose. All the pain he had endured was as nothing compared with the exquisite agony of this. With a roar that was almost lion like in its ferocity, he again hurled himself at the man. But the man, shifting the club from right to left, coolly caught him by the under jaw, at the same time wrenching downward and backward. Buck described a complete circle in the air, and half of another, then crashed to the ground on his head and chest.

For the last time he rushed. The man struck the shrewd blow he had purposely withheld for so long, and Buck crumpled up and went down, knocked utterly senseless.

"He's no slouch at dog-breakin', that's wot I say," one of the men on the wall cried enthusiastically.

"Druther break cayuses any day, and twice on Sundays," was the reply of the driver, as he climbed on the wagon and started the horses.

Buck's senses came back to him, but not his strength. He lay where he had fallen, and from there he watched the man in the red sweater.

"'Answers to the name of Buck,'" the man soliloquized, quoting from the saloon-keeper's letter which had announced the consignment of the crate and contents. "Well, Buck, my boy," he went on in a genial voice, "we've had our little ruction, and the best thing we can do is to let it go at that. You've learned your place, and I know mine. Be a good dog and all 'll go well and the goose hang high. Be a bad dog, and I'll whale the stuffin' outa you. Understand?"

As he spoke he fearlessly patted the head he had so mercilessly pounded, and though Buck's hair involuntarily bristled at touch of the hand, he endured it without protest. When the man brought him water he drank eagerly, and later bolted a generous meal of raw meat, chunk by chunk, from the man's hand.

He was beaten (he knew that); but he was not broken. He saw, once for all, that he stood no chance against a man with a club. He had learned the lesson, and in all his afterlife he never forgot it. That club was a revelation. It was his introduction to the reign of primitive law, and he met the introduction halfway. The facts of life took on a fiercer aspect; and while he faced that aspect uncowed, he faced it with all the latent cunning of his nature aroused. As the days went by, other dogs came, in crates and at the ends of ropes, some docilely, and some raging and roaring as he had come; and, one and all, he watched them pass under the dominion of the man in the red sweater. Again and again, as he looked at each brutal performance, the lesson was driven home to Buck: a man with a club was a lawgiver, a master to be obeyed, though not necessarily conciliated. Of this last Buck was never guilty, though he did see beaten dogs that fawned upon the man, and wagged their tails, and licked his hand. Also he saw one dog, that would neither conciliate nor obey, finally killed in the struggle for mastery.

Now and again men came, strangers, who talked excitedly, wheedlingly, and in all kinds of fashions to the man in the red sweater. And at such times that money passed between them the strangers took one or more of the dogs away with them. Buck wondered where they went, for they never came back; but the fear of the future was strong upon him, and he was glad each time when he was not selected.

Yet his time came, in the end, in the form of a little weazened man who spat broken English and many strange and uncouth exclamations which Buck could not understand.

"Sacredam!" he cried, when his eyes lit upon Buck. "Dat one dam bully dog! Eh? How moch?"

"Three hundred, and a present at that," was the prompt reply of the man in the red sweater. "And seem' it's government money, you ain't got no kick coming, eh, Perrault?"

Perrault grinned. Considering that the price of dogs had been boomed skyward by the unwonted demand, it was not an unfair sum for so fine an animal. The Canadian Government would be no loser, nor would its despatches travel the slower. Perrault knew dogs, and when he looked at Buck he knew that he was one in a thousand—"One in ten t'ousand," he commented mentally.

Buck saw money pass between them, and was not surprised when Curly, a good-natured Newfoundland, and he were led away by the little weazened man. That was the last he saw of the man in the red sweater, and as Curly and he looked at receding Seattle from the deck of the Narwhal, it was the last he saw of the warm Southland. Curly and he were taken below by Perrault and turned over to a black-faced giant called Francois. Perrault was a French-Canadian, and swarthy; but Francois was a French-Canadian half-breed, and twice as swarthy. They were a new kind of men to Buck (of which he was destined to see many more), and while he developed no affection for them, he none the less grew honestly to respect them. He speedily learned that Perrault and Francois were fair men, calm and impartial in administering justice, and too wise in the way of dogs to be fooled by dogs.

In the 'tween-decks of the Narwhal, Buck and Curly joined two other dogs. One of them was a big, snow-white fellow from Spitzbergen who had been brought away by a whaling captain, and who had later accompanied a Geological Survey into the Barrens. He was friendly, in a treacherous sort of way, smiling into one's face the while he meditated some underhand trick, as, for instance, when he stole from Buck's food at the first meal. As Buck sprang to punish him, the lash of Francois's whip sang through the air, reaching the culprit first; and nothing remained to Buck but to recover the bone. That was fair of Francois, he decided, and the half-breed began his rise in Buck's estimation.

The other dog made no advances, nor received any; also, he did not attempt to steal from the newcomers. He was a gloomy, morose fellow, and he showed Curly plainly that all he desired was to be left alone, and further, that there would be trouble if he were not left alone. "Dave" he was called, and he ate and slept, or yawned between times, and took interest in nothing, not even when the Narwhal crossed Queen Charlotte Sound and rolled and pitched and bucked like a thing possessed. When Buck and Curly grew excited, half wild with fear, he raised his head as though annoyed, favored them with an incurious glance, yawned, and went to sleep again.

Day and night the ship throbbed to the tireless pulse of the propeller, and though one day was very like another, it was apparent to Buck that the weather was steadily growing colder. At last, one morning, the propeller was quiet, and the Narwhal was pervaded with an atmosphere of excitement. He felt it, as did the other dogs, and knew that a change was at hand. Francois leashed them and brought them on deck. At the first step upon the cold surface, Buck's feet sank into a white mushy something very like mud. He sprang back with a snort. More of this white stuff was falling through the air. He shook himself, but more of it fell upon him. He sniffed it curiously, then licked some up on his tongue. It bit like fire, and the next instant was gone. This puzzled him. He tried it again, with the same result. The onlookers laughed uproariously, and he felt ashamed, he knew not why, for it was his first snow.

Chapter II. The Law of Club and Fang

Buck's first day on the Dyea beach was like a nightmare. Every hour was filled with shock and surprise. He had been suddenly jerked from the heart of civilization and flung into the heart of things primordial. No lazy, sun-kissed life was this, with nothing to do but loaf and be bored. Here was neither peace, nor rest, nor a moment's safety. All was confusion and action, and every moment life and limb were in peril. There was imperative need to be constantly alert; for these dogs and men were not town dogs and men. They were savages, all of them, who knew no law but the law of club and fang.

He had never seen dogs fight as these wolfish creatures fought, and his first experience taught him an unforgettable lesson. It is true, it was a vicarious experience, else he would not have lived to profit by it. Curly was the victim. They were camped near the log store, where she, in her friendly way, made advances to a husky dog the size of a full-grown wolf, though not half so large as she. There was no warning, only a leap in like a flash, a metallic clip of teeth, a leap out equally swift, and Curly's face was ripped open from eye to jaw.

It was the wolf manner of fighting, to strike and leap away; but there was more to it than this. Thirty or forty huskies ran to the spot and surrounded the combatants in an intent and silent circle. Buck did not comprehend that silent intentness, nor the eager way with which they were licking their chops. Curly rushed her antagonist, who struck again and leaped aside. He met her next rush with his chest, in a peculiar fashion that tumbled her off her feet. She never regained them, This was what the on looking huskies had waited for. They closed in upon her, snarling and yelping, and she was buried, screaming with agony, beneath the bristling mass of bodies.

So sudden was it, and so unexpected, that Buck was taken aback. He saw Spitz run out his scarlet tongue in a way he had of laughing; and he saw Francois, swinging an axe, spring into the mess of dogs. Three men with clubs were helping him to scatter them. It did not take long. Two minutes from the time Curly went down, the last of her assailants were clubbed off. But she lay there limp and lifeless in the bloody, trampled snow, almost literally torn to pieces, the swart half-breed standing over her and cursing horribly. The scene often came back to Buck to trouble him in his sleep. So that was the way. No fair play. Once down, that was the end of you. Well, he would see to it that he never went down. Spitz ran out his tongue and laughed again, and from that moment Buck hated him with a bitter and deathless hatred.

Before he had recovered from the shock caused by the tragic passing of Curly, he received another shock. Francois fastened upon him an arrangement of straps and buckles. It was a harness, such as he had seen the grooms put on the horses at home. And as he had seen horses work, so he was set to work, hauling Francois on a sled to the forest that fringed the valley, and returning with a load of firewood. Though his dignity was sorely hurt by thus being made a draught animal, he was too wise to rebel. He buckled down with a will and did his best, though it was all new and strange. Francois was stern, demanding instant obedience, and by virtue of his whip receiving instant obedience; while Dave, who was an experienced wheeler, nipped Buck's hind quarters whenever he was in error. Spitz was the leader, likewise experienced, and while he could not always get at Buck, he growled sharp reproof now and again, or cunningly threw his weight in the traces to jerk Buck into the way he should go. Buck learned easily, and under the combined tuition of his two mates and Francois made remarkable progress. Ere they returned to camp he knew enough to stop at "ho," to go ahead at "mush," to swing wide on the bends, and to keep clear of the wheeler when the loaded sled shot downhill at their heels.

"T'ree vair' good dogs," Francois told Perrault. "Dat Buck, heem pool lak hell. I tich heem queek as anyt'ing."

By afternoon, Perrault, who was in a hurry to be on the trail with his despatches, returned with two more dogs. "Billee" and "Joe" he called them, two brothers, and true huskies both. Sons of the one mother though they were, they were as different as day and night. Billee's one fault was his excessive good nature, while Joe was the very opposite, sour and introspective, with a perpetual snarl and a malignant eye. Buck received them in comradely fashion, Dave ignored them, while Spitz proceeded to thrash first one and then the other. Billee wagged his tail appeasingly, turned to run when he saw that appeasement was of no avail, and cried (still appeasingly) when Spitz's sharp teeth scored his flank. But no matter how Spitz circled, Joe whirled around on his heels to face him, mane bristling, ears laid back, lips writhing and snarling, jaws clipping together as fast as he could snap, and eyes diabolically gleaming—the incarnation of belligerent fear. So terrible was his appearance that Spitz was forced to forego disciplining him; but to cover his own discomfiture he turned upon the inoffensive and wailing Billee and drove him to the confines of the camp.

By evening Perrault secured another dog, an old husky, long and lean and gaunt, with a battle-scarred face and a single eye which flashed a warning of prowess that commanded respect. He was called Sol-leks, which means the Angry One. Like Dave, he asked nothing, gave nothing, expected nothing; and when he marched slowly and deliberately into their midst, even Spitz left him alone. He had one peculiarity which Buck was unlucky enough to discover. He did not like to be approached on his blind side. Of this offence Buck was unwittingly guilty, and the first knowledge he had of his indiscretion was when Sol-leks whirled upon him and slashed his shoulder to the bone for three inches up and down. Forever after Buck avoided his blind side, and to the last of their comradeship had no more trouble. His only apparent ambition, like Dave's, was to be left alone; though, as Buck was afterward to learn, each of them possessed one other and even more vital ambition.

That night Buck faced the great problem of sleeping. The tent, illumined by a candle, glowed warmly in the midst of the white plain; and when he, as a matter of course, entered it, both Perrault and Francois bombarded him with curses and cooking utensils, till he recovered from his consternation and fled ignominiously into the outer cold. A chill wind was blowing that nipped him sharply and bit with especial venom into his wounded shoulder. He lay down on the snow and attempted to sleep, but the frost soon drove him shivering to his feet. Miserable and disconsolate, he wandered about among the many tents, only to find that one place was as cold as another. Here and there savage dogs rushed upon him, but he bristled his neck-hair and snarled (for he was learning fast), and they let him go his way unmolested.

Finally an idea came to him. He would return and see how his own team-mates were making out. To his astonishment, they had disappeared. Again he wandered about through the great camp, looking for them, and again he returned. Were they in the tent? No, that could not be, else he would not have been driven out. Then where could they possibly be? With drooping tail and shivering body, very forlorn indeed, he aimlessly circled the tent. Suddenly the snow gave way beneath his fore legs and he sank down. Something wriggled under his feet. He sprang back, bristling and snarling, fearful of the unseen and unknown. But a friendly little yelp reassured him, and he went back to investigate. A whiff of warm air ascended to his nostrils, and there, curled up under the snow in a snug ball, lay Billee. He whined placatingly, squirmed and wriggled to show his good will and intentions, and even ventured, as a bribe for peace, to lick Buck's face with his warm wet tongue.

Another lesson. So that was the way they did it, eh? Buck confidently selected a spot, and with much fuss and waste effort proceeded to dig a hole for himself. In a trice the heat from his body filled the confined space and he was asleep. The day had been long and arduous, and he slept soundly and comfortably, though he growled and barked and wrestled with bad dreams.

Nor did he open his eyes till roused by the noises of the waking camp. At first he did not know where he was. It had snowed during the night and he was completely buried. The snow walls pressed him on every side, and a great surge of fear swept through him—the fear of the wild thing for the trap. It was a token that he was harking back through his own life to the lives of his forebears; for he was a civilized dog, an unduly civilized dog, and of his own experience knew no trap and so could not of himself fear it. The muscles of his whole body contracted spasmodically and instinctively, the hair on his neck and shoulders stood on end, and with a ferocious snarl he bounded straight up into the blinding day, the snow flying about him in a flashing cloud. Ere he landed on his feet, he saw the white camp spread out before him and knew where he was and remembered all that had passed from the time he went for a stroll with Manuel to the hole he had dug for himself the night before.

A shout from Francois hailed his appearance. "Wot I say?" the dog-driver cried to Perrault. "Dat Buck for sure learn queek as anyt'ing."

Perrault nodded gravely. As courier for the Canadian Government, bearing important despatches, he was anxious to secure the best dogs, and he was particularly gladdened by the possession of Buck.

Three more huskies were added to the team inside an hour, making a total of nine, and before another quarter of an hour had passed they were in harness and swinging up the trail toward the Dyea Canon. Buck was glad to be gone, and though the work was hard he found he did not particularly despise it. He was surprised at the eagerness which animated the whole team and which was communicated to him; but still more surprising was the change wrought in Dave and Sol-leks. They were new dogs, utterly transformed by the harness. All passiveness and unconcern had dropped from them. They were alert and active, anxious that the work should go well, and fiercely irritable with whatever, by delay or confusion, retarded that work. The toil of the traces seemed the supreme expression of their being, and all that they lived for and the only thing in which they took delight.

Dave was wheeler or sled dog, pulling in front of him was Buck, then came Sol-leks; the rest of the team was strung out ahead, single file, to the leader, which position was filled by Spitz.

Buck had been purposely placed between Dave and Sol-leks so that he might receive instruction. Apt scholar that he was, they were equally apt teachers, never allowing him to linger long in error, and enforcing their teaching with their sharp teeth. Dave was fair and very wise. He never nipped Buck without cause, and he never failed to nip him when he stood in need of it. As Francois's whip backed him up, Buck found it to be cheaper to mend his ways than to retaliate. Once, during a brief halt, when he got tangled in the traces and delayed the start, both Dave and Solleks flew at him and administered a sound trouncing. The resulting tangle was even worse, but Buck took good care to keep the traces clear thereafter; and ere the day was done, so well had he mastered his work, his mates about ceased nagging him. Francois's whip snapped less frequently, and Perrault even honored Buck by lifting up his feet and carefully examining them.

It was a hard day's run, up the Canon, through Sheep Camp, past the Scales and the timber line, across glaciers and snowdrifts hundreds of feet deep, and over the great Chilcoot Divide, which stands between the salt water and the fresh and guards forbiddingly the sad and lonely North. They made good time down the chain of lakes which fills the craters of extinct volcanoes, and late that night pulled into the huge camp at the head of Lake Bennett, where thousands of goldseekers were building boats against the break-up of the ice in the spring. Buck made his hole in the snow and slept the sleep of the exhausted just, but all too early was routed out in the cold darkness and harnessed with his mates to the sled.

That day they made forty miles, the trail being packed; but the next day, and for many days to follow, they broke their own trail, worked harder, and made poorer time. As a rule, Perrault travelled ahead of the team, packing the snow with webbed shoes to make it easier for them. Francois, guiding the sled at the gee-pole, sometimes exchanged places with him, but not often. Perrault was in a hurry, and he prided himself on his knowledge of ice, which knowledge was indispensable, for the fall ice was very thin, and where there was swift water, there was no ice at all.

Day after day, for days unending, Buck toiled in the traces. Always, they broke camp in the dark, and the first gray of dawn found them hitting the trail with fresh miles reeled off behind them. And always they pitched camp after dark, eating their bit of fish, and crawling to sleep into the snow. Buck was ravenous. The pound and a half of sun-dried salmon, which was his ration for each day, seemed to go nowhere. He never had enough, and suffered from perpetual hunger pangs. Yet the other dogs, because they weighed less and were born to the life, received a pound only of the fish and managed to keep in good condition.

He swiftly lost the fastidiousness which had characterized his old life. A dainty eater, he found that his mates, finishing first, robbed him of his unfinished ration. There was no defending it. While he was fighting off two or three, it was disappearing down the throats of the others. To remedy this, he ate as fast as they; and, so greatly did hunger compel him, he was not above taking what did not belong to him. He watched and learned. When he saw Pike, one of the new dogs, a clever malingerer and thief, slyly steal a slice of bacon when Perrault's back was turned, he duplicated the performance the following day, getting away with the whole chunk. A great uproar was raised, but he was unsuspected; while Dub, an awkward blunderer who was always getting caught, was punished for Buck's misdeed.

This first theft marked Buck as fit to survive in the hostile Northland environment. It marked his adaptability, his capacity to adjust himself to changing conditions, the lack of which would have meant swift and terrible death. It marked, further, the decay or going to pieces of his moral nature, a vain thing and a handicap in the ruthless struggle for existence. It was all well enough in the Southland, under the law of love and fellowship, to respect private property and personal feelings; but in the Northland, under the law of club and fang, whoso took such things into account was a fool, and in so far as he observed them he would fail to prosper.

Not that Buck reasoned it out. He was fit, that was all, and unconsciously he accommodated himself to the new mode of life. All his days, no matter what the odds, he had never run from a fight. But the club of the man in the red sweater had beaten into him a more fundamental and primitive code. Civilized, he could have died for a moral consideration, say the defence of Judge Miller's riding-whip; but the completeness of his decivilization was now evidenced by his ability to flee from the defence of a moral consideration and so save his hide. He did not steal for joy of it, but because of the clamor of his stomach. He did not rob openly, but stole secretly and cunningly, out of respect for club and fang. In short, the things he did were done because it was easier to do them than not to do them.

His development (or retrogression) was rapid. His muscles became hard as iron, and he grew callous to all ordinary pain. He achieved an internal as well as external economy. He could eat anything, no matter how loathsome or indigestible; and, once eaten, the juices of his stomach extracted the last least particle of nutriment; and his blood carried it to the farthest reaches of his body, building it into the toughest and stoutest of tissues. Sight and scent became remarkably keen, while his hearing developed such acuteness that in his sleep he heard the faintest sound and knew whether it heralded peace or peril. He learned to bite the ice out with his teeth when it collected between his toes; and when he was thirsty and there was a thick scum of ice over the water hole, he would break it by rearing and striking it with stiff fore legs. His most conspicuous trait was an ability to scent the wind and fore-cast it a night in advance. No matter how breathless the air when he dug his nest by tree or bank, the wind that later blew inevitably found him to leeward, sheltered and snug.

And not only did he learn by experience, but instincts long dead became alive again. The domesticated generations fell from him. In vague ways he remembered back to the youth of the breed, to the time the wild dogs ranged in packs through the primeval forest and killed their meat as they ran it down. It was no task for him to learn to fight with cut and slash and the quick wolf snap. In this manner had fought forgotten ancestors. They quickened the old life within him, and the old tricks which they had stamped into the heredity of the breed were his tricks. They came to him without effort or discovery, as though they had been his always. And when, on the still cold nights, he pointed his nose at a star and howled long and wolflike, it was his ancestors, dead and dust, pointing nose at star and howling down through the centuries and through him. And his cadences were their cadences, the cadences which voiced their woe and what to them was the meaning of the stiffness, and the cold, and dark.

Thus, as token of what a puppet thing life is, the ancient song surged through him and he came into his own again; and he came because men had found a yellow metal in the North, and because Manuel was a gardener's helper whose wages did not lap over the needs of his wife and divers small copies of himself.

Chapter III. The Dominant Primordial Beast

The dominant primordial beast was strong in Buck, and under the fierce conditions of trail life it grew and grew. Yet it was a secret growth. His newborn cunning gave him poise and control. He was too busy adjusting himself to the new life to feel at ease, and not only did he not pick fights, but he avoided them whenever possible. A certain deliberateness characterized his attitude. He was not prone to rashness and precipitate action; and in the bitter hatred between him and Spitz he betrayed no impatience, shunned all offensive acts.

On the other hand, possibly because he divined in Buck a dangerous rival, Spitz never lost an opportunity of showing his teeth. He even went out of his way to bully Buck, striving constantly to start the fight which could end only in the death of one or the other. Early in the trip this might have taken place had it not been for an unwonted accident. At the end of this day they made a bleak and miserable camp on the shore of Lake Le Barge. Driving snow, a wind that cut like a white-hot knife, and darkness had forced them to grope for a camping place. They could hardly have fared worse. At their backs rose a perpendicular wall of rock, and Perrault and Francois were compelled to make their fire and spread their sleeping robes on the ice of the lake itself. The tent they had discarded at Dyea in order to travel light. A few sticks of driftwood furnished them with a fire that thawed down through the ice and left them to eat supper in the dark.

Close in under the sheltering rock Buck made his nest. So snug and warm was it, that he was loath to leave it when Francois distributed the fish which he had first thawed over the fire. But when Buck finished his ration and returned, he found his nest occupied. A warning snarl told him that the trespasser was Spitz. Till now Buck had avoided trouble with his enemy, but this was too much. The beast in him roared. He sprang upon Spitz with a fury which surprised them both, and Spitz particularly, for his whole experience with Buck had gone to teach him that his rival was an unusually timid dog, who managed to hold his own only because of his great weight and size.

Francois was surprised, too, when they shot out in a tangle from the disrupted nest and he divined the cause of the trouble. "A-a-ah!" he cried to Buck. "Gif it to heem, by Gar! Gif it to heem, the dirty t'eef!"

Spitz was equally willing. He was crying with sheer rage and eagerness as he circled back and forth for a chance to spring in. Buck was no less eager, and no less cautious, as he likewise circled back and forth for the advantage. But it was then that the unexpected happened, the thing which projected their struggle for supremacy far into the future, past many a weary mile of trail and toil.

An oath from Perrault, the resounding impact of a club upon a bony frame, and a shrill yelp of pain, heralded the breaking forth of pandemonium. The camp was suddenly discovered to be alive with skulking furry forms,—starving huskies, four or five score of them, who had scented the camp from some Indian village. They had crept in while Buck and Spitz were fighting, and when the two men sprang among them with stout clubs they showed their teeth and fought back. They were crazed by the smell of the food. Perrault found one with head buried in the grub-box. His club landed heavily on the gaunt ribs, and the grub-box was capsized on the ground. On the instant a score of the famished brutes were scrambling for the bread and bacon. The clubs fell upon them unheeded. They yelped and howled under the rain of blows, but struggled none the less madly till the last crumb had been devoured.

In the meantime the astonished team-dogs had burst out of their nests only to be set upon by the fierce invaders. Never had Buck seen such dogs. It seemed as though their bones would burst through their skins. They were mere skeletons, draped loosely in draggled hides, with blazing eyes and slavered fangs. But the hunger-madness made them terrifying, irresistible. There was no opposing them. The team-dogs were swept back against the cliff at the first onset. Buck was beset by three huskies, and in a trice his head and shoulders were ripped and slashed. The din was frightful. Billee was crying as usual. Dave and Sol-leks, dripping blood from a score of wounds, were fighting bravely side by side. Joe was snapping like a demon. Once, his teeth closed on the fore leg of a husky, and he crunched down through the bone. Pike, the malingerer, leaped upon the crippled animal, breaking its neck with a quick flash of teeth and a jerk, Buck got a frothing adversary by the throat, and was sprayed with blood when his teeth sank through the jugular. The warm taste of it in his mouth goaded him to greater fierceness. He flung himself upon another, and at the same time felt teeth sink into his own throat. It was Spitz, treacherously attacking from the side.

Perrault and Francois, having cleaned out their part of the camp, hurried to save their sled-dogs. The wild wave of famished beasts rolled back before them, and Buck shook himself free. But it was only for a moment. The two men were compelled to run back to save the grub, upon which the huskies returned to the attack on the team. Billee, terrified into bravery, sprang through the savage circle and fled away over the ice. Pike and Dub followed on his heels, with the rest of the team behind. As Buck drew himself together to spring after them, out of the tail of his eye he saw Spitz rush upon him with the evident intention of overthrowing him. Once off his feet and under that mass of huskies, there was no hope for him. But he braced himself to the shock of Spitz's charge, then joined the flight out on the lake.

Later, the nine team-dogs gathered together and sought shelter in the forest. Though unpursued, they were in a sorry plight. There was not one who was not wounded in four or five places, while some were wounded grievously. Dub was badly injured in a hind leg; Dolly, the last husky added to the team at Dyea, had a badly torn throat; Joe had lost an eye; while Billee, the good-natured, with an ear chewed and rent to ribbons, cried and whimpered throughout the night. At daybreak they limped warily back to camp, to find the marauders gone and the two men in bad tempers. Fully half their grub supply was gone. The huskies had chewed through the sled lashings and canvas coverings. In fact, nothing, no matter how remotely eatable, had escaped them. They had eaten a pair of Perrault's moose-hide moccasins, chunks out of the leather traces, and even two feet of lash from the end of Francois's whip. He broke from a mournful contemplation of it to look over his wounded dogs.

"Ah, my frien's," he said softly, "mebbe it mek you mad dog, dose many bites. Mebbe all mad dog, sacredam! Wot you t'ink, eh, Perrault?"

The courier shook his head dubiously. With four hundred miles of trail still between him and Dawson, he could ill afford to have madness break out among his dogs. Two hours of cursing and exertion got the harnesses into shape, and the wound-stiffened team was under way, struggling painfully over the hardest part of the trail they had yet encountered, and for that matter, the hardest between them and Dawson.

The Thirty Mile River was wide open. Its wild water defied the frost, and it was in the eddies only and in the quiet places that the ice held at all. Six days of exhausting toil were required to cover those thirty terrible miles. And terrible they were, for every foot of them was accomplished at the risk of life to dog and man. A dozen times, Perrault, nosing the way broke through the ice bridges, being saved by the long pole he carried, which he so held that it fell each time across the hole made by his body. But a cold snap was on, the thermometer registering fifty below zero, and each time he broke through he was compelled for very life to build a fire and dry his garments.

Nothing daunted him. It was because nothing daunted him that he had been chosen for government courier. He took all manner of risks, resolutely thrusting his little weazened face into the frost and struggling on from dim dawn to dark. He skirted the frowning shores on rim ice that bent and crackled under foot and upon which they dared not halt. Once, the sled broke through, with Dave and Buck, and they were half-frozen and all but drowned by the time they were dragged out. The usual fire was necessary to save them. They were coated solidly with ice, and the two men kept them on the run around the fire, sweating and thawing, so close that they were singed by the flames.

At another time Spitz went through, dragging the whole team after him up to Buck, who strained backward with all his strength, his fore paws on the slippery edge and the ice quivering and snapping all around. But behind him was Dave, likewise straining backward, and behind the sled was Francois, pulling till his tendons cracked.

Again, the rim ice broke away before and behind, and there was no escape except up the cliff. Perrault scaled it by a miracle, while Francois prayed for just that miracle; and with every thong and sled lashing and the last bit of harness rove into a long rope, the dogs were hoisted, one by one, to the cliff crest. Francois came up last, after the sled and load. Then came the search for a place to descend, which descent was ultimately made by the aid of the rope, and night found them back on the river with a quarter of a mile to the day's credit.

By the time they made the Hootalinqua and good ice, Buck was played out. The rest of the dogs were in like condition; but Perrault, to make up lost time, pushed them late and early. The first day they covered thirty-five miles to the Big Salmon; the next day thirty-five more to the Little Salmon; the third day forty miles, which brought them well up toward the Five Fingers.

Buck's feet were not so compact and hard as the feet of the huskies. His had softened during the many generations since the day his last wild ancestor was tamed by a cave-dweller or river man. All day long he limped in agony, and camp once made, lay down like a dead dog. Hungry as he was, he would not move to receive his ration of fish, which Francois had to bring to him. Also, the dog-driver rubbed Buck's feet for half an hour each night after supper, and sacrificed the tops of his own moccasins to make four moccasins for Buck. This was a great relief, and Buck caused even the weazened face of Perrault to twist itself into a grin one morning, when Francois forgot the moccasins and Buck lay on his back, his four feet waving appealingly in the air, and refused to budge without them. Later his feet grew hard to the trail, and the worn-out foot-gear was thrown away.

At the Pelly one morning, as they were harnessing up, Dolly, who had never been conspicuous for anything, went suddenly mad. She announced her condition by a long, heartbreaking wolf howl that sent every dog bristling with fear, then sprang straight for Buck. He had never seen a dog go mad, nor did he have any reason to fear madness; yet he knew that here was horror, and fled away from it in a panic. Straight away he raced, with Dolly, panting and frothing, one leap behind; nor could she gain on him, so great was his terror, nor could he leave her, so great was her madness. He plunged through the wooded breast of the island, flew down to the lower end, crossed a back channel filled with rough ice to another island, gained a third island, curved back to the main river, and in desperation started to cross it. And all the time, though he did not look, he could hear her snarling just one leap behind. Francois called to him a quarter of a mile away and he doubled back, still one leap ahead, gasping painfully for air and putting all his faith in that Francois would save him. The dog-driver held the axe poised in his hand, and as Buck shot past him the axe crashed down upon mad Dolly's head.

Buck staggered over against the sled, exhausted, sobbing for breath, helpless. This was Spitz's opportunity. He sprang upon Buck, and twice his teeth sank into his unresisting foe and ripped and tore the flesh to the bone. Then Francois's lash descended, and Buck had the satisfaction of watching Spitz receive the worst whipping as yet administered to any of the teams.

"One devil, dat Spitz," remarked Perrault. "Some dam day heem keel dat Buck."

"Dat Buck two devils," was Francois's rejoinder. "All de tam I watch dat Buck I know for sure. Lissen: some dam fine day heem get mad lak hell an' den heem chew dat Spitz all up an' spit heem out on de snow. Sure. I know."

From then on it was war between them. Spitz, as lead-dog and acknowledged master of the team, felt his supremacy threatened by this strange Southland dog. And strange Buck was to him, for of the many Southland dogs he had known, not one had shown up worthily in camp and on trail. They were all too soft, dying under the toil, the frost, and starvation. Buck was the exception. He alone endured and prospered, matching the husky in strength, savagery, and cunning. Then he was a masterful dog, and what made him dangerous was the fact that the club of the man in the red sweater had knocked all blind pluck and rashness out of his desire for mastery. He was preeminently cunning, and could bide his time with a patience that was nothing less than primitive.

It was inevitable that the clash for leadership should come. Buck wanted it. He wanted it because it was his nature, because he had been gripped tight by that nameless, incomprehensible pride of the trail and trace—that pride which holds dogs in the toil to the last gasp, which lures them to die joyfully in the harness, and breaks their hearts if they are cut out of the harness. This was the pride of Dave as wheel-dog, of Sol-leks as he pulled with all his strength; the pride that laid hold of them at break of camp, transforming them from sour and sullen brutes into straining, eager, ambitious creatures; the pride that spurred them on all day and dropped them at pitch of camp at night, letting them fall back into gloomy unrest and uncontent. This was the pride that bore up Spitz and made him thrash the sled-dogs who blundered and shirked in the traces or hid away at harness-up time in the morning. Likewise it was this pride that made him fear Buck as a possible lead-dog. And this was Buck's pride, too.

He openly threatened the other's leadership. He came between him and the shirks he should have punished. And he did it deliberately. One night there was a heavy snowfall, and in the morning Pike, the malingerer, did not appear. He was securely hidden in his nest under a foot of snow. Francois called him and sought him in vain. Spitz was wild with wrath. He raged through the camp, smelling and digging in every likely place, snarling so frightfully that Pike heard and shivered in his hiding-place.

But when he was at last unearthed, and Spitz flew at him to punish him, Buck flew, with equal rage, in between. So unexpected was it, and so shrewdly managed, that Spitz was hurled backward and off his feet. Pike, who had been trembling abjectly, took heart at this open mutiny, and sprang upon his overthrown leader. Buck, to whom fair play was a forgotten code, likewise sprang upon Spitz. But Francois, chuckling at the incident while unswerving in the administration of justice, brought his lash down upon Buck with all his might. This failed to drive Buck from his prostrate rival, and the butt of the whip was brought into play. Half-stunned by the blow, Buck was knocked backward and the lash laid upon him again and again, while Spitz soundly punished the many times offending Pike.

In the days that followed, as Dawson grew closer and closer, Buck still continued to interfere between Spitz and the culprits; but he did it craftily, when Francois was not around, With the covert mutiny of Buck, a general insubordination sprang up and increased. Dave and Sol-leks were unaffected, but the rest of the team went from bad to worse. Things no longer went right. There was continual bickering and jangling. Trouble was always afoot, and at the bottom of it was Buck. He kept Francois busy, for the dog-driver was in constant apprehension of the life-and-death struggle between the two which he knew must take place sooner or later; and on more than one night the sounds of quarrelling and strife among the other dogs turned him out of his sleeping robe, fearful that Buck and Spitz were at it.

But the opportunity did not present itself, and they pulled into Dawson one dreary afternoon with the great fight still to come. Here were many men, and countless dogs, and Buck found them all at work. It seemed the ordained order of things that dogs should work. All day they swung up and down the main street in long teams, and in the night their jingling bells still went by. They hauled cabin logs and firewood, freighted up to the mines, and did all manner of work that horses did in the Santa Clara Valley. Here and there Buck met Southland dogs, but in the main they were the wild wolf husky breed. Every night, regularly, at nine, at twelve, at three, they lifted a nocturnal song, a weird and eerie chant, in which it was Buck's delight to join.

With the aurora borealis flaming coldly overhead, or the stars leaping in the frost dance, and the land numb and frozen under its pall of snow, this song of the huskies might have been the defiance of life, only it was pitched in minor key, with long-drawn wailings and half-sobs, and was more the pleading of life, the articulate travail of existence. It was an old song, old as the breed itself—one of the first songs of the younger world in a day when songs were sad. It was invested with the woe of unnumbered generations, this plaint by which Buck was so strangely stirred. When he moaned and sobbed, it was with the pain of living that was of old the pain of his wild fathers, and the fear and mystery of the cold and dark that was to them fear and mystery. And that he should be stirred by it marked the completeness with which he harked back through the ages of fire and roof to the raw beginnings of life in the howling ages.

Seven days from the time they pulled into Dawson, they dropped down the steep bank by the Barracks to the Yukon Trail, and pulled for Dyea and Salt Water. Perrault was carrying despatches if anything more urgent than those he had brought in; also, the travel pride had gripped him, and he purposed to make the record trip of the year. Several things favored him in this. The week's rest had recuperated the dogs and put them in thorough trim. The trail they had broken into the country was packed hard by later journeyers. And further, the police had arranged in two or three places deposits of grub for dog and man, and he was travelling light.

They made Sixty Mile, which is a fifty-mile run, on the first day; and the second day saw them booming up the Yukon well on their way to Pelly. But such splendid running was achieved not without great trouble and vexation on the part of Francois. The insidious revolt led by Buck had destroyed the solidarity of the team. It no longer was as one dog leaping in the traces. The encouragement Buck gave the rebels led them into all kinds of petty misdemeanors. No more was Spitz a leader greatly to be feared. The old awe departed, and they grew equal to challenging his authority. Pike robbed him of half a fish one night, and gulped it down under the protection of Buck. Another night Dub and Joe fought Spitz and made him forego the punishment they deserved. And even Billee, the good-natured, was less good-natured, and whined not half so placatingly as in former days. Buck never came near Spitz without snarling and bristling menacingly. In fact, his conduct approached that of a bully, and he was given to swaggering up and down before Spitz's very nose.

The breaking down of discipline likewise affected the dogs in their relations with one another. They quarrelled and bickered more than ever among themselves, till at times the camp was a howling bedlam. Dave and Sol-leks alone were unaltered, though they were made irritable by the unending squabbling. Francois swore strange barbarous oaths, and stamped the snow in futile rage, and tore his hair. His lash was always singing among the dogs, but it was of small avail. Directly his back was turned they were at it again. He backed up Spitz with his whip, while Buck backed up the remainder of the team. Francois knew he was behind all the trouble, and Buck knew he knew; but Buck was too clever ever again to be caught red-handed. He worked faithfully in the harness, for the toil had become a delight to him; yet it was a greater delight slyly to precipitate a fight amongst his mates and tangle the traces.

At the mouth of the Tahkeena, one night after supper, Dub turned up a snowshoe rabbit, blundered it, and missed. In a second the whole team was in full cry. A hundred yards away was a camp of the Northwest Police, with fifty dogs, huskies all, who joined the chase. The rabbit sped down the river, turned off into a small creek, up the frozen bed of which it held steadily. It ran lightly on the surface of the snow, while the dogs ploughed through by main strength. Buck led the pack, sixty strong, around bend after bend, but he could not gain. He lay down low to the race, whining eagerly, his splendid body flashing forward, leap by leap, in the wan white moonlight. And leap by leap, like some pale frost wraith, the snowshoe rabbit flashed on ahead.

All that stirring of old instincts which at stated periods drives men out from the sounding cities to forest and plain to kill things by chemically propelled leaden pellets, the blood lust, the joy to kill—all this was Buck's, only it was infinitely more intimate. He was ranging at the head of the pack, running the wild thing down, the living meat, to kill with his own teeth and wash his muzzle to the eyes in warm blood.

There is an ecstasy that marks the summit of life, and beyond which life cannot rise. And such is the paradox of living, this ecstasy comes when one is most alive, and it comes as a complete forgetfulness that one is alive. This ecstasy, this forgetfulness of living, comes to the artist, caught up and out of himself in a sheet of flame; it comes to the soldier, war-mad on a stricken field and refusing quarter; and it came to Buck, leading the pack, sounding the old wolf-cry, straining after the food that was alive and that fled swiftly before him through the moonlight. He was sounding the deeps of his nature, and of the parts of his nature that were deeper than he, going back into the womb of Time. He was mastered by the sheer surging of life, the tidal wave of being, the perfect joy of each separate muscle, joint, and sinew in that it was everything that was not death, that it was aglow and rampant, expressing itself in movement, flying exultantly under the stars and over the face of dead matter that did not move.

But Spitz, cold and calculating even in his supreme moods, left the pack and cut across a narrow neck of land where the creek made a long bend around. Buck did not know of this, and as he rounded the bend, the frost wraith of a rabbit still flitting before him, he saw another and larger frost wraith leap from the overhanging bank into the immediate path of the rabbit. It was Spitz. The rabbit could not turn, and as the white teeth broke its back in midair it shrieked as loudly as a stricken man may shriek. At sound of this, the cry of Life plunging down from Life's apex in the grip of Death, the fall pack at Buck's heels raised a hell's chorus of delight.

Buck did not cry out. He did not check himself, but drove in upon Spitz, shoulder to shoulder, so hard that he missed the throat. They rolled over and over in the powdery snow. Spitz gained his feet almost as though he had not been overthrown, slashing Buck down the shoulder and leaping clear. Twice his teeth clipped together, like the steel jaws of a trap, as he backed away for better footing, with lean and lifting lips that writhed and snarled.

In a flash Buck knew it. The time had come. It was to the death. As they circled about, snarling, ears laid back, keenly watchful for the advantage, the scene came to Buck with a sense of familiarity. He seemed to remember it all,—the white woods, and earth, and moonlight, and the thrill of battle. Over the whiteness and silence brooded a ghostly calm. There was not the faintest whisper of air—nothing moved, not a leaf quivered, the visible breaths of the dogs rising slowly and lingering in the frosty air. They had made short work of the snowshoe rabbit, these dogs that were ill-tamed wolves; and they were now drawn up in an expectant circle. They, too, were silent, their eyes only gleaming and their breaths drifting slowly upward. To

Buck it was nothing new or strange, this scene of old time. It was as though it had always been, the wonted way of things.

Spitz was a practised fighter. From Spitzbergen through the Arctic, and across Canada and the Barrens, he had held his own with all manner of dogs and achieved to mastery over them. Bitter rage was his, but never blind rage. In passion to rend and destroy, he never forgot that his enemy was in like passion to rend and destroy. He never rushed till he was prepared to receive a rush; never attacked till he had first defended that attack.

In vain Buck strove to sink his teeth in the neck of the big white dog. Wherever his fangs struck for the softer flesh, they were countered by the fangs of Spitz. Fang clashed fang, and lips were cut and bleeding, but Buck could not penetrate his enemy's guard. Then he warmed up and enveloped Spitz in a whirlwind of rushes. Time and time again he tried for the snow-white throat, where life bubbled near to the surface, and each time and every time Spitz slashed him and got away. Then Buck took to rushing, as though for the throat, when, suddenly drawing back his head and curving in from the side, he would drive his shoulder at the shoulder of Spitz, as a ram by which to overthrow him. But instead, Buck's shoulder was slashed down each time as Spitz leaped lightly away.

Spitz was untouched, while Buck was streaming with blood and panting hard. The fight was growing desperate. And all the while the silent and wolfish circle waited to finish off whichever dog went down. As Buck grew winded, Spitz took to rushing, and he kept him staggering for footing. Once Buck went over, and the whole circle of sixty dogs started up; but he recovered himself, almost in mid air, and the circle sank down again and waited.

But Buck possessed a quality that made for greatness—imagination. He fought by instinct, but he could fight by head as well. He rushed, as though attempting the old shoulder trick, but at the last instant swept low to the snow and in. His teeth closed on Spitz's left fore leg. There was a crunch of breaking bone, and the white dog faced him on three legs. Thrice he tried to knock him over, then repeated the trick and broke the right fore leg. Despite the pain and helplessness, Spitz struggled madly to keep up. He saw the silent circle, with gleaming eyes, lolling tongues, and silvery breaths drifting upward, closing in upon him as he had seen similar circles close in upon beaten antagonists in the past. Only this time he was the one who was beaten.

There was no hope for him. Buck was inexorable. Mercy was a thing reserved for gentler climes. He manoeuvred for the final rush. The circle had tightened till he could feel the breaths of the huskies on his flanks. He could see them, beyond Spitz and to either side, half crouching for the spring, their eyes fixed upon him. A pause seemed to fall. Every animal was motionless as though turned to stone. Only Spitz quivered and bristled as he staggered back and forth, snarling with horrible menace, as though to frighten off impending death. Then Buck sprang in and out; but while he was in, shoulder had at last squarely met shoulder. The dark circle became a dot on the moon-flooded snow as Spitz disappeared from view. Buck stood and looked on, the successful champion, the dominant primordial beast who had made his kill and found it good.

Chapter IV. Who Has Won to Mastership

"Eh? Wot I say? I spik true w'en I say dat Buck two devils." This was Francois's speech next morning when he discovered Spitz missing and Buck covered with wounds. He drew him to the fire and by its light pointed them out.

"Dat Spitz fight lak hell," said Perrault, as he surveyed the gaping rips and cuts.

"An' dat Buck fight lak two hells," was Francois's answer. "An' now we make good time. No more Spitz, no more trouble, sure."

While Perrault packed the camp outfit and loaded the sled, the dog-driver proceeded to harness the dogs. Buck trotted up to the place Spitz would have occupied as leader; but Francois, not noticing him, brought Sol-leks to the coveted position. In his judgment, Sol-leks was the best lead-dog left. Buck sprang upon Sol-leks in a fury, driving him back and standing in his place.

"Eh? eh?" Francois cried, slapping his thighs gleefully. "Look at dat Buck. Heem keel dat Spitz, heem t'ink to take de job."

"Go 'way, Chook!" he cried, but Buck refused to budge.

He took Buck by the scruff of the neck, and though the dog growled threateningly, dragged him to one side and replaced Sol-leks. The old dog did not like it, and showed plainly that he was afraid of Buck. Francois was obdurate, but when he turned his back Buck again displaced Sol-leks, who was not at all unwilling to go.

Francois was angry. "Now, by Gar, I feex you!" he cried, coming back with a heavy club in his hand.

Buck remembered the man in the red sweater, and retreated slowly; nor did he attempt to charge in when Sol-leks was once more brought forward. But he circled just beyond the range of the club, snarling with bitterness and rage; and while he circled he watched the club so as to dodge it if thrown by Francois, for he was become wise in the way of clubs. The driver went about his work, and he called to Buck when he was ready to put him in his old place in front of Dave. Buck retreated two or three steps. Francois followed him up, whereupon he again retreated. After some time of this, Francois threw down the club, thinking that Buck feared a thrashing. But Buck was in open revolt. He wanted, not to escape a clubbing, but to have the leadership. It was his by right. He had earned it, and he would not be content with less.

Perrault took a hand. Between them they ran him about for the better part of an hour. They threw clubs at him. He dodged. They cursed him, and his fathers and mothers before him, and all his seed to come after him down to the remotest generation, and every hair on his body and drop of blood in his veins; and he answered curse with snarl and kept out of their reach. He did not try to run away, but retreated around and around the camp, advertising plainly that when his desire was met, he would come in and be good.

Francois sat down and scratched his head. Perrault looked at his watch and swore. Time was flying, and they should have been on the trail an hour gone. Francois scratched his head again. He shook it and grinned sheepishly at the courier, who shrugged his shoulders in sign that they were beaten. Then Francois went up to where Sol-leks stood and called to Buck. Buck laughed, as dogs laugh, yet kept his distance. Francois unfastened Sol-leks's traces and put him back in his old place. The team stood harnessed to the sled in an unbroken line, ready for the trail. There was no place for Buck save at the front. Once more Francois called, and once more Buck laughed and kept away.

"T'row down de club," Perrault commanded.

Francois complied, whereupon Buck trotted in, laughing triumphantly, and swung around into position at the head of the team. His traces were fastened, the sled broken out, and with both men running they dashed out on to the river trail.

Highly as the dog-driver had forevalued Buck, with his two devils, he found, while the day was yet young, that he had undervalued. At a bound Buck took up the duties of leadership; and where judgment was required, and quick thinking and quick acting, he showed himself the superior even of Spitz, of whom Francois had never seen an equal.

But it was in giving the law and making his mates live up to it, that Buck excelled. Dave and Sol-leks did not mind the change in leadership. It was none of their business. Their business was to toil, and toil mightily, in the traces. So long as that were not interfered with, they did not care what happened. Billee, the good-natured, could lead for all they cared, so long as he kept order. The rest of the team, however, had grown unruly during the last days of Spitz, and their surprise was great now that Buck proceeded to lick them into shape.

Pike, who pulled at Buck's heels, and who never put an ounce more of his weight against the breast-band than he was compelled to do, was swiftly and repeatedly shaken for loafing; and ere the first day was done he was pulling more than ever before in his life. The first night in camp, Joe, the sour one, was punished roundly—a thing that Spitz had never succeeded in doing. Buck simply smothered him by virtue of superior weight, and cut him up till he ceased snapping and began to whine for mercy.

The general tone of the team picked up immediately. It recovered its old-time solidarity, and once more the dogs leaped as one dog in the traces. At the Rink Rapids two native huskies, Teek and Koona, were added; and the celerity with which Buck broke them in took away Francois's breath.

"Nevaire such a dog as dat Buck!" he cried. "No, nevaire! Heem worth one t'ousan' dollair, by Gar! Eh? Wot you say, Perrault?"

And Perrault nodded. He was ahead of the record then, and gaining day by day. The trail was in excellent condition, well packed and hard, and there was no new-fallen snow with which to contend. It was not too cold. The temperature dropped to fifty below zero and remained there the whole trip. The men rode and ran by turn, and the dogs were kept on the jump, with but infrequent stoppages.

The Thirty Mile River was comparatively coated with ice, and they covered in one day going out what had taken them ten days coming in. In one run they made a sixty-mile dash from the foot of Lake Le Barge to the White Horse Rapids. Across Marsh, Tagish, and Bennett (seventy miles of lakes), they flew so fast that the man whose turn it was to run towed behind the sled at the end of a rope. And on the last night of the second week they topped White Pass and dropped down the sea slope with the lights of Skaguay and of the shipping at their feet.

It was a record run. Each day for fourteen days they had averaged forty miles. For three days Perrault and Francois threw chests up and down the main street of Skaguay and were deluged with invitations to drink, while the team was the constant centre of a worshipful crowd of dog-busters and mushers. Then three or four western bad men aspired to clean out the town, were riddled like pepper-boxes for their pains, and public interest turned to other idols. Next came official orders. Francois called Buck to him, threw his arms around him, wept over him. And that was the last of Francois and Perrault. Like other men, they passed out of Buck's life for good.

A Scotch half-breed took charge of him and his mates, and in company with a dozen other dog-teams he started back over the weary trail to Dawson. It was no light running now, nor record time, but heavy toil each day, with a heavy load behind; for this was the mail train, carrying word from the world to the men who sought gold under the shadow of the Pole.

Buck did not like it, but he bore up well to the work, taking pride in it after the manner of Dave and Sol-leks, and seeing that his mates, whether they prided in it or not, did their fair share. It was a monotonous life, operating with machine-like regularity. One day was very like another. At a certain time each morning the cooks turned out, fires were built, and breakfast was eaten. Then, while some broke camp, others harnessed the dogs, and they were under way an hour or so before the darkness fell which gave warning of dawn. At night, camp was made. Some pitched the flies, others cut firewood and pine boughs for the beds, and still others carried water or ice for the cooks. Also, the dogs were fed. To them, this was the one feature of the day, though it was good to loaf around, after the fish was eaten, for an hour or so with the other dogs, of which there were fivescore and odd. There were fierce fighters among them, but three battles with the fiercest brought Buck to mastery, so that when he bristled and showed his teeth they got out of his way.

Best of all, perhaps, he loved to lie near the fire, hind legs crouched under him, fore legs stretched out in front, head raised, and eyes blinking dreamily at the flames. Sometimes he thought of Judge Miller's big house in the sun-kissed Santa Clara Valley, and of the cement swimming-tank, and Ysabel, the Mexican hairless, and Toots, the Japanese pug; but oftener he remembered the man in the red sweater, the death of Curly, the great fight with Spitz, and the good things he had eaten or would like to eat. He was not homesick. The Sunland was very dim and distant, and such memories had no power over him. Far more potent were the memories of his heredity that gave things he had never seen before a seeming familiarity; the instincts (which were but the memories of his ancestors become habits) which had lapsed in later days, and still later, in him, quickened and become alive again.

Sometimes as he crouched there, blinking dreamily at the flames, it seemed that the flames were of another fire, and that as he crouched by this other fire he saw another and different man from the half-breed cook before him. This other man was shorter of leg and longer of arm, with muscles that were stringy and knotty rather than rounded and swelling. The hair of this man was long and matted, and his head slanted back under it from the eyes. He uttered strange sounds, and seemed very much afraid of the darkness, into which he peered continually, clutching in his hand, which hung midway between knee and foot, a stick with a heavy stone made fast to the end. He was all but naked, a ragged and fire-scorched skin hanging part way down his back, but on his body there was much hair. In some places, across the chest and shoulders and down the outside of the arms and thighs, it was matted into almost a thick fur. He did not stand erect, but with trunk inclined forward from the hips, on legs that bent at the knees. About his body there was a peculiar springiness, or resiliency, almost catlike, and a quick alertness as of one who lived in perpetual fear of things seen and unseen.

At other times this hairy man squatted by the fire with head between his legs and slept. On such occasions his elbows were on his knees, his hands clasped above his head as though to shed rain by the hairy arms. And beyond that fire, in the circling darkness, Buck could see many gleaming coals, two by two, always two by two, which he knew to be the eyes of great beasts of prey. And he could hear the crashing of their bodies through the undergrowth, and the noises they made in the night. And dreaming there by the Yukon bank, with lazy eyes blinking at the fire, these sounds and sights of another world would make the hair to rise along his back and stand on end across his shoulders and up his neck, till he whimpered low and suppressedly, or growled softly, and the half-breed cook shouted at him, "Hey, you Buck, wake up!" Whereupon the other world would vanish and the real world come into his eyes, and he would get up and yawn and stretch as though he had been asleep.

It was a hard trip, with the mail behind them, and the heavy work wore them down. They were short of weight and in poor condition when they made Dawson, and should have had a ten days' or a week's rest at least. But in two days' time they dropped down the Yukon bank from the Barracks, loaded with letters for the outside. The dogs were tired, the drivers grumbling, and to make matters worse, it snowed every day. This meant a soft trail, greater friction on the runners, and heavier pulling for the dogs; yet the drivers were fair through it all, and did their best for the animals.

Each night the dogs were attended to first. They ate before the drivers ate, and no man sought his sleeping-robe till he had seen to the feet of the dogs he drove. Still, their strength went down. Since the beginning of the winter they had travelled eighteen hundred miles, dragging sleds the whole weary distance; and eighteen hundred miles will tell upon life of the toughest. Buck stood it, keeping his mates up to their work and maintaining discipline, though he, too, was very tired. Billee cried and whimpered regularly in his sleep each night. Joe was sourer than ever, and Solleks was unapproachable, blind side or other side.

But it was Dave who suffered most of all. Something had gone wrong with him. He became more morose and irritable, and when camp was pitched at once made his nest, where his driver fed him. Once out of the harness and down, he did not get on his feet again till harness-up time in the morning. Sometimes, in the traces, when jerked by a sudden stoppage of the sled, or by straining to start it, he would cry out with pain. The driver examined him, but could find nothing. All the drivers became interested in his case. They talked it over at meal-time, and over their last pipes before going to bed, and one night they held a consultation. He was brought from his nest to the fire and was pressed and prodded till he cried out many times. Something was wrong inside, but they could locate no broken bones, could not make it out.

By the time Cassiar Bar was reached, he was so weak that he was falling repeatedly in the traces. The Scotch half-breed called a halt and took him out of the team, making the next dog, Sol-leks, fast to the sled. His intention was to rest Dave, letting him run free behind the sled. Sick as he was, Dave resented being taken out, grunting and growling while the traces were unfastened, and whimpering brokenheartedly when he saw Sol-leks in the position he had held and served so long. For the pride of trace and trail was his, and, sick unto death, he could not bear that another dog should do his work.

When the sled started, he floundered in the soft snow alongside the beaten trail, attacking Sol-leks with his teeth, rushing against him and trying to thrust him off into the soft snow on the other side, striving to leap inside his traces and get between him and the sled, and all the while whining and yelping and crying with grief and pain. The half-breed tried to drive him away with the whip; but he paid no heed to the stinging lash, and the man had not the heart to strike harder. Dave refused to run quietly on the trail behind the sled, where the going was easy, but continued to flounder alongside in the soft snow, where the going was most difficult, till exhausted. Then he fell, and lay where he fell, howling lugubriously as the long train of sleds churned by.

With the last remnant of his strength he managed to stagger along behind till the train made another stop, when he floundered past the sleds to his own, where he stood alongside Sol-leks. His driver lingered a moment to get a light for his pipe from the man behind. Then he returned and started his dogs. They swung out on the trail with remarkable lack of exertion, turned their heads uneasily, and stopped in surprise. The driver was surprised, too; the sled had not moved. He called his comrades to witness the sight. Dave had bitten through both of Sol-leks's traces, and was standing directly in front of the sled in his proper place.

He pleaded with his eyes to remain there. The driver was perplexed. His comrades talked of how a dog could break its heart through being denied the work that killed it, and recalled instances they had known, where dogs, too old for the toil, or injured, had died because they were cut out of the traces. Also, they held it a mercy, since Dave was to die anyway, that he should die in the traces, heart-easy and content. So he was harnessed in again, and proudly he pulled as of old, though more than once he cried out involuntarily from the bite of his inward hurt. Several times he fell down and was dragged in the traces, and once the sled ran upon him so that he limped thereafter in one of his hind legs.

But he held out till camp was reached, when his driver made a place for him by the fire. Morning found him too weak to travel. At harness-up time he tried to crawl to his driver. By convulsive efforts he got on his feet, staggered, and fell. Then he wormed his way forward slowly toward where the harnesses were being put on his mates. He would advance his fore legs and drag up his body with a sort of hitching movement, when he would advance his fore legs and hitch ahead again for a few more inches. His strength left him, and the last his mates saw of him he lay gasping in the snow and yearning toward them. But they could hear him mournfully howling till they passed out of sight behind a belt of river timber.

Here the train was halted. The Scotch half-breed slowly retraced his steps to the camp they had left. The men ceased talking. A revolver-shot rang out. The man came back hurriedly. The whips snapped, the bells tinkled merrily, the sleds churned along the trail; but Buck knew, and every dog knew, what had taken place behind the belt of river trees.

Chapter V. The Toil of Trace and Trail

Thirty days from the time it left Dawson, the Salt Water Mail, with Buck and his mates at the fore, arrived at Skaguay. They were in a wretched state, worn out and worn down. Buck's one hundred and forty pounds had dwindled to one hundred and fifteen. The rest of his mates, though lighter dogs, had relatively lost more weight than he. Pike, the malingerer, who, in his lifetime of deceit, had often successfully feigned a hurt leg, was now limping in earnest. Sol-leks was limping, and Dub was suffering from a wrenched shoulder-blade.

They were all terribly footsore. No spring or rebound was left in them. Their feet fell heavily on the trail, jarring their bodies and doubling the fatigue of a day's travel. There was nothing the matter with them except that they were dead tired. It was not the dead-tiredness that comes through brief and excessive effort, from which recovery is a matter of hours; but it was the dead-tiredness that comes through the slow and prolonged strength drainage of months of toil. There was no power of recuperation left, no reserve strength to call upon. It had been all used, the last least bit of it. Every muscle, every fibre, every cell, was tired, dead tired. And there was reason for it. In less than five months they had travelled twenty-five hundred miles, during the last eighteen hundred of which they had had but five days' rest. When they arrived at Skaguay they were apparently on their last legs. They could barely keep the traces taut, and on the down grades just managed to keep out of the way of the sled.

"Mush on, poor sore feets," the driver encouraged them as they tottered down the main street of Skaguay. "Dis is de las'. Den we get one long res'. Eh? For sure. One bully long res'."

The drivers confidently expected a long stopover. Themselves, they had covered twelve hundred miles with two days' rest, and in the nature of reason and common justice they deserved an interval of loafing. But so many were the men who had rushed into the Klondike, and so many were the sweethearts, wives, and kin that had not rushed in, that the congested mail was taking on Alpine proportions; also, there were official orders. Fresh batches of Hudson Bay dogs were to take the places of those worthless for the trail. The worthless ones were to be got rid of, and, since dogs count for little against dollars, they were to be sold.

Three days passed, by which time Buck and his mates found how really tired and weak they were. Then, on the morning of the fourth day, two men from the

States came along and bought them, harness and all, for a song. The men addressed each other as "Hal" and "Charles." Charles was a middle-aged, lightish-colored man, with weak and watery eyes and a mustache that twisted fiercely and vigorously up, giving the lie to the limply drooping lip it concealed. Hal was a youngster of nineteen or twenty, with a big Colt's revolver and a hunting-knife strapped about him on a belt that fairly bristled with cartridges. This belt was the most salient thing about him. It advertised his callowness—a callowness sheer and unutterable. Both men were manifestly out of place, and why such as they should adventure the North is part of the mystery of things that passes understanding.

Buck heard the chaffering, saw the money pass between the man and the Government agent, and knew that the Scotch half-breed and the mail-train drivers were passing out of his life on the heels of Perrault and Francois and the others who had gone before. When driven with his mates to the new owners' camp, Buck saw a slipshod and slovenly affair, tent half stretched, dishes unwashed, everything in disorder; also, he saw a woman. "Mercedes" the men called her. She was Charles's wife and Hal's sister—a nice family party.

Buck watched them apprehensively as they proceeded to take down the tent and load the sled. There was a great deal of effort about their manner, but no business-like method. The tent was rolled into an awkward bundle three times as large as it should have been. The tin dishes were packed away unwashed. Mercedes continually fluttered in the way of her men and kept up an unbroken chattering of remonstrance and advice. When they put a clothes-sack on the front of the sled, she suggested it should go on the back; and when they had put it on the back, and covered it over with a couple of other bundles, she discovered overlooked articles which could abide nowhere else but in that very sack, and they unloaded again.

Three men from a neighboring tent came out and looked on, grinning and winking at one another.

"You've got a right smart load as it is," said one of them; "and it's not me should tell you your business, but I wouldn't tote that tent along if I was you."

"Undreamed of!" cried Mercedes, throwing up her hands in dainty dismay. "However in the world could I manage without a tent?"

"It's springtime, and you won't get any more cold weather," the man replied.

She shook her head decidedly, and Charles and Hal put the last odds and ends on top the mountainous load.

"Think it'll ride?" one of the men asked.

"Why shouldn't it?" Charles demanded rather shortly.

"Oh, that's all right, that's all right," the man hastened meekly to say. "I was just a-wonderin', that is all. It seemed a mite top-heavy."

Charles turned his back and drew the lashings down as well as he could, which was not in the least well.

"An' of course the dogs can hike along all day with that contraption behind them," affirmed a second of the men.

"Certainly," said Hal, with freezing politeness, taking hold of the gee-pole with one hand and swinging his whip from the other. "Mush!" he shouted. "Mush on there!"

The dogs sprang against the breast-bands, strained hard for a few moments, then relaxed. They were unable to move the sled.

"The lazy brutes, I'll show them," he cried, preparing to lash out at them with the whip.

But Mercedes interfered, crying, "Oh, Hal, you mustn't," as she caught hold of the whip and wrenched it from him. "The poor dears! Now you must promise you won't be harsh with them for the rest of the trip, or I won't go a step."

"Precious lot you know about dogs," her brother sneered; "and I wish you'd leave me alone. They're lazy, I tell you, and you've got to whip them to get anything out of them. That's their way. You ask any one. Ask one of those men."

Mercedes looked at them imploringly, untold repugnance at sight of pain written in her pretty face.

"They're weak as water, if you want to know," came the reply from one of the men. "Plum tuckered out, that's what's the matter. They need a rest."

"Rest be blanked," said Hal, with his beardless lips; and Mercedes said, "Oh!" in pain and sorrow at the oath.

But she was a clannish creature, and rushed at once to the defence of her brother. "Never mind that man," she said pointedly. "You're driving our dogs, and you do what you think best with them."

Again Hal's whip fell upon the dogs. They threw themselves against the breast-bands, dug their feet into the packed snow, got down low to it, and put forth all their strength. The sled held as though it were an anchor. After two efforts, they stood still, panting. The whip was whistling savagely, when once more Mercedes interfered. She dropped on her knees before Buck, with tears in her eyes, and put her arms around his neck.

"You poor, poor dears," she cried sympathetically, "why don't you pull hard?— then you wouldn't be whipped." Buck did not like her, but he was feeling too miserable to resist her, taking it as part of the day's miserable work.

One of the onlookers, who had been clenching his teeth to suppress hot speech, now spoke up:—

"It's not that I care a whoop what becomes of you, but for the dogs' sakes I just want to tell you, you can help them a mighty lot by breaking out that sled. The runners are froze fast. Throw your weight against the gee-pole, right and left, and break it out."

A third time the attempt was made, but this time, following the advice, Hal broke out the runners which had been frozen to the snow. The overloaded and unwieldy sled forged ahead, Buck and his mates struggling frantically under the rain of blows. A hundred yards ahead the path turned and sloped steeply into the main street. It would have required an experienced man to keep the top-heavy sled upright, and Hal was not such a man. As they swung on the turn the sled went over, spilling half its load through the loose lashings. The dogs never stopped. The lightened sled bounded on its side behind them. They were angry because of the ill treatment they had received and the unjust load. Buck was raging. He broke into a run, the team following his lead. Hal cried "Whoa! whoa!" but they gave no heed. He tripped and was pulled off his feet. The capsized sled ground over him, and the dogs dashed on up the street, adding to the gayety of Skaguay as they scattered the remainder of the outfit along its chief thoroughfare.

Kind-hearted citizens caught the dogs and gathered up the scattered belongings. Also, they gave advice. Half the load and twice the dogs, if they ever expected to reach Dawson, was what was said. Hal and his sister and brother-in-law listened unwillingly, pitched tent, and overhauled the outfit. Canned goods were turned out that made men laugh, for canned goods on the Long Trail is a thing to dream about. "Blankets for a hotel" quoth one of the men who laughed and helped. "Half as many is too much; get rid of them. Throw away that tent, and all those dishes,—who's going to wash them, anyway? Good Lord, do you think you're travelling on a Pullman?"

And so it went, the inexorable elimination of the superfluous. Mercedes cried when her clothes-bags were dumped on the ground and article after article was thrown out. She cried in general, and she cried in particular over each discarded thing. She clasped hands about knees, rocking back and forth broken-heartedly. She averred she would not go an inch, not for a dozen Charleses. She appealed to everybody and to everything, finally wiping her eyes and proceeding to cast out even articles of apparel that were imperative necessaries. And in her zeal, when she had finished with her own, she attacked the belongings of her men and went through them like a tornado.

This accomplished, the outfit, though cut in half, was still a formidable bulk. Charles and Hal went out in the evening and bought six Outside dogs. These, added to the six of the original team, and Teek and Koona, the huskies obtained at the Rink Rapids on the record trip, brought the team up to fourteen. But the Outside dogs, though practically broken in since their landing, did not amount to much. Three were short-haired pointers, one was a Newfoundland, and the other two were mongrels of indeterminate breed. They did not seem to know anything, these newcomers. Buck and his comrades looked upon them with disgust, and though he speedily taught them their places and what not to do, he could not teach them what to do. They did not take kindly to trace and trail. With the exception of the two mongrels, they were bewildered and spirit-broken by the strange savage environment in which they found themselves and by the ill treatment they had received. The two mongrels were without spirit at all; bones were the only things breakable about them.

With the newcomers hopeless and forlorn, and the old team worn out by twenty-five hundred miles of continuous trail, the outlook was anything but bright. The two men, however, were quite cheerful. And they were proud, too. They were doing the thing in style, with fourteen dogs. They had seen other sleds depart over the Pass for Dawson, or come in from Dawson, but never had they seen a sled with so many as fourteen dogs. In the nature of Arctic travel there was a reason why fourteen dogs should not drag one sled, and that was that one sled could not carry the food for fourteen dogs. But Charles and Hal did not know this. They had worked the trip out with a pencil, so much to a dog, so many dogs, so many days, Q.E.D. Mercedes looked over their shoulders and nodded comprehensively, it was all so very simple.

Late next morning Buck led the long team up the street. There was nothing lively about it, no snap or go in him and his fellows. They were starting dead weary. Four times he had covered the distance between Salt Water and Dawson, and the knowledge that, jaded and tired, he was facing the same trail once more, made him bitter. His heart was not in the work, nor was the heart of any dog. The Outsides were timid and frightened, the Insides without confidence in their masters.

Buck felt vaguely that there was no depending upon these two men and the woman. They did not know how to do anything, and as the days went by it became apparent that they could not learn. They were slack in all things, without order or discipline. It took them half the night to pitch a slovenly camp, and half the morning to break that camp and get the sled loaded in fashion so slovenly that for the rest of the day they were occupied in stopping and rearranging the load. Some days they did not make ten miles. On other days they were unable to get started at all. And on no day did they succeed in making more than half the distance used by the men as a basis in their dog-food computation.

It was inevitable that they should go short on dog-food. But they hastened it by overfeeding, bringing the day nearer when underfeeding would commence. The Outside dogs, whose digestions had not been trained by chronic famine to make the most of little, had voracious appetites. And when, in addition to this, the worn-out huskies pulled weakly, Hal decided that the orthodox ration was too small. He doubled it. And to cap it all, when Mercedes, with tears in her pretty eyes and a quaver in her throat, could not cajole him into giving the dogs still more, she stole from the fish-sacks and fed them slyly. But it was not food that Buck and the huskies needed, but rest. And though they were making poor time, the heavy load they dragged sapped their strength severely.

Then came the underfeeding. Hal awoke one day to the fact that his dog-food was half gone and the distance only quarter covered; further, that for love or money no additional dog-food was to be obtained. So he cut down even the orthodox ration and tried to increase the day's travel. His sister and brother-in-law seconded him; but they were frustrated by their heavy outfit and their own incompetence. It was a simple matter to give the dogs less food; but it was impossible to make the dogs travel faster, while their own inability to get under way earlier in the morning prevented them from travelling longer hours. Not only did they not know how to work dogs, but they did not know how to work themselves.

The first to go was Dub. Poor blundering thief that he was, always getting caught and punished, he had none the less been a faithful worker. His wrenched shoulder-blade, untreated and unrested, went from bad to worse, till finally Hal shot him with the big Colt's revolver. It is a saying of the country that an Outside dog starves to death on the ration of the husky, so the six Outside dogs under Buck could do no less than die on half the ration of the husky. The Newfoundland went first, followed by the three short-haired pointers, the two mongrels hanging more grittily on to life, but going in the end.

By this time all the amenities and gentlenesses of the Southland had fallen away from the three people. Shorn of its glamour and romance, Arctic travel became to them a reality too harsh for their manhood and womanhood. Mercedes ceased weeping over the dogs, being too occupied with weeping over herself and with quarrelling with her husband and brother. To quarrel was the one thing they were never too weary to do. Their irritability arose out of their misery, increased with it, doubled upon it, outdistanced it. The wonderful patience of the trail which comes to men who toil hard and suffer sore, and remain sweet of speech and kindly, did not come to these two men and the woman. They had no inkling of such a patience. They were stiff and in pain; their muscles ached, their bones ached, their very hearts ached; and because of this they became sharp of speech, and hard words were first on their lips in the morning and last at night.

Charles and Hal wrangled whenever Mercedes gave them a chance. It was the cherished belief of each that he did more than his share of the work, and neither forbore to speak this belief at every opportunity. Sometimes Mercedes sided with her husband, sometimes with her brother. The result was a beautiful and unending family quarrel. Starting from a dispute as to which should chop a few sticks for the fire (a dispute which concerned only Charles and Hal), presently would be lugged in the rest of the family, fathers, mothers, uncles, cousins, people thousands of miles away, and some of them dead. That Hal's views on art, or the sort of society plays his mother's brother wrote, should have anything to do with the chopping of a few sticks of firewood, passes comprehension; nevertheless the quarrel was as likely to tend in that direction as in the direction of Charles's political prejudices. And that Charles's sister's tale-bearing tongue should be relevant to the building of a Yukon fire, was apparent only to Mercedes, who disburdened herself of copious opinions upon that topic, and incidentally upon a few other traits unpleasantly peculiar to her husband's family. In the meantime the fire remained unbuilt, the camp half pitched, and the dogs unfed.

Mercedes nursed a special grievance—the grievance of sex. She was pretty and soft, and had been chivalrously treated all her days. But the present treatment by her husband and brother was everything save chivalrous. It was her custom to be helpless. They complained. Upon which impeachment of what to her was her most essential sex-prerogative, she made their lives unendurable. She no longer considered the dogs, and because she was sore and tired, she persisted in riding on the sled. She was pretty and soft, but she weighed one hundred and twenty pounds—a lusty last straw to the load dragged by the weak and starving animals. She rode for days, till they fell in the traces and the sled stood still. Charles and Hal begged her to get off and walk, pleaded with her, entreated, the while she wept and importuned Heaven with a recital of their brutality.

On one occasion they took her off the sled by main strength. They never did it again. She let her legs go limp like a spoiled child, and sat down on the trail. They went on their way, but she did not move. After they had travelled three miles they unloaded the sled, came back for her, and by main strength put her on the sled again.

In the excess of their own misery they were callous to the suffering of their animals. Hal's theory, which he practised on others, was that one must get hardened. He had started out preaching it to his sister and brother-in-law. Failing there, he hammered it into the dogs with a club. At the Five Fingers the dog-food gave out, and a toothless old squaw offered to trade them a few pounds of frozen horse-hide for the Colt's revolver that kept the big hunting-knife company at Hal's hip. A poor substitute for food was this hide, just as it had been stripped from the starved horses of the cattlemen six months back. In its frozen state it was more like strips of galvanized iron, and when a dog wrestled it into his stomach it thawed into thin and innutritious leathery strings and into a mass of short hair, irritating and indigestible.

And through it all Buck staggered along at the head of the team as in a nightmare. He pulled when he could; when he could no longer pull, he fell down and remained down till blows from whip or club drove him to his feet again. All the stiffness and gloss had gone out of his beautiful furry coat. The hair hung down, limp and draggled, or matted with dried blood where Hal's club had bruised him. His muscles had wasted away to knotty strings, and the flesh pads had disappeared, so that each rib and every bone in his frame were outlined cleanly through the loose hide that was wrinkled in folds of emptiness. It was heartbreaking, only Buck's heart was unbreakable. The man in the red sweater had proved that.

As it was with Buck, so was it with his mates. They were perambulating skeletons. There were seven all together, including him. In their very great misery they had become insensible to the bite of the lash or the bruise of the club. The pain of the beating was dull and distant, just as the things their eyes saw and their ears heard seemed dull and distant. They were not half living, or quarter living. They were simply so many bags of bones in which sparks of life fluttered faintly. When a halt was made, they dropped down in the traces like dead dogs, and the spark dimmed and paled and seemed to go out. And when the club or whip fell upon them, the spark fluttered feebly up, and they tottered to their feet and staggered on.

There came a day when Billee, the good-natured, fell and could not rise. Hal had traded off his revolver, so he took the axe and knocked Billee on the head as he lay in the traces, then cut the carcass out of the harness and dragged it to one side. Buck saw, and his mates saw, and they knew that this thing was very close to them. On the next day Koona went, and but five of them remained: Joe, too far gone to be malignant; Pike, crippled and limping, only half conscious and not conscious enough longer to malinger; Sol-leks, the one-eyed, still faithful to the toil of trace and trail, and mournful in that he had so little strength with which to pull; Teek, who had not travelled so far that winter and who was now beaten more than the others because he was fresher; and Buck, still at the head of the team, but no longer enforcing discipline or striving to enforce it, blind with weakness half the time and keeping the trail by the loom of it and by the dim feel of his feet.

It was beautiful spring weather, but neither dogs nor humans were aware of it. Each day the sun rose earlier and set later. It was dawn by three in the morning, and twilight lingered till nine at night. The whole long day was a blaze of sunshine. The ghostly winter silence had given way to the great spring murmur of awakening life. This murmur arose from all the land, fraught with the joy of living. It came from the things that lived and moved again, things which had been as dead and which had not moved during the long months of frost. The sap was rising in the pines. The willows and aspens were bursting out in young buds. Shrubs and vines were putting on fresh garbs of green. Crickets sang in the nights, and in the days all manner of creeping, crawling things rustled forth into the sun. Partridges and woodpeckers were booming and knocking in the forest. Squirrels were chattering, birds singing, and overhead honked the wild-fowl driving up from the south in cunning wedges that split the air.

From every hill slope came the trickle of running water, the music of unseen fountains. All things were thawing, bending, snapping. The Yukon was straining to break loose the ice that bound it down. It ate away from beneath; the sun ate from above. Air-holes formed, fissures sprang and spread apart, while thin sections of ice fell through bodily into the river. And amid all this bursting, rending, throbbing of awakening life, under the blazing sun and through the soft-sighing breezes, like wayfarers to death, staggered the two men, the woman, and the huskies.

With the dogs falling, Mercedes weeping and riding, Hal swearing innocuously, and Charles's eyes wistfully watering, they staggered into John Thornton's camp at the mouth of White River. When they halted, the dogs dropped down as though they had all been struck dead. Mercedes dried her eyes and looked at John Thornton. Charles sat down on a log to rest. He sat down very slowly and painstakingly what of his great stiffness. Hal did the talking. John Thornton was whittling the last touches on an axe-handle he had made from a stick of birch. He whittled and listened, gave monosyllabic replies, and, when it was asked, terse advice. He knew the breed, and he gave his advice in the certainty that it would not be followed.

"They told us up above that the bottom was dropping out of the trail and that the best thing for us to do was to lay over," Hal said in response to Thornton's warning to take no more chances on the rotten ice. "They told us we couldn't make White River, and here we are." This last with a sneering ring of triumph in it.

"And they told you true," John Thornton answered. "The bottom's likely to drop out at any moment. Only fools, with the blind luck of fools, could have made it. I tell you straight, I wouldn't risk my carcass on that ice for all the gold in Alaska."

"That's because you're not a fool, I suppose," said Hal. "All the same, we'll go on to Dawson." He uncoiled his whip. "Get up there, Buck! Hi! Get up there! Mush on!"

Thornton went on whittling. It was idle, he knew, to get between a fool and his folly; while two or three fools more or less would not alter the scheme of things.

But the team did not get up at the command. It had long since passed into the stage where blows were required to rouse it. The whip flashed out, here and there, on its merciless errands. John Thornton compressed his lips. Sol-leks was the first to crawl to his feet. Teek followed. Joe came next, yelping with pain. Pike made painful efforts. Twice he fell over, when half up, and on the third attempt managed to rise. Buck made no effort. He lay quietly where he had fallen. The lash bit into him again and again, but he neither whined nor struggled. Several times Thornton started, as though to speak, but changed his mind. A moisture came into his eyes, and, as the whipping continued, he arose and walked irresolutely up and down.

This was the first time Buck had failed, in itself a sufficient reason to drive Hal into a rage. He exchanged the whip for the customary club. Buck refused to move under the rain of heavier blows which now fell upon him. Like his mates, he was barely able to get up, but, unlike them, he had made up his mind not to get up. He had a vague feeling of impending doom. This had been strong upon him when he pulled in to the bank, and it had not departed from him. What of the thin and rotten ice he had felt under his feet all day, it seemed that he sensed disaster close at hand, out there ahead on the ice where his master was trying to drive him. He refused to stir. So greatly had he suffered, and so far gone was he, that the blows did not hurt much. And as they continued to fall upon him, the spark of life within flickered and went down. It was nearly out. He felt strangely numb. As though from a great distance, he was aware that he was being beaten. The last sensations of pain left him. He no longer felt anything, though very faintly he could hear the impact of the club upon his body. But it was no longer his body, it seemed so far away.

And then, suddenly, without warning, uttering a cry that was inarticulate and more like the cry of an animal, John Thornton sprang upon the man who wielded the club. Hal was hurled backward, as though struck by a falling tree. Mercedes screamed. Charles looked on wistfully, wiped his watery eyes, but did not get up because of his stiffness.

John Thornton stood over Buck, struggling to control himself, too convulsed with rage to speak.

"If you strike that dog again, I'll kill you," he at last managed to say in a choking voice.

"It's my dog," Hal replied, wiping the blood from his mouth as he came back. "Get out of my way, or I'll fix you. I'm going to Dawson."

Thornton stood between him and Buck, and evinced no intention of getting out of the way. Hal drew his long hunting-knife. Mercedes screamed, cried, laughed, and manifested the chaotic abandonment of hysteria. Thornton rapped Hal's knuckles with the axe-handle, knocking the knife to the ground. He rapped his knuckles again as he tried to pick it up. Then he stooped, picked it up himself, and with two strokes cut Buck's traces.

Hal had no fight left in him. Besides, his hands were full with his sister, or his arms, rather; while Buck was too near dead to be of further use in hauling the sled. A few minutes later they pulled out from the bank and down the river. Buck heard them go and raised his head to see, Pike was leading, Sol-leks was at the wheel, and between were Joe and Teek. They were limping and staggering. Mercedes was riding the loaded sled. Hal guided at the gee-pole, and Charles stumbled along in the rear.

As Buck watched them, Thornton knelt beside him and with rough, kindly hands searched for broken bones. By the time his search had disclosed nothing more than many bruises and a state of terrible starvation, the sled was a quarter of a mile away. Dog and man watched it crawling along over the ice. Suddenly, they saw its back end drop down, as into a rut, and the gee-pole, with Hal clinging to it, jerk into the air. Mercedes's scream came to their ears. They saw Charles turn and make one step to run back, and then a whole section of ice give way and dogs and humans disappear. A yawning hole was all that was to be seen. The bottom had dropped out of the trail.

John Thornton and Buck looked at each other.

"You poor devil," said John Thornton, and Buck licked his hand.

Chapter VI. For the Love of a Man

When John Thornton froze his feet in the previous December his partners had made him comfortable and left him to get well, going on themselves up the river to get out a raft of saw-logs for Dawson. He was still limping slightly at the time he rescued Buck, but with the continued warm weather even the slight limp left him. And here, lying by the river bank through the long spring days, watching the running water, listening lazily to the songs of birds and the hum of nature, Buck slowly won back his strength.

A rest comes very good after one has travelled three thousand miles, and it must be confessed that Buck waxed lazy as his wounds healed, his muscles swelled out, and the flesh came back to cover his bones. For that matter, they were all loafing,— Buck, John Thornton, and Skeet and Nig,—waiting for the raft to come that was to carry them down to Dawson. Skeet was a little Irish setter who early made friends with Buck, who, in a dying condition, was unable to resent her first advances. She had the doctor trait which some dogs possess; and as a mother cat washes her kittens, so she washed and cleansed Buck's wounds. Regularly, each morning after he had finished his breakfast, she performed her self-appointed task, till he came to look for her ministrations as much as he did for Thornton's. Nig, equally friendly, though less demonstrative, was a huge black dog, half bloodhound and half deerhound, with eyes that laughed and a boundless good nature.

To Buck's surprise these dogs manifested no jealousy toward him. They seemed to share the kindliness and largeness of John Thornton. As Buck grew stronger they enticed him into all sorts of ridiculous games, in which Thornton himself could not forbear to join; and in this fashion Buck romped through his convalescence and into a new existence. Love, genuine passionate love, was his for the first time. This he had never experienced at Judge Miller's down in the sun-kissed Santa Clara Valley. With the Judge's sons, hunting and tramping, it had been a working partnership; with the Judge's grandsons, a sort of pompous guardianship; and with the Judge himself, a stately and dignified friendship. But love that was feverish and burning, that was adoration, that was madness, it had taken John Thornton to arouse.

This man had saved his life, which was something; but, further, he was the ideal master. Other men saw to the welfare of their dogs from a sense of duty and business expediency; he saw to the welfare of his as if they were his own children, because he could not help it. And he saw further. He never forgot a kindly greeting or a cheering word, and to sit down for a long talk with them ("gas" he called it) was as much his delight as theirs. He had a way of taking Buck's head roughly between his hands, and resting his own head upon Buck's, of shaking him back and forth, the while calling him ill names that to Buck were love names. Buck knew no greater joy than that rough embrace and the sound of murmured oaths, and at each jerk back and forth it seemed that his heart would be shaken out of his body so great was its ecstasy. And when, released, he sprang to his feet, his mouth laughing, his eyes eloquent, his throat vibrant with unuttered sound, and in that fashion remained without movement, John Thornton would reverently exclaim, "God! you can all but speak!"

Buck had a trick of love expression that was akin to hurt. He would often seize Thornton's hand in his mouth and close so fiercely that the flesh bore the impress of his teeth for some time afterward. And as Buck understood the oaths to be love words, so the man understood this feigned bite for a caress.

For the most part, however, Buck's love was expressed in adoration. While he went wild with happiness when Thornton touched him or spoke to him, he did not seek these tokens. Unlike Skeet, who was wont to shove her nose under Thornton's hand and nudge and nudge till petted, or Nig, who would stalk up and rest his great head on Thornton's knee, Buck was content to adore at a distance. He would lie by the hour, eager, alert, at Thornton's feet, looking up into his face, dwelling upon it, studying it, following with keenest interest each fleeting expression, every movement or change of feature. Or, as chance might have it, he would lie farther away, to the side or rear, watching the outlines of the man and the occasional movements of his body. And often, such was the communion in which they lived, the strength of Buck's gaze would draw John Thornton's head around, and he would return the gaze, without speech, his heart shining out of his eyes as Buck's heart shone out.

For a long time after his rescue, Buck did not like Thornton to get out of his sight. From the moment he left the tent to when he entered it again, Buck would follow at his heels. His transient masters since he had come into the Northland had bred in him a fear that no master could be permanent. He was afraid that Thornton would pass out of his life as Perrault and Francois and the Scotch half-breed had passed out. Even in the night, in his dreams, he was haunted by this fear. At such times he would shake off sleep and creep through the chill to the flap of the tent, where he would stand and listen to the sound of his master's breathing.

But in spite of this great love he bore John Thornton, which seemed to bespeak the soft civilizing influence, the strain of the primitive, which the Northland had aroused in him, remained alive and active. Faithfulness and devotion, things born of fire and roof, were his; yet he retained his wildness and wiliness. He was a thing of the wild, come in from the wild to sit by John Thornton's fire, rather than a dog of the soft Southland stamped with the marks of generations of civilization. Because of his very great love, he could not steal from this man, but from any other man, in any other camp, he did not hesitate an instant; while the cunning with which he stole enabled him to escape detection.

His face and body were scored by the teeth of many dogs, and he fought as fiercely as ever and more shrewdly. Skeet and Nig were too good-natured for quarrelling,—besides, they belonged to John Thornton; but the strange dog, no matter what the breed or valor, swiftly acknowledged Buck's supremacy or found himself struggling for life with a terrible antagonist. And Buck was merciless. He had learned well the law of club and fang, and he never forewent an advantage or drew back from a foe he had started on the way to Death. He had lessoned from Spitz, and from the chief fighting dogs of the police and mail, and knew there was no middle course. He must master or be mastered; while to show mercy was a weakness. Mercy did not exist in the primordial life. It was misunderstood for fear, and such misunderstandings made for death. Kill or be killed, eat or be eaten, was the law; and this mandate, down out of the depths of Time, he obeyed.

He was older than the days he had seen and the breaths he had drawn. He linked the past with the present, and the eternity behind him throbbed through him in a mighty rhythm to which he swayed as the tides and seasons swayed. He sat by John Thornton's fire, a broad-breasted dog, white-fanged and long-furred; but behind him were the shades of all manner of dogs, half-wolves and wild wolves, urgent and prompting, tasting the savor of the meat he ate, thirsting for the water he drank, scenting the wind with him, listening with him and telling him the sounds made by the wild life in the forest, dictating his moods, directing his actions, lying down to sleep with him when he lay down, and dreaming with him and beyond him and becoming themselves the stuff of his dreams.

So peremptorily did these shades beckon him, that each day mankind and the claims of mankind slipped farther from him. Deep in the forest a call was sounding, and as often as he heard this call, mysteriously thrilling and luring, he felt compelled to turn his back upon the fire and the beaten earth around it, and to plunge into the forest, and on and on, he knew not where or why; nor did he wonder where or why, the call sounding imperiously, deep in the forest. But as often as he gained the soft unbroken earth and the green shade, the love for John Thornton drew him back to the fire again.

Thornton alone held him. The rest of mankind was as nothing. Chance travellers might praise or pet him; but he was cold under it all, and from a too demonstrative man he would get up and walk away. When Thornton's partners, Hans and Pete, arrived on the long-expected raft, Buck refused to notice them till he learned they were close to Thornton; after that he tolerated them in a passive sort of way, accepting favors from them as though he favored them by accepting. They were of the same large type as Thornton, living close to the earth, thinking simply and seeing clearly; and ere they swung the raft into the big eddy by the saw-mill at Dawson, they understood Buck and his ways, and did not insist upon an intimacy such as obtained with Skeet and Nig.

For Thornton, however, his love seemed to grow and grow. He, alone among men, could put a pack upon Buck's back in the summer travelling. Nothing was too great for Buck to do, when Thornton commanded. One day (they had grub-staked themselves from the proceeds of the raft and left Dawson for the head-waters of the Tanana) the men and dogs were sitting on the crest of a cliff which fell away, straight down, to naked bed-rock three hundred feet below. John Thornton was sitting near the edge, Buck at his shoulder. A thoughtless whim seized Thornton, and he drew the attention of Hans and Pete to the experiment he had in mind. "Jump, Buck!" he commanded, sweeping his arm out and over the chasm. The next instant he was grappling with Buck on the extreme edge, while Hans and Pete were dragging them back into safety.

"It's uncanny," Pete said, after it was over and they had caught their speech.

Thornton shook his head. "No, it is splendid, and it is terrible, too. Do you know, it sometimes makes me afraid."

"I'm not hankering to be the man that lays hands on you while he's around," Pete announced conclusively, nodding his head toward Buck.

"Py Jingo!" was Hans's contribution. "Not mineself either."

It was at Circle City, ere the year was out, that Pete's apprehensions were realized. "Black" Burton, a man evil-tempered and malicious, had been picking a quarrel with a tenderfoot at the bar, when Thornton stepped good-naturedly between. Buck, as was his custom, was lying in a corner, head on paws, watching his master's every action. Burton struck out, without warning, straight from the shoulder. Thornton was sent spinning, and saved himself from falling only by clutching the rail of the bar.

Those who were looking on heard what was neither bark nor yelp, but a something which is best described as a roar, and they saw Buck's body rise up in the air as he left the floor for Burton's throat. The man saved his life by instinctively throwing out his arm, but was hurled backward to the floor with Buck on top of him. Buck loosed his teeth from the flesh of the arm and drove in again for the throat. This time the man succeeded only in partly blocking, and his throat was torn open. Then the crowd was upon Buck, and he was driven off; but while a surgeon checked the bleeding, he prowled up and down, growling furiously, attempting to rush in, and being forced back by an array of hostile clubs. A "miners' meeting," called on the spot, decided that the dog had sufficient provocation, and Buck was discharged. But his reputation was made, and from that day his name spread through every camp in Alaska.

Later on, in the fall of the year, he saved John Thornton's life in quite another fashion. The three partners were lining a long and narrow poling-boat down a bad stretch of rapids on the Forty-Mile Creek. Hans and Pete moved along the bank, snubbing with a thin Manila rope from tree to tree, while Thornton remained in the boat, helping its descent by means of a pole, and shouting directions to the shore. Buck, on the bank, worried and anxious, kept abreast of the boat, his eyes never off his master.

At a particularly bad spot, where a ledge of barely submerged rocks jutted out into the river, Hans cast off the rope, and, while Thornton poled the boat out into the stream, ran down the bank with the end in his hand to snub the boat when it had cleared the ledge. This it did, and was flying down-stream in a current as swift as a mill-race, when Hans checked it with the rope and checked too suddenly. The boat flirted over and snubbed in to the bank bottom up, while Thornton, flung sheer out of it, was carried down-stream toward the worst part of the rapids, a stretch of wild water in which no swimmer could live.

Buck had sprung in on the instant; and at the end of three hundred yards, amid a mad swirl of water, he overhauled Thornton. When he felt him grasp his tail, Buck headed for the bank, swimming with all his splendid strength. But the progress shoreward was slow; the progress down-stream amazingly rapid. From below came the fatal roaring where the wild current went wilder and was rent in shreds and spray by the rocks which thrust through like the teeth of an enormous comb. The suck of the water as it took the beginning of the last steep pitch was frightful, and Thornton knew that the shore was impossible. He scraped furiously over a rock, bruised across a second, and struck a third with crushing force. He clutched its slippery top with both hands, releasing Buck, and above the roar of the churning water shouted: "Go, Buck! Go!"

Buck could not hold his own, and swept on down-stream, struggling desperately, but unable to win back. When he heard Thornton's command repeated, he partly reared out of the water, throwing his head high, as though for a last look, then turned obediently toward the bank. He swam powerfully and was dragged ashore by Pete and Hans at the very point where swimming ceased to be possible and destruction began.

They knew that the time a man could cling to a slippery rock in the face of that driving current was a matter of minutes, and they ran as fast as they could up the bank to a point far above where Thornton was hanging on. They attached the line with which they had been snubbing the boat to Buck's neck and shoulders, being careful that it should neither strangle him nor impede his swimming, and launched him into the stream. He struck out boldly, but not straight enough into the stream. He discovered the mistake too late, when Thornton was abreast of him and a bare half-dozen strokes away while he was being carried helplessly past.

Hans promptly snubbed with the rope, as though Buck were a boat. The rope thus tightening on him in the sweep of the current, he was jerked under the surface, and under the surface he remained till his body struck against the bank and he was hauled out. He was half drowned, and Hans and Pete threw themselves upon him, pounding the breath into him and the water out of him. He staggered to his feet and fell down. The faint sound of Thornton's voice came to them, and though they could not make out the words of it, they knew that he was in his extremity. His master's voice acted on Buck like an electric shock, He sprang to his feet and ran up the bank ahead of the men to the point of his previous departure.

Again the rope was attached and he was launched, and again he struck out, but this time straight into the stream. He had miscalculated once, but he would not be guilty of it a second time. Hans paid out the rope, permitting no slack, while Pete kept it clear of coils. Buck held on till he was on a line straight above Thornton; then he turned, and with the speed of an express train headed down upon him. Thornton saw him coming, and, as Buck struck him like a battering ram, with the whole force of the current behind him, he reached up and closed with both arms around the shaggy neck. Hans snubbed the rope around the tree, and Buck and Thornton were jerked under the water. Strangling, suffocating, sometimes one uppermost and sometimes the other, dragging over the jagged bottom, smashing against rocks and snags, they veered in to the bank.

Thornton came to, belly downward and being violently propelled back and forth across a drift log by Hans and Pete. His first glance was for Buck, over whose limp and apparently lifeless body Nig was setting up a howl, while Skeet was licking the wet face and closed eyes. Thornton was himself bruised and battered, and he went carefully over Buck's body, when he had been brought around, finding three broken ribs.

"That settles it," he announced. "We camp right here." And camp they did, till Buck's ribs knitted and he was able to travel.

That winter, at Dawson, Buck performed another exploit, not so heroic, perhaps, but one that put his name many notches higher on the totem-pole of Alaskan fame. This exploit was particularly gratifying to the three men; for they stood in need of the outfit which it furnished, and were enabled to make a long-desired trip into the virgin East, where miners had not yet appeared. It was brought about by a conversation in the Eldorado Saloon, in which men waxed boastful of their favorite dogs. Buck, because of his record, was the target for these men, and Thornton was driven stoutly to defend him. At the end of half an hour one man stated that his dog could start a sled with five hundred pounds and walk off with it; a second bragged six hundred for his dog; and a third, seven hundred.

"Pooh! pooh!" said John Thornton; "Buck can start a thousand pounds."

"And break it out? and walk off with it for a hundred yards?" demanded Matthewson, a Bonanza King, he of the seven hundred vaunt.

"And break it out, and walk off with it for a hundred yards," John Thornton said coolly.

"Well," Matthewson said, slowly and deliberately, so that all could hear, "I've got a thousand dollars that says he can't. And there it is." So saying, he slammed a sack of gold dust of the size of a bologna sausage down upon the bar.

Nobody spoke. Thornton's bluff, if bluff it was, had been called. He could feel a flush of warm blood creeping up his face. His tongue had tricked him. He did not know whether Buck could start a thousand pounds. Half a ton! The enormousness of it appalled him. He had great faith in Buck's strength and had often thought him capable of starting such a load; but never, as now, had he faced the possibility of it, the eyes of a dozen men fixed upon him, silent and waiting. Further, he had no thousand dollars; nor had Hans or Pete.

"I've got a sled standing outside now, with twenty fiftypound sacks of flour on it," Matthewson went on with brutal directness; "so don't let that hinder you."

Thornton did not reply. He did not know what to say. He glanced from face to face in the absent way of a man who has lost the power of thought and is seeking somewhere to find the thing that will start it going again. The face of Jim O'Brien, a Mastodon King and old-time comrade, caught his eyes. It was as a cue to him, seeming to rouse him to do what he would never have dreamed of doing.

"Can you lend me a thousand?" he asked, almost in a whisper.

"Sure," answered O'Brien, thumping down a plethoric sack by the side of Matthewson's. "Though it's little faith I'm having, John, that the beast can do the trick."

The Eldorado emptied its occupants into the street to see the test. The tables were deserted, and the dealers and gamekeepers came forth to see the outcome of the wager and to lay odds. Several hundred men, furred and mittened, banked around the sled within easy distance. Matthewson's sled, loaded with a thousand pounds of flour, had been standing for a couple of hours, and in the intense cold (it was sixty below zero) the runners had frozen fast to the hard-packed snow. Men offered odds of two to one that Buck could not budge the sled. A quibble arose concerning the phrase "break out." O'Brien contended it was Thornton's privilege to knock the runners loose, leaving Buck to "break it out" from a dead standstill. Matthewson insisted that the phrase included breaking the runners from the frozen grip of the snow. A majority of the men who had witnessed the making of the bet decided in his favor, whereat the odds went up to three to one against Buck.

There were no takers. Not a man believed him capable of the feat. Thornton had been hurried into the wager, heavy with doubt; and now that he looked at the sled itself, the concrete fact, with the regular team of ten dogs curled up in the snow before it, the more impossible the task appeared. Matthewson waxed jubilant.

"Three to one!" he proclaimed. "I'll lay you another thousand at that figure, Thornton. What d'ye say?"

Thornton's doubt was strong in his face, but his fighting spirit was aroused—the fighting spirit that soars above odds, fails to recognize the impossible, and is deaf to all save the clamor for battle. He called Hans and Pete to him. Their sacks were slim, and with his own the three partners could rake together only two hundred dollars. In the ebb of their fortunes, this sum was their total capital; yet they laid it unhesitatingly against Matthewson's six hundred.

The team of ten dogs was unhitched, and Buck, with his own harness, was put into the sled. He had caught the contagion of the excitement, and he felt that in some way he must do a great thing for John Thornton. Murmurs of admiration at his splendid appearance went up. He was in perfect condition, without an ounce of superfluous flesh, and the one hundred and fifty pounds that he weighed were so many pounds of grit and virility. His furry coat shone with the sheen of silk. Down the neck and across the shoulders, his mane, in repose as it was, half bristled and seemed to lift with every movement, as though excess of vigor made each particular hair alive and active. The great breast and heavy fore legs were no more than in proportion with the rest of the body, where the muscles showed in tight rolls underneath the skin. Men felt these muscles and proclaimed them hard as iron, and the odds went down to two to one.

"Gad, sir! Gad, sir!" stuttered a member of the latest dynasty, a king of the Skookum Benches. "I offer you eight hundred for him, sir, before the test, sir; eight hundred just as he stands."

Thornton shook his head and stepped to Buck's side.

"You must stand off from him," Matthewson protested. "Free play and plenty of room."

The crowd fell silent; only could be heard the voices of the gamblers vainly offering two to one. Everybody acknowledged Buck a magnificent animal, but twenty fifty-pound sacks of flour bulked too large in their eyes for them to loosen their pouch-strings.

Thornton knelt down by Buck's side. He took his head in his two hands and rested cheek on cheek. He did not playfully shake him, as was his wont, or murmur soft love curses; but he whispered in his ear. "As you love me, Buck. As you love me," was what he whispered. Buck whined with suppressed eagerness.

The crowd was watching curiously. The affair was growing mysterious. It seemed like a conjuration. As Thornton got to his feet, Buck seized his mittened hand between his jaws, pressing in with his teeth and releasing slowly, half-reluctantly. It was the answer, in terms, not of speech, but of love. Thornton stepped well back.

"Now, Buck," he said.

Buck tightened the traces, then slacked them for a matter of several inches. It was the way he had learned.

"Gee!" Thornton's voice rang out, sharp in the tense silence.

Buck swung to the right, ending the movement in a plunge that took up the slack and with a sudden jerk arrested his one hundred and fifty pounds. The load quivered, and from under the runners arose a crisp crackling.

"Haw!" Thornton commanded.

Buck duplicated the manoeuvre, this time to the left. The crackling turned into a snapping, the sled pivoting and the runners slipping and grating several inches to the side. The sled was broken out. Men were holding their breaths, intensely unconscious of the fact.

"Now, MUSH!"

Thornton's command cracked out like a pistol-shot. Buck threw himself forward, tightening the traces with a jarring lunge. His whole body was gathered compactly together in the tremendous effort, the muscles writhing and knotting like live things under the silky fur. His great chest was low to the ground, his head forward and down, while his feet were flying like mad, the claws scarring the hard-packed snow in parallel grooves. The sled swayed and trembled, half-started forward. One of his feet slipped, and one man groaned aloud. Then the sled lurched ahead in what appeared a rapid succession of jerks, though it never really came to a dead stop again...half an inch...an inch... two inches... The jerks perceptibly diminished; as the sled gained momentum, he caught them up, till it was moving steadily along.

Men gasped and began to breathe again, unaware that for a moment they had ceased to breathe. Thornton was running behind, encouraging Buck with short, cheery words. The distance had been measured off, and as he neared the pile of firewood which marked the end of the hundred yards, a cheer began to grow and grow, which burst into a roar as he passed the firewood and halted at command. Every man was tearing himself loose, even Matthewson. Hats and mittens were flying in the air. Men were shaking hands, it did not matter with whom, and bubbling over in a general incoherent babel.

But Thornton fell on his knees beside Buck. Head was against head, and he was shaking him back and forth. Those who hurried up heard him cursing Buck, and he cursed him long and fervently, and softly and lovingly.

"Gad, sir! Gad, sir!" spluttered the Skookum Bench king. "I'll give you a thousand for him, sir, a thousand, sir—twelve hundred, sir."

Thornton rose to his feet. His eyes were wet. The tears were streaming frankly down his cheeks. "Sir," he said to the Skookum Bench king, "no, sir. You can go to hell, sir. It's the best I can do for you, sir."

Buck seized Thornton's hand in his teeth. Thornton shook him back and forth. As though animated by a common impulse, the onlookers drew back to a respectful distance; nor were they again indiscreet enough to interrupt.

Chapter VII. The Sounding of the Call

When Buck earned sixteen hundred dollars in five minutes for John Thornton, he made it possible for his master to pay off certain debts and to journey with his partners into the East after a fabled lost mine, the history of which was as old as the history of the country. Many men had sought it; few had found it; and more than a few there were who had never returned from the quest. This lost mine was steeped in tragedy and shrouded in mystery. No one knew of the first man. The oldest tradition stopped before it got back to him. From the beginning there had been an ancient and ramshackle cabin. Dying men had sworn to it, and to the mine the site of which it marked, clinching their testimony with nuggets that were unlike any known grade of gold in the Northland.

But no living man had looted this treasure house, and the dead were dead; wherefore John Thornton and Pete and Hans, with Buck and half a dozen other dogs, faced into the East on an unknown trail to achieve where men and dogs as good as themselves had failed. They sledded seventy miles up the Yukon, swung to the left into the Stewart River, passed the Mayo and the McQuestion, and held on until the Stewart itself became a streamlet, threading the upstanding peaks which marked the backbone of the continent.

John Thornton asked little of man or nature. He was unafraid of the wild. With a handful of salt and a rifle he could plunge into the wilderness and fare wherever he pleased and as long as he pleased. Being in no haste, Indian fashion, he hunted his dinner in the course of the day's travel; and if he failed to find it, like the Indian, he kept on travelling, secure in the knowledge that sooner or later he would come to it. So, on this great journey into the East, straight meat was the bill of fare, ammunition and tools principally made up the load on the sled, and the time-card was drawn upon the limitless future.

To Buck it was boundless delight, this hunting, fishing, and indefinite wandering through strange places. For weeks at a time they would hold on steadily, day after day; and for weeks upon end they would camp, here and there, the dogs loafing and the men burning holes through frozen muck and gravel and washing countless pans of dirt by the heat of the fire. Sometimes they went hungry, sometimes they feasted riotously, all according to the abundance of game and the fortune of hunting. Summer arrived, and dogs and men packed on their backs, rafted across blue mountain lakes, and descended or ascended unknown rivers in slender boats whipsawed from the standing forest.

The months came and went, and back and forth they twisted through the uncharted vastness, where no men were and yet where men had been if the Lost Cabin were true. They went across divides in summer blizzards, shivered under the midnight sun on naked mountains between the timber line and the eternal snows, dropped into summer valleys amid swarming gnats and flies, and in the shadows of glaciers picked strawberries and flowers as ripe and fair as any the Southland could boast. In the fall of the year they penetrated a weird lake country, sad and silent, where wildfowl had been, but where then there was no life nor sign of life—only the blowing of chill winds, the forming of ice in sheltered places, and the melancholy rippling of waves on lonely beaches.

And through another winter they wandered on the obliterated trails of men who had gone before. Once, they came upon a path blazed through the forest, an ancient path, and the Lost Cabin seemed very near. But the path began nowhere and ended nowhere, and it remained mystery, as the man who made it and the reason he made it remained mystery. Another time they chanced upon the time-graven wreckage of a hunting lodge, and amid the shreds of rotted blankets John Thornton found a long-barrelled flint-lock. He knew it for a Hudson Bay Company gun of the young days in the Northwest, when such a gun was worth its height in beaver skins packed flat, And that was all—no hint as to the man who in an early day had reared the lodge and left the gun among the blankets.

Spring came on once more, and at the end of all their wandering they found, not the Lost Cabin, but a shallow placer in a broad valley where the gold showed like yellow butter across the bottom of the washing-pan. They sought no farther. Each day they worked earned them thousands of dollars in clean dust and nuggets, and they worked every day. The gold was sacked in moose-hide bags, fifty pounds to the bag, and piled like so much firewood outside the spruce-bough lodge. Like giants they toiled, days flashing on the heels of days like dreams as they heaped the treasure up.

There was nothing for the dogs to do, save the hauling in of meat now and again that Thornton killed, and Buck spent long hours musing by the fire. The vision of the short-legged hairy man came to him more frequently, now that there was little work to be done; and often, blinking by the fire, Buck wandered with him in that other world which he remembered.

The salient thing of this other world seemed fear. When he watched the hairy man sleeping by the fire, head between his knees and hands clasped above, Buck saw that he slept restlessly, with many starts and awakenings, at which times he would peer fearfully into the darkness and fling more wood upon the fire. Did they walk by the beach of a sea, where the hairy man gathered shellfish and ate them as he gathered, it was with eyes that roved everywhere for hidden danger and with legs prepared to run like the wind at its first appearance. Through the forest they crept noiselessly, Buck at the hairy man's heels; and they were alert and vigilant, the pair of them, ears twitching and moving and nostrils quivering, for the man heard and smelled as keenly as Buck. The hairy man could spring up into the trees and travel ahead as fast as on the ground, swinging by the arms from limb to limb, sometimes a dozen feet apart, letting go and catching, never falling, never missing his grip. In fact, he seemed as much at home among the trees as on the ground; and Buck had memories of nights of vigil spent beneath trees wherein the hairy man roosted, holding on tightly as he slept.

And closely akin to the visions of the hairy man was the call still sounding in the depths of the forest. It filled him with a great unrest and strange desires. It caused him to feel a vague, sweet gladness, and he was aware of wild yearnings and stirrings for he knew not what. Sometimes he pursued the call into the forest, looking for it as though it were a tangible thing, barking softly or defiantly, as the mood might dictate. He would thrust his nose into the cool wood moss, or into the black soil where long grasses grew, and snort with joy at the fat earth smells; or he would crouch for hours, as if in concealment, behind fungus-covered trunks of fallen trees, wide-eyed and wide-eared to all that moved and sounded about him. It might be, lying thus, that he hoped to surprise this call he could not understand. But he did not know why he did these various things. He was impelled to do them, and did not reason about them at all.

Irresistible impulses seized him. He would be lying in camp, dozing lazily in the heat of the day, when suddenly his head would lift and his ears cock up, intent and listening, and he would spring to his feet and dash away, and on and on, for hours, through the forest aisles and across the open spaces where the niggerheads bunched. He loved to run down dry watercourses, and to creep and spy upon the bird life in the woods. For a day at a time he would lie in the underbrush where he could watch the partridges drumming and strutting up and down. But especially he loved to run in the dim twilight of the summer midnights, listening to the subdued and sleepy murmurs of the forest, reading signs and sounds as man may read a book, and seeking for the mysterious something that called—called, waking or sleeping, at all times, for him to come.

One night he sprang from sleep with a start, eager-eyed, nostrils quivering and scenting, his mane bristling in recurrent waves. From the forest came the call (or one note of it, for the call was many noted), distinct and definite as never before,—a long-drawn howl, like, yet unlike, any noise made by husky dog. And he knew it, in the old familiar way, as a sound heard before. He sprang through the sleeping camp and in swift silence dashed through the woods. As he drew closer to the cry he went more slowly, with caution in every movement, till he came to an open place among the trees, and looking out saw, erect on haunches, with nose pointed to the sky, a long, lean, timber wolf.

He had made no noise, yet it ceased from its howling and tried to sense his presence. Buck stalked into the open, half crouching, body gathered compactly together, tail straight and stiff, feet falling with unwonted care. Every movement advertised commingled threatening and overture of friendliness. It was the menacing truce that marks the meeting of wild beasts that prey. But the wolf fled at sight of him. He followed, with wild leapings, in a frenzy to overtake. He ran him into a blind channel, in the bed of the creek where a timber jam barred the way. The wolf whirled about, pivoting on his hind legs after the fashion of Joe and of all cornered husky dogs, snarling and bristling, clipping his teeth together in a continuous and rapid succession of snaps.

Buck did not attack, but circled him about and hedged him in with friendly advances. The wolf was suspicious and afraid; for Buck made three of him in weight, while his head barely reached Buck's shoulder. Watching his chance, he darted away, and the chase was resumed. Time and again he was cornered, and the thing repeated, though he was in poor condition, or Buck could not so easily have overtaken him. He would run till Buck's head was even with his flank, when he would whirl around at bay, only to dash away again at the first opportunity.

But in the end Buck's pertinacity was rewarded; for the wolf, finding that no harm was intended, finally sniffed noses with him. Then they became friendly, and played about in the nervous, half-coy way with which fierce beasts belie their fierceness. After some time of this the wolf started off at an easy lope in a manner that plainly showed he was going somewhere. He made it clear to Buck that he was to come, and they ran side by side through the sombre twilight, straight up the creek bed, into the gorge from which it issued, and across the bleak divide where it took its rise.

On the opposite slope of the watershed they came down into a level country where were great stretches of forest and many streams, and through these great stretches they ran steadily, hour after hour, the sun rising higher and the day growing warmer. Buck was wildly glad. He knew he was at last answering the call, running by the side of his wood brother toward the place from where the call surely came. Old memories were coming upon him fast, and he was stirring to them as of old he stirred to the realities of which they were the shadows. He had done this thing before, somewhere in that other and dimly remembered world, and he was doing it again, now, running free in the open, the unpacked earth underfoot, the wide sky overhead.

They stopped by a running stream to drink, and, stopping, Buck remembered John Thornton. He sat down. The wolf started on toward the place from where the call surely came, then returned to him, sniffing noses and making actions as though to encourage him. But Buck turned about and started slowly on the back track. For the better part of an hour the wild brother ran by his side, whining softly. Then he sat down, pointed his nose upward, and howled. It was a mournful howl, and as Buck held steadily on his way he heard it grow faint and fainter until it was lost in the distance.

John Thornton was eating dinner when Buck dashed into camp and sprang upon him in a frenzy of affection, overturning him, scrambling upon him, licking his face, biting his hand—"playing the general tom-fool," as John Thornton characterized it, the while he shook Buck back and forth and cursed him lovingly.

For two days and nights Buck never left camp, never let Thornton out of his sight. He followed him about at his work, watched him while he ate, saw him into his blankets at night and out of them in the morning. But after two days the call in the forest began to sound more imperiously than ever. Buck's restlessness came back on him, and he was haunted by recollections of the wild brother, and of the smiling land beyond the divide and the run side by side through the wide forest stretches. Once again he took to wandering in the woods, but the wild brother came no more; and though he listened through long vigils, the mournful howl was never raised.

He began to sleep out at night, staying away from camp for days at a time; and once he crossed the divide at the head of the creek and went down into the land of timber and streams. There he wandered for a week, seeking vainly for fresh sign of the wild brother, killing his meat as he travelled and travelling with the long, easy lope that seems never to tire. He fished for salmon in a broad stream that emptied somewhere into the sea, and by this stream he killed a large black bear, blinded by the mosquitoes while likewise fishing, and raging through the forest helpless and terrible. Even so, it was a hard fight, and it aroused the last latent remnants of Buck's ferocity. And two days later, when he returned to his kill and found a dozen wolverenes quarrelling over the spoil, he scattered them like chaff; and those that fled left two behind who would quarrel no more.

The blood-longing became stronger than ever before. He was a killer, a thing that preyed, living on the things that lived, unaided, alone, by virtue of his own strength and prowess, surviving triumphantly in a hostile environment where only the strong survived. Because of all this he became possessed of a great pride in himself, which communicated itself like a contagion to his physical being. It advertised itself in all his movements, was apparent in the play of every muscle, spoke plainly as speech in the way he carried himself, and made his glorious furry coat if anything more glorious. But for the stray brown on his muzzle and above his eyes, and for the splash of white hair that ran midmost down his chest, he might well have been mistaken for a gigantic wolf, larger than the largest of the breed. From his St. Bernard father he had inherited size and weight, but it was his shepherd mother who had given shape to that size and weight. His muzzle was the long wolf muzzle, save that it was larger than the muzzle of any wolf; and his head, somewhat broader, was the wolf head on a massive scale.

His cunning was wolf cunning, and wild cunning; his intelligence, shepherd intelligence and St. Bernard intelligence; and all this, plus an experience gained in the fiercest of schools, made him as formidable a creature as any that roamed the wild. A carnivorous animal living on a straight meat diet, he was in full flower, at the high tide of his life, overspilling with vigor and virility. When Thornton passed a caressing hand along his back, a snapping and crackling followed the hand, each hair discharging its pent magnetism at the contact. Every part, brain and body, nerve tissue and fibre, was keyed to the most exquisite pitch; and between all the parts there was a perfect equilibrium or adjustment. To sights and sounds and events which required action, he responded with lightning-like rapidity. Quickly as a husky dog could leap to defend from attack or to attack, he could leap twice as quickly. He saw the movement, or heard sound, and responded in less time than another dog required to compass the mere seeing or hearing. He perceived and determined and responded in the same instant. In point of fact the three actions of perceiving, determining, and responding were sequential; but so infinitesimal were the intervals of time between them that they appeared simultaneous. His muscles were surcharged with vitality, and snapped into play sharply, like steel springs. Life streamed through him in splendid flood, glad and rampant, until it seemed that it would burst him asunder in sheer ecstasy and pour forth generously over the world.

"Never was there such a dog," said John Thornton one day, as the partners watched Buck marching out of camp.

"When he was made, the mould was broke," said Pete.

"Py jingo! I t'ink so mineself," Hans affirmed.

They saw him marching out of camp, but they did not see the instant and terrible transformation which took place as soon as he was within the secrecy of the forest. He no longer marched. At once he became a thing of the wild, stealing along softly, cat-footed, a passing shadow that appeared and disappeared among the shadows. He knew how to take advantage of every cover, to crawl on his belly like a snake, and like a snake to leap and strike. He could take a ptarmigan from its nest, kill a rabbit as it slept, and snap in mid air the little chipmunks fleeing a second too late for the trees. Fish, in open pools, were not too quick for him; nor were beaver, mending their dams, too wary. He killed to eat, not from wantonness; but he preferred to eat what he killed himself. So a lurking humor ran through his deeds, and it was his delight to steal upon the squirrels, and, when he all but had them, to let them go, chattering in mortal fear to the treetops.

As the fall of the year came on, the moose appeared in greater abundance, moving slowly down to meet the winter in the lower and less rigorous valleys. Buck had already dragged down a stray part-grown calf; but he wished strongly for larger and more formidable quarry, and he came upon it one day on the divide at the head of the creek. A band of twenty moose had crossed over from the land of streams and timber, and chief among them was a great bull. He was in a savage temper, and, standing over six feet from the ground, was as formidable an antagonist as even Buck could desire. Back and forth the bull tossed his great palmated antlers, branching to fourteen points and embracing seven feet within the tips. His small eyes burned with a vicious and bitter light, while he roared with fury at sight of Buck.

From the bull's side, just forward of the flank, protruded a feathered arrow-end, which accounted for his savageness. Guided by that instinct which came from the old hunting days of the primordial world, Buck proceeded to cut the bull out from the herd. It was no slight task. He would bark and dance about in front of the bull, just out of reach of the great antlers and of the terrible splay hoofs which could have stamped his life out with a single blow. Unable to turn his back on the fanged danger and go on, the bull would be driven into paroxysms of rage. At such moments he charged Buck, who retreated craftily, luring him on by a simulated inability to escape. But when he was thus separated from his fellows, two or three of the younger bulls would charge back upon Buck and enable the wounded bull to rejoin the herd.

There is a patience of the wild—dogged, tireless, persistent as life itself—that holds motionless for endless hours the spider in its web, the snake in its coils, the panther in its ambuscade; this patience belongs peculiarly to life when it hunts its living food; and it belonged to Buck as he clung to the flank of the herd, retarding its march, irritating the young bulls, worrying the cows with their half-grown calves, and driving the wounded bull mad with helpless rage. For half a day this continued. Buck multiplied himself, attacking from all sides, enveloping the herd in a whirlwind of menace, cutting out his victim as fast as it could rejoin its mates, wearing out the patience of creatures preyed upon, which is a lesser patience than that of creatures preying.

As the day wore along and the sun dropped to its bed in the northwest (the darkness had come back and the fall nights were six hours long), the young bulls retraced their steps more and more reluctantly to the aid of their beset leader. The down-coming winter was harrying them on to the lower levels, and it seemed they could never shake off this tireless creature that held them back. Besides, it was not the life of the herd, or of the young bulls, that was threatened. The life of only one member was demanded, which was a remoter interest than their lives, and in the end they were content to pay the toll.

As twilight fell the old bull stood with lowered head, watching his mates—the cows he had known, the calves he had fathered, the bulls he had mastered—as they shambled on at a rapid pace through the fading light. He could not follow, for before his nose leaped the merciless fanged terror that would not let him go. Three hundredweight more than half a ton he weighed; he had lived a long, strong life, full of fight and struggle, and at the end he faced death at the teeth of a creature whose head did not reach beyond his great knuckled knees.

From then on, night and day, Buck never left his prey, never gave it a moment's rest, never permitted it to browse the leaves of trees or the shoots of young birch and willow. Nor did he give the wounded bull opportunity to slake his burning thirst in the slender trickling streams they crossed. Often, in desperation, he burst into long stretches of flight. At such times Buck did not attempt to stay him, but loped easily at his heels, satisfied with the way the game was played, lying down when the moose stood still, attacking him fiercely when he strove to eat or drink.

The great head drooped more and more under its tree of horns, and the shambling trot grew weak and weaker. He took to standing for long periods, with nose to the ground and dejected ears dropped limply; and Buck found more time in which to get water for himself and in which to rest. At such moments, panting with red lolling tongue and with eyes fixed upon the big bull, it appeared to Buck that a change was coming over the face of things. He could feel a new stir in the land. As the moose were coming into the land, other kinds of life were coming in. Forest and stream and air seemed palpitant with their presence. The news of it was borne in upon him, not by sight, or sound, or smell, but by some other and subtler sense. He heard nothing, saw nothing, yet knew that the land was somehow different; that through it strange things were afoot and ranging; and he resolved to investigate after he had finished the business in hand.

At last, at the end of the fourth day, he pulled the great moose down. For a day and a night he remained by the kill, eating and sleeping, turn and turn about. Then, rested, refreshed and strong, he turned his face toward camp and John Thornton. He broke into the long easy lope, and went on, hour after hour, never at loss for the tangled way, heading straight home through strange country with a certitude of direction that put man and his magnetic needle to shame.

As he held on he became more and more conscious of the new stir in the land. There was life abroad in it different from the life which had been there throughout the summer. No longer was this fact borne in upon him in some subtle, mysterious way. The birds talked of it, the squirrels chattered about it, the very breeze whispered of it. Several times he stopped and drew in the fresh morning air in great sniffs, reading a message which made him leap on with greater speed. He was oppressed with a sense of calamity happening, if it were not calamity already happened; and as he crossed the last watershed and dropped down into the valley toward camp, he proceeded with greater caution.

Three miles away he came upon a fresh trail that sent his neck hair rippling and bristling, It led straight toward camp and John Thornton. Buck hurried on, swiftly and stealthily, every nerve straining and tense, alert to the multitudinous details which told a story—all but the end. His nose gave him a varying description of the passage of the life on the heels of which he was travelling. He remarked the pregnant silence of the forest. The bird life had flitted. The squirrels were in hiding. One only he saw,—a sleek gray fellow, flattened against a gray dead limb so that he seemed a part of it, a woody excrescence upon the wood itself.

As Buck slid along with the obscureness of a gliding shadow, his nose was jerked suddenly to the side as though a positive force had gripped and pulled it. He followed the new scent into a thicket and found Nig. He was lying on his side, dead where he had dragged himself, an arrow protruding, head and feathers, from either side of his body.

A hundred yards farther on, Buck came upon one of the sled-dogs Thornton had bought in Dawson. This dog was thrashing about in a death-struggle, directly on the trail, and Buck passed around him without stopping. From the camp came the faint sound of many voices, rising and falling in a sing-song chant. Bellying forward to the edge of the clearing, he found Hans, lying on his face, feathered with arrows like a porcupine. At the same instant Buck peered out where the spruce-bough lodge had been and saw what made his hair leap straight up on his neck and shoulders. A gust of overpowering rage swept over him. He did not know that he growled, but he growled aloud with a terrible ferocity. For the last time in his life he allowed passion to usurp cunning and reason, and it was because of his great love for John Thornton that he lost his head.

The Yeehats were dancing about the wreckage of the spruce-bough lodge when they heard a fearful roaring and saw rushing upon them an animal the like of which they had never seen before. It was Buck, a live hurricane of fury, hurling himself upon them in a frenzy to destroy. He sprang at the foremost man (it was the chief of the Yeehats), ripping the throat wide open till the rent jugular spouted a fountain of blood. He did not pause to worry the victim, but ripped in passing, with the next bound tearing wide the throat of a second man. There was no withstanding him. He plunged about in their very midst, tearing, rending, destroying, in constant and terrific motion which defied the arrows they discharged at him. In fact, so inconceivably rapid were his movements, and so closely were the Indians tangled together, that they shot one another with the arrows; and one young hunter, hurling a spear at Buck in mid air, drove it through the chest of another hunter with such force that the point broke through the skin of the back and stood out beyond. Then a panic seized the Yeehats, and they fled in terror to the woods, proclaiming as they fled the advent of the Evil Spirit.

And truly Buck was the Fiend incarnate, raging at their heels and dragging them down like deer as they raced through the trees. It was a fateful day for the Yeehats. They scattered far and wide over the country, and it was not till a week later that the last of the survivors gathered together in a lower valley and counted their losses. As for Buck, wearying of the pursuit, he returned to the desolated camp. He found Pete where he had been killed in his blankets in the first moment of surprise. Thornton's desperate struggle was fresh-written on the earth, and Buck scented every detail of it down to the edge of a deep pool. By the edge, head and fore feet in the water, lay Skeet, faithful to the last. The pool itself, muddy and discolored from the sluice boxes, effectually hid what it contained, and it contained John Thornton; for Buck followed his trace into the water, from which no trace led away.

All day Buck brooded by the pool or roamed restlessly about the camp. Death, as a cessation of movement, as a passing out and away from the lives of the living, he knew, and he knew John Thornton was dead. It left a great void in him, somewhat akin to hunger, but a void which ached and ached, and which food could not fill, At times, when he paused to contemplate the carcasses of the Yeehats, he forgot the pain of it; and at such times he was aware of a great pride in himself,—a pride greater than any he had yet experienced. He had killed man, the noblest game of all, and he had killed in the face of the law of club and fang. He sniffed the bodies curiously. They had died so easily. It was harder to kill a husky dog than them. They were no match at all, were it not for their arrows and spears and clubs. Thenceforward he would be unafraid of them except when they bore in their hands their arrows, spears, and clubs.

Night came on, and a full moon rose high over the trees into the sky, lighting the land till it lay bathed in ghostly day. And with the coming of the night, brooding and mourning by the pool, Buck became alive to a stirring of the new life in the forest other than that which the Yeehats had made, He stood up, listening and scenting. From far away drifted a faint, sharp yelp, followed by a chorus of similar sharp yelps. As the moments passed the yelps grew closer and louder. Again Buck knew them as things heard in that other world which persisted in his memory. He walked to the centre of the open space and listened. It was the call, the many-noted call, sounding more luringly and compellingly than ever before. And as never before, he was ready to obey. John Thornton was dead. The last tie was broken. Man and the claims of man no longer bound him.

Hunting their living meat, as the Yeehats were hunting it, on the flanks of the migrating moose, the wolf pack had at last crossed over from the land of streams and timber and invaded Buck's valley. Into the clearing where the moonlight streamed, they poured in a silvery flood; and in the centre of the clearing stood Buck, motionless as a statue, waiting their coming. They were awed, so still and large he stood, and a moment's pause fell, till the boldest one leaped straight for him. Like a flash Buck struck, breaking the neck. Then he stood, without movement, as before, the stricken wolf rolling in agony behind him. Three others tried it in sharp succession; and one after the other they drew back, streaming blood from slashed throats or shoulders.

This was sufficient to fling the whole pack forward, pell-mell, crowded together, blocked and confused by its eagerness to pull down the prey. Buck's marvellous quickness and agility stood him in good stead. Pivoting on his hind legs, and snapping and gashing, he was everywhere at once, presenting a front which was apparently unbroken so swiftly did he whirl and guard from side to side. But to prevent them from getting behind him, he was forced back, down past the pool and into the creek bed, till he brought up against a high gravel bank. He worked along to a right angle in the bank which the men had made in the course of mining, and in this angle he came to bay, protected on three sides and with nothing to do but face the front.

And so well did he face it, that at the end of half an hour the wolves drew back discomfited. The tongues of all were out and lolling, the white fangs showing cruelly white in the moonlight. Some were lying down with heads raised and ears pricked forward; others stood on their feet, watching him; and still others were lapping water from the pool. One wolf, long and lean and gray, advanced cautiously, in a friendly manner, and Buck recognized the wild brother with whom he had run for a night and a day. He was whining softly, and, as Buck whined, they touched noses.

Then an old wolf, gaunt and battle-scarred, came forward. Buck writhed his lips into the preliminary of a snarl, but sniffed noses with him, Whereupon the old wolf sat down, pointed nose at the moon, and broke out the long wolf howl. The others sat down and howled. And now the call came to Buck in unmistakable accents. He, too, sat down and howled. This over, he came out of his angle and the pack crowded around him, sniffing in half-friendly, half-savage manner. The leaders lifted the yelp of the pack and sprang away into the woods. The wolves swung in behind, yelping in chorus. And Buck ran with them, side by side with the wild brother, yelping as he ran.

And here may well end the story of Buck. The years were not many when the Yeehats noted a change in the breed of timber wolves; for some were seen with splashes of brown on head and muzzle, and with a rift of white centring down the chest. But more remarkable than this, the Yeehats tell of a Ghost Dog that runs at the head of the pack. They are afraid of this Ghost Dog, for it has cunning greater than they, stealing from their camps in fierce winters, robbing their traps, slaying their dogs, and defying their bravest hunters.

Nay, the tale grows worse. Hunters there are who fail to return to the camp, and hunters there have been whom their tribesmen found with throats slashed cruelly open and with wolf prints about them in the snow greater than the prints of any wolf. Each fall, when the Yeehats follow the movement of the moose, there is a certain valley which they never enter. And women there are who become sad when the word goes over the fire of how the Evil Spirit came to select that valley for an abiding-place.

In the summers there is one visitor, however, to that valley, of which the Yeehats do not know. It is a great, gloriously coated wolf, like, and yet unlike, all other wolves. He crosses alone from the smiling timber land and comes down into an open space among the trees. Here a yellow stream flows from rotted moose-hide sacks and sinks into the ground, with long grasses growing through it and vegetable mould overrunning it and hiding its yellow from the sun; and here he muses for a time, howling once, long and mournfully, ere he departs.

But he is not always alone. When the long winter nights come on and the wolves follow their meat into the lower valleys, he may be seen running at the head of the pack through the pale moonlight or glimmering borealis, leaping gigantic above his fellows, his great throat a-bellow as he sings a song of the younger world, which is the song of the pack.

White Fang

PART I

CHAPTER I—THE TRAIL OF THE MEAT

Dark spruce forest frowned on either side the frozen waterway. The trees had been stripped by a recent wind of their white covering of frost, and they seemed to lean towards each other, black and ominous, in the fading light. A vast silence reigned over the land. The land itself was a desolation, lifeless, without movement, so lone and cold that the spirit of it was not even that of sadness. There was a hint in it of laughter, but of a laughter more terrible than any sadness—a laughter that was mirthless as the smile of the sphinx, a laughter cold as the frost and partaking of the grimness of infallibility. It was the masterful and incommunicable wisdom of eternity laughing at the futility of life and the effort of life. It was the Wild, the savage, frozen-hearted Northland Wild.

But there was life, abroad in the land and defiant. Down the frozen waterway toiled a string of wolfish dogs. Their bristly fur was rimed with frost. Their breath froze in the air as it left their mouths, spouting forth in spumes of vapour that settled upon the hair of their bodies and formed into crystals of frost. Leather harness was on the dogs, and leather traces attached them to a sled which dragged along behind. The sled was without runners. It was made of stout birch-bark, and its full surface rested on the snow. The front end of the sled was turned up, like a scroll, in order to force down and under the bore of soft snow that surged like a wave before it. On the sled, securely lashed, was a long and narrow oblong box. There were other things on the sled—blankets, an axe, and a coffee-pot and frying-pan; but prominent, occupying most of the space, was the long and narrow oblong box.

In advance of the dogs, on wide snowshoes, toiled a man. At the rear of the sled toiled a second man. On the sled, in the box, lay a third man whose toil was over,—a man whom the Wild had conquered and beaten down until he would never move nor struggle again. It is not the way of the Wild to like movement. Life is an offence to it, for life is movement; and the Wild aims always to destroy movement. It freezes the water to prevent it running to the sea; it drives the sap out of the trees till they are frozen to their mighty hearts; and most ferociously and terribly of all does the Wild harry and crush into submission man—man who is the most restless of life, ever in revolt against the dictum that all movement must in the end come to the cessation of movement.

But at front and rear, unawed and indomitable, toiled the two men who were not yet dead. Their bodies were covered with fur and soft-tanned leather. Eyelashes and cheeks and lips were so coated with the crystals from their frozen breath that their faces were not discernible. This gave them the seeming of ghostly masques, undertakers in a spectral world at the funeral of some ghost. But under it all they were men, penetrating the land of desolation and mockery and silence, puny adventurers bent on colossal adventure, pitting themselves against the might of a world as remote and alien and pulseless as the abysses of space.

They travelled on without speech, saving their breath for the work of their bodies. On every side was the silence, pressing upon them with a tangible presence. It affected their minds as the many atmospheres of deep water affect the body of the diver. It crushed them with the weight of unending vastness and unalterable decree. It crushed them into the remotest recesses of their own minds, pressing out of them, like juices from the grape, all the false ardours and exaltations and undue self-values of the human soul, until they perceived themselves finite and small, specks and motes, moving with weak cunning and little wisdom amidst the play and inter-play of the great blind elements and forces.

An hour went by, and a second hour. The pale light of the short sunless day was beginning to fade, when a faint far cry arose on the still air. It soared upward with a swift rush, till it reached its topmost note, where it persisted, palpitant and tense, and then slowly died away. It might have been a lost soul wailing, had it not been invested with a certain sad fierceness and hungry eagerness. The front man turned his head until his eyes met the eyes of the man behind. And then, across the narrow oblong box, each nodded to the other.

A second cry arose, piercing the silence with needle-like shrillness. Both men located the sound. It was to the rear, somewhere in the snow expanse they had just traversed. A third and answering cry arose, also to the rear and to the left of the second cry.

"They're after us, Bill," said the man at the front.

His voice sounded hoarse and unreal, and he had spoken with apparent effort.

"Meat is scarce," answered his comrade. "I ain't seen a rabbit sign for days."

Thereafter they spoke no more, though their ears were keen for the hunting-cries that continued to rise behind them.

At the fall of darkness they swung the dogs into a cluster of spruce trees on the edge of the waterway and made a camp. The coffin, at the side of the fire, served for seat and table. The wolf-dogs, clustered on the far side of the fire, snarled and bickered among themselves, but evinced no inclination to stray off into the darkness.

"Seems to me, Henry, they're stayin' remarkable close to camp," Bill commented.

Henry, squatting over the fire and settling the pot of coffee with a piece of ice, nodded. Nor did he speak till he had taken his seat on the coffin and begun to eat.

"They know where their hides is safe," he said. "They'd sooner eat grub than be grub. They're pretty wise, them dogs."

Bill shook his head. "Oh, I don't know."

His comrade looked at him curiously. "First time I ever heard you say anything about their not bein' wise."

"Henry," said the other, munching with deliberation the beans he was eating, "did you happen to notice the way them dogs kicked up when I was a-feedin' 'em?"

"They did cut up more'n usual," Henry acknowledged.

"How many dogs 've we got, Henry?"

"Six."

"Well, Henry . . . " Bill stopped for a moment, in order that his words might gain greater significance. "As I was sayin', Henry, we've got six dogs. I took six fish out of the bag. I gave one fish to each dog, an', Henry, I was one fish short."

"You counted wrong."

"We've got six dogs," the other reiterated dispassionately. "I took out six fish. One Ear didn't get no fish. I came back to the bag afterward an' got 'm his fish."

"We've only got six dogs," Henry said.

"Henry," Bill went on. "I won't say they was all dogs, but there was seven of 'm that got fish."

Henry stopped eating to glance across the fire and count the dogs.

"There's only six now," he said.

"I saw the other one run off across the snow," Bill announced with cool positiveness. "I saw seven."

Henry looked at him commiseratingly, and said, "I'll be almighty glad when this trip's over."

"What d'ye mean by that?" Bill demanded.

"I mean that this load of ourn is gettin' on your nerves, an' that you're beginnin' to see things."

"I thought of that," Bill answered gravely. "An' so, when I saw it run off across the snow, I looked in the snow an' saw its tracks. Then I counted the dogs an' there was still six of 'em. The tracks is there in the snow now. D'ye want to look at 'em? I'll show 'em to you."

Henry did not reply, but munched on in silence, until, the meal finished, he topped it with a final cup of coffee. He wiped his mouth with the back of his hand and said:

"Then you're thinkin' as it was—"

A long wailing cry, fiercely sad, from somewhere in the darkness, had interrupted him. He stopped to listen to it, then he finished his sentence with a wave of his hand toward the sound of the cry, "—one of them?"

Bill nodded. "I'd a blame sight sooner think that than anything else. You noticed yourself the row the dogs made."

Cry after cry, and answering cries, were turning the silence into a bedlam. From every side the cries arose, and the dogs betrayed their fear by huddling together and so close to the fire that their hair was scorched by the heat. Bill threw on more wood, before lighting his pipe.

"I'm thinking you're down in the mouth some," Henry said.

"Henry . . . " He sucked meditatively at his pipe for some time before he went on. "Henry, I was a-thinkin' what a blame sight luckier he is than you an' me'll ever be."

He indicated the third person by a downward thrust of the thumb to the box on which they sat.

"You an' me, Henry, when we die, we'll be lucky if we get enough stones over our carcases to keep the dogs off of us."

"But we ain't got people an' money an' all the rest, like him," Henry rejoined. "Long-distance funerals is somethin' you an' me can't exactly afford."

"What gets me, Henry, is what a chap like this, that's a lord or something in his own country, and that's never had to bother about grub nor blankets; why he comes a-buttin' round the Godforsaken ends of the earth—that's what I can't exactly see."

"He might have lived to a ripe old age if he'd stayed at home," Henry agreed.

Bill opened his mouth to speak, but changed his mind. Instead, he pointed towards the wall of darkness that pressed about them from every side. There was no suggestion of form in the utter blackness; only could be seen a pair of eyes gleaming like live coals. Henry indicated with his head a second pair, and a third. A circle of the gleaming eyes had drawn about their camp. Now and again a pair of eyes moved, or disappeared to appear again a moment later.

The unrest of the dogs had been increasing, and they stampeded, in a surge of sudden fear, to the near side of the fire, cringing and crawling about the legs of the men. In the scramble one of the dogs had been overturned on the edge of the fire, and it had yelped with pain and fright as the smell of its singed coat possessed the air. The commotion caused the circle of eyes to shift restlessly for a moment and even to withdraw a bit, but it settled down again as the dogs became quiet.

"Henry, it's a blame misfortune to be out of ammunition."

Bill had finished his pipe and was helping his companion to spread the bed of fur and blanket upon the spruce boughs which he had laid over the snow before supper. Henry grunted, and began unlacing his moccasins.

"How many cartridges did you say you had left?" he asked.

"Three," came the answer. "An' I wisht 'twas three hundred. Then I'd show 'em what for, damn 'em!"

He shook his fist angrily at the gleaming eyes, and began securely to prop his moccasins before the fire.

"An' I wisht this cold snap'd break," he went on. "It's ben fifty below for two weeks now. An' I wisht I'd never started on this trip, Henry. I don't like the looks of it. I don't feel right, somehow. An' while I'm wishin', I wisht the trip was over an' done with, an' you an' me a-sittin' by the fire in Fort McGurry just about now an' playing cribbage—that's what I wisht."

Henry grunted and crawled into bed. As he dozed off he was aroused by his comrade's voice.

"Say, Henry, that other one that come in an' got a fish—why didn't the dogs pitch into it? That's what's botherin' me."

"You're botherin' too much, Bill," came the sleepy response. "You was never like this before. You jes' shut up now, an' go to sleep, an' you'll be all hunkydory in the mornin'. Your stomach's sour, that's what's botherin' you."

The men slept, breathing heavily, side by side, under the one covering. The fire died down, and the gleaming eyes drew closer the circle they had flung about the camp. The dogs clustered together in fear, now and again snarling menacingly as a pair of eyes drew close. Once their uproar became so loud that Bill woke up. He got out of bed carefully, so as not to disturb the sleep of his comrade, and threw more wood on the fire. As it began to flame up, the circle of eyes drew farther back. He glanced casually at the huddling dogs. He rubbed his eyes and looked at them more sharply. Then he crawled back into the blankets.

"Henry," he said. "Oh, Henry."

Henry groaned as he passed from sleep to waking, and demanded, "What's wrong now?"

"Nothin'," came the answer; "only there's seven of 'em again. I just counted."

Henry acknowledged receipt of the information with a grunt that slid into a snore as he drifted back into sleep.

In the morning it was Henry who awoke first and routed his companion out of bed. Daylight was yet three hours away, though it was already six o'clock; and in the darkness Henry went about preparing breakfast, while Bill rolled the blankets and made the sled ready for lashing.

"Say, Henry," he asked suddenly, "how many dogs did you say we had?"

"Six."

"Wrong," Bill proclaimed triumphantly.

"Seven again?" Henry queried.

"No, five; one's gone."

"The hell!" Henry cried in wrath, leaving the cooking to come and count the dogs.

"You're right, Bill," he concluded. "Fatty's gone."

"An' he went like greased lightnin' once he got started. Couldn't 've seen 'm for smoke."

"No chance at all," Henry concluded. "They jes' swallowed 'm alive. I bet he was yelpin' as he went down their throats, damn 'em!"

"He always was a fool dog," said Bill.

"But no fool dog ought to be fool enough to go off an' commit suicide that way." He looked over the remainder of the team with a speculative eye that summed up instantly the salient traits of each animal. "I bet none of the others would do it."

"Couldn't drive 'em away from the fire with a club," Bill agreed. "I always did think there was somethin' wrong with Fatty anyway."

And this was the epitaph of a dead dog on the Northland trail—less scant than the epitaph of many another dog, of many a man.

CHAPTER II—THE SHE-WOLF

Breakfast eaten and the slim camp-outfit lashed to the sled, the men turned their backs on the cheery fire and launched out into the darkness. At once began to rise the cries that were fiercely sad—cries that called through the darkness and cold to one another and answered back. Conversation ceased. Daylight came at nine o'clock. At midday the sky to the south warmed to rose-colour, and marked where the bulge of the earth intervened between the meridian sun and the northern world. But the rose-colour swiftly faded. The grey light of day that remained lasted until three o'clock, when it, too, faded, and the pall of the Arctic night descended upon the lone and silent land.

As darkness came on, the hunting-cries to right and left and rear drew closer—so close that more than once they sent surges of fear through the toiling dogs, throwing them into short-lived panics.

At the conclusion of one such panic, when he and Henry had got the dogs back in the traces, Bill said:

"I wisht they'd strike game somewheres, an' go away an' leave us alone."

"They do get on the nerves horrible," Henry sympathised.

They spoke no more until camp was made.

Henry was bending over and adding ice to the babbling pot of beans when he was startled by the sound of a blow, an exclamation from Bill, and a sharp snarling cry of pain from among the dogs. He straightened up in time to see a dim form disappearing across the snow into the shelter of the dark. Then he saw Bill, standing amid the dogs, half triumphant, half crestfallen, in one hand a stout club, in the other the tail and part of the body of a sun-cured salmon.

"It got half of it," he announced; "but I got a whack at it jes' the same. D'ye hear it squeal?"

"What'd it look like?" Henry asked.

"Couldn't see. But it had four legs an' a mouth an' hair an' looked like any dog."

"Must be a tame wolf, I reckon."

"It's damned tame, whatever it is, comin' in here at feedin' time an' gettin' its whack of fish."

That night, when supper was finished and they sat on the oblong box and pulled at their pipes, the circle of gleaming eyes drew in even closer than before.

"I wisht they'd spring up a bunch of moose or something, an' go away an' leave us alone," Bill said.

Henry grunted with an intonation that was not all sympathy, and for a quarter of an hour they sat on in silence, Henry staring at the fire, and Bill at the circle of eyes that burned in the darkness just beyond the firelight.

"I wisht we was pullin' into McGurry right now," he began again.

"Shut up your wishin' and your croakin'," Henry burst out angrily. "Your stomach's sour. That's what's ailin' you. Swallow a spoonful of sody, an' you'll sweeten up wonderful an' be more pleasant company."

In the morning Henry was aroused by fervid blasphemy that proceeded from the mouth of Bill. Henry propped himself up on an elbow and looked to see his comrade standing among the dogs beside the replenished fire, his arms raised in objurgation, his face distorted with passion.

"Hello!" Henry called. "What's up now?"

"Frog's gone," came the answer.

"No."

"I tell you yes."

Henry leaped out of the blankets and to the dogs. He counted them with care, and then joined his partner in cursing the power of the Wild that had robbed them of another dog.

"Frog was the strongest dog of the bunch," Bill pronounced finally.

"An' he was no fool dog neither," Henry added.

And so was recorded the second epitaph in two days.

A gloomy breakfast was eaten, and the four remaining dogs were harnessed to the sled. The day was a repetition of the days that had gone before. The men toiled without speech across the face of the frozen world. The silence was unbroken save by the cries of their pursuers, that, unseen, hung upon their rear. With the coming of night in the mid-afternoon, the cries sounded closer as the pursuers drew in according to their custom; and the dogs grew excited and frightened, and were guilty of panics that tangled the traces and further depressed the two men.

"There, that'll fix you fool critters," Bill said with satisfaction that night, standing erect at completion of his task.

Henry left the cooking to come and see. Not only had his partner tied the dogs up, but he had tied them, after the Indian fashion, with sticks. About the neck of each dog he had fastened a leather thong. To this, and so close to the neck that the dog could not get his teeth to it, he had tied a stout stick four or five feet in length. The other end of the stick, in turn, was made fast to a stake in the ground by means of a leather thong. The dog was unable to gnaw through the leather at his own end of the stick. The stick prevented him from getting at the leather that fastened the other end.

Henry nodded his head approvingly.

"It's the only contraption that'll ever hold One Ear," he said. "He can gnaw through leather as clean as a knife an' jes' about half as quick. They all'll be here in the mornin' hunkydory."

"You jes' bet they will," Bill affirmed. "If one of em' turns up missin', I'll go without my coffee."

"They jes' know we ain't loaded to kill," Henry remarked at bed-time, indicating the gleaming circle that hemmed them in. "If we could put a couple of shots into 'em, they'd be more respectful. They come closer every night. Get the firelight out of your eyes an' look hard—there! Did you see that one?"

For some time the two men amused themselves with watching the movement of vague forms on the edge of the firelight. By looking closely and steadily at where a pair of eyes burned in the darkness, the form of the animal would slowly take shape. They could even see these forms move at times.

A sound among the dogs attracted the men's attention. One Ear was uttering quick, eager whines, lunging at the length of his stick toward the darkness, and desisting now and again in order to make frantic attacks on the stick with his teeth.

"Look at that, Bill," Henry whispered.

Full into the firelight, with a stealthy, sidelong movement, glided a doglike animal. It moved with commingled mistrust and daring, cautiously observing the men, its attention fixed on the dogs. One Ear strained the full length of the stick toward the intruder and whined with eagerness.

"That fool One Ear don't seem scairt much," Bill said in a low tone.

"It's a she-wolf," Henry whispered back, "an' that accounts for Fatty an' Frog. She's the decoy for the pack. She draws out the dog an' then all the rest pitches in an' eats 'm up."

The fire crackled. A log fell apart with a loud spluttering noise. At the sound of it the strange animal leaped back into the darkness.

"Henry, I'm a-thinkin'," Bill announced.

"Thinkin' what?"

"I'm a-thinkin' that was the one I lambasted with the club."

"Ain't the slightest doubt in the world," was Henry's response.

"An' right here I want to remark," Bill went on, "that that animal's familyarity with campfires is suspicious an' immoral."

"It knows for certain more'n a self-respectin' wolf ought to know," Henry agreed. "A wolf that knows enough to come in with the dogs at feedin' time has had experiences."

"Ol' Villan had a dog once that run away with the wolves," Bill cogitates aloud. "I ought to know. I shot it out of the pack in a moose pasture over 'on Little Stick. An' Ol' Villan cried like a baby. Hadn't seen it for three years, he said. Ben with the wolves all that time."

"I reckon you've called the turn, Bill. That wolf's a dog, an' it's eaten fish many's the time from the hand of man."

"An if I get a chance at it, that wolf that's a dog'll be jes' meat," Bill declared. "We can't afford to lose no more animals."

"But you've only got three cartridges," Henry objected.

"I'll wait for a dead sure shot," was the reply.

In the morning Henry renewed the fire and cooked breakfast to the accompaniment of his partner's snoring.

"You was sleepin' jes' too comfortable for anything," Henry told him, as he routed him out for breakfast. "I hadn't the heart to rouse you."

Bill began to eat sleepily. He noticed that his cup was empty and started to reach for the pot. But the pot was beyond arm's length and beside Henry.

"Say, Henry," he chided gently, "ain't you forgot somethin'?"

Henry looked about with great carefulness and shook his head. Bill held up the empty cup.

"You don't get no coffee," Henry announced.

"Ain't run out?" Bill asked anxiously.

"Nope."

"Ain't thinkin' it'll hurt my digestion?"

"Nope."

A flush of angry blood pervaded Bill's face.

"Then it's jes' warm an' anxious I am to be hearin' you explain yourself," he said.

"Spanker's gone," Henry answered.

Without haste, with the air of one resigned to misfortune Bill turned his head, and from where he sat counted the dogs.

"How'd it happen?" he asked apathetically.

Henry shrugged his shoulders. "Don't know. Unless One Ear gnawed 'm loose. He couldn't a-done it himself, that's sure."

"The darned cuss." Bill spoke gravely and slowly, with no hint of the anger that was raging within. "Jes' because he couldn't chew himself loose, he chews Spanker loose."

"Well, Spanker's troubles is over anyway; I guess he's digested by this time an' cavortin' over the landscape in the bellies of twenty different wolves," was Henry's epitaph on this, the latest lost dog. "Have some coffee, Bill."

But Bill shook his head.

"Go on," Henry pleaded, elevating the pot.

Bill shoved his cup aside. "I'll be ding-dong-danged if I do. I said I wouldn't if ary dog turned up missin', an' I won't."

"It's darn good coffee," Henry said enticingly.

But Bill was stubborn, and he ate a dry breakfast washed down with mumbled curses at One Ear for the trick he had played.

"I'll tie 'em up out of reach of each other to-night," Bill said, as they took the trail.

They had travelled little more than a hundred yards, when Henry, who was in front, bent down and picked up something with which his snowshoe had collided. It was dark, and he could not see it, but he recognised it by the touch. He flung it back, so that it struck the sled and bounced along until it fetched up on Bill's snowshoes.

"Mebbe you'll need that in your business," Henry said.

Bill uttered an exclamation. It was all that was left of Spanker—the stick with which he had been tied.

"They ate 'm hide an' all," Bill announced. "The stick's as clean as a whistle. They've ate the leather offen both ends. They're damn hungry, Henry, an' they'll have you an' me guessin' before this trip's over."

Henry laughed defiantly. "I ain't been trailed this way by wolves before, but I've gone through a whole lot worse an' kept my health. Takes more'n a handful of them pesky critters to do for yours truly, Bill, my son."

"I don't know, I don't know," Bill muttered ominously.

"Well, you'll know all right when we pull into McGurry."

"I ain't feelin' special enthusiastic," Bill persisted.

"You're off colour, that's what's the matter with you," Henry dogmatised. "What you need is quinine, an' I'm goin' to dose you up stiff as soon as we make McGurry."

Bill grunted his disagreement with the diagnosis, and lapsed into silence. The day was like all the days. Light came at nine o'clock. At twelve o'clock the southern horizon was warmed by the unseen sun; and then began the cold grey of afternoon that would merge, three hours later, into night.

It was just after the sun's futile effort to appear, that Bill slipped the rifle from under the sled-lashings and said:

"You keep right on, Henry, I'm goin' to see what I can see."

"You'd better stick by the sled," his partner protested. "You've only got three cartridges, an' there's no tellin' what might happen."

"Who's croaking now?" Bill demanded triumphantly.

Henry made no reply, and plodded on alone, though often he cast anxious glances back into the grey solitude where his partner had disappeared. An hour later, taking advantage of the cut-offs around which the sled had to go, Bill arrived.

"They're scattered an' rangin' along wide," he said: "keeping up with us an' lookin' for game at the same time. You see, they're sure of us, only they know they've got to wait to get us. In the meantime they're willin' to pick up anything eatable that comes handy."

"You mean they think they're sure of us," Henry objected pointedly.

But Bill ignored him. "I seen some of them. They're pretty thin. They ain't had a bite in weeks I reckon, outside of Fatty an' Frog an' Spanker; an' there's so many of 'em that that didn't go far. They're remarkable thin. Their ribs is like wash-boards, an' their stomachs is right up against their backbones. They're pretty desperate, I can tell you. They'll be goin' mad, yet, an' then watch out."

A few minutes later, Henry, who was now travelling behind the sled, emitted a low, warning whistle. Bill turned and looked, then quietly stopped the dogs. To the rear, from around the last bend and plainly into view, on the very trail they had just covered, trotted a furry, slinking form. Its nose was to the trail, and it trotted with a peculiar, sliding, effortless gait. When they halted, it halted, throwing up its head and regarding them steadily with nostrils that twitched as it caught and studied the scent of them.

"It's the she-wolf," Bill answered.

The dogs had lain down in the snow, and he walked past them to join his partner in the sled. Together they watched the strange animal that had pursued them for days and that had already accomplished the destruction of half their dog-team.

After a searching scrutiny, the animal trotted forward a few steps. This it repeated several times, till it was a short hundred yards away. It paused, head up, close by a clump of spruce trees, and with sight and scent studied the outfit of the watching men. It looked at them in a strangely wistful way, after the manner of a dog; but in its wistfulness there was none of the dog affection. It was a wistfulness bred of hunger, as cruel as its own fangs, as merciless as the frost itself.

It was large for a wolf, its gaunt frame advertising the lines of an animal that was among the largest of its kind.

"Stands pretty close to two feet an' a half at the shoulders," Henry commented. "An' I'll bet it ain't far from five feet long."

"Kind of strange colour for a wolf," was Bill's criticism. "I never seen a red wolf before. Looks almost cinnamon to me."

The animal was certainly not cinnamon-coloured. Its coat was the true wolf-coat. The dominant colour was grey, and yet there was to it a faint reddish hue—a hue that was baffling, that appeared and disappeared, that was more like an illusion of the vision, now grey, distinctly grey, and again giving hints and glints of a vague redness of colour not classifiable in terms of ordinary experience.

"Looks for all the world like a big husky sled-dog," Bill said. "I wouldn't be s'prised to see it wag its tail."

"Hello, you husky!" he called. "Come here, you whatever-your-name-is."

"Ain't a bit scairt of you," Henry laughed.

Bill waved his hand at it threateningly and shouted loudly; but the animal betrayed no fear. The only change in it that they could notice was an accession of

70

alertness. It still regarded them with the merciless wistfulness of hunger. They were meat, and it was hungry; and it would like to go in and eat them if it dared.

"Look here, Henry," Bill said, unconsciously lowering his voice to a whisper because of what he imitated. "We've got three cartridges. But it's a dead shot. Couldn't miss it. It's got away with three of our dogs, an' we oughter put a stop to it. What d'ye say?"

Henry nodded his consent. Bill cautiously slipped the gun from under the sled-lashing. The gun was on the way to his shoulder, but it never got there. For in that instant the she-wolf leaped sidewise from the trail into the clump of spruce trees and disappeared.

The two men looked at each other. Henry whistled long and comprehendingly.

"I might have knowed it," Bill chided himself aloud as he replaced the gun. "Of course a wolf that knows enough to come in with the dogs at feedin' time, 'd know all about shooting-irons. I tell you right now, Henry, that critter's the cause of all our trouble. We'd have six dogs at the present time, 'stead of three, if it wasn't for her. An' I tell you right now, Henry, I'm goin' to get her. She's too smart to be shot in the open. But I'm goin' to lay for her. I'll bushwhack her as sure as my name is Bill."

"You needn't stray off too far in doin' it," his partner admonished. "If that pack ever starts to jump you, them three cartridges'd be wuth no more'n three whoops in hell. Them animals is damn hungry, an' once they start in, they'll sure get you, Bill."

They camped early that night. Three dogs could not drag the sled so fast nor for so long hours as could six, and they were showing unmistakable signs of playing out. And the men went early to bed, Bill first seeing to it that the dogs were tied out of gnawing-reach of one another.

But the wolves were growing bolder, and the men were aroused more than once from their sleep. So near did the wolves approach, that the dogs became frantic with terror, and it was necessary to replenish the fire from time to time in order to keep the adventurous marauders at safer distance.

"I've hearn sailors talk of sharks followin' a ship," Bill remarked, as he crawled back into the blankets after one such replenishing of the fire. "Well, them wolves is land sharks. They know their business better'n we do, an' they ain't a-holdin' our trail this way for their health. They're goin' to get us. They're sure goin' to get us, Henry."

"They've half got you a'ready, a-talkin' like that," Henry retorted sharply. "A man's half licked when he says he is. An' you're half eaten from the way you're goin' on about it."

"They've got away with better men than you an' me," Bill answered.

"Oh, shet up your croakin'. You make me all-fired tired."

Henry rolled over angrily on his side, but was surprised that Bill made no similar display of temper. This was not Bill's way, for he was easily angered by sharp words. Henry thought long over it before he went to sleep, and as his eyelids fluttered down and he dozed off, the thought in his mind was: "There's no mistakin' it, Bill's almighty blue. I'll have to cheer him up to-morrow."

CHAPTER III—THE HUNGER CRY

The day began auspiciously. They had lost no dogs during the night, and they swung out upon the trail and into the silence, the darkness, and the cold with spirits that were fairly light. Bill seemed to have forgotten his forebodings of the previous night, and even waxed facetious with the dogs when, at midday, they overturned the sled on a bad piece of trail.

It was an awkward mix-up. The sled was upside down and jammed between a tree-trunk and a huge rock, and they were forced to unharness the dogs in order to straighten out the tangle. The two men were bent over the sled and trying to right it, when Henry observed One Ear sidling away.

"Here, you, One Ear!" he cried, straightening up and turning around on the dog.

But One Ear broke into a run across the snow, his traces trailing behind him. And there, out in the snow of their back track, was the she-wolf waiting for him. As he neared her, he became suddenly cautious. He slowed down to an alert and mincing walk and then stopped. He regarded her carefully and dubiously, yet desirefully. She seemed to smile at him, showing her teeth in an ingratiating rather than a menacing way. She moved toward him a few steps, playfully, and then halted. One Ear drew near to her, still alert and cautious, his tail and ears in the air, his head held high.

He tried to sniff noses with her, but she retreated playfully and coyly. Every advance on his part was accompanied by a corresponding retreat on her part. Step by step she was luring him away from the security of his human companionship. Once, as though a warning had in vague ways flitted through his intelligence, he turned his head and looked back at the overturned sled, at his team-mates, and at the two men who were calling to him.

But whatever idea was forming in his mind, was dissipated by the she-wolf, who advanced upon him, sniffed noses with him for a fleeting instant, and then resumed her coy retreat before his renewed advances.

In the meantime, Bill had bethought himself of the rifle. But it was jammed beneath the overturned sled, and by the time Henry had helped him to right the load, One Ear and the she-wolf were too close together and the distance too great to risk a shot.

Too late One Ear learned his mistake. Before they saw the cause, the two men saw him turn and start to run back toward them. Then, approaching at right angles to the trail and cutting off his retreat they saw a dozen wolves, lean and grey, bounding across the snow. On the instant, the she-wolf's coyness and playfulness disappeared. With a snarl she sprang upon One Ear. He thrust her off with his shoulder, and, his retreat cut off and still intent on regaining the sled, he altered his course in an attempt to circle around to it. More wolves were appearing every moment and joining in the chase. The she-wolf was one leap behind One Ear and holding her own.

"Where are you goin'?" Henry suddenly demanded, laying his hand on his partner's arm.

Bill shook it off. "I won't stand it," he said. "They ain't a-goin' to get any more of our dogs if I can help it."

Gun in hand, he plunged into the underbrush that lined the side of the trail. His intention was apparent enough. Taking the sled as the centre of the circle that One Ear was making, Bill planned to tap that circle at a point in advance of the pursuit. With his rifle, in the broad daylight, it might be possible for him to awe the wolves and save the dog.

"Say, Bill!" Henry called after him. "Be careful! Don't take no chances!"

Henry sat down on the sled and watched. There was nothing else for him to do. Bill had already gone from sight; but now and again, appearing and disappearing amongst the underbrush and the scattered clumps of spruce, could be seen One Ear. Henry judged his case to be hopeless. The dog was thoroughly alive to its danger, but it was running on the outer circle while the wolf-pack was running on the inner and shorter circle. It was vain to think of One Ear so outdistancing his pursuers as to be able to cut across their circle in advance of them and to regain the sled.

The different lines were rapidly approaching a point. Somewhere out there in the snow, screened from his sight by trees and thickets, Henry knew that the wolf-pack, One Ear, and Bill were coming together. All too quickly, far more quickly than he had expected, it happened. He heard a shot, then two shots, in rapid succession, and he knew that Bill's ammunition was gone. Then he heard a great outcry of snarls and yelps. He recognised One Ear's yell of pain and terror, and he heard a wolf-cry that bespoke a stricken animal. And that was all. The snarls ceased. The yelping died away. Silence settled down again over the lonely land.

He sat for a long while upon the sled. There was no need for him to go and see what had happened. He knew it as though it had taken place before his eyes. Once, he roused with a start and hastily got the axe out from underneath the lashings. But for some time longer he sat and brooded, the two remaining dogs crouching and trembling at his feet.

At last he arose in a weary manner, as though all the resilience had gone out of his body, and proceeded to fasten the dogs to the sled. He passed a rope over his shoulder, a man-trace, and pulled with the dogs. He did not go far. At the first hint of darkness he hastened to make a camp, and he saw to it that he had a generous supply of firewood. He fed the dogs, cooked and ate his supper, and made his bed close to the fire.

But he was not destined to enjoy that bed. Before his eyes closed the wolves had drawn too near for safety. It no longer required an effort of the vision to see them. They were all about him and the fire, in a narrow circle, and he could see them plainly in the firelight lying down, sitting up, crawling forward on their bellies, or slinking back and forth. They even slept. Here and there he could see one curled up in the snow like a dog, taking the sleep that was now denied himself.

He kept the fire brightly blazing, for he knew that it alone intervened between the flesh of his body and their hungry fangs. His two dogs stayed close by him, one on either side, leaning against him for protection, crying and whimpering, and at times snarling desperately when a wolf approached a little closer than usual. At such moments, when his dogs snarled, the whole circle would be agitated, the wolves coming to their feet and pressing tentatively forward, a chorus of snarls and eager yelps rising about him. Then the circle would lie down again, and here and there a wolf would resume its broken nap.

But this circle had a continuous tendency to draw in upon him. Bit by bit, an inch at a time, with here a wolf bellying forward, and there a wolf bellying forward, the circle would narrow until the brutes were almost within springing distance. Then he would seize brands from the fire and hurl them into the pack. A hasty drawing back always resulted, accompanied by angry yelps and frightened snarls when a well-aimed brand struck and scorched a too daring animal.

Morning found the man haggard and worn, wide-eyed from want of sleep. He cooked breakfast in the darkness, and at nine o'clock, when, with the coming of daylight, the wolf-pack drew back, he set about the task he had planned through the long hours of the night. Chopping down young saplings, he made them cross-bars of a scaffold by lashing them high up to the trunks of standing trees. Using the sled-lashing for a heaving rope, and with the aid of the dogs, he hoisted the coffin to the top of the scaffold.

"They got Bill, an' they may get me, but they'll sure never get you, young man," he said, addressing the dead body in its tree-sepulchre.

Then he took the trail, the lightened sled bounding along behind the willing dogs; for they, too, knew that safety lay open in the gaining of Fort McGurry. The wolves were now more open in their pursuit, trotting sedately behind and ranging along on either side, their red tongues lolling out, their lean sides showing the undulating ribs with every movement. They were very lean, mere skin-bags stretched over bony frames, with strings for muscles—so lean that Henry found it in his mind to marvel that they still kept their feet and did not collapse forthright in the snow.

He did not dare travel until dark. At midday, not only did the sun warm the southern horizon, but it even thrust its upper rim, pale and golden, above the sky-line. He received it as a sign. The days were growing longer. The sun was returning. But scarcely had the cheer of its light departed, than he went into camp. There were still several hours of grey daylight and sombre twilight, and he utilised them in chopping an enormous supply of fire-wood.

With night came horror. Not only were the starving wolves growing bolder, but lack of sleep was telling upon Henry. He dozed despite himself, crouching by the fire, the blankets about his shoulders, the axe between his knees, and on either side a dog pressing close against him. He awoke once and saw in front of him, not a dozen feet away, a big grey wolf, one of the largest of the pack. And even as he looked, the brute deliberately stretched himself after the manner of a lazy dog, yawning full in his face and looking upon him with a possessive eye, as if, in truth, he were merely a delayed meal that was soon to be eaten.

This certitude was shown by the whole pack. Fully a score he could count, staring hungrily at him or calmly sleeping in the snow. They reminded him of children gathered about a spread table and awaiting permission to begin to eat. And he was the food they were to eat! He wondered how and when the meal would begin.

As he piled wood on the fire he discovered an appreciation of his own body which he had never felt before. He watched his moving muscles and was interested in the cunning mechanism of his fingers. By the light of the fire he crooked his fingers slowly and repeatedly now one at a time, now all together, spreading them wide or making quick gripping movements. He studied the nail-formation, and prodded the finger-tips, now sharply, and again softly, gauging the while the nerve-sensations produced. It fascinated him, and he grew suddenly fond of this subtle flesh of his that worked so beautifully and smoothly and delicately. Then he would cast a glance of fear at the wolf-circle drawn expectantly about him, and like a blow the realisation would strike him that this wonderful body of his, this living flesh, was no more than so much meat, a quest of ravenous animals, to be torn and slashed by their hungry fangs, to be sustenance to them as the moose and the rabbit had often been sustenance to him.

He came out of a doze that was half nightmare, to see the red-hued she-wolf before him. She was not more than half a dozen feet away sitting in the snow and wistfully regarding him. The two dogs were whimpering and snarling at his feet, but she took no notice of them. She was looking at the man, and for some time he returned her look. There was nothing threatening about her. She looked at him merely with a great wistfulness, but he knew it to be the wistfulness of an equally great hunger. He was the food, and the sight of him excited in her the gustatory sensations. Her mouth opened, the saliva drooled forth, and she licked her chops with the pleasure of anticipation.

A spasm of fear went through him. He reached hastily for a brand to throw at her. But even as he reached, and before his fingers had closed on the missile, she sprang back into safety; and he knew that she was used to having things thrown at her. She had snarled as she sprang away, baring her white fangs to their roots, all her wistfulness vanishing, being replaced by a carnivorous malignity that made him shudder. He glanced at the hand that held the brand, noticing the cunning delicacy of the fingers that gripped it, how they adjusted themselves to all the inequalities of the surface, curling over and under and about the rough wood, and one little finger, too close to the burning portion of the brand, sensitively and automatically writhing back from the hurtful heat to a cooler gripping-place; and in the same instant he seemed to see a vision of those same sensitive and delicate fingers being crushed and torn by the white teeth of the she-wolf. Never had he been so fond of this body of his as now when his tenure of it was so precarious.

All night, with burning brands, he fought off the hungry pack. When he dozed despite himself, the whimpering and snarling of the dogs aroused him. Morning came, but for the first time the light of day failed to scatter the wolves. The man waited in vain for them to go. They remained in a circle about him and his fire, displaying an arrogance of possession that shook his courage born of the morning light.

He made one desperate attempt to pull out on the trail. But the moment he left the protection of the fire, the boldest wolf leaped for him, but leaped short. He saved himself by springing back, the jaws snapping together a scant six inches from his thigh. The rest of the pack was now up and surging upon him, and a throwing of firebrands right and left was necessary to drive them back to a respectful distance.

Even in the daylight he did not dare leave the fire to chop fresh wood. Twenty feet away towered a huge dead spruce. He spent half the day extending his campfire to the tree, at any moment a half dozen burning faggots ready at hand to fling at his enemies. Once at the tree, he studied the surrounding forest in order to fell the tree in the direction of the most firewood.

The night was a repetition of the night before, save that the need for sleep was becoming overpowering. The snarling of his dogs was losing its efficacy. Besides, they were snarling all the time, and his benumbed and drowsy senses no longer took note of changing pitch and intensity. He awoke with a start. The she-wolf was less than a yard from him. Mechanically, at short range, without letting go of it, he thrust a brand full into her open and snarling mouth. She sprang away, yelling with pain, and while he took delight in the smell of burning flesh and hair, he watched her shaking her head and growling wrathfully a score of feet away.

But this time, before he dozed again, he tied a burning pine-knot to his right hand. His eyes were closed but few minutes when the burn of the flame on his flesh awakened him. For several hours he adhered to this programme. Every time he was thus awakened he drove back the wolves with flying brands, replenished the fire, and rearranged the pine-knot on his hand. All worked well, but there came a time when he fastened the pine-knot insecurely. As his eyes closed it fell away from his hand.

He dreamed. It seemed to him that he was in Fort McGurry. It was warm and comfortable, and he was playing cribbage with the Factor. Also, it seemed to him that the fort was besieged by wolves. They were howling at the very gates, and sometimes he and the Factor paused from the game to listen and laugh at the futile efforts of the wolves to get in. And then, so strange was the dream, there was a crash. The door was burst open. He could see the wolves flooding into the big living-room of the fort. They were leaping straight for him and the Factor. With the bursting open of the door, the noise of their howling had increased tremendously. This howling now bothered him. His dream was merging into something else—he knew not what; but through it all, following him, persisted the howling.

And then he awoke to find the howling real. There was a great snarling and yelping. The wolves were rushing him. They were all about him and upon him. The teeth of one had closed upon his arm. Instinctively he leaped into the fire, and as he leaped, he felt the sharp slash of teeth that tore through the flesh of his leg. Then began a fire fight. His stout mittens temporarily protected his hands, and he scooped live coals into the air in all directions, until the campfire took on the semblance of a volcano.

But it could not last long. His face was blistering in the heat, his eyebrows and lashes were singed off, and the heat was becoming unbearable to his feet. With a flaming brand in each hand, he sprang to the edge of the fire. The wolves had been driven back. On every side, wherever the live coals had fallen, the snow was sizzling, and every little while a retiring wolf, with wild leap and snort and snarl, announced that one such live coal had been stepped upon.

Flinging his brands at the nearest of his enemies, the man thrust his smouldering mittens into the snow and stamped about to cool his feet. His two dogs were missing, and he well knew that they had served as a course in the protracted meal which had begun days before with Fatty, the last course of which would likely be himself in the days to follow.

"You ain't got me yet!" he cried, savagely shaking his fist at the hungry beasts; and at the sound of his voice the whole circle was agitated, there was a general snarl, and the she-wolf slid up close to him across the snow and watched him with hungry wistfulness.

He set to work to carry out a new idea that had come to him. He extended the fire into a large circle. Inside this circle he crouched, his sleeping outfit under him as a protection against the melting snow. When he had thus disappeared within his shelter of flame, the whole pack came curiously to the rim of the fire to see what had become of him. Hitherto they had been denied access to the fire, and they now settled down in a close-drawn circle, like so many dogs, blinking and yawning and stretching their lean bodies in the unaccustomed warmth. Then the she-wolf sat down, pointed her nose at a star, and began to howl. One by one the wolves joined her, till the whole pack, on haunches, with noses pointed skyward, was howling its hunger cry.

Dawn came, and daylight. The fire was burning low. The fuel had run out, and there was need to get more. The man attempted to step out of his circle of flame, but the wolves surged to meet him. Burning brands made them spring aside, but they no longer sprang back. In vain he strove to drive them back. As he gave up and stumbled inside his circle, a wolf leaped for him, missed, and landed with all four feet in the coals. It cried out with terror, at the same time snarling, and scrambled back to cool its paws in the snow.

The man sat down on his blankets in a crouching position. His body leaned forward from the hips. His shoulders, relaxed and drooping, and his head on his knees advertised that he had given up the struggle. Now and again he raised his head to note the dying down of the fire. The circle of flame and coals was breaking into segments with openings in between. These openings grew in size, the segments diminished.

"I guess you can come an' get me any time," he mumbled. "Anyway, I'm goin' to sleep."

Once he awakened, and in an opening in the circle, directly in front of him, he saw the she-wolf gazing at him.

Again he awakened, a little later, though it seemed hours to him. A mysterious change had taken place—so mysterious a change that he was shocked wider awake. Something had happened. He could not understand at first. Then he discovered it. The wolves were gone. Remained only the trampled snow to show how closely they had pressed him. Sleep was welling up and gripping him again, his head was sinking down upon his knees, when he roused with a sudden start.

There were cries of men, and churn of sleds, the creaking of harnesses, and the eager whimpering of straining dogs. Four sleds pulled in from the river bed to the camp among the trees. Half a dozen men were about the man who crouched in the centre of the dying fire. They were shaking and prodding him into consciousness. He looked at them like a drunken man and maundered in strange, sleepy speech.

"Red she-wolf. . . . Come in with the dogs at feedin' time. . . . First she ate the dog-food. . . . Then she ate the dogs. . . . An' after that she ate Bill. . . . "

"Where's Lord Alfred?" one of the men bellowed in his ear, shaking him roughly.

He shook his head slowly. "No, she didn't eat him. . . . He's roostin' in a tree at the last camp."

"Dead?" the man shouted.

"An' in a box," Henry answered. He jerked his shoulder petulantly away from the grip of his questioner. "Say, you lemme alone. . . . I'm jes' plump tuckered out. . . . Goo' night, everybody."

His eyes fluttered and went shut. His chin fell forward on his chest. And even as they eased him down upon the blankets his snores were rising on the frosty air.

But there was another sound. Far and faint it was, in the remote distance, the cry of the hungry wolf-pack as it took the trail of other meat than the man it had just missed.

PART II

CHAPTER I—THE BATTLE OF THE FANGS

It was the she-wolf who had first caught the sound of men's voices and the whining of the sled-dogs; and it was the she-wolf who was first to spring away from the cornered man in his circle of dying flame. The pack had been loath to forego the kill it had hunted down, and it lingered for several minutes, making sure of the sounds, and then it, too, sprang away on the trail made by the she-wolf.

Running at the forefront of the pack was a large grey wolf—one of its several leaders. It was he who directed the pack's course on the heels of the she-wolf. It was he who snarled warningly at the younger members of the pack or slashed at them with his fangs when they ambitiously tried to pass him. And it was he who increased the pace when he sighted the she-wolf, now trotting slowly across the snow.

She dropped in alongside by him, as though it were her appointed position, and took the pace of the pack. He did not snarl at her, nor show his teeth, when any leap of hers chanced to put her in advance of him. On the contrary, he seemed kindly disposed toward her—too kindly to suit her, for he was prone to run near to her, and when he ran too near it was she who snarled and showed her teeth. Nor was she above slashing his shoulder sharply on occasion. At such times he betrayed no anger. He merely sprang to the side and ran stiffly ahead for several awkward leaps, in carriage and conduct resembling an abashed country swain.

This was his one trouble in the running of the pack; but she had other troubles. On her other side ran a gaunt old wolf, grizzled and marked with the scars of many battles. He ran always on her right side. The fact that he had but one eye, and that the left eye, might account for this. He, also, was addicted to crowding her, to veering toward her till his scarred muzzle touched her body, or shoulder, or neck. As with the running mate on the left, she repelled these attentions with her teeth; but when both bestowed their attentions at the same time she was roughly jostled, being compelled, with quick snaps to either side, to drive both lovers away and at the same time to maintain her forward leap with the pack and see the way of her feet before her. At such times her running mates flashed their teeth and growled threateningly across at each other. They might have fought, but even wooing and its rivalry waited upon the more pressing hunger-need of the pack.

After each repulse, when the old wolf sheered abruptly away from the sharp-toothed object of his desire, he shouldered against a young three-year-old that ran on his blind right side. This young wolf had attained his full size; and, considering the weak and famished condition of the pack, he possessed more than the average vigour and spirit. Nevertheless, he ran with his head even with the shoulder of his one-eyed elder. When he ventured to run abreast of the older wolf (which was seldom), a snarl and a snap sent him back even with the shoulder again. Sometimes, however, he dropped cautiously and slowly behind and edged in between the old leader and the she-wolf. This was doubly resented, even triply resented. When she snarled her displeasure, the old leader would whirl on the three-year-old. Sometimes she whirled with him. And sometimes the young leader on the left whirled, too.

At such times, confronted by three sets of savage teeth, the young wolf stopped precipitately, throwing himself back on his haunches, with fore-legs stiff, mouth menacing, and mane bristling. This confusion in the front of the moving pack always caused confusion in the rear. The wolves behind collided with the young wolf and expressed their displeasure by administering sharp nips on his hind-legs and flanks. He was laying up trouble for himself, for lack of food and short tempers went together; but with the boundless faith of youth he persisted in repeating the manoeuvre every little while, though it never succeeded in gaining anything for him but discomfiture.

Had there been food, love-making and fighting would have gone on apace, and the pack-formation would have been broken up. But the situation of the pack was desperate. It was lean with long-standing hunger. It ran below its ordinary speed. At the rear limped the weak members, the very young and the very old. At the front were the strongest. Yet all were more like skeletons than full-bodied wolves. Nevertheless, with the exception of the ones that limped, the movements of the animals were effortless and tireless. Their stringy muscles seemed founts of inexhaustible energy. Behind every steel-like contraction of a muscle, lay another steel-like contraction, and another, and another, apparently without end.

They ran many miles that day. They ran through the night. And the next day found them still running. They were running over the surface of a world frozen and dead. No life stirred. They alone moved through the vast inertness. They alone were alive, and they sought for other things that were alive in order that they might devour them and continue to live.

They crossed low divides and ranged a dozen small streams in a lower-lying country before their quest was rewarded. Then they came upon moose. It was a big bull they first found. Here was meat and life, and it was guarded by no mysterious fires nor flying missiles of flame. Splay hoofs and palmated antlers they knew, and they flung their customary patience and caution to the wind. It was a brief fight and fierce. The big bull was beset on every side. He ripped them open or split their skulls with shrewdly driven blows of his great hoofs. He crushed them and broke them on his large horns. He stamped them into the snow under him in the wallowing struggle. But he was foredoomed, and he went down with the she-wolf tearing savagely at his throat, and with other teeth fixed everywhere upon him, devouring him alive, before ever his last struggles ceased or his last damage had been wrought.

There was food in plenty. The bull weighed over eight hundred pounds—fully twenty pounds of meat per mouth for the forty-odd wolves of the pack. But if they could fast prodigiously, they could feed prodigiously, and soon a few scattered bones were all that remained of the splendid live brute that had faced the pack a few hours before.

There was now much resting and sleeping. With full stomachs, bickering and quarrelling began among the younger males, and this continued through the few days that followed before the breaking-up of the pack. The famine was over. The wolves were now in the country of game, and though they still hunted in pack, they hunted more cautiously, cutting out heavy cows or crippled old bulls from the small moose-herds they ran across.

There came a day, in this land of plenty, when the wolf-pack split in half and went in different directions. The she-wolf, the young leader on her left, and the one-eyed elder on her right, led their half of the pack down to the Mackenzie River and across into the lake country to the east. Each day this remnant of the pack dwindled. Two by two, male and female, the wolves were deserting. Occasionally a solitary male was driven out by the sharp teeth of his rivals. In the end there remained only four: the she-wolf, the young leader, the one-eyed one, and the ambitious three-year-old.

The she-wolf had by now developed a ferocious temper. Her three suitors all bore the marks of her teeth. Yet they never replied in kind, never defended themselves against her. They turned their shoulders to her most savage slashes, and with wagging tails and mincing steps strove to placate her wrath. But if they were all mildness toward her, they were all fierceness toward one another. The three-year-old grew too ambitious in his fierceness. He caught the one-eyed elder on his blind side and ripped his ear into ribbons. Though the grizzled old fellow could see only on one side, against the youth and vigour of the other he brought into play the wisdom of long years of experience. His lost eye and his scarred muzzle bore evidence to the nature of his experience. He had survived too many battles to be in doubt for a moment about what to do.

The battle began fairly, but it did not end fairly. There was no telling what the outcome would have been, for the third wolf joined the elder, and together, old leader and young leader, they attacked the ambitious three-year-old and proceeded to destroy him. He was beset on either side by the merciless fangs of his erstwhile comrades. Forgotten were the days they had hunted together, the game they had pulled down, the famine they had suffered. That business was a thing of the past.

The business of love was at hand—ever a sterner and crueller business than that of food-getting.

And in the meanwhile, the she-wolf, the cause of it all, sat down contentedly on her haunches and watched. She was even pleased. This was her day—and it came not often—when manes bristled, and fang smote fang or ripped and tore the yielding flesh, all for the possession of her.

And in the business of love the three-year-old, who had made this his first adventure upon it, yielded up his life. On either side of his body stood his two rivals. They were gazing at the she-wolf, who sat smiling in the snow. But the elder leader was wise, very wise, in love even as in battle. The younger leader turned his head to lick a wound on his shoulder. The curve of his neck was turned toward his rival. With his one eye the elder saw the opportunity. He darted in low and closed with his fangs. It was a long, ripping slash, and deep as well. His teeth, in passing, burst the wall of the great vein of the throat. Then he leaped clear.

The young leader snarled terribly, but his snarl broke midmost into a tickling cough. Bleeding and coughing, already stricken, he sprang at the elder and fought while life faded from him, his legs going weak beneath him, the light of day dulling on his eyes, his blows and springs falling shorter and shorter.

And all the while the she-wolf sat on her haunches and smiled. She was made glad in vague ways by the battle, for this was the love-making of the Wild, the sex-tragedy of the natural world that was tragedy only to those that died. To those that survived it was not tragedy, but realisation and achievement.

When the young leader lay in the snow and moved no more, One Eye stalked over to the she-wolf. His carriage was one of mingled triumph and caution. He was plainly expectant of a rebuff, and he was just as plainly surprised when her teeth did not flash out at him in anger. For the first time she met him with a kindly manner. She sniffed noses with him, and even condescended to leap about and frisk and play with him in quite puppyish fashion. And he, for all his grey years and sage experience, behaved quite as puppyishly and even a little more foolishly.

Forgotten already were the vanquished rivals and the love-tale red-written on the snow. Forgotten, save once, when old One Eye stopped for a moment to lick his stiffening wounds. Then it was that his lips half writhed into a snarl, and the hair of his neck and shoulders involuntarily bristled, while he half crouched for a spring, his claws spasmodically clutching into the snow-surface for firmer footing. But it was all forgotten the next moment, as he sprang after the she-wolf, who was coyly leading him a chase through the woods.

After that they ran side by side, like good friends who have come to an understanding. The days passed by, and they kept together, hunting their meat and killing and eating it in common. After a time the she-wolf began to grow restless. She seemed to be searching for something that she could not find. The hollows under fallen trees seemed to attract her, and she spent much time nosing about among the larger snow-piled crevices in the rocks and in the caves of overhanging banks. Old One Eye was not interested at all, but he followed her good-naturedly in her quest, and when her investigations in particular places were unusually protracted, he would lie down and wait until she was ready to go on.

They did not remain in one place, but travelled across country until they regained the Mackenzie River, down which they slowly went, leaving it often to hunt game along the small streams that entered it, but always returning to it again. Sometimes they chanced upon other wolves, usually in pairs; but there was no friendliness of intercourse displayed on either side, no gladness at meeting, no desire to return to the pack-formation. Several times they encountered solitary wolves. These were always males, and they were pressingly insistent on joining with One Eye and his mate. This he resented, and when she stood shoulder to shoulder with him, bristling and showing her teeth, the aspiring solitary ones would back off, turn-tail, and continue on their lonely way.

One moonlight night, running through the quiet forest, One Eye suddenly halted. His muzzle went up, his tail stiffened, and his nostrils dilated as he scented the air. One foot also he held up, after the manner of a dog. He was not satisfied, and he continued to smell the air, striving to understand the message borne upon it to him. One careless sniff had satisfied his mate, and she trotted on to reassure him. Though he followed her, he was still dubious, and he could not forbear an occasional halt in order more carefully to study the warning.

She crept out cautiously on the edge of a large open space in the midst of the trees. For some time she stood alone. Then One Eye, creeping and crawling, every sense on the alert, every hair radiating infinite suspicion, joined her. They stood side by side, watching and listening and smelling.

To their ears came the sounds of dogs wrangling and scuffling, the guttural cries of men, the sharper voices of scolding women, and once the shrill and plaintive cry of a child. With the exception of the huge bulks of the skin-lodges, little could be seen save the flames of the fire, broken by the movements of intervening bodies, and the smoke rising slowly on the quiet air. But to their nostrils came the myriad smells of an Indian camp, carrying a story that was largely incomprehensible to One Eye, but every detail of which the she-wolf knew.

She was strangely stirred, and sniffed and sniffed with an increasing delight. But old One Eye was doubtful. He betrayed his apprehension, and started tentatively to go. She turned and touched his neck with her muzzle in a reassuring way, then regarded the camp again. A new wistfulness was in her face, but it was not the wistfulness of hunger. She was thrilling to a desire that urged her to go forward, to be in closer to that fire, to be squabbling with the dogs, and to be avoiding and dodging the stumbling feet of men.

One Eye moved impatiently beside her; her unrest came back upon her, and she knew again her pressing need to find the thing for which she searched. She turned and trotted back into the forest, to the great relief of One Eye, who trotted a little to the fore until they were well within the shelter of the trees.

As they slid along, noiseless as shadows, in the moonlight, they came upon a run-way. Both noses went down to the footprints in the snow. These footprints were very fresh. One Eye ran ahead cautiously, his mate at his heels. The broad pads of their feet were spread wide and in contact with the snow were like velvet. One Eye caught sight of a dim movement of white in the midst of the white. His sliding gait had been deceptively swift, but it was as nothing to the speed at which he now ran. Before him was bounding the faint patch of white he had discovered.

They were running along a narrow alley flanked on either side by a growth of young spruce. Through the trees the mouth of the alley could be seen, opening out on a moonlit glade. Old One Eye was rapidly overhauling the fleeing shape of white. Bound by bound he gained. Now he was upon it. One leap more and his teeth would be sinking into it. But that leap was never made. High in the air, and straight up, soared the shape of white, now a struggling snowshoe rabbit that leaped and bounded, executing a fantastic dance there above him in the air and never once returning to earth.

One Eye sprang back with a snort of sudden fright, then shrank down to the snow and crouched, snarling threats at this thing of fear he did not understand. But the she-wolf coolly thrust past him. She poised for a moment, then sprang for the dancing rabbit. She, too, soared high, but not so high as the quarry, and her teeth clipped emptily together with a metallic snap. She made another leap, and another.

Her mate had slowly relaxed from his crouch and was watching her. He now evinced displeasure at her repeated failures, and himself made a mighty spring upward. His teeth closed upon the rabbit, and he bore it back to earth with him. But at the same time there was a suspicious crackling movement beside him, and his astonished eye saw a young spruce sapling bending down above him to strike him. His jaws let go their grip, and he leaped backward to escape this strange danger, his lips drawn back from his fangs, his throat snarling, every hair bristling with rage and fright. And in that moment the sapling reared its slender length upright and the rabbit soared dancing in the air again.

The she-wolf was angry. She sank her fangs into her mate's shoulder in reproof; and he, frightened, unaware of what constituted this new onslaught, struck back ferociously and in still greater fright, ripping down the side of the she-wolf's muzzle. For him to resent such reproof was equally unexpected to her, and she sprang upon him in snarling indignation. Then he discovered his mistake and tried to placate her. But she proceeded to punish him roundly, until he gave over all attempts at placation, and whirled in a circle, his head away from her, his shoulders receiving the punishment of her teeth.

In the meantime the rabbit danced above them in the air. The she-wolf sat down in the snow, and old One Eye, now more in fear of his mate than of the mysterious sapling, again sprang for the rabbit. As he sank back with it between his teeth, he kept his eye on the sapling. As before, it followed him back to earth. He crouched down under the impending blow, his hair bristling, but his teeth still keeping tight hold of the rabbit. But the blow did not fall. The sapling remained bent above him. When he moved it moved, and he growled at it through his clenched jaws; when he remained still, it remained still, and he concluded it was safer to continue remaining still. Yet the warm blood of the rabbit tasted good in his mouth.

It was his mate who relieved him from the quandary in which he found himself. She took the rabbit from him, and while the sapling swayed and teetered threateningly above her she calmly gnawed off the rabbit's head. At once the sapling shot up, and after that gave no more trouble, remaining in the decorous and perpendicular position in which nature had intended it to grow. Then, between them, the she-wolf and One Eye devoured the game which the mysterious sapling had caught for them.

There were other run-ways and alleys where rabbits were hanging in the air, and the wolf-pair prospected them all, the she-wolf leading the way, old One Eye following and observant, learning the method of robbing snares—a knowledge destined to stand him in good stead in the days to come.

CHAPTER II—THE LAIR

For two days the she-wolf and One Eye hung about the Indian camp. He was worried and apprehensive, yet the camp lured his mate and she was loath to depart. But when, one morning, the air was rent with the report of a rifle close at hand, and a bullet smashed against a tree trunk several inches from One Eye's head, they hesitated no more, but went off on a long, swinging lope that put quick miles between them and the danger.

They did not go far—a couple of days' journey. The she-wolf's need to find the thing for which she searched had now become imperative. She was getting very heavy, and could run but slowly. Once, in the pursuit of a rabbit, which she ordinarily would have caught with ease, she gave over and lay down and rested. One Eye came to her; but when he touched her neck gently with his muzzle she snapped at him with such quick fierceness that he tumbled over backward and cut a ridiculous figure in his effort to escape her teeth. Her temper was now shorter than ever; but he had become more patient than ever and more solicitous.

And then she found the thing for which she sought. It was a few miles up a small stream that in the summer time flowed into the Mackenzie, but that then was frozen over and frozen down to its rocky bottom—a dead stream of solid white from source to mouth. The she-wolf was trotting wearily along, her mate well in advance, when she came upon the overhanging, high clay-bank. She turned aside and trotted over to it. The wear and tear of spring storms and melting snows had underwashed the bank and in one place had made a small cave out of a narrow fissure.

She paused at the mouth of the cave and looked the wall over carefully. Then, on one side and the other, she ran along the base of the wall to where its abrupt bulk merged from the softer-lined landscape. Returning to the cave, she entered its narrow mouth. For a short three feet she was compelled to crouch, then the walls widened and rose higher in a little round chamber nearly six feet in diameter. The roof barely cleared her head. It was dry and cosey. She inspected it with painstaking care, while One Eye, who had returned, stood in the entrance and patiently watched her. She dropped her head, with her nose to the ground and directed toward a point near to her closely bunched feet, and around this point she circled several times; then, with a tired sigh that was almost a grunt, she curled her body in, relaxed her legs, and dropped down, her head toward the entrance. One Eye, with pointed, interested ears, laughed at her, and beyond, outlined against the white light, she could see the brush of his tail waving good-naturedly. Her own ears, with a snuggling

84

movement, laid their sharp points backward and down against the head for a moment, while her mouth opened and her tongue lolled peaceably out, and in this way she expressed that she was pleased and satisfied.

One Eye was hungry. Though he lay down in the entrance and slept, his sleep was fitful. He kept awaking and cocking his ears at the bright world without, where the April sun was blazing across the snow. When he dozed, upon his ears would steal the faint whispers of hidden trickles of running water, and he would rouse and listen intently. The sun had come back, and all the awakening Northland world was calling to him. Life was stirring. The feel of spring was in the air, the feel of growing life under the snow, of sap ascending in the trees, of buds bursting the shackles of the frost.

He cast anxious glances at his mate, but she showed no desire to get up. He looked outside, and half a dozen snow-birds fluttered across his field of vision. He started to get up, then looked back to his mate again, and settled down and dozed. A shrill and minute singing stole upon his hearing. Once, and twice, he sleepily brushed his nose with his paw. Then he woke up. There, buzzing in the air at the tip of his nose, was a lone mosquito. It was a full-grown mosquito, one that had lain frozen in a dry log all winter and that had now been thawed out by the sun. He could resist the call of the world no longer. Besides, he was hungry.

He crawled over to his mate and tried to persuade her to get up. But she only snarled at him, and he walked out alone into the bright sunshine to find the snow-surface soft under foot and the travelling difficult. He went up the frozen bed of the stream, where the snow, shaded by the trees, was yet hard and crystalline. He was gone eight hours, and he came back through the darkness hungrier than when he had started. He had found game, but he had not caught it. He had broken through the melting snow crust, and wallowed, while the snowshoe rabbits had skimmed along on top lightly as ever.

He paused at the mouth of the cave with a sudden shock of suspicion. Faint, strange sounds came from within. They were sounds not made by his mate, and yet they were remotely familiar. He bellied cautiously inside and was met by a warning snarl from the she-wolf. This he received without perturbation, though he obeyed it by keeping his distance; but he remained interested in the other sounds—faint, muffled sobbings and slubberings.

His mate warned him irritably away, and he curled up and slept in the entrance. When morning came and a dim light pervaded the lair, he again sought after the source of the remotely familiar sounds. There was a new note in his mate's warning snarl. It was a jealous note, and he was very careful in keeping a respectful distance. Nevertheless, he made out, sheltering between her legs against the length of her body, five strange little bundles of life, very feeble, very helpless, making tiny whimpering noises, with eyes that did not open to the light. He was surprised. It was not the first time in his long and successful life that this thing had happened. It had happened many times, yet each time it was as fresh a surprise as ever to him.

His mate looked at him anxiously. Every little while she emitted a low growl, and at times, when it seemed to her he approached too near, the growl shot up in her throat to a sharp snarl. Of her own experience she had no memory of the thing happening; but in her instinct, which was the experience of all the mothers of wolves, there lurked a memory of fathers that had eaten their new-born and helpless progeny. It manifested itself as a fear strong within her, that made her prevent One Eye from more closely inspecting the cubs he had fathered.

But there was no danger. Old One Eye was feeling the urge of an impulse, that was, in turn, an instinct that had come down to him from all the fathers of wolves. He did not question it, nor puzzle over it. It was there, in the fibre of his being; and it was the most natural thing in the world that he should obey it by turning his back on his new-born family and by trotting out and away on the meat-trail whereby he lived.

Five or six miles from the lair, the stream divided, its forks going off among the mountains at a right angle. Here, leading up the left fork, he came upon a fresh track. He smelled it and found it so recent that he crouched swiftly, and looked in the direction in which it disappeared. Then he turned deliberately and took the right fork. The footprint was much larger than the one his own feet made, and he knew that in the wake of such a trail there was little meat for him.

Half a mile up the right fork, his quick ears caught the sound of gnawing teeth. He stalked the quarry and found it to be a porcupine, standing upright against a tree and trying his teeth on the bark. One Eye approached carefully but hopelessly. He knew the breed, though he had never met it so far north before; and never in his long life had porcupine served him for a meal. But he had long since learned that there was such a thing as Chance, or Opportunity, and he continued to draw near. There was never any telling what might happen, for with live things events were somehow always happening differently.

The porcupine rolled itself into a ball, radiating long, sharp needles in all directions that defied attack. In his youth One Eye had once sniffed too near a similar, apparently inert ball of quills, and had the tail flick out suddenly in his face. One quill he had carried away in his muzzle, where it had remained for weeks, a rankling flame, until it finally worked out. So he lay down, in a comfortable crouching position, his nose fully a foot away, and out of the line of the tail. Thus he waited, keeping perfectly quiet. There was no telling. Something might happen. The porcupine might unroll. There might be opportunity for a deft and ripping thrust of paw into the tender, unguarded belly.

But at the end of half an hour he arose, growled wrathfully at the motionless ball, and trotted on. He had waited too often and futilely in the past for porcupines to unroll, to waste any more time. He continued up the right fork. The day wore along, and nothing rewarded his hunt.

The urge of his awakened instinct of fatherhood was strong upon him. He must find meat. In the afternoon he blundered upon a ptarmigan. He came out of a thicket and found himself face to face with the slow-witted bird. It was sitting on a log, not a foot beyond the end of his nose. Each saw the other. The bird made a startled rise, but he struck it with his paw, and smashed it down to earth, then pounced upon it, and caught it in his teeth as it scuttled across the snow trying to rise in the air again. As his teeth crunched through the tender flesh and fragile bones, he began naturally to eat. Then he remembered, and, turning on the back-track, started for home, carrying the ptarmigan in his mouth.

A mile above the forks, running velvet-footed as was his custom, a gliding shadow that cautiously prospected each new vista of the trail, he came upon later imprints of the large tracks he had discovered in the early morning. As the track led his way, he followed, prepared to meet the maker of it at every turn of the stream.

He slid his head around a corner of rock, where began an unusually large bend in the stream, and his quick eyes made out something that sent him crouching swiftly down. It was the maker of the track, a large female lynx. She was crouching as he had crouched once that day, in front of her the tight-rolled ball of quills. If he had been a gliding shadow before, he now became the ghost of such a shadow, as he crept and circled around, and came up well to leeward of the silent, motionless pair.

He lay down in the snow, depositing the ptarmigan beside him, and with eyes peering through the needles of a low-growing spruce he watched the play of life before him—the waiting lynx and the waiting porcupine, each intent on life; and, such was the curiousness of the game, the way of life for one lay in the eating of the other, and the way of life for the other lay in being not eaten. While old One Eye, the wolf crouching in the covert, played his part, too, in the game, waiting for some strange freak of Chance, that might help him on the meat-trail which was his way of life.

Half an hour passed, an hour; and nothing happened. The ball of quills might have been a stone for all it moved; the lynx might have been frozen to marble; and old One Eye might have been dead. Yet all three animals were keyed to a tenseness of living that was almost painful, and scarcely ever would it come to them to be more alive than they were then in their seeming petrifaction.

One Eye moved slightly and peered forth with increased eagerness. Something was happening. The porcupine had at last decided that its enemy had gone away. Slowly, cautiously, it was unrolling its ball of impregnable armour. It was agitated by no tremor of anticipation. Slowly, slowly, the bristling ball straightened out and lengthened. One Eye watching, felt a sudden moistness in his mouth and a drooling of saliva, involuntary, excited by the living meat that was spreading itself like a repast before him.

Not quite entirely had the porcupine unrolled when it discovered its enemy. In that instant the lynx struck. The blow was like a flash of light. The paw, with rigid claws curving like talons, shot under the tender belly and came back with a swift ripping movement. Had the porcupine been entirely unrolled, or had it not discovered its enemy a fraction of a second before the blow was struck, the paw would have escaped unscathed; but a side-flick of the tail sank sharp quills into it as it was withdrawn.

Everything had happened at once—the blow, the counter-blow, the squeal of agony from the porcupine, the big cat's squall of sudden hurt and astonishment. One Eye half arose in his excitement, his ears up, his tail straight out and quivering behind him. The lynx's bad temper got the best of her. She sprang savagely at the thing that had hurt her. But the porcupine, squealing and grunting, with disrupted anatomy trying feebly to roll up into its ball-protection, flicked out its tail again, and again the big cat squalled with hurt and astonishment. Then she fell to backing away and sneezing, her nose bristling with quills like a monstrous pin-cushion. She brushed her nose with her paws, trying to dislodge the fiery darts, thrust it into the snow, and rubbed it against twigs and branches, and all the time leaping about, ahead, sidewise, up and down, in a frenzy of pain and fright.

She sneezed continually, and her stub of a tail was doing its best toward lashing about by giving quick, violent jerks. She quit her antics, and quieted down for a long minute. One Eye watched. And even he could not repress a start and an involuntary bristling of hair along his back when she suddenly leaped, without warning, straight up in the air, at the same time emitting a long and most terrible squall. Then she sprang away, up the trail, squalling with every leap she made.

It was not until her racket had faded away in the distance and died out that One Eye ventured forth. He walked as delicately as though all the snow were carpeted with porcupine quills, erect and ready to pierce the soft pads of his feet. The porcupine met his approach with a furious squealing and a clashing of its long teeth. It had managed to roll up in a ball again, but it was not quite the old compact ball; its muscles were too much torn for that. It had been ripped almost in half, and was still bleeding profusely.

One Eye scooped out mouthfuls of the blood-soaked snow, and chewed and tasted and swallowed. This served as a relish, and his hunger increased mightily; but he was too old in the world to forget his caution. He waited. He lay down and waited, while the porcupine grated its teeth and uttered grunts and sobs and occasional sharp little squeals. In a little while, One Eye noticed that the quills were drooping and that a great quivering had set up. The quivering came to an end suddenly. There was a final defiant clash of the long teeth. Then all the quills drooped quite down, and the body relaxed and moved no more.

With a nervous, shrinking paw, One Eye stretched out the porcupine to its full length and turned it over on its back. Nothing had happened. It was surely dead. He studied it intently for a moment, then took a careful grip with his teeth and started off down the stream, partly carrying, partly dragging the porcupine, with head turned to the side so as to avoid stepping on the prickly mass. He recollected something, dropped the burden, and trotted back to where he had left the ptarmigan. He did not hesitate a moment. He knew clearly what was to be done, and this he did by promptly eating the ptarmigan. Then he returned and took up his burden.

When he dragged the result of his day's hunt into the cave, the she-wolf inspected it, turned her muzzle to him, and lightly licked him on the neck. But the next instant she was warning him away from the cubs with a snarl that was less harsh than usual and that was more apologetic than menacing. Her instinctive fear of the father of her progeny was toning down. He was behaving as a wolf-father should, and manifesting no unholy desire to devour the young lives she had brought into the world.

CHAPTER III—THE GREY CUB

He was different from his brothers and sisters. Their hair already betrayed the reddish hue inherited from their mother, the she-wolf; while he alone, in this particular, took after his father. He was the one little grey cub of the litter. He had bred true to the straight wolf-stock—in fact, he had bred true to old One Eye himself, physically, with but a single exception, and that was he had two eyes to his father's one.

The grey cub's eyes had not been open long, yet already he could see with steady clearness. And while his eyes were still closed, he had felt, tasted, and smelled. He knew his two brothers and his two sisters very well. He had begun to romp with them in a feeble, awkward way, and even to squabble, his little throat vibrating with a queer rasping noise (the forerunner of the growl), as he worked himself into a passion. And long before his eyes had opened he had learned by touch, taste, and smell to know his mother—a fount of warmth and liquid food and tenderness. She possessed a gentle, caressing tongue that soothed him when it passed over his soft little body, and that impelled him to snuggle close against her and to doze off to sleep.

Most of the first month of his life had been passed thus in sleeping; but now he could see quite well, and he stayed awake for longer periods of time, and he was coming to learn his world quite well. His world was gloomy; but he did not know that, for he knew no other world. It was dim-lighted; but his eyes had never had to adjust themselves to any other light. His world was very small. Its limits were the walls of the lair; but as he had no knowledge of the wide world outside, he was never oppressed by the narrow confines of his existence.

But he had early discovered that one wall of his world was different from the rest. This was the mouth of the cave and the source of light. He had discovered that it was different from the other walls long before he had any thoughts of his own, any conscious volitions. It had been an irresistible attraction before ever his eyes opened and looked upon it. The light from it had beat upon his sealed lids, and the eyes and the optic nerves had pulsated to little, sparklike flashes, warm-coloured and strangely pleasing. The life of his body, and of every fibre of his body, the life that was the very substance of his body and that was apart from his own personal life, had yearned toward this light and urged his body toward it in the same way that the cunning chemistry of a plant urges it toward the sun.

Always, in the beginning, before his conscious life dawned, he had crawled toward the mouth of the cave. And in this his brothers and sisters were one with him. Never, in that period, did any of them crawl toward the dark corners of the back-wall. The light drew them as if they were plants; the chemistry of the life that composed them demanded the light as a necessity of being; and their little puppet-bodies crawled blindly and chemically, like the tendrils of a vine. Later on, when each developed individuality and became personally conscious of impulses and desires, the attraction of the light increased. They were always crawling and sprawling toward it, and being driven back from it by their mother.

It was in this way that the grey cub learned other attributes of his mother than the soft, soothing, tongue. In his insistent crawling toward the light, he discovered in her a nose that with a sharp nudge administered rebuke, and later, a paw, that crushed him down and rolled him over and over with swift, calculating stroke. Thus he learned hurt; and on top of it he learned to avoid hurt, first, by not incurring the risk of it; and second, when he had incurred the risk, by dodging and by retreating. These were conscious actions, and were the results of his first generalisations upon the world. Before that he had recoiled automatically from hurt, as he had crawled automatically toward the light. After that he recoiled from hurt because he knew that it was hurt.

He was a fierce little cub. So were his brothers and sisters. It was to be expected. He was a carnivorous animal. He came of a breed of meat-killers and meat-eaters. His father and mother lived wholly upon meat. The milk he had sucked with his first flickering life, was milk transformed directly from meat, and now, at a month old, when his eyes had been open for but a week, he was beginning himself to eat meat—meat half-digested by the she-wolf and disgorged for the five growing cubs that already made too great demand upon her breast.

But he was, further, the fiercest of the litter. He could make a louder rasping growl than any of them. His tiny rages were much more terrible than theirs. It was he that first learned the trick of rolling a fellow-cub over with a cunning paw-stroke. And it was he that first gripped another cub by the ear and pulled and tugged and growled through jaws tight-clenched. And certainly it was he that caused the mother the most trouble in keeping her litter from the mouth of the cave.

The fascination of the light for the grey cub increased from day to day. He was perpetually departing on yard-long adventures toward the cave's entrance, and as perpetually being driven back. Only he did not know it for an entrance. He did not know anything about entrances—passages whereby one goes from one place to another place. He did not know any other place, much less of a way to get there. So to him the entrance of the cave was a wall—a wall of light. As the sun was to the outside dweller, this wall was to him the sun of his world. It attracted him as a candle attracts a moth. He was always striving to attain it. The life that was so swiftly expanding within him, urged him continually toward the wall of light. The life that was within him knew that it was the one way out, the way he was predestined to tread. But he himself did not know anything about it. He did not know there was any outside at all.

There was one strange thing about this wall of light. His father (he had already come to recognise his father as the one other dweller in the world, a creature like his mother, who slept near the light and was a bringer of meat)—his father had a way of walking right into the white far wall and disappearing. The grey cub could not understand this. Though never permitted by his mother to approach that wall, he had approached the other walls, and encountered hard obstruction on the end of his tender nose. This hurt. And after several such adventures, he left the walls alone. Without thinking about it, he accepted this disappearing into the wall as a peculiarity of his father, as milk and half-digested meat were peculiarities of his mother.

In fact, the grey cub was not given to thinking—at least, to the kind of thinking customary of men. His brain worked in dim ways. Yet his conclusions were as sharp and distinct as those achieved by men. He had a method of accepting things, without questioning the why and wherefore. In reality, this was the act of classification. He was never disturbed over why a thing happened. How it happened was sufficient for him. Thus, when he had bumped his nose on the back-wall a few times, he accepted that he would not disappear into walls. In the same way he accepted that his father could disappear into walls. But he was not in the least disturbed by desire to find out the reason for the difference between his father and himself. Logic and physics were no part of his mental make-up.

Like most creatures of the Wild, he early experienced famine. There came a time when not only did the meat-supply cease, but the milk no longer came from his mother's breast. At first, the cubs whimpered and cried, but for the most part they slept. It was not long before they were reduced to a coma of hunger. There were no more spats and squabbles, no more tiny rages nor attempts at growling; while the adventures toward the far white wall ceased altogether. The cubs slept, while the life that was in them flickered and died down.

One Eye was desperate. He ranged far and wide, and slept but little in the lair that had now become cheerless and miserable. The she-wolf, too, left her litter and went out in search of meat. In the first days after the birth of the cubs, One Eye had journeyed several times back to the Indian camp and robbed the rabbit snares; but, with the melting of the snow and the opening of the streams, the Indian camp had moved away, and that source of supply was closed to him.

When the grey cub came back to life and again took interest in the far white wall, he found that the population of his world had been reduced. Only one sister remained to him. The rest were gone. As he grew stronger, he found himself compelled to play alone, for the sister no longer lifted her head nor moved about. His little body rounded out with the meat he now ate; but the food had come too late for her. She slept continuously, a tiny skeleton flung round with skin in which the flame flickered lower and lower and at last went out.

Then there came a time when the grey cub no longer saw his father appearing and disappearing in the wall nor lying down asleep in the entrance. This had happened at the end of a second and less severe famine. The she-wolf knew why One Eye never came back, but there was no way by which she could tell what she had seen to the grey cub. Hunting herself for meat, up the left fork of the stream where lived the lynx, she had followed a day-old trail of One Eye. And she had found him, or what remained of him, at the end of the trail. There were many signs of the battle that had been fought, and of the lynx's withdrawal to her lair after having won the victory. Before she went away, the she-wolf had found this lair, but the signs told her that the lynx was inside, and she had not dared to venture in.

After that, the she-wolf in her hunting avoided the left fork. For she knew that in the lynx's lair was a litter of kittens, and she knew the lynx for a fierce, bad-tempered creature and a terrible fighter. It was all very well for half a dozen wolves to drive a lynx, spitting and bristling, up a tree; but it was quite a different matter for a lone wolf to encounter a lynx—especially when the lynx was known to have a litter of hungry kittens at her back.

But the Wild is the Wild, and motherhood is motherhood, at all times fiercely protective whether in the Wild or out of it; and the time was to come when the she-wolf, for her grey cub's sake, would venture the left fork, and the lair in the rocks, and the lynx's wrath.

CHAPTER IV—THE WALL OF THE WORLD

By the time his mother began leaving the cave on hunting expeditions, the cub had learned well the law that forbade his approaching the entrance. Not only had this law been forcibly and many times impressed on him by his mother's nose and paw, but in him the instinct of fear was developing. Never, in his brief cave-life, had he encountered anything of which to be afraid. Yet fear was in him. It had come down to him from a remote ancestry through a thousand thousand lives. It was a heritage he had received directly from One Eye and the she-wolf; but to them, in turn, it had been passed down through all the generations of wolves that had gone before. Fear!—that legacy of the Wild which no animal may escape nor exchange for pottage.

So the grey cub knew fear, though he knew not the stuff of which fear was made. Possibly he accepted it as one of the restrictions of life. For he had already learned that there were such restrictions. Hunger he had known; and when he could not appease his hunger he had felt restriction. The hard obstruction of the cave-wall, the sharp nudge of his mother's nose, the smashing stroke of her paw, the hunger unappeased of several famines, had borne in upon him that all was not freedom in the world, that to life there was limitations and restraints. These limitations and re-straints were laws. To be obedient to them was to escape hurt and make for happiness.

He did not reason the question out in this man fashion. He merely classified the things that hurt and the things that did not hurt. And after such classification he avoided the things that hurt, the restrictions and restraints, in order to enjoy the sat-isfactions and the remunerations of life.

Thus it was that in obedience to the law laid down by his mother, and in obedi-ence to the law of that unknown and nameless thing, fear, he kept away from the mouth of the cave. It remained to him a white wall of light. When his mother was absent, he slept most of the time, while during the intervals that he was awake he kept very quiet, suppressing the whimpering cries that tickled in his throat and strove for noise.

Once, lying awake, he heard a strange sound in the white wall. He did not know that it was a wolverine, standing outside, all a-trembling with its own daring, and cautiously scenting out the contents of the cave. The cub knew only that the sniff was strange, a something unclassified, therefore unknown and terrible—for the un-known was one of the chief elements that went into the making of fear.

The hair bristled upon the grey cub's back, but it bristled silently. How was he to know that this thing that sniffed was a thing at which to bristle? It was not born of any knowledge of his, yet it was the visible expression of the fear that was in him, and for which, in his own life, there was no accounting. But fear was accompanied by another instinct—that of concealment. The cub was in a frenzy of terror, yet he lay without movement or sound, frozen, petrified into immobility, to all appearances dead. His mother, coming home, growled as she smelt the wolverine's track, and bounded into the cave and licked and nozzled him with undue vehemence of affection. And the cub felt that somehow he had escaped a great hurt.

But there were other forces at work in the cub, the greatest of which was growth. Instinct and law demanded of him obedience. But growth demanded disobedience. His mother and fear impelled him to keep away from the white wall. Growth is life, and life is for ever destined to make for light. So there was no damming up the tide of life that was rising within him—rising with every mouthful of meat he swallowed, with every breath he drew. In the end, one day, fear and obedience were swept away by the rush of life, and the cub straddled and sprawled toward the entrance.

Unlike any other wall with which he had had experience, this wall seemed to recede from him as he approached. No hard surface collided with the tender little nose he thrust out tentatively before him. The substance of the wall seemed as permeable and yielding as light. And as condition, in his eyes, had the seeming of form, so he entered into what had been wall to him and bathed in the substance that composed it.

It was bewildering. He was sprawling through solidity. And ever the light grew brighter. Fear urged him to go back, but growth drove him on. Suddenly he found himself at the mouth of the cave. The wall, inside which he had thought himself, as suddenly leaped back before him to an immeasurable distance. The light had become painfully bright. He was dazzled by it. Likewise he was made dizzy by this abrupt and tremendous extension of space. Automatically, his eyes were adjusting themselves to the brightness, focusing themselves to meet the increased distance of objects. At first, the wall had leaped beyond his vision. He now saw it again; but it had taken upon itself a remarkable remoteness. Also, its appearance had changed. It was now a variegated wall, composed of the trees that fringed the stream, the opposing mountain that towered above the trees, and the sky that out-towered the mountain.

A great fear came upon him. This was more of the terrible unknown. He crouched down on the lip of the cave and gazed out on the world. He was very much afraid. Because it was unknown, it was hostile to him. Therefore the hair stood up on end along his back and his lips wrinkled weakly in an attempt at a ferocious and intimidating snarl. Out of his puniness and fright he challenged and menaced the whole wide world.

Nothing happened. He continued to gaze, and in his interest he forgot to snarl. Also, he forgot to be afraid. For the time, fear had been routed by growth, while growth had assumed the guise of curiosity. He began to notice near objects—an open portion of the stream that flashed in the sun, the blasted pine-tree that stood at the base of the slope, and the slope itself, that ran right up to him and ceased two feet beneath the lip of the cave on which he crouched.

Now the grey cub had lived all his days on a level floor. He had never experienced the hurt of a fall. He did not know what a fall was. So he stepped boldly out upon the air. His hind-legs still rested on the cave-lip, so he fell forward head downward. The earth struck him a harsh blow on the nose that made him yelp. Then he began rolling down the slope, over and over. He was in a panic of terror. The unknown had caught him at last. It had gripped savagely hold of him and was about to wreak upon him some terrific hurt. Growth was now routed by fear, and he ki-yi'd like any frightened puppy.

The unknown bore him on he knew not to what frightful hurt, and he yelped and ki-yi'd unceasingly. This was a different proposition from crouching in frozen fear while the unknown lurked just alongside. Now the unknown had caught tight hold of him. Silence would do no good. Besides, it was not fear, but terror, that convulsed him.

But the slope grew more gradual, and its base was grass-covered. Here the cub lost momentum. When at last he came to a stop, he gave one last agonised yell and then a long, whimpering wail. Also, and quite as a matter of course, as though in his life he had already made a thousand toilets, he proceeded to lick away the dry clay that soiled him.

After that he sat up and gazed about him, as might the first man of the earth who landed upon Mars. The cub had broken through the wall of the world, the unknown had let go its hold of him, and here he was without hurt. But the first man on Mars would have experienced less unfamiliarity than did he. Without any antecedent knowledge, without any warning whatever that such existed, he found himself an explorer in a totally new world.

Now that the terrible unknown had let go of him, he forgot that the unknown had any terrors. He was aware only of curiosity in all the things about him. He inspected the grass beneath him, the moss-berry plant just beyond, and the dead trunk of the blasted pine that stood on the edge of an open space among the trees. A squirrel, running around the base of the trunk, came full upon him, and gave him a great fright. He cowered down and snarled. But the squirrel was as badly scared. It ran up the tree, and from a point of safety chattered back savagely.

This helped the cub's courage, and though the woodpecker he next encountered gave him a start, he proceeded confidently on his way. Such was his confidence, that when a moose-bird impudently hopped up to him, he reached out at it with a playful paw. The result was a sharp peck on the end of his nose that made him cower down and ki-yi. The noise he made was too much for the moose-bird, who sought safety in flight.

But the cub was learning. His misty little mind had already made an unconscious classification. There were live things and things not alive. Also, he must watch out for the live things. The things not alive remained always in one place, but the live things moved about, and there was no telling what they might do. The thing to expect of them was the unexpected, and for this he must be prepared.

He travelled very clumsily. He ran into sticks and things. A twig that he thought a long way off, would the next instant hit him on the nose or rake along his ribs. There were inequalities of surface. Sometimes he overstepped and stubbed his nose. Quite as often he understepped and stubbed his feet. Then there were the pebbles and stones that turned under him when he trod upon them; and from them he came to know that the things not alive were not all in the same state of stable equilibrium as was his cave—also, that small things not alive were more liable than large things to fall down or turn over. But with every mishap he was learning. The longer he walked, the better he walked. He was adjusting himself. He was learning to calculate his own muscular movements, to know his physical limitations, to measure distances between objects, and between objects and himself.

His was the luck of the beginner. Born to be a hunter of meat (though he did not know it), he blundered upon meat just outside his own cave-door on his first foray into the world. It was by sheer blundering that he chanced upon the shrewdly hidden ptarmigan nest. He fell into it. He had essayed to walk along the trunk of a fallen pine. The rotten bark gave way under his feet, and with a despairing yelp he pitched down the rounded crescent, smashed through the leafage and stalks of a small bush, and in the heart of the bush, on the ground, fetched up in the midst of seven ptarmigan chicks.

They made noises, and at first he was frightened at them. Then he perceived that they were very little, and he became bolder. They moved. He placed his paw on one, and its movements were accelerated. This was a source of enjoyment to him. He smelled it. He picked it up in his mouth. It struggled and tickled his tongue. At the same time he was made aware of a sensation of hunger. His jaws closed together. There was a crunching of fragile bones, and warm blood ran in his mouth. The taste of it was good. This was meat, the same as his mother gave him, only it was alive between his teeth and therefore better. So he ate the ptarmigan. Nor did he stop till he had devoured the whole brood. Then he licked his chops in quite the same way his mother did, and began to crawl out of the bush.

He encountered a feathered whirlwind. He was confused and blinded by the rush of it and the beat of angry wings. He hid his head between his paws and yelped. The blows increased. The mother ptarmigan was in a fury. Then he became angry. He rose up, snarling, striking out with his paws. He sank his tiny teeth into one of the wings and pulled and tugged sturdily. The ptarmigan struggled against him, showering blows upon him with her free wing. It was his first battle. He was elated. He forgot all about the unknown. He no longer was afraid of anything. He was fighting, tearing at a live thing that was striking at him. Also, this live thing was meat. The lust to kill was on him. He had just destroyed little live things. He would now destroy a big live thing. He was too busy and happy to know that he was happy. He was thrilling and exulting in ways new to him and greater to him than any he had known before.

He held on to the wing and growled between his tight-clenched teeth. The ptarmigan dragged him out of the bush. When she turned and tried to drag him back into the bush's shelter, he pulled her away from it and on into the open. And all the time she was making outcry and striking with her free wing, while feathers were flying like a snow-fall. The pitch to which he was aroused was tremendous. All the fighting blood of his breed was up in him and surging through him. This was living, though he did not know it. He was realising his own meaning in the world; he was doing that for which he was made—killing meat and battling to kill it. He was justifying his existence, than which life can do no greater; for life achieves its summit when it does to the uttermost that which it was equipped to do.

After a time, the ptarmigan ceased her struggling. He still held her by the wing, and they lay on the ground and looked at each other. He tried to growl threateningly, ferociously. She pecked on his nose, which by now, what of previous adventures was sore. He winced but held on. She pecked him again and again. From wincing he went to whimpering. He tried to back away from her, oblivious to the fact that by his hold on her he dragged her after him. A rain of pecks fell on his ill-used nose. The flood of fight ebbed down in him, and, releasing his prey, he turned tail and scampered on across the open in inglorious retreat.

He lay down to rest on the other side of the open, near the edge of the bushes, his tongue lolling out, his chest heaving and panting, his nose still hurting him and causing him to continue his whimper. But as he lay there, suddenly there came to him a feeling as of something terrible impending. The unknown with all its terrors rushed upon him, and he shrank back instinctively into the shelter of the bush. As he did so, a draught of air fanned him, and a large, winged body swept ominously and silently past. A hawk, driving down out of the blue, had barely missed him.

While he lay in the bush, recovering from his fright and peering fearfully out, the mother-ptarmigan on the other side of the open space fluttered out of the ravaged nest. It was because of her loss that she paid no attention to the winged bolt of the sky. But the cub saw, and it was a warning and a lesson to him—the swift downward swoop of the hawk, the short skim of its body just above the ground, the strike of its talons in the body of the ptarmigan, the ptarmigan's squawk of agony and fright, and the hawk's rush upward into the blue, carrying the ptarmigan away with it.

It was a long time before the cub left its shelter. He had learned much. Live things were meat. They were good to eat. Also, live things when they were large enough, could give hurt. It was better to eat small live things like ptarmigan chicks, and to let alone large live things like ptarmigan hens. Nevertheless he felt a little prick of ambition, a sneaking desire to have another battle with that ptarmigan hen—only the hawk had carried her away. May be there were other ptarmigan hens. He would go and see.

He came down a shelving bank to the stream. He had never seen water before. The footing looked good. There were no inequalities of surface. He stepped boldly out on it; and went down, crying with fear, into the embrace of the unknown. It was cold, and he gasped, breathing quickly. The water rushed into his lungs instead of the air that had always accompanied his act of breathing. The suffocation he experienced was like the pang of death. To him it signified death. He had no conscious knowledge of death, but like every animal of the Wild, he possessed the instinct of death. To him it stood as the greatest of hurts. It was the very essence of the unknown; it was the sum of the terrors of the unknown, the one culminating and unthinkable catastrophe that could happen to him, about which he knew nothing and about which he feared everything.

He came to the surface, and the sweet air rushed into his open mouth. He did not go down again. Quite as though it had been a long-established custom of his he struck out with all his legs and began to swim. The near bank was a yard away; but he had come up with his back to it, and the first thing his eyes rested upon was the opposite bank, toward which he immediately began to swim. The stream was a small one, but in the pool it widened out to a score of feet.

Midway in the passage, the current picked up the cub and swept him downstream. He was caught in the miniature rapid at the bottom of the pool. Here was little chance for swimming. The quiet water had become suddenly angry. Sometimes he was under, sometimes on top. At all times he was in violent motion, now being turned over or around, and again, being smashed against a rock. And with every rock he struck, he yelped. His progress was a series of yelps, from which might have been adduced the number of rocks he encountered.

Below the rapid was a second pool, and here, captured by the eddy, he was gently borne to the bank, and as gently deposited on a bed of gravel. He crawled frantically clear of the water and lay down. He had learned some more about the world. Water was not alive. Yet it moved. Also, it looked as solid as the earth, but was without any solidity at all. His conclusion was that things were not always what they appeared to be. The cub's fear of the unknown was an inherited distrust, and it had now been strengthened by experience. Thenceforth, in the nature of things, he would possess an abiding distrust of appearances. He would have to learn the reality of a thing before he could put his faith into it.

One other adventure was destined for him that day. He had recollected that there was such a thing in the world as his mother. And then there came to him a feeling that he wanted her more than all the rest of the things in the world. Not only was his body tired with the adventures it had undergone, but his little brain was equally tired. In all the days he had lived it had not worked so hard as on this one day. Furthermore, he was sleepy. So he started out to look for the cave and his mother, feeling at the same time an overwhelming rush of loneliness and helplessness.

He was sprawling along between some bushes, when he heard a sharp intimidating cry. There was a flash of yellow before his eyes. He saw a weasel leaping swiftly away from him. It was a small live thing, and he had no fear. Then, before him, at his feet, he saw an extremely small live thing, only several inches long, a young weasel, that, like himself, had disobediently gone out adventuring. It tried to retreat before him. He turned it over with his paw. It made a queer, grating noise. The next moment the flash of yellow reappeared before his eyes. He heard again the intimidating cry, and at the same instant received a sharp blow on the side of the neck and felt the sharp teeth of the mother-weasel cut into his flesh.

While he yelped and ki-yi'd and scrambled backward, he saw the mother-weasel leap upon her young one and disappear with it into the neighbouring thicket. The cut of her teeth in his neck still hurt, but his feelings were hurt more grievously, and he sat down and weakly whimpered. This mother-weasel was so small and so savage. He was yet to learn that for size and weight the weasel was the most ferocious, vindictive, and terrible of all the killers of the Wild. But a portion of this knowledge was quickly to be his.

He was still whimpering when the mother-weasel reappeared. She did not rush him, now that her young one was safe. She approached more cautiously, and the cub had full opportunity to observe her lean, snakelike body, and her head, erect, eager, and snake-like itself. Her sharp, menacing cry sent the hair bristling along his back, and he snarled warningly at her. She came closer and closer. There was a leap, swifter than his unpractised sight, and the lean, yellow body disappeared for a moment out of the field of his vision. The next moment she was at his throat, her teeth buried in his hair and flesh.

At first he snarled and tried to fight; but he was very young, and this was only his first day in the world, and his snarl became a whimper, his fight a struggle to escape. The weasel never relaxed her hold. She hung on, striving to press down with her teeth to the great vein where his life-blood bubbled. The weasel was a drinker of blood, and it was ever her preference to drink from the throat of life itself.

The grey cub would have died, and there would have been no story to write about him, had not the she-wolf come bounding through the bushes. The weasel let go the cub and flashed at the she-wolf's throat, missing, but getting a hold on the jaw instead. The she-wolf flirted her head like the snap of a whip, breaking the weasel's hold and flinging it high in the air. And, still in the air, the she-wolf's jaws closed on the lean, yellow body, and the weasel knew death between the crunching teeth.

The cub experienced another access of affection on the part of his mother. Her joy at finding him seemed even greater than his joy at being found. She nozzled him and caressed him and licked the cuts made in him by the weasel's teeth. Then, between them, mother and cub, they ate the blood-drinker, and after that went back to the cave and slept.

CHAPTER V—THE LAW OF MEAT

The cub's development was rapid. He rested for two days, and then ventured forth from the cave again. It was on this adventure that he found the young weasel whose mother he had helped eat, and he saw to it that the young weasel went the way of its mother. But on this trip he did not get lost. When he grew tired, he found his way back to the cave and slept. And every day thereafter found him out and ranging a wider area.

He began to get accurate measurement of his strength and his weakness, and to know when to be bold and when to be cautious. He found it expedient to be cautious all the time, except for the rare moments, when, assured of his own intrepidity, he abandoned himself to petty rages and lusts.

He was always a little demon of fury when he chanced upon a stray ptarmigan. Never did he fail to respond savagely to the chatter of the squirrel he had first met on the blasted pine. While the sight of a moose-bird almost invariably put him into the wildest of rages; for he never forgot the peck on the nose he had received from the first of that ilk he encountered.

But there were times when even a moose-bird failed to affect him, and those were times when he felt himself to be in danger from some other prowling meat hunter. He never forgot the hawk, and its moving shadow always sent him crouching into the nearest thicket. He no longer sprawled and straddled, and already he was developing the gait of his mother, slinking and furtive, apparently without exertion, yet sliding along with a swiftness that was as deceptive as it was imperceptible.

In the matter of meat, his luck had been all in the beginning. The seven ptarmigan chicks and the baby weasel represented the sum of his killings. His desire to kill strengthened with the days, and he cherished hungry ambitions for the squirrel that chattered so volubly and always informed all wild creatures that the wolf-cub was approaching. But as birds flew in the air, squirrels could climb trees, and the cub could only try to crawl unobserved upon the squirrel when it was on the ground.

The cub entertained a great respect for his mother. She could get meat, and she never failed to bring him his share. Further, she was unafraid of things. It did not occur to him that this fearlessness was founded upon experience and knowledge. Its effect on him was that of an impression of power. His mother represented power; and as he grew older he felt this power in the sharper admonishment of her paw; while the reproving nudge of her nose gave place to the slash of her fangs. For this, likewise, he respected his mother. She compelled obedience from him, and the older he grew the shorter grew her temper.

Famine came again, and the cub with clearer consciousness knew once more the bite of hunger. The she-wolf ran herself thin in the quest for meat. She rarely slept any more in the cave, spending most of her time on the meat-trail, and spending it vainly. This famine was not a long one, but it was severe while it lasted. The cub found no more milk in his mother's breast, nor did he get one mouthful of meat for himself.

Before, he had hunted in play, for the sheer joyousness of it; now he hunted in deadly earnestness, and found nothing. Yet the failure of it accelerated his development. He studied the habits of the squirrel with greater carefulness, and strove with greater craft to steal upon it and surprise it. He studied the wood-mice and tried to dig them out of their burrows; and he learned much about the ways of moose-birds and woodpeckers. And there came a day when the hawk's shadow did not drive him crouching into the bushes. He had grown stronger and wiser, and more confident. Also, he was desperate. So he sat on his haunches, conspicuously in an open space, and challenged the hawk down out of the sky. For he knew that there, floating in the blue above him, was meat, the meat his stomach yearned after so insistently. But the hawk refused to come down and give battle, and the cub crawled away into a thicket and whimpered his disappointment and hunger.

The famine broke. The she-wolf brought home meat. It was strange meat, different from any she had ever brought before. It was a lynx kitten, partly grown, like the cub, but not so large. And it was all for him. His mother had satisfied her hunger elsewhere; though he did not know that it was the rest of the lynx litter that had gone to satisfy her. Nor did he know the desperateness of her deed. He knew only that the velvet-furred kitten was meat, and he ate and waxed happier with every mouthful.

A full stomach conduces to inaction, and the cub lay in the cave, sleeping against his mother's side. He was aroused by her snarling. Never had he heard her snarl so terribly. Possibly in her whole life it was the most terrible snarl she ever gave. There was reason for it, and none knew it better than she. A lynx's lair is not despoiled with impunity. In the full glare of the afternoon light, crouching in the entrance of the cave, the cub saw the lynx-mother. The hair rippled up along his back at the sight. Here was fear, and it did not require his instinct to tell him of it. And if sight alone were not sufficient, the cry of rage the intruder gave, beginning with a snarl and rushing abruptly upward into a hoarse screech, was convincing enough in itself.

The cub felt the prod of the life that was in him, and stood up and snarled valiantly by his mother's side. But she thrust him ignominiously away and behind her. Because of the low-roofed entrance the lynx could not leap in, and when she made a crawling rush of it the she-wolf sprang upon her and pinned her down. The cub saw little of the battle. There was a tremendous snarling and spitting and screeching. The two animals threshed about, the lynx ripping and tearing with her claws and using her teeth as well, while the she-wolf used her teeth alone.

Once, the cub sprang in and sank his teeth into the hind leg of the lynx. He clung on, growling savagely. Though he did not know it, by the weight of his body he clogged the action of the leg and thereby saved his mother much damage. A change in the battle crushed him under both their bodies and wrenched loose his hold. The next moment the two mothers separated, and, before they rushed together again, the lynx lashed out at the cub with a huge fore-paw that ripped his shoulder open to the bone and sent him hurtling sidewise against the wall. Then was added to the uproar the cub's shrill yelp of pain and fright. But the fight lasted so long that he had time to cry himself out and to experience a second burst of courage; and the end of the battle found him again clinging to a hind-leg and furiously growling between his teeth.

The lynx was dead. But the she-wolf was very weak and sick. At first she caressed the cub and licked his wounded shoulder; but the blood she had lost had taken with it her strength, and for all of a day and a night she lay by her dead foe's side, without movement, scarcely breathing. For a week she never left the cave, except for water, and then her movements were slow and painful. At the end of that time the lynx was devoured, while the she-wolf's wounds had healed sufficiently to permit her to take the meat-trail again.

The cub's shoulder was stiff and sore, and for some time he limped from the terrible slash he had received. But the world now seemed changed. He went about in it with greater confidence, with a feeling of prowess that had not been his in the days before the battle with the lynx. He had looked upon life in a more ferocious aspect; he had fought; he had buried his teeth in the flesh of a foe; and he had survived. And because of all this, he carried himself more boldly, with a touch of defiance that was new in him. He was no longer afraid of minor things, and much of his timidity had vanished, though the unknown never ceased to press upon him with its mysteries and terrors, intangible and ever-menacing.

He began to accompany his mother on the meat-trail, and he saw much of the killing of meat and began to play his part in it. And in his own dim way he learned the law of meat. There were two kinds of life—his own kind and the other kind. His own kind included his mother and himself. The other kind included all live things that moved. But the other kind was divided. One portion was what his own kind killed and ate. This portion was composed of the non-killers and the small killers. The other portion killed and ate his own kind, or was killed and eaten by his own kind. And out of this classification arose the law. The aim of life was meat. Life itself was meat. Life lived on life. There were the eaters and the eaten. The law was: EAT OR BE EATEN. He did not formulate the law in clear, set terms and moralise about it. He did not even think the law; he merely lived the law without thinking about it at all.

He saw the law operating around him on every side. He had eaten the ptarmigan chicks. The hawk had eaten the ptarmigan-mother. The hawk would also have eaten him. Later, when he had grown more formidable, he wanted to eat the hawk. He had eaten the lynx kitten. The lynx-mother would have eaten him had she not herself been killed and eaten. And so it went. The law was being lived about him by all live things, and he himself was part and parcel of the law. He was a killer. His only food was meat, live meat, that ran away swiftly before him, or flew into the air, or climbed trees, or hid in the ground, or faced him and fought with him, or turned the tables and ran after him.

Had the cub thought in man-fashion, he might have epitomised life as a voracious appetite and the world as a place wherein ranged a multitude of appetites, pursuing and being pursued, hunting and being hunted, eating and being eaten, all in blindness and confusion, with violence and disorder, a chaos of gluttony and slaughter, ruled over by chance, merciless, planless, endless.

But the cub did not think in man-fashion. He did not look at things with wide vision. He was single-purposed, and entertained but one thought or desire at a time. Besides the law of meat, there were a myriad other and lesser laws for him to learn and obey. The world was filled with surprise. The stir of the life that was in him, the play of his muscles, was an unending happiness. To run down meat was to experience thrills and elations. His rages and battles were pleasures. Terror itself, and the mystery of the unknown, led to his living.

And there were easements and satisfactions. To have a full stomach, to doze lazily in the sunshine—such things were remuneration in full for his ardours and toils, while his ardours and tolls were in themselves self-remunerative. They were expressions of life, and life is always happy when it is expressing itself. So the cub had no quarrel with his hostile environment. He was very much alive, very happy, and very proud of himself.

PART III

CHAPTER I—THE MAKERS OF FIRE

The cub came upon it suddenly. It was his own fault. He had been careless. He had left the cave and run down to the stream to drink. It might have been that he took no notice because he was heavy with sleep. (He had been out all night on the meat-trail, and had but just then awakened.) And his carelessness might have been due to the familiarity of the trail to the pool. He had travelled it often, and nothing had ever happened on it.

He went down past the blasted pine, crossed the open space, and trotted in amongst the trees. Then, at the same instant, he saw and smelt. Before him, sitting silently on their haunches, were five live things, the like of which he had never seen before. It was his first glimpse of mankind. But at the sight of him the five men did not spring to their feet, nor show their teeth, nor snarl. They did not move, but sat there, silent and ominous.

Nor did the cub move. Every instinct of his nature would have impelled him to dash wildly away, had there not suddenly and for the first time arisen in him another and counter instinct. A great awe descended upon him. He was beaten down to movelessness by an overwhelming sense of his own weakness and littleness. Here was mastery and power, something far and away beyond him.

The cub had never seen man, yet the instinct concerning man was his. In dim ways he recognised in man the animal that had fought itself to primacy over the other animals of the Wild. Not alone out of his own eyes, but out of the eyes of all his ancestors was the cub now looking upon man—out of eyes that had circled in the darkness around countless winter camp-fires, that had peered from safe distances and from the hearts of thickets at the strange, two-legged animal that was lord over living things. The spell of the cub's heritage was upon him, the fear and the respect born of the centuries of struggle and the accumulated experience of the generations. The heritage was too compelling for a wolf that was only a cub. Had he been full-grown, he would have run away. As it was, he cowered down in a paralysis of fear, already half proffering the submission that his kind had proffered from the first time a wolf came in to sit by man's fire and be made warm.

One of the Indians arose and walked over to him and stooped above him. The cub cowered closer to the ground. It was the unknown, objectified at last, in concrete flesh and blood, bending over him and reaching down to seize hold of him. His hair bristled involuntarily; his lips writhed back and his little fangs were bared. The hand, poised like doom above him, hesitated, and the man spoke laughing, "Wabam wabisca ip pit tah." ("Look! The white fangs!")

The other Indians laughed loudly, and urged the man on to pick up the cub. As the hand descended closer and closer, there raged within the cub a battle of the instincts. He experienced two great impulsions—to yield and to fight. The resulting action was a compromise. He did both. He yielded till the hand almost touched him.

Then he fought, his teeth flashing in a snap that sank them into the hand. The next moment he received a clout alongside the head that knocked him over on his side. Then all fight fled out of him. His puppyhood and the instinct of submission took charge of him. He sat up on his haunches and ki-yi'd. But the man whose hand he had bitten was angry. The cub received a clout on the other side of his head. Whereupon he sat up and ki-yi'd louder than ever.

The four Indians laughed more loudly, while even the man who had been bitten began to laugh. They surrounded the cub and laughed at him, while he wailed out his terror and his hurt. In the midst of it, he heard something. The Indians heard it too. But the cub knew what it was, and with a last, long wail that had in it more of triumph than grief, he ceased his noise and waited for the coming of his mother, of his ferocious and indomitable mother who fought and killed all things and was never afraid. She was snarling as she ran. She had heard the cry of her cub and was dashing to save him.

She bounded in amongst them, her anxious and militant motherhood making her anything but a pretty sight. But to the cub the spectacle of her protective rage was pleasing. He uttered a glad little cry and bounded to meet her, while the man-animals went back hastily several steps. The she-wolf stood over against her cub, facing the men, with bristling hair, a snarl rumbling deep in her throat. Her face was distorted and malignant with menace, even the bridge of the nose wrinkling from tip to eyes so prodigious was her snarl.

Then it was that a cry went up from one of the men. "Kiche!" was what he uttered. It was an exclamation of surprise. The cub felt his mother wilting at the sound.

"Kiche!" the man cried again, this time with sharpness and authority.

And then the cub saw his mother, the she-wolf, the fearless one, crouching down till her belly touched the ground, whimpering, wagging her tail, making peace signs. The cub could not understand. He was appalled. The awe of man rushed over him again. His instinct had been true. His mother verified it. She, too, rendered submission to the man-animals.

The man who had spoken came over to her. He put his hand upon her head, and she only crouched closer. She did not snap, nor threaten to snap. The other men came up, and surrounded her, and felt her, and pawed her, which actions she made no attempt to resent. They were greatly excited, and made many noises with their mouths. These noises were not indication of danger, the cub decided, as he crouched near his mother still bristling from time to time but doing his best to submit.

"It is not strange," an Indian was saying. "Her father was a wolf. It is true, her mother was a dog; but did not my brother tie her out in the woods all of three nights in the mating season? Therefore was the father of Kiche a wolf."

"It is a year, Grey Beaver, since she ran away," spoke a second Indian.

"It is not strange, Salmon Tongue," Grey Beaver answered. "It was the time of the famine, and there was no meat for the dogs."

"She has lived with the wolves," said a third Indian.

"So it would seem, Three Eagles," Grey Beaver answered, laying his hand on the cub; "and this be the sign of it."

The cub snarled a little at the touch of the hand, and the hand flew back to administer a clout. Whereupon the cub covered its fangs, and sank down submissively, while the hand, returning, rubbed behind his ears, and up and down his back.

"This be the sign of it," Grey Beaver went on. "It is plain that his mother is Kiche. But his father was a wolf. Wherefore is there in him little dog and much wolf. His fangs be white, and White Fang shall be his name. I have spoken. He is my dog. For was not Kiche my brother's dog? And is not my brother dead?"

The cub, who had thus received a name in the world, lay and watched. For a time the man-animals continued to make their mouth-noises. Then Grey Beaver took a knife from a sheath that hung around his neck, and went into the thicket and cut a stick. White Fang watched him. He notched the stick at each end and in the notches fastened strings of raw-hide. One string he tied around the throat of Kiche. Then he led her to a small pine, around which he tied the other string.

White Fang followed and lay down beside her. Salmon Tongue's hand reached out to him and rolled him over on his back. Kiche looked on anxiously. White Fang felt fear mounting in him again. He could not quite suppress a snarl, but he made no offer to snap. The hand, with fingers crooked and spread apart, rubbed his stomach in a playful way and rolled him from side to side. It was ridiculous and ungainly, lying there on his back with legs sprawling in the air. Besides, it was a position of such utter helplessness that White Fang's whole nature revolted against it. He could do nothing to defend himself. If this man-animal intended harm, White Fang knew that he could not escape it. How could he spring away with his four legs in the air above him? Yet submission made him master his fear, and he only growled softly. This growl he could not suppress; nor did the man-animal resent it by giving him a blow on the head. And furthermore, such was the strangeness of it, White Fang experienced an unaccountable sensation of pleasure as the hand rubbed back and forth. When he was rolled on his side he ceased to growl, when the fingers pressed and prodded at the base of his ears the pleasurable sensation increased; and when, with a final rub and scratch, the man left him alone and went away, all fear had died out of White Fang. He was to know fear many times in his dealing with man; yet it was a token of the fearless companionship with man that was ultimately to be his.

After a time, White Fang heard strange noises approaching. He was quick in his classification, for he knew them at once for man-animal noises. A few minutes later the remainder of the tribe, strung out as it was on the march, trailed in. There were more men and many women and children, forty souls of them, and all heavily burdened with camp equipage and outfit. Also there were many dogs; and these, with the exception of the part-grown puppies, were likewise burdened with camp outfit. On their backs, in bags that fastened tightly around underneath, the dogs carried from twenty to thirty pounds of weight.

White Fang had never seen dogs before, but at sight of them he felt that they were his own kind, only somehow different. But they displayed little difference from the wolf when they discovered the cub and his mother. There was a rush. White Fang bristled and snarled and snapped in the face of the open-mouthed oncoming wave of dogs, and went down and under them, feeling the sharp slash of teeth in his body, himself biting and tearing at the legs and bellies above him. There was a great uproar. He could hear the snarl of Kiche as she fought for him; and he could hear the cries of the man-animals, the sound of clubs striking upon bodies, and the yelps of pain from the dogs so struck.

Only a few seconds elapsed before he was on his feet again. He could now see the man-animals driving back the dogs with clubs and stones, defending him, saving him from the savage teeth of his kind that somehow was not his kind. And though there was no reason in his brain for a clear conception of so abstract a thing as justice, nevertheless, in his own way, he felt the justice of the man-animals, and he knew them for what they were—makers of law and executors of law. Also, he appreciated the power with which they administered the law. Unlike any animals he had ever encountered, they did not bite nor claw. They enforced their live strength with the power of dead things. Dead things did their bidding. Thus, sticks and stones, directed by these strange creatures, leaped through the air like living things, inflicting grievous hurts upon the dogs.

To his mind this was power unusual, power inconceivable and beyond the natural, power that was godlike. White Fang, in the very nature of him, could never know anything about gods; at the best he could know only things that were beyond knowing—but the wonder and awe that he had of these man-animals in ways resembled what would be the wonder and awe of man at sight of some celestial creature, on a mountain top, hurling thunderbolts from either hand at an astonished world.

The last dog had been driven back. The hubbub died down. And White Fang licked his hurts and meditated upon this, his first taste of pack-cruelty and his introduction to the pack. He had never dreamed that his own kind consisted of more than One Eye, his mother, and himself. They had constituted a kind apart, and here, abruptly, he had discovered many more creatures apparently of his own kind. And there was a subconscious resentment that these, his kind, at first sight had pitched upon him and tried to destroy him. In the same way he resented his mother being tied with a stick, even though it was done by the superior man-animals. It savoured of the trap, of bondage. Yet of the trap and of bondage he knew nothing. Freedom to roam and run and lie down at will, had been his heritage; and here it was being infringed upon. His mother's movements were restricted to the length of a stick, and by the length of that same stick was he restricted, for he had not yet got beyond the need of his mother's side.

He did not like it. Nor did he like it when the man-animals arose and went on with their march; for a tiny man-animal took the other end of the stick and led Kiche captive behind him, and behind Kiche followed White Fang, greatly perturbed and worried by this new adventure he had entered upon.

They went down the valley of the stream, far beyond White Fang's widest ranging, until they came to the end of the valley, where the stream ran into the Mackenzie River. Here, where canoes were cached on poles high in the air and where stood fish-racks for the drying of fish, camp was made; and White Fang looked on with wondering eyes. The superiority of these man-animals increased with every moment. There was their mastery over all these sharp-fanged dogs. It breathed of power. But greater than that, to the wolf-cub, was their mastery over things not alive; their capacity to communicate motion to unmoving things; their capacity to change the very face of the world.

It was this last that especially affected him. The elevation of frames of poles caught his eye; yet this in itself was not so remarkable, being done by the same creatures that flung sticks and stones to great distances. But when the frames of poles were made into tepees by being covered with cloth and skins, White Fang was astounded. It was the colossal bulk of them that impressed him. They arose around him, on every side, like some monstrous quick-growing form of life. They occupied nearly the whole circumference of his field of vision. He was afraid of them. They loomed ominously above him; and when the breeze stirred them into huge movements, he cowered down in fear, keeping his eyes warily upon them, and prepared to spring away if they attempted to precipitate themselves upon him.

But in a short while his fear of the tepees passed away. He saw the women and children passing in and out of them without harm, and he saw the dogs trying often to get into them, and being driven away with sharp words and flying stones. After a time, he left Kiche's side and crawled cautiously toward the wall of the nearest tepee. It was the curiosity of growth that urged him on—the necessity of learning and living and doing that brings experience. The last few inches to the wall of the tepee were crawled with painful slowness and precaution. The day's events had prepared him for the unknown to manifest itself in most stupendous and unthinkable ways. At last his nose touched the canvas. He waited. Nothing happened. Then he smelled the strange fabric, saturated with the man-smell. He closed on the canvas with his teeth and gave a gentle tug. Nothing happened, though the adjacent portions of the tepee moved. He tugged harder. There was a greater movement. It was delightful. He tugged still harder, and repeatedly, until the whole tepee was in motion. Then the sharp cry of a squaw inside sent him scampering back to Kiche. But after that he was afraid no more of the looming bulks of the tepees.

A moment later he was straying away again from his mother. Her stick was tied to a peg in the ground and she could not follow him. A part-grown puppy, somewhat larger and older than he, came toward him slowly, with ostentatious and belligerent importance. The puppy's name, as White Fang was afterward to hear him called, was Lip-lip. He had had experience in puppy fights and was already something of a bully.

Lip-lip was White Fang's own kind, and, being only a puppy, did not seem dangerous; so White Fang prepared to meet him in a friendly spirit. But when the strangers walk became stiff-legged and his lips lifted clear of his teeth, White Fang stiffened too, and answered with lifted lips. They half circled about each other, tentatively, snarling and bristling. This lasted several minutes, and White Fang was beginning to enjoy it, as a sort of game. But suddenly, with remarkable swiftness, Lip-lip leaped in, delivering a slashing snap, and leaped away again. The snap had taken effect on the shoulder that had been hurt by the lynx and that was still sore deep down near the bone. The surprise and hurt of it brought a yelp out of White Fang; but the next moment, in a rush of anger, he was upon Lip-lip and snapping viciously.

But Lip-lip had lived his life in camp and had fought many puppy fights. Three times, four times, and half a dozen times, his sharp little teeth scored on the new-comer, until White Fang, yelping shamelessly, fled to the protection of his mother. It was the first of the many fights he was to have with Lip-lip, for they were enemies from the start, born so, with natures destined perpetually to clash.

Kiche licked White Fang soothingly with her tongue, and tried to prevail upon him to remain with her. But his curiosity was rampant, and several minutes later he was venturing forth on a new quest. He came upon one of the man-animals, Grey Beaver, who was squatting on his hams and doing something with sticks and dry moss spread before him on the ground. White Fang came near to him and watched. Grey Beaver made mouth-noises which White Fang interpreted as not hostile, so he came still nearer.

Women and children were carrying more sticks and branches to Grey Beaver. It was evidently an affair of moment. White Fang came in until he touched Grey Beaver's knee, so curious was he, and already forgetful that this was a terrible man-animal. Suddenly he saw a strange thing like mist beginning to arise from the sticks and moss beneath Grey Beaver's hands. Then, amongst the sticks themselves, appeared a live thing, twisting and turning, of a colour like the colour of the sun in the sky. White Fang knew nothing about fire. It drew him as the light, in the mouth of the cave had drawn him in his early puppyhood. He crawled the several steps toward the flame. He heard Grey Beaver chuckle above him, and he knew the sound was not hostile. Then his nose touched the flame, and at the same instant his little tongue went out to it.

For a moment he was paralysed. The unknown, lurking in the midst of the sticks and moss, was savagely clutching him by the nose. He scrambled backward, bursting out in an astonished explosion of ki-yi's. At the sound, Kiche leaped snarling to the end of her stick, and there raged terribly because she could not come to his aid. But Grey Beaver laughed loudly, and slapped his thighs, and told the happening to all the rest of the camp, till everybody was laughing uproariously. But White Fang sat on his haunches and ki-yi'd and ki-yi'd, a forlorn and pitiable little figure in the midst of the man-animals.

It was the worst hurt he had ever known. Both nose and tongue had been scorched by the live thing, sun-coloured, that had grown up under Grey Beaver's hands. He cried and cried interminably, and every fresh wail was greeted by bursts of laughter on the part of the man-animals. He tried to soothe his nose with his tongue, but the tongue was burnt too, and the two hurts coming together produced greater hurt; whereupon he cried more hopelessly and helplessly than ever.

And then shame came to him. He knew laughter and the meaning of it. It is not given us to know how some animals know laughter, and know when they are being laughed at; but it was this same way that White Fang knew it. And he felt shame that the man-animals should be laughing at him. He turned and fled away, not from the hurt of the fire, but from the laughter that sank even deeper, and hurt in the spirit of him. And he fled to Kiche, raging at the end of her stick like an animal gone mad—to Kiche, the one creature in the world who was not laughing at him.

Twilight drew down and night came on, and White Fang lay by his mother's side. His nose and tongue still hurt, but he was perplexed by a greater trouble. He was homesick. He felt a vacancy in him, a need for the hush and quietude of the stream and the cave in the cliff. Life had become too populous. There were so many of the man-animals, men, women, and children, all making noises and irritations. And there were the dogs, ever squabbling and bickering, bursting into uproars and creating confusions. The restful loneliness of the only life he had known was gone. Here the very air was palpitant with life. It hummed and buzzed unceasingly. Continually changing its intensity and abruptly variant in pitch, it impinged on his nerves and senses, made him nervous and restless and worried him with a perpetual imminence of happening.

He watched the man-animals coming and going and moving about the camp. In fashion distantly resembling the way men look upon the gods they create, so looked White Fang upon the man-animals before him. They were superior creatures, of a verity, gods. To his dim comprehension they were as much wonder-workers as gods are to men. They were creatures of mastery, possessing all manner of unknown and impossible potencies, overlords of the alive and the not alive—making obey that which moved, imparting movement to that which did not move, and making life, sun-coloured and biting life, to grow out of dead moss and wood. They were fire-makers! They were gods.

CHAPTER II—THE BONDAGE

The days were thronged with experience for White Fang. During the time that Kiche was tied by the stick, he ran about over all the camp, inquiring, investigating, learning. He quickly came to know much of the ways of the man-animals, but familiarity did not breed contempt. The more he came to know them, the more they vindicated their superiority, the more they displayed their mysterious powers, the greater loomed their god-likeness.

To man has been given the grief, often, of seeing his gods overthrown and his altars crumbling; but to the wolf and the wild dog that have come in to crouch at man's feet, this grief has never come. Unlike man, whose gods are of the unseen and the overguessed, vapours and mists of fancy eluding the garmenture of reality, wandering wraiths of desired goodness and power, intangible out-croppings of self into the realm of spirit—unlike man, the wolf and the wild dog that have come in to the fire find their gods in the living flesh, solid to the touch, occupying earth-space and requiring time for the accomplishment of their ends and their existence. No effort of faith is necessary to believe in such a god; no effort of will can possibly induce disbelief in such a god. There is no getting away from it. There it stands, on its two hind-legs, club in hand, immensely potential, passionate and wrathful and loving, god and mystery and power all wrapped up and around by flesh that bleeds when it is torn and that is good to eat like any flesh.

And so it was with White Fang. The man-animals were gods unmistakable and unescapable. As his mother, Kiche, had rendered her allegiance to them at the first cry of her name, so he was beginning to render his allegiance. He gave them the trail as a privilege indubitably theirs. When they walked, he got out of their way. When they called, he came. When they threatened, he cowered down. When they commanded him to go, he went away hurriedly. For behind any wish of theirs was power to enforce that wish, power that hurt, power that expressed itself in clouts and clubs, in flying stones and stinging lashes of whips.

He belonged to them as all dogs belonged to them. His actions were theirs to command. His body was theirs to maul, to stamp upon, to tolerate. Such was the lesson that was quickly borne in upon him. It came hard, going as it did, counter to much that was strong and dominant in his own nature; and, while he disliked it in the learning of it, unknown to himself he was learning to like it. It was a placing of his destiny in another's hands, a shifting of the responsibilities of existence. This in itself was compensation, for it is always easier to lean upon another than to stand alone.

But it did not all happen in a day, this giving over of himself, body and soul, to the man-animals. He could not immediately forego his wild heritage and his memories of the Wild. There were days when he crept to the edge of the forest and stood and listened to something calling him far and away. And always he returned, restless and uncomfortable, to whimper softly and wistfully at Kiche's side and to lick her face with eager, questioning tongue.

White Fang learned rapidly the ways of the camp. He knew the injustice and greediness of the older dogs when meat or fish was thrown out to be eaten. He came to know that men were more just, children more cruel, and women more kindly and more likely to toss him a bit of meat or bone. And after two or three painful adventures with the mothers of part-grown puppies, he came into the knowledge that it was always good policy to let such mothers alone, to keep away from them as far as possible, and to avoid them when he saw them coming.

But the bane of his life was Lip-lip. Larger, older, and stronger, Lip-lip had selected White Fang for his special object of persecution. White Fang fought willingly enough, but he was outclassed. His enemy was too big. Lip-lip became a nightmare to him. Whenever he ventured away from his mother, the bully was sure to appear, trailing at his heels, snarling at him, picking upon him, and watchful of an opportunity, when no man-animal was near, to spring upon him and force a fight. As Lip-lip invariably won, he enjoyed it hugely. It became his chief delight in life, as it became White Fang's chief torment.

But the effect upon White Fang was not to cow him. Though he suffered most of the damage and was always defeated, his spirit remained unsubdued. Yet a bad effect was produced. He became malignant and morose. His temper had been savage by birth, but it became more savage under this unending persecution. The genial, playful, puppyish side of him found little expression. He never played and gambolled about with the other puppies of the camp. Lip-lip would not permit it. The moment White Fang appeared near them, Lip-lip was upon him, bullying and hectoring him, or fighting with him until he had driven him away.

The effect of all this was to rob White Fang of much of his puppyhood and to make him in his comportment older than his age. Denied the outlet, through play, of his energies, he recoiled upon himself and developed his mental processes. He became cunning; he had idle time in which to devote himself to thoughts of trickery. Prevented from obtaining his share of meat and fish when a general feed was given to the camp-dogs, he became a clever thief. He had to forage for himself, and he foraged well, though he was oft-times a plague to the squaws in consequence. He learned to sneak about camp, to be crafty, to know what was going on everywhere, to see and to hear everything and to reason accordingly, and successfully to devise ways and means of avoiding his implacable persecutor.

It was early in the days of his persecution that he played his first really big crafty game and got there from his first taste of revenge. As Kiche, when with the wolves, had lured out to destruction dogs from the camps of men, so White Fang, in manner somewhat similar, lured Lip-lip into Kiche's avenging jaws. Retreating before Lip-lip, White Fang made an indirect flight that led in and out and around the various tepees of the camp. He was a good runner, swifter than any puppy of his size, and swifter than Lip-lip. But he did not run his best in this chase. He barely held his own, one leap ahead of his pursuer.

Lip-lip, excited by the chase and by the persistent nearness of his victim, forgot caution and locality. When he remembered locality, it was too late. Dashing at top speed around a tepee, he ran full tilt into Kiche lying at the end of her stick. He gave one yelp of consternation, and then her punishing jaws closed upon him. She was tied, but he could not get away from her easily. She rolled him off his legs so that he could not run, while she repeatedly ripped and slashed him with her fangs.

When at last he succeeded in rolling clear of her, he crawled to his feet, badly dishevelled, hurt both in body and in spirit. His hair was standing out all over him in tufts where her teeth had mauled. He stood where he had arisen, opened his mouth, and broke out the long, heart-broken puppy wail. But even this he was not allowed to complete. In the middle of it, White Fang, rushing in, sank his teeth into Lip-lip's hind leg. There was no fight left in Lip-lip, and he ran away shamelessly, his victim hot on his heels and worrying him all the way back to his own tepee. Here the squaws came to his aid, and White Fang, transformed into a raging demon, was finally driven off only by a fusillade of stones.

Came the day when Grey Beaver, deciding that the liability of her running away was past, released Kiche. White Fang was delighted with his mother's freedom. He accompanied her joyfully about the camp; and, so long as he remained close by her side, Lip-lip kept a respectful distance. White-Fang even bristled up to him and walked stiff-legged, but Lip-lip ignored the challenge. He was no fool himself, and whatever vengeance he desired to wreak, he could wait until he caught White Fang alone.

Later on that day, Kiche and White Fang strayed into the edge of the woods next to the camp. He had led his mother there, step by step, and now when she stopped, he tried to inveigle her farther. The stream, the lair, and the quiet woods were calling to him, and he wanted her to come. He ran on a few steps, stopped, and looked back. She had not moved. He whined pleadingly, and scurried playfully in and out of the underbrush. He ran back to her, licked her face, and ran on again. And still she did not move. He stopped and regarded her, all of an intentness and eagerness, physically expressed, that slowly faded out of him as she turned her head and gazed back at the camp.

There was something calling to him out there in the open. His mother heard it too. But she heard also that other and louder call, the call of the fire and of man— the call which has been given alone of all animals to the wolf to answer, to the wolf and the wild-dog, who are brothers.

Kiche turned and slowly trotted back toward camp. Stronger than the physical restraint of the stick was the clutch of the camp upon her. Unseen and occultly, the gods still gripped with their power and would not let her go. White Fang sat down in the shadow of a birch and whimpered softly. There was a strong smell of pine, and subtle wood fragrances filled the air, reminding him of his old life of freedom before the days of his bondage. But he was still only a part-grown puppy, and stronger than the call either of man or of the Wild was the call of his mother. All the hours of his short life he had depended upon her. The time was yet to come for independence. So he arose and trotted forlornly back to camp, pausing once, and twice, to sit down and whimper and to listen to the call that still sounded in the depths of the forest.

In the Wild the time of a mother with her young is short; but under the dominion of man it is sometimes even shorter. Thus it was with White Fang. Grey Beaver was in the debt of Three Eagles. Three Eagles was going away on a trip up the Mackenzie to the Great Slave Lake. A strip of scarlet cloth, a bearskin, twenty cartridges, and Kiche, went to pay the debt. White Fang saw his mother taken aboard Three Eagles' canoe, and tried to follow her. A blow from Three Eagles knocked him backward to the land. The canoe shoved off. He sprang into the water and swam after it, deaf to the sharp cries of Grey Beaver to return. Even a man-animal, a god, White Fang ignored, such was the terror he was in of losing his mother.

But gods are accustomed to being obeyed, and Grey Beaver wrathfully launched a canoe in pursuit. When he overtook White Fang, he reached down and by the nape of the neck lifted him clear of the water. He did not deposit him at once in the bottom of the canoe. Holding him suspended with one hand, with the other hand he proceeded to give him a beating. And it was a beating. His hand was heavy. Every blow was shrewd to hurt; and he delivered a multitude of blows.

Impelled by the blows that rained upon him, now from this side, now from that, White Fang swung back and forth like an erratic and jerky pendulum. Varying were the emotions that surged through him. At first, he had known surprise. Then came a momentary fear, when he yelped several times to the impact of the hand. But this was quickly followed by anger. His free nature asserted itself, and he showed his teeth and snarled fearlessly in the face of the wrathful god. This but served to make the god more wrathful. The blows came faster, heavier, more shrewd to hurt.

Grey Beaver continued to beat, White Fang continued to snarl. But this could not last for ever. One or the other must give over, and that one was White Fang. Fear surged through him again. For the first time he was being really man-handled. The occasional blows of sticks and stones he had previously experienced were as caresses compared with this. He broke down and began to cry and yelp. For a time each blow brought a yelp from him; but fear passed into terror, until finally his yelps were voiced in unbroken succession, unconnected with the rhythm of the punishment.

At last Grey Beaver withheld his hand. White Fang, hanging limply, continued to cry. This seemed to satisfy his master, who flung him down roughly in the bottom of the canoe. In the meantime the canoe had drifted down the stream. Grey Beaver picked up the paddle. White Fang was in his way. He spurned him savagely with his foot. In that moment White Fang's free nature flashed forth again, and he sank his teeth into the moccasined foot.

The beating that had gone before was as nothing compared with the beating he now received. Grey Beaver's wrath was terrible; likewise was White Fang's fright. Not only the hand, but the hard wooden paddle was used upon him; and he was bruised and sore in all his small body when he was again flung down in the canoe. Again, and this time with purpose, did Grey Beaver kick him. White Fang did not repeat his attack on the foot. He had learned another lesson of his bondage. Never, no matter what the circumstance, must he dare to bite the god who was lord and master over him; the body of the lord and master was sacred, not to be defiled by the teeth of such as he. That was evidently the crime of crimes, the one offence there was no condoning nor overlooking.

When the canoe touched the shore, White Fang lay whimpering and motionless, waiting the will of Grey Beaver. It was Grey Beaver's will that he should go ashore, for ashore he was flung, striking heavily on his side and hurting his bruises afresh. He crawled tremblingly to his feet and stood whimpering. Lip-lip, who had watched the whole proceeding from the bank, now rushed upon him, knocking him over and sinking his teeth into him. White Fang was too helpless to defend himself, and it would have gone hard with him had not Grey Beaver's foot shot out, lifting Lip-lip into the air with its violence so that he smashed down to earth a dozen feet away. This was the man-animal's justice; and even then, in his own pitiable plight, White Fang experienced a little grateful thrill. At Grey Beaver's heels he limped obediently through the village to the tepee. And so it came that White Fang learned that the right to punish was something the gods reserved for themselves and denied to the lesser creatures under them.

That night, when all was still, White Fang remembered his mother and sorrowed for her. He sorrowed too loudly and woke up Grey Beaver, who beat him. After that he mourned gently when the gods were around. But sometimes, straying off to the edge of the woods by himself, he gave vent to his grief, and cried it out with loud whimperings and wailings.

It was during this period that he might have harkened to the memories of the lair and the stream and run back to the Wild. But the memory of his mother held him. As the hunting man-animals went out and came back, so she would come back to the village some time. So he remained in his bondage waiting for her.

But it was not altogether an unhappy bondage. There was much to interest him. Something was always happening. There was no end to the strange things these gods did, and he was always curious to see. Besides, he was learning how to get along with Grey Beaver. Obedience, rigid, undeviating obedience, was what was exacted of him; and in return he escaped beatings and his existence was tolerated.

Nay, Grey Beaver himself sometimes tossed him a piece of meat, and defended him against the other dogs in the eating of it. And such a piece of meat was of value. It was worth more, in some strange way, then a dozen pieces of meat from the hand of a squaw. Grey Beaver never petted nor caressed. Perhaps it was the weight of his hand, perhaps his justice, perhaps the sheer power of him, and perhaps it was all these things that influenced White Fang; for a certain tie of attachment was forming between him and his surly lord.

Insidiously, and by remote ways, as well as by the power of stick and stone and clout of hand, were the shackles of White Fang's bondage being riveted upon him. The qualities in his kind that in the beginning made it possible for them to come in to the fires of men, were qualities capable of development. They were developing in him, and the camp-life, replete with misery as it was, was secretly endearing itself to him all the time. But White Fang was unaware of it. He knew only grief for the loss of Kiche, hope for her return, and a hungry yearning for the free life that had been his.

CHAPTER III—THE OUTCAST

Lip-lip continued so to darken his days that White Fang became wickeder and more ferocious than it was his natural right to be. Savageness was a part of his make-up, but the savageness thus developed exceeded his make-up. He acquired a reputation for wickedness amongst the man-animals themselves. Wherever there was trouble and uproar in camp, fighting and squabbling or the outcry of a squaw over a bit of stolen meat, they were sure to find White Fang mixed up in it and usually at the bottom of it. They did not bother to look after the causes of his conduct. They saw only the effects, and the effects were bad. He was a sneak and a thief, a mischief-maker, a fomenter of trouble; and irate squaws told him to his face, the while he eyed them alert and ready to dodge any quick-flung missile, that he was a wolf and worthless and bound to come to an evil end.

He found himself an outcast in the midst of the populous camp. All the young dogs followed Lip-lip's lead. There was a difference between White Fang and them. Perhaps they sensed his wild-wood breed, and instinctively felt for him the enmity that the domestic dog feels for the wolf. But be that as it may, they joined with Lip-lip in the persecution. And, once declared against him, they found good reason to continue declared against him. One and all, from time to time, they felt his teeth; and to his credit, he gave more than he received. Many of them he could whip in single fight; but single fight was denied him. The beginning of such a fight was a signal for all the young dogs in camp to come running and pitch upon him.

Out of this pack-persecution he learned two important things: how to take care of himself in a mass-fight against him—and how, on a single dog, to inflict the greatest amount of damage in the briefest space of time. To keep one's feet in the midst of the hostile mass meant life, and this he learnt well. He became cat-like in his ability to stay on his feet. Even grown dogs might hurtle him backward or sideways with the impact of their heavy bodies; and backward or sideways he would go, in the air or sliding on the ground, but always with his legs under him and his feet downward to the mother earth.

When dogs fight, there are usually preliminaries to the actual combat—snarlings and bristlings and stiff-legged struttings. But White Fang learned to omit these preliminaries. Delay meant the coming against him of all the young dogs. He must do his work quickly and get away. So he learnt to give no warning of his intention. He rushed in and snapped and slashed on the instant, without notice, before his foe could prepare to meet him. Thus he learned how to inflict quick and severe damage. Also he learned the value of surprise. A dog, taken off its guard, its shoulder slashed open or its ear ripped in ribbons before it knew what was happening, was a dog half whipped.

Furthermore, it was remarkably easy to overthrow a dog taken by surprise; while a dog, thus overthrown, invariably exposed for a moment the soft underside of its neck—the vulnerable point at which to strike for its life. White Fang knew this point. It was a knowledge bequeathed to him directly from the hunting generation of wolves. So it was that White Fang's method when he took the offensive, was: first to find a young dog alone; second, to surprise it and knock it off its feet; and third, to drive in with his teeth at the soft throat.

Being but partly grown his jaws had not yet become large enough nor strong enough to make his throat-attack deadly; but many a young dog went around camp with a lacerated throat in token of White Fang's intention. And one day, catching one of his enemies alone on the edge of the woods, he managed, by repeatedly overthrowing him and attacking the throat, to cut the great vein and let out the life. There was a great row that night. He had been observed, the news had been carried to the dead dog's master, the squaws remembered all the instances of stolen meat, and Grey Beaver was beset by many angry voices. But he resolutely held the door of his tepee, inside which he had placed the culprit, and refused to permit the vengeance for which his tribespeople clamoured.

White Fang became hated by man and dog. During this period of his development he never knew a moment's security. The tooth of every dog was against him, the hand of every man. He was greeted with snarls by his kind, with curses and stones by his gods. He lived tensely. He was always keyed up, alert for attack, wary of being attacked, with an eye for sudden and unexpected missiles, prepared to act precipitately and coolly, to leap in with a flash of teeth, or to leap away with a menacing snarl.

As for snarling he could snarl more terribly than any dog, young or old, in camp. The intent of the snarl is to warn or frighten, and judgment is required to know when it should be used. White Fang knew how to make it and when to make it. Into his snarl he incorporated all that was vicious, malignant, and horrible. With nose serrulated by continuous spasms, hair bristling in recurrent waves, tongue whipping out like a red snake and whipping back again, ears flattened down, eyes gleaming hatred, lips wrinkled back, and fangs exposed and dripping, he could compel a pause on the part of almost any assailant. A temporary pause, when taken off his guard, gave him the vital moment in which to think and determine his action. But often a pause so gained lengthened out until it evolved into a complete cessation from the attack. And before more than one of the grown dogs White Fang's snarl enabled him to beat an honourable retreat.

An outcast himself from the pack of the part-grown dogs, his sanguinary methods and remarkable efficiency made the pack pay for its persecution of him. Not permitted himself to run with the pack, the curious state of affairs obtained that no member of the pack could run outside the pack. White Fang would not permit it. What of his bushwhacking and waylaying tactics, the young dogs were afraid to run by themselves. With the exception of Lip-lip, they were compelled to hunch together for mutual protection against the terrible enemy they had made. A puppy alone by the river bank meant a puppy dead or a puppy that aroused the camp with its shrill pain and terror as it fled back from the wolf-cub that had waylaid it.

But White Fang's reprisals did not cease, even when the young dogs had learned thoroughly that they must stay together. He attacked them when he caught them alone, and they attacked him when they were bunched. The sight of him was sufficient to start them rushing after him, at which times his swiftness usually carried him into safety. But woe the dog that outran his fellows in such pursuit! White Fang had learned to turn suddenly upon the pursuer that was ahead of the pack and thoroughly to rip him up before the pack could arrive. This occurred with great frequency, for, once in full cry, the dogs were prone to forget themselves in the excitement of the chase, while White Fang never forgot himself. Stealing backward glances as he ran, he was always ready to whirl around and down the overzealous pursuer that outran his fellows.

Young dogs are bound to play, and out of the exigencies of the situation they realised their play in this mimic warfare. Thus it was that the hunt of White Fang became their chief game—a deadly game, withal, and at all times a serious game. He, on the other hand, being the fastest-footed, was unafraid to venture anywhere. During the period that he waited vainly for his mother to come back, he led the pack many a wild chase through the adjacent woods. But the pack invariably lost him. Its noise and outcry warned him of its presence, while he ran alone, velvet-footed, silently, a moving shadow among the trees after the manner of his father and mother before him. Further he was more directly connected with the Wild than they; and he knew more of its secrets and stratagems. A favourite trick of his was to lose his trail in running water and then lie quietly in a near-by thicket while their baffled cries arose around him.

Hated by his kind and by mankind, indomitable, perpetually warred upon and himself waging perpetual war, his development was rapid and one-sided. This was no soil for kindliness and affection to blossom in. Of such things he had not the faintest glimmering. The code he learned was to obey the strong and to oppress the weak. Grey Beaver was a god, and strong. Therefore White Fang obeyed him. But the dog younger or smaller than himself was weak, a thing to be destroyed. His development was in the direction of power. In order to face the constant danger of hurt and even of destruction, his predatory and protective faculties were unduly developed. He became quicker of movement than the other dogs, swifter of foot, craftier, deadlier, more lithe, more lean with ironlike muscle and sinew, more enduring, more cruel, more ferocious, and more intelligent. He had to become all these things, else he would not have held his own nor survive the hostile environment in which he found himself.

CHAPTER IV—THE TRAIL OF THE GODS

In the fall of the year, when the days were shortening and the bite of the frost was coming into the air, White Fang got his chance for liberty. For several days there had been a great hubbub in the village. The summer camp was being dismantled, and the tribe, bag and baggage, was preparing to go off to the fall hunting. White Fang watched it all with eager eyes, and when the tepees began to come down and the canoes were loading at the bank, he understood. Already the canoes were departing, and some had disappeared down the river.

Quite deliberately he determined to stay behind. He waited his opportunity to slink out of camp to the woods. Here, in the running stream where ice was beginning to form, he hid his trail. Then he crawled into the heart of a dense thicket and waited. The time passed by, and he slept intermittently for hours. Then he was aroused by Grey Beaver's voice calling him by name. There were other voices. White Fang could hear Grey Beaver's squaw taking part in the search, and Mit-sah, who was Grey Beaver's son.

White Fang trembled with fear, and though the impulse came to crawl out of his hiding-place, he resisted it. After a time the voices died away, and some time after that he crept out to enjoy the success of his undertaking. Darkness was coming on, and for a while he played about among the trees, pleasuring in his freedom. Then, and quite suddenly, he became aware of loneliness. He sat down to consider, listening to the silence of the forest and perturbed by it. That nothing moved nor sounded, seemed ominous. He felt the lurking of danger, unseen and unguessed. He was suspicious of the looming bulks of the trees and of the dark shadows that might conceal all manner of perilous things.

Then it was cold. Here was no warm side of a tepee against which to snuggle. The frost was in his feet, and he kept lifting first one fore-foot and then the other. He curved his bushy tail around to cover them, and at the same time he saw a vision. There was nothing strange about it. Upon his inward sight was impressed a succession of memory-pictures. He saw the camp again, the tepees, and the blaze of the fires. He heard the shrill voices of the women, the gruff basses of the men, and the snarling of the dogs. He was hungry, and he remembered pieces of meat and fish that had been thrown him. Here was no meat, nothing but a threatening and inedible silence.

His bondage had softened him. Irresponsibility had weakened him. He had forgotten how to shift for himself. The night yawned about him. His senses, accustomed to the hum and bustle of the camp, used to the continuous impact of sights and sounds, were now left idle. There was nothing to do, nothing to see nor hear. They strained to catch some interruption of the silence and immobility of nature. They were appalled by inaction and by the feel of something terrible impending.

He gave a great start of fright. A colossal and formless something was rushing across the field of his vision. It was a tree-shadow flung by the moon, from whose face the clouds had been brushed away. Reassured, he whimpered softly; then he suppressed the whimper for fear that it might attract the attention of the lurking dangers.

A tree, contracting in the cool of the night, made a loud noise. It was directly above him. He yelped in his fright. A panic seized him, and he ran madly toward the village. He knew an overpowering desire for the protection and companionship of man. In his nostrils was the smell of the camp-smoke. In his ears the camp-sounds and cries were ringing loud. He passed out of the forest and into the moonlit open where were no shadows nor darknesses. But no village greeted his eyes. He had forgotten. The village had gone away.

His wild flight ceased abruptly. There was no place to which to flee. He slunk forlornly through the deserted camp, smelling the rubbish-heaps and the discarded rags and tags of the gods. He would have been glad for the rattle of stones about him, flung by an angry squaw, glad for the hand of Grey Beaver descending upon him in wrath; while he would have welcomed with delight Lip-lip and the whole snarling, cowardly pack.

He came to where Grey Beaver's tepee had stood. In the centre of the space it had occupied, he sat down. He pointed his nose at the moon. His throat was afflicted by rigid spasms, his mouth opened, and in a heart-broken cry bubbled up his loneliness and fear, his grief for Kiche, all his past sorrows and miseries as well as his apprehension of sufferings and dangers to come. It was the long wolf-howl, full-throated and mournful, the first howl he had ever uttered.

The coming of daylight dispelled his fears but increased his loneliness. The naked earth, which so shortly before had been so populous; thrust his loneliness more forcibly upon him. It did not take him long to make up his mind. He plunged into the forest and followed the river bank down the stream. All day he ran. He did not rest. He seemed made to run on for ever. His iron-like body ignored fatigue. And even after fatigue came, his heritage of endurance braced him to endless endeavour and enabled him to drive his complaining body onward.

Where the river swung in against precipitous bluffs, he climbed the high mountains behind. Rivers and streams that entered the main river he forded or swam. Often he took to the rim-ice that was beginning to form, and more than once he crashed through and struggled for life in the icy current. Always he was on the lookout for the trail of the gods where it might leave the river and proceed inland.

White Fang was intelligent beyond the average of his kind; yet his mental vision was not wide enough to embrace the other bank of the Mackenzie. What if the trail of the gods led out on that side? It never entered his head. Later on, when he had travelled more and grown older and wiser and come to know more of trails and rivers, it might be that he could grasp and apprehend such a possibility. But that mental power was yet in the future. Just now he ran blindly, his own bank of the Mackenzie alone entering into his calculations.

All night he ran, blundering in the darkness into mishaps and obstacles that delayed but did not daunt. By the middle of the second day he had been running continuously for thirty hours, and the iron of his flesh was giving out. It was the endurance of his mind that kept him going. He had not eaten in forty hours, and he was weak with hunger. The repeated drenchings in the icy water had likewise had their effect on him. His handsome coat was draggled. The broad pads of his feet were bruised and bleeding. He had begun to limp, and this limp increased with the hours. To make it worse, the light of the sky was obscured and snow began to fall— a raw, moist, melting, clinging snow, slippery under foot, that hid from him the landscape he traversed, and that covered over the inequalities of the ground so that the way of his feet was more difficult and painful.

Grey Beaver had intended camping that night on the far bank of the Mackenzie, for it was in that direction that the hunting lay. But on the near bank, shortly before dark, a moose coming down to drink, had been espied by Kloo-kooch, who was Grey Beaver's squaw. Now, had not the moose come down to drink, had not Mit-sah been steering out of the course because of the snow, had not Kloo-kooch sighted the moose, and had not Grey Beaver killed it with a lucky shot from his rifle, all subsequent things would have happened differently. Grey Beaver would not have camped on the near side of the Mackenzie, and White Fang would have passed by and gone on, either to die or to find his way to his wild brothers and become one of them—a wolf to the end of his days.

Night had fallen. The snow was flying more thickly, and White Fang, whimpering softly to himself as he stumbled and limped along, came upon a fresh trail in the snow. So fresh was it that he knew it immediately for what it was. Whining with eagerness, he followed back from the river bank and in among the trees. The camp-sounds came to his ears. He saw the blaze of the fire, Kloo-kooch cooking, and Grey Beaver squatting on his hams and mumbling a chunk of raw tallow. There was fresh meat in camp!

White Fang expected a beating. He crouched and bristled a little at the thought of it. Then he went forward again. He feared and disliked the beating he knew to be waiting for him. But he knew, further, that the comfort of the fire would be his, the protection of the gods, the companionship of the dogs—the last, a companionship of enmity, but none the less a companionship and satisfying to his gregarious needs.

He came cringing and crawling into the firelight. Grey Beaver saw him, and stopped munching the tallow. White Fang crawled slowly, cringing and grovelling in the abjectness of his abasement and submission. He crawled straight toward Grey Beaver, every inch of his progress becoming slower and more painful. At last he lay at the master's feet, into whose possession he now surrendered himself, voluntarily, body and soul. Of his own choice, he came in to sit by man's fire and to be ruled by him. White Fang trembled, waiting for the punishment to fall upon him. There was a movement of the hand above him. He cringed involuntarily under the expected blow. It did not fall. He stole a glance upward. Grey Beaver was breaking the lump of tallow in half! Grey Beaver was offering him one piece of the tallow! Very gently and somewhat suspiciously, he first smelled the tallow and then proceeded to eat it. Grey Beaver ordered meat to be brought to him, and guarded him from the other dogs while he ate. After that, grateful and content, White Fang lay at Grey Beaver's feet, gazing at the fire that warmed him, blinking and dozing, secure in the knowledge that the morrow would find him, not wandering forlorn through bleak forest-stretches, but in the camp of the man-animals, with the gods to whom he had given himself and upon whom he was now dependent.

CHAPTER V—THE COVENANT

When December was well along, Grey Beaver went on a journey up the Mackenzie. Mit-sah and Kloo-kooch went with him. One sled he drove himself, drawn by dogs he had traded for or borrowed. A second and smaller sled was driven by Mit-sah, and to this was harnessed a team of puppies. It was more of a toy affair than anything else, yet it was the delight of Mit-sah, who felt that he was beginning to do a man's work in the world. Also, he was learning to drive dogs and to train dogs; while the puppies themselves were being broken in to the harness. Furthermore, the sled was of some service, for it carried nearly two hundred pounds of outfit and food.

White Fang had seen the camp-dogs toiling in the harness, so that he did not resent overmuch the first placing of the harness upon himself. About his neck was put a moss-stuffed collar, which was connected by two pulling-traces to a strap that passed around his chest and over his back. It was to this that was fastened the long rope by which he pulled at the sled.

There were seven puppies in the team. The others had been born earlier in the year and were nine and ten months old, while White Fang was only eight months old. Each dog was fastened to the sled by a single rope. No two ropes were of the same length, while the difference in length between any two ropes was at least that of a dog's body. Every rope was brought to a ring at the front end of the sled. The sled itself was without runners, being a birch-bark toboggan, with upturned forward end to keep it from ploughing under the snow. This construction enabled the weight of the sled and load to be distributed over the largest snow-surface; for the snow was crystal-powder and very soft. Observing the same principle of widest distribution of weight, the dogs at the ends of their ropes radiated fan-fashion from the nose of the sled, so that no dog trod in another's footsteps.

There was, furthermore, another virtue in the fan-formation. The ropes of varying length prevented the dogs attacking from the rear those that ran in front of them. For a dog to attack another, it would have to turn upon one at a shorter rope. In which case it would find itself face to face with the dog attacked, and also it would find itself facing the whip of the driver. But the most peculiar virtue of all lay in the fact that the dog that strove to attack one in front of him must pull the sled faster, and that the faster the sled travelled, the faster could the dog attacked run away. Thus, the dog behind could never catch up with the one in front. The faster he ran, the faster ran the one he was after, and the faster ran all the dogs. Incidentally, the sled went faster, and thus, by cunning indirection, did man increase his mastery over the beasts.

Mit-sah resembled his father, much of whose grey wisdom he possessed. In the past he had observed Lip-lip's persecution of White Fang; but at that time Lip-lip was another man's dog, and Mit-sah had never dared more than to shy an occasional stone at him. But now Lip-lip was his dog, and he proceeded to wreak his vengeance on him by putting him at the end of the longest rope. This made Lip-lip the leader, and was apparently an honour! but in reality it took away from him all honour, and instead of being bully and master of the pack, he now found himself hated and persecuted by the pack.

Because he ran at the end of the longest rope, the dogs had always the view of him running away before them. All that they saw of him was his bushy tail and fleeing hind legs—a view far less ferocious and intimidating than his bristling mane and gleaming fangs. Also, dogs being so constituted in their mental ways, the sight of him running away gave desire to run after him and a feeling that he ran away from them.

The moment the sled started, the team took after Lip-lip in a chase that extended throughout the day. At first he had been prone to turn upon his pursuers, jealous of his dignity and wrathful; but at such times Mit-sah would throw the stinging lash of the thirty-foot cariboo-gut whip into his face and compel him to turn tail and run on. Lip-lip might face the pack, but he could not face that whip, and all that was left him to do was to keep his long rope taut and his flanks ahead of the teeth of his mates.

But a still greater cunning lurked in the recesses of the Indian mind. To give point to unending pursuit of the leader, Mit-sah favoured him over the other dogs. These favours aroused in them jealousy and hatred. In their presence Mit-sah would give him meat and would give it to him only. This was maddening to them. They would rage around just outside the throwing-distance of the whip, while Lip-lip devoured the meat and Mit-sah protected him. And when there was no meat to give, Mit-sah would keep the team at a distance and make believe to give meat to Lip-lip.

White Fang took kindly to the work. He had travelled a greater distance than the other dogs in the yielding of himself to the rule of the gods, and he had learned more thoroughly the futility of opposing their will. In addition, the persecution he had suffered from the pack had made the pack less to him in the scheme of things, and man more. He had not learned to be dependent on his kind for companionship. Besides, Kiche was well-nigh forgotten; and the chief outlet of expression that remained to him was in the allegiance he tendered the gods he had accepted as masters. So he worked hard, learned discipline, and was obedient. Faithfulness and willingness characterised his toil. These are essential traits of the wolf and the wild-dog when they have become domesticated, and these traits White Fang possessed in unusual measure.

A companionship did exist between White Fang and the other dogs, but it was one of warfare and enmity. He had never learned to play with them. He knew only how to fight, and fight with them he did, returning to them a hundred-fold the snaps and slashes they had given him in the days when Lip-lip was leader of the pack. But Lip-lip was no longer leader—except when he fled away before his mates at the end of his rope, the sled bounding along behind. In camp he kept close to Mit-sah or Grey Beaver or Kloo-kooch. He did not dare venture away from the gods, for now the fangs of all dogs were against him, and he tasted to the dregs the persecution that had been White Fang's.

With the overthrow of Lip-lip, White Fang could have become leader of the pack. But he was too morose and solitary for that. He merely thrashed his team-mates. Otherwise he ignored them. They got out of his way when he came along; nor did the boldest of them ever dare to rob him of his meat. On the contrary, they devoured their own meat hurriedly, for fear that he would take it away from them. White Fang knew the law well: to oppress the weak and obey the strong. He ate his share of meat as rapidly as he could. And then woe the dog that had not yet fin-ished! A snarl and a flash of fangs, and that dog would wail his indignation to the uncomforting stars while White Fang finished his portion for him.

Every little while, however, one dog or another would flame up in revolt and be promptly subdued. Thus White Fang was kept in training. He was jealous of the isolation in which he kept himself in the midst of the pack, and he fought often to maintain it. But such fights were of brief duration. He was too quick for the others. They were slashed open and bleeding before they knew what had happened, were whipped almost before they had begun to fight.

As rigid as the sled-discipline of the gods, was the discipline maintained by White Fang amongst his fellows. He never allowed them any latitude. He compelled them to an unremitting respect for him. They might do as they pleased amongst themselves. That was no concern of his. But it was his concern that they leave him alone in his isolation, get out of his way when he elected to walk among them, and at all times acknowledge his mastery over them. A hint of stiff-leggedness on their part, a lifted lip or a bristle of hair, and he would be upon them, merciless and cruel, swiftly convincing them of the error of their way.

He was a monstrous tyrant. His mastery was rigid as steel. He oppressed the weak with a vengeance. Not for nothing had he been exposed to the pitiless strug-gles for life in the day of his cubhood, when his mother and he, alone and unaided, held their own and survived in the ferocious environment of the Wild. And not for nothing had he learned to walk softly when superior strength went by. He oppressed the weak, but he respected the strong. And in the course of the long journey with Grey Beaver he walked softly indeed amongst the full-grown dogs in the camps of the strange man-animals they encountered.

The months passed by. Still continued the journey of Grey Beaver. White Fang's strength was developed by the long hours on trail and the steady toil at the sled; and it would have seemed that his mental development was well-nigh complete. He had come to know quite thoroughly the world in which he lived. His outlook was bleak and materialistic. The world as he saw it was a fierce and brutal world, a world without warmth, a world in which caresses and affection and the bright sweetnesses of the spirit did not exist.

He had no affection for Grey Beaver. True, he was a god, but a most savage god. White Fang was glad to acknowledge his lordship, but it was a lordship based upon superior intelligence and brute strength. There was something in the fibre of White Fang's being that made his lordship a thing to be desired, else he would not have come back from the Wild when he did to tender his allegiance. There were deeps in his nature which had never been sounded. A kind word, a caressing touch of the hand, on the part of Grey Beaver, might have sounded these deeps; but Grey Beaver did not caress, nor speak kind words. It was not his way. His primacy was savage, and savagely he ruled, administering justice with a club, punishing transgression with the pain of a blow, and rewarding merit, not by kindness, but by withholding a blow.

So White Fang knew nothing of the heaven a man's hand might contain for him. Besides, he did not like the hands of the man-animals. He was suspicious of them. It was true that they sometimes gave meat, but more often they gave hurt. Hands were things to keep away from. They hurled stones, wielded sticks and clubs and whips, administered slaps and clouts, and, when they touched him, were cunning to hurt with pinch and twist and wrench. In strange villages he had encountered the hands of the children and learned that they were cruel to hurt. Also, he had once nearly had an eye poked out by a toddling papoose. From these experiences he became suspicious of all children. He could not tolerate them. When they came near with their ominous hands, he got up.

It was in a village at the Great Slave Lake, that, in the course of resenting the evil of the hands of the man-animals, he came to modify the law that he had learned from Grey Beaver: namely, that the unpardonable crime was to bite one of the gods. In this village, after the custom of all dogs in all villages, White Fang went foraging, for food. A boy was chopping frozen moose-meat with an axe, and the chips were flying in the snow. White Fang, sliding by in quest of meat, stopped and began to eat the chips. He observed the boy lay down the axe and take up a stout club. White Fang sprang clear, just in time to escape the descending blow. The boy pursued him, and he, a stranger in the village, fled between two tepees to find himself cornered against a high earth bank.

There was no escape for White Fang. The only way out was between the two tepees, and this the boy guarded. Holding his club prepared to strike, he drew in on his cornered quarry. White Fang was furious. He faced the boy, bristling and snarling, his sense of justice outraged. He knew the law of forage. All the wastage of meat, such as the frozen chips, belonged to the dog that found it. He had done no wrong, broken no law, yet here was this boy preparing to give him a beating. White Fang scarcely knew what happened. He did it in a surge of rage. And he did it so quickly that the boy did not know either. All the boy knew was that he had in some unaccountable way been overturned into the snow, and that his club-hand had been ripped wide open by White Fang's teeth.

But White Fang knew that he had broken the law of the gods. He had driven his teeth into the sacred flesh of one of them, and could expect nothing but a most terrible punishment. He fled away to Grey Beaver, behind whose protecting legs he crouched when the bitten boy and the boy's family came, demanding vengeance. But they went away with vengeance unsatisfied. Grey Beaver defended White Fang. So did Mit-sah and Kloo-kooch. White Fang, listening to the wordy war and watching the angry gestures, knew that his act was justified. And so it came that he learned there were gods and gods. There were his gods, and there were other gods, and between them there was a difference. Justice or injustice, it was all the same, he must take all things from the hands of his own gods. But he was not compelled to take injustice from the other gods. It was his privilege to resent it with his teeth. And this also was a law of the gods.

Before the day was out, White Fang was to learn more about this law. Mit-sah, alone, gathering firewood in the forest, encountered the boy that had been bitten. With him were other boys. Hot words passed. Then all the boys attacked Mit-sah. It was going hard with him. Blows were raining upon him from all sides. White Fang looked on at first. This was an affair of the gods, and no concern of his. Then he realised that this was Mit-sah, one of his own particular gods, who was being mal-treated. It was no reasoned impulse that made White Fang do what he then did. A mad rush of anger sent him leaping in amongst the combatants. Five minutes later the landscape was covered with fleeing boys, many of whom dripped blood upon the snow in token that White Fang's teeth had not been idle. When Mit-sah told the story in camp, Grey Beaver ordered meat to be given to White Fang. He ordered much meat to be given, and White Fang, gorged and sleepy by the fire, knew that the law had received its verification.

It was in line with these experiences that White Fang came to learn the law of property and the duty of the defence of property. From the protection of his god's body to the protection of his god's possessions was a step, and this step he made. What was his god's was to be defended against all the world—even to the extent of biting other gods. Not only was such an act sacrilegious in its nature, but it was fraught with peril. The gods were all-powerful, and a dog was no match against them; yet White Fang learned to face them, fiercely belligerent and unafraid. Duty rose above fear, and thieving gods learned to leave Grey Beaver's property alone.

One thing, in this connection, White Fang quickly learnt, and that was that a thieving god was usually a cowardly god and prone to run away at the sounding of the alarm. Also, he learned that but brief time elapsed between his sounding of the alarm and Grey Beaver coming to his aid. He came to know that it was not fear of him that drove the thief away, but fear of Grey Beaver. White Fang did not give the alarm by barking. He never barked. His method was to drive straight at the intruder, and to sink his teeth in if he could. Because he was morose and solitary, having nothing to do with the other dogs, he was unusually fitted to guard his master's property; and in this he was encouraged and trained by Grey Beaver. One result of this was to make White Fang more ferocious and indomitable, and more solitary.

The months went by, binding stronger and stronger the covenant between dog and man. This was the ancient covenant that the first wolf that came in from the Wild entered into with man. And, like all succeeding wolves and wild dogs that had done likewise, White Fang worked the covenant out for himself. The terms were simple. For the possession of a flesh-and-blood god, he exchanged his own liberty. Food and fire, protection and companionship, were some of the things he received from the god. In return, he guarded the god's property, defended his body, worked for him, and obeyed him.

The possession of a god implies service. White Fang's was a service of duty and awe, but not of love. He did not know what love was. He had no experience of love. Kiche was a remote memory. Besides, not only had he abandoned the Wild and his kind when he gave himself up to man, but the terms of the covenant were such that if ever he met Kiche again he would not desert his god to go with her. His allegiance to man seemed somehow a law of his being greater than the love of liberty, of kind and kin.

CHAPTER VI—THE FAMINE

The spring of the year was at hand when Grey Beaver finished his long journey. It was April, and White Fang was a year old when he pulled into the home villages and was loosed from the harness by Mit-sah. Though a long way from his full growth, White Fang, next to Lip-lip, was the largest yearling in the village. Both from his father, the wolf, and from Kiche, he had inherited stature and strength, and already he was measuring up alongside the full-grown dogs. But he had not yet grown compact. His body was slender and rangy, and his strength more stringy than massive, His coat was the true wolf-grey, and to all appearances he was true wolf himself. The quarter-strain of dog he had inherited from Kiche had left no mark on him physically, though it had played its part in his mental make-up.

He wandered through the village, recognising with staid satisfaction the various gods he had known before the long journey. Then there were the dogs, puppies growing up like himself, and grown dogs that did not look so large and formidable as the memory pictures he retained of them. Also, he stood less in fear of them than formerly, stalking among them with a certain careless ease that was as new to him as it was enjoyable.

There was Baseek, a grizzled old fellow that in his younger days had but to uncover his fangs to send White Fang cringing and crouching to the right about. From him White Fang had learned much of his own insignificance; and from him he was now to learn much of the change and development that had taken place in himself. While Baseek had been growing weaker with age, White Fang had been growing stronger with youth.

It was at the cutting-up of a moose, fresh-killed, that White Fang learned of the changed relations in which he stood to the dog-world. He had got for himself a hoof and part of the shin-bone, to which quite a bit of meat was attached. Withdrawn from the immediate scramble of the other dogs—in fact out of sight behind a thicket—he was devouring his prize, when Baseek rushed in upon him. Before he knew what he was doing, he had slashed the intruder twice and sprung clear. Baseek was surprised by the other's temerity and swiftness of attack. He stood, gazing stupidly across at White Fang, the raw, red shin-bone between them.

Baseek was old, and already he had come to know the increasing valour of the dogs it had been his wont to bully. Bitter experiences these, which, perforce, he swallowed, calling upon all his wisdom to cope with them. In the old days he would have sprung upon White Fang in a fury of righteous wrath. But now his waning powers would not permit such a course. He bristled fiercely and looked ominously across the shin-bone at White Fang. And White Fang, resurrecting quite a deal of the old awe, seemed to wilt and to shrink in upon himself and grow small, as he cast about in his mind for a way to beat a retreat not too inglorious.

And right here Baseek erred. Had he contented himself with looking fierce and ominous, all would have been well. White Fang, on the verge of retreat, would have retreated, leaving the meat to him. But Baseek did not wait. He considered the victory already his and stepped forward to the meat. As he bent his head carelessly to smell it, White Fang bristled slightly. Even then it was not too late for Baseek to retrieve the situation. Had he merely stood over the meat, head up and glowering, White Fang would ultimately have slunk away. But the fresh meat was strong in Baseek's nostrils, and greed urged him to take a bite of it.

This was too much for White Fang. Fresh upon his months of mastery over his own team-mates, it was beyond his self-control to stand idly by while another devoured the meat that belonged to him. He struck, after his custom, without warning. With the first slash, Baseek's right ear was ripped into ribbons. He was astounded at the suddenness of it. But more things, and most grievous ones, were happening with equal suddenness. He was knocked off his feet. His throat was bitten. While he was struggling to his feet the young dog sank teeth twice into his shoulder. The swiftness of it was bewildering. He made a futile rush at White Fang, clipping the empty air with an outraged snap. The next moment his nose was laid open, and he was staggering backward away from the meat.

The situation was now reversed. White Fang stood over the shin-bone, bristling and menacing, while Baseek stood a little way off, preparing to retreat. He dared not risk a fight with this young lightning-flash, and again he knew, and more bitterly, the enfeeblement of oncoming age. His attempt to maintain his dignity was heroic. Calmly turning his back upon young dog and shin-bone, as though both were beneath his notice and unworthy of his consideration, he stalked grandly away. Nor, until well out of sight, did he stop to lick his bleeding wounds.

The effect on White Fang was to give him a greater faith in himself, and a greater pride. He walked less softly among the grown dogs; his attitude toward them was less compromising. Not that he went out of his way looking for trouble. Far from it. But upon his way he demanded consideration. He stood upon his right to go his way unmolested and to give trail to no dog. He had to be taken into account, that was all. He was no longer to be disregarded and ignored, as was the lot of puppies, and as continued to be the lot of the puppies that were his team-mates. They got out of the way, gave trail to the grown dogs, and gave up meat to them under compulsion. But White Fang, uncompanionable, solitary, morose, scarcely looking to right or left, redoubtable, forbidding of aspect, remote and alien, was accepted as an equal by his puzzled elders. They quickly learned to leave him alone, neither venturing hostile acts nor making overtures of friendliness. If they left him alone, he left them alone—a state of affairs that they found, after a few encounters, to be pre-eminently desirable.

In midsummer White Fang had an experience. Trotting along in his silent way to investigate a new tepee which had been erected on the edge of the village while he was away with the hunters after moose, he came full upon Kiche. He paused and looked at her. He remembered her vaguely, but he remembered her, and that was more than could be said for her. She lifted her lip at him in the old snarl of menace, and his memory became clear. His forgotten cubhood, all that was associated with that familiar snarl, rushed back to him. Before he had known the gods, she had been to him the centre-pin of the universe. The old familiar feelings of that time came back upon him, surged up within him. He bounded towards her joyously, and she met him with shrewd fangs that laid his cheek open to the bone. He did not understand. He backed away, bewildered and puzzled.

But it was not Kiche's fault. A wolf-mother was not made to remember her cubs of a year or so before. So she did not remember White Fang. He was a strange animal, an intruder; and her present litter of puppies gave her the right to resent such intrusion.

One of the puppies sprawled up to White Fang. They were half-brothers, only they did not know it. White Fang sniffed the puppy curiously, whereupon Kiche rushed upon him, gashing his face a second time. He backed farther away. All the old memories and associations died down again and passed into the grave from which they had been resurrected. He looked at Kiche licking her puppy and stopping now and then to snarl at him. She was without value to him. He had learned to get along without her. Her meaning was forgotten. There was no place for her in his scheme of things, as there was no place for him in hers.

He was still standing, stupid and bewildered, the memories forgotten, wondering what it was all about, when Kiche attacked him a third time, intent on driving him away altogether from the vicinity. And White Fang allowed himself to be driven away. This was a female of his kind, and it was a law of his kind that the males must not fight the females. He did not know anything about this law, for it was no generalisation of the mind, not a something acquired by experience of the world. He knew it as a secret prompting, as an urge of instinct—of the same instinct that made him howl at the moon and stars of nights, and that made him fear death and the unknown.

The months went by. White Fang grew stronger, heavier, and more compact, while his character was developing along the lines laid down by his heredity and his environment. His heredity was a life-stuff that may be likened to clay. It possessed many possibilities, was capable of being moulded into many different forms. Environment served to model the clay, to give it a particular form. Thus, had White Fang never come in to the fires of man, the Wild would have moulded him into a true wolf. But the gods had given him a different environment, and he was moulded into a dog that was rather wolfish, but that was a dog and not a wolf.

And so, according to the clay of his nature and the pressure of his surroundings, his character was being moulded into a certain particular shape. There was no escaping it. He was becoming more morose, more uncompanionable, more solitary, more ferocious; while the dogs were learning more and more that it was better to be at peace with him than at war, and Grey Beaver was coming to prize him more greatly with the passage of each day.

White Fang, seeming to sum up strength in all his qualities, nevertheless suffered from one besetting weakness. He could not stand being laughed at. The laughter of men was a hateful thing. They might laugh among themselves about anything they pleased except himself, and he did not mind. But the moment laughter was turned upon him he would fly into a most terrible rage. Grave, dignified, sombre, a laugh made him frantic to ridiculousness. It so outraged him and upset him that for hours he would behave like a demon. And woe to the dog that at such times ran foul of him. He knew the law too well to take it out of Grey Beaver; behind Grey Beaver were a club and godhead. But behind the dogs there was nothing but space, and into this space they flew when White Fang came on the scene, made mad by laughter.

In the third year of his life there came a great famine to the Mackenzie Indians. In the summer the fish failed. In the winter the cariboo forsook their accustomed track. Moose were scarce, the rabbits almost disappeared, hunting and preying animals perished. Denied their usual food-supply, weakened by hunger, they fell upon and devoured one another. Only the strong survived. White Fang's gods were always hunting animals. The old and the weak of them died of hunger. There was wailing in the village, where the women and children went without in order that what little they had might go into the bellies of the lean and hollow-eyed hunters who trod the forest in the vain pursuit of meat.

To such extremity were the gods driven that they ate the soft-tanned leather of their mocassins and mittens, while the dogs ate the harnesses off their backs and the very whip-lashes. Also, the dogs ate one another, and also the gods ate the dogs. The weakest and the more worthless were eaten first. The dogs that still lived, looked on and understood. A few of the boldest and wisest forsook the fires of the gods, which had now become a shambles, and fled into the forest, where, in the end, they starved to death or were eaten by wolves.

In this time of misery, White Fang, too, stole away into the woods. He was better fitted for the life than the other dogs, for he had the training of his cubhood to guide him. Especially adept did he become in stalking small living things. He would lie concealed for hours, following every movement of a cautious tree-squirrel, waiting, with a patience as huge as the hunger he suffered from, until the squirrel ventured out upon the ground. Even then, White Fang was not premature. He waited until he was sure of striking before the squirrel could gain a tree-refuge. Then, and not until then, would he flash from his hiding-place, a grey projectile, incredibly swift, never failing its mark—the fleeing squirrel that fled not fast enough.

Successful as he was with squirrels, there was one difficulty that prevented him from living and growing fat on them. There were not enough squirrels. So he was driven to hunt still smaller things. So acute did his hunger become at times that he was not above rooting out wood-mice from their burrows in the ground. Nor did he scorn to do battle with a weasel as hungry as himself and many times more ferocious.

In the worst pinches of the famine he stole back to the fires of the gods. But he did not go into the fires. He lurked in the forest, avoiding discovery and robbing the snares at the rare intervals when game was caught. He even robbed Grey Beaver's snare of a rabbit at a time when Grey Beaver staggered and tottered through the forest, sitting down often to rest, what of weakness and of shortness of breath.

One day While Fang encountered a young wolf, gaunt and scrawny, loose-jointed with famine. Had he not been hungry himself, White Fang might have gone with him and eventually found his way into the pack amongst his wild brethren. As it was, he ran the young wolf down and killed and ate him.

Fortune seemed to favour him. Always, when hardest pressed for food, he found something to kill. Again, when he was weak, it was his luck that none of the larger preying animals chanced upon him. Thus, he was strong from the two days' eating a lynx had afforded him when the hungry wolf-pack ran full tilt upon him. It was a long, cruel chase, but he was better nourished than they, and in the end outran them. And not only did he outrun them, but, circling widely back on his track, he gathered in one of his exhausted pursuers.

After that he left that part of the country and journeyed over to the valley where-in he had been born. Here, in the old lair, he encountered Kiche. Up to her old tricks, she, too, had fled the inhospitable fires of the gods and gone back to her old refuge to give birth to her young. Of this litter but one remained alive when White Fang came upon the scene, and this one was not destined to live long. Young life had little chance in such a famine.

Kiche's greeting of her grown son was anything but affectionate. But White Fang did not mind. He had outgrown his mother. So he turned tail philosophically and trotted on up the stream. At the forks he took the turning to the left, where he found the lair of the lynx with whom his mother and he had fought long before. Here, in the abandoned lair, he settled down and rested for a day.

During the early summer, in the last days of the famine, he met Lip-lip, who had likewise taken to the woods, where he had eked out a miserable existence.

White Fang came upon him unexpectedly. Trotting in opposite directions along the base of a high bluff, they rounded a corner of rock and found themselves face to face. They paused with instant alarm, and looked at each other suspiciously.

White Fang was in splendid condition. His hunting had been good, and for a week he had eaten his fill. He was even gorged from his latest kill. But in the mo-ment he looked at Lip-lip his hair rose on end all along his back. It was an involuntary bristling on his part, the physical state that in the past had always ac-companied the mental state produced in him by Lip-lip's bullying and persecution. As in the past he had bristled and snarled at sight of Lip-lip, so now, and automati-cally, he bristled and snarled. He did not waste any time. The thing was done thoroughly and with despatch. Lip-lip essayed to back away, but White Fang struck him hard, shoulder to shoulder. Lip-lip was overthrown and rolled upon his back. White Fang's teeth drove into the scrawny throat. There was a death-struggle, dur-ing which White Fang walked around, stiff-legged and observant. Then he resumed his course and trotted on along the base of the bluff.

One day, not long after, he came to the edge of the forest, where a narrow stretch of open land sloped down to the Mackenzie. He had been over this ground before, when it was bare, but now a village occupied it. Still hidden amongst the trees, he paused to study the situation. Sights and sounds and scents were familiar to him. It was the old village changed to a new place. But sights and sounds and smells were different from those he had last had when he fled away from it. There was no whimpering nor wailing. Contented sounds saluted his ear, and when he heard the angry voice of a woman he knew it to be the anger that proceeds from a full stomach. And there was a smell in the air of fish. There was food. The famine was gone. He came out boldly from the forest and trotted into camp straight to Grey Beaver's tepee. Grey Beaver was not there; but Kloo-kooch welcomed him with glad cries and the whole of a fresh-caught fish, and he lay down to wait Grey Beaver's coming.

PART IV

CHAPTER I—THE ENEMY OF HIS KIND

Had there been in White Fang's nature any possibility, no matter how remote, of his ever coming to fraternise with his kind, such possibility was irretrievably destroyed when he was made leader of the sled-team. For now the dogs hated him—hated him for the extra meat bestowed upon him by Mit-sah; hated him for all the real and fancied favours he received; hated him for that he fled always at the head of the team, his waving brush of a tail and his perpetually retreating hind-quarters for ever maddening their eyes.

And White Fang just as bitterly hated them back. Being sled-leader was anything but gratifying to him. To be compelled to run away before the yelling pack, every dog of which, for three years, he had thrashed and mastered, was almost more than he could endure. But endure it he must, or perish, and the life that was in him had no desire to perish out. The moment Mit-sah gave his order for the start, that moment the whole team, with eager, savage cries, sprang forward at White Fang.

There was no defence for him. If he turned upon them, Mit-sah would throw the stinging lash of the whip into his face. Only remained to him to run away. He could not encounter that howling horde with his tail and hind-quarters. These were scarcely fit weapons with which to meet the many merciless fangs. So run away he did, violating his own nature and pride with every leap he made, and leaping all day long.

One cannot violate the promptings of one's nature without having that nature recoil upon itself. Such a recoil is like that of a hair, made to grow out from the body, turning unnaturally upon the direction of its growth and growing into the body—a rankling, festering thing of hurt. And so with White Fang. Every urge of his being impelled him to spring upon the pack that cried at his heels, but it was the will of the gods that this should not be; and behind the will, to enforce it, was the whip of cariboo-gut with its biting thirty-foot lash. So White Fang could only eat his heart in bitterness and develop a hatred and malice commensurate with the ferocity and indomitability of his nature.

If ever a creature was the enemy of its kind, White Fang was that creature. He asked no quarter, gave none. He was continually marred and scarred by the teeth of the pack, and as continually he left his own marks upon the pack. Unlike most leaders, who, when camp was made and the dogs were unhitched, huddled near to the gods for protection, White Fang disdained such protection. He walked boldly about the camp, inflicting punishment in the night for what he had suffered in the day. In the time before he was made leader of the team, the pack had learned to get out of his way. But now it was different. Excited by the day-long pursuit of him, swayed subconsciously by the insistent iteration on their brains of the sight of him fleeing away, mastered by the feeling of mastery enjoyed all day, the dogs could not bring themselves to give way to him. When he appeared amongst them, there was always a squabble. His progress was marked by snarl and snap and growl. The very atmosphere he breathed was surcharged with hatred and malice, and this but served to increase the hatred and malice within him.

When Mit-sah cried out his command for the team to stop, White Fang obeyed. At first this caused trouble for the other dogs. All of them would spring upon the hated leader only to find the tables turned. Behind him would be Mit-sah, the great whip singing in his hand. So the dogs came to understand that when the team stopped by order, White Fang was to be let alone. But when White Fang stopped without orders, then it was allowed them to spring upon him and destroy him if they could. After several experiences, White Fang never stopped without orders. He learned quickly. It was in the nature of things, that he must learn quickly if he were to survive the unusually severe conditions under which life was vouchsafed him.

But the dogs could never learn the lesson to leave him alone in camp. Each day, pursuing him and crying defiance at him, the lesson of the previous night was erased, and that night would have to be learned over again, to be as immediately forgotten. Besides, there was a greater consistence in their dislike of him. They sensed between themselves and him a difference of kind—cause sufficient in itself for hostility. Like him, they were domesticated wolves. But they had been domesticated for generations. Much of the Wild had been lost, so that to them the Wild was the unknown, the terrible, the ever-menacing and ever warring. But to him, in appearance and action and impulse, still clung the Wild. He symbolised it, was its personification: so that when they showed their teeth to him they were defending themselves against the powers of destruction that lurked in the shadows of the forest and in the dark beyond the camp-fire.

But there was one lesson the dogs did learn, and that was to keep together. White Fang was too terrible for any of them to face single-handed. They met him with the mass-formation, otherwise he would have killed them, one by one, in a night. As it was, he never had a chance to kill them. He might roll a dog off its feet, but the pack would be upon him before he could follow up and deliver the deadly throat-stroke. At the first hint of conflict, the whole team drew together and faced him. The dogs had quarrels among themselves, but these were forgotten when trouble was brewing with White Fang.

On the other hand, try as they would, they could not kill White Fang. He was too quick for them, too formidable, too wise. He avoided tight places and always backed out of it when they bade fair to surround him. While, as for getting him off his feet, there was no dog among them capable of doing the trick. His feet clung to the earth with the same tenacity that he clung to life. For that matter, life and footing were synonymous in this unending warfare with the pack, and none knew it better than White Fang.

So he became the enemy of his kind, domesticated wolves that they were, softened by the fires of man, weakened in the sheltering shadow of man's strength. White Fang was bitter and implacable. The clay of him was so moulded. He declared a vendetta against all dogs. And so terribly did he live this vendetta that Grey Beaver, fierce savage himself, could not but marvel at White Fang's ferocity. Never, he swore, had there been the like of this animal; and the Indians in strange villages swore likewise when they considered the tale of his killings amongst their dogs.

When White Fang was nearly five years old, Grey Beaver took him on another great journey, and long remembered was the havoc he worked amongst the dogs of the many villages along the Mackenzie, across the Rockies, and down the Porcupine to the Yukon. He revelled in the vengeance he wreaked upon his kind. They were ordinary, unsuspecting dogs. They were not prepared for his swiftness and directness, for his attack without warning. They did not know him for what he was, a lightning-flash of slaughter. They bristled up to him, stiff-legged and challenging, while he, wasting no time on elaborate preliminaries, snapping into action like a steel spring, was at their throats and destroying them before they knew what was happening and while they were yet in the throes of surprise.

He became an adept at fighting. He economised. He never wasted his strength, never tussled. He was in too quickly for that, and, if he missed, was out again too quickly. The dislike of the wolf for close quarters was his to an unusual degree. He could not endure a prolonged contact with another body. It smacked of danger. It made him frantic. He must be away, free, on his own legs, touching no living thing. It was the Wild still clinging to him, asserting itself through him. This feeling had been accentuated by the Ishmaelite life he had led from his puppyhood. Danger lurked in contacts. It was the trap, ever the trap, the fear of it lurking deep in the life of him, woven into the fibre of him.

In consequence, the strange dogs he encountered had no chance against him. He eluded their fangs. He got them, or got away, himself untouched in either event. In the natural course of things there were exceptions to this. There were times when several dogs, pitching on to him, punished him before he could get away; and there were times when a single dog scored deeply on him. But these were accidents. In the main, so efficient a fighter had he become, he went his way unscathed.

Another advantage he possessed was that of correctly judging time and distance. Not that he did this consciously, however. He did not calculate such things. It was all automatic. His eyes saw correctly, and the nerves carried the vision correctly to his brain. The parts of him were better adjusted than those of the average dog. They worked together more smoothly and steadily. His was a better, far better, nervous, mental, and muscular co-ordination. When his eyes conveyed to his brain the moving image of an action, his brain without conscious effort, knew the space that limited that action and the time required for its completion. Thus, he could avoid the leap of another dog, or the drive of its fangs, and at the same moment could seize the infinitesimal fraction of time in which to deliver his own attack. Body and brain, his was a more perfected mechanism. Not that he was to be praised for it. Nature had been more generous to him than to the average animal, that was all.

It was in the summer that White Fang arrived at Fort Yukon. Grey Beaver had crossed the great watershed between Mackenzie and the Yukon in the late winter, and spent the spring in hunting among the western outlying spurs of the Rockies. Then, after the break-up of the ice on the Porcupine, he had built a canoe and paddled down that stream to where it effected its junction with the Yukon just under the Artic circle. Here stood the old Hudson's Bay Company fort; and here were many Indians, much food, and unprecedented excitement. It was the summer of 1898, and thousands of gold-hunters were going up the Yukon to Dawson and the Klondike. Still hundreds of miles from their goal, nevertheless many of them had been on the way for a year, and the least any of them had travelled to get that far was five thousand miles, while some had come from the other side of the world.

Here Grey Beaver stopped. A whisper of the gold-rush had reached his ears, and he had come with several bales of furs, and another of gut-sewn mittens and moccasins. He would not have ventured so long a trip had he not expected generous profits. But what he had expected was nothing to what he realised. His wildest dreams had not exceeded a hundred per cent. profit; he made a thousand per cent. And like a true Indian, he settled down to trade carefully and slowly, even if it took all summer and the rest of the winter to dispose of his goods.

It was at Fort Yukon that White Fang saw his first white men. As compared with the Indians he had known, they were to him another race of beings, a race of superior gods. They impressed him as possessing superior power, and it is on power that godhead rests. White Fang did not reason it out, did not in his mind make the sharp generalisation that the white gods were more powerful. It was a feeling, nothing more, and yet none the less potent. As, in his puppyhood, the looming bulks of the tepees, man-reared, had affected him as manifestations of power, so was he affected now by the houses and the huge fort all of massive logs. Here was power. Those white gods were strong. They possessed greater mastery over matter than the gods he had known, most powerful among which was Grey Beaver. And yet Grey Beaver was as a child-god among these white-skinned ones.

To be sure, White Fang only felt these things. He was not conscious of them. Yet it is upon feeling, more often than thinking, that animals act; and every act White Fang now performed was based upon the feeling that the white men were the superior gods. In the first place he was very suspicious of them. There was no telling what unknown terrors were theirs, what unknown hurts they could administer. He was curious to observe them, fearful of being noticed by them. For the first few hours he was content with slinking around and watching them from a safe distance. Then he saw that no harm befell the dogs that were near to them, and he came in closer.

In turn he was an object of great curiosity to them. His wolfish appearance caught their eyes at once, and they pointed him out to one another. This act of pointing put White Fang on his guard, and when they tried to approach him he showed his teeth and backed away. Not one succeeded in laying a hand on him, and it was well that they did not.

White Fang soon learned that very few of these gods—not more than a dozen—lived at this place. Every two or three days a steamer (another and colossal manifestation of power) came into the bank and stopped for several hours. The white men came from off these steamers and went away on them again. There seemed untold numbers of these white men. In the first day or so, he saw more of them than he had seen Indians in all his life; and as the days went by they continued to come up the river, stop, and then go on up the river out of sight.

But if the white gods were all-powerful, their dogs did not amount to much. This White Fang quickly discovered by mixing with those that came ashore with their masters. They were irregular shapes and sizes. Some were short-legged—too short; others were long-legged—too long. They had hair instead of fur, and a few had very little hair at that. And none of them knew how to fight.

As an enemy of his kind, it was in White Fang's province to fight with them. This he did, and he quickly achieved for them a mighty contempt. They were soft and helpless, made much noise, and floundered around clumsily trying to accomplish by main strength what he accomplished by dexterity and cunning. They rushed bellowing at him. He sprang to the side. They did not know what had become of him; and in that moment he struck them on the shoulder, rolling them off their feet and delivering his stroke at the throat.

Sometimes this stroke was successful, and a stricken dog rolled in the dirt, to be pounced upon and torn to pieces by the pack of Indian dogs that waited. White Fang was wise. He had long since learned that the gods were made angry when their dogs were killed. The white men were no exception to this. So he was content, when he had overthrown and slashed wide the throat of one of their dogs, to drop back and let the pack go in and do the cruel finishing work. It was then that the white men rushed in, visiting their wrath heavily on the pack, while White Fang went free. He would stand off at a little distance and look on, while stones, clubs, axes, and all sorts of weapons fell upon his fellows. White Fang was very wise.

But his fellows grew wise in their own way; and in this White Fang grew wise with them. They learned that it was when a steamer first tied to the bank that they had their fun. After the first two or three strange dogs had been downed and destroyed, the white men hustled their own animals back on board and wrecked savage vengeance on the offenders. One white man, having seen his dog, a setter, torn to pieces before his eyes, drew a revolver. He fired rapidly, six times, and six of the pack lay dead or dying—another manifestation of power that sank deep into White Fang's consciousness.

White Fang enjoyed it all. He did not love his kind, and he was shrewd enough to escape hurt himself. At first, the killing of the white men's dogs had been a diversion. After a time it became his occupation. There was no work for him to do. Grey Beaver was busy trading and getting wealthy. So White Fang hung around the landing with the disreputable gang of Indian dogs, waiting for steamers. With the arrival of a steamer the fun began. After a few minutes, by the time the white men had got over their surprise, the gang scattered. The fun was over until the next steamer should arrive.

But it can scarcely be said that White Fang was a member of the gang. He did not mingle with it, but remained aloof, always himself, and was even feared by it. It is true, he worked with it. He picked the quarrel with the strange dog while the gang waited. And when he had overthrown the strange dog the gang went in to finish it. But it is equally true that he then withdrew, leaving the gang to receive the punishment of the outraged gods.

It did not require much exertion to pick these quarrels. All he had to do, when the strange dogs came ashore, was to show himself. When they saw him they rushed for him. It was their instinct. He was the Wild—the unknown, the terrible, the ever-menacing, the thing that prowled in the darkness around the fires of the primeval world when they, cowering close to the fires, were reshaping their instincts, learning to fear the Wild out of which they had come, and which they had deserted and betrayed. Generation by generation, down all the generations, had this fear of the Wild been stamped into their natures. For centuries the Wild had stood for terror and destruction. And during all this time free licence had been theirs, from their masters, to kill the things of the Wild. In doing this they had protected both themselves and the gods whose companionship they shared.

And so, fresh from the soft southern world, these dogs, trotting down the gang-plank and out upon the Yukon shore had but to see White Fang to experience the irresistible impulse to rush upon him and destroy him. They might be town-reared dogs, but the instinctive fear of the Wild was theirs just the same. Not alone with their own eyes did they see the wolfish creature in the clear light of day, standing before them. They saw him with the eyes of their ancestors, and by their inherited memory they knew White Fang for the wolf, and they remembered the ancient feud.

All of which served to make White Fang's days enjoyable. If the sight of him drove these strange dogs upon him, so much the better for him, so much the worse for them. They looked upon him as legitimate prey, and as legitimate prey he looked upon them.

Not for nothing had he first seen the light of day in a lonely lair and fought his first fights with the ptarmigan, the weasel, and the lynx. And not for nothing had his puppyhood been made bitter by the persecution of Lip-lip and the whole puppy pack. It might have been otherwise, and he would then have been otherwise. Had Lip-lip not existed, he would have passed his puppyhood with the other puppies and grown up more doglike and with more liking for dogs. Had Grey Beaver possessed the plummet of affection and love, he might have sounded the deeps of White Fang's nature and brought up to the surface all manner of kindly qualities. But these things had not been so. The clay of White Fang had been moulded until he became what he was, morose and lonely, unloving and ferocious, the enemy of all his kind.

CHAPTER II—THE MAD GOD

A small number of white men lived in Fort Yukon. These men had been long in the country. They called themselves Sour-doughs, and took great pride in so classifying themselves. For other men, new in the land, they felt nothing but disdain. The men who came ashore from the steamers were newcomers. They were known as chechaquos, and they always wilted at the application of the name. They made their bread with baking-powder. This was the invidious distinction between them and the Sour-doughs, who, forsooth, made their bread from sour-dough because they had no baking-powder.

All of which is neither here nor there. The men in the fort disdained the newcomers and enjoyed seeing them come to grief. Especially did they enjoy the havoc worked amongst the newcomers' dogs by White Fang and his disreputable gang. When a steamer arrived, the men of the fort made it a point always to come down to the bank and see the fun. They looked forward to it with as much anticipation as did the Indian dogs, while they were not slow to appreciate the savage and crafty part played by White Fang.

But there was one man amongst them who particularly enjoyed the sport. He would come running at the first sound of a steamboat's whistle; and when the last fight was over and White Fang and the pack had scattered, he would return slowly to the fort, his face heavy with regret. Sometimes, when a soft southland dog went down, shrieking its death-cry under the fangs of the pack, this man would be unable to contain himself, and would leap into the air and cry out with delight. And always he had a sharp and covetous eye for White Fang.

This man was called "Beauty" by the other men of the fort. No one knew his first name, and in general he was known in the country as Beauty Smith. But he was anything save a beauty. To antithesis was due his naming. He was pre-eminently unbeautiful. Nature had been niggardly with him. He was a small man to begin with; and upon his meagre frame was deposited an even more strikingly meagre head. Its apex might be likened to a point. In fact, in his boyhood, before he had been named Beauty by his fellows, he had been called "Pinhead."

Backward, from the apex, his head slanted down to his neck and forward it slanted uncompromisingly to meet a low and remarkably wide forehead. Beginning here, as though regretting her parsimony, Nature had spread his features with a lavish hand. His eyes were large, and between them was the distance of two eyes. His face, in relation to the rest of him, was prodigious. In order to discover the necessary area, Nature had given him an enormous prognathous jaw. It was wide and heavy, and protruded outward and down until it seemed to rest on his chest. Possibly this appearance was due to the weariness of the slender neck, unable properly to support so great a burden.

This jaw gave the impression of ferocious determination. But something lacked. Perhaps it was from excess. Perhaps the jaw was too large. At any rate, it was a lie. Beauty Smith was known far and wide as the weakest of weak-kneed and snivelling cowards. To complete his description, his teeth were large and yellow, while the two eye-teeth, larger than their fellows, showed under his lean lips like fangs. His eyes were yellow and muddy, as though Nature had run short on pigments and squeezed together the dregs of all her tubes. It was the same with his hair, sparse and irregular of growth, muddy-yellow and dirty-yellow, rising on his head and sprouting out of his face in unexpected tufts and bunches, in appearance like clumped and wind-blown grain.

In short, Beauty Smith was a monstrosity, and the blame of it lay elsewhere. He was not responsible. The clay of him had been so moulded in the making. He did the cooking for the other men in the fort, the dish-washing and the drudgery. They did not despise him. Rather did they tolerate him in a broad human way, as one tolerates any creature evilly treated in the making. Also, they feared him. His cowardly rages made them dread a shot in the back or poison in their coffee. But somebody had to do the cooking, and whatever else his shortcomings, Beauty Smith could cook.

This was the man that looked at White Fang, delighted in his ferocious prowess, and desired to possess him. He made overtures to White Fang from the first. White Fang began by ignoring him. Later on, when the overtures became more insistent, White Fang bristled and bared his teeth and backed away. He did not like the man. The feel of him was bad. He sensed the evil in him, and feared the extended hand and the attempts at soft-spoken speech. Because of all this, he hated the man.

With the simpler creatures, good and bad are things simply understood. The good stands for all things that bring easement and satisfaction and surcease from pain. Therefore, the good is liked. The bad stands for all things that are fraught with discomfort, menace, and hurt, and is hated accordingly. White Fang's feel of Beauty Smith was bad. From the man's distorted body and twisted mind, in occult ways, like mists rising from malarial marshes, came emanations of the unhealth within. Not by reasoning, not by the five senses alone, but by other and remoter and uncharted senses, came the feeling to White Fang that the man was ominous with evil, pregnant with hurtfulness, and therefore a thing bad, and wisely to be hated.

White Fang was in Grey Beaver's camp when Beauty Smith first visited it. At the faint sound of his distant feet, before he came in sight, White Fang knew who was coming and began to bristle. He had been lying down in an abandon of comfort, but he arose quickly, and, as the man arrived, slid away in true wolf-fashion to the edge of the camp. He did not know what they said, but he could see the man and Grey Beaver talking together. Once, the man pointed at him, and White Fang snarled back as though the hand were just descending upon him instead of being, as it was, fifty feet away. The man laughed at this; and White Fang slunk away to the sheltering woods, his head turned to observe as he glided softly over the ground.

Grey Beaver refused to sell the dog. He had grown rich with his trading and stood in need of nothing. Besides, White Fang was a valuable animal, the strongest sled-dog he had ever owned, and the best leader. Furthermore, there was no dog like him on the Mackenzie nor the Yukon. He could fight. He killed other dogs as easily as men killed mosquitoes. (Beauty Smith's eyes lighted up at this, and he licked his thin lips with an eager tongue). No, White Fang was not for sale at any price.

But Beauty Smith knew the ways of Indians. He visited Grey Beaver's camp often, and hidden under his coat was always a black bottle or so. One of the potencies of whisky is the breeding of thirst. Grey Beaver got the thirst. His fevered membranes and burnt stomach began to clamour for more and more of the scorching fluid; while his brain, thrust all awry by the unwonted stimulant, permitted him to go any length to obtain it. The money he had received for his furs and mittens and moccasins began to go. It went faster and faster, and the shorter his money-sack grew, the shorter grew his temper.

In the end his money and goods and temper were all gone. Nothing remained to him but his thirst, a prodigious possession in itself that grew more prodigious with every sober breath he drew. Then it was that Beauty Smith had talk with him again about the sale of White Fang; but this time the price offered was in bottles, not dollars, and Grey Beaver's ears were more eager to hear.

"You ketch um dog you take um all right," was his last word.

The bottles were delivered, but after two days. "You ketch um dog," were Beauty Smith's words to Grey Beaver.

White Fang slunk into camp one evening and dropped down with a sigh of content. The dreaded white god was not there. For days his manifestations of desire to lay hands on him had been growing more insistent, and during that time White Fang had been compelled to avoid the camp. He did not know what evil was threatened by those insistent hands. He knew only that they did threaten evil of some sort, and that it was best for him to keep out of their reach.

But scarcely had he lain down when Grey Beaver staggered over to him and tied a leather thong around his neck. He sat down beside White Fang, holding the end of the thong in his hand. In the other hand he held a bottle, which, from time to time, was inverted above his head to the accompaniment of gurgling noises.

An hour of this passed, when the vibrations of feet in contact with the ground foreran the one who approached. White Fang heard it first, and he was bristling with recognition while Grey Beaver still nodded stupidly. White Fang tried to draw the thong softly out of his master's hand; but the relaxed fingers closed tightly and Grey Beaver roused himself.

Beauty Smith strode into camp and stood over White Fang. He snarled softly up at the thing of fear, watching keenly the deportment of the hands. One hand extended outward and began to descend upon his head. His soft snarl grew tense and harsh. The hand continued slowly to descend, while he crouched beneath it, eyeing it malignantly, his snarl growing shorter and shorter as, with quickening breath, it approached its culmination. Suddenly he snapped, striking with his fangs like a snake. The hand was jerked back, and the teeth came together emptily with a sharp click. Beauty Smith was frightened and angry. Grey Beaver clouted White Fang alongside the head, so that he cowered down close to the earth in respectful obedience.

White Fang's suspicious eyes followed every movement. He saw Beauty Smith go away and return with a stout club. Then the end of the thong was given over to him by Grey Beaver. Beauty Smith started to walk away. The thong grew taut. White Fang resisted it. Grey Beaver clouted him right and left to make him get up and follow. He obeyed, but with a rush, hurling himself upon the stranger who was dragging him away. Beauty Smith did not jump away. He had been waiting for this. He swung the club smartly, stopping the rush midway and smashing White Fang down upon the ground. Grey Beaver laughed and nodded approval. Beauty Smith tightened the thong again, and White Fang crawled limply and dizzily to his feet.

He did not rush a second time. One smash from the club was sufficient to convince him that the white god knew how to handle it, and he was too wise to fight the inevitable. So he followed morosely at Beauty Smith's heels, his tail between his legs, yet snarling softly under his breath. But Beauty Smith kept a wary eye on him, and the club was held always ready to strike.

At the fort Beauty Smith left him securely tied and went in to bed. White Fang waited an hour. Then he applied his teeth to the thong, and in the space of ten seconds was free. He had wasted no time with his teeth. There had been no useless gnawing. The thong was cut across, diagonally, almost as clean as though done by a knife. White Fang looked up at the fort, at the same time bristling and growling. Then he turned and trotted back to Grey Beaver's camp. He owed no allegiance to this strange and terrible god. He had given himself to Grey Beaver, and to Grey Beaver he considered he still belonged.

But what had occurred before was repeated—with a difference. Grey Beaver again made him fast with a thong, and in the morning turned him over to Beauty Smith. And here was where the difference came in. Beauty Smith gave him a beating. Tied securely, White Fang could only rage futilely and endure the punishment. Club and whip were both used upon him, and he experienced the worst beating he had ever received in his life. Even the big beating given him in his puppyhood by Grey Beaver was mild compared with this.

Beauty Smith enjoyed the task. He delighted in it. He gloated over his victim, and his eyes flamed dully, as he swung the whip or club and listened to White Fang's cries of pain and to his helpless bellows and snarls. For Beauty Smith was cruel in the way that cowards are cruel. Cringing and snivelling himself before the blows or angry speech of a man, he revenged himself, in turn, upon creatures weaker than he. All life likes power, and Beauty Smith was no exception. Denied the expression of power amongst his own kind, he fell back upon the lesser creatures and there vindicated the life that was in him. But Beauty Smith had not created himself, and no blame was to be attached to him. He had come into the world with a twisted body and a brute intelligence. This had constituted the clay of him, and it had not been kindly moulded by the world.

White Fang knew why he was being beaten. When Grey Beaver tied the thong around his neck, and passed the end of the thong into Beauty Smith's keeping, White Fang knew that it was his god's will for him to go with Beauty Smith. And when Beauty Smith left him tied outside the fort, he knew that it was Beauty Smith's will that he should remain there. Therefore, he had disobeyed the will of both the gods, and earned the consequent punishment. He had seen dogs change owners in the past, and he had seen the runaways beaten as he was being beaten. He was wise, and yet in the nature of him there were forces greater than wisdom. One of these was fidelity. He did not love Grey Beaver, yet, even in the face of his will and his anger, he was faithful to him. He could not help it. This faithfulness was a quality of the clay that composed him. It was the quality that was peculiarly the possession of his kind; the quality that set apart his species from all other species; the quality that has enabled the wolf and the wild dog to come in from the open and be the companions of man.

After the beating, White Fang was dragged back to the fort. But this time Beauty Smith left him tied with a stick. One does not give up a god easily, and so with White Fang. Grey Beaver was his own particular god, and, in spite of Grey Beaver's will, White Fang still clung to him and would not give him up. Grey Beaver had betrayed and forsaken him, but that had no effect upon him. Not for nothing had he surrendered himself body and soul to Grey Beaver. There had been no reservation on White Fang's part, and the bond was not to be broken easily.

So, in the night, when the men in the fort were asleep, White Fang applied his teeth to the stick that held him. The wood was seasoned and dry, and it was tied so closely to his neck that he could scarcely get his teeth to it. It was only by the severest muscular exertion and neck-arching that he succeeded in getting the wood between his teeth, and barely between his teeth at that; and it was only by the exercise of an immense patience, extending through many hours, that he succeeded in gnawing through the stick. This was something that dogs were not supposed to do. It was unprecedented. But White Fang did it, trotting away from the fort in the early morning, with the end of the stick hanging to his neck.

He was wise. But had he been merely wise he would not have gone back to Grey Beaver who had already twice betrayed him. But there was his faithfulness, and he went back to be betrayed yet a third time. Again he yielded to the tying of a thong around his neck by Grey Beaver, and again Beauty Smith came to claim him. And this time he was beaten even more severely than before.

Grey Beaver looked on stolidly while the white man wielded the whip. He gave no protection. It was no longer his dog. When the beating was over White Fang was sick. A soft southland dog would have died under it, but not he. His school of life had been sterner, and he was himself of sterner stuff. He had too great vitality. His clutch on life was too strong. But he was very sick. At first he was unable to drag himself along, and Beauty Smith had to wait half-an-hour for him. And then, blind and reeling, he followed at Beauty Smith's heels back to the fort.

But now he was tied with a chain that defied his teeth, and he strove in vain, by lunging, to draw the staple from the timber into which it was driven. After a few days, sober and bankrupt, Grey Beaver departed up the Porcupine on his long journey to the Mackenzie. White Fang remained on the Yukon, the property of a man more than half mad and all brute. But what is a dog to know in its consciousness of madness? To White Fang, Beauty Smith was a veritable, if terrible, god. He was a mad god at best, but White Fang knew nothing of madness; he knew only that he must submit to the will of this new master, obey his every whim and fancy.

CHAPTER III—THE REIGN OF HATE

Under the tutelage of the mad god, White Fang became a fiend. He was kept chained in a pen at the rear of the fort, and here Beauty Smith teased and irritated and drove him wild with petty torments. The man early discovered White Fang's susceptibility to laughter, and made it a point after painfully tricking him, to laugh at him. This laughter was uproarious and scornful, and at the same time the god pointed his finger derisively at White Fang. At such times reason fled from White Fang, and in his transports of rage he was even more mad than Beauty Smith.

Formerly, White Fang had been merely the enemy of his kind, withal a ferocious enemy. He now became the enemy of all things, and more ferocious than ever. To such an extent was he tormented, that he hated blindly and without the faintest spark of reason. He hated the chain that bound him, the men who peered in at him through the slats of the pen, the dogs that accompanied the men and that snarled malignantly at him in his helplessness. He hated the very wood of the pen that confined him. And, first, last, and most of all, he hated Beauty Smith.

But Beauty Smith had a purpose in all that he did to White Fang. One day a number of men gathered about the pen. Beauty Smith entered, club in hand, and took the chain off from White Fang's neck. When his master had gone out, White Fang turned loose and tore around the pen, trying to get at the men outside. He was magnificently terrible. Fully five feet in length, and standing two and one-half feet at the shoulder, he far outweighed a wolf of corresponding size. From his mother he had inherited the heavier proportions of the dog, so that he weighed, without any fat and without an ounce of superfluous flesh, over ninety pounds. It was all muscle, bone, and sinew-fighting flesh in the finest condition.

The door of the pen was being opened again. White Fang paused. Something unusual was happening. He waited. The door was opened wider. Then a huge dog was thrust inside, and the door was slammed shut behind him. White Fang had never seen such a dog (it was a mastiff); but the size and fierce aspect of the intruder did not deter him. Here was some thing, not wood nor iron, upon which to wreak his hate. He leaped in with a flash of fangs that ripped down the side of the mastiff's neck. The mastiff shook his head, growled hoarsely, and plunged at White Fang. But White Fang was here, there, and everywhere, always evading and eluding, and always leaping in and slashing with his fangs and leaping out again in time to escape punishment.

The men outside shouted and applauded, while Beauty Smith, in an ecstasy of delight, gloated over the ripping and mangling performed by White Fang. There was no hope for the mastiff from the first. He was too ponderous and slow. In the end, while Beauty Smith beat White Fang back with a club, the mastiff was dragged out by its owner. Then there was a payment of bets, and money clinked in Beauty Smith's hand.

White Fang came to look forward eagerly to the gathering of the men around his pen. It meant a fight; and this was the only way that was now vouchsafed him of expressing the life that was in him. Tormented, incited to hate, he was kept a prisoner so that there was no way of satisfying that hate except at the times his master saw fit to put another dog against him. Beauty Smith had estimated his powers well, for he was invariably the victor. One day, three dogs were turned in upon him in succession. Another day a full-grown wolf, fresh-caught from the Wild, was shoved in through the door of the pen. And on still another day two dogs were set against him at the same time. This was his severest fight, and though in the end he killed them both he was himself half killed in doing it.

In the fall of the year, when the first snows were falling and mush-ice was running in the river, Beauty Smith took passage for himself and White Fang on a steamboat bound up the Yukon to Dawson. White Fang had now achieved a reputation in the land. As "the Fighting Wolf" he was known far and wide, and the cage in which he was kept on the steam-boat's deck was usually surrounded by curious men. He raged and snarled at them, or lay quietly and studied them with cold hatred. Why should he not hate them? He never asked himself the question. He knew only hate and lost himself in the passion of it. Life had become a hell to him. He had not been made for the close confinement wild beasts endure at the hands of men. And yet it was in precisely this way that he was treated. Men stared at him, poked sticks between the bars to make him snarl, and then laughed at him.

They were his environment, these men, and they were moulding the clay of him into a more ferocious thing than had been intended by Nature. Nevertheless, Nature had given him plasticity. Where many another animal would have died or had its spirit broken, he adjusted himself and lived, and at no expense of the spirit. Possibly Beauty Smith, arch-fiend and tormentor, was capable of breaking White Fang's spirit, but as yet there were no signs of his succeeding.

If Beauty Smith had in him a devil, White Fang had another; and the two of them raged against each other unceasingly. In the days before, White Fang had had the wisdom to cower down and submit to a man with a club in his hand; but this wisdom now left him. The mere sight of Beauty Smith was sufficient to send him into transports of fury. And when they came to close quarters, and he had been beaten back by the club, he went on growling and snarling, and showing his fangs. The last growl could never be extracted from him. No matter how terribly he was beaten, he had always another growl; and when Beauty Smith gave up and withdrew, the defiant growl followed after him, or White Fang sprang at the bars of the cage bellowing his hatred.

When the steamboat arrived at Dawson, White Fang went ashore. But he still lived a public life, in a cage, surrounded by curious men. He was exhibited as "the Fighting Wolf," and men paid fifty cents in gold dust to see him. He was given no rest. Did he lie down to sleep, he was stirred up by a sharp stick—so that the audience might get its money's worth. In order to make the exhibition interesting, he was kept in a rage most of the time. But worse than all this, was the atmosphere in which he lived. He was regarded as the most fearful of wild beasts, and this was borne in to him through the bars of the cage. Every word, every cautious action, on the part of the men, impressed upon him his own terrible ferocity. It was so much added fuel to the flame of his fierceness. There could be but one result, and that was that his ferocity fed upon itself and increased. It was another instance of the plasticity of his clay, of his capacity for being moulded by the pressure of environment.

In addition to being exhibited he was a professional fighting animal. At irregular intervals, whenever a fight could be arranged, he was taken out of his cage and led off into the woods a few miles from town. Usually this occurred at night, so as to avoid interference from the mounted police of the Territory. After a few hours of waiting, when daylight had come, the audience and the dog with which he was to fight arrived. In this manner it came about that he fought all sizes and breeds of dogs. It was a savage land, the men were savage, and the fights were usually to the death.

Since White Fang continued to fight, it is obvious that it was the other dogs that died. He never knew defeat. His early training, when he fought with Lip-lip and the whole puppy-pack, stood him in good stead. There was the tenacity with which he clung to the earth. No dog could make him lose his footing. This was the favourite trick of the wolf breeds—to rush in upon him, either directly or with an unexpected swerve, in the hope of striking his shoulder and overthrowing him. Mackenzie hounds, Eskimo and Labrador dogs, huskies and Malemutes—all tried it on him, and all failed. He was never known to lose his footing. Men told this to one another, and looked each time to see it happen; but White Fang always disappointed them.

Then there was his lightning quickness. It gave him a tremendous advantage over his antagonists. No matter what their fighting experience, they had never encountered a dog that moved so swiftly as he. Also to be reckoned with, was the immediateness of his attack. The average dog was accustomed to the preliminaries of snarling and bristling and growling, and the average dog was knocked off his feet and finished before he had begun to fight or recovered from his surprise. So often did this happen, that it became the custom to hold White Fang until the other dog went through its preliminaries, was good and ready, and even made the first attack.

But greatest of all the advantages in White Fang's favour, was his experience. He knew more about fighting than did any of the dogs that faced him. He had fought more fights, knew how to meet more tricks and methods, and had more tricks himself, while his own method was scarcely to be improved upon.

As the time went by, he had fewer and fewer fights. Men despaired of matching him with an equal, and Beauty Smith was compelled to pit wolves against him. These were trapped by the Indians for the purpose, and a fight between White Fang and a wolf was always sure to draw a crowd. Once, a full-grown female lynx was secured, and this time White Fang fought for his life. Her quickness matched his; her ferocity equalled his; while he fought with his fangs alone, and she fought with her sharp-clawed feet as well.

But after the lynx, all fighting ceased for White Fang. There were no more animals with which to fight—at least, there was none considered worthy of fighting with him. So he remained on exhibition until spring, when one Tim Keenan, a faro-dealer, arrived in the land. With him came the first bull-dog that had ever entered the Klondike. That this dog and White Fang should come together was inevitable, and for a week the anticipated fight was the mainspring of conversation in certain quarters of the town.

CHAPTER IV—THE CLINGING DEATH

Beauty Smith slipped the chain from his neck and stepped back.

For once White Fang did not make an immediate attack. He stood still, ears pricked forward, alert and curious, surveying the strange animal that faced him. He had never seen such a dog before. Tim Keenan shoved the bull-dog forward with a muttered "Go to it." The animal waddled toward the centre of the circle, short and squat and ungainly. He came to a stop and blinked across at White Fang.

There were cries from the crowd of, "Go to him, Cherokee! Sick 'm, Cherokee! Eat 'm up!"

But Cherokee did not seem anxious to fight. He turned his head and blinked at the men who shouted, at the same time wagging his stump of a tail good-naturedly. He was not afraid, but merely lazy. Besides, it did not seem to him that it was intended he should fight with the dog he saw before him. He was not used to fighting with that kind of dog, and he was waiting for them to bring on the real dog.

Tim Keenan stepped in and bent over Cherokee, fondling him on both sides of the shoulders with hands that rubbed against the grain of the hair and that made slight, pushing-forward movements. These were so many suggestions. Also, their effect was irritating, for Cherokee began to growl, very softly, deep down in his throat. There was a correspondence in rhythm between the growls and the movements of the man's hands. The growl rose in the throat with the culmination of each forward-pushing movement, and ebbed down to start up afresh with the beginning of the next movement. The end of each movement was the accent of the rhythm, the movement ending abruptly and the growling rising with a jerk.

This was not without its effect on White Fang. The hair began to rise on his neck and across the shoulders. Tim Keenan gave a final shove forward and stepped back again. As the impetus that carried Cherokee forward died down, he continued to go forward of his own volition, in a swift, bow-legged run. Then White Fang struck. A cry of startled admiration went up. He had covered the distance and gone in more like a cat than a dog; and with the same cat-like swiftness he had slashed with his fangs and leaped clear.

The bull-dog was bleeding back of one ear from a rip in his thick neck. He gave no sign, did not even snarl, but turned and followed after White Fang. The display on both sides, the quickness of the one and the steadiness of the other, had excited the partisan spirit of the crowd, and the men were making new bets and increasing original bets. Again, and yet again, White Fang sprang in, slashed, and got away untouched, and still his strange foe followed after him, without too great haste, not slowly, but deliberately and determinedly, in a businesslike sort of way. There was purpose in his method—something for him to do that he was intent upon doing and from which nothing could distract him.

His whole demeanour, every action, was stamped with this purpose. It puzzled White Fang. Never had he seen such a dog. It had no hair protection. It was soft, and bled easily. There was no thick mat of fur to baffle White Fang's teeth as they were often baffled by dogs of his own breed. Each time that his teeth struck they sank easily into the yielding flesh, while the animal did not seem able to defend itself. Another disconcerting thing was that it made no outcry, such as he had been accustomed to with the other dogs he had fought. Beyond a growl or a grunt, the dog took its punishment silently. And never did it flag in its pursuit of him.

Not that Cherokee was slow. He could turn and whirl swiftly enough, but White Fang was never there. Cherokee was puzzled, too. He had never fought before with a dog with which he could not close. The desire to close had always been mutual.

But here was a dog that kept at a distance, dancing and dodging here and there and all about. And when it did get its teeth into him, it did not hold on but let go instantly and darted away again.

But White Fang could not get at the soft underside of the throat. The bull-dog stood too short, while its massive jaws were an added protection. White Fang darted in and out unscathed, while Cherokee's wounds increased. Both sides of his neck and head were ripped and slashed. He bled freely, but showed no signs of being disconcerted. He continued his plodding pursuit, though once, for the moment baffled, he came to a full stop and blinked at the men who looked on, at the same time wagging his stump of a tail as an expression of his willingness to fight.

In that moment White Fang was in upon him and out, in passing ripping his trimmed remnant of an ear. With a slight manifestation of anger, Cherokee took up the pursuit again, running on the inside of the circle White Fang was making, and striving to fasten his deadly grip on White Fang's throat. The bull-dog missed by a hair's-breadth, and cries of praise went up as White Fang doubled suddenly out of danger in the opposite direction.

The time went by. White Fang still danced on, dodging and doubling, leaping in and out, and ever inflicting damage. And still the bull-dog, with grim certitude, toiled after him. Sooner or later he would accomplish his purpose, get the grip that would win the battle. In the meantime, he accepted all the punishment the other could deal him. His tufts of ears had become tassels, his neck and shoulders were slashed in a score of places, and his very lips were cut and bleeding—all from these lightning snaps that were beyond his foreseeing and guarding.

Time and again White Fang had attempted to knock Cherokee off his feet; but the difference in their height was too great. Cherokee was too squat, too close to the ground. White Fang tried the trick once too often. The chance came in one of his quick doublings and counter-circlings. He caught Cherokee with head turned away as he whirled more slowly. His shoulder was exposed. White Fang drove in upon it: but his own shoulder was high above, while he struck with such force that his momentum carried him on across over the other's body. For the first time in his fighting history, men saw White Fang lose his footing. His body turned a half-somersault in the air, and he would have landed on his back had he not twisted, cat-like, still in the air, in the effort to bring his feet to the earth. As it was, he struck heavily on his side. The next instant he was on his feet, but in that instant Cherokee's teeth closed on his throat.

It was not a good grip, being too low down toward the chest; but Cherokee held on. White Fang sprang to his feet and tore wildly around, trying to shake off the bull-dog's body. It made him frantic, this clinging, dragging weight. It bound his movements, restricted his freedom. It was like the trap, and all his instinct resented it and revolted against it. It was a mad revolt. For several minutes he was to all intents insane. The basic life that was in him took charge of him. The will to exist of his body surged over him. He was dominated by this mere flesh-love of life. All intelligence was gone. It was as though he had no brain. His reason was unseated by the blind yearning of the flesh to exist and move, at all hazards to move, to continue to move, for movement was the expression of its existence.

Round and round he went, whirling and turning and reversing, trying to shake off the fifty-pound weight that dragged at his throat. The bull-dog did little but keep his grip. Sometimes, and rarely, he managed to get his feet to the earth and for a moment to brace himself against White Fang. But the next moment his footing would be lost and he would be dragging around in the whirl of one of White Fang's mad gyrations. Cherokee identified himself with his instinct. He knew that he was doing the right thing by holding on, and there came to him certain blissful thrills of satisfaction. At such moments he even closed his eyes and allowed his body to be hurled hither and thither, willy-nilly, careless of any hurt that might thereby come to it. That did not count. The grip was the thing, and the grip he kept.

White Fang ceased only when he had tired himself out. He could do nothing, and he could not understand. Never, in all his fighting, had this thing happened. The dogs he had fought with did not fight that way. With them it was snap and slash and get away, snap and slash and get away. He lay partly on his side, panting for breath. Cherokee still holding his grip, urged against him, trying to get him over entirely on his side. White Fang resisted, and he could feel the jaws shifting their grip, slightly relaxing and coming together again in a chewing movement. Each shift brought the grip closer to his throat. The bull-dog's method was to hold what he had, and when opportunity favoured to work in for more. Opportunity favoured when White Fang remained quiet. When White Fang struggled, Cherokee was content merely to hold on.

The bulging back of Cherokee's neck was the only portion of his body that White Fang's teeth could reach. He got hold toward the base where the neck comes out from the shoulders; but he did not know the chewing method of fighting, nor were his jaws adapted to it. He spasmodically ripped and tore with his fangs for a space. Then a change in their position diverted him. The bull-dog had managed to roll him over on his back, and still hanging on to his throat, was on top of him. Like a cat, White Fang bowed his hind-quarters in, and, with the feet digging into his enemy's abdomen above him, he began to claw with long tearing-strokes. Cherokee might well have been disembowelled had he not quickly pivoted on his grip and got his body off of White Fang's and at right angles to it.

There was no escaping that grip. It was like Fate itself, and as inexorable. Slowly it shifted up along the jugular. All that saved White Fang from death was the loose skin of his neck and the thick fur that covered it. This served to form a large roll in Cherokee's mouth, the fur of which well-nigh defied his teeth. But bit by bit, whenever the chance offered, he was getting more of the loose skin and fur in his mouth. The result was that he was slowly throttling White Fang. The latter's breath was drawn with greater and greater difficulty as the moments went by.

It began to look as though the battle were over. The backers of Cherokee waxed jubilant and offered ridiculous odds. White Fang's backers were correspondingly depressed, and refused bets of ten to one and twenty to one, though one man was rash enough to close a wager of fifty to one. This man was Beauty Smith. He took a step into the ring and pointed his finger at White Fang. Then he began to laugh derisively and scornfully. This produced the desired effect. White Fang went wild with rage. He called up his reserves of strength, and gained his feet. As he struggled around the ring, the fifty pounds of his foe ever dragging on his throat, his anger passed on into panic. The basic life of him dominated him again, and his intelligence fled before the will of his flesh to live. Round and round and back again, stumbling and falling and rising, even uprearing at times on his hind-legs and lifting his foe clear of the earth, he struggled vainly to shake off the clinging death.

At last he fell, toppling backward, exhausted; and the bull-dog promptly shifted his grip, getting in closer, mangling more and more of the fur-folded flesh, throttling White Fang more severely than ever. Shouts of applause went up for the victor, and there were many cries of "Cherokee!" "Cherokee!" To this Cherokee responded by vigorous wagging of the stump of his tail. But the clamour of approval did not distract him. There was no sympathetic relation between his tail and his massive jaws. The one might wag, but the others held their terrible grip on White Fang's throat.

It was at this time that a diversion came to the spectators. There was a jingle of bells. Dog-mushers' cries were heard. Everybody, save Beauty Smith, looked apprehensively, the fear of the police strong upon them. But they saw, up the trail, and not down, two men running with sled and dogs. They were evidently coming down the creek from some prospecting trip. At sight of the crowd they stopped their dogs and came over and joined it, curious to see the cause of the excitement. The dog-musher wore a moustache, but the other, a taller and younger man, was smooth-shaven, his skin rosy from the pounding of his blood and the running in the frosty air.

White Fang had practically ceased struggling. Now and again he resisted spasmodically and to no purpose. He could get little air, and that little grew less and less under the merciless grip that ever tightened. In spite of his armour of fur, the great vein of his throat would have long since been torn open, had not the first grip of the bull-dog been so low down as to be practically on the chest. It had taken Cherokee a long time to shift that grip upward, and this had also tended further to clog his jaws with fur and skin-fold.

In the meantime, the abysmal brute in Beauty Smith had been rising into his brain and mastering the small bit of sanity that he possessed at best. When he saw White Fang's eyes beginning to glaze, he knew beyond doubt that the fight was lost. Then he broke loose. He sprang upon White Fang and began savagely to kick him. There were hisses from the crowd and cries of protest, but that was all. While this went on, and Beauty Smith continued to kick White Fang, there was a commotion in the crowd. The tall young newcomer was forcing his way through, shouldering men right and left without ceremony or gentleness. When he broke through into the ring, Beauty Smith was just in the act of delivering another kick. All his weight was on one foot, and he was in a state of unstable equilibrium. At that moment the newcomer's fist landed a smashing blow full in his face. Beauty Smith's remaining leg left the ground, and his whole body seemed to lift into the air as he turned over backward and struck the snow. The newcomer turned upon the crowd.

"You cowards!" he cried. "You beasts!"

He was in a rage himself—a sane rage. His grey eyes seemed metallic and steel-like as they flashed upon the crowd. Beauty Smith regained his feet and came toward him, sniffling and cowardly. The new-comer did not understand. He did not know how abject a coward the other was, and thought he was coming back intent on fighting. So, with a "You beast!" he smashed Beauty Smith over backward with a second blow in the face. Beauty Smith decided that the snow was the safest place for him, and lay where he had fallen, making no effort to get up.

"Come on, Matt, lend a hand," the newcomer called the dog-musher, who had followed him into the ring.

Both men bent over the dogs. Matt took hold of White Fang, ready to pull when Cherokee's jaws should be loosened. This the younger man endeavoured to accomplish by clutching the bulldog's jaws in his hands and trying to spread them. It was a vain undertaking. As he pulled and tugged and wrenched, he kept exclaiming with every expulsion of breath, "Beasts!"

The crowd began to grow unruly, and some of the men were protesting against the spoiling of the sport; but they were silenced when the newcomer lifted his head from his work for a moment and glared at them.

"You damn beasts!" he finally exploded, and went back to his task.

"It's no use, Mr. Scott, you can't break 'm apart that way," Matt said at last.

The pair paused and surveyed the locked dogs.

"Ain't bleedin' much," Matt announced. "Ain't got all the way in yet."

"But he's liable to any moment," Scott answered. "There, did you see that! He shifted his grip in a bit."

The younger man's excitement and apprehension for White Fang was growing. He struck Cherokee about the head savagely again and again. But that did not loosen the jaws. Cherokee wagged the stump of his tail in advertisement that he understood the meaning of the blows, but that he knew he was himself in the right and only doing his duty by keeping his grip.

"Won't some of you help?" Scott cried desperately at the crowd.

But no help was offered. Instead, the crowd began sarcastically to cheer him on and showered him with facetious advice.

"You'll have to get a pry," Matt counselled.

The other reached into the holster at his hip, drew his revolver, and tried to thrust its muzzle between the bull-dog's jaws. He shoved, and shoved hard, till the grating of the steel against the locked teeth could be distinctly heard. Both men were on their knees, bending over the dogs. Tim Keenan strode into the ring. He paused beside Scott and touched him on the shoulder, saying ominously:

"Don't break them teeth, stranger."

"Then I'll break his neck," Scott retorted, continuing his shoving and wedging with the revolver muzzle.

"I said don't break them teeth," the faro-dealer repeated more ominously than before.

But if it was a bluff he intended, it did not work. Scott never desisted from his efforts, though he looked up coolly and asked:

"Your dog?"

The faro-dealer grunted.

"Then get in here and break this grip."

"Well, stranger," the other drawled irritatingly, "I don't mind telling you that's something I ain't worked out for myself. I don't know how to turn the trick."

"Then get out of the way," was the reply, "and don't bother me. I'm busy."

Tim Keenan continued standing over him, but Scott took no further notice of his presence. He had managed to get the muzzle in between the jaws on one side, and was trying to get it out between the jaws on the other side. This accomplished, he pried gently and carefully, loosening the jaws a bit at a time, while Matt, a bit at a time, extricated White Fang's mangled neck.

"Stand by to receive your dog," was Scott's peremptory order to Cherokee's owner.

The faro-dealer stooped down obediently and got a firm hold on Cherokee.

"Now!" Scott warned, giving the final pry.

The dogs were drawn apart, the bull-dog struggling vigorously.

"Take him away," Scott commanded, and Tim Keenan dragged Cherokee back into the crowd.

White Fang made several ineffectual efforts to get up. Once he gained his feet, but his legs were too weak to sustain him, and he slowly wilted and sank back into the snow. His eyes were half closed, and the surface of them was glassy. His jaws were apart, and through them the tongue protruded, draggled and limp. To all appearances he looked like a dog that had been strangled to death. Matt examined him.

"Just about all in," he announced; "but he's breathin' all right."

Beauty Smith had regained his feet and come over to look at White Fang.

"Matt, how much is a good sled-dog worth?" Scott asked.

The dog-musher, still on his knees and stooped over White Fang, calculated for a moment.

"Three hundred dollars," he answered.

"And how much for one that's all chewed up like this one?" Scott asked, nudging White Fang with his foot.

"Half of that," was the dog-musher's judgment. Scott turned upon Beauty Smith.

"Did you hear, Mr. Beast? I'm going to take your dog from you, and I'm going to give you a hundred and fifty for him."

He opened his pocket-book and counted out the bills.

Beauty Smith put his hands behind his back, refusing to touch the proffered money.

"I ain't a-sellin'," he said.

"Oh, yes you are," the other assured him. "Because I'm buying. Here's your money. The dog's mine."

Beauty Smith, his hands still behind him, began to back away.

Scott sprang toward him, drawing his fist back to strike. Beauty Smith cowered down in anticipation of the blow.

"I've got my rights," he whimpered.

"You've forfeited your rights to own that dog," was the rejoinder. "Are you going to take the money? or do I have to hit you again?"

"All right," Beauty Smith spoke up with the alacrity of fear. "But I take the money under protest," he added. "The dog's a mint. I ain't a-goin' to be robbed. A man's got his rights."

"Correct," Scott answered, passing the money over to him. "A man's got his rights. But you're not a man. You're a beast."

"Wait till I get back to Dawson," Beauty Smith threatened. "I'll have the law on you."

"If you open your mouth when you get back to Dawson, I'll have you run out of town. Understand?"

Beauty Smith replied with a grunt.

"Understand?" the other thundered with abrupt fierceness.

"Yes," Beauty Smith grunted, shrinking away.

"Yes what?"

"Yes, sir," Beauty Smith snarled.

"Look out! He'll bite!" some one shouted, and a guffaw of laughter went up.

Scott turned his back on him, and returned to help the dog-musher, who was working over White Fang.

Some of the men were already departing; others stood in groups, looking on and talking. Tim Keenan joined one of the groups.

"Who's that mug?" he asked.

"Weedon Scott," some one answered.

"And who in hell is Weedon Scott?" the faro-dealer demanded.

"Oh, one of them crackerjack minin' experts. He's in with all the big bugs. If you want to keep out of trouble, you'll steer clear of him, that's my talk. He's all hunky with the officials. The Gold Commissioner's a special pal of his."

"I thought he must be somebody," was the faro-dealer's comment. "That's why I kept my hands offen him at the start."

CHAPTER V—THE INDOMITABLE

"It's hopeless," Weedon Scott confessed.

He sat on the step of his cabin and stared at the dog-musher, who responded with a shrug that was equally hopeless.

Together they looked at White Fang at the end of his stretched chain, bristling, snarling, ferocious, straining to get at the sled-dogs. Having received sundry lessons from Matt, said lessons being imparted by means of a club, the sled-dogs had learned to leave White Fang alone; and even then they were lying down at a distance, apparently oblivious of his existence.

"It's a wolf and there's no taming it," Weedon Scott announced.

"Oh, I don't know about that," Matt objected. "Might be a lot of dog in 'm, for all you can tell. But there's one thing I know sure, an' that there's no gettin' away from."

The dog-musher paused and nodded his head confidentially at Moosehide Mountain.

"Well, don't be a miser with what you know," Scott said sharply, after waiting a suitable length of time. "Spit it out. What is it?"

The dog-musher indicated White Fang with a backward thrust of his thumb.

"Wolf or dog, it's all the same—he's ben tamed 'ready."

"No!"

"I tell you yes, an' broke to harness. Look close there. D'ye see them marks across the chest?"

"You're right, Matt. He was a sled-dog before Beauty Smith got hold of him."

"And there's not much reason against his bein' a sled-dog again."

"What d'ye think?" Scott queried eagerly. Then the hope died down as he added, shaking his head, "We've had him two weeks now, and if anything he's wilder than ever at the present moment."

"Give 'm a chance," Matt counselled. "Turn 'm loose for a spell."

The other looked at him incredulously.

"Yes," Matt went on, "I know you've tried to, but you didn't take a club."

"You try it then."

The dog-musher secured a club and went over to the chained animal. White Fang watched the club after the manner of a caged lion watching the whip of its trainer.

"See 'm keep his eye on that club," Matt said. "That's a good sign. He's no fool. Don't dast tackle me so long as I got that club handy. He's not clean crazy, sure."

As the man's hand approached his neck, White Fang bristled and snarled and crouched down. But while he eyed the approaching hand, he at the same time contrived to keep track of the club in the other hand, suspended threateningly above him. Matt unsnapped the chain from the collar and stepped back.

White Fang could scarcely realise that he was free. Many months had gone by since he passed into the possession of Beauty Smith, and in all that period he had never known a moment of freedom except at the times he had been loosed to fight with other dogs. Immediately after such fights he had always been imprisoned again.

He did not know what to make of it. Perhaps some new devilry of the gods was about to be perpetrated on him. He walked slowly and cautiously, prepared to be assailed at any moment. He did not know what to do, it was all so unprecedented. He took the precaution to sheer off from the two watching gods, and walked carefully to the corner of the cabin. Nothing happened. He was plainly perplexed, and he came back again, pausing a dozen feet away and regarding the two men intently.

"Won't he run away?" his new owner asked.

Matt shrugged his shoulders. "Got to take a gamble. Only way to find out is to find out."

"Poor devil," Scott murmured pityingly. "What he needs is some show of human kindness," he added, turning and going into the cabin.

He came out with a piece of meat, which he tossed to White Fang. He sprang away from it, and from a distance studied it suspiciously.

"Hi-yu, Major!" Matt shouted warningly, but too late.

Major had made a spring for the meat. At the instant his jaws closed on it, White Fang struck him. He was overthrown. Matt rushed in, but quicker than he was White Fang. Major staggered to his feet, but the blood spouting from his throat reddened the snow in a widening path.

"It's too bad, but it served him right," Scott said hastily.

But Matt's foot had already started on its way to kick White Fang. There was a leap, a flash of teeth, a sharp exclamation. White Fang, snarling fiercely, scrambled backward for several yards, while Matt stooped and investigated his leg.

"He got me all right," he announced, pointing to the torn trousers and undercloths, and the growing stain of red.

"I told you it was hopeless, Matt," Scott said in a discouraged voice. "I've thought about it off and on, while not wanting to think of it. But we've come to it now. It's the only thing to do."

As he talked, with reluctant movements he drew his revolver, threw open the cylinder, and assured himself of its contents.

"Look here, Mr. Scott," Matt objected; "that dog's ben through hell. You can't expect 'm to come out a white an' shinin' angel. Give 'm time."

"Look at Major," the other rejoined.

The dog-musher surveyed the stricken dog. He had sunk down on the snow in the circle of his blood and was plainly in the last gasp.

"Served 'm right. You said so yourself, Mr. Scott. He tried to take White Fang's meat, an' he's dead-O. That was to be expected. I wouldn't give two whoops in hell for a dog that wouldn't fight for his own meat."

"But look at yourself, Matt. It's all right about the dogs, but we must draw the line somewhere."

"Served me right," Matt argued stubbornly. "What'd I want to kick 'm for? You said yourself that he'd done right. Then I had no right to kick 'm."

"It would be a mercy to kill him," Scott insisted. "He's untamable."

"Now look here, Mr. Scott, give the poor devil a fightin' chance. He ain't had no chance yet. He's just come through hell, an' this is the first time he's ben loose. Give 'm a fair chance, an' if he don't deliver the goods, I'll kill 'm myself. There!"

"God knows I don't want to kill him or have him killed," Scott answered, putting away the revolver. "We'll let him run loose and see what kindness can do for him. And here's a try at it."

He walked over to White Fang and began talking to him gently and soothingly.

"Better have a club handy," Matt warned.

Scott shook his head and went on trying to win White Fang's confidence.

White Fang was suspicious. Something was impending. He had killed this god's dog, bitten his companion god, and what else was to be expected than some terrible punishment? But in the face of it he was indomitable. He bristled and showed his teeth, his eyes vigilant, his whole body wary and prepared for anything. The god had no club, so he suffered him to approach quite near. The god's hand had come out and was descending upon his head. White Fang shrank together and grew tense as he crouched under it. Here was danger, some treachery or something. He knew the hands of the gods, their proved mastery, their cunning to hurt. Besides, there was his old antipathy to being touched. He snarled more menacingly, crouched still lower, and still the hand descended. He did not want to bite the hand, and he endured the peril of it until his instinct surged up in him, mastering him with its insatiable yearning for life.

Weedon Scott had believed that he was quick enough to avoid any snap or slash. But he had yet to learn the remarkable quickness of White Fang, who struck with the certainty and swiftness of a coiled snake.

Scott cried out sharply with surprise, catching his torn hand and holding it tightly in his other hand. Matt uttered a great oath and sprang to his side. White Fang crouched down, and backed away, bristling, showing his fangs, his eyes malignant with menace. Now he could expect a beating as fearful as any he had received from Beauty Smith.

"Here! What are you doing?" Scott cried suddenly.

Matt had dashed into the cabin and come out with a rifle.

"Nothin'," he said slowly, with a careless calmness that was assumed, "only goin' to keep that promise I made. I reckon it's up to me to kill 'm as I said I'd do."

"No you don't!"

"Yes I do. Watch me."

As Matt had pleaded for White Fang when he had been bitten, it was now Weedon Scott's turn to plead.

"You said to give him a chance. Well, give it to him. We've only just started, and we can't quit at the beginning. It served me right, this time. And—look at him!"

White Fang, near the corner of the cabin and forty feet away, was snarling with blood-curdling viciousness, not at Scott, but at the dog-musher.

"Well, I'll be everlastingly gosh-swoggled!" was the dog-musher's expression of astonishment.

"Look at the intelligence of him," Scott went on hastily. "He knows the meaning of firearms as well as you do. He's got intelligence and we've got to give that intelligence a chance. Put up the gun."

"All right, I'm willin'," Matt agreed, leaning the rifle against the woodpile.

"But will you look at that!" he exclaimed the next moment.

White Fang had quieted down and ceased snarling. "This is worth investigatin'. Watch."

Matt, reached for the rifle, and at the same moment White Fang snarled. He stepped away from the rifle, and White Fang's lifted lips descended, covering his teeth.

"Now, just for fun."

Matt took the rifle and began slowly to raise it to his shoulder. White Fang's snarling began with the movement, and increased as the movement approached its culmination. But the moment before the rifle came to a level on him, he leaped sidewise behind the corner of the cabin. Matt stood staring along the sights at the empty space of snow which had been occupied by White Fang.

The dog-musher put the rifle down solemnly, then turned and looked at his employer.

"I agree with you, Mr. Scott. That dog's too intelligent to kill."

CHAPTER VI—THE LOVE-MASTER

As White Fang watched Weedon Scott approach, he bristled and snarled to advertise that he would not submit to punishment. Twenty-four hours had passed since he had slashed open the hand that was now bandaged and held up by a sling to keep the blood out of it. In the past White Fang had experienced delayed punishments, and he apprehended that such a one was about to befall him. How could it be otherwise? He had committed what was to him sacrilege, sunk his fangs into the holy flesh of a god, and of a white-skinned superior god at that. In the nature of things, and of intercourse with gods, something terrible awaited him.

The god sat down several feet away. White Fang could see nothing dangerous in that. When the gods administered punishment they stood on their legs. Besides, this god had no club, no whip, no firearm. And furthermore, he himself was free. No chain nor stick bound him. He could escape into safety while the god was scrambling to his feet. In the meantime he would wait and see.

The god remained quiet, made no movement; and White Fang's snarl slowly dwindled to a growl that ebbed down in his throat and ceased. Then the god spoke, and at the first sound of his voice, the hair rose on White Fang's neck and the growl rushed up in his throat. But the god made no hostile movement, and went on calmly talking. For a time White Fang growled in unison with him, a correspondence of rhythm being established between growl and voice. But the god talked on interminably. He talked to White Fang as White Fang had never been talked to before. He talked softly and soothingly, with a gentleness that somehow, somewhere, touched White Fang. In spite of himself and all the pricking warnings of his instinct, White Fang began to have confidence in this god. He had a feeling of security that was belied by all his experience with men.

After a long time, the god got up and went into the cabin. White Fang scanned him apprehensively when he came out. He had neither whip nor club nor weapon. Nor was his uninjured hand behind his back hiding something. He sat down as before, in the same spot, several feet away. He held out a small piece of meat. White Fang pricked his ears and investigated it suspiciously, managing to look at the same time both at the meat and the god, alert for any overt act, his body tense and ready to spring away at the first sign of hostility.

Still the punishment delayed. The god merely held near to his nose a piece of meat. And about the meat there seemed nothing wrong. Still White Fang suspected; and though the meat was proffered to him with short inviting thrusts of the hand, he refused to touch it. The gods were all-wise, and there was no telling what masterful treachery lurked behind that apparently harmless piece of meat. In past experience, especially in dealing with squaws, meat and punishment had often been disastrously related.

In the end, the god tossed the meat on the snow at White Fang's feet. He smelled the meat carefully; but he did not look at it. While he smelled it he kept his eyes on the god. Nothing happened. He took the meat into his mouth and swallowed it. Still nothing happened. The god was actually offering him another piece of meat. Again he refused to take it from the hand, and again it was tossed to him. This was repeated a number of times. But there came a time when the god refused to toss it. He kept it in his hand and steadfastly proffered it.

The meat was good meat, and White Fang was hungry. Bit by bit, infinitely cautious, he approached the hand. At last the time came that he decided to eat the meat from the hand. He never took his eyes from the god, thrusting his head forward with ears flattened back and hair involuntarily rising and cresting on his neck. Also a low growl rumbled in his throat as warning that he was not to be trifled with. He ate the meat, and nothing happened. Piece by piece, he ate all the meat, and nothing happened. Still the punishment delayed.

He licked his chops and waited. The god went on talking. In his voice was kindness—something of which White Fang had no experience whatever. And within him it aroused feelings which he had likewise never experienced before. He was aware of a certain strange satisfaction, as though some need were being gratified, as though some void in his being were being filled. Then again came the prod of his instinct and the warning of past experience. The gods were ever crafty, and they had unguessed ways of attaining their ends.

Ah, he had thought so! There it came now, the god's hand, cunning to hurt, thrusting out at him, descending upon his head. But the god went on talking. His voice was soft and soothing. In spite of the menacing hand, the voice inspired confidence. And in spite of the assuring voice, the hand inspired distrust. White Fang was torn by conflicting feelings, impulses. It seemed he would fly to pieces, so terrible was the control he was exerting, holding together by an unwonted indecision the counter-forces that struggled within him for mastery.

He compromised. He snarled and bristled and flattened his ears. But he neither snapped nor sprang away. The hand descended. Nearer and nearer it came. It touched the ends of his upstanding hair. He shrank down under it. It followed down after him, pressing more closely against him. Shrinking, almost shivering, he still managed to hold himself together. It was a torment, this hand that touched him and violated his instinct. He could not forget in a day all the evil that had been wrought him at the hands of men. But it was the will of the god, and he strove to submit.

The hand lifted and descended again in a patting, caressing movement. This continued, but every time the hand lifted, the hair lifted under it. And every time the hand descended, the ears flattened down and a cavernous growl surged in his throat. White Fang growled and growled with insistent warning. By this means he announced that he was prepared to retaliate for any hurt he might receive. There was no telling when the god's ulterior motive might be disclosed. At any moment that soft, confidence-inspiring voice might break forth in a roar of wrath, that gentle and caressing hand transform itself into a vice-like grip to hold him helpless and administer punishment.

But the god talked on softly, and ever the hand rose and fell with non-hostile pats. White Fang experienced dual feelings. It was distasteful to his instinct. It restrained him, opposed the will of him toward personal liberty. And yet it was not physically painful. On the contrary, it was even pleasant, in a physical way. The patting movement slowly and carefully changed to a rubbing of the ears about their bases, and the physical pleasure even increased a little. Yet he continued to fear, and he stood on guard, expectant of unguessed evil, alternately suffering and enjoying as one feeling or the other came uppermost and swayed him.

"Well, I'll be gosh-swoggled!"

So spoke Matt, coming out of the cabin, his sleeves rolled up, a pan of dirty dish-water in his hands, arrested in the act of emptying the pan by the sight of Weedon Scott patting White Fang.

At the instant his voice broke the silence, White Fang leaped back, snarling savagely at him.

Matt regarded his employer with grieved disapproval.

"If you don't mind my expressin' my feelin's, Mr. Scott, I'll make free to say you're seventeen kinds of a damn fool an' all of 'em different, an' then some."

Weedon Scott smiled with a superior air, gained his feet, and walked over to White Fang. He talked soothingly to him, but not for long, then slowly put out his hand, rested it on White Fang's head, and resumed the interrupted patting. White Fang endured it, keeping his eyes fixed suspiciously, not upon the man that patted him, but upon the man that stood in the doorway.

"You may be a number one, tip-top minin' expert, all right all right," the dog-musher delivered himself oracularly, "but you missed the chance of your life when you was a boy an' didn't run off an' join a circus."

White Fang snarled at the sound of his voice, but this time did not leap away from under the hand that was caressing his head and the back of his neck with long, soothing strokes.

It was the beginning of the end for White Fang—the ending of the old life and the reign of hate. A new and incomprehensibly fairer life was dawning. It required much thinking and endless patience on the part of Weedon Scott to accomplish this. And on the part of White Fang it required nothing less than a revolution. He had to ignore the urges and promptings of instinct and reason, defy experience, give the lie to life itself.

Life, as he had known it, not only had had no place in it for much that he now did; but all the currents had gone counter to those to which he now abandoned himself. In short, when all things were considered, he had to achieve an orientation far vaster than the one he had achieved at the time he came voluntarily in from the Wild and accepted Grey Beaver as his lord. At that time he was a mere puppy, soft from the making, without form, ready for the thumb of circumstance to begin its work upon him. But now it was different. The thumb of circumstance had done its work only too well. By it he had been formed and hardened into the Fighting Wolf, fierce and implacable, unloving and unlovable. To accomplish the change was like a reflux of being, and this when the plasticity of youth was no longer his; when the fibre of him had become tough and knotty; when the warp and the woof of him had made of him an adamantine texture, harsh and unyielding; when the face of his spirit had become iron and all his instincts and axioms had crystallised into set rules, cautions, dislikes, and desires.

Yet again, in this new orientation, it was the thumb of circumstance that pressed and prodded him, softening that which had become hard and remoulding it into fairer form. Weedon Scott was in truth this thumb. He had gone to the roots of White

Fang's nature, and with kindness touched to life potencies that had languished and well-nigh perished. One such potency was love. It took the place of like, which latter had been the highest feeling that thrilled him in his intercourse with the gods.

But this love did not come in a day. It began with like and out of it slowly developed. White Fang did not run away, though he was allowed to remain loose, because he liked this new god. This was certainly better than the life he had lived in the cage of Beauty Smith, and it was necessary that he should have some god. The lordship of man was a need of his nature. The seal of his dependence on man had been set upon him in that early day when he turned his back on the Wild and crawled to Grey Beaver's feet to receive the expected beating. This seal had been stamped upon him again, and ineradicably, on his second return from the Wild, when the long famine was over and there was fish once more in the village of Grey Beaver.

And so, because he needed a god and because he preferred Weedon Scott to Beauty Smith, White Fang remained. In acknowledgment of fealty, he proceeded to take upon himself the guardianship of his master's property. He prowled about the cabin while the sled-dogs slept, and the first night-visitor to the cabin fought him off with a club until Weedon Scott came to the rescue. But White Fang soon learned to differentiate between thieves and honest men, to appraise the true value of step and carriage. The man who travelled, loud-stepping, the direct line to the cabin door, he let alone—though he watched him vigilantly until the door opened and he received the endorsement of the master. But the man who went softly, by circuitous ways, peering with caution, seeking after secrecy—that was the man who received no suspension of judgment from White Fang, and who went away abruptly, hurriedly, and without dignity.

Weedon Scott had set himself the task of redeeming White Fang—or rather, of redeeming mankind from the wrong it had done White Fang. It was a matter of principle and conscience. He felt that the ill done White Fang was a debt incurred by man and that it must be paid. So he went out of his way to be especially kind to the Fighting Wolf. Each day he made it a point to caress and pet White Fang, and to do it at length.

At first suspicious and hostile, White Fang grew to like this petting. But there was one thing that he never outgrew—his growling. Growl he would, from the moment the petting began till it ended. But it was a growl with a new note in it. A stranger could not hear this note, and to such a stranger the growling of White Fang was an exhibition of primordial savagery, nerve-racking and blood-curdling. But White Fang's throat had become harsh-fibred from the making of ferocious sounds through the many years since his first little rasp of anger in the lair of his cubhood, and he could not soften the sounds of that throat now to express the gentleness he felt. Nevertheless, Weedon Scott's ear and sympathy were fine enough to catch the new note all but drowned in the fierceness—the note that was the faintest hint of a croon of content and that none but he could hear.

As the days went by, the evolution of like into love was accelerated. White Fang himself began to grow aware of it, though in his consciousness he knew not what love was. It manifested itself to him as a void in his being—a hungry, aching, yearn-

156

ing void that clamoured to be filled. It was a pain and an unrest; and it received easement only by the touch of the new god's presence. At such times love was joy to him, a wild, keen-thrilling satisfaction. But when away from his god, the pain and the unrest returned; the void in him sprang up and pressed against him with its emptiness, and the hunger gnawed and gnawed unceasingly.

White Fang was in the process of finding himself. In spite of the maturity of his years and of the savage rigidity of the mould that had formed him, his nature was undergoing an expansion. There was a burgeoning within him of strange feelings and unwonted impulses. His old code of conduct was changing. In the past he had liked comfort and surcease from pain, disliked discomfort and pain, and he had adjusted his actions accordingly. But now it was different. Because of this new feeling within him, he ofttimes elected discomfort and pain for the sake of his god. Thus, in the early morning, instead of roaming and foraging, or lying in a sheltered nook, he would wait for hours on the cheerless cabin-stoop for a sight of the god's face. At night, when the god returned home, White Fang would leave the warm sleeping-place he had burrowed in the snow in order to receive the friendly snap of fingers and the word of greeting. Meat, even meat itself, he would forego to be with his god, to receive a caress from him or to accompany him down into the town.

Like had been replaced by love. And love was the plummet dropped down into the deeps of him where like had never gone. And responsive out of his deeps had come the new thing—love. That which was given unto him did he return. This was a god indeed, a love-god, a warm and radiant god, in whose light White Fang's nature expanded as a flower expands under the sun.

But White Fang was not demonstrative. He was too old, too firmly moulded, to become adept at expressing himself in new ways. He was too self-possessed, too strongly poised in his own isolation. Too long had he cultivated reticence, aloofness, and moroseness. He had never barked in his life, and he could not now learn to bark a welcome when his god approached. He was never in the way, never extravagant nor foolish in the expression of his love. He never ran to meet his god. He waited at a distance; but he always waited, was always there. His love partook of the nature of worship, dumb, inarticulate, a silent adoration. Only by the steady regard of his eyes did he express his love, and by the unceasing following with his eyes of his god's every movement. Also, at times, when his god looked at him and spoke to him, he betrayed an awkward self-consciousness, caused by the struggle of his love to express itself and his physical inability to express it.

He learned to adjust himself in many ways to his new mode of life. It was borne in upon him that he must let his master's dogs alone. Yet his dominant nature asserted itself, and he had first to thrash them into an acknowledgment of his superiority and leadership. This accomplished, he had little trouble with them. They gave trail to him when he came and went or walked among them, and when he asserted his will they obeyed.

In the same way, he came to tolerate Matt—as a possession of his master. His master rarely fed him. Matt did that, it was his business; yet White Fang divined that it was his master's food he ate and that it was his master who thus fed him vicariously. Matt it was who tried to put him into the harness and make him haul sled with the other dogs. But Matt failed. It was not until Weedon Scott put the harness on White Fang and worked him, that he understood. He took it as his master's will that Matt should drive him and work him just as he drove and worked his master's other dogs.

Different from the Mackenzie toboggans were the Klondike sleds with runners under them. And different was the method of driving the dogs. There was no fan-formation of the team. The dogs worked in single file, one behind another, hauling on double traces. And here, in the Klondike, the leader was indeed the leader. The wisest as well as strongest dog was the leader, and the team obeyed him and feared him. That White Fang should quickly gain this post was inevitable. He could not be satisfied with less, as Matt learned after much inconvenience and trouble. White Fang picked out the post for himself, and Matt backed his judgment with strong language after the experiment had been tried. But, though he worked in the sled in the day, White Fang did not forego the guarding of his master's property in the night. Thus he was on duty all the time, ever vigilant and faithful, the most valuable of all the dogs.

"Makin' free to spit out what's in me," Matt said one day, "I beg to state that you was a wise guy all right when you paid the price you did for that dog. You clean swindled Beauty Smith on top of pushin' his face in with your fist."

A recrudescence of anger glinted in Weedon Scott's grey eyes, and he muttered savagely, "The beast!"

In the late spring a great trouble came to White Fang. Without warning, the love-master disappeared. There had been warning, but White Fang was unversed in such things and did not understand the packing of a grip. He remembered afterwards that his packing had preceded the master's disappearance; but at the time he suspected nothing. That night he waited for the master to return. At midnight the chill wind that blew drove him to shelter at the rear of the cabin. There he drowsed, only half asleep, his ears keyed for the first sound of the familiar step. But, at two in the morning, his anxiety drove him out to the cold front stoop, where he crouched, and waited.

But no master came. In the morning the door opened and Matt stepped outside. White Fang gazed at him wistfully. There was no common speech by which he might learn what he wanted to know. The days came and went, but never the master. White Fang, who had never known sickness in his life, became sick. He became very sick, so sick that Matt was finally compelled to bring him inside the cabin. Also, in writing to his employer, Matt devoted a postscript to White Fang.

Weedon Scott reading the letter down in Circle City, came upon the following:

"That dam wolf won't work. Won't eat. Aint got no spunk left. All the dogs is licking him. Wants to know what has become of you, and I don't know how to tell him. Mebbe he is going to die."

It was as Matt had said. White Fang had ceased eating, lost heart, and allowed every dog of the team to thrash him. In the cabin he lay on the floor near the stove, without interest in food, in Matt, nor in life. Matt might talk gently to him or swear at him, it was all the same; he never did more than turn his dull eyes upon the man, then drop his head back to its customary position on his fore-paws.

And then, one night, Matt, reading to himself with moving lips and mumbled sounds, was startled by a low whine from White Fang. He had got upon his feet, his ears cocked towards the door, and he was listening intently. A moment later, Matt heard a footstep. The door opened, and Weedon Scott stepped in. The two men shook hands. Then Scott looked around the room.

"Where's the wolf?" he asked.

Then he discovered him, standing where he had been lying, near to the stove. He had not rushed forward after the manner of other dogs. He stood, watching and waiting.

"Holy smoke!" Matt exclaimed. "Look at 'm wag his tail!"

Weedon Scott strode half across the room toward him, at the same time calling him. White Fang came to him, not with a great bound, yet quickly. He was awakened from self-consciousness, but as he drew near, his eyes took on a strange expression. Something, an incommunicable vastness of feeling, rose up into his eyes as a light and shone forth.

"He never looked at me that way all the time you was gone!" Matt commented.

Weedon Scott did not hear. He was squatting down on his heels, face to face with White Fang and petting him—rubbing at the roots of the ears, making long caressing strokes down the neck to the shoulders, tapping the spine gently with the balls of his fingers. And White Fang was growling responsively, the crooning note of the growl more pronounced than ever.

But that was not all. What of his joy, the great love in him, ever surging and struggling to express itself, succeeded in finding a new mode of expression. He suddenly thrust his head forward and nudged his way in between the master's arm and body. And here, confined, hidden from view all except his ears, no longer growling, he continued to nudge and snuggle.

The two men looked at each other. Scott's eyes were shining.

"Gosh!" said Matt in an awe-stricken voice.

A moment later, when he had recovered himself, he said, "I always insisted that wolf was a dog. Look at 'm!"

With the return of the love-master, White Fang's recovery was rapid. Two nights and a day he spent in the cabin. Then he sallied forth. The sled-dogs had forgotten his prowess. They remembered only the latest, which was his weakness and sickness. At the sight of him as he came out of the cabin, they sprang upon him.

"Talk about your rough-houses," Matt murmured gleefully, standing in the doorway and looking on.

"Give 'm hell, you wolf! Give 'm hell!—an' then some!"

White Fang did not need the encouragement. The return of the love-master was enough. Life was flowing through him again, splendid and indomitable. He fought from sheer joy, finding in it an expression of much that he felt and that otherwise was without speech. There could be but one ending. The team dispersed in ignominious defeat, and it was not until after dark that the dogs came sneaking back, one by one, by meekness and humility signifying their fealty to White Fang.

Having learned to snuggle, White Fang was guilty of it often. It was the final word. He could not go beyond it. The one thing of which he had always been particularly jealous was his head. He had always disliked to have it touched. It was the Wild in him, the fear of hurt and of the trap, that had given rise to the panicky impulses to avoid contacts. It was the mandate of his instinct that that head must be free. And now, with the love-master, his snuggling was the deliberate act of putting himself into a position of hopeless helplessness. It was an expression of perfect confidence, of absolute self-surrender, as though he said: "I put myself into thy hands. Work thou thy will with me."

One night, not long after the return, Scott and Matt sat at a game of cribbage preliminary to going to bed. "Fifteen-two, fifteen-four an' a pair makes six," Mat was pegging up, when there was an outcry and sound of snarling without. They looked at each other as they started to rise to their feet.

"The wolf's nailed somebody," Matt said.

A wild scream of fear and anguish hastened them.

"Bring a light!" Scott shouted, as he sprang outside.

Matt followed with the lamp, and by its light they saw a man lying on his back in the snow. His arms were folded, one above the other, across his face and throat. Thus he was trying to shield himself from White Fang's teeth. And there was need for it. White Fang was in a rage, wickedly making his attack on the most vulnerable spot. From shoulder to wrist of the crossed arms, the coat-sleeve, blue flannel shirt and undershirt were ripped in rags, while the arms themselves were terribly slashed and streaming blood.

All this the two men saw in the first instant. The next instant Weedon Scott had White Fang by the throat and was dragging him clear. White Fang struggled and snarled, but made no attempt to bite, while he quickly quieted down at a sharp word from the master.

Matt helped the man to his feet. As he arose he lowered his crossed arms, exposing the bestial face of Beauty Smith. The dog-musher let go of him precipitately, with action similar to that of a man who has picked up live fire. Beauty Smith blinked in the lamplight and looked about him. He caught sight of White Fang and terror rushed into his face.

At the same moment Matt noticed two objects lying in the snow. He held the lamp close to them, indicating them with his toe for his employer's benefit—a steel dog-chain and a stout club.

Weedon Scott saw and nodded. Not a word was spoken. The dog-musher laid his hand on Beauty Smith's shoulder and faced him to the right about. No word needed to be spoken. Beauty Smith started.

In the meantime the love-master was patting White Fang and talking to him.

"Tried to steal you, eh? And you wouldn't have it! Well, well, he made a mistake, didn't he?"

"Must 'a' thought he had hold of seventeen devils," the dog-musher sniggered.

White Fang, still wrought up and bristling, growled and growled, the hair slowly lying down, the crooning note remote and dim, but growing in his throat.

PART V

CHAPTER I—THE LONG TRAIL

It was in the air. White Fang sensed the coming calamity, even before there was tangible evidence of it. In vague ways it was borne in upon him that a change was impending. He knew not how nor why, yet he got his feel of the oncoming event from the gods themselves. In ways subtler than they knew, they betrayed their intentions to the wolf-dog that haunted the cabin-stoop, and that, though he never came inside the cabin, knew what went on inside their brains.

"Listen to that, will you!" the dug-musher exclaimed at supper one night.

Weedon Scott listened. Through the door came a low, anxious whine, like a sobbing under the breath that had just grown audible. Then came the long sniff, as White Fang reassured himself that his god was still inside and had not yet taken himself off in mysterious and solitary flight.

"I do believe that wolf's on to you," the dog-musher said.

Weedon Scott looked across at his companion with eyes that almost pleaded, though this was given the lie by his words.

"What the devil can I do with a wolf in California?" he demanded.

"That's what I say," Matt answered. "What the devil can you do with a wolf in California?"

But this did not satisfy Weedon Scott. The other seemed to be judging him in a non-committal sort of way.

"White man's dogs would have no show against him," Scott went on. "He'd kill them on sight. If he didn't bankrupt me with damaged suits, the authorities would take him away from me and electrocute him."

"He's a downright murderer, I know," was the dog-musher's comment.

Weedon Scott looked at him suspiciously.

"It would never do," he said decisively.

"It would never do!" Matt concurred. "Why you'd have to hire a man 'specially to take care of 'm."

The other suspicion was allayed. He nodded cheerfully. In the silence that followed, the low, half-sobbing whine was heard at the door and then the long, questing sniff.

"There's no denyin' he thinks a hell of a lot of you," Matt said.

The other glared at him in sudden wrath. "Damn it all, man! I know my own mind and what's best!"

"I'm agreein' with you, only . . . "

"Only what?" Scott snapped out.

"Only . . . " the dog-musher began softly, then changed his mind and betrayed a rising anger of his own. "Well, you needn't get so all-fired het up about it. Judgin' by your actions one'd think you didn't know your own mind."

Weedon Scott debated with himself for a while, and then said more gently: "You are right, Matt. I don't know my own mind, and that's what's the trouble."

"Why, it would be rank ridiculousness for me to take that dog along," he broke out after another pause.

"I'm agreein' with you," was Matt's answer, and again his employer was not quite satisfied with him.

"But how in the name of the great Sardanapolis he knows you're goin' is what gets me," the dog-musher continued innocently.

"It's beyond me, Matt," Scott answered, with a mournful shake of the head.

Then came the day when, through the open cabin door, White Fang saw the fatal grip on the floor and the love-master packing things into it. Also, there were comings and goings, and the erstwhile placid atmosphere of the cabin was vexed with strange perturbations and unrest. Here was indubitable evidence. White Fang had already scented it. He now reasoned it. His god was preparing for another flight. And since he had not taken him with him before, so, now, he could look to be left behind.

That night he lifted the long wolf-howl. As he had howled, in his puppy days, when he fled back from the Wild to the village to find it vanished and naught but a rubbish-heap to mark the site of Grey Beaver's tepee, so now he pointed his muzzle to the cold stars and told to them his woe.

Inside the cabin the two men had just gone to bed.

"He's gone off his food again," Matt remarked from his bunk.

There was a grunt from Weedon Scott's bunk, and a stir of blankets.

"From the way he cut up the other time you went away, I wouldn't wonder this time but what he died."

The blankets in the other bunk stirred irritably.

"Oh, shut up!" Scott cried out through the darkness. "You nag worse than a woman."

"I'm agreein' with you," the dog-musher answered, and Weedon Scott was not quite sure whether or not the other had snickered.

The next day White Fang's anxiety and restlessness were even more pronounced. He dogged his master's heels whenever he left the cabin, and haunted the front stoop when he remained inside. Through the open door he could catch glimpses of the luggage on the floor. The grip had been joined by two large canvas bags and a box. Matt was rolling the master's blankets and fur robe inside a small tarpaulin. White Fang whined as he watched the operation.

Later on two Indians arrived. He watched them closely as they shouldered the luggage and were led off down the hill by Matt, who carried the bedding and the grip. But White Fang did not follow them. The master was still in the cabin. After a time, Matt returned. The master came to the door and called White Fang inside.

"You poor devil," he said gently, rubbing White Fang's ears and tapping his spine. "I'm hitting the long trail, old man, where you cannot follow. Now give me a growl—the last, good, good-bye growl."

But White Fang refused to growl. Instead, and after a wistful, searching look, he snuggled in, burrowing his head out of sight between the master's arm and body.

"There she blows!" Matt cried. From the Yukon arose the hoarse bellowing of a river steamboat. "You've got to cut it short. Be sure and lock the front door. I'll go out the back. Get a move on!"

The two doors slammed at the same moment, and Weedon Scott waited for Matt to come around to the front. From inside the door came a low whining and sobbing. Then there were long, deep-drawn sniffs.

"You must take good care of him, Matt," Scott said, as they started down the hill. "Write and let me know how he gets along."

"Sure," the dog-musher answered. "But listen to that, will you!"

Both men stopped. White Fang was howling as dogs howl when their masters lie dead. He was voicing an utter woe, his cry bursting upward in great heart-breaking rushes, dying down into quavering misery, and bursting upward again with a rush upon rush of grief.

The Aurora was the first steamboat of the year for the Outside, and her decks were jammed with prosperous adventurers and broken gold seekers, all equally as mad to get to the Outside as they had been originally to get to the Inside. Near the gang-plank, Scott was shaking hands with Matt, who was preparing to go ashore. But Matt's hand went limp in the other's grasp as his gaze shot past and remained fixed on something behind him. Scott turned to see. Sitting on the deck several feet away and watching wistfully was White Fang.

The dog-musher swore softly, in awe-stricken accents. Scott could only look in wonder.

"Did you lock the front door?" Matt demanded. The other nodded, and asked, "How about the back?"

"You just bet I did," was the fervent reply.

White Fang flattened his ears ingratiatingly, but remained where he was, making no attempt to approach.

"I'll have to take 'm ashore with me."

Matt made a couple of steps toward White Fang, but the latter slid away from him. The dog-musher made a rush of it, and White Fang dodged between the legs of a group of men. Ducking, turning, doubling, he slid about the deck, eluding the other's efforts to capture him.

But when the love-master spoke, White Fang came to him with prompt obedience.

"Won't come to the hand that's fed 'm all these months," the dog-musher muttered resentfully. "And you—you ain't never fed 'm after them first days of gettin' acquainted. I'm blamed if I can see how he works it out that you're the boss."

Scott, who had been patting White Fang, suddenly bent closer and pointed out fresh-made cuts on his muzzle, and a gash between the eyes.

Matt bent over and passed his hand along White Fang's belly.

"We plump forgot the window. He's all cut an' gouged underneath. Must 'a' butted clean through it, b'gosh!"

But Weedon Scott was not listening. He was thinking rapidly. The Aurora's whistle hooted a final announcement of departure. Men were scurrying down the gang-plank to the shore. Matt loosened the bandana from his own neck and started to put it around White Fang's. Scott grasped the dog-musher's hand.

"Good-bye, Matt, old man. About the wolf—you needn't write. You see, I've . . . !"

"What!" the dog-musher exploded. "You don't mean to say . . .?"

"The very thing I mean. Here's your bandana. I'll write to you about him."

Matt paused halfway down the gang-plank.

"He'll never stand the climate!" he shouted back. "Unless you clip 'm in warm weather!"

The gang-plank was hauled in, and the Aurora swung out from the bank. Weedon Scott waved a last good-bye. Then he turned and bent over White Fang, standing by his side.

"Now growl, damn you, growl," he said, as he patted the responsive head and rubbed the flattening ears.

CHAPTER II—THE SOUTHLAND

White Fang landed from the steamer in San Francisco. He was appalled. Deep in him, below any reasoning process or act of consciousness, he had associated power with godhead. And never had the white men seemed such marvellous gods as now, when he trod the slimy pavement of San Francisco. The log cabins he had known were replaced by towering buildings. The streets were crowded with perils— waggons, carts, automobiles; great, straining horses pulling huge trucks; and monstrous cable and electric cars hooting and clanging through the midst, screeching their insistent menace after the manner of the lynxes he had known in the northern woods.

All this was the manifestation of power. Through it all, behind it all, was man, governing and controlling, expressing himself, as of old, by his mastery over matter. It was colossal, stunning. White Fang was awed. Fear sat upon him. As in his cubhood he had been made to feel his smallness and puniness on the day he first came in from the Wild to the village of Grey Beaver, so now, in his full-grown stature and pride of strength, he was made to feel small and puny. And there were so many gods! He was made dizzy by the swarming of them. The thunder of the streets smote upon his ears. He was bewildered by the tremendous and endless rush and movement of things. As never before, he felt his dependence on the love-master, close at whose heels he followed, no matter what happened never losing sight of him.

But White Fang was to have no more than a nightmare vision of the city—an experience that was like a bad dream, unreal and terrible, that haunted him for long after in his dreams. He was put into a baggage-car by the master, chained in a corner in the midst of heaped trunks and valises. Here a squat and brawny god held sway, with much noise, hurling trunks and boxes about, dragging them in through the door and tossing them into the piles, or flinging them out of the door, smashing and crashing, to other gods who awaited them.

164

And here, in this inferno of luggage, was White Fang deserted by the master. Or at least White Fang thought he was deserted, until he smelled out the master's canvas clothes-bags alongside of him, and proceeded to mount guard over them.

"'Bout time you come," growled the god of the car, an hour later, when Weedon Scott appeared at the door. "That dog of yourn won't let me lay a finger on your stuff."

White Fang emerged from the car. He was astonished. The nightmare city was gone. The car had been to him no more than a room in a house, and when he had entered it the city had been all around him. In the interval the city had disappeared. The roar of it no longer dinned upon his ears. Before him was smiling country, streaming with sunshine, lazy with quietude. But he had little time to marvel at the transformation. He accepted it as he accepted all the unaccountable doings and manifestations of the gods. It was their way.

There was a carriage waiting. A man and a woman approached the master. The woman's arms went out and clutched the master around the neck—a hostile act! The next moment Weedon Scott had torn loose from the embrace and closed with White Fang, who had become a snarling, raging demon.

"It's all right, mother," Scott was saying as he kept tight hold of White Fang and placated him. "He thought you were going to injure me, and he wouldn't stand for it. It's all right. It's all right. He'll learn soon enough."

"And in the meantime I may be permitted to love my son when his dog is not around," she laughed, though she was pale and weak from the fright.

She looked at White Fang, who snarled and bristled and glared malevolently.

"He'll have to learn, and he shall, without postponement," Scott said.

He spoke softly to White Fang until he had quieted him, then his voice became firm.

"Down, sir! Down with you!"

This had been one of the things taught him by the master, and White Fang obeyed, though he lay down reluctantly and sullenly.

"Now, mother."

Scott opened his arms to her, but kept his eyes on White Fang.

"Down!" he warned. "Down!"

White Fang, bristling silently, half-crouching as he rose, sank back and watched the hostile act repeated. But no harm came of it, nor of the embrace from the strange man-god that followed. Then the clothes-bags were taken into the carriage, the strange gods and the love-master followed, and White Fang pursued, now running vigilantly behind, now bristling up to the running horses and warning them that he was there to see that no harm befell the god they dragged so swiftly across the earth.

At the end of fifteen minutes, the carriage swung in through a stone gateway and on between a double row of arched and interlacing walnut trees. On either side stretched lawns, their broad sweep broken here and there by great sturdy-limbed oaks. In the near distance, in contrast with the young-green of the tended grass, sunburnt hay-fields showed tan and gold; while beyond were the tawny hills and upland pastures. From the head of the lawn, on the first soft swell from the valley-level, looked down the deep-porched, many-windowed house.

Little opportunity was given White Fang to see all this. Hardly had the carriage entered the grounds, when he was set upon by a sheep-dog, bright-eyed, sharp-muzzled, righteously indignant and angry. It was between him and the master, cutting him off. White Fang snarled no warning, but his hair bristled as he made his silent and deadly rush. This rush was never completed. He halted with awkward abruptness, with stiff fore-legs bracing himself against his momentum, almost sitting down on his haunches, so desirous was he of avoiding contact with the dog he was in the act of attacking. It was a female, and the law of his kind thrust a barrier between. For him to attack her would require nothing less than a violation of his instinct.

But with the sheep-dog it was otherwise. Being a female, she possessed no such instinct. On the other hand, being a sheep-dog, her instinctive fear of the Wild, and especially of the wolf, was unusually keen. White Fang was to her a wolf, the hereditary marauder who had preyed upon her flocks from the time sheep were first herded and guarded by some dim ancestor of hers. And so, as he abandoned his rush at her and braced himself to avoid the contact, she sprang upon him. He snarled involuntarily as he felt her teeth in his shoulder, but beyond this made no offer to hurt her. He backed away, stiff-legged with self-consciousness, and tried to go around her. He dodged this way and that, and curved and turned, but to no purpose. She remained always between him and the way he wanted to go.

"Here, Collie!" called the strange man in the carriage.

Weedon Scott laughed.

"Never mind, father. It is good discipline. White Fang will have to learn many things, and it's just as well that he begins now. He'll adjust himself all right."

The carriage drove on, and still Collie blocked White Fang's way. He tried to outrun her by leaving the drive and circling across the lawn but she ran on the inner and smaller circle, and was always there, facing him with her two rows of gleaming teeth. Back he circled, across the drive to the other lawn, and again she headed him off.

The carriage was bearing the master away. White Fang caught glimpses of it disappearing amongst the trees. The situation was desperate. He essayed another circle. She followed, running swiftly. And then, suddenly, he turned upon her. It was his old fighting trick. Shoulder to shoulder, he struck her squarely. Not only was she overthrown. So fast had she been running that she rolled along, now on her back, now on her side, as she struggled to stop, clawing gravel with her feet and crying shrilly her hurt pride and indignation.

White Fang did not wait. The way was clear, and that was all he had wanted. She took after him, never ceasing her outcry. It was the straightaway now, and when it came to real running, White Fang could teach her things. She ran frantically, hysterically, straining to the utmost, advertising the effort she was making with every leap: and all the time White Fang slid smoothly away from her silently, without effort, gliding like a ghost over the ground.

As he rounded the house to the porte-cochère, he came upon the carriage. It had stopped, and the master was alighting. At this moment, still running at top speed, White Fang became suddenly aware of an attack from the side. It was a deer-hound rushing upon him. White Fang tried to face it. But he was going too fast, and the hound was too close. It struck him on the side; and such was his forward momentum and the unexpectedness of it, White Fang was hurled to the ground and rolled clear over. He came out of the tangle a spectacle of malignancy, ears flattened back, lips writhing, nose wrinkling, his teeth clipping together as the fangs barely missed the hound's soft throat.

The master was running up, but was too far away; and it was Collie that saved the hound's life. Before White Fang could spring in and deliver the fatal stroke, and just as he was in the act of springing in, Collie arrived. She had been out-manoeuvred and out-run, to say nothing of her having been unceremoniously tumbled in the gravel, and her arrival was like that of a tornado—made up of offended dignity, justifiable wrath, and instinctive hatred for this marauder from the Wild. She struck White Fang at right angles in the midst of his spring, and again he was knocked off his feet and rolled over.

The next moment the master arrived, and with one hand held White Fang, while the father called off the dogs.

"I say, this is a pretty warm reception for a poor lone wolf from the Arctic," the master said, while White Fang calmed down under his caressing hand. "In all his life he's only been known once to go off his feet, and here he's been rolled twice in thirty seconds."

The carriage had driven away, and other strange gods had appeared from out the house. Some of these stood respectfully at a distance; but two of them, women, perpetrated the hostile act of clutching the master around the neck. White Fang, however, was beginning to tolerate this act. No harm seemed to come of it, while the noises the gods made were certainly not threatening. These gods also made overtures to White Fang, but he warned them off with a snarl, and the master did likewise with word of mouth. At such times White Fang leaned in close against the master's legs and received reassuring pats on the head.

The hound, under the command, "Dick! Lie down, sir!" had gone up the steps and lain down to one side of the porch, still growling and keeping a sullen watch on the intruder. Collie had been taken in charge by one of the woman-gods, who held arms around her neck and petted and caressed her; but Collie was very much perplexed and worried, whining and restless, outraged by the permitted presence of this wolf and confident that the gods were making a mistake.

All the gods started up the steps to enter the house. White Fang followed closely at the master's heels. Dick, on the porch, growled, and White Fang, on the steps, bristled and growled back.

"Take Collie inside and leave the two of them to fight it out," suggested Scott's father. "After that they'll be friends."

"Then White Fang, to show his friendship, will have to be chief mourner at the funeral," laughed the master.

The elder Scott looked incredulously, first at White Fang, then at Dick, and finally at his son.

"You mean . . .?"

Weedon nodded his head. "I mean just that. You'd have a dead Dick inside one minute—two minutes at the farthest."

He turned to White Fang. "Come on, you wolf. It's you that'll have to come inside."

White Fang walked stiff-legged up the steps and across the porch, with tail rigidly erect, keeping his eyes on Dick to guard against a flank attack, and at the same time prepared for whatever fierce manifestation of the unknown that might pounce out upon him from the interior of the house. But no thing of fear pounced out, and when he had gained the inside he scouted carefully around, looking at it and finding it not. Then he lay down with a contented grunt at the master's feet, observing all that went on, ever ready to spring to his feet and fight for life with the terrors he felt must lurk under the trap-roof of the dwelling.

CHAPTER III—THE GOD'S DOMAIN

Not only was White Fang adaptable by nature, but he had travelled much, and knew the meaning and necessity of adjustment. Here, in Sierra Vista, which was the name of Judge Scott's place, White Fang quickly began to make himself at home. He had no further serious trouble with the dogs. They knew more about the ways of the Southland gods than did he, and in their eyes he had qualified when he accompanied the gods inside the house. Wolf that he was, and unprecedented as it was, the gods had sanctioned his presence, and they, the dogs of the gods, could only recognise this sanction.

Dick, perforce, had to go through a few stiff formalities at first, after which he calmly accepted White Fang as an addition to the premises. Had Dick had his way, they would have been good friends. All but White Fang was averse to friendship. All he asked of other dogs was to be let alone. His whole life he had kept aloof from his kind, and he still desired to keep aloof. Dick's overtures bothered him, so he snarled Dick away. In the north he had learned the lesson that he must let the master's dogs alone, and he did not forget that lesson now. But he insisted on his own privacy and self-seclusion, and so thoroughly ignored Dick that that good-natured creature finally gave him up and scarcely took as much interest in him as in the hitching-post near the stable.

Not so with Collie. While she accepted him because it was the mandate of the gods, that was no reason that she should leave him in peace. Woven into her being was the memory of countless crimes he and his had perpetrated against her ancestry. Not in a day nor a generation were the ravaged sheepfolds to be forgotten. All this was a spur to her, pricking her to retaliation. She could not fly in the face of the gods who permitted him, but that did not prevent her from making life miserable for him in petty ways. A feud, ages old, was between them, and she, for one, would see to it that he was reminded.

So Collie took advantage of her sex to pick upon White Fang and maltreat him. His instinct would not permit him to attack her, while her persistence would not permit him to ignore her. When she rushed at him he turned his fur-protected shoulder to her sharp teeth and walked away stiff-legged and stately. When she forced him too hard, he was compelled to go about in a circle, his shoulder presented to her, his head turned from her, and on his face and in his eyes a patient and bored expression. Sometimes, however, a nip on his hind-quarters hastened his retreat and made it anything but stately. But as a rule he managed to maintain a dignity that was almost solemnity. He ignored her existence whenever it was possible, and made it a point to keep out of her way. When he saw or heard her coming, he got up and walked off.

There was much in other matters for White Fang to learn. Life in the Northland was simplicity itself when compared with the complicated affairs of Sierra Vista. First of all, he had to learn the family of the master. In a way he was prepared to do this. As Mit-sah and Kloo-kooch had belonged to Grey Beaver, sharing his food, his fire, and his blankets, so now, at Sierra Vista, belonged to the love-master all the denizens of the house.

But in this matter there was a difference, and many differences. Sierra Vista was a far vaster affair than the tepee of Grey Beaver. There were many persons to be considered. There was Judge Scott, and there was his wife. There were the master's two sisters, Beth and Mary. There was his wife, Alice, and then there were his children, Weedon and Maud, toddlers of four and six. There was no way for anybody to tell him about all these people, and of blood-ties and relationship he knew nothing whatever and never would be capable of knowing. Yet he quickly worked it out that all of them belonged to the master. Then, by observation, whenever opportunity offered, by study of action, speech, and the very intonations of the voice, he slowly learned the intimacy and the degree of favour they enjoyed with the master. And by this ascertained standard, White Fang treated them accordingly. What was of value to the master he valued; what was dear to the master was to be cherished by White Fang and guarded carefully.

Thus it was with the two children. All his life he had disliked children. He hated and feared their hands. The lessons were not tender that he had learned of their tyranny and cruelty in the days of the Indian villages. When Weedon and Maud had first approached him, he growled warningly and looked malignant. A cuff from the master and a sharp word had then compelled him to permit their caresses, though he growled and growled under their tiny hands, and in the growl there was no crooning note. Later, he observed that the boy and girl were of great value in the master's eyes. Then it was that no cuff nor sharp word was necessary before they could pat him.

Yet White Fang was never effusively affectionate. He yielded to the master's children with an ill but honest grace, and endured their fooling as one would endure a painful operation. When he could no longer endure, he would get up and stalk determinedly away from them. But after a time, he grew even to like the children. Still he was not demonstrative. He would not go up to them. On the other hand, instead of walking away at sight of them, he waited for them to come to him. And still later, it was noticed that a pleased light came into his eyes when he saw them approaching, and that he looked after them with an appearance of curious regret when they left him for other amusements.

All this was a matter of development, and took time. Next in his regard, after the children, was Judge Scott. There were two reasons, possibly, for this. First, he was evidently a valuable possession of the master's, and next, he was undemonstrative. White Fang liked to lie at his feet on the wide porch when he read the newspaper, from time to time favouring White Fang with a look or a word—untroublesome tokens that he recognised White Fang's presence and existence. But this was only when the master was not around. When the master appeared, all other beings ceased to exist so far as White Fang was concerned.

White Fang allowed all the members of the family to pet him and make much of him; but he never gave to them what he gave to the master. No caress of theirs could put the love-croon into his throat, and, try as they would, they could never persuade him into snuggling against them. This expression of abandon and surrender, of absolute trust, he reserved for the master alone. In fact, he never regarded the members of the family in any other light than possessions of the love-master.

Also White Fang had early come to differentiate between the family and the servants of the household. The latter were afraid of him, while he merely refrained from attacking them. This because he considered that they were likewise possessions of the master. Between White Fang and them existed a neutrality and no more. They cooked for the master and washed the dishes and did other things just as Matt had done up in the Klondike. They were, in short, appurtenances of the household.

Outside the household there was even more for White Fang to learn. The master's domain was wide and complex, yet it had its metes and bounds. The land itself ceased at the county road. Outside was the common domain of all gods—the roads and streets. Then inside other fences were the particular domains of other gods. A myriad laws governed all these things and determined conduct; yet he did not know the speech of the gods, nor was there any way for him to learn save by experience. He obeyed his natural impulses until they ran him counter to some law. When this had been done a few times, he learned the law and after that observed it.

But most potent in his education was the cuff of the master's hand, the censure of the master's voice. Because of White Fang's very great love, a cuff from the master hurt him far more than any beating Grey Beaver or Beauty Smith had ever given him. They had hurt only the flesh of him; beneath the flesh the spirit had still raged, splendid and invincible. But with the master the cuff was always too light to hurt the flesh. Yet it went deeper. It was an expression of the master's disapproval, and White Fang's spirit wilted under it.

In point of fact, the cuff was rarely administered. The master's voice was sufficient. By it White Fang knew whether he did right or not. By it he trimmed his conduct and adjusted his actions. It was the compass by which he steered and learned to chart the manners of a new land and life.

In the Northland, the only domesticated animal was the dog. All other animals lived in the Wild, and were, when not too formidable, lawful spoil for any dog. All his days White Fang had foraged among the live things for food. It did not enter his head that in the Southland it was otherwise. But this he was to learn early in his residence in Santa Clara Valley. Sauntering around the corner of the house in the early morning, he came upon a chicken that had escaped from the chicken-yard.

White Fang's natural impulse was to eat it. A couple of bounds, a flash of teeth and a frightened squawk, and he had scooped in the adventurous fowl. It was farm-bred and fat and tender; and White Fang licked his chops and decided that such fare was good.

Later in the day, he chanced upon another stray chicken near the stables. One of the grooms ran to the rescue. He did not know White Fang's breed, so for weapon he took a light buggy-whip. At the first cut of the whip, White Fang left the chicken for the man. A club might have stopped White Fang, but not a whip. Silently, without flinching, he took a second cut in his forward rush, and as he leaped for the throat the groom cried out, "My God!" and staggered backward. He dropped the whip and shielded his throat with his arms. In consequence, his forearm was ripped open to the bone.

The man was badly frightened. It was not so much White Fang's ferocity as it was his silence that unnerved the groom. Still protecting his throat and face with his torn and bleeding arm, he tried to retreat to the barn. And it would have gone hard with him had not Collie appeared on the scene. As she had saved Dick's life, she now saved the groom's. She rushed upon White Fang in frenzied wrath. She had been right. She had known better than the blundering gods. All her suspicions were justified. Here was the ancient marauder up to his old tricks again.

The groom escaped into the stables, and White Fang backed away before Collie's wicked teeth, or presented his shoulder to them and circled round and round. But Collie did not give over, as was her wont, after a decent interval of chastisement. On the contrary, she grew more excited and angry every moment, until, in the end, White Fang flung dignity to the winds and frankly fled away from her across the fields.

"He'll learn to leave chickens alone," the master said. "But I can't give him the lesson until I catch him in the act."

Two nights later came the act, but on a more generous scale than the master had anticipated. White Fang had observed closely the chicken-yards and the habits of the chickens. In the night-time, after they had gone to roost, he climbed to the top of a pile of newly hauled lumber. From there he gained the roof of a chicken-house, passed over the ridgepole and dropped to the ground inside. A moment later he was inside the house, and the slaughter began.

In the morning, when the master came out on to the porch, fifty white Leghorn hens, laid out in a row by the groom, greeted his eyes. He whistled to himself, softly, first with surprise, and then, at the end, with admiration. His eyes were likewise greeted by White Fang, but about the latter there were no signs of shame nor guilt. He carried himself with pride, as though, forsooth, he had achieved a deed praiseworthy and meritorious. There was about him no consciousness of sin. The master's lips tightened as he faced the disagreeable task. Then he talked harshly to the unwitting culprit, and in his voice there was nothing but godlike wrath. Also, he held White Fang's nose down to the slain hens, and at the same time cuffed him soundly.

White Fang never raided a chicken-roost again. It was against the law, and he had learned it. Then the master took him into the chicken-yards. White Fang's natural impulse, when he saw the live food fluttering about him and under his very nose, was to spring upon it. He obeyed the impulse, but was checked by the master's voice. They continued in the yards for half an hour. Time and again the impulse surged over White Fang, and each time, as he yielded to it, he was checked by the master's voice. Thus it was he learned the law, and ere he left the domain of the chickens, he had learned to ignore their existence.

"You can never cure a chicken-killer." Judge Scott shook his head sadly at luncheon table, when his son narrated the lesson he had given White Fang. "Once they've got the habit and the taste of blood . . ." Again he shook his head sadly.

But Weedon Scott did not agree with his father. "I'll tell you what I'll do," he challenged finally. "I'll lock White Fang in with the chickens all afternoon."

"But think of the chickens," objected the judge.

"And furthermore," the son went on, "for every chicken he kills, I'll pay you one dollar gold coin of the realm."

"But you should penalise father, too," interpose Beth.

Her sister seconded her, and a chorus of approval arose from around the table. Judge Scott nodded his head in agreement.

"All right." Weedon Scott pondered for a moment. "And if, at the end of the afternoon White Fang hasn't harmed a chicken, for every ten minutes of the time he has spent in the yard, you will have to say to him, gravely and with deliberation, just as if you were sitting on the bench and solemnly passing judgment, 'White Fang, you are smarter than I thought.'"

From hidden points of vantage the family watched the performance. But it was a fizzle. Locked in the yard and there deserted by the master, White Fang lay down and went to sleep. Once he got up and walked over to the trough for a drink of water. The chickens he calmly ignored. So far as he was concerned they did not exist. At four o'clock he executed a running jump, gained the roof of the chicken-house and leaped to the ground outside, whence he sauntered gravely to the house. He had learned the law. And on the porch, before the delighted family, Judge Scott, face to face with White Fang, said slowly and solemnly, sixteen times, "White Fang, you are smarter than I thought."

But it was the multiplicity of laws that befuddled White Fang and often brought him into disgrace. He had to learn that he must not touch the chickens that belonged to other gods. Then there were cats, and rabbits, and turkeys; all these he must let alone. In fact, when he had but partly learned the law, his impression was that he must leave all live things alone. Out in the back-pasture, a quail could flutter up under his nose unharmed. All tense and trembling with eagerness and desire, he mastered his instinct and stood still. He was obeying the will of the gods.

And then, one day, again out in the back-pasture, he saw Dick start a jackrabbit and run it. The master himself was looking on and did not interfere. Nay, he encouraged White Fang to join in the chase. And thus he learned that there was no taboo on jackrabbits. In the end he worked out the complete law. Between him and all domestic animals there must be no hostilities. If not amity, at least neutrality must obtain. But the other animals—the squirrels, and quail, and cottontails, were creatures of the Wild who had never yielded allegiance to man. They were the lawful prey of any dog. It was only the tame that the gods protected, and between the tame

172

deadly strife was not permitted. The gods held the power of life and death over their subjects, and the gods were jealous of their power.

Life was complex in the Santa Clara Valley after the simplicities of the North-land. And the chief thing demanded by these intricacies of civilisation was control, restraint—a poise of self that was as delicate as the fluttering of gossamer wings and at the same time as rigid as steel. Life had a thousand faces, and White Fang found he must meet them all—thus, when he went to town, in to San Jose, running behind the carriage or loafing about the streets when the carriage stopped. Life flowed past him, deep and wide and varied, continually impinging upon his senses, demanding of him instant and endless adjustments and correspondences, and compelling him, almost always, to suppress his natural impulses.

There were butcher-shops where meat hung within reach. This meat he must not touch. There were cats at the houses the master visited that must be let alone. And there were dogs everywhere that snarled at him and that he must not attack. And then, on the crowded sidewalks there were persons innumerable whose attention he attracted. They would stop and look at him, point him out to one another, examine him, talk of him, and, worst of all, pat him. And these perilous contacts from all these strange hands he must endure. Yet this endurance he achieved. Furthermore, he got over being awkward and self-conscious. In a lofty way he received the atten-tions of the multitudes of strange gods. With condescension he accepted their condescension. On the other hand, there was something about him that prevented great familiarity. They patted him on the head and passed on, contented and pleased with their own daring.

But it was not all easy for White Fang. Running behind the carriage in the out-skirts of San Jose, he encountered certain small boys who made a practice of flinging stones at him. Yet he knew that it was not permitted him to pursue and drag them down. Here he was compelled to violate his instinct of self-preservation, and violate it he did, for he was becoming tame and qualifying himself for civilisation.

Nevertheless, White Fang was not quite satisfied with the arrangement. He had no abstract ideas about justice and fair play. But there is a certain sense of equity that resides in life, and it was this sense in him that resented the unfairness of his being permitted no defence against the stone-throwers. He forgot that in the cove-nant entered into between him and the gods they were pledged to care for him and defend him. But one day the master sprang from the carriage, whip in hand, and gave the stone-throwers a thrashing. After that they threw stones no more, and White Fang understood and was satisfied.

One other experience of similar nature was his. On the way to town, hanging around the saloon at the cross-roads, were three dogs that made a practice of rushing out upon him when he went by. Knowing his deadly method of fighting, the master had never ceased impressing upon White Fang the law that he must not fight. As a result, having learned the lesson well, White Fang was hard put whenever he passed the cross-roads saloon. After the first rush, each time, his snarl kept the three dogs at a distance but they trailed along behind, yelping and bickering and insulting him. This endured for some time. The men at the saloon even urged the dogs on to attack

White Fang. One day they openly sicked the dogs on him. The master stopped the carriage.

"Go to it," he said to White Fang.

But White Fang could not believe. He looked at the master, and he looked at the dogs. Then he looked back eagerly and questioningly at the master.

The master nodded his head. "Go to them, old fellow. Eat them up."

White Fang no longer hesitated. He turned and leaped silently among his enemies. All three faced him. There was a great snarling and growling, a clashing of teeth and a flurry of bodies. The dust of the road arose in a cloud and screened the battle. But at the end of several minutes two dogs were struggling in the dirt and the third was in full flight. He leaped a ditch, went through a rail fence, and fled across a field. White Fang followed, sliding over the ground in wolf fashion and with wolf speed, swiftly and without noise, and in the centre of the field he dragged down and slew the dog.

With this triple killing his main troubles with dogs ceased. The word went up and down the valley, and men saw to it that their dogs did not molest the Fighting Wolf.

CHAPTER IV—THE CALL OF KIND

The months came and went. There was plenty of food and no work in the Southland, and White Fang lived fat and prosperous and happy. Not alone was he in the geographical Southland, for he was in the Southland of life. Human kindness was like a sun shining upon him, and he flourished like a flower planted in good soil.

And yet he remained somehow different from other dogs. He knew the law even better than did the dogs that had known no other life, and he observed the law more punctiliously; but still there was about him a suggestion of lurking ferocity, as though the Wild still lingered in him and the wolf in him merely slept.

He never chummed with other dogs. Lonely he had lived, so far as his kind was concerned, and lonely he would continue to live. In his puppyhood, under the persecution of Lip-lip and the puppy-pack, and in his fighting days with Beauty Smith, he had acquired a fixed aversion for dogs. The natural course of his life had been diverted, and, recoiling from his kind, he had clung to the human.

Besides, all Southland dogs looked upon him with suspicion. He aroused in them their instinctive fear of the Wild, and they greeted him always with snarl and growl and belligerent hatred. He, on the other hand, learned that it was not necessary to use his teeth upon them. His naked fangs and writhing lips were uniformly efficacious, rarely failing to send a bellowing on-rushing dog back on its haunches.

But there was one trial in White Fang's life—Collie. She never gave him a moment's peace. She was not so amenable to the law as he. She defied all efforts of the master to make her become friends with White Fang. Ever in his ears was sounding her sharp and nervous snarl. She had never forgiven him the chicken-killing episode, and persistently held to the belief that his intentions were bad. She found him guilty before the act, and treated him accordingly. She became a pest to him, like a policeman following him around the stable and the hounds, and, if he even so much as glanced curiously at a pigeon or chicken, bursting into an outcry of indignation and wrath. His favourite way of ignoring her was to lie down, with his head on his fore-paws, and pretend sleep. This always dumfounded and silenced her.

With the exception of Collie, all things went well with White Fang. He had learned control and poise, and he knew the law. He achieved a staidness, and calmness, and philosophic tolerance. He no longer lived in a hostile environment. Danger and hurt and death did not lurk everywhere about him. In time, the unknown, as a thing of terror and menace ever impending, faded away. Life was soft and easy. It flowed along smoothly, and neither fear nor foe lurked by the way.

He missed the snow without being aware of it. "An unduly long summer," would have been his thought had he thought about it; as it was, he merely missed the snow in a vague, subconscious way. In the same fashion, especially in the heat of summer when he suffered from the sun, he experienced faint longings for the Northland. Their only effect upon him, however, was to make him uneasy and restless without his knowing what was the matter.

White Fang had never been very demonstrative. Beyond his snuggling and the throwing of a crooning note into his love-growl, he had no way of expressing his love. Yet it was given him to discover a third way. He had always been susceptible to the laughter of the gods. Laughter had affected him with madness, made him frantic with rage. But he did not have it in him to be angry with the love-master, and when that god elected to laugh at him in a good-natured, bantering way, he was nonplussed. He could feel the pricking and stinging of the old anger as it strove to rise up in him, but it strove against love. He could not be angry; yet he had to do something. At first he was dignified, and the master laughed the harder. Then he tried to be more dignified, and the master laughed harder than before. In the end, the master laughed him out of his dignity. His jaws slightly parted, his lips lifted a little, and a quizzical expression that was more love than humour came into his eyes. He had learned to laugh.

Likewise he learned to romp with the master, to be tumbled down and rolled over, and be the victim of innumerable rough tricks. In return he feigned anger, bristling and growling ferociously, and clipping his teeth together in snaps that had all the seeming of deadly intention. But he never forgot himself. Those snaps were always delivered on the empty air. At the end of such a romp, when blow and cuff and snap and snarl were last and furious, they would break off suddenly and stand several feet apart, glaring at each other. And then, just as suddenly, like the sun rising on a stormy sea, they would begin to laugh. This would always culminate with the master's arms going around White Fang's neck and shoulders while the latter crooned and growled his love-song.

But nobody else ever romped with White Fang. He did not permit it. He stood on his dignity, and when they attempted it, his warning snarl and bristling mane were anything but playful. That he allowed the master these liberties was no reason that he should be a common dog, loving here and loving there, everybody's property for a romp and good time. He loved with single heart and refused to cheapen himself or his love.

The master went out on horseback a great deal, and to accompany him was one of White Fang's chief duties in life. In the Northland he had evidenced his fealty by toiling in the harness; but there were no sleds in the Southland, nor did dogs pack burdens on their backs. So he rendered fealty in the new way, by running with the master's horse. The longest day never played White Fang out. His was the gait of the wolf, smooth, tireless and effortless, and at the end of fifty miles he would come in jauntily ahead of the horse.

It was in connection with the riding, that White Fang achieved one other mode of expression—remarkable in that he did it but twice in all his life. The first time occurred when the master was trying to teach a spirited thoroughbred the method of opening and closing gates without the rider's dismounting. Time and again and many times he ranged the horse up to the gate in the effort to close it and each time the horse became frightened and backed and plunged away. It grew more nervous and excited every moment. When it reared, the master put the spurs to it and made it drop its fore-legs back to earth, whereupon it would begin kicking with its hind-legs. White Fang watched the performance with increasing anxiety until he could contain himself no longer, when he sprang in front of the horse and barked savagely and warningly.

Though he often tried to bark thereafter, and the master encouraged him, he succeeded only once, and then it was not in the master's presence. A scamper across the pasture, a jackrabbit rising suddenly under the horse's feet, a violent sheer, a stumble, a fall to earth, and a broken leg for the master, was the cause of it. White Fang sprang in a rage at the throat of the offending horse, but was checked by the master's voice.

"Home! Go home!" the master commanded when he had ascertained his injury.

White Fang was disinclined to desert him. The master thought of writing a note, but searched his pockets vainly for pencil and paper. Again he commanded White Fang to go home.

The latter regarded him wistfully, started away, then returned and whined softly. The master talked to him gently but seriously, and he cocked his ears, and listened with painful intentness.

"That's all right, old fellow, you just run along home," ran the talk. "Go on home and tell them what's happened to me. Home with you, you wolf. Get along home!"

White Fang knew the meaning of "home," and though he did not understand the remainder of the master's language, he knew it was his will that he should go home. He turned and trotted reluctantly away. Then he stopped, undecided, and looked back over his shoulder.

"Go home!" came the sharp command, and this time he obeyed.

The family was on the porch, taking the cool of the afternoon, when White Fang arrived. He came in among them, panting, covered with dust.

"Weedon's back," Weedon's mother announced.

The children welcomed White Fang with glad cries and ran to meet him. He avoided them and passed down the porch, but they cornered him against a rocking-chair and the railing. He growled and tried to push by them. Their mother looked apprehensively in their direction.

"I confess, he makes me nervous around the children," she said. "I have a dread that he will turn upon them unexpectedly some day."

Growling savagely, White Fang sprang out of the corner, overturning the boy and the girl. The mother called them to her and comforted them, telling them not to bother White Fang.

"A wolf is a wolf!" commented Judge Scott. "There is no trusting one."

"But he is not all wolf," interposed Beth, standing for her brother in his absence.

"You have only Weedon's opinion for that," rejoined the judge. "He merely surmises that there is some strain of dog in White Fang; but as he will tell you himself, he knows nothing about it. As for his appearance—"

He did not finish his sentence. White Fang stood before him, growling fiercely.

"Go away! Lie down, sir!" Judge Scott commanded.

White Fang turned to the love-master's wife. She screamed with fright as he seized her dress in his teeth and dragged on it till the frail fabric tore away. By this time he had become the centre of interest.

He had ceased from his growling and stood, head up, looking into their faces. His throat worked spasmodically, but made no sound, while he struggled with all his body, convulsed with the effort to rid himself of the incommunicable something that strained for utterance.

"I hope he is not going mad," said Weedon's mother. "I told Weedon that I was afraid the warm climate would not agree with an Arctic animal."

"He's trying to speak, I do believe," Beth announced.

At this moment speech came to White Fang, rushing up in a great burst of barking.

"Something has happened to Weedon," his wife said decisively.

They were all on their feet now, and White Fang ran down the steps, looking back for them to follow. For the second and last time in his life he had barked and made himself understood.

After this event he found a warmer place in the hearts of the Sierra Vista people, and even the groom whose arm he had slashed admitted that he was a wise dog even if he was a wolf. Judge Scott still held to the same opinion, and proved it to everybody's dissatisfaction by measurements and descriptions taken from the encyclopaedia and various works on natural history.

The days came and went, streaming their unbroken sunshine over the Santa Clara Valley. But as they grew shorter and White Fang's second winter in the Southland came on, he made a strange discovery. Collie's teeth were no longer sharp. There was a playfulness about her nips and a gentleness that prevented them from really hurting him. He forgot that she had made life a burden to him, and when she disported herself around him he responded solemnly, striving to be playful and becoming no more than ridiculous.

One day she led him off on a long chase through the back-pasture land into the woods. It was the afternoon that the master was to ride, and White Fang knew it. The horse stood saddled and waiting at the door. White Fang hesitated. But there was that in him deeper than all the law he had learned, than the customs that had moulded him, than his love for the master, than the very will to live of himself; and when, in the moment of his indecision, Collie nipped him and scampered off, he turned and followed after. The master rode alone that day; and in the woods, side by side, White Fang ran with Collie, as his mother, Kiche, and old One Eye had run long years before in the silent Northland forest.

CHAPTER V—THE SLEEPING WOLF

It was about this time that the newspapers were full of the daring escape of a convict from San Quentin prison. He was a ferocious man. He had been ill-made in the making. He had not been born right, and he had not been helped any by the moulding he had received at the hands of society. The hands of society are harsh, and this man was a striking sample of its handiwork. He was a beast—a human beast, it is true, but nevertheless so terrible a beast that he can best be characterised as carnivorous.

In San Quentin prison he had proved incorrigible. Punishment failed to break his spirit. He could die dumb-mad and fighting to the last, but he could not live and be beaten. The more fiercely he fought, the more harshly society handled him, and the only effect of harshness was to make him fiercer. Strait-jackets, starvation, and beatings and clubbings were the wrong treatment for Jim Hall; but it was the treatment he received. It was the treatment he had received from the time he was a little pulpy boy in a San Francisco slum—soft clay in the hands of society and ready to be formed into something.

It was during Jim Hall's third term in prison that he encountered a guard that was almost as great a beast as he. The guard treated him unfairly, lied about him to the warden, lost his credits, persecuted him. The difference between them was that the guard carried a bunch of keys and a revolver. Jim Hall had only his naked hands and his teeth. But he sprang upon the guard one day and used his teeth on the other's throat just like any jungle animal.

After this, Jim Hall went to live in the incorrigible cell. He lived there three years. The cell was of iron, the floor, the walls, the roof. He never left this cell. He never saw the sky nor the sunshine. Day was a twilight and night was a black silence. He was in an iron tomb, buried alive. He saw no human face, spoke to no human thing. When his food was shoved in to him, he growled like a wild animal. He hated all things. For days and nights he bellowed his rage at the universe. For weeks and months he never made a sound, in the black silence eating his very soul. He was a man and a monstrosity, as fearful a thing of fear as ever gibbered in the visions of a maddened brain.

And then, one night, he escaped. The warders said it was impossible, but nevertheless the cell was empty, and half in half out of it lay the body of a dead guard. Two other dead guards marked his trail through the prison to the outer walls, and he had killed with his hands to avoid noise.

He was armed with the weapons of the slain guards—a live arsenal that fled through the hills pursued by the organised might of society. A heavy price of gold was upon his head. Avaricious farmers hunted him with shot-guns. His blood might pay off a mortgage or send a son to college. Public-spirited citizens took down their rifles and went out after him. A pack of bloodhounds followed the way of his bleeding feet. And the sleuth-hounds of the law, the paid fighting animals of society, with telephone, and telegraph, and special train, clung to his trail night and day.

Sometimes they came upon him, and men faced him like heroes, or stampeded through barbed-wire fences to the delight of the commonwealth reading the account at the breakfast table. It was after such encounters that the dead and wounded were carted back to the towns, and their places filled by men eager for the man-hunt.

And then Jim Hall disappeared. The bloodhounds vainly quested on the lost trail. Inoffensive ranchers in remote valleys were held up by armed men and compelled to identify themselves. While the remains of Jim Hall were discovered on a dozen mountain-sides by greedy claimants for blood-money.

In the meantime the newspapers were read at Sierra Vista, not so much with interest as with anxiety. The women were afraid. Judge Scott pooh-poohed and laughed, but not with reason, for it was in his last days on the bench that Jim Hall had stood before him and received sentence. And in open court-room, before all men, Jim Hall had proclaimed that the day would come when he would wreak vengeance on the Judge that sentenced him.

For once, Jim Hall was right. He was innocent of the crime for which he was sentenced. It was a case, in the parlance of thieves and police, of "rail-roading." Jim Hall was being "rail-roaded" to prison for a crime he had not committed. Because of the two prior convictions against him, Judge Scott imposed upon him a sentence of fifty years.

Judge Scott did not know all things, and he did not know that he was party to a police conspiracy, that the evidence was hatched and perjured, that Jim Hall was guiltless of the crime charged. And Jim Hall, on the other hand, did not know that Judge Scott was merely ignorant. Jim Hall believed that the judge knew all about it and was hand in glove with the police in the perpetration of the monstrous injustice. So it was, when the doom of fifty years of living death was uttered by Judge Scott, that Jim Hall, hating all things in the society that misused him, rose up and raged in the court-room until dragged down by half a dozen of his blue-coated enemies. To him, Judge Scott was the keystone in the arch of injustice, and upon Judge Scott he emptied the vials of his wrath and hurled the threats of his revenge yet to come. Then Jim Hall went to his living death . . . and escaped.

Of all this White Fang knew nothing. But between him and Alice, the master's wife, there existed a secret. Each night, after Sierra Vista had gone to bed, she rose and let in White Fang to sleep in the big hall. Now White Fang was not a house-dog, nor was he permitted to sleep in the house; so each morning, early, she slipped down and let him out before the family was awake.

On one such night, while all the house slept, White Fang awoke and lay very quietly. And very quietly he smelled the air and read the message it bore of a strange god's presence. And to his ears came sounds of the strange god's movements. White Fang burst into no furious outcry. It was not his way. The strange god walked softly, but more softly walked White Fang, for he had no clothes to rub against the flesh of his body. He followed silently. In the Wild he had hunted live meat that was infinitely timid, and he knew the advantage of surprise.

The strange god paused at the foot of the great staircase and listened, and White Fang was as dead, so without movement was he as he watched and waited. Up that staircase the way led to the love-master and to the love-master's dearest possessions. White Fang bristled, but waited. The strange god's foot lifted. He was beginning the ascent.

Then it was that White Fang struck. He gave no warning, with no snarl anticipated his own action. Into the air he lifted his body in the spring that landed him on the strange god's back. White Fang clung with his fore-paws to the man's shoulders, at the same time burying his fangs into the back of the man's neck. He clung on for a moment, long enough to drag the god over backward. Together they crashed to the floor. White Fang leaped clear, and, as the man struggled to rise, was in again with the slashing fangs.

Sierra Vista awoke in alarm. The noise from downstairs was as that of a score of battling fiends. There were revolver shots. A man's voice screamed once in horror and anguish. There was a great snarling and growling, and over all arose a smashing and crashing of furniture and glass.

But almost as quickly as it had arisen, the commotion died away. The struggle had not lasted more than three minutes. The frightened household clustered at the top of the stairway. From below, as from out an abyss of blackness, came up a gurgling sound, as of air bubbling through water. Sometimes this gurgle became sibilant, almost a whistle. But this, too, quickly died down and ceased. Then naught came up out of the blackness save a heavy panting of some creature struggling sorely for air.

Weedon Scott pressed a button, and the staircase and downstairs hall were flooded with light. Then he and Judge Scott, revolvers in hand, cautiously descended. There was no need for this caution. White Fang had done his work. In the midst of the wreckage of overthrown and smashed furniture, partly on his side, his face hidden by an arm, lay a man. Weedon Scott bent over, removed the arm and turned the man's face upward. A gaping throat explained the manner of his death.

"Jim Hall," said Judge Scott, and father and son looked significantly at each other.

Then they turned to White Fang. He, too, was lying on his side. His eyes were closed, but the lids slightly lifted in an effort to look at them as they bent over him, and the tail was perceptibly agitated in a vain effort to wag. Weedon Scott patted him, and his throat rumbled an acknowledging growl. But it was a weak growl at best, and it quickly ceased. His eyelids drooped and went shut, and his whole body seemed to relax and flatten out upon the floor.

"He's all in, poor devil," muttered the master.

"We'll see about that," asserted the Judge, as he started for the telephone.

"Frankly, he has one chance in a thousand," announced the surgeon, after he had worked an hour and a half on White Fang.

180

Dawn was breaking through the windows and dimming the electric lights. With the exception of the children, the whole family was gathered about the surgeon to hear his verdict.

"One broken hind-leg," he went on. "Three broken ribs, one at least of which has pierced the lungs. He has lost nearly all the blood in his body. There is a large likelihood of internal injuries. He must have been jumped upon. To say nothing of three bullet holes clear through him. One chance in a thousand is really optimistic. He hasn't a chance in ten thousand."

"But he mustn't lose any chance that might be of help to him," Judge Scott exclaimed. "Never mind expense. Put him under the X-ray—anything. Weedon, telegraph at once to San Francisco for Doctor Nichols. No reflection on you, doctor, you understand; but he must have the advantage of every chance."

The surgeon smiled indulgently. "Of course I understand. He deserves all that can be done for him. He must be nursed as you would nurse a human being, a sick child. And don't forget what I told you about temperature. I'll be back at ten o'clock again."

White Fang received the nursing. Judge Scott's suggestion of a trained nurse was indignantly clamoured down by the girls, who themselves undertook the task. And White Fang won out on the one chance in ten thousand denied him by the surgeon.

The latter was not to be censured for his misjudgment. All his life he had tended and operated on the soft humans of civilisation, who lived sheltered lives and had descended out of many sheltered generations. Compared with White Fang, they were frail and flabby, and clutched life without any strength in their grip. White Fang had come straight from the Wild, where the weak perish early and shelter is vouchsafed to none. In neither his father nor his mother was there any weakness, nor in the generations before them. A constitution of iron and the vitality of the Wild were White Fang's inheritance, and he clung to life, the whole of him and every part of him, in spirit and in flesh, with the tenacity that of old belonged to all creatures.

Bound down a prisoner, denied even movement by the plaster casts and bandages, White Fang lingered out the weeks. He slept long hours and dreamed much, and through his mind passed an unending pageant of Northland visions. All the ghosts of the past arose and were with him. Once again he lived in the lair with Kiche, crept trembling to the knees of Grey Beaver to tender his allegiance, ran for his life before Lip-lip and all the howling bedlam of the puppy-pack.

He ran again through the silence, hunting his living food through the months of famine; and again he ran at the head of the team, the gut-whips of Mit-sah and Grey Beaver snapping behind, their voices crying "Ra! Raa!" when they came to a narrow passage and the team closed together like a fan to go through. He lived again all his days with Beauty Smith and the fights he had fought. At such times he whimpered and snarled in his sleep, and they that looked on said that his dreams were bad.

But there was one particular nightmare from which he suffered—the clanking, clanging monsters of electric cars that were to him colossal screaming lynxes. He would lie in a screen of bushes, watching for a squirrel to venture far enough out on the ground from its tree-refuge. Then, when he sprang out upon it, it would transform itself into an electric car, menacing and terrible, towering over him like a mountain, screaming and clanging and spitting fire at him. It was the same when he challenged the hawk down out of the sky. Down out of the blue it would rush, as it dropped upon him changing itself into the ubiquitous electric car. Or again, he would be in the pen of Beauty Smith. Outside the pen, men would be gathering, and he knew that a fight was on. He watched the door for his antagonist to enter. The door would open, and thrust in upon him would come the awful electric car. A thousand times this occurred, and each time the terror it inspired was as vivid and great as ever.

Then came the day when the last bandage and the last plaster cast were taken off. It was a gala day. All Sierra Vista was gathered around. The master rubbed his ears, and he crooned his love-growl. The master's wife called him the "Blessed Wolf," which name was taken up with acclaim and all the women called him the Blessed Wolf.

He tried to rise to his feet, and after several attempts fell down from weakness. He had lain so long that his muscles had lost their cunning, and all the strength had gone out of them. He felt a little shame because of his weakness, as though, forsooth, he were failing the gods in the service he owed them. Because of this he made heroic efforts to arise and at last he stood on his four legs, tottering and swaying back and forth.

"The Blessed Wolf!" chorused the women.

Judge Scott surveyed them triumphantly.

"Out of your own mouths be it," he said. "Just as I contended right along. No mere dog could have done what he did. He's a wolf."

"A Blessed Wolf," amended the Judge's wife.

"Yes, Blessed Wolf," agreed the Judge. "And henceforth that shall be my name for him."

"He'll have to learn to walk again," said the surgeon; "so he might as well start in right now. It won't hurt him. Take him outside."

And outside he went, like a king, with all Sierra Vista about him and tending on him. He was very weak, and when he reached the lawn he lay down and rested for a while.

Then the procession started on, little spurts of strength coming into White Fang's muscles as he used them and the blood began to surge through them. The stables were reached, and there in the doorway, lay Collie, a half-dozen pudgy puppies playing about her in the sun.

White Fang looked on with a wondering eye. Collie snarled warningly at him, and he was careful to keep his distance. The master with his toe helped one sprawling puppy toward him. He bristled suspiciously, but the master warned him that all was well. Collie, clasped in the arms of one of the women, watched him jealously and with a snarl warned him that all was not well.

The puppy sprawled in front of him. He cocked his ears and watched it curiously. Then their noses touched, and he felt the warm little tongue of the puppy on his jowl. White Fang's tongue went out, he knew not why, and he licked the puppy's face.

Hand-clapping and pleased cries from the gods greeted the performance. He was surprised, and looked at them in a puzzled way. Then his weakness asserted itself, and he lay down, his ears cocked, his head on one side, as he watched the puppy. The other puppies came sprawling toward him, to Collie's great disgust; and he gravely permitted them to clamber and tumble over him. At first, amid the applause of the gods, he betrayed a trifle of his old self-consciousness and awkwardness. This passed away as the puppies' antics and mauling continued, and he lay with half-shut patient eyes, drowsing in the sun.

A Day's Lodging

It was the gosh-dangdest stampede I ever seen. A thousand dog-teams hittin' the ice. You couldn't see 'm fer smoke. Two white men an' a Swede froze to death that night, an' there was a dozen busted their lungs. But didn't I see with my own eyes the bottom of the water-hole? It was yellow with gold like a mustard-plaster. That's why I staked the Yukon for a minin' claim. That's what made the stampede. An' then there was nothin' to it. That's what I said—*nothin'* to it. An' I ain't got over guessin' yet.—Narrative of Shorty.

John Messner clung with mittened hand to the bucking gee-pole and held the sled in the trail. With the other mittened hand he rubbed his cheeks and nose. He rubbed his cheeks and nose every little while. In point of fact, he rarely ceased from rubbing them, and sometimes, as their numbness increased, he rubbed fiercely. His forehead was covered by the visor of his fur cap, the flaps of which went over his ears. The rest of his face was protected by a thick beard, golden-brown under its coating of frost.

Behind him churned a heavily loaded Yukon sled, and before him toiled a string of five dogs. The rope by which they dragged the sled rubbed against the side of Messner's leg. When the dogs swung on a bend in the trail, he stepped over the rope. There were many bends, and he was compelled to step over it often. Sometimes he tripped on the rope, or stumbled, and at all times he was awkward, betraying a weariness so great that the sled now and again ran upon his heels.

When he came to a straight piece of trail, where the sled could get along for a moment without guidance, he let go the gee-pole and batted his right hand sharply upon the hard wood. He found it difficult to keep up the circulation in that hand. But while he pounded the one hand, he never ceased from rubbing his nose and cheeks with the other.

"It's too cold to travel, anyway," he said. He spoke aloud, after the manner of men who are much by themselves. "Only a fool would travel at such a temperature. If it isn't eighty below, it's because it's seventy-nine."

He pulled out his watch, and after some fumbling got it back into the breast pocket of his thick woollen jacket. Then he surveyed the heavens and ran his eye along the white sky-line to the south.

"Twelve o'clock," he mumbled, "A clear sky, and no sun."

He plodded on silently for ten minutes, and then, as though there had been no lapse in his speech, he added:

"And no ground covered, and it's too cold to travel."

Suddenly he yelled "Whoa!" at the dogs, and stopped. He seemed in a wild panic over his right hand, and proceeded to hammer it furiously against the gee-pole.

"You—poor—devils!" he addressed the dogs, which had dropped down heavily on the ice to rest. His was a broken, jerky utterance, caused by the violence with which he hammered his numb hand upon the wood. "What have you done anyway that a two-legged other animal should come along, break you to harness, curb all your natural proclivities, and make slave-beasts out of you?"

He rubbed his nose, not reflectively, but savagely, in order to drive the blood into it, and urged the dogs to their work again. He travelled on the frozen surface of a great river. Behind him it stretched away in a mighty curve of many miles, losing itself in a fantastic jumble of mountains, snow-covered and silent. Ahead of him the river split into many channels to accommodate the freight of islands it carried on its breast. These islands were silent and white. No animals nor humming insects broke the silence. No birds flew in the chill air. There was no sound of man, no mark of the handiwork of man. The world slept, and it was like the sleep of death.

John Messner seemed succumbing to the apathy of it all. The frost was benumbing his spirit. He plodded on with bowed head, unobservant, mechanically rubbing nose and cheeks, and batting his steering hand against the gee-pole in the straight trail-stretches.

But the dogs were observant, and suddenly they stopped, turning their heads and looking back at their master out of eyes that were wistful and questioning. Their eyelashes were frosted white, as were their muzzles, and they had all the seeming of decrepit old age, what of the frost-rime and exhaustion.

The man was about to urge them on, when he checked himself, roused up with an effort, and looked around. The dogs had stopped beside a water-hole, not a fissure, but a hole man-made, chopped laboriously with an axe through three and a half feet of ice. A thick skin of new ice showed that it had not been used for some time. Messner glanced about him. The dogs were already pointing the way, each wistful and hoary muzzle turned toward the dim snow-path that left the main river trail and climbed the bank of the island.

"All right, you sore-footed brutes," he said. "I'll investigate. You're not a bit more anxious to quit than I am."

He climbed the bank and disappeared. The dogs did not lie down, but on their feet eagerly waited his return. He came back to them, took a hauling-rope from the front of the sled, and put it around his shoulders. Then he gee'd the dogs to the right and put them at the bank on the run. It was a stiff pull, but their weariness fell from them as they crouched low to the snow, whining with eagerness and gladness as they struggled upward to the last ounce of effort in their bodies. When a dog slipped or faltered, the one behind nipped his hind quarters. The man shouted encouragement and threats, and threw all his weight on the hauling-rope.

They cleared the bank with a rush, swung to the left, and dashed up to a small log cabin. It was a deserted cabin of a single room, eight feet by ten on the inside. Messner unharnessed the animals, unloaded his sled and took possession. The last chance wayfarer had left a supply of firewood. Messner set up his light sheet-iron stove and starred a fire. He put five sun-cured salmon into the oven to thaw out for the dogs, and from the water-hole filled his coffee-pot and cooking-pail.

While waiting for the water to boil, he held his face over the stove. The moisture from his breath had collected on his beard and frozen into a great mass of ice, and this he proceeded to thaw out. As it melted and dropped upon the stove it sizzled and rose about him in steam. He helped the process with his fingers, working loose small ice-chunks that fell rattling to the floor.

A wild outcry from the dogs without did not take him from his task. He heard the wolfish snarling and yelping of strange dogs and the sound of voices. A knock came on the door.

"Come in," Messner called, in a voice muffled because at the moment he was sucking loose a fragment of ice from its anchorage on his upper lip.

The door opened, and, gazing out of his cloud of steam, he saw a man and a woman pausing on the threshold.

"Come in," he said peremptorily, "and shut the door!"

Peering through the steam, he could make out but little of their personal appearance. The nose and cheek strap worn by the woman and the trail-wrappings about her head allowed only a pair of black eyes to be seen. The man was dark-eyed and smooth-shaven all except his mustache, which was so iced up as to hide his mouth.

"We just wanted to know if there is any other cabin around here," he said, at the same time glancing over the unfurnished state of the room. "We thought this cabin was empty."

"It isn't my cabin," Messner answered. "I just found it a few minutes ago. Come right in and camp. Plenty of room, and you won't need your stove. There's room for all."

At the sound of his voice the woman peered at him with quick curiousness.

"Get your things off," her companion said to her. "I'll unhitch and get the water so we can start cooking."

Messner took the thawed salmon outside and fed his dogs. He had to guard them against the second team of dogs, and when he had reëntered the cabin the other man had unpacked the sled and fetched water. Messner's pot was boiling. He threw in the coffee, settled it with half a cup of cold water, and took the pot from the stove. He thawed some sour-dough biscuits in the oven, at the same time heating a pot of beans he had boiled the night before and that had ridden frozen on the sled all morning.

Removing his utensils from the stove, so as to give the newcomers a chance to cook, he proceeded to take his meal from the top of his grub-box, himself sitting on his bed-roll. Between mouthfuls he talked trail and dogs with the man, who, with head over the stove, was thawing the ice from his mustache. There were two bunks in the cabin, and into one of them, when he had cleared his lip, the stranger tossed his bed-roll.

"We'll sleep here," he said, "unless you prefer this bunk. You're the first comer and you have first choice, you know."

"That's all right," Messner answered. "One bunk's just as good as the other."

He spread his own bedding in the second bunk, and sat down on the edge. The stranger thrust a physician's small travelling case under his blankets at one end to serve for a pillow.

"Doctor?" Messner asked.

"Yes," came the answer, "but I assure you I didn't come into the Klondike to practise."

The woman busied herself with cooking, while the man sliced bacon and fired the stove. The light in the cabin was dim, filtering through in a small window made of onion-skin writing paper and oiled with bacon grease, so that John Messner could not make out very well what the woman looked like. Not that he tried. He seemed to have no interest in her. But she glanced curiously from time to time into the dark corner where he sat.

"Oh, it's a great life," the doctor proclaimed enthusiastically, pausing from sharpening his knife on the stovepipe. "What I like about it is the struggle, the endeavor with one's own hands, the primitiveness of it, the realness."

"The temperature is real enough," Messner laughed.

"Do you know how cold it actually is?" the doctor demanded.

The other shook his head.

"Well, I'll tell you. Seventy-four below zero by spirit thermometer on the sled."

"That's one hundred and six below freezing point—too cold for travelling, eh?"

"Practically suicide," was the doctor's verdict. "One exerts himself. He breathes heavily, taking into his lungs the frost itself. It chills his lungs, freezes the edges of the tissues. He gets a dry, hacking cough as the dead tissue sloughs away, and dies the following summer of pneumonia, wondering what it's all about. I'll stay in this cabin for a week, unless the thermometer rises at least to fifty below."

"I say, Tess," he said, the next moment, "don't you think that coffee's boiled long enough!"

At the sound of the woman's name, John Messner became suddenly alert. He looked at her quickly, while across his face shot a haunting expression, the ghost of some buried misery achieving swift resurrection. But the next moment, and by an effort of will, the ghost was laid again. His face was as placid as before, though he was still alert, dissatisfied with what the feeble light had shown him of the woman's face.

Automatically, her first act had been to set the coffee-pot back. It was not until she had done this that she glanced at Messner. But already he had composed himself. She saw only a man sitting on the edge of the bunk and incuriously studying the toes of his moccasins. But, as she turned casually to go about her cooking, he shot another swift look at her, and she, glancing as swiftly back, caught his look. He shifted on past her to the doctor, though the slightest smile curled his lip in appreciation of the way she had trapped him.

She drew a candle from the grub-box and lighted it. One look at her illuminated face was enough for Messner. In the small cabin the widest limit was only a matter of several steps, and the next moment she was alongside of him. She deliberately held the candle close to his face and stared at him out of eyes wide with fear and recognition. He smiled quietly back at her.

"What are you looking for, Tess?" the doctor called.

"Hairpins," she replied, passing on and rummaging in a clothes-bag on the bunk.

They served their meal on their grub-box, sitting on Messner's grub-box and facing him. He had stretched out on his bunk to rest, lying on his side, his head on his arm. In the close quarters it was as though the three were together at table.

"What part of the States do you come from?" Messner asked.

"San Francisco," answered the doctor. "I've been in here two years, though."

"I hail from California myself," was Messner's announcement.

The woman looked at him appealingly, but he smiled and went on:

"Berkeley, you know."

The other man was becoming interested.

"U. C.?" he asked.

"Yes, Class of '86."

"I meant faculty," the doctor explained. "You remind me of the type."

"Sorry to hear you say so," Messner smiled back. "I'd prefer being taken for a prospector or a dog-musher."

"I don't think he looks any more like a professor than you do a doctor," the woman broke in.

"Thank you," said Messner. Then, turning to her companion, "By the way, Doctor, what is your name, if I may ask?"

"Haythorne, if you'll take my word for it. I gave up cards with civilization."

"And Mrs. Haythorne," Messner smiled and bowed.

She flashed a look at him that was more anger than appeal.

Haythorne was about to ask the other's name. His mouth had opened to form the question when Messner cut him off.

"Come to think of it, Doctor, you may possibly be able to satisfy my curiosity. There was a sort of scandal in faculty circles some two or three years ago. The wife of one of the English professors—er, if you will pardon me, Mrs. Haythorne—disappeared with some San Francisco doctor, I understood, though his name does not just now come to my lips. Do you remember the incident?"

Haythorne nodded his head. "Made quite a stir at the time. His name was Womble—Graham Womble. He had a magnificent practice. I knew him somewhat."

"Well, what I was trying to get at was what had become of them. I was wondering if you had heard. They left no trace, hide nor hair."

"He covered his tracks cunningly." Haythorne cleared his throat. "There was rumor that they went to the South Seas—were lost on a trading schooner in a typhoon, or something like that."

"I never heard that," Messner said. "You remember the case, Mrs. Haythorne?"

"Perfectly," she answered, in a voice the control of which was in amazing contrast to the anger that blazed in the face she turned aside so that Haythorne might not see.

The latter was again on the verge of asking his name, when Messner remarked:

"This Dr. Womble, I've heard he was very handsome, and—er—quite a success, so to say, with the ladies."

"Well, if he was, he finished himself off by that affair," Haythorne grumbled.

"And the woman was a termagant—at least so I've been told. It was generally accepted in Berkeley that she made life—er—not exactly paradise for her husband."

"I never heard that," Haythorne rejoined. "In San Francisco the talk was all the other way."

"Woman sort of a martyr, eh?—crucified on the cross of matrimony?"

The doctor nodded. Messner's gray eyes were mildly curious as he went on:

"That was to be expected—two sides to the shield. Living in Berkeley I only got the one side. She was a great deal in San Francisco, it seems."

"Some coffee, please," Haythorne said.

The woman refilled his mug, at the same time breaking into light laughter.

"You're gossiping like a pair of beldames," she chided them.

"It's so interesting," Messner smiled at her, then returned to the doctor. "The husband seems then to have had a not very savory reputation in San Francisco?"

"On the contrary, he was a moral prig," Haythorne blurted out, with apparently undue warmth. "He was a little scholastic shrimp without a drop of red blood in his body."

"Did you know him?"

"Never laid eyes on him. I never knocked about in university circles."

"One side of the shield again," Messner said, with an air of weighing the matter judicially. "While he did not amount to much, it is true—that is, physically—I'd hardly say he was as bad as all that. He did take an active interest in student athletics. And he had some talent. He once wrote a Nativity play that brought him quite a bit of local appreciation. I have heard, also, that he was slated for the head of the English department, only the affair happened and he resigned and went away. It quite broke his career, or so it seemed. At any rate, on our side the shield, it was considered a knock-out blow to him. It was thought he cared a great deal for his wife."

Haythorne, finishing his mug of coffee, grunted uninterestedly and lighted his pipe.

"It was fortunate they had no children," Messner continued.

But Haythorne, with a glance at the stove, pulled on his cap and mittens.

"I'm going out to get some wood," he said. "Then I can take off my moccasins and he comfortable."

The door slammed behind him. For a long minute there was silence. The man continued in the same position on the bed. The woman sat on the grub-box, facing him.

"What are you going to do?" she asked abruptly.

Messner looked at her with lazy indecision. "What do you think I ought to do? Nothing scenic, I hope. You see I am stiff and trail-sore, and this bunk is so restful."

She gnawed her lower lip and fumed dumbly.

"But—" she began vehemently, then clenched her hands and stopped.

"I hope you don't want me to kill Mr.—er—Haythorne," he said gently, almost pleadingly. "It would be most distressing, and, I assure you, really it is unnecessary."

"But you must do something," she cried.

"On the contrary, it is quite conceivable that I do not have to do anything."

"You would stay here?"

He nodded.

She glanced desperately around the cabin and at the bed unrolled on the other bunk. "Night is coming on. You can't stop here. You can't! I tell you, you simply can't!"

"Of course I can. I might remind you that I found this cabin first and that you are my guests."

Again her eyes travelled around the room, and the terror in them leaped up at sight of the other bunk.

"Then we'll have to go," she announced decisively.

"Impossible. You have a dry, hacking cough—the sort Mr.—er—Haythorne so aptly described. You've already slightly chilled your lungs. Besides, he is a physician and knows. He would never permit it."

"Then what are you going to do?" she demanded again, with a tense, quiet utterance that boded an outbreak.

Messner regarded her in a way that was almost paternal, what of the profundity of pity and patience with which he contrived to suffuse it.

"My dear Theresa, as I told you before, I don't know. I really haven't thought about it."

"Oh! You drive me mad!" She sprang to her feet, wringing her hands in impotent wrath. "You never used to be this way."

"I used to be all softness and gentleness," he nodded concurrence. "Was that why you left me?"

"You are so different, so dreadfully calm. You frighten me. I feel you have something terrible planned all the while. But whatever you do, don't do anything rash. Don't get excited—"

"I don't get excited any more," he interrupted. "Not since you went away."

"You have improved—remarkably," she retorted.

He smiled acknowledgment. "While I am thinking about what I shall do, I'll tell you what you will have to do—tell Mr.—er—Haythorne who I am. It may make our stay in this cabin more—may I say, sociable?"

"Why have you followed me into this frightful country?" she asked irrelevantly.

"Don't think I came here looking for you, Theresa. Your vanity shall not be tickled by any such misapprehension. Our meeting is wholly fortuitous. I broke with the life academic and I had to go somewhere. To be honest, I came into the Klondike because I thought it the place you were least liable to be in."

There was a fumbling at the latch, then the door swung in and Haythorne entered with an armful of firewood. At the first warning, Theresa began casually to clear away the dishes. Haythorne went out again after more wood.

"Why didn't you introduce us?" Messner queried.

"I'll tell him," she replied, with a toss of her head. "Don't think I'm afraid."

"I never knew you to be afraid, very much, of anything."

"And I'm not afraid of confession, either," she said, with softening face and voice.

"In your case, I fear, confession is exploitation by indirection, profit-making by ruse, self-aggrandizement at the expense of God."

"Don't be literary," she pouted, with growing tenderness. "I never did like epigrammatic discussion. Besides, I'm not afraid to ask you to forgive me."

"There is nothing to forgive, Theresa. I really should thank you. True, at first I suffered; and then, with all the graciousness of spring, it dawned upon me that I was happy, very happy. It was a most amazing discovery."

"But what if I should return to you?" she asked.

"I should" (he looked at her whimsically), "be greatly perturbed."

"I am your wife. You know you have never got a divorce."

"I see," he meditated. "I have been careless. It will be one of the first things I attend to."

She came over to his side, resting her hand on his arm. "You don't want me, John?" Her voice was soft and caressing, her hand rested like a lure. "If I told you I had made a mistake? If I told you that I was very unhappy?—and I am. And I did make a mistake."

Fear began to grow on Messner. He felt himself wilting under the lightly laid hand. The situation was slipping away from him, all his beautiful calmness was going. She looked at him with melting eyes, and he, too, seemed all dew and melting. He felt himself on the edge of an abyss, powerless to withstand the force that was drawing him over.

"I am coming back to you, John. I am coming back to-day . . . now."

As in a nightmare, he strove under the hand. While she talked, he seemed to hear, rippling softly, the song of the Lorelei. It was as though, somewhere, a piano were playing and the actual notes were impinging on his ear-drums.

Suddenly he sprang to his feet, thrust her from him as her arms attempted to clasp him, and retreated backward to the door. He was in a panic.

"I'll do something desperate!" he cried.

"I warned you not to get excited." She laughed mockingly, and went about washing the dishes. "Nobody wants you. I was just playing with you. I am happier where I am."

But Messner did not believe. He remembered her facility in changing front. She had changed front now. It was exploitation by indirection. She was not happy with the other man. She had discovered her mistake. The flame of his ego flared up at the thought. She wanted to come back to him, which was the one thing he did not want. Unwittingly, his hand rattled the door-latch.

"Don't run away," she laughed. "I won't bite you."

"I am not running away," he replied with child-like defiance, at the same time pulling on his mittens. "I'm only going to get some water."

He gathered the empty pails and cooking pots together and opened the door. He looked back at her.

"Don't forget you're to tell Mr.—er—Haythorne who I am."

Messner broke the skin that had formed on the water-hole within the hour, and filled his pails. But he did not return immediately to the cabin. Leaving the pails standing in the trail, he walked up and down, rapidly, to keep from freezing, for the frost bit into the flesh like fire. His beard was white with his frozen breath when the perplexed and frowning brows relaxed and decision came into his face. He had made up his mind to his course of action, and his frigid lips and cheeks crackled into a chuckle over it. The pails were already skinned over with young ice when he picked them up and made for the cabin.

When he entered he found the other man waiting, standing near the stove, a certain stiff awkwardness and indecision in his manner. Messner set down his water-pails.

"Glad to meet you, Graham Womble," he said in conventional tones, as though acknowledging an introduction.

Messner did not offer his hand. Womble stirred uneasily, feeling for the other the hatred one is prone to feel for one he has wronged.

"And so you're the chap," Messner said in marvelling accents. "Well, well. You see, I really am glad to meet you. I have been—er—curious to know what Theresa found in you—where, I may say, the attraction lay. Well, well."

And he looked the other up and down as a man would look a horse up and down.

"I know how you must feel about me," Womble began.

"Don't mention it," Messner broke in with exaggerated cordiality of voice and manner. "Never mind that. What I want to know is how do you find her? Up to expectations? Has she worn well? Life been all a happy dream ever since?"

"Don't be silly," Theresa interjected.

"I can't help being natural," Messner complained.

"You can be expedient at the same time, and practical," Womble said sharply. "What we want to know is what are you going to do?"

Messner made a well-feigned gesture of helplessness. "I really don't know. It is one of those impossible situations against which there can be no provision."

"All three of us cannot remain the night in this cabin."

Messner nodded affirmation.

"Then somebody must get out."

"That also is incontrovertible," Messner agreed. "When three bodies cannot occupy the same space at the same time, one must get out."

"And you're that one," Womble announced grimly. "It's a ten-mile pull to the next camp, but you can make it all right."

"And that's the first flaw in your reasoning," the other objected. "Why, necessarily, should I be the one to get out? I found this cabin first."

"But Tess can't get out," Womble explained. "Her lungs are already slightly chilled."

"I agree with you. She can't venture ten miles of frost. By all means she must remain."

"Then it is as I said," Womble announced with finality.

Messner cleared his throat. "Your lungs are all right, aren't they?"

"Yes, but what of it?"

Again the other cleared his throat and spoke with painstaking and judicial slowness. "Why, I may say, nothing of it, except, ah, according to your own reasoning, there is nothing to prevent your getting out, hitting the frost, so to speak, for a matter of ten miles. You can make it all right."

Womble looked with quick suspicion at Theresa and caught in her eyes a glint of pleased surprise.

"Well?" he demanded of her.

She hesitated, and a surge of anger darkened his face. He turned upon Messner.

"Enough of this. You can't stop here."

"Yes, I can."

"I won't let you." Womble squared his shoulders. "I'm running things."

"I'll stay anyway," the other persisted.

"I'll put you out."

"I'll come back."

Womble stopped a moment to steady his voice and control himself. Then he spoke slowly, in a low, tense voice.

"Look here, Messner, if you refuse to get out, I'll thrash you. This isn't California. I'll beat you to a jelly with my two fists."

Messner shrugged his shoulders. "If you do, I'll call a miners' meeting and see you strung up to the nearest tree. As you said, this is not California. They're a simple folk, these miners, and all I'll have to do will be to show them the marks of the beating, tell them the truth about you, and present my claim for my wife."

The woman attempted to speak, but Womble turned upon her fiercely.

"You keep out of this," he cried.

In marked contrast was Messner's "Please don't intrude, Theresa."

What of her anger and pent feelings, her lungs were irritated into the dry, hacking cough, and with blood-suffused face and one hand clenched against her chest, she waited for the paroxysm to pass.

Womble looked gloomily at her, noting her cough.

"Something must be done," he said. "Yet her lungs can't stand the exposure. She can't travel till the temperature rises. And I'm not going to give her up."

Messner hemmed, cleared his throat, and hemmed again, semi-apologetically, and said, "I need some money."

Contempt showed instantly in Womble's face. At last, beneath him in vileness, had the other sunk himself.

"You've got a fat sack of dust," Messner went on. "I saw you unload it from the sled."

"How much do you want?" Womble demanded, with a contempt in his voice equal to that in his face.

"I made an estimate of the sack, and I—ah—should say it weighed about twenty pounds. What do you say we call it four thousand?"

"But it's all I've got, man!" Womble cried out.

"You've got her," the other said soothingly. "She must be worth it. Think what I'm giving up. Surely it is a reasonable price."

"All right." Womble rushed across the floor to the gold-sack. "Can't put this deal through too quick for me, you—you little worm!"

"Now, there you err," was the smiling rejoinder. "As a matter of ethics isn't the man who gives a bribe as bad as the man who takes a bribe? The receiver is as bad as the thief, you know; and you needn't console yourself with any fictitious moral superiority concerning this little deal."

"To hell with your ethics!" the other burst out. "Come here and watch the weighing of this dust. I might cheat you."

And the woman, leaning against the bunk, raging and impotent, watched herself weighed out in yellow dust and nuggets in the scales erected on the grub-box. The scales were small, making necessary many weighings, and Messner with precise care verified each weighing.

"There's too much silver in it," he remarked as he tied up the gold-sack. "I don't think it will run quite sixteen to the ounce. You got a trifle the better of me, Womble."

He handled the sack lovingly, and with due appreciation of its preciousness carried it out to his sled.

Returning, he gathered his pots and pans together, packed his grub-box, and rolled up his bed. When the sled was lashed and the complaining dogs harnessed, he returned into the cabin for his mittens.

"Good-by, Tess," he said, standing at the open door.

She turned on him, struggling for speech but too frantic to word the passion that burned in her.

"Good-by, Tess," he repeated gently.

"Beast!" she managed to articulate.

She turned and tottered to the bunk, flinging herself face down upon it, sobbing: "You beasts! You beasts!"

John Messner closed the door softly behind him, and, as he started the dogs, looked back at the cabin with a great relief in his face. At the bottom of the bank, beside the water-hole, he halted the sled. He worked the sack of gold out between the lashings and carried it to the water-hole. Already a new skin of ice had formed. This he broke with his fist. Untying the knotted mouth with his teeth, he emptied the contents of the sack into the water. The river was shallow at that point, and two feet beneath the surface he could see the bottom dull-yellow in the fading light. At the sight of it, he spat into the hole.

He started the dogs along the Yukon trail. Whining spiritlessly, they were reluctant to work. Clinging to the gee-pole with his right band and with his left rubbing cheeks and nose, he stumbled over the rope as the dogs swung on a bend.

"Mush-on, you poor, sore-footed brutes!" he cried. "That's it, mush-on!"

John Barleycorn

CHAPTER I

It all came to me one election day. It was on a warm California afternoon, and I had ridden down into the Valley of the Moon from the ranch to the little village to vote Yes and No to a host of proposed amendments to the Constitution of the State of California. Because of the warmth of the day I had had several drinks before casting my ballot, and divers drinks after casting it. Then I had ridden up through the vine-clad hills and rolling pastures of the ranch, and arrived at the farm-house in time for another drink and supper.

"How did you vote on the suffrage amendment?" Charmian asked.

"I voted for it."

She uttered an exclamation of surprise. For, be it known, in my younger days, despite my ardent democracy, I had been opposed to woman suffrage. In my later and more tolerant years I had been unenthusiastic in my acceptance of it as an inevitable social phenomenon.

"Now just why did you vote for it?" Charmian asked.

I answered. I answered at length. I answered indignantly. The more I answered, the more indignant I became. (No; I was not drunk. The horse I had ridden was well named "The Outlaw." I'd like to see any drunken man ride her.)

And yet—how shall I say?—I was lighted up, I was feeling "good," I was pleasantly jingled.

"When the women get the ballot, they will vote for prohibition," I said. "It is the wives, and sisters, and mothers, and they only, who will drive the nails into the coffin of John Barleycorn——"

"But I thought you were a friend to John Barleycorn," Charmian interpolated.

"I am. I was. I am not. I never am. I am never less his friend than when he is with me and when I seem most his friend. He is the king of liars. He is the frankest truthsayer. He is the august companion with whom one walks with the gods. He is also in league with the Noseless One. His way leads to truth naked, and to death. He gives clear vision, and muddy dreams. He is the enemy of life, and the teacher of wisdom beyond life's wisdom. He is a red-handed killer, and he slays youth."

And Charmian looked at me, and I knew she wondered where I had got it.

I continued to talk. As I say, I was lighted up. In my brain every thought was at home. Every thought, in its little cell, crouched ready-dressed at the door, like prisoners at midnight waiting a jail-break. And every thought was a vision, bright-imaged, sharp-cut, unmistakable. My brain was illuminated by the clear, white light of alcohol. John Barleycorn was on a truth-telling rampage, giving away the choicest secrets on himself. And I was his spokesman. There moved the multitudes of memories of my past life, all orderly arranged like soldiers in some vast review. It was mine to pick and choose. I was a lord of thought, the master of my vocabulary and of the totality of my experience, unerringly capable of selecting my data and building my exposition. For so John Barleycorn tricks and lures, setting the maggots of intelligence gnawing, whispering his fatal intuitions of truth, flinging purple passages into the monotony of one's days.

196

I outlined my life to Charmian, and expounded the make-up of my constitution. I was no hereditary alcoholic. I had been born with no organic, chemical predisposition toward alcohol. In this matter I was normal in my generation. Alcohol was an acquired taste. It had been painfully acquired. Alcohol had been a dreadfully repugnant thing—more nauseous than any physic. Even now I did not like the taste of it. I drank it only for its "kick." And from the age of five to that of twenty-five I had not learned to care for its kick. Twenty years of unwilling apprenticeship had been required to make my system rebelliously tolerant of alcohol, to make me, in the heart and the deeps of me, desirous of alcohol.

I sketched my first contacts with alcohol, told of my first intoxications and revulsions, and pointed out always the one thing that in the end had won me over— namely, the accessibility of alcohol. Not only had it always been accessible, but every interest of my developing life had drawn me to it. A newsboy on the streets, a sailor, a miner, a wanderer in far lands, always where men came together to exchange ideas, to laugh and boast and dare, to relax, to forget the dull toil of tiresome nights and days, always they came together over alcohol. The saloon was the place of congregation. Men gathered to it as primitive men gathered about the fire of the squatting place or the fire at the mouth of the cave.

I reminded Charmian of the canoe houses from which she had been barred in the South Pacific, where the kinky-haired cannibals escaped from their womenkind and feasted and drank by themselves, the sacred precincts taboo to women under pain of death. As a youth, by way of the saloon I had escaped from the narrowness of woman's influence into the wide free world of men. All ways led to the saloon. The thousand roads of romance and adventure drew together in the saloon, and thence led out and on over the world.

"The point is," I concluded my sermon, "that it is the accessibility of alcohol that has given me my taste for alcohol. I did not care for it. I used to laugh at it. Yet here I am, at the last, possessed with the drinker's desire. It took twenty years to implant that desire; and for ten years more that desire has grown. And the effect of satisfying that desire is anything but good. Temperamentally I am wholesome-hearted and merry. Yet when I walk with John Barleycorn I suffer all the damnation of intellectual pessimism.

"But," I hastened to add (I always hasten to add), "John Barleycorn must have his due. He does tell the truth. That is the curse of it. The so-called truths of life are not true. They are the vital lies by which life lives, and John Barleycorn gives them the lie."

"Which does not make toward life," Charmian said.

"Very true," I answered. "And that is the perfectest hell of it. John Barleycorn makes toward death. That is why I voted for the amendment to-day. I read back in my life and saw how the accessibility of alcohol had given me the taste for it. You see, comparatively few alcoholics are born in a generation. And by alcoholic I mean a man whose chemistry craves alcohol and drives him resistlessly to it. The great majority of habitual drinkers are born not only without desire for alcohol, but with actual repugnance toward it. Not the first, nor the twentieth, nor the hundredth drink, succeeded in giving them the liking. But they learned, just as men learn to smoke; though it is far easier to learn to smoke than to learn to drink. They learned because alcohol was so accessible. The women know the game. They pay for it—the wives and sisters and mothers. And when they come to vote, they will vote for prohibition. And the best of it is that there will be no hardship worked on the coming generation. Not having access to alcohol, not being predisposed toward alcohol, it will never miss alcohol. It will mean life more abundant for the manhood of the young boys born and growing up—ay, and life more abundant for the young girls born and growing up to share the lives of the young men."

"Why not write all this up for the sake of the men and women coming?" Charmian asked. "Why not write it so as to help the wives and sisters and mothers to the way they should vote?"

"The 'Memoirs of an Alcoholic,'" I sneered—or, rather, John Barleycorn sneered; for he sat with me there at table in my pleasant, philanthropic jingle, and it is a trick of John Barleycorn to turn the smile to a sneer without an instant's warning.

"No," said Charmian, ignoring John Barleycorn's roughness, as so many women have learned to do. "You have shown yourself no alcoholic, no dipsomaniac, but merely an habitual drinker, one who has made John Barleycorn's acquaintance through long years of rubbing shoulders with him. Write it up and call it 'Alcoholic Memoirs.'"

CHAPTER II

And, ere I begin, I must ask the reader to walk with me in all sympathy; and, since sympathy is merely understanding, begin by understanding me and whom and what I write about. In the first place, I am a seasoned drinker. I have no constitutional predisposition for alcohol. I am not stupid. I am not a swine. I know the drinking game from A to Z, and I have used my judgment in drinking. I never have to be put to bed. Nor do I stagger. In short, I am a normal, average man; and I drink in the normal, average way, as drinking goes. And this is the very point: I am writing of the effects of alcohol on the normal, average man. I have no word to say for or about the microscopically unimportant excessivist, the dipsomaniac.

There are, broadly speaking, two types of drinkers. There is the man whom we all know, stupid, unimaginative, whose brain is bitten numbly by numb maggots; who walks generously with wide-spread, tentative legs, falls frequently in the gutter, and who sees, in the extremity of his ecstasy, blue mice and pink elephants. He is the type that gives rise to the jokes in the funny papers.

The other type of drinker has imagination, vision. Even when most pleasantly jingled, he walks straight and naturally, never staggers nor falls, and knows just where he is and what he is doing. It is not his body but his brain that is drunken. He may bubble with wit, or expand with good fellowship. Or he may see intellectual spectres and phantoms that are cosmic and logical and that take the forms of syllogisms. It is when in this condition that he strips away the husks of life's healthiest illusions and gravely considers the iron collar of necessity welded about the neck of his soul. This is the hour of John Barleycorn's subtlest power. It is easy for any man to roll in the gutter. But it is a terrible ordeal for a man to stand upright on his two legs unswaying, and decide that in all the universe he finds for himself but one freedom—namely, the anticipating of the day of his death. With this man this is the hour of the white logic (of which more anon), when he knows that he may know only the laws of things—the meaning of things never. This is his danger hour. His feet are taking hold of the pathway that leads down into the grave.

All is clear to him. All these baffling head-reaches after immortality are but the panics of souls frightened by the fear of death, and cursed with the thrice-cursed gift of imagination. They have not the instinct for death; they lack the will to die when the time to die is at hand. They trick themselves into believing they will outwit the game and win to a future, leaving the other animals to the darkness of the grave or the annihilating heats of the crematory. But he, this man in the hour of his white logic, knows that they trick and outwit themselves. The one event happeneth to all alike. There is no new thing under the sun, not even that yearned-for bauble of feeble souls—immortality. But he knows, *he* knows, standing upright on his two legs unswaying. He is compounded of meat and wine and sparkle, of sun-mote and world-dust, a frail mechanism made to run for a span, to be tinkered at by doctors of divinity and doctors of physic, and to be flung into the scrap-heap at the end.

Of course, all this is soul-sickness, life-sickness. It is the penalty the imaginative man must pay for his friendship with John Barleycorn. The penalty paid by the stupid man is simpler, easier. He drinks himself into sottish unconsciousness. He sleeps a drugged sleep, and, if he dream, his dreams are dim and inarticulate. But to the imaginative man, John Barleycorn sends the pitiless, spectral syllogisms of the white logic. He looks upon life and all its affairs with the jaundiced eye of a pessimistic German philosopher. He sees through all illusions. He transvalues all values. Good is bad, truth is a cheat, and life is a joke. From his calm-mad heights, with the certitude of a god, he beholds all life as evil. Wife, children, friends—in the clear, white light of his logic they are exposed as frauds and shams. He sees through them, and all that he sees is their frailty, their meagreness, their sordidness, their pitifulness. No longer do they fool him. They are miserable little egotisms, like all the other little humans, fluttering their May-fly life-dance of an hour. They are without freedom. They are puppets of chance. So is he. He realises that. But there is one difference. He sees; he knows. And he knows his one freedom: he may anticipate the day of his death. All of which is not good for a man who is made to live and love and be loved. Yet suicide, quick or slow, a sudden spill or a gradual oozing away through the years, is the price John Barleycorn exacts. No friend of his ever escapes making the just, due payment.

CHAPTER III

I was five years old the first time I got drunk. It was on a hot day, and my father was ploughing in the field. I was sent from the house, half a mile away, to carry to him a pail of beer. "And be sure you don't spill it," was the parting injunction.

It was, as I remember it, a lard pail, very wide across the top, and without a cover. As I toddled along, the beer slopped over the rim upon my legs. And as I toddled, I pondered. Beer was a very precious thing. Come to think of it, it must be wonderfully good. Else why was I never permitted to drink of it in the house? Other things kept from me by the grown-ups I had found good. Then this, too, was good. Trust the grown-ups. They knew. And, anyway, the pail was too full. I was slopping it against my legs and spilling it on the ground. Why waste it? And no one would know whether I had drunk or spilled it.

I was so small that, in order to negotiate the pail, I sat down and gathered it into my lap. First I sipped the foam. I was disappointed. The preciousness evaded me. Evidently it did not reside in the foam. Besides, the taste was not good. Then I remembered seeing the grown-ups blow the foam away before they drank. I buried my face in the foam and lapped the solid liquid beneath. It wasn't good at all. But still I drank. The grown-ups knew what they were about. Considering my diminutiveness, the size of the pail in my lap, and my drinking out of it my breath held and my face buried to the ears in foam, it was rather difficult to estimate how much I drank. Also, I was gulping it down like medicine, in nauseous haste to get the ordeal over.

I shuddered when I started on, and decided that the good taste would come afterward. I tried several times more in the course of that long half-mile. Then, astounded by the quantity of beer that was lacking, and remembering having seen stale beer made to foam afresh, I took a stick and stirred what was left till it foamed to the brim.

And my father never noticed. He emptied the pail with the wide thirst of the sweating ploughman, returned it to me, and started up the plough. I endeavoured to walk beside the horses. I remember tottering and falling against their heels in front of the shining share, and that my father hauled back on the lines so violently that the horses nearly sat down on me. He told me afterward that it was by only a matter of inches that I escaped disembowelling. Vaguely, too, I remember, my father carried me in his arms to the trees on the edge of the field, while all the world reeled and swung about me, and I was aware of deadly nausea mingled with an appalling conviction of sin.

I slept the afternoon away under the trees, and when my father roused me at sundown it was a very sick little boy that got up and dragged wearily homeward. I was exhausted, oppressed by the weight of my limbs, and in my stomach was a harp-like vibrating that extended to my throat and brain. My condition was like that of one who had gone through a battle with poison. In truth, I had been poisoned.

In the weeks and months that followed I had no more interest in beer than in the kitchen stove after it had burned me. The grown-ups were right. Beer was not for children. The grown-ups didn't mind it; but neither did they mind taking pills and castor oil. As for me, I could manage to get along quite well without beer. Yes, and to the day of my death I could have managed to get along quite well without it. But circumstance decreed otherwise. At every turn in the world in which I lived, John Barleycorn beckoned. There was no escaping him. All paths led to him. And it took twenty years of contact, of exchanging greetings and passing on with my tongue in my cheek, to develop in me a sneaking liking for the rascal.

CHAPTER IV

My next bout with John Barleycorn occurred when I was seven. This time my imagination was at fault, and I was frightened into the encounter. Still farming, my family had moved to a ranch on the bleak sad coast of San Mateo County, south of San Francisco. It was a wild, primitive countryside in those days; and often I heard my mother pride herself that we were old American stock and not immigrant Irish and Italians like our neighbours. In all our section there was only one other old American family.

One Sunday morning found me, how or why I cannot now remember, at the Morrisey ranch. A number of young people had gathered there from the nearer ranches. Besides, the oldsters had been there, drinking since early dawn, and, some of them, since the night before. The Morriseys were a huge breed, and there were many strapping great sons and uncles, heavy-booted, big-fisted, rough-voiced.

Suddenly there were screams from the girls and cries of "Fight!" There was a rush. Men hurled themselves out of the kitchen. Two giants, flush-faced, with grey-ing hair, were locked in each other's arms. One was Black Matt, who, everybody said, had killed two men in his time. The women screamed softly, crossed them-selves, or prayed brokenly, hiding their eyes and peeping through their fingers. But not I. It is a fair presumption that I was the most interested spectator. Maybe I would see that wonderful thing, a man killed. Anyway, I would see a man-fight. Great was my disappointment. Black Matt and Tom Morrisey merely held on to each other and lifted their clumsy-booted feet in what seemed a grotesque, elephan-tine dance. They were too drunk to fight. Then the peacemakers got hold of them and led them back to cement the new friendship in the kitchen.

Soon they were all talking at once, rumbling and roaring as big-chested open-air men will, when whisky has whipped their taciturnity. And I, a little shaver of seven, my heart in my mouth, my trembling body strung tense as a deer's on the verge of flight, peered wonderingly in at the open door and learned more of the strangeness of men. And I marvelled at Black Matt and Tom Morrisey, sprawled over the table, arms about each other's necks, weeping lovingly.

The kitchen-drinking continued, and the girls outside grew timorous. They knew the drink game, and all were certain that something terrible was going to happen. They protested that they did not wish to be there when it happened, and some one suggested going to a big Italian rancho four miles away, where they could get up a dance. Immediately they paired off, lad and lassie, and started down the sandy road. And each lad walked with his sweetheart—trust a child of seven to listen and to know the love-affairs of his countryside. And behold, I, too, was a lad with a lassie. A little Irish girl of my own age had been paired off with me. We were the only children in this spontaneous affair. Perhaps the oldest couple might have been twenty. There were chits of girls, quite grown up, of fourteen and sixteen, walking with their fellows. But we were uniquely young, this little Irish girl and I, and we walked hand in hand, and, sometimes, under the tutelage of our elders, with my arm around her waist. Only that wasn't comfortable. And I was very proud, on that bright Sunday morning, going down the long bleak road among the sandhills. I, too, had my girl, and was a little man.

The Italian rancho was a bachelor establishment. Our visit was hailed with delight. The red wine was poured in tumblers for all, and the long dining-room was partly cleared for dancing. And the young fellows drank and danced with the girls to the strains of an accordion. To me that music was divine. I had never heard anything so glorious. The young Italian who furnished it would even get up and dance, his arms around his girl, playing the accordion behind her back. All of which was very wonderful for me, who did not dance, but who sat at a table and gazed wide-eyed at the amazingness of life. I was only a little lad, and there was so much of life for me to learn. As the time passed, the Irish lads began helping themselves to the wine, and jollity and high spirits reigned. I noted that some of them staggered and fell down in the dances, and that one had gone to sleep in a corner. Also, some of the girls were complaining, and wanting to leave, and others of the girls were titteringly complacent, willing for anything to happen.

When our Italian hosts had offered me wine in a general sort of way, I had declined. My beer experience had been enough for me, and I had no inclination to traffic further in the stuff, or in anything related to it. Unfortunately, one young Italian, Peter, an impish soul, seeing me sitting solitary, stirred by a whim of the moment, half-filled a tumbler with wine and passed it to me. He was sitting across the table from me. I declined. His face grew stern, and he insistently proffered the wine. And then terror descended upon me—a terror which I must explain.

My mother had theories. First, she steadfastly maintained that brunettes and all the tribe of dark-eyed humans were deceitful. Needless to say, my mother was a blonde. Next, she was convinced that the dark-eyed Latin races were profoundly sensitive, profoundly treacherous, and profoundly murderous. Again and again, drinking in the strangeness and the fearsomeness of the world from her lips, I had heard her state that if one offended an Italian, no matter how slightly and unintentionally, he was certain to retaliate by stabbing one in the back. That was her particular phrase—"stab you in the back."

Now, although I had been eager to see Black Matt kill Tom Morrisey that morning, I did not care to furnish to the dancers the spectacle of a knife sticking in my back. I had not yet learned to distinguish between facts and theories. My faith was implicit in my mother's exposition of the Italian character. Besides, I had some glimmering inkling of the sacredness of hospitality. Here was a treacherous, sensitive, murderous Italian, offering me hospitality. I had been taught to believe that if I offended him he would strike at me with a knife precisely as a horse kicked out when one got too close to its heels and worried it. Then, too, this Italian, Peter, had those terrible black eyes I had heard my mother talk about. They were eyes different from the eyes I knew, from the blues and greys and hazels of my own family, from the pale and genial blues of the Irish. Perhaps Peter had had a few drinks. At any rate, his eyes were brilliantly black and sparkling with devilry. They were the mysterious, the unknown, and who was I, a seven-year-old, to analyse them and know their prankishness? In them I visioned sudden death, and I declined the wine half-heartedly. The expression in his eyes changed. They grew stern and imperious as he shoved the tumbler of wine closer.

What could I do? I have faced real death since in my life, but never have I known the fear of death as I knew it then. I put the glass to my lips, and Peter's eyes relented. I knew he would not kill me just then. That was a relief. But the wine was not. It was cheap, new wine, bitter and sour, made of the leavings and scrapings of the vineyards and the vats, and it tasted far worse than beer. There is only one way to take medicine, and that is to take it. And that is the way I took that wine. I threw my head back and gulped it down. I had to gulp again and hold the poison down, for poison it was to my child's tissues and membranes.

Looking back now, I can realise that Peter was astounded. He half-filled a second tumbler and shoved it across the table. Frozen with fear, in despair at the fate which had befallen me, I gulped the second glass down like the first. This was too much for Peter. He must share the infant prodigy he had discovered. He called Dominick, a young moustached Italian, to see the sight. This time it was a full tumbler that was given me. One will do anything to live. I gripped myself, mastered the qualms that rose in my throat, and downed the stuff.

Dominick had never seen an infant of such heroic calibre. Twice again he refilled the tumbler, each time to the brim, and watched it disappear down my throat. By this time my exploits were attracting attention. Middle-aged Italian labourers, old-country peasants who did not talk English, and who could not dance with the Irish girls, surrounded me. They were swarthy and wild-looking; they wore belts and red shirts; and I knew they carried knives; and they ringed me around like a pirate chorus. And Peter and Dominick made me show off for them.

Had I lacked imagination, had I been stupid, had I been stubbornly mulish in having my own way, I should never have got in this pickle. And the lads and lassies were dancing, and there was no one to save me from my fate. How much I drank I do not know. My memory of it is of an age-long suffering of fear in the midst of a murderous crew, and of an infinite number of glasses of red wine passing across the bare boards of a wine-drenched table and going down my burning throat. Bad as the wine was, a knife in the back was worse, and I must survive at any cost.

Looking back with the drinker's knowledge, I know now why I did not collapse stupefied upon the table. As I have said, I was frozen, I was paralysed, with fear. The only movement I made was to convey that never-ending procession of glasses to my lips. I was a poised and motionless receptacle for all that quantity of wine. It lay inert in my fear-inert stomach. I was too frightened, even, for my stomach to turn. So all that Italian crew looked on and marvelled at the infant phenomenon that downed wine with the sang-froid of an automaton. It is not in the spirit of braggadocio that I dare to assert they had never seen anything like it.

The time came to go. The tipsy antics of the lads had led a majority of the soberer-minded lassies to compel a departure. I found myself, at the door, beside my little maiden. She had not had my experience, so she was sober. She was fascinated by the titubations of the lads who strove to walk beside their girls, and began to mimic them. I thought this a great game, and I, too, began to stagger tipsily. But she had no wine to stir up, while my movements quickly set the fumes rising to my head. Even at the start, I was more realistic than she. In several minutes I was astonishing myself. I saw one lad, after reeling half a dozen steps, pause at the side of the road, gravely peer into the ditch, and gravely, and after apparent deep thought, fall into it. To me this was excruciatingly funny. I staggered to the edge of the ditch, fully intending to stop on the edge. I came to myself, in the ditch, in process of being hauled out by several anxious-faced girls.

I didn't care to play at being drunk any more. There was no more fun in me. My eyes were beginning to swim, and with wide-open mouth I panted for air. A girl led me by the hand on either side, but my legs were leaden. The alcohol I had drunk was striking my heart and brain like a club. Had I been a weakling of a child, I am confident that it would have killed me. As it was, I know I was nearer death than any of the scared girls dreamed. I could hear them bickering among themselves as to whose fault it was; some were weeping—for themselves, for me, and for the disgraceful way their lads had behaved. But I was not interested. I was suffocating, and I wanted air. To move was agony. It made me pant harder. Yet those girls persisted in making me walk, and it was four miles home. Four miles! I remember my swimming eyes saw a small bridge across the road an infinite distance away. In fact, it was not a hundred feet distant. When I reached it, I sank down and lay on my back panting. The girls tried to lift me, but I was helpless and suffocating. Their cries of alarm brought Larry, a drunken youth of seventeen, who proceeded to resuscitate me by jumping on my chest. Dimly I remember this, and the squalling of the girls as they struggled with him and dragged him away. And then I knew nothing, though I learned afterward that Larry wound up under the bridge and spent the night there.

When I came to, it was dark. I had been carried unconscious for four miles and been put to bed. I was a sick child, and, despite the terrible strain on my heart and tissues, I continually relapsed into the madness of delirium. All the contents of the terrible and horrible in my child's mind spilled out. The most frightful visions were realities to me. I saw murders committed, and I was pursued by murderers. I screamed and raved and fought. My sufferings were prodigious. Emerging from such delirium, I would hear my mother's voice: "But the child's brain. He will lose his reason." And sinking back into delirium, I would take the idea with me and be immured in madhouses, and be beaten by keepers, and surrounded by screeching lunatics.

One thing that had strongly impressed my young mind was the talk of my elders about the dens of iniquity in San Francisco's Chinatown. In my delirium I wandered deep beneath the ground through a thousand of these dens, and behind locked doors of iron I suffered and died a thousand deaths. And when I would come upon my father, seated at table in these subterranean crypts, gambling with Chinese for great stakes of gold, all my outrage gave vent in the vilest cursing. I would rise in bed, struggling against the detaining hands, and curse my father till the rafters rang. All the inconceivable filth a child running at large in a primitive countryside may hear men utter was mine; and though I had never dared utter such oaths, they now poured from me, at the top of my lungs, as I cursed my father sitting there underground and gambling with long-haired, long-nailed Chinamen.

It is a wonder that I did not burst my heart or brain that night. A seven-year-old child's arteries and nerve-centres are scarcely fitted to endure the terrific paroxysms that convulsed me. No one slept in the thin, frame farm-house that night when John Barleycorn had his will of me. And Larry, under the bridge, had no delirium like mine. I am confident that his sleep was stupefied and dreamless, and that he awoke next day merely to heaviness and moroseness, and that if he lives to-day he does not remember that night, so passing was it as an incident. But my brain was seared for ever by that experience. Writing now, thirty years afterward, every vision is as distinct, as sharp-cut, every pain as vital and terrible, as on that night.

I was sick for days afterward, and I needed none of my mother's injunctions to avoid John Barleycorn in the future. My mother had been dreadfully shocked. She held that I had done wrong, very wrong, and that I had gone contrary to all her teaching. And how was I, who was never allowed to talk back, who lacked the very words with which to express my psychology—how was I to tell my mother that it was her teaching that was directly responsible for my drunkenness? Had it not been for her theories about dark eyes and Italian character, I should never have wet my lips with the sour, bitter wine. And not until man-grown did I tell her the true inwardness of that disgraceful affair.

In those after days of sickness, I was confused on some points, and very clear on others. I felt guilty of sin, yet smarted with a sense of injustice. It had not been my fault, yet I had done wrong. But very clear was my resolution never to touch liquor again. No mad dog was ever more afraid of water than was I of alcohol.

Yet the point I am making is that this experience, terrible as it was, could not in the end deter me from forming John Barleycorn's cheek-by-jowl acquaintance. All about me, even then, were the forces moving me toward him. In the first place, barring my mother, ever extreme in her views, it seemed to me all the grown-ups looked upon the affair with tolerant eyes. It was a joke, something funny that had happened. There was no shame attached. Even the lads and lassies giggled and snickered over their part in the affair, narrating with gusto how Larry had jumped on my chest and slept under the bridge, how So-and-So had slept out in the sandhills that night, and what had happened to the other lad who fell in the ditch. As I say, so far as I could see, there was no shame anywhere. It had been something ticklishly, devilishly fine—a bright and gorgeous episode in the monotony of life and labour on that bleak, fog-girt coast.

The Irish ranchers twitted me good-naturedly on my exploit, and patted me on the back until I felt that I had done something heroic. Peter and Dominick and the other Italians were proud of my drinking prowess. The face of morality was not set against drinking. Besides, everybody drank. There was not a teetotaler in the community. Even the teacher of our little country school, a greying man of fifty, gave us vacations on the occasions when he wrestled with John Barleycorn and was thrown. Thus there was no spiritual deterrence. My loathing for alcohol was purely physiological. I didn't like the damned stuff.

CHAPTER V

This physical loathing for alcohol I have never got over. But I have conquered it. To this day I conquer it every time I take a drink. The palate never ceases to rebel, and the palate can be trusted to know what is good for the body. But men do not drink for the effect alcohol produces on the body. What they drink for is the brain-effect; and if it must come through the body, so much the worse for the body.

And yet, despite my physical loathing for alcohol, the brightest spots in my child life were the saloons. Sitting on the heavy potato wagons, wrapped in fog, feet stinging from inactivity, the horses plodding slowly along the deep road through the sandhills, one bright vision made the way never too long. The bright vision was the saloon at Colma, where my father, or whoever drove, always got out to get a drink. And I got out to warm by the great stove and get a soda cracker. Just one soda cracker, but a fabulous luxury. Saloons were good for something. Back behind the plodding horses, I would take an hour in consuming that one cracker. I took the smallest nibbles, never losing a crumb, and chewed the nibble till it became the thinnest and most delectable of pastes. I never voluntarily swallowed this paste. I just tasted it, and went on tasting it, turning it over with my tongue, spreading it on the inside of this cheek, then on the inside of the other cheek, until, at the end, it eluded me and in tiny drops and oozelets, slipped and dribbled down my throat. Horace Fletcher had nothing on me when it came to soda crackers.

I liked saloons. Especially I liked the San Francisco saloons. They had the most delicious dainties for the taking—strange breads and crackers, cheeses, sausages, sardines—wonderful foods that I never saw on our meagre home-table. And once, I remember, a barkeeper mixed me a sweet temperance drink of syrup and soda-water. My father did not pay for it. It was the barkeeper's treat, and he became my ideal of a good, kind man. I dreamed day-dreams of him for years. Although I was seven years old at the time, I can see him now with undiminished clearness, though I never laid eyes on him but that one time. The saloon was south of Market Street in San Francisco. It stood on the west side of the street. As you entered, the bar was on the left. On the right, against the wall, was the free lunch counter. It was a long, narrow room, and at the rear, beyond the beer kegs on tap, were small, round tables and chairs. The barkeeper was blue-eyed, and had fair, silky hair peeping out from under a black silk skull-cap. I remember he wore a brown Cardigan jacket, and I know precisely the spot, in the midst of the array of bottles, from which he took the bottle of red-coloured syrup. He and my father talked long, and I sipped my sweet drink and worshipped him. And for years afterward I worshipped the memory of him.

Despite my two disastrous experiences, here was John Barleycorn, prevalent and accessible everywhere in the community, luring and drawing me. Here were connotations of the saloon making deep indentations in a child's mind. Here was a child, forming its first judgments of the world, finding the saloon a delightful and desirable place. Stores, nor public buildings, nor all the dwellings of men ever opened their doors to me and let me warm by their fires or permitted me to eat the food of the gods from narrow shelves against the wall. Their doors were ever closed to me; the saloon's doors were ever open. And always and everywhere I found saloons, on highway and byway, up narrow alleys and on busy thoroughfares, bright-lighted and cheerful, warm in winter, and in summer dark and cool. Yes, the saloon was a mighty fine place, and it was more than that.

By the time I was ten years old, my family had abandoned ranching and gone to live in the city. And here, at ten, I began on the streets as a newsboy. One of the reasons for this was that we needed the money. Another reason was that I needed the exercise. I had found my way to the free public library, and was reading myself into nervous prostration. On the poor ranches on which I had lived there had been no books. In ways truly miraculous, I had been lent four books, marvellous books, and them I had devoured. One was the life of Garfield; the second, Paul du Chaillu's African travels; the third, a novel by Ouida with the last forty pages missing; and the fourth, Irving's "Alhambra." This last had been lent me by a school-teacher. I was not a forward child. Unlike Oliver Twist, I was incapable of asking for more. When I returned the "Alhambra" to the teacher I hoped she would lend me another book. And because she did not—most likely she deemed me unappreciative—I cried all the way home on the three-mile tramp from the school to the ranch. I waited and yearned for her to lend me another book. Scores of times I nerved myself almost to the point of asking her, but never quite reached the necessary pitch of effrontery.

And then came the city of Oakland, and on the shelves of that free library I discovered all the great world beyond the skyline. Here were thousands of books as good as my four wonder-books, and some were even better. Libraries were not concerned with children in those days, and I had strange adventures. I remember, in the catalogue, being impressed by the title, "The Adventures of Peregrine Pickle." I filled an application blank and the librarian handed me the collected and entirely unexpurgated works of Smollett in one huge volume. I read everything, but principally history and adventure, and all the old travels and voyages. I read mornings, afternoons, and nights. I read in bed, I read at table, I read as I walked to and from school, and I read at recess while the other boys were playing. I began to get the "jerks." To everybody I replied: "Go away. You make me nervous."

And so, at ten, I was out on the streets, a newsboy. I had no time to read. I was busy getting exercise and learning how to fight, busy learning forwardness, and brass and bluff. I had an imagination and a curiosity about all things that made me plastic. Not least among the things I was curious about was the saloon. And I was in and out of many a one. I remember, in those days, on the east side of Broadway, between Sixth and Seventh, from corner to corner, there was a solid block of saloons.

In the saloons life was different. Men talked with great voices, laughed great laughs, and there was an atmosphere of greatness. Here was something more than common every-day where nothing happened. Here life was always very live, and, sometimes, even lurid, when blows were struck, and blood was shed, and big policemen came shouldering in. Great moments, these, for me, my head filled with all the wild and valiant fighting of the gallant adventurers on sea and land. There were no big moments when I trudged along the street throwing my papers in at doors. But in the saloons, even the sots, stupefied, sprawling across the tables or in the sawdust, were objects of mystery and wonder.

And more, the saloons were right. The city fathers sanctioned them and licensed them. They were not the terrible places I heard boys deem them who lacked my opportunities to know. Terrible they might be, but then that only meant they were terribly wonderful, and it is the terribly wonderful that a boy desires to know. In the same way pirates, and shipwrecks, and battles were terrible; and what healthy boy wouldn't give his immortal soul to participate in such affairs?

Besides, in saloons I saw reporters, editors, lawyers, judges, whose names and faces I knew. They put the seal of social approval on the saloon. They verified my own feeling of fascination in the saloon. They, too, must have found there that something different, that something beyond, which I sensed and groped after. What it was, I did not know; yet there it must be, for there men focused like buzzing flies about a honey pot. I had no sorrows, and the world was very bright, so I could not guess that what these men sought was forgetfulness of jaded toil and stale grief.

Not that I drank at that time. From ten to fifteen I rarely tasted liquor, but I was intimately in contact with drinkers and drinking places. The only reason I did not drink was because I didn't like the stuff. As the time passed, I worked as boy-helper on an ice-wagon, set up pins in a bowling alley with a saloon attached, and swept out saloons at Sunday picnic grounds.

Big jovial Josie Harper ran a road house at Telegraph Avenue and Thirty-ninth Street. Here for a year I delivered an evening paper, until my route was changed to the water-front and tenderloin of Oakland. The first month, when I collected Josie Harper's bill, she poured me a glass of wine. I was ashamed to refuse, so I drank it. But after that I watched the chance when she wasn't around so as to collect from her barkeeper.

The first day I worked in the bowling alley, the barkeeper, according to custom, called us boys up to have a drink after we had been setting up pins for several hours. The others asked for beer. I said I'd take ginger ale. The boys snickered, and I noticed the barkeeper favoured me with a strange, searching scrutiny. Nevertheless, he opened a bottle of ginger ale. Afterward, back in the alleys, in the pauses between games, the boys enlightened me. I had offended the barkeeper. A bottle of ginger ale cost the saloon ever so much more than a glass of steam beer; and it was up to me, if I wanted to hold my job, to drink beer. Besides, beer was food. I could work better on it. There was no food in ginger ale. After that, when I couldn't sneak out of it, I drank beer and wondered what men found in it that was so good. I was always aware that I was missing something.

What I really liked in those days was candy. For five cents I could buy five "cannon-balls"—big lumps of the most delicious lastingness. I could chew and worry a single one for an hour. Then there was a Mexican who sold big slabs of brown chewing taffy for five cents each. It required a quarter of a day properly to absorb one of them. And many a day I made my entire lunch off one of those slabs. In truth, I found food there, but not in beer.

CHAPTER VI

But the time was rapidly drawing near when I was to begin my second series of bouts with John Barleycorn. When I was fourteen, my head filled with the tales of the old voyagers, my vision with tropic isles and far sea-rims, I was sailing a small centreboard skiff around San Francisco Bay and on the Oakland Estuary. I wanted to go to sea. I wanted to get away from monotony and the commonplace. I was in the flower of my adolescence, a-thrill with romance and adventure, dreaming of wild life in the wild man-world. Little I guessed how all the warp and woof of that man-world was entangled with alcohol.

So, one day, as I hoisted sail on my skiff, I met Scotty. He was a husky youngster of seventeen, a runaway apprentice, he told me, from an English ship in Australia. He had just worked his way on another ship to San Francisco; and now he wanted to see about getting a berth on a whaler. Across the estuary, near where the whalers lay, was lying the sloop-yacht *Idler*. The caretaker was a harpooner who intended sailing next voyage on the whale ship *Bonanza*. Would I take him, Scotty, over in my skiff to call upon the harpooner?

Would I! Hadn't I heard the stories and rumours about the *Idler*?—the big sloop that had come up from the Sandwich Islands where it had been engaged in smuggling opium. And the harpooner who was caretaker! How often had I seen him and envied him his freedom. He never had to leave the water. He slept aboard the *Idler* each night, while I had to go home upon the land to go to bed. The harpooner was only nineteen years old (and I have never had anything but his own word that he was a harpooner); but he had been too shining and glorious a personality for me ever to address as I paddled around the yacht at a wistful distance. Would I take Scotty, the runaway sailor, to visit the harpooner, on the opium-smuggler *Idler*? *Would I!*

The harpooner came on deck to answer our hail, and invited us aboard. I played the sailor and the man, fending off the skiff so that it would not mar the yacht's white paint, dropping the skiff astern on a long painter, and making the painter fast with two nonchalant half-hitches.

We went below. It was the first sea-interior I had ever seen. The clothing on the wall smelled musty. But what of that? Was it not the sea-gear of men?—leather jackets lined with corduroy, blue coats of pilot cloth, sou'westers, sea-boots, oilskins. And everywhere was in evidence the economy of space—the narrow bunks, the swinging tables, the incredible lockers. There were the tell-tale compass, the sea-lamps in their gimbals, the blue-backed charts carelessly rolled and tucked away, the signal-flags in alphabetical order, and a mariner's dividers jammed into the woodwork to hold a calendar. At last I was living. Here I sat, inside my first ship, a smuggler, accepted as a comrade by a harpooner and a runaway English sailor who said his name was Scotty.

The first thing that the harpooner, aged nineteen, and the sailor, aged seventeen, did to show that they were men was to behave like men. The harpooner suggested the eminent desirableness of a drink, and Scotty searched his pockets for dimes and nickels. Then the harpooner carried away a pink flask to be filled in some blind pig, for there were no licensed saloons in that locality. We drank the cheap rotgut out of tumblers. Was I any the less strong, any the less valiant, than the harpooner and the sailor? They were men. They proved it by the way they drank. Drink was the badge of manhood. So I drank with them, drink by drink, raw and straight, though the damned stuff couldn't compare with a stick of chewing taffy or a delectable "cannon-ball." I shuddered and swallowed my gorge with every drink, though I manfully hid all such symptoms.

Divers times we filled the flask that afternoon. All I had was twenty cents, but I put it up like a man, though with secret regret at the enormous store of candy it could have bought. The liquor mounted in the heads of all of us, and the talk of Scotty and the harpooner was upon running the Easting down, gales off the Horn and pamperos off the Plate, lower topsail breezes, southerly busters, North Pacific gales, and of smashed whaleboats in the Arctic ice.

"You can't swim in that ice water," said the harpooner confidentially to me. "You double up in a minute and go down. When a whale smashes your boat, the thing to do is to get your belly across an oar, so that when the cold doubles you you'll float."

"Sure," I said, with a grateful nod and an air of certitude that I, too, would hunt whales and be in smashed boats in the Arctic Ocean. And, truly, I registered his advice as singularly valuable information, and filed it away in my brain, where it persists to this day.

But I couldn't talk—at first. Heavens! I was only fourteen, and had never been on the ocean in my life. I could only listen to the two sea-dogs, and show my manhood by drinking with them, fairly and squarely, drink and drink.

The liquor worked its will with me; the talk of Scotty and the harpooner poured through the pent space of the *Idler's* cabin and through my brain like great gusts of wide, free wind; and in imagination I lived my years to come and rocked over the wild, mad, glorious world on multitudinous adventures.

We unbent. Our inhibitions and taciturnities vanished. We were as if we had known each other for years and years, and we pledged ourselves to years of future voyagings together. The harpooner told of misadventures and secret shames. Scotty wept over his poor old mother in Edinburgh—a lady, he insisted, gently born—who was in reduced circumstances, who had pinched herself to pay the lump sum to the ship-owners for his apprenticeship, whose sacrificing dream had been to see him a merchantman officer and a gentleman, and who was heartbroken because he had deserted his ship in Australia and joined another as a common sailor before the mast. And Scotty proved it. He drew her last sad letter from his pocket and wept

210

over it as he read it aloud. The harpooner and I wept with him, and swore that all three of us would ship on the whaleship *Bonanza*, win a big pay-day, and, still together, make a pilgrimage to Edinburgh and lay our store of money in the dear lady's lap.

And, as John Barleycorn heated his way into my brain, thawing my reticence, melting my modesty, talking through me and with me and as me, my adopted twin brother and alter ego, I, too, raised my voice to show myself a man and an adventurer, and bragged in detail and at length of how I had crossed San Francisco Bay in my open skiff in a roaring southwester when even the schooner sailors doubted my exploit. Further, I—or John Barleycorn, for it was the same thing—told Scotty that he might be a deep-sea sailor and know the last rope on the great deep-sea ships, but that when it came to small-boat sailing I could beat him hands down and sail circles around him.

The best of it was that my assertion and brag were true. With reticence and modesty present, I could never have dared tell Scotty my small-boat estimate of him. But it is ever the way of John Barleycorn to loosen the tongue and babble the secret thought.

Scotty, or John Barleycorn, or the pair, was very naturally offended by my remarks. Nor was I loath. I could whip any runaway sailor seventeen years old. Scotty and I flared and raged like young cockerels, until the harpooner poured another round of drinks to enable us to forgive and make up. Which we did, arms around each other's necks, protesting vows of eternal friendship—just like Black Matt and Tom Morrisey, I remembered, in the ranch kitchen in San Mateo. And, remembering, I knew that I was at last a man—despite my meagre fourteen years—a man as big and manly as those two strapping giants who had quarrelled and made up on that memorable Sunday morning of long ago.

By this time the singing stage was reached, and I joined Scotty and the harpooner in snatches of sea songs and chanties. It was here, in the cabin of the *Idler*, that I first heard "Blow the Man Down," "Flying Cloud," and "Whisky, Johnny, Whisky." Oh, it was brave. I was beginning to grasp the meaning of life. Here was no commonplace, no Oakland Estuary, no weary round of throwing newspapers at front doors, delivering ice, and setting up ninepins. All the world was mine, all its paths were under my feet, and John Barleycorn, tricking my fancy, enabled me to anticipate the life of adventure for which I yearned.

We were not ordinary. We were three tipsy young gods, incredibly wise, gloriously genial, and without limit to our powers. Ah!—and I say it now, after the years—could John Barleycorn keep one at such a height, I should never draw a sober breath again. But this is not a world of free freights. One pays according to an iron schedule—for every strength the balanced weakness; for every high a corresponding low; for every fictitious god-like moment an equivalent time in reptilian slime. For every feat of telescoping long days and weeks of life into mad magnificent instants, one must pay with shortened life, and, oft-times, with savage usury added.

Intenseness and duration are as ancient enemies as fire and water. They are mutually destructive. They cannot co-exist. And John Barleycorn, mighty necromancer though he be, is as much a slave to organic chemistry as we mortals are. We pay for every nerve marathon we run, nor can John Barleycorn intercede and fend off the just payment. He can lead us to the heights, but he cannot keep us there, else would we all be devotees. And there is no devotee but pays for the mad dances John Barleycorn pipes.

Yet the foregoing is all in after wisdom spoken. It was no part of the knowledge of the lad, fourteen years old, who sat in the *Idler*'s cabin between the harpooner and the sailor, the air rich in his nostrils with the musty smell of men's sea-gear, roaring in chorus: "Yankee ship come down de ribber—pull, my bully boys, pull!"

We grew maudlin, and all talked and shouted at once. I had a splendid constitution, a stomach that would digest scrap-iron, and I was still running my marathon in full vigour when Scotty began to fail and fade. His talk grew incoherent. He groped for words and could not find them, while the ones he found his lips were unable to form. His poisoned consciousness was leaving him. The brightness went out of his eyes, and he looked as stupid as were his efforts to talk. His face and body sagged as his consciousness sagged. (A man cannot sit upright save by an act of will.) Scotty's reeling brain could not control his muscles. All his correlations were breaking down. He strove to take another drink, and feebly dropped the tumbler on the floor. Then, to my amazement, weeping bitterly, he rolled into a bunk on his back and immediately snored off to sleep.

The harpooner and I drank on, grinning in a superior way to each other over Scotty's plight. The last flask was opened, and we drank it between us, to the accompaniment of Scotty's stertorous breathing. Then the harpooner faded away into his bunk, and I was left alone, unthrown, on the field of battle.

I was very proud, and John Barleycorn was proud with me. I could carry my drink. I was a man. I had drunk two men, drink for drink, into unconsciousness. And I was still on my two feet, upright, making my way on deck to get air into my scorching lungs. It was in this bout on the *Idler* that I discovered what a good stomach and a strong head I had for drink—a bit of knowledge that was to be a source of pride in succeeding years, and that ultimately I was to come to consider a great affliction. The fortunate man is the one who cannot take more than a couple of drinks without becoming intoxicated. The unfortunate wight is the one who can take many glasses without betraying a sign, who must take numerous glasses in order to get the "kick."

The sun was setting when I came on the *Idler*'s deck. There were plenty of bunks below. I did not need to go home. But I wanted to demonstrate to myself how much I was a man. There lay my skiff astern. The last of a strong ebb was running out in channel in the teeth of an ocean breeze of forty miles an hour. I could see the stiff whitecaps, and the suck and run of the current was plainly visible in the face and trough of each one.

I set sail, cast off, took my place at the tiller, the sheet in my hand, and headed across channel. The skiff heeled over and plunged into it madly. The spray began to fly. I was at the pinnacle of exaltation. I sang "Blow the Man Down" as I sailed. I was no boy of fourteen, living the mediocre ways of the sleepy town called Oakland. I was a man, a god, and the very elements rendered me allegiance as I bitted them to my will.

The tide was out. A full hundred yards of soft mud intervened between the boat-wharf and the water. I pulled up my centreboard, ran full tilt into the mud, took in sail, and, standing in the stern, as I had often done at low tide, I began to shove the skiff with an oar. It was then that my correlations began to break down. I lost my balance and pitched head-foremost into the ooze. Then, and for the first time, as I floundered to my feet covered with slime, the blood running down my arms from a scrape against a barnacled stake, I knew that I was drunk. But what of it? Across the channel two strong sailormen lay unconscious in their bunks where I had drunk them. I *was* a man. I was still on my legs, if they were knee-deep in mud. I disdained to get back into the skiff. I waded through the mud, shoving the skiff before me and yammering the chant of my manhood to the world.

I paid for it. I was sick for a couple of days, meanly sick, and my arms were painfully poisoned from the barnacle scratches. For a week I could not use them, and it was a torture to put on and take off my clothes.

I swore, "Never again!" The game wasn't worth it. The price was too stiff. I had no moral qualms. My revulsion was purely physical. No exalted moments were worth such hours of misery and wretchedness. When I got back to my skiff, I shunned the *Idler*. I would cross the opposite side of the channel to go around her. Scotty had disappeared. The harpooner was still about, but him I avoided. Once, when he landed on the boat-wharf, I hid in a shed so as to escape seeing him. I was afraid he would propose some more drinking, maybe have a flask full of whisky in his pocket.

And yet—and here enters the necromancy of John Barleycorn—that afternoon's drunk on the *Idler* had been a purple passage flung into the monotony of my days. It was memorable. My mind dwelt on it continually. I went over the details, over and over again. Among other things, I had got into the cogs and springs of men's actions. I had seen Scotty weep about his own worthlessness and the sad case of his Edinburgh mother who was a lady. The harpooner had told me terribly wonderful things of himself. I had caught a myriad enticing and inflammatory hints of a world beyond my world, and for which I was certainly as fitted as the two lads who had drunk with me. I had got behind men's souls. I had got behind my own soul and found unguessed potencies and greatnesses.

Yes, that day stood out above all my other days. To this day it so stands out. The memory of it is branded in my brain. But the price exacted was too high. I refused to play and pay, and returned to my cannon-balls and taffy-slabs. The point is that all the chemistry of my healthy, normal body drove me away from alcohol. The stuff didn't agree with me. It was abominable. But, despite this, circumstance was to continue to drive me toward John Barleycorn, to drive me again and again, until, after long years, the time should come when I would look up John Barleycorn in every haunt of men—look him up and hail him gladly as benefactor and friend. And detest and hate him all the time. Yes, he is a strange friend, John Barleycorn.

CHAPTER VII

I was barely turned fifteen, and working long hours in a cannery. Month in and month out, the shortest day I ever worked was ten hours. When to ten hours of actual work at a machine is added the noon hour; the walking to work and walking home from work; the getting up in the morning, dressing, and eating; the eating at night, undressing, and going to bed, there remains no more than the nine hours out of the twenty-four required by a healthy youngster for sleep. Out of those nine hours, after I was in bed and ere my eyes drowsed shut, I managed to steal a little time for reading.

But many a night I did not knock off work until midnight. On occasion I worked eighteen and twenty hours on a stretch. Once I worked at my machine for thirty-six consecutive hours. And there were weeks on end when I never knocked off work earlier than eleven o'clock, got home and in bed at half after midnight, and was called at half-past five to dress, eat, walk to work, and be at my machine at seven o'clock whistle blow.

No moments here to be stolen for my beloved books. And what had John Barleycorn to do with such strenuous, Stoic toil of a lad just turned fifteen? He had everything to do with it. Let me show you. I asked myself if this were the meaning of life—to be a work-beast? I knew of no horse in the city of Oakland that worked the hours I worked. If this were living, I was entirely unenamoured of it. I remembered my skiff, lying idle and accumulating barnacles at the boat-wharf; I remembered the wind that blew every day on the bay, the sunrises and sunsets I never saw; the bite of the salt air in my nostrils, the bite of the salt water on my flesh when I plunged overside; I remembered all the beauty and the wonder and the sense-delights of the world denied me. There was only one way to escape my deadening toil. I must get out and away on the water. I must earn my bread on the water. And the way of the water led inevitably to John Barleycorn. I did not know this. And when I did learn it, I was courageous enough not to retreat back to my bestial life at the machine.

I wanted to be where the winds of adventure blew. And the winds of adventure blew the oyster pirate sloops up and down San Francisco Bay, from raided oyster-beds and fights at night on shoal and flat, to markets in the morning against city wharves, where peddlers and saloon-keepers came down to buy. Every raid on an oyster-bed was a felony. The penalty was State imprisonment, the stripes and the lockstep. And what of that? The men in stripes worked a shorter day than I at my machine. And there was vastly more romance in being an oyster pirate or a convict than in being a machine slave. And behind it all, behind all of me with youth abubble, whispered Romance, Adventure.

So I interviewed my Mammy Jennie, my old nurse at whose black breast I had suckled. She was more prosperous than my folks. She was nursing sick people at a good weekly wage. Would she lend her "white child" the money? *Would she?* What she had was mine.

Then I sought out French Frank, the oyster pirate, who wanted to sell, I had heard, his sloop, the *Razzle Dazzle*. I found him lying at anchor on the Alameda side of the estuary near the Webster Street bridge, with visitors aboard, whom he was entertaining with afternoon wine. He came on deck to talk business. He was willing to sell. But it was Sunday. Besides, he had guests. On the morrow he would make out the bill of sale and I could enter into possession. And in the meantime I must come below and meet his friends. They were two sisters, Mamie and Tess; a Mrs. Hadley, who chaperoned them; "Whisky" Bob, a youthful oyster pirate of sixteen; and "Spider" Healey, a black-whiskered wharf-rat of twenty. Mamie, who was Spider's niece, was called the Queen of the Oyster Pirates, and, on occasion, presided at their revels. French Frank was in love with her, though I did not know it at the time; and she steadfastly refused to marry him.

French Frank poured a tumbler of red wine from a big demijohn to drink to our transaction. I remembered the red wine of the Italian rancho, and shuddered inwardly. Whisky and beer were not quite so repulsive. But the Queen of the Oyster Pirates was looking at me, a part-emptied glass in her own hand. I had my pride. If I was only fifteen, at least I could not show myself any less a man than she. Besides, there were her sister, and Mrs. Hadley, and the young oyster pirate, and the whiskered wharf-rat, all with glasses in their hands. Was I a milk-and-water sop? No; a thousand times no, and a thousand glasses no. I downed the tumblerful like a man.

French Frank was elated by the sale, which I had bound with a twenty-dollar goldpiece. He poured more wine. I had learned my strong head and stomach, and I was certain I could drink with them in a temperate way and not poison myself for a week to come. I could stand as much as they; and besides, they had already been drinking for some time.

We got to singing. Spider sang "The Boston Burglar" and "Black Lulu." The Queen sang "Then I Wisht I Were a Little Bird." And her sister Tess sang "Oh, Treat My Daughter Kindily." The fun grew fast and furious. I found myself able to miss drinks without being noticed or called to account. Also, standing in the companionway, head and shoulders out and glass in hand, I could fling the wine overboard.

I reasoned something like this: It is a queerness of these people that they like this vile-tasting wine. Well, let them. I cannot quarrel with their tastes. My manhood, according to their queer notions, must compel me to appear to like this wine. Very well. I shall so appear. But I shall drink no more than is unavoidable.

And the Queen began to make love to me, the latest recruit to the oyster pirate fleet, and no mere hand, but a master and owner. She went upon deck to take the air, and took me with her. She knew, of course, but I never dreamed, how French Frank was raging down below. Then Tess joined us, sitting on the cabin; and Spider, and Bob; and at the last, Mrs. Hadley and French Frank. And we sat there, glasses in hand, and sang, while the big demijohn went around; and I was the only strictly sober one.

And I enjoyed it as no one of them was able to enjoy it. Here, in this atmosphere of bohemianism, I could not but contrast the scene with my scene of the day before, sitting at my machine, in the stifling, shut-in air, repeating, endlessly repeating, at top speed, my series of mechanical motions. And here I sat now, glass in hand, in warm-glowing camaraderie, with the oyster pirates, adventurers who refused to be slaves to petty routine, who flouted restrictions and the law, who carried their lives and their liberty in their hands. And it was through John Barleycorn that I came to join this glorious company of free souls, unashamed and unafraid.

And the afternoon seabreeze blew its tang into my lungs, and curled the waves in mid-channel. Before it came the scow schooners, wing-and-wing, blowing their horns for the drawbridges to open. Red-stacked tugs tore by, rocking the *Razzle Dazzle* in the waves of their wake. A sugar barque towed from the "boneyard" to sea. The sun-wash was on the crisping water, and life was big. And Spider sang:

"Oh, it's Lulu, black Lulu, my darling,
Oh, it's where have you been so long?
Been layin' in jail,
A-waitin' for bail,
Till my bully comes rollin' along."

There it was, the smack and slap of the spirit of revolt, of adventure, of romance, of the things forbidden and done defiantly and grandly. And I knew that on the morrow I would not go back to my machine at the cannery. To-morrow I would be an oyster pirate, as free a freebooter as the century and the waters of San Francisco Bay would permit. Spider had already agreed to sail with me as my crew of one, and, also, as cook while I did the deck work. We would outfit our grub and water in the morning, hoist the big mainsail (which was a bigger piece of canvas than any I had ever sailed under), and beat our way out the estuary on the first of the seabreeze and the last of the ebb. Then we would slack sheets, and on the first of the flood run down the bay to the Asparagus Islands, where we would anchor miles off shore. And at last my dream would be realised: I would sleep upon the water. And next morning I would wake upon the water; and thereafter all my days and nights would be on the water.

And the Queen asked me to row her ashore in my skiff, when at sunset French Frank prepared to take his guests ashore. Nor did I catch the significance of his abrupt change of plan when he turned the task of rowing his skiff over to Whisky Bob, himself remaining on board the sloop. Nor did I understand Spider's grinning side-remark to me: "Gee! There's nothin' slow about *you*." How could it possibly enter my boy's head that a grizzled man of fifty should be jealous of me?

CHAPTER VIII

We met by appointment, early Monday morning, to complete the deal, in Johnny Heinhold's "Last Chance"—a saloon, of course, for the transactions of men. I paid the money over, received the bill of sale, and French Frank treated. This struck me as an evident custom, and a logical one—the seller, who receives the money, to wet a piece of it in the establishment where the trade was consummated. But, to my surprise, French Frank treated the house. He and I drank, which seemed just; but why should Johnny Heinhold, who owned the saloon and waited behind the bar, be invited to drink? I figured it immediately that he made a profit on the very drink he drank. I could, in a way, considering that they were friends and shipmates, understand Spider and Whisky Bob being asked to drink; but why should the longshoremen, Bill Kelley and Soup Kennedy, be asked?

Then there was Pat, the Queen's brother, making a total of eight of us. It was early morning, and all ordered whisky. What could I do, here in this company of big men, all drinking whisky? "Whisky," I said, with the careless air of one who had said it a thousand times. And such whisky! I tossed it down. A-r-r-r-gh! I can taste it yet.

And I was appalled at the price French Frank had paid—eighty cents. *Eighty cents*! It was an outrage to my thrifty soul. Eighty cents—the equivalent of eight long hours of my toil at the machine, gone down our throats, and gone like that, in a twinkling, leaving only a bad taste in the mouth. There was no discussion that French Frank was a waster.

I was anxious to be gone, out into the sunshine, out over the water to my glorious boat. But all hands lingered. Even Spider, my crew, lingered. No hint broke through my obtuseness of why they lingered. I have often thought since of how they must have regarded me, the newcomer being welcomed into their company standing at bar with them, and not standing for a single round of drinks.

French Frank, who, unknown to me, had swallowed his chagrin since the day before, now that the money for the *Razzle Dazzle* was in his pocket, began to behave curiously toward me. I sensed the change in his attitude, saw the forbidding glitter in his eyes, and wondered. The more I saw of men, the queerer they became. Johnny Heinhold leaned across the bar and whispered in my ear, "He's got it in for you. Watch out."

I nodded comprehension of his statement, and acquiescence in it, as a man should nod who knows all about men. But secretly I was perplexed. Heavens! How was I, who had worked hard and read books of adventure, and who was only fifteen years old, who had not dreamed of giving the Queen of the Oyster Pirates a second thought, and who did not know that French Frank was madly and Latinly in love with her—how was I to guess that I had done him shame? And how was I to guess that the story of how the Queen had thrown him down on his own boat, the moment I hove in sight, was already the gleeful gossip of the water-front? And by the same token, how was I to guess that her brother Pat's offishness with me was anything else than temperamental gloominess of spirit?

Whisky Bob got me aside a moment. "Keep your eyes open," he muttered. "Take my tip. French Frank's ugly. I'm going up river with him to get a schooner for oystering. When he gets down on the beds, watch out. He says he'll run you down. After dark, any time he's around, change your anchorage and douse your riding light. Savve?"

Oh, certainly, I savve'd. I nodded my head, and, as one man to another, thanked him for his tip; and drifted back to the group at the bar. No; I did not treat. I never dreamed that I was expected to treat. I left with Spider, and my ears burn now as I try to surmise the things they must have said about me.

I asked Spider, in an off-hand way, what was eating French Frank. "He's crazy jealous of you," was the answer. "Do you think so?" I said, and dismissed the matter as not worth thinking about.

But I leave it to any one—the swell of my fifteen-years-old manhood at learning that French Frank, the adventurer of fifty, the sailor of all the seas of all the world, was jealous of me—and jealous over a girl most romantically named the Queen of the Oyster Pirates. I had read of such things in books, and regarded them as personal probabilities of a distant maturity. Oh, I felt a rare young devil, as we hoisted the big mainsail that morning, broke out anchor, and filled away close-hauled on the three-mile beat to windward out into the bay.

Such was my escape from the killing machine-toil, and my introduction to the oyster pirates. True, the introduction had begun with drink, and the life promised to continue with drink. But was I to stay away from it for such reason? Wherever life ran free and great, there men drank. Romance and Adventure seemed always to go down the street locked arm in arm with John Barleycorn. To know the two, I must know the third. Or else I must go back to my free library books and read of the deeds of other men and do no deeds of my own save slave for ten cents an hour at a machine in a cannery.

No; I was not to be deterred from this brave life on the water by the fact that the water-dwellers had queer and expensive desires for beer and wine and whisky. What if their notions of happiness included the strange one of seeing me drink? When they persisted in buying the stuff and thrusting it upon me, why, I would drink it. It was the price I would pay for their comradeship. And I didn't have to get drunk. I had not got drunk the Sunday afternoon I arranged to buy the *Razzle Dazzle*, despite the fact that not one of the rest was sober. Well, I could go on into the future that way, drinking the stuff when it gave them pleasure that I should drink it, but carefully avoiding over-drinking.

CHAPTER IX

Gradual as was my development as a heavy drinker among the oyster pirates, the real heavy drinking came suddenly, and was the result, not of desire for alcohol, but of an intellectual conviction.

The more I saw of the life, the more I was enamoured of it. I can never forget my thrills the first night I took part in a concerted raid, when we assembled on board the Annie—rough men, big and unafraid, and weazened wharf-rats, some of

218

them ex-convicts, all of them enemies of the law and meriting jail, in sea-boots and sea-gear, talking in gruff low voices, and "Big" George with revolvers strapped about his waist to show that he meant business.

Oh, I know, looking back, that the whole thing was sordid and silly. But I was not looking back in those days when I was rubbing shoulders with John Barleycorn and beginning to accept him. The life was brave and wild, and I was living the adventure I had read so much about.

Nelson, "Young Scratch" they called him, to distinguish him from "Old Scratch," his father, sailed in the sloop *Reindeer*, partners with one "Clam." Clam was a dare-devil, but Nelson was a reckless maniac. He was twenty years old, with the body of a Hercules. When he was shot in Benicia, a couple of years later, the coroner said he was the greatest-shouldered man he had ever seen laid on a slab.

Nelson could not read or write. He had been "dragged" up by his father on San Francisco Bay, and boats were second nature with him. His strength was prodigious, and his reputation along the water-front for violence was anything but savoury. He had Berserker rages and did mad, terrible things. I made his acquaintance the first cruise of the *Razzle Dazzle*, and saw him sail the *Reindeer* in a blow and dredge oysters all around the rest of us as we lay at two anchors, troubled with fear of going ashore.

He was some man, this Nelson; and when, passing by the Last Chance saloon, he spoke to me, I felt very proud. But try to imagine my pride when he promptly asked me in to have a drink. I stood at the bar and drank a glass of beer with him, and talked manfully of oysters, and boats, and of the mystery of who had put the load of buckshot through the *Annie*'s mainsail.

We talked and lingered at the bar. It seemed to me strange that we lingered. We had had our beer. But who was I to lead the way outside when great Nelson chose to lean against the bar? After a few minutes, to my surprise, he asked me to have another drink, which I did. And still we talked, and Nelson evinced no intention of leaving the bar.

Bear with me while I explain the way of my reasoning and of my innocence. First of all, I was very proud to be in the company of Nelson, who was the most heroic figure among the oyster pirates and bay adventurers. Unfortunately for my stomach and mucous membranes, Nelson had a strange quirk of nature that made him find happiness in treating me to beer. I had no moral disinclination for beer, and just because I didn't like the taste of it and the weight of it was no reason I should forgo the honour of his company. It was his whim to drink beer, and to have me drink beer with him. Very well, I would put up with the passing discomfort.

So we continued to talk at the bar, and to drink beer ordered and paid for by Nelson. I think, now, when I look back upon it, that Nelson was curious. He wanted to find out just what kind of a gink I was. He wanted to see how many times I'd let him treat without offering to treat in return.

After I had drunk half a dozen glasses, my policy of temperateness in mind, I decided that I had had enough for that time. So I mentioned that I was going aboard the *Razzle Dazzle*, then lying at the city wharf, a hundred yards away.

I said good-bye to Nelson, and went on down the wharf. But, John Barleycorn, to the extent of six glasses, went with me. My brain tingled and was very much alive. I was uplifted by my sense of manhood. I, a truly-true oyster pirate, was going aboard my own boat after hob-nobbing in the Last Chance with Nelson, the greatest oyster pirate of us all. Strong in my brain was the vision of us leaning against the bar and drinking beer. And curious it was, I decided, this whim of nature that made men happy in spending good money for beer for a fellow like me who didn't want it.

As I pondered this, I recollected that several times other men, in couples, had entered the Last Chance, and first one, then the other, had treated to drinks. I remembered, on the drunk on the *Idler*, how Scotty and the harpooner and myself had raked and scraped dimes and nickels with which to buy the whisky. Then came my boy code: when on a day a fellow gave another a "cannon-ball" or a chunk of taffy, on some other day he would expect to receive back a cannon-ball or a chunk of taffy.

That was why Nelson had lingered at the bar. Having bought a drink, he had waited for me to buy one. *I had let him buy six drinks and never once offered to treat.* And he was the great Nelson! I could feel myself blushing with shame. I sat down on the stringer-piece of the wharf and buried my face in my hands. And the heat of my shame burned up my neck and into my cheeks and forehead. I have blushed many times in my life, but never have I experienced so terrible a blush as that one.

And sitting there on the stringer-piece in my shame, I did a great deal of thinking and transvaluing of values. I had been born poor. Poor I had lived. I had gone hungry on occasion. I had never had toys nor playthings like other children. My first memories of life were pinched by poverty. The pinch of poverty had been chronic. I was eight years old when I wore my first little undershirt actually sold in a store across the counter. And then it had been only one little undershirt. When it was soiled I had to return to the awful home-made things until it was washed. I had been so proud of it that I insisted on wearing it without any outer garment. For the first time I mutinied against my mother—mutinied myself into hysteria, until she let me wear the store undershirt so all the world could see.

Only a man who has undergone famine can properly value food; only sailors and desert-dwellers know the meaning of fresh water. And only a child, with a child's imagination, can come to know the meaning of things it has been long denied. I early discovered that the only things I could have were those I got for myself. My meagre childhood developed meagreness. The first things I had been able to get for myself had been cigarette pictures, cigarette posters, and cigarette albums. I had not had the spending of the money I earned, so I traded "extra" newspapers for these treasures. I traded duplicates with the other boys, and circulating, as I did, all about town, I had greater opportunities for trading and acquiring.

It was not long before I had complete every series issued by every cigarette manufacturer—such as the Great Race Horses, Parisian Beauties, Women of All Nations, Flags of All Nations, Noted Actors, Champion Prize Fighters, etc. And each series I had three different ways: in the card from the cigarette package, in the poster, and in the album.

Then I began to accumulate duplicate sets, duplicate albums. I traded for other things that boys valued and which they usually bought with money given them by their parents. Naturally, they did not have the keen sense of values that I had, who was never given money to buy anything. I traded for postage-stamps, for minerals, for curios, for birds' eggs, for marbles (I had a more magnificent collection of agates than I have ever seen any boy possess—and the nucleus of the collection was a handful worth at least three dollars, which I had kept as security for twenty cents I loaned to a messenger-boy who was sent to reform school before he could redeem them).

I'd trade anything and everything for anything else, and turn it over in a dozen more trades until it was transmuted into something that was worth something. I was famous as a trader. I was notorious as a miser. I could even make a junkman weep when I had dealings with him. Other boys called me in to sell for them their collections of bottles, rags, old iron, grain, and gunny-sacks, and five-gallon oil-cans—aye, and gave me a commission for doing it.

And this was the thrifty, close-fisted boy, accustomed to slave at a machine for ten cents an hour, who sat on the stringer-piece and considered the matter of beer at five cents a glass and gone in a moment with nothing to show for it. I was now with men I admired. I was proud to be with them. Had all my pinching and saving brought me the equivalent of one of the many thrills which had been mine since I came among the oyster pirates? Then what was worth while—money or thrills? These men had no horror of squandering a nickel, or many nickels. They were magnificently careless of money, calling up eight men to drink whisky at ten cents a glass, as French Frank had done. Why, Nelson had just spent sixty cents on beer for the two of us.

Which was it to be? I was aware that I was making a grave decision. I was deciding between money and men, between niggardliness and romance. Either I must throw overboard all my old values of money and look upon it as something to be flung about wastefully, or I must throw overboard my comradeship with these men whose peculiar quirks made them like strong drink.

I retraced my steps up the wharf to the Last Chance, where Nelson still stood outside. "Come on and have a beer," I invited. Again we stood at the bar and drank and talked, but this time it was I who paid ten cents! a whole hour of my labour at a machine for a drink of something I didn't want and which tasted rotten. But it wasn't difficult. I had achieved a concept. Money no longer counted. It was comradeship that counted. "Have another?" I said. And we had another, and I paid for it. Nelson, with the wisdom of the skilled drinker, said to the barkeeper, "Make mine a small one, Johnny." Johnny nodded and gave him a glass that contained only a third as much as the glasses we had been drinking. Yet the charge was the same—five cents.

By this time I was getting nicely jingled, so such extravagance didn't hurt me much. Besides, I was learning. There was more in this buying of drinks than mere quantity. I got my finger on it. There was a stage when the beer didn't count at all, but just the spirit of comradeship of drinking together. And, ha!—another thing! I, too, could call for small beers and minimise by two-thirds the detestable freightage with which comradeship burdened one.

"I had to go aboard to get some money," I remarked casually, as we drank, in the hope Nelson would take it as an explanation of why I had let him treat six consecutive times.

"Oh, well, you didn't have to do that," he answered. "Johnny'll trust a fellow like you—won't you, Johnny!"

"Sure," Johnny agreed, with a smile.

"How much you got down against me?" Nelson queried.

Johnny pulled out the book he kept behind the bar, found Nelson's page, and added up the account of several dollars. At once I became possessed with a desire to have a page in that book. Almost it seemed the final badge of manhood.

After a couple more drinks, for which I insisted on paying, Nelson decided to go. We parted true comradely, and I wandered down the wharf to the *Razzle Dazzle*. Spider was just building the fire for supper.

"Where'd you get it?" he grinned up at me through the open companion.

"Oh, I've been with Nelson," I said carelessly, trying to hide my pride.

Then an idea came to me. Here was another one of them. Now that I had achieved my concept, I might as well practise it thoroughly. "Come on," I said, "up to Johnny's and have a drink."

Going up the wharf, we met Clam coming down. Clam was Nelson's partner, and he was a fine, brave, handsome, moustached man of thirty—everything, in short, that his nickname did not connote. "Come on," I said, "and have a drink." He came. As we turned into the Last Chance, there was Pat, the Queen's brother, coming out.

"What's your hurry?" I greeted him. "We're having a drink. Come on along." "I've just had one," he demurred. "What of it?—we're having one now," I retorted. And Pat consented to join us, and I melted my way into his good graces with a couple of glasses of beer. Oh! I was learning things that afternoon about John Barleycorn. There was more in him than the bad taste when you swallowed him. Here, at the absurd cost of ten cents, a gloomy, grouchy individual, who threatened to become an enemy, was made into a good friend. He became even genial, his looks were kindly, and our voices mellowed together as we talked water-front and oyster-bed gossip.

"Small beer for me, Johnny," I said, when the others had ordered schooners. Yes, and I said it like the accustomed drinker, carelessly, casually, as a sort of spontaneous thought that had just occurred to me. Looking back, I am confident that the only one there who guessed I was a tyro at bar-drinking was Johnny Heinhold.

"Where'd he get it?" I overheard Spider confidentially ask Johnny.

"Oh, he's been sousin' here with Nelson all afternoon," was Johnny's answer.

I never let on that I'd heard, but *proud*? Aye, even the barkeeper was giving me a recommendation as a man. *"He's been sousin' here with nelson all afternoon."* Magic words! The accolade delivered by a barkeeper with a beer glass!

I remembered that French Frank had treated Johnny the day I bought the *Razzle Dazzle*. The glasses were filled and we were ready to drink. "Have something yourself, Johnny," I said, with an air of having intended to say it all the time, but of having been a trifle remiss because of the interesting conversation I had been holding with Clam and Pat.

Johnny looked at me with quick sharpness, divining, I am positive, the strides I was making in my education, and poured himself whisky from his private bottle. This hit me for a moment on my thrifty side. He had taken a ten-cent drink when the rest of us were drinking five-cent drinks! But the hurt was only for a moment. I dismissed it as ignoble, remembered my concept, and did not give myself away.

"You'd better put me down in the book for this," I said, when we had finished the drink. And I had the satisfaction of seeing a fresh page devoted to my name and a charge pencilled for a round of drinks amounting to thirty cents. And I glimpsed, as through a golden haze, a future wherein that page would be much charged, and crossed off, and charged again.

I treated a second time around, and then, to my amazement, Johnny redeemed himself in that matter of the ten-cent drink. He treated us around from behind the bar, and I decided that he had arithmetically evened things up handsomely.

"Let's go around to the St. Louis House," Spider suggested when we got outside. Pat, who had been shovelling coal all day, had gone home, and Clam had gone upon the *Reindeer* to cook supper.

So around Spider and I went to the St. Louis House—my first visit—a huge barroom, where perhaps fifty men, mostly longshoremen, were congregated. And there I met Soup Kennedy for the second time, and Bill Kelley. And Smith, of the Annie, drifted in—he of the belt-buckled revolvers. And Nelson showed up. And I met others, including the Vigy brothers, who ran the place, and, chiefest of all, Joe Goose, with the wicked eyes, the twisted nose, and the flowered vest, who played the harmonica like a roystering angel and went on the most atrocious tears that even the Oakland water-front could conceive of and admire.

As I bought drinks—others treated as well—the thought flickered across my mind that Mammy Jennie wasn't going to be repaid much on her loan out of that week's earnings of the *Razzle Dazzle*. "But what of it?" I thought, or rather, John Barleycorn thought it for me. "You're a man and you're getting acquainted with men. Mammy Jennie doesn't need the money as promptly as all that. She isn't starving. You know that. She's got other money in the bank. Let her wait, and pay her back gradually."

And thus it was I learned another trait of John Barleycorn. He inhibits morality. Wrong conduct that it is impossible for one to do sober, is done quite easily when one is not sober. In fact, it is the only thing one can do, for John Barleycorn's inhibition rises like a wall between one's immediate desires and long-learned morality.

I dismissed my thought of debt to Mammy Jennie and proceeded to get acquainted at the trifling expense of some trifling money and a jingle that was growing unpleasant. Who took me on board and put me to bed that night I do not know, but I imagine it must have been Spider.

CHAPTER X

And so I won my manhood's spurs. My status on the water-front and with the oyster pirates became immediately excellent. I was looked upon as a good fellow, as well as no coward. And somehow, from the day I achieved that concept sitting on the stringer-piece of the Oakland City Wharf, I have never cared much for money. No one has ever considered me a miser since, while my carelessness of money is a source of anxiety and worry to some that know me.

So completely did I break with my parsimonious past that I sent word home to my mother to call in the boys of the neighbourhood and give to them all my collections. I never even cared to learn what boys got what collections. I was a man now, and I made a clean sweep of everything that bound me to my boyhood.

My reputation grew. When the story went around the water-front of how French Frank had tried to run me down with his schooner, and of how I had stood on the deck of the *Razzle Dazzle*, a cocked double-barrelled shotgun in my hands, steering with my feet and holding her to her course, and compelled him to put up his wheel and keep away, the water-front decided that there was something in me despite my youth. And I continued to show what was in me. There were the times I brought the *Razzle Dazzle* in with a bigger load of oysters than any other two-man craft; there was the time when we raided far down in Lower Bay, and mine was the only craft back at daylight to the anchorage off Asparagus Island; there was the Thursday night we raced for market and I brought the *Razzle Dazzle* in without a rudder, first of the fleet, and skimmed the cream of the Friday morning trade; and there was the time I brought her in from Upper Bay under a jib, when Scotty burned my mainsail. (Yes; it was Scotty of the *Idler* adventure. Irish had followed Spider on board the *Razzle Dazzle*, and Scotty, turning up, had taken Irish's place.)

But the things I did on the water only partly counted. What completed everything, and won for me the title of "Prince of the Oyster Beds," was that I was a good fellow ashore with my money, buying drinks like a man. I little dreamed that the time would come when the Oakland water-front, which had shocked me at first would be shocked and annoyed by the devilry of the things I did.

But always the life was tied up with drinking. The saloons are poor men's clubs. Saloons are congregating places. We engaged to meet one another in saloons. We celebrated our good fortune or wept our grief in saloons. We got acquainted in saloons.

Can I ever forget the afternoon I met "Old Scratch," Nelson's father? It was in the Last Chance. Johnny Heinhold introduced us. That Old Scratch was Nelson's father was noteworthy enough. But there was more in it than that. He was owner and master of the scow-schooner *Annie Mine*, and some day I might ship as a sailor with him. Still more, he was romance. He was a blue-eyed, yellow-haired, raw-boned Viking, big-bodied and strong-muscled despite his age. And he had sailed the seas in ships of all nations in the old savage sailing days.

I had heard many weird tales about him, and worshipped him from a distance. It took the saloon to bring us together. Even so, our acquaintance might have been no more than a hand-grip and a word—he was a laconic old fellow—had it not been for the drinking.

"Have a drink," I said, with promptitude, after the pause which I had learned good form in drinking dictates. Of course, while we drank our beer, which I had paid for, it was incumbent on him to listen to me and to talk to me. And Johnny, like a true host, made the tactful remarks that enabled us to find mutual topics of conversation. And of course, having drunk my beer, Captain Nelson must now buy beer in turn. This led to more talking, and Johnny drifted out of the conversation to wait on other customers.

The more beer Captain Nelson and I drank, the better we got acquainted. In me he found an appreciative listener, who, by virtue of book-reading, knew much about the sea-life he had lived. So he drifted back to his wild young days, and spun many a rare yarn for me, while we downed beer, treat by treat, all through a blessed summer afternoon. And it was only John Barleycorn that made possible that long afternoon with the old sea-dog.

It was Johnny Heinhold who secretly warned me across the bar that I was getting pickled and advised me to take small beers. But as long as Captain Nelson drank large beers, my pride forbade anything else than large beers. And not until the skipper ordered his first small beer did I order one for myself. Oh, when we came to a lingering fond farewell, I was drunk. But I had the satisfaction of seeing Old Scratch as drunk as I. My youthful modesty scarcely let me dare believe that the hardened old buccaneer was even more drunk.

And afterwards, from Spider, and Pat, and Clam, and Johnny Heinhold, and others, came the tips that Old Scratch liked me and had nothing but good words for the fine lad I was. Which was the more remarkable, because he was known as a savage, cantankerous old cuss who never liked anybody. (His very nickname, "Scratch," arose from a Berserker trick of his, in fighting, of tearing off his opponent's face.) And that I had won his friendship, all thanks were due to John Barleycorn. I have given the incident merely as an example of the multitudinous lures and draws and services by which John Barleycorn wins his followers.

CHAPTER XI

And still there arose in me no desire for alcohol, no chemical demand. In years and years of heavy drinking, drinking did not beget the desire. Drinking was the way of the life I led, the way of the men with whom I lived. While away on my cruises on the bay, I took no drink along; and while out on the bay the thought of the desirableness of a drink never crossed my mind. It was not until I tied the *Razzle Dazzle* up to the wharf and got ashore in the congregating places of men, where drink flowed, that the buying of drinks for other men, and the accepting of drinks from other men, devolved upon me as a social duty and a manhood rite.

Then, too, there were the times, lying at the city wharf or across the estuary on the sand-spit, when the Queen, and her sister, and her brother Pat, and Mrs. Hadley came aboard. It was my boat, I was host, and I could only dispense hospitality in the terms of their understanding of it. So I would rush Spider, or Irish, or Scotty, or whoever was my crew, with the can for beer and the demijohn for red wine. And again, lying at the wharf disposing of my oysters, there were dusky twilights when big policemen and plain-clothes men stole on board. And because we lived in the shadow of the police, we opened oysters and fed them to them with squirts of pepper sauce, and rushed the growler or got stronger stuff in bottles.

Drink as I would, I couldn't come to like John Barleycorn. I valued him extremely well for his associations, but not for the taste of him. All the time I was striving to be a man amongst men, and all the time I nursed secret and shameful desires for candy. But I would have died before I'd let anybody guess it. I used to indulge in lonely debauches, on nights when I knew my crew was going to sleep ashore. I would go up to the Free Library, exchange my books, buy a quarter's worth of all sorts of candy that chewed and lasted, sneak aboard the *Razzle Dazzle*, lock myself in the cabin, go to bed, and lie there long hours of bliss, reading and chewing candy. And those were the only times I felt that I got my real money's worth. Dollars and dollars, across the bar, couldn't buy the satisfaction that twenty-five cents did in a candy store.

As my drinking grew heavier, I began to note more and more that it was in the drinking bouts the purple passages occurred. Drunks were always memorable. At such times things happened. Men like Joe Goose dated existence from drunk to drunk. The longshoremen all looked forward to their Saturday night drunk. We of the oyster boats waited until we had disposed of our cargoes before we got really started, though a scattering of drinks and a meeting of a chance friend sometimes precipitated an accidental drunk.

In ways, the accidental drunks were the best. Stranger and more exciting things happened at such times. As, for instance, the Sunday when Nelson and French Frank and Captain Spink stole the stolen salmon boat from Whisky Bob and Nicky the Greek. Changes had taken place in the personnel of the oyster boats. Nelson had got into a fight with Bill Kelley on the *Annie* and was carrying a bullet-hole through his left hand. Also, having quarrelled with Clam and broken partnership, Nelson had sailed the *Reindeer*, his arm in a sling, with a crew of two deep-water sailors, and he had sailed so madly as to frighten them ashore. Such was the tale of his recklessness they spread, that no one on the water-front would go out with Nelson. So the *Reindeer*, crewless, lay across the estuary at the sandspit. Beside her lay the *Razzle Dazzle* with a burned mainsail and Scotty and me on board. Whisky Bob had fallen out with French Frank and gone on a raid "up river" with Nicky the Greek.

The result of this raid was a brand-new Columbia River salmon boat, stolen from an Italian fisherman. We oyster pirates were all visited by the searching Italian, and we were convinced, from what we knew of their movements, that Whisky Bob and Nicky the Greek were the guilty parties. But where was the salmon boat? Hundreds of Greek and Italian fishermen, up river and down bay, had searched every slough and tule patch for it. When the owner despairingly offered a reward of fifty dollars, our interest increased and the mystery deepened.

One Sunday morning old Captain Spink paid me a visit. The conversation was confidential. He had just been fishing in his skiff in the old Alameda ferry slip. As the tide went down, he had noticed a rope tied to a pile under water and leading downward. In vain he had tried to heave up what was fast on the other end. Farther along, to another pile, was a similar rope, leading downward and unheavable. Without doubt, it was the missing salmon boat. If we restored it to its rightful owner there was fifty dollars in it for us. But I had queer ethical notions about honour amongst thieves, and declined to have anything to do with the affair.

But French Frank had quarrelled with Whisky Bob, and Nelson was also an enemy. (Poor Whisky Bob!—without viciousness, good-natured, generous, born weak, raised poorly, with an irresistible chemical demand for alcohol, still prosecuting his vocation of bay pirate, his body was picked up, not long afterward, beside a dock where it had sunk full of gunshot wounds.) Within an hour after I had rejected Captain Spink's proposal, I saw him sail down the estuary on board the *Reindeer* with Nelson. Also, French Frank went by on his schooner.

It was not long ere they sailed back up the estuary, curiously side by side. As they headed in for the sandspit, the submerged salmon boat could be seen, gunwales awash and held up from sinking by ropes fast to the schooner and the sloop. The tide was half out, and they sailed squarely in on the sand, grounding in a row, with the salmon boat in the middle.

Immediately Hans, one of French Frank's sailors, was into a skiff and pulling rapidly for the north shore. The big demijohn in the stern-sheets told his errand. They couldn't wait a moment to celebrate the fifty dollars they had so easily earned. It is the way of the devotees of John Barleycorn. When good fortune comes, they drink. When they have no fortune, they drink to the hope of good fortune. If fortune be ill, they drink to forget it. If they meet a friend, they drink. If they quarrel with a friend and lose him, they drink. If their love-making be crowned with success, they are so happy they needs must drink. If they be jilted, they drink for the contrary reason. And if they haven't anything to do at all, why, they take a drink, secure in the knowledge that when they have taken a sufficient number of drinks the maggots will start crawling in their brains and they will have their hands full with things to do. When they are sober they want to drink; and when they have drunk they want to drink more.

Of course, as fellow comrades, Scotty and I were called in for the drinking. We helped to make a hole in that fifty dollars not yet received. The afternoon, from just an ordinary common summer Sunday afternoon, became a gorgeous, purple afternoon. We all talked and sang and ranted and bragged, and ever French Frank and Nelson sent more drinks around. We lay in full sight of the Oakland water-front, and the noise of our revels attracted friends. Skiff after skiff crossed the estuary and hauled up on the sandspit, while Hans' work was cut out for him—ever to row back and forth for more supplies of booze.

Then Whisky Bob and Nicky the Greek arrived, sober, indignant, outraged in that their fellow pirates had raised their plant. French Frank, aided by John Barleycorn, orated hypocritically about virtue and honesty, and, despite his fifty years, got Whisky Bob out on the sand and proceeded to lick him. When Nicky the Greek jumped in with a short-handled shovel to Whisky Bob's assistance, short work was made of him by Hans. And of course, when the bleeding remnants of Bob and Nicky were sent packing in their skiff, the event must needs be celebrated in further carousal.

By this time, our visitors being numerous, we were a large crowd compounded of many nationalities and diverse temperaments, all aroused by John Barleycorn, all restraints cast off. Old quarrels revived, ancient hates flared up. Fight was in the air. And whenever a longshoreman remembered something against a scow-schooner sailor, or vice versa, or an oyster pirate remembered or was remembered, a fist shot out and another fight was on. And every fight was made up in more rounds of drinks, wherein the combatants, aided and abetted by the rest of us, embraced each other and pledged undying friendship.

And, of all times, Soup Kennedy selected this time to come and retrieve an old shirt of his, left aboard the *Reindeer* from the trip he sailed with Clam. He had espoused Clam's side of the quarrel with Nelson. Also, he had been drinking in the St. Louis House, so that it was John Barleycorn who led him to the sandspit in quest of his old shirt. Few words started the fray. He locked with Nelson in the cockpit of the *Reindeer*, and in the mix-up barely escaped being brained by an iron bar wielded by irate French Frank—irate because a two-handed man had attacked a one-handed man. (If the *Reindeer* still floats, the dent of the iron bar remains in the hard-wood rail of her cockpit.)

But Nelson pulled his bandaged hand, bullet-perforated, out of its sling, and, held by us, wept and roared his Berserker belief that he could lick Soup Kennedy one-handed. And we let them loose on the sand. Once, when it looked as if Nelson were getting the worst of it, French Frank and John Barleycorn sprang unfairly into the fight. Scotty protested and reached for French Frank, who whirled upon him and fell on top of him in a pummelling clinch after a sprawl of twenty feet across the sand. In the course of separating these two, half a dozen fights started amongst the rest of us. These fights were finished, one way or the other, or we separated them with drinks, while all the time Nelson and Soup Kennedy fought on. Occasionally we returned to them and gave advice, such as, when they lay exhausted in the sand, unable to strike a blow, "Throw sand in his eyes." And they threw sand in each other's eyes, recuperated, and fought on to successive exhaustions.

And now, of all this that is squalid, and ridiculous, and bestial, try to think what it meant to me, a youth not yet sixteen, burning with the spirit of adventure, fancy-filled with tales of buccaneers and sea-rovers, sacks of cities and conflicts of armed men, and imagination-maddened by the stuff I had drunk. It was life raw and naked, wild and free—the only life of that sort which my birth in time and space permitted me to attain. And more than that. It carried a promise. It was the beginning. From the sandspit the way led out through the Golden Gate to the vastness of adventure of all the world, where battles would be fought, not for old shirts and over stolen salmon boats, but for high purposes and romantic ends.

And because I told Scotty what I thought of his letting an old man like French Frank get away with him, we, too, brawled and added to the festivity of the sandspit. And Scotty threw up his job as crew, and departed in the night with a pair of blankets belonging to me. During the night, while the oyster pirates lay stupefied in their bunks, the schooner and the *Reindeer* floated on the high water and swung about to their anchors. The salmon boat, still filled with rocks and water, rested on the bottom.

In the morning, early, I heard wild cries from the *Reindeer*, and tumbled out in the chill grey to see a spectacle that made the water-front laugh for days. The beautiful salmon boat lay on the hard sand, squashed flat as a pancake, while on it were perched French Frank's schooner and the *Reindeer*. Unfortunately two of the *Reindeer*'s planks had been crushed in by the stout oak stem of the salmon boat. The rising tide had flowed through the hole, and just awakened Nelson by getting into his bunk with him. I lent a hand, and we pumped the *Reindeer* out and repaired the damage.

Then Nelson cooked breakfast, and while we ate we considered the situation. He was broke. So was I. The fifty dollars reward would never be paid for that pitiful mess of splinters on the sand beneath us. He had a wounded hand and no crew. I had a burned main sail and no crew.

"What d'ye say, you and me?" Nelson queried. "I'll go you," was my answer. And thus I became partners with "Young Scratch" Nelson, the wildest, maddest of them all. We borrowed the money for an outfit of grub from Johnny Heinhold, filled our water-barrels, and sailed away that day for the oyster-beds.

CHAPTER XII

Nor have I ever regretted those months of mad devilry I put in with Nelson. He *could* sail, even if he did frighten every man that sailed with him. To steer to miss destruction by an inch or an instant was his joy. To do what everybody else did not dare attempt to do, was his pride. Never to reef down was his mania, and in all the time I spent with him, blow high or low, the *Reindeer* was never reefed. Nor was she ever dry. We strained her open and sailed her open and sailed her open continually. And we abandoned the Oakland water-front and went wider afield for our adventures.

And all this glorious passage in my life was made possible for me by John Barleycorn. And this is my complaint against John Barleycorn. Here I was, thirsting for the wild life of adventure, and the only way for me to win to it was through John Barleycorn's mediation. It was the way of the men who lived the life. Did I wish to live the life, I must live it the way they did. It was by virtue of drinking that I gained that partnership and comradeship with Nelson. Had I drunk only the beer he paid for, or had I declined to drink at all, I should never have been selected by him as a partner. He wanted a partner who would meet him on the social side, as well as the work side of life.

I abandoned myself to the life, and developed the misconception that the secret of John Barleycorn lay in going on mad drunks, rising through the successive stages that only an iron constitution could endure to final stupefaction and swinish unconsciousness. I did not like the taste, so I drank for the sole purpose of getting drunk, of getting hopelessly, helplessly drunk. And I, who had saved and scraped, traded like a Shylock and made junkmen weep; I, who had stood aghast when French Frank, at a single stroke, spent eighty cents for whisky for eight men, I turned myself loose with a more lavish disregard for money than any of them.

I remember going ashore one night with Nelson. In my pocket were one hundred and eighty dollars. It was my intention, first, to buy me some clothes, after that, some drinks. I needed the clothes. All I possessed were on me, and they were as follows: a pair of sea-boots that providentially leaked the water out as fast as it ran in, a pair of fifty-cent overalls, a forty-cent cotton shirt, and a sou'wester. I had no hat, so I had to wear the sou'wester, and it will be noted that I have listed neither underclothes nor socks. I didn't own any.

To reach the stores where clothes could be bought, we had to pass a dozen saloons. So I bought me the drinks first. I never got to the clothing stores. In the morning, broke, poisoned, but contented, I came back on board, and we set sail. I possessed only the clothes I had gone ashore in, and not a cent remained of the one hundred and eighty dollars. It might well be deemed impossible, by those who have never tried it, that in twelve hours a lad can spend all of one hundred and eighty dollars for drinks. I know otherwise.

And I had no regrets. I was proud. I had shown them I could spend with the best of them. Amongst strong men I had proved myself strong. I had clinched again, as I had often clinched, my right to the title of "Prince." Also, my attitude may be considered, in part, as a reaction from my childhood's meagreness and my childhood's excessive toil. Possibly my inchoate thought was: Better to reign among booze-fighters a prince than to toil twelve hours a day at a machine for ten cents an hour. There are no purple passages in machine toil. But if the spending of one hundred and eighty dollars in twelve hours isn't a purple passage, then I'd like to know what is.

Oh, I skip much of the details of my trafficking with John Barleycorn during this period, and shall only mention events that will throw light on John Barleycorn's ways. There were three things that enabled me to pursue this heavy drinking: first, a magnificent constitution far better than the average; second, the healthy open-air life on the water; and third, the fact that I drank irregularly. While out on the water, we never carried any drink along.

The world was opening up to me. Already I knew several hundred miles of the water-ways of it, and of the towns and cities and fishing hamlets on the shores. Came the whisper to range farther. I had not found it yet. There was more behind. But even this much of the world was too wide for Nelson. He wearied for his beloved Oakland water-front, and when he elected to return to it we separated in all friendliness.

I now made the old town of Benicia, on the Carquinez Straits, my headquarters. In a cluster of fishermen's arks, moored in the tules on the water-front, dwelt a congenial crowd of drinkers and vagabonds, and I joined them. I had longer spells ashore, between fooling with salmon fishing and making raids up and down bay and rivers as a deputy fish patrolman, and I drank more and learned more about drinking. I held my own with any one, drink for drink; and often drank more than my share to show the strength of my manhood. When, on a morning, my unconscious carcass was disentangled from the nets on the drying-frames, whither I had stupidly, blindly crawled the night before; and when the water-front talked it over with many a giggle and laugh and another drink, I was proud indeed. It was an exploit.

And when I never drew a sober breath, on one stretch, for three solid weeks, I was certain I had reached the top. Surely, in that direction, one could go no farther. It was time for me to move on. For always, drunk or sober, at the back of my consciousness something whispered that this carousing and bay-adventuring was not all of life. This whisper was my good fortune. I happened to be so made that I could hear it calling, always calling, out and away over the world. It was not canniness on my part. It was curiosity, desire to know, an unrest and a seeking for things wonderful that I seemed somehow to have glimpsed or guessed. What was this life for, I demanded, if this were all? No; there was something more, away and beyond. (And, in relation to my much later development as a drinker, this whisper, this promise of the things at the back of life, must be noted, for it was destined to play a dire part in my more recent wrestlings with John Barleycorn.)

But what gave immediacy to my decision to move on was a trick John Barleycorn played me—a monstrous, incredible trick that showed abysses of intoxication hitherto undreamed. At one o'clock in the morning, after a prodigious drunk, I was tottering aboard a sloop at the end of the wharf, intending to go to sleep. The tides sweep through Carquinez Straits as in a mill-race, and the full ebb was on when I stumbled overboard. There was nobody on the wharf, nobody on the sloop. I was borne away by the current. I was not startled. I thought the misadventure delightful. I was a good swimmer, and in my inflamed condition the contact of the water with my skin soothed me like cool linen.

And then John Barleycorn played me his maniacal trick. Some maundering fancy of going out with the tide suddenly obsessed me. I had never been morbid. Thoughts of suicide had never entered my head. And now that they entered, I thought it fine, a splendid culminating, a perfect rounding off of my short but exciting career. I, who had never known girl's love, nor woman's love, nor the love of children; who had never played in the wide joy-fields of art, nor climbed the star-cool heights of philosophy, nor seen with my eyes more than a pin-point's surface of the gorgeous world; I decided that this was all, that I had seen all, lived all, been all, that was worth while, and that now was the time to cease. This was the trick of John Barleycorn, laying me by the heels of my imagination and in a drug-dream dragging me to death.

Oh, he was convincing. I had really experienced all of life, and it didn't amount to much. The swinish drunkenness in which I had lived for months (this was accompanied by the sense of degradation and the old feeling of conviction of sin) was the last and best, and I could see for myself what it was worth. There were all the broken-down old bums and loafers I had bought drinks for. That was what remained of life. Did I want to become like them? A thousand times no; and I wept tears of sweet sadness over my glorious youth going out with the tide. (And who has not seen the weeping drunk, the melancholic drunk? They are to be found in all the bar-rooms, if they can find no other listener telling their sorrows to the barkeeper, who is paid to listen.)

The water was delicious. It was a man's way to die. John Barleycorn changed the tune he played in my drink-maddened brain. Away with tears and regret. It was a hero's death, and by the hero's own hand and will. So I struck up my death-chant and was singing it lustily, when the gurgle and splash of the current-riffles in my ears reminded me of my more immediate situation.

Below the town of Benicia, where the Solano wharf projects, the Straits widen out into what bay-farers call the "Bight of Turner's Shipyard." I was in the shore-tide that swept under the Solano wharf and on into the bight. I knew of old the power of the suck which developed when the tide swung around the end of Dead Man's Island and drove straight for the wharf. I didn't want to go through those piles. It wouldn't be nice, and I might lose an hour in the bight on my way out with the tide.

I undressed in the water and struck out with a strong, single-overhand stroke, crossing the current at right-angles. Nor did I cease until, by the wharf lights, I knew I was safe to sweep by the end. Then I turned over and rested. The stroke had been a telling one, and I was a little time in recovering my breath.

I was elated, for I had succeeded in avoiding the suck. I started to raise my death-chant again—a purely extemporised farrago of a drug-crazed youth. "Don't sing—yet," whispered John Barleycorn. "The Solano runs all night. There are railroad men on the wharf. They will hear you, and come out in a boat and rescue you, and you don't want to be rescued." I certainly didn't. What? Be robbed of my hero's death? Never. And I lay on my back in the starlight, watching the familiar wharf-lights go by, red and green and white, and bidding sad sentimental farewell to them, each and all.

When I was well clear, in mid-channel, I sang again. Sometimes I swam a few strokes, but in the main I contented myself with floating and dreaming long drunken dreams. Before daylight, the chill of the water and the passage of the hours had sobered me sufficiently to make me wonder what portion of the Straits I was in, and also to wonder if the turn of the tide wouldn't catch me and take me back ere I had drifted out into San Pablo Bay.

Next I discovered that I was very weary and very cold, and quite sober, and that I didn't in the least want to be drowned. I could make out the Selby Smelter on the Contra Costa shore and the Mare Island lighthouse. I started to swim for the Solano shore, but was too weak and chilled, and made so little headway, and at the cost of such painful effort, that I gave it up and contented myself with floating, now and then giving a stroke to keep my balance in the tide-rips which were increasing their commotion on the surface of the water. And I knew fear. I was sober now, and I didn't want to die. I discovered scores of reasons for living. And the more reasons I discovered, the more liable it seemed that I was going to drown anyway.

Daylight, after I had been four hours in the water, found me in a parlous condition in the tide-rips off Mare Island light, where the swift ebbs from Vallejo Straits and Carquinez Straits were fighting with each other, and where, at that particular moment, they were fighting the flood tide setting up against them from San Pablo Bay. A stiff breeze had sprung up, and the crisp little waves were persistently lapping into my mouth, and I was beginning to swallow salt water. With my swimmer's knowledge, I knew the end was near. And then the boat came—a Greek fisherman running in for Vallejo; and again I had been saved from John Barleycorn by my constitution and physical vigour.

And, in passing, let me note that this maniacal trick John Barleycorn played me is nothing uncommon. An absolute statistic of the percentage of suicides due to John Barleycorn would be appalling. In my case, healthy, normal, young, full of the joy of life, the suggestion to kill myself was unusual; but it must be taken into account that it came on the heels of a long carouse, when my nerves and brain were fearfully poisoned, and that the dramatic, romantic side of my imagination, drink-maddened to lunacy, was delighted with the suggestion. And yet, the older, more morbid drinkers, more jaded with life and more disillusioned, who kill themselves, do so usually after a long debauch, when their nerves and brains are thoroughly poison-soaked.

CHAPTER XIII

So I left Benicia, where John Barleycorn had nearly got me, and ranged wider afield in pursuit of the whisper from the back of life to come and find. And wherever I ranged, the way lay along alcohol-drenched roads. Men still congregated in saloons. They were the poor-man's clubs, and they were the only clubs to which I had access. I could get acquainted in saloons. I could go into a saloon and talk with any man. In the strange towns and cities I wandered through, the only place for me to go was the saloon. I was no longer a stranger in any town the moment I had entered a saloon.

And right here let me break in with experiences no later than last year. I harnessed four horses to a light trap, took Charmian along, and drove for three months and a half over the wildest mountain parts of California and Oregon. Each morning I did my regular day's work of writing fiction. That completed, I drove on through the middle of the day and the afternoon to the next stop. But the irregularity of occurrence of stopping-places, coupled with widely varying road conditions, made it necessary to plan, the day before, each day's drive and my work. I must know when I was to start driving in order to start writing in time to finish my day's output. Thus, on occasion, when the drive was to be long, I would be up and at my writing by five in the morning. On easier driving days I might not start writing till nine o'clock.

But how to plan? As soon as I arrived in a town, and put the horses up, on the way from the stable to the hotel I dropped into the saloons. First thing, a drink—oh, I wanted the drink, but also it must not be forgotten that, because of wanting to know things, it was in this very way I had learned to want a drink. Well, the first thing, a drink. "Have something yourself," to the barkeeper. And then, as we drink, my opening query about roads and stopping-places on ahead.

"Let me see," the barkeeper will say, "there's the road across Tarwater Divide. That used to be good. I was over it three years ago. But it was blocked this spring. Say, I'll tell you what. I'll ask Jerry——" And the barkeeper turns and addresses some man sitting at a table or leaning against the bar farther along, and who may be Jerry, or Tom, or Bill. "Say, Jerry, how about the Tarwater road? You was down to Wilkins last week."

And while Bill or Jerry or Tom is beginning to unlimber his thinking and speaking apparatus, I suggest that he join us in the drink. Then discussions arise about the advisability of this road or that, what the best stopping-places may be, what running time I may expect to make, where the best trout streams are, and so forth, in which other men join, and which are punctuated with more drinks.

Two or three more saloons, and I accumulate a warm jingle and come pretty close to knowing everybody in town, all about the town, and a fair deal about the surrounding country. I know the lawyers, editors, business men, local politicians, and the visiting ranchers, hunters, and miners, so that by evening, when Charmian and I stroll down the main street and back, she is astounded by the number of my acquaintances in that totally strange town.

And thus is demonstrated a service John Barleycorn renders, a service by which he increases his power over men. And over the world, wherever I have gone, during all the years, it has been the same. It may be a cabaret in the Latin Quarter, a cafe in some obscure Italian village, a boozing ken in sailor-town, and it may be up at the club over Scotch and soda; but always it will be where John Barleycorn makes fellowship that I get immediately in touch, and meet, and know. And in the good days coming, when John Barleycorn will have been banished out of existence along with the other barbarisms, some other institution than the saloon will have to obtain, some other congregating place of men where strange men and stranger men may get in touch, and meet, and know.

But to return to my narrative. When I turned my back on Benicia, my way led through saloons. I had developed no moral theories against drinking, and I disliked as much as ever the taste of the stuff. But I had grown respectfully suspicious of John Barleycorn. I could not forget that trick he had played on me—on me who did not want to die. So I continued to drink, and to keep a sharp eye on John Barleycorn, resolved to resist all future suggestions of self-destruction.

In strange towns I made immediate acquaintances in the saloons. When I hoboed, and hadn't the price of a bed, a saloon was the only place that would receive me and give me a chair by the fire. I could go into a saloon and wash up, brush my clothes, and comb my hair. And saloons were always so damnably convenient. They were everywhere in my western country.

I couldn't go into the dwellings of strangers that way. Their doors were not open to me; no seats were there for me by their fires. Also, churches and preachers I had never known. And from what I didn't know I was not attracted toward them. Besides, there was no glamour about them, no haze of romance, no promise of adventure. They were the sort with whom things never happened. They lived and remained always in the one place, creatures of order and system, narrow, limited, restrained. They were without greatness, without imagination, without camaraderie. It was the good fellows, easy and genial, daring, and, on occasion, mad, that I wanted to know—the fellows, generous-hearted and -handed, and not rabbit-hearted.

And here is another complaint I bring against John Barleycorn. It is these good fellows that he gets—the fellows with the fire and the go in them, who have bigness, and warmness, and the best of the human weaknesses. And John Barleycorn puts out the fire, and soddens the agility, and, when he does not more immediately kill them or make maniacs of them, he coarsens and grossens them, twists and malforms them out of the original goodness and fineness of their natures.

Oh!—and I speak out of later knowledge—Heaven forefend me from the most of the average run of male humans who are not good fellows, the ones cold of heart and cold of head who don't smoke, drink, or swear, or do much of anything else that is brase, and resentful, and stinging, because in their feeble fibres there has never been the stir and prod of life to well over its boundaries and be devilish and daring. One doesn't meet these in saloons, nor rallying to lost causes, nor flaming on the adventure-paths, nor loving as God's own mad lovers. They are too busy keeping their feet dry, conserving their heart-beats, and making unlovely life-successes of their spirit-mediocrity.

And so I draw the indictment home to John Barleycorn. It is just those, the good fellows, the worth while, the fellows with the weakness of too much strength, too much spirit, too much fire and flame of fine devilishness, that he solicits and ruins. Of course, he ruins weaklings; but with them, the worst we breed, I am not here concerned. My concern is that it is so much of the best we breed whom John Barleycorn destroys. And the reason why these best are destroyed is because John Barleycorn stands on every highway and byway, accessible, law-protected, saluted by the policeman on the beat, speaking to them, leading them by the hand to the places where the good fellows and daring ones forgather and drink deep. With John Barleycorn out of the way, these daring ones would still be born, and they would do things instead of perishing.

Always I encountered the camaraderie of drink. I might be walking down the track to the water-tank to lie in wait for a passing freight-train, when I would chance upon a bunch of "alki-stiffs." An alki-stiff is a tramp who drinks druggist's alcohol. Immediately, with greeting and salutation, I am taken into the fellowship. The alcohol, shrewdly blended with water, is handed to me, and soon I am caught up in the revelry, with maggots crawling in my brain and John Barleycorn whispering to me that life is big, and that we are all brave and fine—free spirits sprawling like careless gods upon the turf and telling the two-by-four, cut-and-dried, conventional world to go hang.

CHAPTER XIV

Back in Oakland from my wanderings, I returned to the water-front and renewed my comradeship with Nelson, who was now on shore all the time and living more madly than before. I, too, spent my time on shore with him, only occasionally going for cruises of several days on the bay to help out on short-handed scow-schooners.

The result was that I was no longer reinvigorated by periods of open-air abstinence and healthy toil. I drank every day, and whenever opportunity offered I drank to excess; for I still laboured under the misconception that the secret of John Barleycorn lay in drinking to bestiality and unconsciousness. I became pretty thoroughly alcohol-soaked during this period. I practically lived in saloons; became a bar-room loafer, and worse.

And right here was John Barleycorn getting me in a more insidious though no less deadly way than when he nearly sent me out with the tide. I had a few months still to run before I was seventeen; I scorned the thought of a steady job at anything; I felt myself a pretty tough individual in a group of pretty tough men; and I drank because these men drank and because I had to make good with them. I had never had a real boyhood, and in this, my precocious manhood, I was very hard and woefully wise. Though I had never known girl's love even, I had crawled through such depths that I was convinced absolutely that I knew the last word about love and life. And it wasn't a pretty knowledge. Without being pessimistic, I was quite satisfied that life was a rather cheap and ordinary affair.

You see, John Barleycorn was blunting me. The old stings and prods of the spirit were no longer sharp. Curiosity was leaving me. What did it matter what lay on the other side of the world? Men and women, without doubt, very much like the men and women I knew; marrying and giving in marriage and all the petty run of petty human concerns; and drinks, too. But the other side of the world was a long way to go for a drink. I had but to step to the corner and get all I wanted at Joe Vigy's. Johnny Heinhold still ran the Last Chance. And there were saloons on all the corners and between the corners.

The whispers from the back of life were growing dim as my mind and body soddened. The old unrest was drowsy. I might as well rot and die here in Oakland as anywhere else. And I should have so rotted and died, and not in very long order either, at the pace John Barleycorn was leading me, had the matter depended wholly on him. I was learning what it was to have no appetite. I was learning what it was to get up shaky in the morning, with a stomach that quivered, with fingers touched with palsy, and to know the drinker's need for a stiff glass of whisky neat in order to brace up. (Oh! John Barleycorn is a wizard dopester. Brain and body, scorched and jangled and poisoned, return to be tuned up by the very poison that caused the damage.)

There is no end to John Barleycorn's tricks. He had tried to inveigle me into killing myself. At this period he was doing his best to kill me at a fairly rapid pace. But, not satisfied with that, he tried another dodge. He very nearly got me, too, and right there I learned a lesson about him—became a wiser, a more skilful drinker. I learned there were limits to my gorgeous constitution, and that there were no limits to John Barleycorn. I learned that in a short hour or two he could master my strong head, my broad shoulders and deep chest, put me on my back, and with a devil's grip on my throat proceed to choke the life out of me.

Nelson and I were sitting in the Overland House. It was early in the evening, and the only reason we were there was because we were broke and it was election time. You see, in election time local politicians, aspirants for office, have a way of making the rounds of the saloons to get votes. One is sitting at a table, in a dry condition, wondering who is going to turn up and buy him a drink, or if his credit is good at some other saloon and if it's worth while to walk that far to find out, when suddenly the saloon doors swing wide, and enters a bevy of well-dressed men, themselves usually wide and exhaling an atmosphere of prosperity and fellowship.

They have smiles and greetings for everybody—for you, without the price of a glass of beer in your pocket, for the timid hobo who lurks in the corner and who certainly hasn't a vote, but who may establish a lodging-house registration. And do you know, when these politicians swing wide the doors and come in, with their broad shoulders, their deep chests, and their generous stomachs which cannot help making them optimists and masters of life, why, you perk right up. It's going to be a warm evening after all, and you know you'll get a souse started at the very least.

And—who knows?—the gods may be kind, other drinks may come, and the night culminate in glorious greatness. And the next thing you know, you are lined up at the bar, pouring drinks down your throat and learning the gentlemen's names and the offices which they hope to fill.

It was during this period, when the politicians went their saloon rounds, that I was getting bitter bits of education and having illusions punctured—I, who had pored and thrilled over "The Rail-Splitter," and "From Canal Boy to President." Yes, I was learning how noble politics and politicians are.

Well, on this night, broke, thirsty, but with the drinker's faith in the unexpected drink, Nelson and I sat in the Overland House waiting for something to turn up, especially politicians. And there entered Joe Goose—he of the unquenchable thirst, the wicked eyes, the crooked nose, the flowered vest.

"Come on, fellows—free booze—all you want of it. I didn't want you to miss it."

"Where?" we wanted to know.

"Come on. I'll tell you as we go along. We haven't a minute to lose." And as we hurried up town, Joe Goose explained: "It's the Hancock Fire Brigade. All you have to do is wear a red shirt and a helmet, and carry a torch.

"They're going down on a special train to Haywards to parade."

(I think the place was Haywards. It may have been San Leandro or Niles. And, to save me, I can't remember whether the Hancock Fire Brigade was a republican or a democratic organisation. But anyway, the politicians who ran it were short of torch-bearers, and anybody who would parade could get drunk if he wanted to.)

"The town'll be wide open," Joe Goose went on. "Booze? It'll run like water. The politicians have bought the stocks of the saloons. There'll be no charge. All you got to do is walk right up and call for it. We'll raise hell."

At the hall, on Eighth Street near Broadway, we got into the firemen's shirts and helmets, were equipped with torches, and, growling because we weren't given at least one drink before we started, were herded aboard the train. Oh, those politicians had handled our kind before. At Haywards there were no drinks either. Parade first, and earn your booze, was the order of the night.

We paraded. Then the saloons were opened. Extra barkeepers had been engaged, and the drinkers jammed six deep before every drink-drenched and unwiped bar. There was no time to wipe the bar, nor wash glasses, nor do anything save fill glasses. The Oakland water-front can be real thirsty on occasion.

This method of jamming and struggling in front of the bar was too slow for us. The drink was ours. The politicians had bought it for us. We'd paraded and earned it, hadn't we? So we made a flank attack around the end of the bar, shoved the protesting barkeepers aside, and helped ourselves to bottles.

Outside, we knocked the necks of the bottles off against the concrete curbs, and drank. Now Joe Goose and Nelson had learned discretion with straight whisky, drunk in quantity. I hadn't. I still laboured under the misconception that one was to drink all he could get—especially when it didn't cost anything. We shared our bottles with others, and drank a good portion ourselves, while I drank most of all. And I didn't like the stuff. I drank it as I had drunk beer at five, and wine at seven. I mastered my qualms and downed it like so much medicine. And when we wanted more bottles, we went into other saloons where the free drink was flowing, and helped ourselves.

I haven't the slightest idea of how much I drank—whether it was two quarts or five. I do know that I began the orgy with half-pint draughts and with no water afterward to wash the taste away or to dilute the whisky.

Now the politicians were too wise to leave the town filled with drunks from the water-front of Oakland. When train time came, there was a round-up of the saloons. Already I was feeling the impact of the whisky. Nelson and I were hustled out of a saloon, and found ourselves in the very last rank of a disorderly parade. I struggled along heroically, my correlations breaking down, my legs tottering under me, my head swimming, my heart pounding, my lungs panting for air.

My helplessness was coming on so rapidly that my reeling brain told me I would go down and out and never reach the train if I remained at the rear of the procession. I left the ranks and ran down a pathway beside the road under broad-spreading trees. Nelson pursued me, laughing. Certain things stand out, as in memories of nightmare. I remember those trees especially, and my desperate running along under them, and how, every time I fell, roars of laughter went up from the other drunks. They thought I was merely antic drunk. They did not dream that John Barleycorn had me by the throat in a death-clutch. But I knew it. And I remember the fleeting bitterness that was mine as I realised that I was in a struggle with death, and that these others did not know. It was as if I were drowning before a crowd of spectators who thought I was cutting up tricks for their entertainment.

And running there under the trees, I fell and lost consciousness. What happened afterward, with one glimmering exception, I had to be told. Nelson, with his enormous strength, picked me up and dragged me on and aboard the train. When he had got me into a seat, I fought and panted so terribly for air that even with his obtuseness he knew I was in a bad way. And right there, at any moment, I know now, I might have died. I often think it is the nearest to death I have ever been. I have only Nelson's description of my behaviour to go by.

I was scorching up, burning alive internally, in an agony of fire and suffocation, and I wanted air. I madly wanted air. My efforts to raise a window were vain, for all the windows in the car were screwed down. Nelson had seen drink-crazed men, and thought I wanted to throw myself out. He tried to restrain me, but I fought on. I seized some man's torch and smashed the glass.

Now there were pro-Nelson and anti-Nelson factions on the Oakland water-front, and men of both factions, with more drink in them than was good, filled the car. My smashing of the window was the signal for the antis. One of them reached for me, and dropped me, and started the fight, of all of which I have no knowledge save what was told me afterward, and a sore jaw next day from the blow that put me out. The man who struck me went down across my body, Nelson followed him, and they say there were few unbroken windows in the wreckage of the car that followed as the free-for-all fight had its course.

This being knocked cold and motionless was perhaps the best thing that could have happened to me. My violent struggles had only accelerated my already dangerously accelerated heart, and increased the need for oxygen in my suffocating lungs.

After the fight was over and I came to, I did not come to myself. I was no more myself than a drowning man is who continues to struggle after he has lost consciousness. I have no memory of my actions, but I cried "Air! Air!" so insistently, that it dawned on Nelson that I did not contemplate self-destruction. So he cleared the jagged glass from the window-ledge and let me stick my head and shoulders out. He realised, partially, the seriousness of my condition, and held me by the waist to prevent me from crawling farther out. And for the rest of the run in to Oakland I kept my head and shoulders out, fighting like a maniac whenever he tried to draw me inside.

And here my one glimmering streak of true consciousness came. My sole recollection, from the time I fell under the trees until I awoke the following evening, is of my head out of the window, facing the wind caused by the train, cinders striking and burning and blinding me, while I breathed with will. All my will was concentrated on breathing—on breathing the air in the hugest lung-full gulps I could, pumping the greatest amount of air into my lungs in the shortest possible time. It was that or death, and I was a swimmer and diver, and I knew it; and in the most intolerable agony of prolonged suffocation, during those moments I was conscious, I faced the wind and the cinders and breathed for life.

All the rest is a blank. I came to the following evening, in a water-front lodging-house. I was alone. No doctor had been called in. And I might well have died there, for Nelson and the others, deeming me merely "sleeping off my drunk," had let me lie there in a comatose condition for seventeen hours. Many a man, as every doctor knows, has died of the sudden impact of a quart or more of whisky. Usually one reads of them so dying, strong drinkers, on account of a wager. But I didn't know—then. And so I learned; and by no virtue nor prowess, but simply through good fortune and constitution. Again my constitution had triumphed over John Barleycorn. I had escaped from another death-pit, dragged myself through another morass, and perilously acquired the discretion that would enable me to drink wisely for many another year to come.

Heavens! That was twenty years ago, and I am still very much and wisely alive; and I have seen much, done much, lived much, in that intervening score of years; and I shudder when I think how close a shave I ran, how near I was to missing that splendid fifth of a century that has been mine. And, oh, it wasn't John Barleycorn's fault that he didn't get me that night of the Hancock Fire Brigade.

CHAPTER XV

It was during the early winter of 1892 that I resolved to go to sea. My Hancock Fire Brigade experience was very little responsible for this. I still drank and frequented saloons—practically lived in saloons. Whisky was dangerous, in my opinion, but not wrong. Whisky was dangerous like other dangerous things in the natural world. Men died of whisky; but then, too, fishermen were capsized and drowned, hoboes fell under trains and were cut to pieces. To cope with winds and waves, railroad trains, and bar-rooms, one must use judgment. To get drunk after the manner of men was all right, but one must do it with discretion. No more quarts of whisky for me.

What really decided me to go to sea was that I had caught my first vision of the death-road which John Barleycorn maintains for his devotees. It was not a clear vision, however, and there were two phases of it, somewhat jumbled at the time. It struck me, from watching those with whom I associated, that the life we were living was more destructive than that lived by the average man.

John Barleycorn, by inhibiting morality, incited to crime. Everywhere I saw men doing, drunk, what they would never dream of doing sober. And this wasn't the worst of it. It was the penalty that must be paid. Crime was destructive. Saloon-mates I drank with, who were good fellows and harmless, sober, did most violent and lunatic things when they were drunk. And then the police gathered them in and they vanished from our ken. Sometimes I visited them behind the bars and said good-bye ere they journeyed across the bay to put on the felon's stripes. And time and again I heard the one explanation *"If i hadn't been drunk i wouldn't a-done it."* And sometimes, under the spell of John Barleycorn, the most frightful things were done—things that shocked even my case-hardened soul.

The other phase of the death-road was that of the habitual drunkards, who had a way of turning up their toes without apparent provocation. When they took sick, even with trifling afflictions that any ordinary man could pull through, they just pegged out. Sometimes they were found unattended and dead in their beds; on occasion their bodies were dragged out of the water; and sometimes it was just plain accident, as when Bill Kelley, unloading cargo while drunk, had a finger jerked off, which, under the circumstances, might just as easily have been his head.

So I considered my situation and knew that I was getting into a bad way of living. It made toward death too quickly to suit my youth and vitality. And there was only one way out of this hazardous manner of living, and that was to get out. The sealing fleet was wintering in San Francisco Bay, and in the saloons I met skippers, mates, hunters, boat-steerers, and boat-pullers. I met the seal-hunter, Pete Holt, and agreed to be his boat-puller and to sign on any schooner he signed on. And I had to have half a dozen drinks with Pete Holt there and then to seal our agreement.

And at once awoke all my old unrest that John Barleycorn had put to sleep. I found myself actually bored with the saloon life of the Oakland water-front, and wondered what I had ever found fascinating in it. Also, with this death-road concept in my brain, I began to grow afraid that something would happen to me before sailing day, which was set for some time in January. I lived more circumspectly, drank less deeply, and went home more frequently. When drinking grew too wild, I got out. When Nelson was in his maniacal cups, I managed to get separated from him.

On the 12th of January, 1893, I was seventeen, and the 20th of January I signed before the shipping commissioner the articles of the Sophie Sutherland, a three topmast sealing schooner bound on a voyage to the coast of Japan. And of course we had to drink on it. Joe Vigy cashed my advance note, and Pete Holt treated, and I treated, and Joe Vigy treated, and other hunters treated. Well, it was the way of men, and who was I, just turned seventeen, that I should decline the way of life of these fine, chesty, man-grown men?

CHAPTER XVI

There was nothing to drink on the Sophie Sutherland, and we had fifty-one days of glorious sailing, taking the southern passage in the north-east trades to Bonin Islands. This isolated group, belonging to Japan, had been selected as the rendezvous of the Canadian and American sealing fleets. Here they filled their water-barrels and made repairs before starting on the hundred days' harrying of the seal-herd along the northern coasts of Japan to Behring Sea.

Those fifty-one days of fine sailing and intense sobriety had put me in splendid fettle. The alcohol had been worked out of my system, and from the moment the voyage began I had not known the desire for a drink. I doubt if I even thought once about a drink. Often, of course, the talk in the forecastle turned on drink, and the men told of their more exciting or humorous drunks, remembering such passages more keenly, with greater delight, than all the other passages of their adventurous lives.

In the forecastle, the oldest man, fat and fifty, was Louis. He was a broken skipper. John Barleycorn had thrown him, and he was winding up his career where he had begun it, in the forecastle. His case made quite an impression on me. John Barleycorn did other things beside kill a man. He hadn't killed Louis. He had done much worse. He had robbed him of power and place and comfort, crucified his pride, and condemned him to the hardship of the common sailor that would last as long as his healthy breath lasted, which promised to be for a long time.

We completed our run across the Pacific, lifted the volcanic peaks, jungle-clad, of the Bonin Islands, sailed in among the reefs to the land-locked harbour, and let our anchor rumble down where lay a score or more of sea-gypsies like ourselves. The scents of strange vegetation blew off the tropic land. Aborigines, in queer outrigger canoes, and Japanese, in queerer sampans, paddled about the bay and came aboard. It was my first foreign land; I had won to the other side of the world, and I would see all I had read in the books come true. I was wild to get ashore.

Victor and Axel, a Swede and a Norwegian, and I planned to keep together. (And so well did we, that for the rest of the cruise we were known as the "Three Sports.") Victor pointed out a pathway that disappeared up a wild canyon, emerged on a steep bare lava slope, and thereafter appeared and disappeared, ever climbing, among the palms and flowers. We would go over that path, he said, and we agreed, and we would see beautiful scenery, and strange native villages, and find, Heaven alone knew, what adventure at the end. And Axel was keen to go fishing. The three of us agreed to that, too. We would get a sampan, and a couple of Japanese fishermen who knew the fishing grounds, and we would have great sport. As for me, I was keen for anything.

And then, our plans made, we rowed ashore over the banks of living coral and pulled our boat up the white beach of coral sand. We walked across the fringe of beach under the cocoanut-palms and into the little town, and found several hundred riotous seamen from all the world, drinking prodigiously, singing prodigiously, dancing prodigiously—and all on the main street to the scandal of a helpless handful of Japanese police.

Victor and Axel said that we'd have a drink before we started on our long walk. Could I decline to drink with these two chesty shipmates? Drinking together, glass in hand, put the seal on comradeship. It was the way of life. Our teetotaler owner-captain was laughed at, and sneered at, by all of us because of his teetotalism. I didn't in the least want a drink, but I did want to be a good fellow and a good comrade. Nor did Louis' case deter me, as I poured the biting, scorching stuff down my throat. John Barleycorn had thrown Louis to a nasty fall, but I was young. My blood ran full and red; I had a constitution of iron; and—well, youth ever grins scornfully at the wreckage of age.

Queer, fierce, alcoholic stuff it was that we drank. There was no telling where or how it had been manufactured—some native concoction most likely. But it was hot as fire, pale as water, and quick as death with its kick. It had been filled into empty "square-face" bottles which had once contained Holland gin, and which still bore the fitting legend "Anchor Brand." It certainly anchored us. We never got out of the town. We never went fishing in the sampan. And though we were there ten days, we never trod that wild path along the lava cliffs and among the flowers.

We met old acquaintances from other schooners, fellows we had met in the saloons of San Francisco before we sailed. And each meeting meant a drink; and there was much to talk about; and more drinks; and songs to be sung; and pranks and antics to be performed, until the maggots of imagination began to crawl, and it all seemed great and wonderful to me, these lusty hard-bitten sea-rovers, of whom I made one, gathered in wassail on a coral strand. Old lines about knights at table in the great banquet halls, and of those above the salt and below the salt, and of Vikings feasting fresh from sea and ripe for battle, came to me; and I knew that the old times were not dead and that we belonged to that selfsame ancient breed.

By mid-afternoon Victor went mad with drink, and wanted to fight everybody and everything. I have since seen lunatics in the violent wards of asylums that seemed to behave in no wise different from Victor's way, save that perhaps he was more violent. Axel and I interfered as peacemakers, were roughed and jostled in the mix-ups, and finally, with infinite precaution and intoxicated cunning, succeeded in inveigling our chum down to the boat and in rowing him aboard our schooner.

But no sooner did Victor's feet touch the deck than he began to clean up the ship. He had the strength of several men, and he ran amuck with it. I remember especially one man whom he got into the chain-boxes but failed to damage through inability to hit him. The man dodged and ducked, and Victor broke all the knuckles of both his fists against the huge links of the anchor chain. By the time we dragged him out of that, his madness had shifted to the belief that he was a great swimmer, and the next moment he was overboard and demonstrating his ability by floundering like a sick porpoise and swallowing much salt water.

We rescued him, and by the time we got him below, undressed, and into his bunk, we were wrecks ourselves. But Axel and I wanted to see more of shore, and away we went, leaving Victor snoring. It was curious, the judgment passed on Victor by his shipmates, drinkers themselves. They shook their heads disapprovingly and muttered: "A man like that oughtn't to drink." Now Victor was the smartest sailor and best-tempered shipmate in the forecastle. He was an all-round splendid type of seaman; his mates recognised his worth, and respected him and liked him. Yet John Barleycorn metamorphosed him into a violent lunatic. And that was the very point these drinkers made. They knew that drink—and drink with a sailor is always excessive—made them mad, but only mildly mad. Violent madness was objectionable because it spoiled the fun of others and often culminated in tragedy. From their standpoint, mild madness was all right. But from the standpoint of the whole human race, is not all madness objectionable? And is there a greater maker of madness of all sorts than John Barleycorn?

But to return. Ashore, snugly ensconced in a Japanese house of entertainment, Axel and I compared bruises, and over a comfortable drink talked of the afternoon's happenings. We liked the quietness of that drink and took another. A shipmate dropped in, several shipmates dropped in, and we had more quiet drinks. Finally, just as we had engaged a Japanese orchestra, and as the first strains of the samisens and taikos were rising, through the paper-walls came a wild howl from the street. We recognised it. Still howling, disdaining doorways, with blood-shot eyes and wildly waving muscular arms, Victor burst upon us through the fragile walls. The old amuck rage was on him, and he wanted blood, anybody's blood. The orchestra fled; so did we. We went through doorways, and we went through paper-walls—anything to get away.

And after the place was half wrecked, and we had agreed to pay the damage, leaving Victor partly subdued and showing symptoms of lapsing into a comatose state, Axel and I wandered away in quest of a quieter drinking-place. The main street was a madness. Hundreds of sailors rollicked up and down. Because the chief of police with his small force was helpless, the governor of the colony had issued orders to the captains to have all their men on board by sunset.

What! To be treated in such fashion! As the news spread among the schooners, they were emptied. Everybody came ashore. Men who had had no intention of coming ashore climbed into the boats. The unfortunate governor's ukase had precipitated a general debauch for all hands. It was hours after sunset, and the men wanted to see anybody try to put them on board. They went around inviting the authorities to try to put them on board. In front of the governor's house they were gathered thickest, bawling sea-songs, circulating square faces, and dancing uproarious Virginia reels and old-country dances. The police, including the reserves, stood in little forlorn groups, waiting for the command the governor was too wise to issue. And I thought this saturnalia was great. It was like the old days of the Spanish Main come back. It was license; it was adventure. And I was part of it, a chesty sea-rover along with all these other chesty sea-rovers among the paper houses of Japan.

The governor never issued the order to clear the streets, and Axel and I wandered on from drink to drink. After a time, in some of the antics, getting hazy myself, I lost him. I drifted along, making new acquaintances, downing more drinks, getting hazier and hazier. I remember, somewhere, sitting in a circle with Japanese fishermen, Kanaka boat-steerers from our own vessels, and a young Danish sailor fresh from cowboying in the Argentine and with a penchant for native customs and ceremonials. And with due and proper and most intricate Japanese ceremonial we of the circle drank saki, pale, mild, and lukewarm, from tiny porcelain bowls.

And, later, I remember the runaway apprentices—boys of eighteen and twenty, of middle class English families, who had jumped their ships and apprenticeships in various ports of the world and drifted into the forecastles of the sealing schooners. They were healthy, smooth-skinned, clear-eyed, and they were young—youths like me, learning the way of their feet in the world of men. And they *were* men. No mild saki for them, but square faces illicitly refilled with corrosive fire that flamed through their veins and burst into conflagrations in their heads. I remember a melting song they sang, the refrain of which was:

"'Tis but a little golden ring,
I give it to thee with pride,
Wear it for your mother's sake
When you are on the tide."

They wept over it as they sang it, the graceless young scamps who had all broken their mothers' prides, and I sang with them, and wept with them, and luxuriated in the pathos and the tragedy of it, and struggled to make glimmering inebriated generalisations on life and romance. And one last picture I have, standing out very clear and bright in the midst of vagueness before and blackness afterward. We—the apprentices and I—are swaying and clinging to one another under the stars. We are singing a rollicking sea song, all save one who sits on the ground and weeps; and we are marking the rhythm with waving square faces. From up and down the street come far choruses of sea-voices similarly singing, and life is great, and beautiful and romantic, and magnificently mad.

And next, after the blackness, I open my eyes in the early dawn to see a Japanese woman, solicitously anxious, bending over me. She is the port pilot's wife and

244

I am lying in her doorway. I am chilled and shivering, sick with the after-sickness of debauch. And I feel lightly clad. Those rascals of runaway apprentices! They have acquired the habit of running away. They have run away with my possessions. My watch is gone. My few dollars are gone. My coat is gone. So is my belt. And yes, my shoes.

And the foregoing is a sample of the ten days I spent in the Bonin Islands. Victor got over his lunacy, rejoined Axel and me, and after that we caroused somewhat more discreetly. And we never climbed that lava path among the flowers. The town and the square faces were all we saw.

One who has been burned by fire must preach about the fire. I might have seen and healthily enjoyed a whole lot more of the Bonin Islands, if I had done what I ought to have done. But, as I see it, it is not a matter of what one ought to do, or ought not to do. It is what one *does* do. That is the everlasting, irrefragable fact. I did just what I did. I did what all those men did in the Bonin Islands. I did what millions of men over the world were doing at that particular point in time. I did it because the way led to it, because I was only a human boy, a creature of my environment, and neither an anaemic nor a god. I was just human, and I was taking the path in the world that men took—men whom I admired, if you please; full-blooded men, lusty, breedy, chesty men, free spirits and anything but niggards in the way they foamed life away.

And the way was open. It was like an uncovered well in a yard where children play. It is small use to tell the brave little boys toddling their way along into knowledge of life that they mustn't play near the uncovered well. They'll play near it. Any parent knows that. And we know that a certain percentage of them, the livest and most daring, will fall into the well. The thing to do—we all know it—is to cover up the well. The case is the same with John Barleycorn. All the no-saying and no-preaching in the world will fail to keep men, and youths growing into manhood, away from John Barleycorn when John Barleycorn is everywhere accessible, and where John Barleycorn is everywhere the connotation of manliness, and daring, and great-spiritedness.

The only rational thing for the twentieth-century folk to do is to cover up the well; to make the twentieth century in truth the twentieth century, and to relegate to the nineteenth century and all the preceding centuries the things of those centuries, the witch-burnings, the intolerances, the fetiches, and, not least among such barbarisms, John Barleycorn.

CHAPTER XVII

North we raced from the Bonin Islands to pick up the seal-herd, and north we hunted it for a hundred days into frosty, mitten weather and into and through vast fogs which hid the sun from us for a week at a time. It was wild and heavy work, without a drink or thought of drink. Then we sailed south to Yokohama, with a big catch of skins in our salt and a heavy pay-day coming.

I was eager to be ashore and see Japan, but the first day was devoted to ship's work, and not until evening did we sailors land. And here, by the very system of things, by the way life was organised and men transacted affairs, John Barleycorn reached out and tucked my arm in his. The captain had given money for us to the hunters, and the hunters were waiting in a certain Japanese public house for us to come and get it. We rode to the place in rickshaws. Our own crowd had taken possession of it. Drink was flowing. Everybody had money, and everybody was treating. After the hundred days of hard toil and absolute abstinence, in the pink of physical condition, bulging with health, over-spilling with spirits that had long been pent by discipline and circumstance, of course we would have a drink or two. And after that we would see the town.

It was the old story. There were so many drinks to be drunk, and as the warm magic poured through our veins and mellowed our voices and affections we knew it was no time to make invidious distinctions—to drink with this shipmate and to decline to drink with that shipmate. We were all shipmates who had been through stress and storm together, who had pulled and hauled on the same sheets and tackles, relieved one another's wheels, laid out side by side on the same jib-boom when she was plunging into it and looked to see who was missing when she cleared and lifted. So we drank with all, and all treated, and our voices rose, and we remembered a myriad kindly acts of comradeship, and forgot our fights and wordy squabbles, and knew one another for the best fellows in the world.

Well, the night was young when we arrived in that public house, and for all of that first night that public house was what I saw of Japan—a drinking-place which was very like a drinking-place at home or anywhere else over the world.

We lay in Yokohama harbour for two weeks, and about all we saw of Japan was its drinking-places where sailors congregated. Occasionally, some one of us varied the monotony with a more exciting drunk. In such fashion I managed a real exploit by swimming off to the schooner one dark midnight and going soundly to sleep while the water-police searched the harbour for my body and brought my clothes out for identification.

Perhaps it was for things like that, I imagined, that men got drunk. In our little round of living what I had done was a noteworthy event. All the harbour talked about it. I enjoyed several days of fame among the Japanese boatmen and ashore in the pubs. It was a red-letter event. It was an event to be remembered and narrated with pride. I remember it to-day, twenty years afterward, with a secret glow of pride. It was a purple passage, just as Victor's wrecking of the tea-house in the Bonin Islands and my being looted by the runaway apprentices were purple passages.

The point is that the charm of John Barleycorn was still a mystery to me. I was so organically a non-alcoholic that alcohol itself made no appeal; the chemical reactions it produced in me were not satisfying because I possessed no need for such chemical satisfaction. I drank because the men I was with drank, and because my nature was such that I could not permit myself to be less of a man than other men at their favourite pastime. And I still had a sweet tooth, and on privy occasions when there was no man to see, bought candy and blissfully devoured it.

We hove up anchor to a jolly chanty, and sailed out of Yokohama harbour for San Francisco. We took the northern passage, and with the stout west wind at our back made the run across the Pacific in thirty-seven days of brave sailing. We still had a big pay-day coming to us, and for thirty-seven days, without a drink to addle our mental processes, we incessantly planned the spending of our money.

The first statement of each man—ever an ancient one in homeward-bound forecastles—was: "No boarding-house sharks in mine." Next, in parentheses, was regret at having spent so much money in Yokohama. And after that, each man proceeded to paint his favourite phantom. Victor, for instance, said that immediately he landed in San Francisco he would pass right through the water-front and the Barbary Coast, and put an advertisement in the papers. His advertisement would be for board and room in some simple working-class family. "Then," said Victor, "I shall go to some dancing-school for a week or two, just to meet and get acquainted with the girls and fellows. Then I'll get the run of the different dancing crowds, and be invited to their homes, and to parties, and all that, and with the money I've got I can last out till next January, when I'll go sealing again."

No; he wasn't going to drink. He knew the way of it, particularly his way of it, wine in, wit out, and his money would be gone in no time. He had his choice, based on bitter experience, between three days' debauch among the sharks and harpies of the Barbary Coast and a whole winter of wholesome enjoyment and sociability, and there wasn't any doubt of the way he was going to choose.

Said Axel Gunderson, who didn't care for dancing and social functions: "I've got a good pay-day. Now I can go home. It is fifteen years since I've seen my mother and all the family. When I pay off, I shall send my money home to wait for me. Then I'll pick a good ship bound for Europe, and arrive there with another pay-day. Put them together, and I'll have more money than ever in my life before. I'll be a prince at home. You haven't any idea how cheap everything is in Norway. I can make presents to everybody, and spend my money like what would seem to them a millionaire, and live a whole year there before I'd have to go back to sea."

"The very thing I'm going to do," declared Red John. "It's three years since I've received a line from home and ten years since I was there. Things are just as cheap in Sweden, Axel, as in Norway, and my folks are real country folk and farmers. I'll send my pay-day home and ship on the same ship with you for around the Horn. We'll pick a good one."

And as Axel Gunderson and Red John painted the pastoral delights and festive customs of their respective countries, each fell in love with the other's home place, and they solemnly pledged to make the journey together, and to spend, together, six months in the one's Swedish home and six months in the other's Norwegian home. And for the rest of the voyage they could hardly be pried apart, so infatuated did they become with discussing their plans.

Long John was not a home-body. But he was tired of the forecastle. No boarding-house sharks in his. He, too, would get a room in a quiet family, and he would go to a navigation school and study to be a captain. And so it went. Each man swore that for once he would be sensible and not squander his money. No boarding-house sharks, no sailor-town, no drink, was the slogan of our forecastle.

The men became stingy. Never was there such economy. They refused to buy anything more from the slopchest. Old rags had to last, and they sewed patch upon patch, turning out what are called "homeward-bound patches" of the most amazing proportions. They saved on matches, even, waiting till two or three were ready to light their pipes from the same match.

As we sailed up the San Francisco water-front, the moment the port doctors passed us, the boarding-house runners were alongside in whitehall boats. They swarmed on board, each drumming for his own boarding-house, and each with a bottle of free whisky inside his shirt. But we waved them grandly and blasphemously away. We wanted none of their boarding-houses and none of their whisky. We were sober, thrifty sailormen, with better use for our money.

Came the paying off before the shipping commissioner. We emerged upon the sidewalk, each with a pocketful of money. About us, like buzzards, clustered the sharks and harpies. And we looked at each other. We had been seven months together, and our paths were separating. One last farewell rite of comradeship remained. (Oh, it was the way, the custom.) "Come on, boys," said our sailing master. There stood the inevitable adjacent saloon. There were a dozen saloons all around. And when we had followed the sailing master into the one of his choice, the sharks were thick on the sidewalk outside. Some of them even ventured inside, but we would have nothing to do with them.

There we stood at the long bar—the sailing master, the mate, the six hunters, the six boat-steerers, and the five boat-pullers. There were only five of the last, for one of our number had been dropped overboard, with a sack of coal at his feet, between two snow squalls in a driving gale off Cape Jerimo. There were nineteen of us and it was to be our last drink together. With seven months of men's work in the world, blow high, blow low, behind us, we were looking on each other for the last time. We knew it, for sailors' ways go wide. And the nineteen of us drank the sailing master's treat. Then the mate looked at us with eloquent eyes and called another round. We liked the mate just as well as the sailing master, and we liked them both. Could we drink with one, and not the other?

And Pete Holt, my own hunter (lost next year in the Mary Thomas, with all hands), called a round. The time passed, the drinks continued to come on the bar, our voices rose, and the maggots began to crawl. There were six hunters, and each insisted, in the sacred name of comradeship, that all hands drink with him just once. There were six boat-steerers and five boat-pullers and the same logic held with them. There was money in all our pockets, and our money was as good as any man's, and our hearts were as free and generous.

Nineteen rounds of drinks. What more would John Barleycorn ask in order to have his will with men? They were ripe to forget their dearly cherished plans. They rolled out of the saloon and into the arms of the sharks and harpies. They didn't last long. From two days to a week saw the end of their money and saw them being carted by the boarding-house masters on board outward-bound ships. Victor was a fine body of a man, and through a lucky friendship managed to get into the life-saving service. He never saw the dancing-school nor placed his advertisement for a room in a working-class family. Nor did Long John win to navigation school. By the end of the week he was a transient lumper on a river steamboat. Red John and Axel did not send their pay-days home to the old country. Instead, and along with the rest, they were scattered on board sailing ships bound for the four quarters of the globe, where they had been placed by the boarding-house masters, and where they were working out advance money which they had neither seen nor spent.

What saved me was that I had a home and people to go to. I crossed the bay to Oakland, and, among other things, took a look at the death-road. Nelson was gone—shot to death while drunk and resisting the officers. His partner in that affair was lying in prison. Whisky Bob was gone. Old Cole, Old Smoudge, and Bob Smith were gone. Another Smith, he of the belted guns and the Annie, was drowned. French Frank, they said, was lurking up river, afraid to come down because of something he had done. Others were wearing the stripes in San Quentin or Folsom. Big Alec, the King of the Greeks, whom I had known well in the old Benicia days, and with whom I had drunk whole nights through, had killed two men and fled to foreign parts. Fitzsimmons, with whom I had sailed on the Fish Patrol, had been stabbed in the lung through the back and had died a lingering death complicated with tuberculosis. And so it went, a very lively and well-patronised road, and, from what I knew of all of them, John Barleycorn was responsible, with the sole exception of Smith of the Annie.

CHAPTER XVIII

My infatuation for the Oakland water-front was quite dead. I didn't like the looks of it, nor the life. I didn't care for the drinking, nor the vagrancy of it, and I wandered back to the Oakland Free Library and read the books with greater understanding. Then, too, my mother said I had sown my wild oats and it was time I settled down to a regular job. Also, the family needed the money. So I got a job at the jute mills—a ten-hour day at ten cents an hour. Despite my increase in strength and general efficiency, I was receiving no more than when I worked in the cannery several years before. But, then, there was a promise of a rise to a dollar and a quarter a day after a few months. And here, so far as John Barleycorn is concerned, began a period of innocence. I did not know what it was to take a drink from month end to month end. Not yet eighteen years old, healthy and with labour-hardened but unhurt muscles, like any young animal I needed diversion, excitement, something beyond the books and the mechanical toil.

I strayed into Young Men's Christian Associations. The life there was healthful and athletic, but too juvenile. For me it was too late. I was not boy, nor youth, despite my paucity of years. I had bucked big with men. I knew mysterious and violent things. I was from the other side of life so far as concerned the young men I encountered in the Y.M.C.A. I spoke another language, possessed a sadder and more terrible wisdom. (When I come to think it over, I realise now that I have never had a boyhood.) At any rate, the Y.M.C.A. young men were too juvenile for me, too unsophisticated. This I would not have minded, could they have met me and helped me mentally. But I had got more out of the books than they. Their meagre physical experiences, plus their meagre intellectual experiences, made a negative sum so vast that it overbalanced their wholesome morality and healthful sports.

In short, I couldn't play with the pupils of a lower grade. All the clean splendid young life that was theirs was denied me—thanks to my earlier tutelage under John Barleycorn. I knew too much too young. And yet, in the good time coming when alcohol is eliminated from the needs and the institutions of men, it will be the Y.M.C.A., and similar unthinkably better and wiser and more virile congregating-places, that will receive the men who now go to saloons to find themselves and one another. In the meantime, we live to-day, here and now, and we discuss to-day, here and now.

I was working ten hours a day in the jute mills. It was hum-drum machine toil. I wanted life. I wanted to realise myself in other ways than at a machine for ten cents an hour. And yet I had had my fill of saloons. I wanted something new. I was growing up. I was developing unguessed and troubling potencies and proclivities. And at this very stage, fortunately, I met Louis Shattuck and we became chums.

Louis Shattuck, without one vicious trait, was a real innocently devilish young fellow, who was quite convinced that he was a sophisticated town boy. And I wasn't a town boy at all. Louis was handsome, and graceful, and filled with love for the girls. With him it was an exciting and all-absorbing pursuit. I didn't know anything about girls. I had been too busy being a man. This was an entirely new phase of existence which had escaped me. And when I saw Louis say good-bye to me, raise his hat to a girl of his acquaintance, and walk on with her side by side down the sidewalk, I was made excited and envious. I, too, wanted to play this game.

"Well, there's only one thing to do," said Louis, "and that is, you must get a girl."

Which is more difficult than it sounds. Let me show you, at the expense of a slight going aside. Louis did not know girls in their home life. He had the entree to no girl's home. And of course, I, a stranger in this new world, was similarly circumstanced. But, further, Louis and I were unable to go to dancing-schools, or to public dances, which were very good places for getting acquainted. We didn't have the money. He was a blacksmith's apprentice, and was earning but slightly more than I. We both lived at home and paid our way. When we had done this, and bought our cigarettes, and the inevitable clothes and shoes, there remained to each of us, for personal spending, a sum that varied between seventy cents and a dollar for the week. We whacked this up, shared it, and sometimes loaned all of what was left of it when one of us needed it for some more gorgeous girl-adventure, such as car-fare out to Blair's Park and back—twenty cents, bang, just like that; and ice-cream for two—thirty cents; or tamales in a tamale-parlour, which came cheaper and which for two cost only twenty cents.

I did not mind this money meagreness. The disdain I had learned for money from the oyster pirates had never left me. I didn't care over-weeningly for it for personal gratification; and in my philosophy I completed the circle, finding myself as equable with the lack of a ten-cent piece as I was with the squandering of scores of dollars in calling all men and hangers-on up to the bar to drink with me.

But how to get a girl? There was no girl's home to which Louis could take me and where I might be introduced to girls. I knew none. And Louis' several girls he wanted for himself; and anyway, in the very human nature of boys' and girls' ways, he couldn't turn any of them over to me. He did persuade them to bring girl-friends for me; but I found them weak sisters, pale and ineffectual alongside the choice specimens he had.

"You'll have to do like I did," he said finally. "I got these by getting them. You'll have to get one the same way."

And he initiated me. It must be remembered that Louis and I were hard situated. We really had to struggle to pay our board and maintain a decent appearance. We met each other in the evening, after the day's work, on the street corner, or in a little candy store on a side street, our sole frequenting-place. Here we bought our cigarettes, and, occasionally, a nickel's worth of "red-hots." (Oh, yes; Louis and I unblushingly ate candy—all we could get. Neither of us drank. Neither of us ever went into a saloon.)

But the girl. In quite primitive fashion, as Louis advised me, I was to select her and make myself acquainted with her. We strolled the streets in the early evenings. The girls, like us, strolled in pairs. And strolling girls will look at strolling boys who look. (And to this day, in any town, city, or village, in which I, in my middle age, find myself, I look on with the eye trained of old experience, and watch the sweet innocent game played by the strolling boys and girls who just must stroll when the spring and summer evenings call.)

The trouble was that in this Arcadian phase of my history, I, who had come through, case-hardened, from the other side of life, was timid and bashful. Again and again Louis nerved me up. But I didn't know girls. They were strange and wonderful to me after my precocious man's life. I failed of the bold front and the necessary forwardness when the crucial moment came.

Then Louis would show me how—a certain, eloquent glance of eye, a smile, a daring, a lifted hat, a spoken word, hesitancies, giggles, coy nervousnesses—and, behold, Louis acquainted and nodding me up to be introduced. But when we paired off to stroll along boy and girl together, I noted that Louis had invariably picked the good-looker and left to me the little lame sister.

I improved, of course, after experiences too numerous to enter upon, so that there were divers girls to whom I could lift my hat and who would walk beside me in the early evenings. But girl's love did not immediately come to me. I was excited, interested, and I pursued the quest. And the thought of drink never entered my mind. Some of Louis' and my adventures have since given me serious pause when casting sociological generalisations. But it was all good and innocently youthful, and I learned one generalisation, biological rather than sociological, namely, that the "Colonel's lady and Judy O'Grady are sisters under their skins."

And before long I learned girl's love, all the dear fond deliciousness of it, all the glory and the wonder. I shall call her Haydee. She was between fifteen and sixteen. Her little skirt reached her shoe-tops. We sat side by side in a Salvation Army meeting. She was not a convert, nor was her aunt who sat on the other side of her, and who, visiting from the country where at that time the Salvation Army was not, had dropped in to the meeting for half an hour out of curiosity. And Louis sat beside me and observed—I do believe he did no more than observe, because Haydee was not his style of girl.

We did not speak, but in that great half-hour we glanced shyly at each other, and shyly avoided or as shyly returned and met each other's glances more than several times. She had a slender oval face. Her brown eyes were beautiful. Her nose was a dream, as was her sweet-lipped, petulant-hinting mouth. She wore a tam-o'-shanter, and I thought her brown hair the prettiest shade of brown I had ever seen. And from that single experience of half an hour I have ever since been convinced of the reality of love at first sight.

All too soon the aunt and Haydee departed. (This is permissible at any stage of a Salvation Army meeting.) I was no longer interested in the meeting, and, after an appropriate interval of a couple of minutes or less, started to leave with Louis. As we passed out, at the back of the hall a woman recognised me with her eyes, arose, and followed me. I shall not describe her. She was of my own kind and friendship of the old time on the water-front. When Nelson was shot, he had died in her arms, and she knew me as his one comrade. And she must tell me how Nelson had died, and I did want to know; so I went with her across the width of life from dawning boy's love for a brown-haired girl in a tam-o'-shanter back to the old sad savagery I had known.

And when I had heard the tale, I hurried away to find Louis, fearing that I had lost my first love with the first glimpse of her. But Louis was dependable. Her name was—Haydee. He knew where she lived. Each day she passed the blacksmith's shop where he worked, going to or from the Lafayette School. Further, he had seen her on occasion with Ruth, another schoolgirl, and, still further, Nita, who sold us red-hots at the candy store, was a friend of Ruth. The thing to do was to go around to the candy store and see if we could get Nita to give a note to Ruth to give to Haydee. If this could be arranged, all I had to do was write the note.

And it so happened. And in stolen half-hours of meeting I came to know all the sweet madness of boy's love and girl's love. So far as it goes it is not the biggest love in the world, but I do dare to assert that it is the sweetest. Oh, as I look back on it! Never did girl have more innocent boy-lover than I who had been so wicked-wise and violent beyond my years. I didn't know the first thing about girls. I, who had been hailed Prince of the Oyster Pirates, who could go anywhere in the world as a man amongst men; who could sail boats, lay aloft in black and storm, or go into the toughest hang-outs in sailor town and play my part in any rough-house that started or call all hands to the bar—I didn't know the first thing I might say or do with this slender little chit of a girl-woman whose scant skirt just reached her shoe-tops and who was as abysmally ignorant of life as I was, or thought I was, profoundly wise.

I remember we sat on a bench in the starlight. There was fully a foot of space between us. We slightly faced each other, our near elbows on the back of the bench; and once or twice our elbows just touched. And all the time, deliriously happy, talking in the gentlest and most delicate terms that might not offend her sensitive ears, I was cudgelling my brains in an effort to divine what I was expected to do. What did girls expect of boys, sitting on a bench and tentatively striving to find out what love

252

was? What did she expect me to do? Was I expected to kiss her? Did she expect me to try? And if she did expect me, and I didn't what would she think of me?

Ah, she was wiser than I—I know it now—the little innocent girl-woman in her shoe-top skirt. She had known boys all her life. She encouraged me in the ways a girl may. Her gloves were off and in one hand, and I remember, lightly and daringly, in mock reproof for something I had said, how she tapped my lips with a tiny flirt of those gloves. I was like to swoon with delight. It was the most wonderful thing that had ever happened to me. And I remember yet the faint scent that clung to those gloves and that I breathed in the moment they touched my lips.

Then came the agony of apprehension and doubt. Should I imprison in my hand that little hand with the dangling, scented gloves which had just tapped my lips? Should I dare to kiss her there and then, or slip my arm around her waist? Or dared I even sit closer?

Well, I didn't dare. I did nothing. I merely continued to sit there and love with all my soul. And when we parted that evening I had not kissed her. I do remember the first time I kissed her, on another evening, at parting—a mighty moment, when I took all my heart of courage and dared. We never succeeded in managing more than a dozen stolen meetings, and we kissed perhaps a dozen times—as boys and girls kiss, briefly and innocently, and wonderingly. We never went anywhere—not even to a matinee. We once shared together five cents worth of red-hots. But I have always fondly believed that she loved me. I know I loved her; and I dreamed daydreams of her for a year and more, and the memory of her is very dear.

CHAPTER XIX

When I was with people who did not drink, I never thought of drinking. Louis did not drink. Neither he nor I could afford it; but, more significant than that, we had no desire to drink. We were healthy, normal, non-alcoholic. Had we been alcoholic, we would have drunk whether or not we could have afforded it.

Each night, after the day's work, washed up, clothes changed, and supper eaten, we met on the street corner or in the little candy store. But the warm fall weather passed, and on bitter nights of frost or damp nights of drizzle, the street corner was not a comfortable meeting-place. And the candy store was unheated. Nita, or whoever waited on the counter, between waitings lurked in a back living-room that was heated. We were not admitted to this room, and in the store it was as cold as out-of-doors.

Louis and I debated the situation. There was only one solution: the saloon, the congregating-place of men, the place where men hobnobbed with John Barleycorn. Well do I remember the damp and draughty evening, shivering without overcoats because we could not afford them, that Louis and I started out to select our saloon. Saloons are always warm and comfortable. Now Louis and I did not go into this saloon because we wanted a drink. Yet we knew that saloons were not charitable institutions. A man could not make a lounging-place of a saloon without occasionally buying something over the bar.

Our dimes and nickels were few. We could ill spare any of them when they were so potent in paying car-fare for oneself and a girl. (We never paid car-fare when by ourselves, being content to walk.) So, in this saloon, we desired to make the most of our expenditure. We called for a deck of cards and sat down at a table and played euchre for an hour, in which time Louis treated once, and I treated once, to beer—the cheapest drink, ten cents for two. Prodigal! How we grudged it!

We studied the men who came into the place. They seemed all middle-aged and elderly work-men, most of them Germans, who flocked by themselves in old-acquaintance groups, and with whom we could have only the slightest contacts. We voted against that saloon, and went out cast down with the knowledge that we had lost an evening and wasted twenty cents for beer that we didn't want.

We made several more tries on succeeding nights, and at last found our way into the National, a saloon on Tenth and Franklin. Here was a more congenial crowd. Here Louis met a fellow or two he knew, and here I met fellows I had gone to school with when a little lad in knee pants. We talked of old days, and of what had become of this fellow, and what that fellow was doing now, and of course we talked it over drinks. They treated, and we drank. Then, according to the code of drinking, we had to treat. It hurt, for it meant forty to fifty cents a clatter.

We felt quite enlivened when the short evening was over; but at the same time we were bankrupt. Our week's spending money was gone. We decided that that was the saloon for us, and we agreed to be more circumspect thereafter in our drink-buying. Also, we had to economise for the rest of the week. We didn't even have car-fare. We were compelled to break an engagement with two girls from West Oakland with whom we were attempting to be in love. They were to meet us up town the next evening, and we hadn't the car-fare necessary to take them home. Like many others financially embarrassed, we had to disappear for a time from the gay whirl—at least until Saturday night pay-day. So Louis and I rendezvoused in a livery stable, and with coats buttoned and chattering teeth played euchre and casino until the time of our exile was over.

Then we returned to the National Saloon and spent no more than we could decently avoid spending for the comfort and warmth. Sometimes we had mishaps, as when one got stuck twice in succession in a five-handed game of Sancho Pedro for the drinks. Such a disaster meant anywhere between twenty-five to eighty cents, just according to how many of the players ordered ten-cent drinks. But we could temporarily escape the evil effects of such disaster, by virtue of an account we ran behind the bar. Of course, this only set back the day of reckoning and seduced us into spending more than we would have spent on a cash basis. (When I left Oakland suddenly for the adventure-path the following spring, I well remember I owed that saloon-keeper one dollar and seventy cents. Long after, when I returned, he was gone. I still owe him that dollar and seventy cents, and if he should chance to read these lines I want him to know that I'll pay on demand.)

The foregoing incident of the National Saloon I have given in order again to show the lure, or draw, or compulsion, toward John Barleycorn in society as at present organised with saloons on all the corners. Louis and I were two healthy youths. We didn't want to drink. We couldn't afford to drink. And yet we were driven by the circumstance of cold and rainy weather to seek refuge in a saloon, where we had to spend part of our pitiful dole for drink. It will be urged by some critics that we might have gone to the Y.M.C.A., to night school, and to the social circles and homes of young people. The only reply is that we didn't. That is the irrefragable fact. We didn't. And to-day, at this moment, there are hundreds of thousands of boys like Louis and me doing just what Louis and I did with John Barleycorn, warm and comfortable, beckoning and welcoming, tucking their arms in his and beginning to teach them his mellow ways.

CHAPTER XX

The jute mills failed of its agreement to increase my pay to a dollar and a quarter a day, and I, a free-born American boy whose direct ancestors had fought in all the wars from the old pre-Revolutionary Indian wars down, exercised my sovereign right of free contract by quitting the job.

I was still resolved to settle down, and I looked about me. One thing was clear. Unskilled labour didn't pay. I must learn a trade, and I decided on electricity. The need for electricians was constantly growing. But how to become an electrician? I hadn't the money to go to a technical school or university; besides, I didn't think much of schools. I was a practical man in a practical world. Also, I still believed in the old myths which were the heritage of the American boy when I was a boy.

A canal boy could become a President. Any boy who took employment with any firm could, by thrift, energy, and sobriety, learn the business and rise from position to position until he was taken in as a junior partner. After that the senior partnership was only a matter of time. Very often—so ran the myth—the boy, by reason of his steadiness and application, married his employer's daughter. By this time I had been encouraged to such faith in myself in the matter of girls that I was quite certain I would marry my employer's daughter. There wasn't a doubt of it. All the little boys in the myths did it as soon as they were old enough.

So I bade farewell for ever to the adventure-path, and went out to the power plant of one of our Oakland street railways. I saw the superintendent himself, in a private office so fine that it almost stunned me. But I talked straight up. I told him I wanted to become a practical electrician, that I was unafraid of work, that I was used to hard work, and that all he had to do was look at me to see I was fit and strong. I told him that I wanted to begin right at the bottom and work up, that I wanted to devote my life to this one occupation and this one employment.

The superintendent beamed as he listened. He told me that I was the right stuff for success, and that he believed in encouraging American youth that wanted to rise. Why, employers were always on the lookout for young fellows like me, and alas, they found them all too rarely. My ambition was fine and worthy, and he would see to it that I got my chance. (And as I listened with swelling heart, I wondered if it was his daughter I was to marry.)

"Before you can go out on the road and learn the more complicated and higher details of the profession," he said, "you will, of course, have to work in the car-house with the men who install and repair the motors. (By this time I was sure that it was his daughter, and I was wondering how much stock he might own in the company.)

"But," he said, "as you yourself so plainly see, you couldn't expect to begin as a helper to the car-house electricians. That will come when you have worked up to it. You will really begin at the bottom. In the car-house your first employment will be sweeping up, washing the windows, keeping things clean. And after you have shown yourself satisfactory at that, then you may become a helper to the car-house electricians."

I didn't see how sweeping and scrubbing a building was any preparation for the trade of electrician; but I did know that in the books all the boys started with the most menial tasks and by making good ultimately won to the ownership of the whole concern.

"When shall I come to work?" I asked, eager to launch on this dazzling career.

"But," said the superintendent, "as you and I have already agreed, you must begin at the bottom. Not immediately can you in any capacity enter the car-house. Before that you must pass through the engine-room as an oiler."

My heart went down slightly and for the moment as I saw the road lengthen between his daughter and me; then it rose again. I would be a better electrician with knowledge of steam engines. As an oiler in the great engine-room I was confident that few things concerning steam would escape me. Heavens! My career shone more dazzling than ever.

"When shall I come to work?" I asked gratefully.

"But," said the superintendent, "you could not expect to enter immediately into the engine-room. There must be preparation for that. And through the fire-room, of course. Come, you see the matter clearly, I know. And you will see that even the mere handling of coal is a scientific matter and not to be sneered at. Do you know that we weigh every pound of coal we burn? Thus, we learn the value of the coal we buy; we know to a tee the last penny of cost of every item of production, and we learn which firemen are the most wasteful, which firemen, out of stupidity or carelessness, get the least out of the coal they fire." The superintendent beamed again. "You see how very important the little matter of coal is, and by as much as you learn of this little matter you will become that much better a workman—more valuable to us, more valuable to yourself. Now, are you prepared to begin?"

"Any time," I said valiantly. "The sooner the better."

"Very well," he answered. "You will come to-morrow morning at seven o'clock."

I was taken out and shown my duties. Also, I was told the terms of my employment—a ten-hour day, every day in the month including Sundays and holidays, with one day off each month, with a salary of thirty dollars a month. It wasn't exciting. Years before, at the cannery, I had earned a dollar a day for a ten-hour day. I consoled myself with the thought that the reason my earning capacity had not increased with my years and strength was because I had remained an unskilled labourer. But it was different now. I was beginning to work for skill, for a trade, for career and fortune, and the superintendent's daughter.

And I was beginning in the right way—right at the beginning. That was the thing. I was passing coal to the firemen, who shovelled it into the furnaces, where its energy was transformed into steam, which, in the engine-room, was transformed into the electricity with which the electricians worked. This passing coal was surely the very beginning-unless the superintendent should take it into his head to send me to work in the mines from which the coal came in order to get a completer understanding of the genesis of electricity for street railways.

Work! I, who had worked with men, found that I didn't know the first thing about real work. A ten-hour day! I had to pass coal for the day and night shifts, and, despite working through the noon-hour, I never finished my task before eight at night. I was working a twelve-to thirteen-hour day, and I wasn't being paid overtime as in the cannery.

I might as well give the secret away right here. I was doing the work of two men. Before me, one mature able-bodied labourer had done the day shift and another equally mature able-bodied labourer had done the night-shift. They had received forty dollars a month each. The superintendent, bent on an economical administration, had persuaded me to do the work of both men for thirty dollars a month. I thought he was making an electrician of me. In truth and fact, he was saving fifty dollars a month operating expenses to the company.

But I didn't know I was displacing two men. Nobody told me. On the contrary, the superintendent warned everybody not to tell me. How valiantly I went at it that first day. I worked at top speed, filling the iron wheelbarrow with coal, running it on the scales and weighing the load, then trundling it into the fire-room and dumping it on the plates before the fires.

Work! I did more than the two men whom I had displaced. They had merely wheeled in the coal and dumped it on the plates. But while I did this for the day coal, the night coal I had to pile against the wall of the fire-room. Now the fire-room was small. It had been planned for a night coal-passer. So I had to pile the night coal higher and higher, buttressing up the heap with stout planks. Toward the top of the heap I had to handle the coal a second time, tossing it up with a shovel.

I dripped with sweat, but I never ceased from my stride, though I could feel exhaustion coming on. By ten o'clock in the morning, so much of my body's energy had I consumed, I felt hungry and snatched a thick double-slice of bread and butter from my dinner pail. This I devoured, standing, grimed with coal-dust, my knees trembling under me. By eleven o'clock, in this fashion I had consumed my whole lunch. But what of it? I realised that it would enable me to continue working through the noon hour. And I worked all the afternoon. Darkness came on, and I worked under the electric lights. The day fireman went off and the night fireman came on. I plugged away.

At half-past eight, famished, tottering, I washed up, changed my clothes, and dragged my weary body to the car. It was three miles to where I lived, and I had received a pass with the stipulation that I could sit down as long as there were no paying passengers in need of a seat. As I sank into a corner outside seat I prayed that no passenger might require my seat. But the car filled up, and, half-way in, a woman came on board, and there was no seat for her. I started to get up, and to my astonishment found that I could not. With the chill wind blowing on me, my spent body had stiffened into the seat. It took me the rest of the run in to unkink my complaining joints and muscles and get into a standing position on the lower step. And when the car stopped at my corner I nearly fell to the ground when I stepped off.

I hobbled two blocks to the house and limped into the kitchen. While my mother started to cook, I plunged into bread and butter; but before my appetite was appeased, or the steak fried, I was sound asleep. In vain my mother strove to shake me awake enough to eat the meat. Failing in this, with the assistance of my father she managed to get me to my room, where I collapsed dead asleep on the bed. They undressed me and covered me up. In the morning came the agony of being awakened. I was terribly sore, and, worst of all, my wrists were swelling. But I made up for my lost supper, eating an enormous breakfast, and when I hobbled to catch my car I carried a lunch twice as big as the one the day before.

Work! Let any youth just turned eighteen try to out-shovel two man-grown coal-shovellers. Work! Long before midday I had eaten the last scrap of my huge lunch. But I was resolved to show them what a husky young fellow determined to rise could do. The worst of it was that my wrists were swelling and going back on me. There are few who do not know the pain of walking on a sprained ankle. Then imagine the pain of shovelling coal and trundling a loaded wheelbarrow with two sprained wrists.

Work! More than once I sank down on the coal where no one could see me, and cried with rage, and mortification, and exhaustion, and despair. That second day was my hardest, and all that enabled me to survive it and get in the last of the night coal at the end of thirteen hours was the day fireman, who bound both my wrists with broad leather straps. So tightly were they buckled that they were like slightly flexible plaster casts. They took the stresses and pressures which hitherto had been borne by my wrists, and they were so tight that there was no room for the inflammation to rise in the sprains.

And in this fashion I continued to learn to be an electrician. Night after night I limped home, fell asleep before I could eat my supper, and was helped into bed and undressed. Morning after morning, always with huger lunches in my dinner pail, I limped out of the house on my way to work.

I no longer read my library books. I made no dates with the girls. I was a proper work beast. I worked, and ate, and slept, while my mind slept all the time. The whole thing was a nightmare. I worked every day, including Sunday, and I looked far ahead to my one day off at the end of a month, resolved to lie abed all that day and just sleep and rest up.

The strangest part of this experience was that I never took a drink nor thought of taking a drink. Yet I knew that men under hard pressure almost invariably drank. I had seen them do it, and in the past had often done it myself. But so sheerly non-alcoholic was I that it never entered my mind that a drink might be good for me. I instance this to show how entirely lacking from my make-up was any predisposition toward alcohol. And the point of this instance is that later on, after more years had passed, contact with John Barleycorn at last did induce in me the alcoholic desire.

I had often noticed the day fireman staring at me in a curious way. At last, one day, he spoke. He began by swearing me to secrecy. He had been warned by the superintendent not to tell me, and in telling me he was risking his job. He told me of the day coal-passer and the night coal-passer, and of the wages they had received. I was doing for thirty dollars a month what they had received eighty dollars for doing. He would have told me sooner, the fireman said, had he not been so certain that I would break down under the work and quit. As it was, I was killing myself, and all to no good purpose. I was merely cheapening the price of labour, he argued, and keeping two men out of a job.

Being an American boy, and a proud American boy, I did not immediately quit. This was foolish of me, I know; but I resolved to continue the work long enough to prove to the superintendent that I could do it without breaking down. Then I would quit, and he would realise what a fine young fellow he had lost.

All of which I faithfully and foolishly did. I worked on until the time came when I got in the last of the night coal by six o'clock. Then I quit the job of learning electricity by doing more than two men's work for a boy's wages, went home, and proceeded to sleep the clock around.

Fortunately, I had not stayed by the job long enough to injure myself—though I was compelled to wear straps on my wrists for a year afterward. But the effect of this work orgy in which I had indulged was to sicken me with work. I just wouldn't work. The thought of work was repulsive. I didn't care if I never settled down. Learning a trade could go hang. It was a whole lot better to royster and frolic over the world in the way I had previously done. So I headed out on the adventure-path again, starting to tramp East by beating my way on the railroads.

CHAPTER XXI

But behold! As soon as I went out on the adventure-path I met John Barleycorn again. I moved through a world of strangers, and the act of drinking together made one acquainted with men and opened the way to adventures. It might be in a saloon with jingled townsmen, or with a genial railroad man well lighted up and armed with pocket flasks, or with a bunch of alki stiffs in a hang-out. Yes; and it might be in a prohibition state, such as Iowa was in 1894, when I wandered up the main street of Des Moines and was variously invited by strangers into various blind pigs—I remember drinking in barber-shops, plumbing establishments, and furniture stores.

Always it was John Barleycorn. Even a tramp, in those halcyon days, could get most frequently drunk. I remember, inside the prison at Buffalo, how some of us got magnificently jingled, and how, on the streets of Buffalo after our release, another jingle was financed with pennies begged on the main-drag.

I had no call for alcohol, but when I was with those who drank, I drank with them. I insisted on travelling or loafing with the livest, keenest men, and it was just these live, keen ones that did most of the drinking. They were the more comradely men, the more venturous, the more individual. Perhaps it was too much temperament that made them turn from the commonplace and humdrum to find relief in the lying and fantastic sureties of John Barleycorn. Be that as it may, the men I liked best, desired most to be with, were invariably to be found in John Barleycorn's company.

In the course of my tramping over the United States I achieved a new concept. As a tramp, I was behind the scenes of society—aye, and down in the cellar. I could watch the machinery work. I saw the wheels of the social machine go around, and I learned that the dignity of manual labour wasn't what I had been told it was by the teachers, preachers, and politicians. The men without trades were helpless cattle. If one learned a trade, he was compelled to belong to a union in order to work at his trade. And his union was compelled to bully and slug the employers' unions in order to hold up wages or hold down hours. The employers' unions like-wise bullied and slugged. I couldn't see any dignity at all. And when a workman got old, or had an accident, he was thrown into the scrap-heap like any worn-out machine. I saw too many of this sort who were making anything but dignified ends of life.

So my new concept was that manual labour was undignified, and that it didn't pay. No trade for me, was my decision, and no superintendent's daughters. And no criminality, I also decided. That would be almost as disastrous as to be a labourer. Brains paid, not brawn, and I resolved never again to offer my muscles for sale in the brawn market. Brain, and brain only, would I sell.

I returned to California with the firm intention of developing my brain. This meant school education. I had gone through the grammar school long ago, so I entered the Oakland High School. To pay my way I worked as a janitor. My sister helped me, too; and I was not above mowing anybody's lawn or taking up and beating carpets when I had half a day to spare. I was working to get away from work, and I buckled down to it with a grim realisation of the paradox.

Boy and girl love was left behind, and, along with it, Haydee and Louis Shattuck, and the early evening strolls. I hadn't the time. I joined the Henry Clay Debating Society. I was received into the homes of some of the members, where I met nice girls whose skirts reached the ground. I dallied with little home clubs wherein we discussed poetry and art and the nuances of grammar. I joined the socialist local where we studied and orated political economy, philosophy, and politics. I kept half a dozen membership cards working in the free library and did an immense amount of collateral reading.

And for a year and a half on end I never took a drink, nor thought of taking a drink. I hadn't the time, and I certainly did not have the inclination. Between my janitor-work, my studies, and innocent amusements such as chess, I hadn't a moment to spare. I was discovering a new world, and such was the passion of my exploration that the old world of John Barleycorn held no inducements for me.

Come to think of it, I did enter a saloon. I went to see Johnny Heinhold in the Last Chance, and I went to borrow money. And right here is another phase of John

Barleycorn. Saloon-keepers are notoriously good fellows. On an average they perform vastly greater generosities than do business men. When I simply had to have ten dollars, desperate, with no place to turn, I went to Johnny Heinhold. Several years had passed since I had been in his place or spent a cent across his bar. And when I went to borrow the ten dollars I didn't buy a drink, either. And Johnny Heinhold let me have the ten dollars without security or interest.

More than once, in the brief days of my struggle for an education, I went to Johnny Heinhold to borrow money. When I entered the university, I borrowed forty dollars from him, without interest, without security, without buying a drink. And yet—and here is the point, the custom, and the code—in the days of my prosperity, after the lapse of years, I have gone out of my way by many a long block to spend across Johnny Heinhold's bar deferred interest on the various loans. Not that Johnny Heinhold asked me to do it, or expected me to do it. I did it, as I have said, in obedience to the code I had learned along with all the other things connected with John Barleycorn. In distress, when a man has no other place to turn, when he hasn't the slightest bit of security which a savage-hearted pawn-broker would consider, he can go to some saloon-keeper he knows. Gratitude is inherently human. When the man so helped has money again, depend upon it that a portion will be spent across the bar of the saloon-keeper who befriended him.

Why, I recollect the early days of my writing career, when the small sums of money I earned from the magazines came with tragic irregularity, while at the same time I was staggering along with a growing family—a wife, children, a mother, a nephew, and my Mammy Jennie and her old husband fallen on evil days. There were two places at which I could borrow money; a barber shop and a saloon. The barber charged me five per cent. per month in advance. That is to say, when I borrowed one hundred dollars, he handed me ninety-five. The other five dollars he retained as advance interest for the first month. And on the second month I paid him five dollars more, and continued so to do each month until I made a ten strike with the editors and lifted the loan.

The other place to which I came in trouble was the saloon. This saloon-keeper I had known by sight for a couple of years. I had never spent my money in his saloon, and even when I borrowed from him I didn't spend any money. Yet never did he refuse me any sum I asked of him. Unfortunately, before I became prosperous, he moved away to another city. And to this day I regret that he is gone. It is the code I have learned. The right thing to do, and the thing I'd do right now did I know where he is, would be to drop in on occasion and spend a few dollars across his bar for old sake's sake and gratitude.

This is not to exalt saloon-keepers. I have written it to exalt the power of John Barleycorn and to illustrate one more of the myriad ways by which a man is brought in contact with John Barleycorn until in the end he finds he cannot get along without him.

But to return to the run of my narrative. Away from the adventure-path, up to my ears in study, every moment occupied, I lived oblivious to John Barleycorn's existence. Nobody about me drank. If any had drunk, and had they offered it to me, I surely would have drunk. As it was, when I had spare moments I spent them playing chess, or going with nice girls who were themselves students, or in riding a bi-cycle whenever I was fortunate enough to have it out of the pawnbroker's posses-possession.

What I am insisting upon all the time is this: in me was not the slightest trace of alcoholic desire, and this despite the long and severe apprenticeship I had served under John Barleycorn. I had come back from the other side of life to be delighted with this Arcadian simplicity of student youths and student maidens. Also, I had found my way into the realm of the mind, and I was intellectually intoxicated. (Alas! as I was to learn at a later period, intellectual intoxication too, has its katzen-jammer.)

CHAPTER XXII

Three years was the time required to go through the high school. I grew impa-tient. Also, my schooling was becoming financially impossible. At such rate I could not last out, and I did greatly want to go to the state university. When I had done a year of high school, I decided to attempt a short cut. I borrowed the money and paid to enter the senior class of a "cramming joint" or academy. I was scheduled to grad-uate right into the university at the end of four months, thus saving two years.

And how I did cram! I had two years' new work to do in a third of a year. For five weeks I crammed, until simultaneous quadratic equations and chemical formu-las fairly oozed from my ears. And then the master of the academy took me aside. He was very sorry, but he was compelled to give me back my tuition fee and to ask me to leave the school. It wasn't a matter of scholarship. I stood well in my classes, and did he graduate me into the university he was confident that in that institution I would continue to stand well. The trouble was that tongues were gossiping about my case. What! In four months accomplished two years' work! It would be a scan-dal, and the universities were becoming severer in their treatment of accredited prep schools. He couldn't afford such a scandal, therefore I must gracefully depart.

I did. And I paid back the borrowed money, and gritted my teeth, and started to cram by myself. There were three months yet before the university entrance exami-nations. Without laboratories, without coaching, sitting in my bedroom, I proceeded to compress that two years' work into three months and to keep reviewed on the previous year's work.

Nineteen hours a day I studied. For three months I kept this pace, only breaking it on several occasions. My body grew weary, my mind grew weary, but I stayed with it. My eyes grew weary and began to twitch, but they did not break down. Per-haps, toward the last, I got a bit dotty. I know that at the time I was confident, I had discovered the formula for squaring the circle; but I resolutely deferred the working of it out until after the examinations. Then I would show them.

Came the several days of the examinations, during which time I scarcely closed my eyes in sleep, devoting every moment to cramming and reviewing. And when I turned in my last examination paper I was in full possession of a splendid case of brain-fag. I didn't want to see a book. I didn't want to think or to lay eyes on anybody who was liable to think.

There was but one prescription for such a condition, and I gave it to myself—the adventure-path. I didn't wait to learn the result of my examinations. I stowed a roll of blankets and some cold food into a borrowed whitehall boat and set sail. Out of the Oakland Estuary I drifted on the last of an early morning ebb, caught the first of the flood up bay, and raced along with a spanking breeze. San Pablo Bay was smoking, and the Carquinez Straits off the Selby Smelter were smoking, as I picked up ahead and left astern the old landmarks I had first learned with Nelson in the unreefer *Reindeer*.

Benicia showed before me. I opened the bight of Turner's Shipyard, rounded the Solano wharf, and surged along abreast of the patch of tules and the clustering fishermen's arks where in the old days I had lived and drunk deep.

And right here something happened to me, the gravity of which I never dreamed for many a long year to come. I had had no intention of stopping at Benicia. The tide favoured, the wind was fair and howling—glorious sailing for a sailor. Bull Head and Army Points showed ahead, marking the entrance to Suisun Bay which I knew was smoking. And yet, when I laid eyes on those fishing arks lying in the water-front tules, without debate, on the instant, I put down my tiller, came in on the sheet, and headed for the shore. On the instant, out of the profound of my brain-fag, I knew what I wanted. I wanted to drink. I wanted to get drunk.

The call was imperative. There was no uncertainty about it. More than anything else in the world, my frayed and frazzled mind wanted surcease from weariness in the way it knew surcease would come. And right here is the point. For the first time in my life I consciously, deliberately, desired to get drunk. It was a new, a totally different manifestation of John Barleycorn's power. It was not a body need for alcohol. It was a mental desire. My over-worked and jaded mind wanted to forget.

And here the point is drawn to its sharpest. Granted my prodigious brain-fag, nevertheless, had I never drunk in the past, the thought would never have entered my mind to get drunk now. Beginning with physical intolerance for alcohol, for years drinking only for the sake of comradeship and because alcohol was everywhere on the adventure-path, I had now reached the stage where my brain cried out, not merely for a drink, but for a drunk. And had I not been so long used to alcohol, my brain would not have so cried out. I should have sailed on past Bull Head, and in the smoking white of Suisun Bay, and in the wine of wind that filled my sail and poured through me, I should have forgotten my weary brain and rested and refreshed it.

So I sailed in to shore, made all fast, and hurried up among the arks. Charley Le Grant fell on my neck. His wife, Lizzie, folded me to her capacious breast. Billy Murphy, and Joe Lloyd, and all the survivors of the old guard, got around me and their arms around me. Charley seized the can and started for Jorgensen's saloon across the railroad tracks. That meant beer. I wanted whisky, so I called after him to bring a flask.

Many times that flask journeyed across the railroad tracks and back. More old friends of the old free and easy times dropped in, fishermen, Greeks, and Russians, and French. They took turns in treating, and treated all around in turn again. They came and went, but I stayed on and drank with all. I guzzled. I swilled. I ran the liquor down and joyed as the maggots mounted in my brain.

And Clam came in, Nelson's partner before me, handsome as ever, but more reckless, half insane, burning himself out with whisky. He had just had a quarrel with his partner on the sloop *Gazelle*, and knives had been drawn, and blows struck, and he was bent on maddening the fever of the memory with more whisky. And while we downed it, we remembered Nelson and that he had stretched out his great shoulders for the last long sleep in this very town of Benicia; and we wept over the memory of him, and remembered only the good things of him, and sent out the flask to be filled and drank again.

They wanted me to stay over, but through the open door I could see the brave wind on the water, and my ears were filled with the roar of it. And while I forgot that I had plunged into the books nineteen hours a day for three solid months, Charley Le Grant shifted my outfit into a big Columbia River salmon boat. He added charcoal and a fisherman's brazier, a coffee pot and frying pan, and the coffee and the meat, and a black bass fresh from the water that day.

They had to help me down the rickety wharf and into the salmon boat. Likewise they stretched my boom and sprit until the sail set like a board. Some feared to set the sprit; but I insisted, and Charley had no doubts. He knew me of old, and knew that I could sail as long as I could see. They cast off my painter. I put the tiller up, filled away before it, and with dizzy eyes checked and steadied the boat on her course and waved farewell.

The tide had turned, and the fierce ebb, running in the teeth of a fiercer wind, kicked up a stiff, upstanding sea. Suisun Bay was white with wrath and sea-lump. But a salmon boat can sail, and I knew how to sail a salmon boat. So I drove her into it, and through it, and across, and maundered aloud and chanted my disdain for all the books and schools. Cresting seas filled me a foot or so with water, but I laughed at it sloshing about my feet, and chanted my disdain for the wind and the water. I hailed myself a master of life, riding on the back of the unleashed elements, and John Barleycorn rode with me. Amid dissertations on mathematics and philosophy and spoutings and quotations, I sang all the old songs learned in the days when I went from the cannery to the oyster boats to be a pirate—such songs as: "Black Lulu," "Flying Cloud," "Treat my Daughter Kind-i-ly," "The Boston Burglar," "Come all you Rambling, Gambling Men," "I Wisht I was a Little Bird," "Shenandoah," and "Ranzo, Boys, Ranzo."

Hours afterward, in the fires of sunset, where the Sacramento and the San Joaquin tumble their muddy floods together, I took the New York Cut-Off, skimmed across the smooth land-locked water past Black Diamond, on into the San Joaquin, and on to Antioch, where, somewhat sobered and magnificently hungry, I laid alongside a big potato sloop that had a familiar rig. Here were old friends aboard, who fried my black bass in olive oil. Then, too, there was a meaty fisherman's stew, delicious with garlic, and crusty Italian bread without butter, and all washed down with pint mugs of thick and heady claret.

My salmon boat was a-soak, but in the snug cabin of the sloop dry blankets and a dry bunk were mine; and we lay and smoked and yarned of old days, while overhead the wind screamed through the rigging and taut halyards drummed against the mast.

CHAPTER XXIII

My cruise in the salmon boat lasted a week, and I returned ready to enter the university. During the week's cruise I did not drink again. To accomplish this I was compelled to avoid looking up old friends, for as ever the adventure-path was beset with John Barleycorn. I had wanted the drink that first day, and in the days that followed I did not want it. My tired brain had recuperated. I had no moral scruples in the matter. I was not ashamed nor sorry because of that first day's orgy at Benicia, and I thought no more about it, returning gladly to my books and studies.

Long years were to pass ere I looked back upon that day and realised its significance. At the time, and for a long time afterward, I was to think of it only as a frolic. But still later, in the slough of brain-fag and intellectual weariness, I was to remember and know the craving for the anodyne that resides in alcohol.

In the meantime, after this one relapse at Benicia, I went on with my abstemiousness, primarily because I didn't want to drink. And next, I was abstemious because my way led among books and students where no drinking was. Had I been out on the adventure-path, I should as a matter of course have been drinking. For that is the pity of the adventure-path, which is one of John Barleycorn's favourite stamping grounds.

I completed the first half of my freshman year, and in January of 1897 took up my courses for the second half. But the pressure from lack of money, plus a conviction that the university was not giving me all that I wanted in the time I could spare for it, forced me to leave. I was not very disappointed. For two years I had studied, and in those two years, what was far more valuable, I had done a prodigious amount of reading. Then, too, my grammar had improved. It is true, I had not yet learned that I must say "It is I"; but I no longer was guilty of a double negative in writing, though still prone to that error in excited speech.

I decided immediately to embark on my career. I had four preferences: first, music; second, poetry; third, the writing of philosophic, economic, and political essays; and, fourth, and last, and least, fiction writing. I resolutely cut out music as impossible, settled down in my bedroom, and tackled my second, third, and fourth choices simultaneously. Heavens, how I wrote! Never was there a creative fever such as mine from which the patient escaped fatal results. The way I worked was enough to soften my brain and send me to a mad-house. I wrote, I wrote everything— ponderous essays, scientific and sociological short stories, humorous verse, verse of all sorts from triolets and sonnets to blank verse tragedy and elephantine epics in Spenserian stanzas. On occasion I composed steadily, day after day, for fifteen hours a day. At times I forgot to eat, or refused to tear myself away from my passionate outpouring in order to eat.

And then there was the matter of typewriting. My brother-in-law owned a machine which he used in the day-time. In the night I was free to use it. That machine was a wonder. I could weep now as I recollect my wrestlings with it. It must have been a first model in the year one of the typewriter era. Its alphabet was all capitals. It was informed with an evil spirit. It obeyed no known laws of physics, and overthrew the hoary axiom that like things performed to like things produce like results. I'll swear that machine never did the same thing in the same way twice. Again and again it demonstrated that unlike actions produce like results.

How my back used to ache with it! Prior to that experience, my back had been good for every violent strain put upon it in a none too gentle career. But that typewriter proved to me that I had a pipe-stem for a back. Also, it made me doubt my shoulders. They ached as with rheumatism after every bout. The keys of that machine had to be hit so hard that to one outside the house it sounded like distant thunder or some one breaking up the furniture. I had to hit the keys so hard that I strained my first fingers to the elbows, while the ends of my fingers were blisters burst and blistered again. Had it been my machine I'd have operated it with a carpenter's hammer.

The worst of it was that I was actually typing my manuscripts at the same time I was trying to master that machine. It was a feat of physical endurance and a brain storm combined to type a thousand words, and I was composing thousands of words every day which just had to be typed for the waiting editors.

Oh, between the writing and the typewriting I was well a-weary. I had brain and nerve fag, and body fag as well, and yet the thought of drink never suggested itself. I was living too high to stand in need of an anodyne. All my waking hours, except those with that infernal typewriter, were spent in a creative heaven. And along with this I had no desire for drink because I still believed in many things—in the love of all men and women in the matter of man and woman love; in fatherhood; in human justice; in art—in the whole host of fond illusions that keep the world turning around.

But the waiting editors elected to keep on waiting. My manuscripts made amazing round-trip records between the Pacific and the Atlantic. It might have been the weirdness of the typewriting that prevented the editors from accepting at least one little offering of mine. I don't know, and goodness knows the stuff I wrote was as weird as its typing. I sold my hard-bought school books for ridiculous sums to second-hand bookmen. I borrowed small sums of money wherever I could, and suffered my old father to feed me with the meagre returns of his failing strength.

It didn't last long, only a few weeks, when I had to surrender and go to work. Yet I was unaware of any need for the drink anodyne. I was not disappointed. My career was retarded, that was all. Perhaps I did need further preparation. I had learned enough from the books to realise that I had only touched the hem of knowledge's garment. I still lived on the heights. My waking hours, and most of the hours I should have used for sleep, were spent with the books.

CHAPTER XXIV

Out in the country, at the Belmont Academy, I went to work in a small, perfectly appointed steam laundry. Another fellow and myself did all the work from sorting and washing to ironing the white shirts, collars and cuffs, and the "fancy starch" of the wives of the professors. We worked like tigers, especially as summer came on and the academy boys took to the wearing of duck trousers. It consumes a dreadful lot of time to iron one pair of duck trousers. And there were so many pairs of them. We sweated our way through long sizzling weeks at a task that was never done; and many a night, while the students snored in bed, my partner and I toiled on under the electric light at steam mangle or ironing board.

The hours were long, the work was arduous, despite the fact that we became past masters in the art of eliminating waste motion. And I was receiving thirty dollars a month and board—a slight increase over my coal-shovelling and cannery days, at least to the extent of board, which cost my employer little (we ate in the kitchen), but which was to me the equivalent of twenty dollars a month. My robuster strength of added years, my increased skill, and all I had learned from the books, were responsible for this increase of twenty dollars. Judging by my rate of development, I might hope before I died to be a night watchman for sixty dollars a month, or a policeman actually receiving a hundred dollars with pickings.

So relentlessly did my partner and I spring into our work throughout the week that by Saturday night we were frazzled wrecks. I found myself in the old familiar work-beast condition, toiling longer hours than the horses toiled, thinking scarcely more frequent thoughts than horses think. The books were closed to me. I had brought a trunkful to the laundry, but found myself unable to read them. I fell asleep the moment I tried to read; and if I did manage to keep my eyes open for several pages, I could not remember the contents of those pages. I gave over attempts on heavy study, such as jurisprudence, political economy, and biology, and tried lighter stuff, such as history. I fell asleep. I tried literature, and fell asleep. And finally, when I fell asleep over lively novels, I gave up. I never succeeded in reading one book in all the time I spent in the laundry.

And when Saturday night came, and the week's work was over until Monday morning, I knew only one desire besides the desire to sleep, and that was to get drunk. This was the second time in my life that I had heard the unmistakable call of John Barleycorn. The first time it had been because of brain-fag. But I had no overworked brain now. On the contrary, all I knew was the dull numbness of a brain that was not worked at all. That was the trouble. My brain had become so alert and eager, so quickened by the wonder of the new world the books had discovered to it, that it now suffered all the misery of stagnancy and inaction.

And I, the long time intimate of John Barleycorn, knew just what he promised me—maggots of fancy, dreams of power, forgetfulness, anything and everything save whirling washers, revolving mangles, humming centrifugal wringers, and fancy starch and interminable processions of duck trousers moving in steam under my flying iron. And that's it. John Barleycorn makes his appeal to weakness and failure, to weariness and exhaustion. He is the easy way out. And he is lying all the time. He offers false strength to the body, false elevation to the spirit, making things seem what they are not and vastly fairer than what they are.

But it must not be forgotten that John Barleycorn is protean. As well as to weakness and exhaustion, does he appeal to too much strength, to superabundant vitality, to the ennui of idleness. He can tuck in his arm the arm of any man in any mood. He can throw the net of his lure over all men. He exchanges new lamps for old, the spangles of illusion for the drabs of reality, and in the end cheats all who traffic with him.

I didn't get drunk, however, for the simple reason that it was a mile and a half to the nearest saloon. And this, in turn, was because the call to get drunk was not very loud in my ears. Had it been loud, I would have travelled ten times the distance to win to the saloon. On the other hand, had the saloon been just around the corner, I should have got drunk. As it was, I would sprawl out in the shade on my one day of rest and dally with the Sunday papers. But I was too weary even for their froth. The comic supplement might bring a pallid smile to my face, and then I would fall asleep.

Although I did not yield to John Barleycorn while working in the laundry, a certain definite result was produced. I had heard the call, felt the gnaw of desire, yearned for the anodyne. I was being prepared for the stronger desire of later years.

And the point is that this development of desire was entirely in my brain. My body did not cry out for alcohol. As always, alcohol was repulsive to my body. When I was bodily weary from shovelling coal the thought of taking a drink had never flickered into my consciousness. When I was brain-wearied after taking the entrance examinations to the university, I promptly got drunk. At the laundry I was suffering physical exhaustion again, and physical exhaustion that was not nearly so profound as that of the coal-shovelling. But there was a difference. When I went coal-shovelling my mind had not yet awakened. Between that time and the laundry my mind had found the kingdom of the mind. While shovelling coal my mind was somnolent. While toiling in the laundry my mind, informed and eager to do and be, was crucified.

And whether I yielded to drink, as at Benicia, or whether I refrained, as at the laundry, in my brain the seeds of desire for alcohol were germinating.

CHAPTER XXV

After the laundry my sister and her husband grubstaked me into the Klondike. It was the first gold rush into that region, the early fall rush of 1897. I was twenty-one years old, and in splendid physical condition. I remember, at the end of the twenty-eight-mile portage across Chilcoot from Dyea Beach to Lake Linderman, I was packing up with the Indians and out-packing many an Indian. The last pack into Linderman was three miles. I back-tripped it four times a day, and on each forward trip carried one hundred and fifty pounds. This means that over the worst trails I daily travelled twenty-four miles, twelve of which were under a burden of one hundred and fifty pounds.

Yes, I had let career go hang, and was on the adventure-path again in quest of fortune. And of course, on the adventure-path, I met John Barleycorn. Here were the chesty men again, rovers and adventurers, and while they didn't mind a grub famine, whisky they could not do without. Whisky went over the trail, while the flour lay cached and untouched by the trail-side.

As good fortune would have it, the three men in my party were not drinkers. Therefore I didn't drink save on rare occasions and disgracefully when with other men. In my personal medicine chest was a quart of whisky. I never drew the cork till six months afterward, in a lonely camp, where, without anaesthetics, a doctor was compelled to operate on a man. The doctor and the patient emptied my bottle between them and then proceeded to the operation.

Back in California a year later, recovering from scurvy, I found that my father was dead and that I was the head and the sole bread-winner of a household. When I state that I had passed coal on a steamship from Behring Sea to British Columbia, and travelled in the steerage from there to San Francisco, it will be understood that I brought nothing back from the Klondike but my scurvy.

Times were hard. Work of any sort was difficult to get. And work of any sort was what I had to take, for I was still an unskilled labourer. I had no thought of career. That was over and done with. I had to find food for two mouths beside my own and keep a roof over our heads—yes, and buy a winter suit, my one suit being decidedly summery. I had to get some sort of work immediately. After that, when I had caught my breath, I might think about my future.

Unskilled labour is the first to feel the slackness of hard times, and I had no trades save those of sailor and laundryman. With my new responsibilities I didn't dare go to sea, and I failed to find a job at laundrying. I failed to find a job at anything. I had my name down in five employment bureaux. I advertised in three newspapers. I sought out the few friends I knew who might be able to get me work; but they were either uninterested or unable to find anything for me.

The situation was desperate. I pawned my watch, my bicycle, and a mackintosh of which my father had been very proud and which he had left to me. It was and is my sole legacy in this world. It had cost fifteen dollars, and the pawnbroker let me have two dollars on it. And—oh, yes—a water-front comrade of earlier years drifted along one day with a dress suit wrapped in newspapers. He could give no adequate explanation of how he had come to possess it, nor did I press for an explanation. I wanted the suit myself. No; not to wear. I traded him a lot of rubbish which, being unpawnable, was useless to me. He peddled the rubbish for several dollars, while I pledged the dress-suit with my pawnbroker for five dollars. And for all I know the pawnbroker still has the suit. I had never intended to redeem it.

But I couldn't get any work. Yet I was a bargain in the labour market. I was twenty-two years old, weighed one hundred and sixty-five pounds stripped, every pound of which was excellent for toil; and the last traces of my scurvy were vanishing before a treatment of potatoes chewed raw. I tackled every opening for employment. I tried to become a studio model, but there were too many fine-bodied young fellows out of jobs. I answered advertisements of elderly invalids in need of companions. And I almost became a sewing machine agent, on commission, without salary. But poor people don't buy sewing machines in hard times, so I was forced to forgo that employment.

Of course, it must be remembered that along with such frivolous occupations I was trying to get work as wop, lumper, and roustabout. But winter was coming on, and the surplus labour army was pouring into the cities. Also I, who had romped along carelessly through the countries of the world and the kingdom of the mind, was not a member of any union.

I sought odd jobs. I worked days, and half-days, at anything I could get. I mowed lawns, trimmed hedges, took up carpets, beat them, and laid them again. Further, I took the civil service examinations for mail carrier and passed first. But alas! there was no vacancy, and I must wait. And while I waited, and in between the odd jobs I managed to procure, I started to earn ten dollars by writing a newspaper account of a voyage I had made, in an open boat down the Yukon, of nineteen hundred miles in nineteen days. I didn't know the first thing about the newspaper game, but I was confident I'd get ten dollars for my article.

But I didn't. The first San Francisco newspaper to which I mailed it never acknowledged receipt of the manuscript, but held on to it. The longer it held on to it the more certain I was that the thing was accepted.

And here is the funny thing. Some are born to fortune, and some have fortune thrust upon them. But in my case I was clubbed into fortune, and bitter necessity wielded the club. I had long since abandoned all thought of writing as a career. My honest intention in writing that article was to earn ten dollars. And that was the limit of my intention. It would help to tide me along until I got steady employment. Had a vacancy occurred in the post office at that time, I should have jumped at it.

But the vacancy did not occur, nor did a steady job; and I employed the time between odd jobs with writing a twenty-one-thousand-word serial for the "Youth's Companion." I turned it out and typed it in seven days. I fancy that was what was the matter with it, for it came back.

It took some time for it to go and come, and in the meantime I tried my hand at short stories. I sold one to the "Overland Monthly" for five dollars. The "Black Cat" gave me forty dollars for another. The "Overland Monthly" offered me seven dollars and a half, pay on publication, for all the stories I should deliver. I got my bicycle, my watch, and my father's mackintosh out of pawn and rented a typewriter. Also, I paid up the bills I owed to the several groceries that allowed me a small credit. I recall the Portuguese groceryman who never permitted my bill to go beyond four dollars. Hopkins, another grocer, could not be budged beyond five dollars.

And just then came the call from the post office to go to work. It placed me in a most trying predicament. The sixty-five dollars I could earn regularly every month was a terrible temptation. I couldn't decide what to do. And I'll never be able to forgive the postmaster of Oakland. I answered the call, and I talked to him like a man. I frankly told him the situation. It looked as if I might win out at writing. The chance was good, but not certain. Now, if he would pass me by and select the next man on the eligible list and give me a call at the next vacancy—

But he shut me off with: "Then you don't want the position?"

"But I do," I protested. "Don't you see, if you will pass me over this time—"

"If you want it you will take it," he said coldly.

Happily for me, the cursed brutality of the man made me angry.

"Very well," I said. "I won't take it."

CHAPTER XXVI

Having burned my ship, I plunged into writing. I am afraid I always was an extremist. Early and late I was at it—writing, typing, studying grammar, studying writing and all the forms of writing, and studying the writers who succeeded in order to find out how they succeeded. I managed on five hours' sleep in the twenty-four, and came pretty close to working the nineteen waking hours left to me. My light burned till two and three in the morning, which led a good neighbour woman into a bit of sentimental Sherlock-Holmes deduction. Never seeing me in the daytime, she concluded that I was a gambler, and that the light in my window was placed there by my mother to guide her erring son home.

The trouble with the beginner at the writing game is the long, dry spells, when there is never an editor's cheque and everything pawnable is pawned. I wore my summer suit pretty well through that winter, and the following summer experienced the longest, dryest spell of all, in the period when salaried men are gone on vacation and manuscripts lie in editorial offices until vacation is over.

My difficulty was that I had no one to advise me. I didn't know a soul who had written or who had ever tried to write. I didn't even know one reporter. Also, to succeed at the writing game, I found I had to unlearn about everything the teachers and professors of literature of the high school and university had taught me. I was very indignant about this at the time; though now I can understand it. They did not know the trick of successful writing in the years 1895 and 1896. They knew all about "Snow Bound" and "Sartor Resartus"; but the American editors of 1899 did not want such truck. They wanted the 1899 truck, and offered to pay so well for it that the teachers and professors of literature would have quit their jobs could they have supplied it.

I struggled along, stood off the butcher and the grocer, pawned my watch and bicycle and my father's mackintosh, and I worked. I really did work, and went on short commons of sleep. Critics have complained about the swift education one of my characters, Martin Eden, achieved. In three years, from a sailor with a common school education, I made a successful writer of him. The critics say this is impossible. Yet I was Martin Eden. At the end of three working years, two of which were spent in high school and the university and one spent at writing, and all three in studying immensely and intensely, I was publishing stories in magazines such as the "Atlantic Monthly," was correcting proofs of my first book (issued by Houghton, Mifflin Co.), was selling sociological articles to "Cosmopolitan" and "McClure's," had declined an associate editorship proffered me by telegraph from New York City, and was getting ready to marry.

Now the foregoing means work, especially the last year of it, when I was learning my trade as a writer. And in that year, running short on sleep and tasking my brain to its limit, I neither drank nor cared to drink. So far as I was concerned, alcohol did not exist. I did suffer from brain-fag on occasion, but alcohol never suggested itself as an ameliorative. Heavens! Editorial acceptances and cheques were all the amelioratives I needed. A thin envelope from an editor in the morning's mail was more stimulating than half a dozen cocktails. And if a cheque of decent amount came out of the envelope, such incident in itself was a whole drunk.

Furthermore, at that time in my life I did not know what a cocktail was. I remember, when my first book was published, several Alaskans, who were members of the Bohemian Club, entertained me one evening at the club in San Francisco. We sat in most wonderful leather chairs, and drinks were ordered. Never had I heard such an ordering of liqueurs and of highballs of particular brands of Scotch. I didn't know what a liqueur or a highball was, and I didn't know that "Scotch" meant whisky. I knew only poor men's drinks, the drinks of the frontier and of sailor-town— cheap beer and cheaper whisky that was just called whisky and nothing else. I was embarrassed to make a choice, and the steward nearly collapsed when I ordered claret as an after-dinner drink.

CHAPTER XXVII

As I succeeded with my writing, my standard of living rose and my horizon broadened. I confined myself to writing and typing a thousand words a day, including Sundays and holidays; and I still studied hard, but not so hard as formerly. I allowed myself five and one-half hours of actual sleep. I added this half-hour because I was compelled. Financial success permitted me more time for exercise. I rode my wheel more, chiefly because it was permanently out of pawn; and I boxed and fenced, walked on my hands, jumped high and broad, put the shot and tossed the caber, and went swimming. And I learned that more sleep is required for physical exercise than for mental exercise. There were tired nights, bodily, when I slept six hours; and on occasion of very severe exercise I actually slept seven hours. But such sleep orgies were not frequent. There was so much to learn, so much to be done, that I felt wicked when I slept seven hours. And I blessed the man who invented alarm clocks.

And still no desire to drink. I possessed too many fine faiths, was living at too keen a pitch. I was a socialist, intent on saving the world, and alcohol could not give me the fervours that were mine from my ideas and ideals. My voice, on account of my successful writing, had added weight, or so I thought. At any rate, my reputation as a writer drew me audiences that my reputation as a speaker never could have drawn. I was invited before clubs and organisations of all sorts to deliver my message. I fought the good fight, and went on studying and writing, and was very busy.

Up to this time I had had a very restricted circle of friends. But now I began to go about. I was invited out, especially to dinner, and I made many friends and acquaintances whose economic lives were easier than mine had been. And many of them drank. In their own houses they drank and offered me drink. They were not drunkards any of them. They just drank temperately, and I drank temperately with them as an act of comradeship and accepted hospitality. I did not care for it, neither wanted it nor did not want it, and so small was the impression made by it that I do not remember my first cocktail nor my first Scotch highball.

Well, I had a house. When one is asked into other houses, he naturally asks others into his house. Behold the rising standard of living. Having been given drink in other houses, I could expect nothing else of myself than to give drink in my own house. So I laid in a supply of beer and whisky and table claret. Never since that has my house not been well supplied.

And still, through all this period, I did not care in the slightest for John Barleycorn. I drank when others drank, and with them, as a social act. And I had so little choice in the matter that I drank whatever they drank. If they elected whisky, then whisky it was for me. If they drank root beer or sarsaparilla, I drank root beer or sarsaparilla with them. And when there were no friends in the house, why, I didn't drink anything. Whisky decanters were always in the room where I wrote, and for months and years I never knew what it was, when by myself, to take a drink.

When out at dinner I noticed the kindly, genial glow of the preliminary cocktail. It seemed a very fitting and gracious thing. Yet so little did I stand in need of it, with my own high intensity and vitality, that I never thought it worth while to have a cocktail before my own meal when I ate alone.

On the other hand, I well remember a very brilliant man, somewhat older than I, who occasionally visited me. He liked whisky, and I recall sitting whole afternoons in my den, drinking steadily with him, drink for drink, until he was mildly lighted up and I was slightly aware that I had drunk some whisky. Now why did I do this? I don't know, save that the old schooling held, the training of the old days and nights glass in hand with men, the drinking ways of drink and drinkers.

Besides, I no longer feared John Barleycorn. Mine was that most dangerous stage when a man believes himself John Barleycorn's master. I had proved it to my satisfaction in the long years of work and study. I could drink when I wanted, refrain when I wanted, drink without getting drunk, and to cap everything I was thoroughly conscious that I had no liking for the stuff. During this period I drank precisely for the same reason I had drunk with Scotty and the harpooner and with the oyster pirates—because it was an act that men performed with whom I wanted to behave as a man. These brilliant ones, these adventurers of the mind, drank. Very well. There was no reason I should not drink with them—I who knew so confidently that I had nothing to fear from John Barleycorn.

And the foregoing was my attitude of mind for years. Occasionally I got well jingled, but such occasions were rare. It interfered with my work, and I permitted nothing to interfere with my work. I remember, when spending several months in the East End of London, during which time I wrote a book and adventured much amongst the worst of the slum classes, that I got drunk several times and was mightily wroth with myself because it interfered with my writing. Yet these very times were because I was out on the adventure-path where John Barleycorn is always to be found.

Then, too, with the certitude of long training and unholy intimacy, there were occasions when I engaged in drinking bouts with men. Of course, this was on the adventure-path in various parts of the world, and it was a matter of pride. It is a queer man-pride that leads one to drink with men in order to show as strong a head as they. But this queer man-pride is no theory. It is a fact.

For instance, a wild band of young revolutionists invited me as the guest of honour to a beer bust. It is the only technical beer bust I ever attended. I did not know the true inwardness of the affair when I accepted. I imagined that the talk would be wild and high, that some of them might drink more than they ought, and that I would drink discreetly. But it seemed these beer busts were a diversion of these high-spirited young fellows whereby they whiled away the tedium of existence by making fools of their betters. As I learned afterward, they had got their previous guest of honour, a brilliant young radical, unskilled in drinking, quite pipped.

When I found myself with them, and the situation dawned on me, up rose my queer man-pride. I'd show them, the young rascals. I'd show them who was husky and chesty, who had the vitality and the constitution, the stomach and the head, who could make most of a swine of himself and show it least. These unlicked cubs who thought they could out-drink *me*!

You see, it was an endurance test, and no man likes to give another best. Faugh! it was steam beer. I had learned more expensive brews. Not for years had I drunk steam beer; but when I had, I had drunk with men, and I guessed I could show these youngsters some ability in beer-guzzling. And the drinking began, and I had to drink with the best of them. Some of them might lag, but the guest of honour was not permitted to lag.

And all my austere nights of midnight oil, all the books I had read, all the wisdom I had gathered, went glimmering before the ape and tiger in me that crawled up from the abysm of my heredity, atavistic, competitive and brutal, lustful with strength and desire to outswine the swine.

And when the session broke up I was still on my feet, and I walked, erect, unswaying—which was more than can be said of some of my hosts. I recall one of them in indignant tears on the street corner, weeping as he pointed out my sober condition. Little he dreamed the iron clutch, born of old training, with which I held to my consciousness in my swimming brain, kept control of my muscles and my qualms, kept my voice unbroken and easy and my thoughts consecutive and logical. Yes, and mixed up with it all I was privily a-grin. They hadn't made a fool of me in that drinking bout. And I was proud of myself for the achievement. Darn it, I am still proud, so strangely is man compounded.

But I didn't write my thousand words next morning. I was sick, poisoned. It was a day of wretchedness. In the afternoon I had to give a public speech. I gave it, and I am confident it was as bad as I felt. Some of my hosts were there in the front rows to mark any signs on me of the night before. I don't know what signs they marked, but I marked signs on them and took consolation in the knowledge that they were just as sick as I.

Never again, I swore. And I have never been inveigled into another beer bust. For that matter, that was my last drinking bout of any sort. Oh, I have drunk ever since, but with more wisdom, more discretion, and never in a competitive spirit. It is thus that the seasoned drinker grows seasoned.

To show that at this period in my life drinking was wholly a matter of companionship, I remember crossing the Atlantic in the old Teutonic. It chanced, at the start, that I chummed with an English cable operator and a younger member of a Spanish shipping firm. Now the only thing they drank was "horse's neck"—a long, soft, cool drink with an apple peel or an orange peel floating in it. And for that whole voyage I drank horse's necks with my two companions. On the other hand, had they drunk whisky, I should have drunk whisky with them. From this it must not be concluded that I was merely weak. I didn't care. I had no morality in the matter. I was strong with youth, and unafraid, and alcohol was an utterly negligible question so far as I was concerned.

CHAPTER XXVIII

Not yet was I ready to tuck my arm in John Barleycorn's. The older I got, the greater my success, the more money I earned, the wider was the command of the world that became mine and the more prominently did John Barleycorn bulk in my life. And still I maintained no more than a nodding acquaintance with him. I drank for the sake of sociability, and when alone I did not drink. Sometimes I got jingled, but I considered such jingles the mild price I paid for sociability.

To show how unripe I was for John Barleycorn, when, at this time, I descended into my slough of despond, I never dreamed of turning to John Barleycorn for a helping hand. I had life troubles and heart troubles which are neither here nor there in this narrative. But, combined with them, were intellectual troubles which are indeed germane.

Mine was no uncommon experience. I had read too much positive science and lived too much positive life. In the eagerness of youth I had made the ancient mistake of pursuing Truth too relentlessly. I had torn her veils from her, and the sight was too terrible for me to stand. In brief, I lost my fine faiths in pretty well everything except humanity, and the humanity I retained faith in was a very stark humanity indeed.

This long sickness of pessimism is too well known to most of us to be detailed here. Let it suffice to state that I had it very bad. I meditated suicide coolly, as a Greek philosopher might. My regret was that there were too many dependent directly upon me for food and shelter for me to quit living. But that was sheer morality. What really saved me was the one remaining illusion—the *people*.

The things I had fought for and burned my midnight oil for had failed me. Success—I despised it. Recognition—it was dead ashes. Society, men and women above the ruck and the muck of the water-front and the forecastle—I was appalled by their unlovely mental mediocrity. Love of woman—it was like all the rest. Money—I could sleep in only one bed at a time, and of what worth was an income of a hundred porterhouses a day when I could eat only one? Art, culture—in the face of the iron facts of biology such things were ridiculous, the exponents of such things only the more ridiculous.

From the foregoing it can be seen how very sick I was. I was born a fighter. The things I had fought for had proved not worth the fight. Remained the *people*. My fight was finished, yet something was left still to fight for—the *people*.

But while I was discovering this one last tie to bind me to life, in my extremity, in the depths of despond, walking in the valley of the shadow, my ears were deaf to John Barleycorn. Never the remotest whisper arose in my consciousness that John Barleycorn was the anodyne, that he could lie me along to live. One way only was uppermost in my thought—my revolver, the crashing eternal darkness of a bullet. There was plenty of whisky in the house—for my guests. I never touched it. I grew afraid of my revolver—afraid during the period in which the radiant, flashing vision of the *people* was forming in my mind and will. So obsessed was I with the desire to die that I feared I might commit the act in my sleep, and I was compelled to give my revolver away to others who were to lose it for me where my subconscious hand might not find it.

But the *people* saved me. By the *people* was I handcuffed to life. There was still one fight left in me, and here was the thing for which to fight. I threw all precaution to the winds, threw myself with fiercer zeal into the fight for socialism, laughed at the editors and publishers who warned me and who were the sources of my hundred porterhouses a day, and was brutally careless of whose feelings I hurt and of how savagely I hurt them. As the "well-balanced radicals" charged at the time, my efforts were so strenuous, so unsafe and unsane, so ultra-revolutionary, that I retarded the socialist development in the United States by five years. In passing, I wish to remark, at this late date, that it is my fond belief that I accelerated the socialist development in the United States by at least five minutes.

It was the *people*, and no thanks to John Barleycorn, who pulled me through my long sickness. And when I was convalescent came the love of woman to complete the cure and lull my pessimism asleep for many a long day, until John Barleycorn again awoke it. But in the meantime, I pursued Truth less relentlessly, refraining from tearing her last veils aside even when I clutched them in my hand. I no longer cared to look upon Truth naked. I refused to permit myself to see a second time what I had once seen. And the memory of what I had that time seen I resolutely blotted from my mind.

And I was very happy. Life went well with me, I took delight in little things. The big things I declined to take too seriously. I still read the books, but not with the old eagerness. I still read the books to-day, but never again shall I read them with that old glory of youthful passion when I harked to the call from over and beyond that whispered me on to win to the mystery at the back of life and behind the stars.

The point of this chapter is that, in the long sickness that at some time comes to most of us, I came through without any appeal for aid to John Barleycorn. Love, socialism, the *people*—healthful figments of man's mind—were the things that cured and saved me. If ever a man was not a born alcoholic, I believe that I am that man. And yet—well, let the succeeding chapters tell their tale, for in them will be shown how I paid for my previous quarter of a century of contact with ever-accessible John Barleycorn.

CHAPTER XXIX

After my long sickness my drinking continued to be convivial. I drank when others drank and I was with them. But, imperceptibly, my need for alcohol took form and began to grow. It was not a body need. I boxed, swam, sailed, rode horses, lived in the open an arrantly healthful life, and passed life insurance examinations with flying colours. In its inception, now that I look back upon it, this need for alcohol was a mental need, a nerve need, a good-spirits need. How can I explain?

It was something like this. Physiologically, from the standpoint of palate and stomach, alcohol was, as it had always been, repulsive. It tasted no better than beer did when I was five, than bitter claret did when I was seven. When I was alone, writing or studying, I had no need for it. But—I was growing old, or wise, or both, or senile as an alternative. When I was in company I was less pleased, less excited, with the things said and done. Erstwhile worth-while fun and stunts seemed no longer worth while; and it was a torment to listen to the insipidities and stupidities of women, to the pompous, arrogant sayings of the little half-baked men. It is the penalty one pays for reading the books too much, or for being oneself a fool. In my case it does not matter which was my trouble. The trouble itself was the fact. The condition of the fact was mine. For me the life, and light, and sparkle of human intercourse were dwindling.

I had climbed too high among the stars, or, maybe, I had slept too hard. Yet I was not hysterical nor in any way overwrought. My pulse was normal. My heart was an amazement of excellence to the insurance doctors. My lungs threw the said doctors into ecstasies. I wrote a thousand words every day. I was punctiliously exact in dealing with all the affairs of life that fell to my lot. I exercised in joy and gladness. I slept at night like a babe. But—

Well, as soon as I got out in the company of others I was driven to melancholy and spiritual tears. I could neither laugh with nor at the solemn utterances of men I esteemed ponderous asses; nor could I laugh, nor engage in my old-time lightsome persiflage, with the silly superficial chatterings of women, who, underneath all their silliness and softness, were as primitive, direct, and deadly in their pursuit of biological destiny as the monkeys women were before they shed their furry coats and replaced them with the furs of other animals.

And I was not pessimistic. I swear I was not pessimistic. I was merely bored. I had seen the same show too often, listened too often to the same songs and the same jokes. I knew too much about the box office receipts. I knew the cogs of the machinery behind the scenes so well that the posing on the stage, and the laughter and the song, could not drown the creaking of the wheels behind.

It doesn't pay to go behind the scenes and see the angel-voiced tenor beat his wife. Well, I'd been behind, and I was paying for it. Or else I was a fool. It is immaterial which was my situation. The situation is what counts, and the situation was that social intercourse for me was getting painful and difficult. On the other hand, it must be stated that on rare occasions, on very rare occasions, I did meet rare souls, or fools like me, with whom I could spend magnificent hours among the stars, or in the paradise of fools. I was married to a rare soul, or a fool, who never bored me and who was always a source of new and unending surprise and delight. But I could not spend all my hours solely in her company.

Nor would it have been fair, nor wise, to compel her to spend all her hours in my company. Besides, I had written a string of successful books, and society demands some portion of the recreative hours of a fellow that writes books. And any normal man, of himself and his needs, demands some hours of his fellow men.

And now we begin to come to it. How to face the social intercourse game with the glamour gone? John Barleycorn. The ever patient one had waited a quarter of a century and more for me to reach my hand out in need of him. His thousand tricks had failed, thanks to my constitution and good luck, but he had more tricks in his bag. A cocktail or two, or several, I found, cheered me up for the foolishness of foolish people. A cocktail, or several, before dinner, enabled me to laugh wholeheartedly at things which had long since ceased being laughable. The cocktail was a prod, a spur, a kick, to my jaded mind and bored spirits. It recrudesced the laughter and the song, and put a lilt into my own imagination so that I could laugh and sing and say foolish things with the liveliest of them, or platitudes with verve and intensity to the satisfaction of the pompous mediocre ones who knew no other way to talk.

A poor companion without a cocktail, I became a very good companion with one. I achieved a false exhilaration, drugged myself to merriment. And the thing began so imperceptibly that I, old intimate of John Barleycorn, never dreamed whither it was leading me. I was beginning to call for music and wine; soon I should be calling for madder music and more wine.

It was at this time I became aware of waiting with expectancy for the pre-dinner cocktail. I *wanted* it, and I was *conscious* that I wanted it. I remember, while war-corresponding in the Far East, of being irresistibly attracted to a certain home. Besides accepting all invitations to dinner, I made a point of dropping in almost every afternoon. Now, the hostess was a charming woman, but it was not for her sake that I was under her roof so frequently. It happened that she made by far the finest cocktail procurable in that large city where drink-mixing on the part of the foreign population was indeed an art. Up at the club, down at the hotels, and in other private houses, no such cocktails were created. Her cocktails were subtle. They were masterpieces. They were the least repulsive to the palate and carried the most "kick." And yet, I desired her cocktails only for sociability's sake, to key myself to sociable moods. When I rode away from that city, across hundreds of miles of rice-fields and mountains, and through months of campaigning, and on with the victorious Japanese into Manchuria, I did not drink. Several bottles of whisky were always to be found on the backs of my pack-horses. Yet I never broached a bottle for myself, never took a drink by myself, and never knew a desire to take such a drink. Oh, if a white man came into my camp, I opened a bottle and we drank together according to the way of men, just as he would open a bottle and drink with me if I came into his camp. I carried that whisky for social purposes, and I so charged it up in my expense account to the newspaper for which I worked.

Only in retrospect can I mark the almost imperceptible growth of my desire. There were little hints then that I did not take, little straws in the wind that I did not see, little incidents the gravity of which I did not realise.

For instance, for some years it had been my practice each winter to cruise for six or eight weeks on San Francisco Bay. My stout sloop yacht, the *Spray*, had a comfortable cabin and a coal stove. A Korean boy did the cooking, and I usually took a friend or so along to share the joys of the cruise. Also, I took my machine along and did my thousand words a day. On the particular trip I have in mind, Cloudesley and Toddy came along. This was Toddy's first trip. On previous trips Cloudesley had elected to drink beer; so I had kept the yacht supplied with beer and had drunk beer with him.

But on this cruise the situation was different. Toddy was so nicknamed because of his diabolical cleverness in concocting toddies. So I brought whisky along—a couple of gallons. Alas! Many another gallon I bought, for Cloudesley and I got into the habit of drinking a certain hot toddy that actually tasted delicious going down and that carried the most exhilarating kick imaginable.

I liked those toddies. I grew to look forward to the making of them. We drank them regularly, one before breakfast, one before dinner, one before supper, and a final one when we went to bed. We never got drunk. But I will say that four times a day we were very genial. And when, in the middle of the cruise, Toddy was called back to San Francisco on business, Cloudesley and I saw to it that the Korean boy mixed toddies regularly for us according to formula.

But that was only on the boat. Back on the land, in my house, I took no before breakfast eye-opener, no bed-going nightcap. And I haven't drunk hot toddies since, and that was many a year ago. But the point is, I *liked* those toddies. The geniality of which they were provocative was marvellous. They were eloquent proselyters for John Barleycorn in their own small insidious way. They were tickles of the something destined to grow into daily and deadly desire. And I didn't know, never dreamed—I, who had lived with John Barleycorn for so many years and laughed at all his unavailing attempts to win me.

CHAPTER XXX

Part of the process of recovering from my long sickness was to find delight in little things, in things unconnected with books and problems, in play, in games of tag in the swimming pool, in flying kites, in fooling with horses, in working out mechanical puzzles. As a result, I grew tired of the city. On the ranch, in the Valley of the Moon, I found my paradise. I gave up living in cities. All the cities held for me were music, the theatre, and Turkish baths.

And all went well with me. I worked hard, played hard, and was very happy. I read more fiction and less fact. I did not study a tithe as much as I had studied in the past. I still took an interest in the fundamental problems of existence, but it was a very cautious interest; for I had burned my fingers that time I clutched at the veils of Truth and wrested them from her. There was a bit of lie in this attitude of mine, a bit of hypocrisy; but the lie and the hypocrisy were those of a man desiring to live. I deliberately blinded myself to what I took to be the savage interpretation of biological fact. After all, I was merely forswearing a bad habit, forgoing a bad frame of mind. And I repeat, I was very happy. And I add, that in all my days, measuring them with cold, considerative judgment, this was, far and away beyond all other periods, the happiest period of my life.

But the time was at hand, rhymeless and reasonless so far as I can see, when I was to begin to pay for my score of years of dallying with John Barleycorn. Occasionally guests journeyed to the ranch and remained a few days. Some did not drink. But to those who did drink, the absence of all alcohol on the ranch was a hardship. I could not violate my sense of hospitality by compelling them to endure this hardship. I ordered in a stock—for my guests.

I was never interested enough in cocktails to know how they were made. So I got a bar-keeper in Oakland to make them in bulk and ship them to me. When I had no guests I didn't drink. But I began to notice, when I finished my morning's work, that I was glad if there were a guest, for then I could drink a cocktail with him.

Now I was so clean of alcohol that even a single cocktail was provocative of pitch. A single cocktail would glow the mind and tickle a laugh for the few minutes prior to sitting down to table and starting the delightful process of eating. On the other hand, such was the strength of my stomach, of my alcoholic resistance, that the single cocktail was only the glimmer of a glow, the faintest tickle of a laugh. One day, a friend frankly and shamelessly suggested a second cocktail. I drank the second one with him. The glow was appreciably longer and warmer, the laughter deeper and more resonant. One does not forget such experiences. Sometimes I almost think that it was because I was so very happy that I started on my real drinking.

I remember one day Charmian and I took a long ride over the mountains on our horses. The servants had been dismissed for the day, and we returned late at night to a jolly chafing-dish supper. Oh, it was good to be alive that night while the supper was preparing, the two of us alone in the kitchen. I, personally, was at the top of life. Such things as the books and ultimate truth did not exist. My body was gloriously healthy, and healthily tired from the long ride. It had been a splendid day. The night was splendid. I was with the woman who was my mate, picnicking in gleeful abandon. I had no troubles. The bills were all paid, and a surplus of money was rolling in on me. The future ever-widened before me. And right there, in the kitchen, delicious things bubbled in the chafing-dish, our laughter bubbled, and my stomach was keen with a most delicious edge of appetite.

I felt so good, that somehow, somewhere, in me arose an insatiable greed to feel better. I was so happy that I wanted to pitch my happiness even higher. And I knew the way. Ten thousand contacts with John Barleycorn had taught me. Several times I wandered out of the kitchen to the cocktail bottle, and each time I left it diminished by one man's size cocktail. The result was splendid. I wasn't jingled, I wasn't lighted up; but I was warmed, I glowed, my happiness was pyramided. Munificent as life was to me, I added to that munificence. It was a great hour—one of my greatest. But I paid for it, long afterwards, as you will see. One does not forget such experiences, and, in human stupidity, cannot be brought to realise that there is no immutable law which decrees that same things shall produce same results. For they don't, else would the thousandth pipe of opium be provocative of similar delights to the first, else would one cocktail, instead of several, produce an equivalent glow after a year of cocktails.

One day, just before I ate midday dinner, after my morning's writing was done, when I had no guest, I took a cocktail by myself. Thereafter, when there were no guests, I took this daily pre-dinner cocktail. And right there John Barleycorn had me. I was beginning to drink regularly. I was beginning to drink alone. And I was beginning to drink, not for hospitality's sake, not for the sake of the taste, but for the effect of the drink.

I *wanted* that daily pre-dinner cocktail. And it never crossed my mind that there was any reason I should not have it. I paid for it. I could pay for a thousand cocktails each day if I wanted. And what was a cocktail—one cocktail—to me who on so many occasions for so many years had drunk inordinate quantities of stiffer stuff and been unharmed?

The programme of my ranch life was as follows: Each morning, at eight-thirty, having been reading or correcting proofs in bed since four or five, I went to my desk. Odds and ends of correspondence and notes occupied me till nine, and at nine sharp, invariably, I began my writing. By eleven, sometimes a few minutes earlier or later, my thousand words were finished. Another half-hour at cleaning up my desk, and my day's work was done, so that at eleven-thirty I got into a hammock under the trees with my mail-bag and the morning newspaper. At twelve-thirty I ate dinner and in the afternoon I swam and rode.

One morning, at eleven-thirty, before I got into the hammock, I took a cocktail. I repeated this on subsequent mornings, of course, taking another cocktail just before I ate at twelve-thirty. Soon I found myself, seated at my desk in the midst of my thousand words, looking forward to that eleven-thirty cocktail.

At last, now, I was thoroughly conscious that I desired alcohol. But what of it? I wasn't afraid of John Barleycorn. I had associated with him too long. I was wise in the matter of drink. I was discreet. Never again would I drink to excess. I knew the dangers and the pitfalls of John Barleycorn, the various ways by which he had tried to kill me in the past. But all that was past, long past. Never again would I drink myself to stupefaction. Never again would I get drunk. All I wanted, and all I would take, was just enough to glow and warm me, to kick geniality alive in me and put laughter in my throat and stir the maggots of imagination slightly in my brain. Oh, I was thoroughly master of myself, and of John Barleycorn.

CHAPTER XXXI

But the same stimulus to the human organism will not continue to produce the same response. By and by I discovered there was no kick at all in one cocktail. One cocktail left me dead. There was no glow, no laughter tickle. Two or three cocktails were required to produce the original effect of one. And I wanted that effect. I drank my first cocktail at eleven-thirty when I took the morning's mail into the hammock, and I drank my second cocktail an hour later just before I ate. I got into the habit of crawling out of the hammock ten minutes earlier so as to find time and decency for two more cocktails ere I ate. This became schedule—three cocktails in the hour that intervened between my desk and dinner. And these are two of the deadliest drinking habits: regular drinking and solitary drinking.

I was always willing to drink when any one was around. I drank by myself when no one was around. Then I made another step. When I had for guest a man of limited drinking calibre, I took two drinks to his one—one drink with him, the other drink without him and of which he did not know. I *stole* that other drink, and, worse than that, I began the habit of drinking alone when there was a guest, a man, a comrade, with whom I could have drunk. But John Barleycorn furnished the extenuation. It was a wrong thing to trip a guest up with excess of hospitality and get him drunk. If I persuaded him, with his limited calibre, into drinking up with me, I'd surely get him drunk. What could I do but steal that every second drink, or else deny myself the kick equivalent to what he got out of half the number?

Please remember, as I recite this development of my drinking, that I am no fool, no weakling. As the world measures such things, I am a success—I dare to say a success more conspicuous than the success of the average successful man, and a success that required a pretty fair amount of brains and will power. My body is a strong body. It has survived where weaklings died like flies. And yet these things which I am relating happened to my body and to me. I am a fact. My drinking is a fact. My drinking is a thing that has happened, and is no theory nor speculation; and, as I see it, it but lays the emphasis on the power of John Barleycorn—a savagery that we still permit to exist, a deadly institution that lingers from the mad old brutal days and that takes its heavy toll of youth and strength, and high spirit, and of very much of all of the best we breed.

To return. After a boisterous afternoon in the swimming pool, followed by a glorious ride on horseback over the mountains or up or down the Valley of the Moon, I found myself so keyed and splendid that I desired to be more highly keyed, to feel more splendid. I knew the way. A cocktail before supper was not the way. Two or three, at the very least, was what was needed. I took them. Why not? It was living. I had always dearly loved to live. This also became part of the daily schedule.

Then, too, I was perpetually finding excuses for extra cocktails. It might be the assembling of a particularly jolly crowd; a touch of anger against my architect or against a thieving stone-mason working on my barn; the death of my favourite horse in a barbed wire fence; or news of good fortune in the morning mail from my dealings with editors and publishers. It was immaterial what the excuse might be, once the desire had germinated in me. The thing was: I *wanted* alcohol. At last, after a score and more of years of dallying and of not wanting, now I wanted it. And my strength was my weakness. I required two, three, or four drinks to get an effect commensurate with the effect the average man got out of one drink.

One rule I observed. I never took a drink until my day's work of writing a thousand words was done. And, when done, the cocktails reared a wall of inhibition in my brain between the day's work done and the rest of the day of fun to come. My work ceased from my consciousness. No thought of it flickered in my brain till next morning at nine o'clock when I sat at my desk and began my next thousand words. This was a desirable condition of mind to achieve. I conserved my energy by means of this alcoholic inhibition. John Barleycorn was not so black as he was painted. He did a fellow many a good turn, and this was one of them.

And I turned out work that was healthful, and wholesome, and sincere. It was never pessimistic. The way to life I had learned in my long sickness. I knew the illusions were right, and I exalted the illusions. Oh, I still turn out the same sort of work, stuff that is clean, alive, optimistic, and that makes toward life. And I am always assured by the critics of my super-abundant and abounding vitality, and of how thoroughly I am deluded by these very illusions I exploit.

And while on this digression, let me repeat the question I have repeated to myself ten thousand times. *Why did I drink?* What need was there for it? I was happy. Was it because I was too happy? I was strong. Was it because I was too strong? Did I possess too much vitality? I don't know why I drank. I cannot answer, though I can voice the suspicion that ever grows in me. I had been in too-familiar contact with John Barleycorn through too many years. A left-handed man, by long practice, can become a right-handed man. Had I, a non-alcoholic, by long practice become an alcoholic?

I was so happy. I had won through my long sickness to the satisfying love of woman. I earned more money with less endeavour. I glowed with health. I slept like a babe. I continued to write successful books, and in sociological controversy I saw my opponents confuted with the facts of the times that daily reared new buttresses to my intellectual position. From day's end to day's end I never knew sorrow, disappointment, nor regret. I was happy all the time. Life was one unending song. I begrudged the very hours of blessed sleep because by that much was I robbed of the joy that would have been mine had I remained awake. And yet I drank. And John Barleycorn, all unguessed by me, was setting the stage for a sickness all his own.

The more I drank the more I was required to drink to get an equivalent effect. When I left the Valley of the Moon, and went to the city, and dined out, a cocktail served at table was a wan and worthless thing. There was no pre-dinner kick in it. On my way to dinner I was compelled to accumulate the kick—two cocktails, three, and, if I met some fellows, four or five, or six, it didn't matter within several. Once, I was in a rush. I had no time decently to accumulate the several drinks. A brilliant idea came to me. I told the barkeeper to mix me a double cocktail. Thereafter, whenever I was in a hurry, I ordered double cocktails. It saved time.

One result of this regular heavy drinking was to jade me. My mind grew so accustomed to spring and liven by artificial means that without artificial means it refused to spring and liven. Alcohol became more and more imperative in order to meet people, in order to become sociably fit. I had to get the kick and the hit of the stuff, the crawl of the maggots, the genial brain glow, the laughter tickle, the touch of devilishness and sting, the smile over the face of things, ere I could join my fellows and make one with them.

Another result was that John Barleycorn was beginning to trip me up. He was thrusting my long sickness back upon me, inveigling me into again pursuing Truth and snatching her veils away from her, tricking me into looking reality stark in the face. But this came on gradually. My thoughts were growing harsh again, though they grew harsh slowly.

Sometimes warning thoughts crossed my mind. Where was this steady drinking leading? But trust John Barleycorn to silence such questions. "Come on and have a drink and I'll tell you all about it," is his way. And it works. For instance, the following is a case in point, and one which John Barleycorn never wearied of reminding me:

I had suffered an accident which required a ticklish operation. One morning, a week after I had come off the table, I lay on my hospital bed, weak and weary. The sunburn of my face, what little of it could be seen through a scraggly growth of beard, had faded to a sickly yellow. My doctor stood at my bedside on the verge of departure. He glared disapprovingly at the cigarette I was smoking.

"That's what you ought to quit," he lectured. "It will get you in the end. Look at me."

I looked. He was about my own age, broad-shouldered, deep-chested, eyes sparkling, and ruddy-cheeked with health. A finer specimen of manhood one would not ask.

"I used to smoke," he went on. "Cigars. But I gave even them up. And look at me."

The man was arrogant, and rightly arrogant, with conscious well-being. And within a month he was dead. It was no accident. Half a dozen different bugs of long scientific names had attacked and destroyed him. The complications were astonishing and painful, and for days before he died the screams of agony of that splendid manhood could be heard for a block around. He died screaming.

"You see," said John Barleycorn. "He took care of himself. He even stopped smoking cigars. And that's what he got for it. Pretty rotten, eh? But the bugs will jump. There's no forefending them. Your magnificent doctor took every precaution, yet they got him. When the bug jumps you can't tell where it will land. It may be you. Look what he missed. Will you miss all I can give you, only to have a bug jump on you and drag you down? There is no equity in life. It's all a lottery. But I put the lying smile on the face of life and laugh at the facts. Smile with me and laugh. You'll get yours in the end, but in the meantime laugh. It's a pretty dark world. I illuminate it for you. It's a rotten world, when things can happen such as happened to your doctor. There's only one thing to do: take another drink and forget it."

And, of course, I took another drink for the inhibition that accompanied it. I took another drink every time John Barleycorn reminded me of what had happened. Yet I drank rationally, intelligently. I saw to it that the quality of the stuff was of the best. I sought the kick and the inhibition, and avoided the penalties of poor quality and of drunkenness. It is to be remarked, in passing, that when a man begins to drink rationally and intelligently that he betrays a grave symptom of how far along the road he has travelled.

But I continued to observe my rule of never taking my first drink of the day until the last word of my thousand words was written. On occasion, however, I took a day's vacation from my writing. At such times, since it was no violation of my rule, I didn't mind how early in the day I took that first drink. And persons who have never been through the drinking game wonder how the drinking habit grows!

CHAPTER XXXII

When the Snark sailed on her long cruise from San Francisco there was nothing to drink on board. Or, rather, we were all of us unaware that there was anything to drink, nor did we discover it for many a month. This sailing with a "dry" boat was malice aforethought on my part. I had played John Barleycorn a trick. And it showed that I was listening ever so slightly to the faint warnings that were beginning to arise in my consciousness.

Of course, I veiled the situation to myself and excused myself to John Barleycorn. And I was very scientific about it. I said that I would drink only while in ports. During the dry sea-stretches my system would be cleansed of the alcohol that soaked it, so that when I reached a port I should be in shape to enjoy John Barleycorn more thoroughly. His bite would be sharper, his kick keener and more delicious.

We were twenty-seven days on the traverse between San Francisco and Honolulu. After the first day out, the thought of a drink never troubled me. This I take to show how intrinsically I am not an alcoholic. Sometimes, during the traverse, looking ahead and anticipating the delightful lanai luncheons and dinners of Hawaii (I had been there a couple of times before), I thought, naturally, of the drinks that would precede those meals. I did not think of those drinks with any yearning, with any irk at the length of the voyage. I merely thought they would be nice and jolly, part of the atmosphere of a proper meal.

Thus, once again I proved to my complete satisfaction that I was John Barleycorn's master. I could drink when I wanted, refrain when I wanted. Therefore I would continue to drink when I wanted.

Some five months were spent in the various islands of the Hawaiian group. Being ashore, I drank. I even drank a bit more than I had been accustomed to drink in California prior to the voyage. The people in Hawaii seemed to drink a bit more, on the average, than the people in more temperate latitudes. I do not intend the pun, and can awkwardly revise the statement to "latitudes more remote from the equator." Yet Hawaii is only sub-tropical. The deeper I got into the tropics, the deeper I found men drank, the deeper I drank myself.

From Hawaii we sailed for the Marquesas. The traverse occupied sixty days. For sixty days we never raised land, a sail, nor a steamer smoke. But early in those sixty days the cook, giving an overhauling to the galley, made a find. Down in the bottom of a deep locker he found a dozen bottles of angelica and muscatel. These had come down from the kitchen cellar of the ranch along with the home-preserved fruits and jellies. Six months in the galley heat had effected some sort of a change in the thick sweet wine—branded it, I imagine.

I took a taste. Delicious! And thereafter, once each day, at twelve o'clock, after our observations were worked up and the Snark's position charted, I drank half a tumbler of the stuff. It had a rare kick to it. It warmed the cockles of my geniality and put a fairer face on the truly fair face of the sea. Each morning, below, sweating out my thousand words, I found myself looking forward to that twelve o'clock event of the day.

The trouble was I had to share the stuff, and the length of the traverse was doubtful. I regretted that there were not more than a dozen bottles. And when they were gone I even regretted that I had shared any of it. I was thirsty for the alcohol, and eager to arrive in the Marquesas.

So it was that I reached the Marquesas the possessor of a real man's size thirst. And in the Marquesas were several white men, a lot of sickly natives, much magnificent scenery, plenty of trade rum, an immense quantity of absinthe, but neither whisky nor gin. The trade rum scorched the skin off one's mouth. I know, because I tried it. But I had ever been plastic, and I accepted the absinthe. The trouble with the stuff was that I had to take such inordinate quantities in order to feel the slightest effect.

From the Marquesas I sailed with sufficient absinthe in ballast to last me to Tahiti, where I outfitted with Scotch and American whisky, and thereafter there were no dry stretches between ports. But please do not misunderstand. There was no drunkenness, as drunkenness is ordinarily understood—no staggering and rolling around, no befuddlement of the senses. The skilled and seasoned drinker, with a strong constitution, never descends to anything like that. He drinks to feel good, to get a pleasant jingle, and no more than that. The things he carefully avoids are the nausea of over-drinking, the after-effect of over-drinking, the helplessness and loss of pride of over-drinking.

What the skilled and seasoned drinker achieves is a discreet and canny semi-intoxication. And he does it by the twelve-month around without any apparent penalty. There are hundreds of thousands of men of this sort in the United States to-day, in clubs, hotels, and in their own homes—men who are never drunk, and who, though most of them will indignantly deny it, are rarely sober. And all of them fondly believe, as I fondly believed, that they are beating the game.

On the sea-stretches I was fairly abstemious; but ashore I drank more. I seemed to need more, anyway, in the tropics. This is a common experience, for the excessive consumption of alcohol in the tropics by white men is a notorious fact. The tropics is no place for white-skinned men. Their skin-pigment does not protect them against the excessive white light of the sun. The ultra-violet rays, and other high-velocity and invisible rays from the upper end of the spectrum, rip and tear through their tissues, just as the X-ray ripped and tore through the tissues of so many experimenters before they learned the danger.

White men in the tropics undergo radical changes of nature. They become savage, merciless. They commit monstrous acts of cruelty that they would never dream of committing in their original temperate climate. They become nervous, irritable, and less moral. And they drink as they never drank before. Drinking is one form of the many forms of degeneration that set in when white men are exposed too long to too much white light. The increase of alcoholic consumption is automatic. The tropics is no place for a long sojourn. They seem doomed to die anyway, and the heavy drinking expedites the process. They don't reason about it. They just do it.

The sun sickness got me, despite the fact that I had been in the tropics only a couple of years. I drank heavily during this time, but right here I wish to forestall misunderstanding. The drinking was not the cause of the sickness, nor of the abandonment of the voyage. I was strong as a bull, and for many months I fought the sun sickness that was ripping and tearing my surface and nervous tissues to pieces. All through the New Hebrides and the Solomons and up among the atolls on the Line, during this period under a tropic sun, rotten with malaria, and suffering from a few minor afflictions such as Biblical leprosy with the silvery skin, I did the work of five men.

To navigate a vessel through the reefs and shoals and passages and unlighted coasts of the coral seas is a man's work in itself. I was the only navigator on board. There was no one to check me up on the working out of my observations, nor with whom I could advise in the ticklish darkness among uncharted reefs and shoals. And I stood all watches. There was no sea-man on board whom I could trust to stand a mate's watch. I was mate as well as captain. Twenty-four hours a day were the watches I stood at sea, catching cat-naps when I might. Third, I was doctor. And let me say right here that the doctor's job on the Snark at that time was a man's job. All on board suffered from malaria—the real, tropical malaria that can kill in three months. All on board suffered from perforating ulcers and from the maddening itch of ngari-ngari. A Japanese cook went insane from his too numerous afflictions. One of my Polynesian sailors lay at death's door with blackwater fever. Oh, yes, it was a full man's job, and I dosed and doctored, and pulled teeth, and dragged my patients through mild little things like ptomaine poisoning.

Fourth, I was a writer. I sweated out my thousand words a day, every day, except when the shock of fever smote me, or a couple of nasty squalls smote the

Snark, in the morning. Fifth, I was a traveller and a writer, eager to see things and to gather material into my note-books. And, sixth, I was master and owner of the craft that was visiting strange places where visitors are rare and where visitors are made much of. So here I had to hold up the social end, entertain on board, be entertained ashore by planters, traders, governors, captains of war vessels, kinky-headed cannibal kings, and prime ministers sometimes fortunate enough to be clad in cotton shifts.

Of course I drank. I drank with my guests and hosts. Also, I drank by myself. Doing the work of five men, I thought, entitled me to drink. Alcohol was good for a man who over-worked. I noted its effect on my small crew, when, breaking their backs and hearts at heaving up anchor in forty fathoms, they knocked off gasping and trembling at the end of half an hour and had new life put into them by stiff jolts of rum. They caught their breaths, wiped their mouths, and went to it again with a will. And when we careened the Snark and had to work in the water to our necks between shocks of fever, I noted how raw trade rum helped the work along.

And here again we come to another side of many-sided John Barleycorn. On the face of it, he gives something for nothing. Where no strength remains he finds new strength. The wearied one rises to greater effort. For the time being there is an actual accession of strength. I remember passing coal on an ocean steamer through eight days of hell, during which time we coal-passers were kept to the job by being fed with whisky. We toiled half drunk all the time. And without the whisky we could not have passed the coal.

This strength John Barleycorn gives is not fictitious strength. It is real strength. But it is manufactured out of the sources of strength, and it must ultimately be paid for, and with interest. But what weary human will look so far ahead? He takes this apparently miraculous accession of strength at its face value. And many an over-worked business and professional man, as well as a harried common labourer, has travelled John Barleycorn's death road because of this mistake.

CHAPTER XXXIII

I went to Australia to go into hospital and get tinkered up, after which I planned to go on with the voyage. And during the long weeks I lay in hospital, from the first day I never missed alcohol. I never thought about it. I knew I should have it again when I was on my feet. But when I regained my feet I was not cured of my major afflictions. Naaman's silvery skin was still mine. The mysterious sun-sickness, which the experts of Australia could not fathom, still ripped and tore my tissues. Malaria still festered in me and put me on my back in shivering delirium at the most unexpected moments, compelling me to cancel a double lecture tour which had been arranged.

So I abandoned the Snark voyage and sought a cooler climate. The day I came out of hospital I took up drinking again as a matter of course. I drank wine at meals. I drank cocktails before meals. I drank Scotch highballs when anybody I chanced to be with was drinking them. I was so thoroughly the master of John Barleycorn I could take up with him or let go of him whenever I pleased, just as I had done all my life.

After a time, for cooler climate, I went down to southermost Tasmania in forty-three South. And I found myself in a place where there was nothing to drink. It didn't mean anything. I didn't drink. It was no hardship. I soaked in the cool air, rode horseback, and did my thousand words a day save when the fever shock came in the morning.

And for fear that the idea may still lurk in some minds that my preceding years of drinking were the cause of my disabilities, I here point out that my Japanese cabin boy, Nakata, still with me, was rotten with fever, as was Charmian, who in addition was in the slough of a tropical neurasthenia that required several years of temperate climates to cure, and that neither she nor Nakata drank or ever had drunk.

When I returned to Hobart Town, where drink was obtainable, I drank as of old. The same when I arrived back in Australia. On the contrary, when I sailed from Australia on a tramp steamer commanded by an abstemious captain, I took no drink along, and had no drink for the forty-three days' passage. Arrived in Ecuador, squarely under the equatorial sun, where the humans were dying of yellow fever, smallpox, and the plague, I promptly drank again—every drink of every sort that had a kick in it. I caught none of these diseases. Neither did Charmian nor Nakata who did not drink.

Enamoured of the tropics, despite the damage done me, I stopped in various places, and was a long while getting back to the splendid, temperate climate of California. I did my thousand words a day, travelling or stopping over, suffered my last faint fever shock, saw my silvery skin vanish and my sun-torn tissues healthily knit again, and drank as a broad-shouldered chesty man may drink.

CHAPTER XXXIV

Back on the ranch, in the Valley of the Moon, I resumed my steady drinking. My programme was no drink in the morning; first drink-time came with the completion of my thousand words. Then, between that and the midday meal, were drinks numerous enough to develop a pleasant jingle. Again, in the hour preceding the evening meal, I developed another pleasant jingle. Nobody ever saw me drunk, for the simple reason that I never was drunk. But I did get a jingle twice each day; and the amount of alcohol I consumed every day, if loosed in the system of one unaccustomed to drink, would have put such a one on his back and out.

It was the old proposition. The more I drank, the more I was compelled to drink in order to get an effect. The time came when cocktails were inadequate. I had neither the time in which to drink them nor the space to accommodate them. Whisky had a more powerful jolt. It gave quicker action with less quantity. Bourbon or rye, or cunningly aged blends, constituted the pre-midday drinking. In the late afternoon it was Scotch and soda.

My sleep, always excellent, now became not quite so excellent. I had been accustomed to read myself back asleep when I chanced to awake. But now this began to fail me. When I had read two or three of the small hours away and was as wide awake as ever, I found that a drink furnished the soporific effect. Sometimes two or three drinks were required.

So short a period of sleep then intervened before early morning rising that my system did not have time to work off the alcohol. As a result I awoke with mouth parched and dry, with a slight heaviness of head, and with a mild nervous palpitation in the stomach. In fact I did not feel good. I was suffering from the morning sickness of the steady, heavy drinker. What I needed was a pick-me-up, a bracer. Trust John Barleycorn, once he has broken down a man's defences! So it was a drink before breakfast to put me right for breakfast—the old poison of the snake that has bitten one! Another custom begun at this time was that of the pitcher of water by the bedside to furnish relief to my scorched and sizzling membranes.

I achieved a condition in which my body was never free from alcohol. Nor did I permit myself to be away from alcohol. If I travelled to out-of-the-way places, I declined to run the risk of finding them dry. I took a quart, or several quarts, along in my grip. In the past I had been amazed by other men guilty of this practice. Now I did it myself unblushingly. And when I got out with the fellows, I cast all rules by the board. I drank when they drank, what they drank, and in the same way they drank.

I was carrying a beautiful alcoholic conflagration around with me. The thing fed on its own heat and flamed the fiercer. There was no time, in all my waking time, that I didn't want a drink. I began to anticipate the completion of my daily thousand words by taking a drink when only five hundred words were written. It was not long until I prefaced the beginning of the thousand words with a drink.

The gravity of this I realised too well. I made new rules. Resolutely I would refrain from drinking until my work was done. But a new and most diabolical complication arose. The work refused to be done without drinking. It just couldn't be done. I had to drink in order to do it. I was beginning to fight now. I had the craving at last, and it was mastering me. I would sit at my desk and dally with pad and pen, but words refused to flow. My brain could not think the proper thoughts because continually it was obsessed with the one thought that across the room in the liquor cabinet stood John Barleycorn. When, in despair, I took my drink, at once my brain loosened up and began to roll off the thousand words.

In my town house, in Oakland, I finished the stock of liquor and wilfully refused to purchase more. It was no use, because, unfortunately, there remained in the bottom of the liquor cabinet a case of beer. In vain I tried to write. Now beer is a poor substitute for strong waters: besides, I didn't like beer, yet all I could think of was that beer so singularly accessible in the bottom of the cabinet. Not until I had drunk a pint of it did the words begin to reel off, and the thousand were reeled off to the tune of numerous pints. The worst of it was that the beer caused me severe heartburn; but despite the discomfort I soon finished off the case.

The liquor cabinet was now bare. I did not replenish it. By truly heroic perseverance I finally forced myself to write the daily thousand words without the spur of

John Barleycorn. But all the time I wrote I was keenly aware of the craving for a drink. And as soon as the morning's work was done, I was out of the house and away down-town to get my first drink. Merciful goodness!—if John Barleycorn could get such sway over me, a non-alcoholic, what must be the sufferings of the true alcoholic, battling against the organic demands of his chemistry while those closest to him sympathise little, understand less, and despise and deride him!

CHAPTER XXXV

But the freight has to be paid. John Barleycorn began to collect, and he collected not so much from the body as from the mind. The old long sickness, which had been purely an intellectual sickness, recrudesced. The old ghosts, long laid, lifted their heads again. But they were different and more deadly ghosts. The old ghosts, intellectual in their inception, had been laid by a sane and normal logic. But now they were raised by the White Logic of John Barleycorn, and John Barleycorn never lays the ghosts of his raising. For this sickness of pessimism, caused by drink, one must drink further in quest of the anodyne that John Barleycorn promises but never delivers.

How to describe this White Logic to those who have never experienced it! It is perhaps better first to state how impossible such a description is. Take Hasheesh Land, for instance, the land of enormous extensions of time and space. In past years I have made two memorable journeys into that far land. My adventures there are seared in sharpest detail on my brain. Yet I have tried vainly, with endless words, to describe any tiny particular phase to persons who have not travelled there.

I use all the hyperbole of metaphor, and tell what centuries of time and profounds of unthinkable agony and horror can obtain in each interval of all the intervals between the notes of a quick jig played quickly on the piano. I talk for an hour, elaborating that one phase of Hasheesh Land, and at the end I have told them nothing. And when I cannot tell them this one thing of all the vastness of terrible and wonderful things, I know I have failed to give them the slightest concept of Hasheesh Land.

But let me talk with some other traveller in that weird region, and at once am I understood. A phrase, a word, conveys instantly to his mind what hours of words and phrases could not convey to the mind of the non-traveller. So it is with John Barleycorn's realm where the White Logic reigns. To those untravelled there, the traveller's account must always seem unintelligible and fantastic. At the best, I may only beg of the untravelled ones to strive to take on faith the narrative I shall relate.

For there are fatal intuitions of truth that reside in alcohol. Philip sober vouches for Philip drunk in this matter. There seem to be various orders of truth in this world. Some sorts of truth are truer than others. Some sorts of truth are lies, and these sorts are the very ones that have the greatest use-value to life that desires to realise and live. At once, O untravelled reader, you see how lunatic and blasphemous is the realm I am trying to describe to you in the language of John

Barleycorn's tribe. It is not the language of your tribe, all of whose members resolutely shun the roads that lead to death and tread only the roads that lead to life. For there are roads and roads, and of truth there are orders and orders. But have patience. At least, through what seems no more than verbal yammerings, you may, perchance, glimpse faint far vistas of other lands and tribes.

Alcohol tells truth, but its truth is not normal. What is normal is healthful. What is healthful tends toward life. Normal truth is a different order, and a lesser order, of truth. Take a dray horse. Through all the vicissitudes of its life, from first to last, somehow, in unguessably dim ways, it must believe that life is good; that the drudgery in harness is good; that death, no matter how blind-instinctively apprehended, is a dread giant; that life is beneficent and worth while; that, in the end, with fading life, it will not be knocked about and beaten and urged beyond its sprained and spavined best; that old age, even, is decent, dignified, and valuable, though old age means a ribby scare-crow in a hawker's cart, stumbling a step to every blow, stumbling dizzily on through merciless servitude and slow disintegration to the end—the end, the apportionment of its parts (of its subtle flesh, its pink and springy bone, its juices and ferments, and all the sensateness that informed it) to the chicken farm, the hide-house, the glue-rendering works, and the bone-meal fertiliser factory. To the last stumble of its stumbling end this dray horse must abide by the mandates of the lesser truth that is the truth of life and that makes life possible to persist.

This dray horse, like all other horses, like all other animals, including man, is life-blinded and sense-struck. It will live, no matter what the price. The game of life is good, though all of life may be hurt, and though all lives lose the game in the end. This is the order of truth that obtains, not for the universe, but for the live things in it if they for a little space will endure ere they pass. This order of truth, no matter how erroneous it may be, is the sane and normal order of truth, the rational order of truth that life must believe in order to live.

To man, alone among the animals, has been given the awful privilege of reason. Man, with his brain, can penetrate the intoxicating show of things and look upon the universe brazen with indifference toward him and his dreams. He can do this, but it is not well for him to do it. To live, and live abundantly, to sting with life, to be alive (which is to be what he is), it is good that man be life-blinded and sense-struck. What is good is true. And this is the order of truth, lesser though it be, that man must know and guide his actions by with unswerving certitude that it is absolute truth and that in the universe no other order of truth can obtain. It is good that man should accept at face value the cheats of sense and snares of flesh and through the fogs of sentiency pursue the lures and lies of passion. It is good that he shall see neither shadows nor futilities, nor be appalled by his lusts and rapacities.

And man does this. Countless men have glimpsed that other and truer order of truth and recoiled from it. Countless men have passed through the long sickness and lived to tell of it and deliberately to forget it to the end of their days. They lived. They realised life, for life is what they were. They did right.

And now comes John Barleycorn with the curse he lays upon the imaginative man who is lusty with life and desire to live. John Barleycorn sends his White Logic, the argent messenger of truth beyond truth, the antithesis of life, cruel and bleak as interstellar space, pulseless and frozen as absolute zero, dazzling with the frost of irrefragable logic and unforgettable fact. John Barleycorn will not let the dreamer dream, the liver live. He destroys birth and death, and dissipates to mist the paradox of being, until his victim cries out, as in "The City of Dreadful Night": "Our life's a cheat, our death a black abyss." And the feet of the victim of such dreadful intimacy take hold of the way of death.

CHAPTER XXXVI

Back to personal experiences and the effects in the past of John Barleycorn's White Logic on me. On my lovely ranch in the Valley of the Moon, brain-soaked with many months of alcohol, I am oppressed by the cosmic sadness that has always been the heritage of man. In vain do I ask myself why I should be sad. My nights are warm. My roof does not leak. I have food galore for all the caprices of appetite. Every creature comfort is mine. In my body are no aches nor pains. The good old flesh-machine is running smoothly on. Neither brain nor muscle is overworked. I have land, money, power, recognition from the world, a consciousness that I do my meed of good in serving others, a mate whom I love, children that are of my own fond flesh. I have done, and am doing, what a good citizen of the world should do. I have built houses, many houses, and tilled many a hundred acres. And as for trees, have I not planted a hundred thousand? Everywhere, from any window of my house, I can gaze forth upon these trees of my planting, standing valiantly erect and aspiring toward the sun.

My life has indeed fallen in pleasant places. Not a hundred men in a million have been so lucky as I. Yet, with all this vast good fortune, am I sad. And I am sad because John Barleycorn is with me. And John Barleycorn is with me because I was born in what future ages will call the dark ages before the ages of rational civilisation. John Barleycorn is with me because in all the unwitting days of my youth John Barleycorn was accessible, calling to me and inviting me on every corner and on every street between the corners. The pseudo-civilisation into which I was born permitted everywhere licensed shops for the sale of soul-poison. The system of life was so organised that I (and millions like me) was lured and drawn and driven to the poison shops.

Wander with me through one mood of the myriad moods of sadness into which one is plunged by John Barleycorn. I ride out over my beautiful ranch. Between my legs is a beautiful horse. The air is wine. The grapes on a score of rolling hills are red with autumn flame. Across Sonoma Mountain wisps of sea fog are stealing. The afternoon sun smoulders in the drowsy sky. I have everything to make me glad I am alive. I am filled with dreams and mysteries. I am all sun and air and sparkle. I am vitalised, organic. I move, I have the power of movement, I command movement of the live thing I bestride. I am possessed with the pomps of being, and know proud passions and inspirations. I have ten thousand august connotations. I am a king in the kingdom of sense, and trample the face of the uncomplaining dust....

And yet, with jaundiced eye I gaze upon all the beauty and wonder about me, and with jaundiced brain consider the pitiful figure I cut in this world that endured so long without me and that will again endure without me. I remember the men who broke their hearts and their backs over this stubborn soil that now belongs to me. As if anything imperishable could belong to the perishable! These men passed. I, too, shall pass. These men toiled, and cleared, and planted, gazed with aching eyes, while they rested their labour-stiffened bodies on these same sunrises and sunsets, at the autumn glory of the grape, and at the fog-wisps stealing across the mountain. And they are gone. And I know that I, too, shall some day, and soon, be gone.

Gone? I am going now. In my jaw are cunning artifices of the dentists which replace the parts of me already gone. Never again will I have the thumbs of my youth. Old fights and wrestlings have injured them irreparably. That punch on the head of a man whose very name is forgotten settled this thumb finally and for ever. A slip-grip at catch-as-catch-can did for the other. My lean runner's stomach has passed into the limbo of memory. The joints of the legs that bear me up are not so adequate as they once were, when, in wild nights and days of toil and frolic, I strained and snapped and ruptured them. Never again can I swing dizzily aloft and trust all the proud quick that is I to a single rope-clutch in the driving blackness of storm. Never again can I run with the sled-dogs along the endless miles of Arctic trail.

I am aware that within this disintegrating body which has been dying since I was born I carry a skeleton, that under the rind of flesh which is called my face is a bony, noseless death's head. All of which does not shudder me. To be afraid is to be healthy. Fear of death makes for life. But the curse of the White Logic is that it does not make one afraid. The world-sickness of the White Logic makes one grin jocosely into the face of the Noseless One and to sneer at all the phantasmagoria of living.

I look about me as I ride and on every hand I see the merciless and infinite waste of natural selection. The White Logic insists upon opening the long-closed books, and by paragraph and chapter states the beauty and wonder I behold in terms of futility and dust. About me is murmur and hum, and I know it for the gnat-swarm of the living, piping for a little space its thin plaint of troubled air.

I return across the ranch. Twilight is on, and the hunting animals are out. I watch the piteous tragic play of life feeding on life. Here is no morality. Only in man is morality, and man created it—a code of action that makes toward living and that is of the lesser order of truth. Yet all this I knew before, in the weary days of my long sickness. These were the greater truths that I so successfully schooled myself to forget; the truths that were so serious that I refused to take them seriously, and played with gently, oh! so gently, as sleeping dogs at the back of consciousness which I did not care to waken. I did but stir them, and let them lie. I was too wise, too wicked wise, to wake them. But now White Logic willy-nilly wakes them for me, for White Logic, most valiant, is unafraid of all the monsters of the earthly dream.

"Let the doctors of all the schools condemn me," White Logic whispers as I ride along. "What of it? I am truth. You know it. You cannot combat me. They say I make for death. What of it? It is truth. Life lies in order to live. Life is a perpetual lie-telling process. Life is a mad dance in the domain of flux, wherein appearances in mighty tides ebb and flow, chained to the wheels of moons beyond our ken. Appearances are ghosts. Life is ghost land, where appearances change, transfuse, permeate each the other and all the others, that are, that are not, that always flicker, fade, and pass, only to come again as new appearances, as other appearances. You are such an appearance, composed of countless appearances out of the past. All an appearance can know is mirage. You know mirages of desire. These very mirages are the unthinkable and incalculable congeries of appearances that crowd in upon you and form you out of the past, and that sweep you on into dissemination into other unthinkable and incalculable congeries of appearances to people the ghost land of the future. Life is apparitional, and passes. You are an apparition. Through all the apparitions that preceded you and that compose the parts of you, you rose gibbering from the evolutionary mire, and gibbering you will pass on, interfusing, permeating the procession of apparitions that will succeed you."

And of course it is all unanswerable, and as I ride along through the evening shadows I sneer at that Great Fetish which Comte called the world. And I remember what another pessimist of sentiency has uttered: "Transient are all. They, being born, must die, and, being dead, are glad to be at rest."

But here through the dusk comes one who is not glad to be at rest. He is a workman on the ranch, an old man, an immigrant Italian. He takes his hat off to me in all servility, because, forsooth, I am to him a lord of life. I am food to him, and shelter, and existence. He has toiled like a beast all his days, and lived less comfortably than my horses in their deep-strawed stalls. He is labour-crippled. He shambles as he walks. One shoulder is twisted higher than the other. His hands are gnarled claws, repulsive, horrible. As an apparition he is a pretty miserable specimen. His brain is as stupid as his body is ugly.

"His brain is so stupid that he does not know he is an apparition," the White Logic chuckles to me. "He is sense-drunk. He is the slave of the dream of life. His brain is filled with superrational sanctions and obsessions. He believes in a transcendent over-world. He has listened to the vagaries of the prophets, who have given to him the sumptuous bubble of Paradise. He feels inarticulate self-affinities, with self-conjured non-realities. He sees penumbral visions of himself titubating fantastically through days and nights of space and stars. Beyond the shadow of any doubt he is convinced that the universe was made for him, and that it is his destiny to live for ever in the immaterial and supersensuous realms he and his kind have builded of the stuff of semblance and deception.

"But you, who have opened the books and who share my awful confidence—you know him for what he is, brother to you and the dust, a cosmic joke, a sport of chemistry, a garmented beast that arose out of the ruck of screaming beastliness by virtue and accident of two opposable great toes. He is brother as well to the gorilla and the chimpanzee. He thumps his chest in anger, and roars and quivers with cataleptic ferocity. He knows monstrous, atavistic promptings, and he is composed of all manner of shreds of abysmal and forgotten instincts."

"Yet he dreams he is immortal," I argue feebly. "It is vastly wonderful for so stupid a clod to bestride the shoulders of time and ride the eternities."

"Pah!" is the retort. "Would you then shut the books and exchange places with this thing that is only an appetite and a desire, a marionette of the belly and the loins?"

"To be stupid is to be happy," I contend.

"Then your ideal of happiness is a jelly-like organism floating in a tideless, tepid twilight sea, eh?"

Oh, the victim cannot combat John Barleycorn!

"One step removed from the annihilating bliss of Buddha's Nirvana," the White Logic adds. "Oh well, here's the house. Cheer up and take a drink. We know, we illuminated, you and I, all the folly and the farce."

And in my book-walled den, the mausoleum of the thoughts of men, I take my drink, and other drinks, and roust out the sleeping dogs from the recesses of my brain and hallo them on over the walls of prejudice and law and through all the cunning labyrinths of superstition and belief.

"Drink," says the White Logic. "The Greeks believed that the gods gave them wine so that they might forget the miserableness of existence. And remember what Heine said."

Well do I remember that flaming Jew's "With the last breath all is done: joy, love, sorrow, macaroni, the theatre, lime-trees, raspberry drops, the power of human relations, gossip, the barking of dogs, champagne."

"Your clear white light is sickness," I tell the White Logic. "You lie."

"By telling too strong a truth," he quips back.

"Alas, yes, so topsy-turvy is existence," I acknowledge sadly.

"Ah, well, Liu Ling was wiser than you," the White Logic girds. "You remember him?"

I nod my head—Liu Ling, a hard drinker, one of the group of bibulous poets who called themselves the Seven Sages of the Bamboo Grove and who lived in China many an ancient century ago.

"It was Liu Ling," prompts the White Logic, "who declared that to a drunken man the affairs of this world appear but as so much duckweed on a river. Very well. Have another Scotch, and let semblance and deception become duck-weed on a river."

And while I pour and sip my Scotch, I remember another Chinese philosopher, Chuang Tzu, who, four centuries before Christ, challenged this dreamland of the world, saying: "How then do I know but that the dead repent of having previously clung to life? Those who dream of the banquet, wake to lamentation and sorrow. Those who dream of lamentation and sorrow, wake to join the hunt. While they dream, they do not know that they dream. Some will even interpret the very dream they are dreaming; and only when they awake do they know it was a dream.... Fools think they are awake now, and flatter themselves they know if they are really princes or peasants. Confucius and you are both dreams; and I who say you are dreams— I am but a dream myself.

"Once upon a time, I, Chuang Tzu, dreamt I was a butterfly, fluttering hither and thither, to all intents and purposes a butterfly. I was conscious only of following my fancies as a butterfly, and was unconscious of my individuality as a man. Suddenly,

I awaked, and there I lay, myself again. Now I do not know whether I was then a man dreaming I was a butterfly, or whether I am now a butterfly dreaming I am a man."

CHAPTER XXXVII

"Come," says the White Logic, "and forget these Asian dreamers of old time. Fill your glass and let us look at the parchments of the dreamers of yesterday who dreamed their dreams on your own warm hills."

I pore over the abstract of title of the vineyard called Tokay on the rancho called Petaluma. It is a sad long list of the names of men, beginning with Manuel Micheltoreno, one time Mexican "Governor, Commander-in-Chief, and Inspector of the Department of the Californias," who deeded ten square leagues of stolen Indian land to Colonel Don Mariano Guadalupe Vallejo for services rendered his country and for moneys paid by him for ten years to his soldiers.

Immediately this musty record of man's land lust assumes the formidableness of a battle—the quick struggling with the dust. There are deeds of trust, mortgages, certificates of release, transfers, judgments, foreclosures, writs of attachment, orders of sale, tax liens, petitions for letters of administration, and decrees of distribution. It is like a monster ever unsubdued, this stubborn land that drowses in this Indian summer weather and that survives them all, the men who scratched its surface and passed.

Who was this James King of William, so curiously named? The oldest surviving settler in the Valley of the Moon knows him not. Yet only sixty years ago he loaned Mariano G. Vallejo eighteen thousand dollars on security of certain lands including the vineyard yet to be and to be called Tokay. Whence came Peter O'Connor, and whither vanished, after writing his little name of a day on the woodland that was to become a vineyard? Appears Louis Csomortanyi, a name to conjure with. He lasts through several pages of this record of the enduring soil.

Comes old American stock, thirsting across the Great American Desert, mule-backing across the Isthmus, wind-jamming around the Horn, to write brief and forgotten names where ten thousand generations of wild Indians are equally forgotten—names like Halleck, Hastings, Swett, Tait, Denman, Tracy, Grimwood, Carlton, Temple. There are no names like those to-day in the Valley of the Moon.

The names begin to appear fast and furiously, flashing from legal page to legal page and in a flash vanishing. But ever the persistent soil remains for others to scrawl themselves across. Come the names of men of whom I have vaguely heard but whom I have never known. Kohler and Frohling—who built the great stone winery on the vineyard called Tokay, but who built upon a hill up which other vineyardists refused to haul their grapes. So Kohler and Frohling lost the land; the earthquake of 1906 threw down the winery; and I now live in its ruins.

La Motte—he broke the soil, planted vines and orchards, instituted commercial fish culture, built a mansion renowned in its day, was defeated by the soil, and passed. And my name of a day appears. On the site of his orchards and vine-yards, of his proud mansion, of his very fish ponds, I have scrawled myself with half a hundred thousand eucalyptus trees.

Cooper and Greenlaw—on what is called the Hill Ranch they left two of their dead, "Little Lillie" and "Little David," who rest to-day inside a tiny square of hand-hewn palings. Also, Cooper and Greenlaw in their time cleared the virgin forest from three fields of forty acres. To-day I have those three fields sown with Canada peas, and in the spring they shall be ploughed under for green manure.

Haska—a dim legendary figure of a generation ago, who went back up the mountain and cleared six acres of brush in the tiny valley that took his name. He broke the soil, reared stone walls and a house, and planted apple trees. And already the site of the house is undiscoverable, the location of the stone walls may be deduced from the configuration of the landscape, and I am renewing the battle, putting in angora goats to browse away the brush that has overrun Haska's clearing and choked Haska's apple trees to death. So I, too, scratch the land with my brief endeavour and flash my name across a page of legal script ere I pass and the page grows musty.

"Dreamers and ghosts," the White Logic chuckles.

"But surely the striving was not altogether vain," I contend.

"It was based on illusion and is a lie."

"A vital lie," I retort.

"And pray what is a vital lie but a lie?" the White Logic challenges. "Come. Fill your glass and let us examine these vital liars who crowd your bookshelves. Let us dabble in William James a bit."

"A man of health," I say. "From him we may expect no philosopher's stone, but at least we will find a few robust tonic things to which to tie."

"Rationality gelded to sentiment," the White Logic grins. "At the end of all his thinking he still clung to the sentiment of immortality. Facts transmuted in the alembic of hope into terms of faith. The ripest fruit of reason the stultification of reason. From the topmost peak of reason James teaches to cease reasoning and to have faith that all is well and will be well—the old, oh, ancient old, acrobatic flip of the metaphysicians whereby they reasoned reason quite away in order to escape the pessimism consequent upon the grim and honest exercise of reason.

"Is this flesh of yours you? Or is it an extraneous something possessed by you? Your body—what is it? A machine for converting stimuli into reactions. Stimuli and reactions are remembered. They constitute experience. Then you are in your consciousness these experiences. You are at any moment what you are thinking at that moment. Your I is both subject and object; it predicates things of itself and is the things predicated. The thinker is the thought, the knower is what is known, the possessor is the things possessed.

"After all, as you know well, man is a flux of states of consciousness, a flow of passing thoughts, each thought of self another self, a myriad thoughts, a myriad selves, a continual becoming but never being, a will-of-the-wisp flitting of ghosts in ghostland. But this, man will not accept of himself. He refuses to accept his own passing. He will not pass. He will live again if he has to die to do it.

"He shuffles atoms and jets of light, remotest nebulae, drips of water, prickpoints of sensation, slime-oozings and cosmic bulks, all mixed with pearls of faith, love of woman, imagined dignities, frightened surmises, and pompous arrogances, and of the stuff builds himself an immortality to startle the heavens and baffle the immensities. He squirms on his dunghill, and like a child lost in the dark among goblins, calls to the gods that he is their younger brother, a prisoner of the quick that is destined to be as free as they—monuments of egotism reared by the epiphenomena; dreams and the dust of dreams, that vanish when the dreamer vanishes and are no more when he is not.

"It is nothing new, these vital lies men tell themselves, muttering and mumbling them like charms and incantations against the powers of Night. The voodoos and medicine men and the devil-devil doctors were the fathers of metaphysics. Night and the Noseless One were ogres that beset the way of light and life. And the metaphysicians would win by if they had to tell lies to do it. They were vexed by the brazen law of the Ecclesiast that men die like the beasts of the field and their end is the same. Their creeds were their schemes, their religions their nostrums, their philosophies their devices, by which they half-believed they would outwit the Noseless One and the Night.

"Bog-lights, vapours of mysticism, psychic overtones, soul orgies, wailings among the shadows, weird gnosticisms, veils and tissues of words, gibbering subjectivisms, gropings and maunderings, ontological fantasies, pan-psychic hallucinations—this is the stuff, the phantasms of hope, that fills your bookshelves. Look at them, all the sad wraiths of sad mad men and passionate rebels—your Schopenhauers, your Strindbergs, your Tolstois and Nietzsches.

"Come. Your glass is empty. Fill and forget."

I obey, for my brain is now well a-crawl with the maggots of alcohol, and as I drink to the sad thinkers on my shelves I quote Richard Hovey:

"Abstain not! Life and Love like night and day
Offer themselves to us on their own terms,
Not ours. Accept their bounty while ye may,
Before we be accepted by the worms,"

"I will cap you," cries the White Logic.

"No," I answer, while the maggots madden me. "I know you for what you are, and I am unafraid. Under your mask of hedonism you are yourself the Noseless One and your way leads to the Night. Hedonism has no meaning. It, too, is a lie, at best the coward's smug compromise."

"Now will I cap you!" the White Logic breaks in.
"But if you would not this poor life fulfil,
Lo, you are free to end it when you will,
Without the fear of waking after death."

And I laugh my defiance; for now, and for the moment, I know the White Logic to be the arch-impostor of them all, whispering his whispers of death. And he is guilty of his own unmasking, with his own genial chemistry turning the tables on himself, with his own maggots biting alive the old illusions, resurrecting and making to sound again the old voice from beyond of my youth, telling me again that still are mine the possibilities and powers which life and the books had taught me did not exist.

And the dinner gong sounds to the reversed bottom of my glass. Jeering at the White Logic, I go out to join my guests at table, and with assumed seriousness to discuss the current magazines and the silly doings of the world's day, whipping every trick and ruse of controversy through all the paces of paradox and persiflage. And, when the whim changes, it is most easy and delightfully disconcerting to play with the respectable and cowardly bourgeois fetishes and to laugh and epigram at the flitting god-ghosts and the debaucheries and follies of wisdom.

The clown's the thing! The clown! If one must be a philosopher, let him be Aristophanes. And no one at the table thinks I am jingled. I am in fine fettle, that is all. I tire of the labour of thinking, and, when the table is finished, start practical jokes and set all playing at games, which we carry on with bucolic boisterousness.

And when the evening is over and good-night said, I go back through my book-walled den to my sleeping porch and to myself and to the White Logic which, undefeated, has never left me. And as I fall to fuddled sleep I hear youth crying, as Harry Kemp heard it:

"I heard Youth calling in the night:
'Gone is my former world-delight;
For there is naught my feet may stay;
The morn suffuses into day,
It dare not stand a moment still
But must the world with light fulfil.
More evanescent than the rose
My sudden rainbow comes and goes,
Plunging bright ends across the sky—
Yea, I am Youth because I die!'"

CHAPTER XXXVIII

The foregoing is a sample roaming with the White Logic through the dusk of my soul.

To the best of my power I have striven to give the reader a glimpse of a man's secret dwelling when it is shared with John Barleycorn. And the reader must remember that this mood, which he has read in a quarter of an hour, is but one mood of the myriad moods of John Barleycorn, and that the procession of such moods may well last the clock around through many a day and week and month.

My alcoholic reminiscences draw to a close. I can say, as any strong, chesty drinker can say, that all that leaves me alive to-day on the planet is my unmerited luck—the luck of chest, and shoulders, and constitution. I dare to say that a not large percentage of youths, in the formative stage of fifteen to seventeen, could have survived the stress of heavy drinking that I survived between my fifteenth and seventeenth years; that a not large percentage of men could have punished the alcohol I have punished in my manhood years and lived to tell the tale. I survived, through no personal virtue, but because I did not have the chemistry of a dipsomaniac and because I possessed an organism unusually resistant to the ravages of John Barleycorn. And, surviving, I have watched the others die, not so lucky, down all the long sad road.

It was my unmitigated and absolute good fortune, good luck, chance, call it what you will, that brought me through the fires of John Barleycorn. My life, my career, my joy in living, have not been destroyed. They have been scorched, it is true; like the survivors of forlorn hopes, they have by unthinkably miraculous ways come through the fight to marvel at the tally of the slain.

And like such a survivor of old red war who cries out, "Let there be no more war!" so I cry out, "Let there be no more poison-fighting by our youths!" The way to stop war is to stop it. The way to stop drinking is to stop it. The way China stopped the general use of opium was by stopping the cultivation and importation of opium. The philosophers, priests, and doctors of China could have preached themselves breathless against opium for a thousand years, and the use of opium, so long as opium was ever accessible and obtainable, would have continued unabated. We are so made, that is all.

We have with great success made a practice of not leaving arsenic and strychnine, and typhoid and tuberculosis germs lying around for our children to be destroyed by. Treat John Barleycorn the same way. Stop him. Don't let him lie around, licensed and legal, to pounce upon our youth. Not of alcoholics nor for alcoholics do I write, but for our youths, for those who possess no more than the adventure-stings and the genial predispositions, the social man-impulses, which are twisted all awry by our barbarian civilisation which feeds them poison on all the corners. It is the healthy, normal boys, now born or being born, for whom I write.

It was for this reason, more than any other, and more ardently than any other, that I rode down into the Valley of the Moon, all a-jingle, and voted for equal suffrage. I voted that women might vote, because I knew that they, the wives and mothers of the race, would vote John Barleycorn out of existence and back into the historical limbo of our vanished customs of savagery. If I thus seem to cry out as one hurt, please remember that I have been sorely bruised and that I do dislike the thought that any son or daughter of mine or yours should be similarly bruised.

The women are the true conservators of the race. The men are the wastrels, the adventure-lovers and gamblers, and in the end it is by their women that they are saved. About man's first experiment in chemistry was the making of alcohol, and down all the generations to this day man has continued to manufacture and drink it.

And there has never been a day when the women have not resented man's use of alcohol, though they have never had the power to give weight to their resentment. The moment women get the vote in any community, the first thing they proceed to do is to close the saloons. In a thousand generations to come men of themselves will not close the saloons. As well expect the morphine victims to legislate the sale of morphine out of existence.

The women know. They have paid an incalculable price of sweat and tears for man's use of alcohol. Ever jealous for the race, they will legislate for the babes of boys yet to be born; and for the babes of girls, too, for they must be the mothers, wives, and sisters of these boys.

And it will be easy. The only ones that will be hurt will be the topers and sea-soned drinkers of a single generation. I am one of these, and I make solemn assurance, based upon long traffic with John Barleycorn, that it won't hurt me very much to stop drinking when no one else drinks and when no drink is obtainable. On the other hand, the overwhelming proportion of young men are so normally non-alcoholic, that, never having had access to alcohol, they will never miss it. They will know of the saloon only in the pages of history, and they will think of the saloon as a quaint old custom similar to bull-baiting and the burning of witches.

CHAPTER XXXIX

Of course, no personal tale is complete without bringing the narrative of the person down to the last moment. But mine is no tale of a reformed drunkard. I was never a drunkard, and I have not reformed.

It chanced, some time ago, that I made a voyage of one hundred and forty-eight days in a windjammer around the Horn. I took no private supply of alcohol along, and, though there was no day of those one hundred and forty-eight days that I could not have got a drink from the captain, I did not take a drink. I did not take a drink because I did not desire a drink. No one else drank on board. The atmosphere for drinking was not present, and in my system there was no organic need for alcohol. My chemistry did not demand alcohol.

So there arose before me a problem, a clear and simple problem: *this is so easy, why not keep it up when you get back on land?* I weighed this problem carefully. I weighed it for five months, in a state of absolute non-contact with alcohol. And out of the data of past experience, I reached certain conclusions.

In the first place, I am convinced that not one man in ten thousand or in a hundred thousand is a genuine, chemical dipsomaniac. Drinking, as I deem it, is practically entirely a habit of mind. It is unlike tobacco, or cocaine, or morphine, or all the rest of the long list of drugs. The desire for alcohol is quite peculiarly mental in its origin. It is a matter of mental training and growth, and it is cultivated in social soil. Not one drinker in a million began drinking alone. All drinkers begin socially, and this drinking is accompanied by a thousand social connotations such as I have described out of my own experience in the first part of this narrative. These social connotations are the stuff of which the drink habit is largely composed. The part that alcohol itself plays is inconsiderable when compared with the part played by the social atmosphere in which it is drunk. The human is rarely born these days, who, without long training in the social associations of drinking, feels the irresistible chemical propulsion of his system toward alcohol. I do assume that such rare individuals are born, but I have never encountered one.

On this long, five-months' voyage, I found that among all my bodily needs not the slightest shred of a bodily need for alcohol existed. But this I did find: my need was mental and social. When I thought of alcohol, the connotation was fellowship. When I thought of fellowship, the connotation was alcohol. Fellowship and alcohol were Siamese twins. They always occurred linked together.

Thus, when reading in my deck chair or when talking with others, practically any mention of any part of the world I knew instantly aroused the connotation of drinking and good fellows. Big nights and days and moments, all purple passages and freedoms, thronged my memory. "Venice" stares at me from the printed page, and I remember the cafe tables on the sidewalks. "The Battle of Santiago," some one says, and I answer, "Yes, I've been over the ground." But I do not see the ground, nor Kettle Hill, nor the Peace Tree. What I see is the Cafe Venus, on the plaza of Santiago, where one hot night I drank and talked with a dying consumptive.

The East End of London, I read, or some one says; and first of all, under my eyelids, leap the visions of the shining pubs, and in my ears echo the calls for "two of bitter" and "three of Scotch." The Latin Quarter—at once I am in the student cabarets, bright faces and keen spirits around me, sipping cool, well-dripped absinthe while our voices mount and soar in Latin fashion as we settle God and art and democracy and the rest of the simple problems of existence.

In a pampero off the River Plate we speculate, if we are disabled, of running in to Buenos Ayres, the "Paris of America," and I have visions of bright congregating places of men, of the jollity of raised glasses, and of song and cheer and the hum of genial voices. When we have picked up the North-east Trades in the Pacific we try to persuade our dying captain to run for Honolulu, and while I persuade I see myself again drinking cocktails on the cool lanais and fizzes out at Waikiki where the surf rolls in. Some one mentions the way wild ducks are cooked in the restaurants of San Francisco, and at once I am transported to the light and clatter of many tables, where I gaze at old friends across the golden brims of long-stemmed Rhine-wine glasses.

And so I pondered my problem. I should not care to revisit all these fair places of the world except in the fashion I visited them before. *Glass in hand!* There is a magic in the phrase. It means more than all the words in the dictionary can be made to mean. It is a habit of mind to which I have been trained all my life. It is now part of the stuff that composes me. I like the bubbling play of wit, the chesty laughs, the resonant voices of men, when, glass in hand, they shut the grey world outside and prod their brains with the fun and folly of an accelerated pulse.

No, I decided; I shall take my drink on occasion. With all the books on my shelves, with all the thoughts of the thinkers shaded by my particular temperament, I decided coolly and deliberately that I should continue to do what I had been trained to want to do. I would drink—but oh, more skilfully, more discreetly, than ever before. Never again would I be a peripatetic conflagration. Never again would I invoke the White Logic. I had learned how not to invoke him.

The White Logic now lies decently buried alongside the Long Sickness. Neither will afflict me again. It is many a year since I laid the Long Sickness away; his sleep is sound. And just as sound is the sleep of the White Logic. And yet, in conclusion, I can well say that I wish my forefathers had banished John Barleycorn before my time. I regret that John Barleycorn flourished everywhere in the system of society in which I was born, else I should not have made his acquaintance, and I was long trained in his acquaintance.

Love of Life

"This out of all will remain—
They have lived and have tossed:
So much of the game will be gain,
Though the gold of the dice has been lost."

They limped painfully down the bank, and once the foremost of the two men staggered among the rough-strewn rocks. They were tired and weak, and their faces had the drawn expression of patience which comes of hardship long endured. They were heavily burdened with blanket packs which were strapped to their shoulders. Head-straps, passing across the forehead, helped support these packs. Each man carried a rifle. They walked in a stooped posture, the shoulders well forward, the head still farther forward, the eyes bent upon the ground.

"I wish we had just about two of them cartridges that's layin' in that cache of ourn," said the second man.

His voice was utterly and drearily expressionless. He spoke without enthusiasm; and the first man, limping into the milky stream that foamed over the rocks, vouchsafed no reply.

The other man followed at his heels. They did not remove their foot-gear, though the water was icy cold—so cold that their ankles ached and their feet went numb. In places the water dashed against their knees, and both men staggered for footing.

The man who followed slipped on a smooth boulder, nearly fell, but recovered himself with a violent effort, at the same time uttering a sharp exclamation of pain. He seemed faint and dizzy and put out his free hand while he reeled, as though seeking support against the air. When he had steadied himself he stepped forward, but reeled again and nearly fell. Then he stood still and looked at the other man, who had never turned his head.

The man stood still for fully a minute, as though debating with himself. Then he called out:

"I say, Bill, I've sprained my ankle."

Bill staggered on through the milky water. He did not look around. The man watched him go, and though his face was expressionless as ever, his eyes were like the eyes of a wounded deer.

The other man limped up the farther bank and continued straight on without looking back. The man in the stream watched him. His lips trembled a little, so that the rough thatch of brown hair which covered them was visibly agitated. His tongue even strayed out to moisten them.

"Bill!" he cried out.

It was the pleading cry of a strong man in distress, but Bill's head did not turn. The man watched him go, limping grotesquely and lurching forward with stammering gait up the slow slope toward the soft sky-line of the low-lying hill. He watched him go till he passed over the crest and disappeared. Then he turned his gaze and slowly took in the circle of the world that remained to him now that Bill was gone.

Near the horizon the sun was smouldering dimly, almost obscured by formless mists and vapors, which gave an impression of mass and density without outline or tangibility. The man pulled out his watch, the while resting his weight on one leg. It was four o'clock, and as the season was near the last of July or first of August,—he did not know the precise date within a week or two,—he knew that the sun roughly marked the northwest. He looked to the south and knew that somewhere beyond those bleak hills lay the Great Bear Lake; also, he knew that in that direction the Arctic Circle cut its forbidding way across the Canadian Barrens. This stream in which he stood was a feeder to the Coppermine River, which in turn flowed north and emptied into Coronation Gulf and the Arctic Ocean. He had never been there, but he had seen it, once, on a Hudson Bay Company chart.

Again his gaze completed the circle of the world about him. It was not a heartening spectacle. Everywhere was soft sky-line. The hills were all low-lying. There were no trees, no shrubs, no grasses—naught but a tremendous and terrible desolation that sent fear swiftly dawning into his eyes.

"Bill!" he whispered, once and twice; "Bill!"

He cowered in the midst of the milky water, as though the vastness were pressing in upon him with overwhelming force, brutally crushing him with its complacent awfulness. He began to shake as with an ague-fit, till the gun fell from his hand with a splash. This served to rouse him. He fought with his fear and pulled himself together, groping in the water and recovering the weapon. He hitched his pack farther over on his left shoulder, so as to take a portion of its weight from off the injured ankle. Then he proceeded, slowly and carefully, wincing with pain, to the bank.

He did not stop. With a desperation that was madness, unmindful of the pain, he hurried up the slope to the crest of the hill over which his comrade had disappeared—more grotesque and comical by far than that limping, jerking comrade. But at the crest he saw a shallow valley, empty of life. He fought with his fear again, overcame it, hitched the pack still farther over on his left shoulder, and lurched on down the slope.

The bottom of the valley was soggy with water, which the thick moss held, spongelike, close to the surface. This water squirted out from under his feet at every step, and each time he lifted a foot the action culminated in a sucking sound as the wet moss reluctantly released its grip. He picked his way from muskeg to muskeg, and followed the other man's footsteps along and across the rocky ledges which thrust like islets through the sea of moss.

Though alone, he was not lost. Farther on he knew he would come to where dead spruce and fir, very small and weazened, bordered the shore of a little lake, the titchin-nichilie, in the tongue of the country, the "land of little sticks." And into that lake flowed a small stream, the water of which was not milky. There was rush-grass on that stream—this he remembered well—but no timber, and he would follow it till its first trickle ceased at a divide. He would cross this divide to the first trickle of another stream, flowing to the west, which he would follow until it emptied into the river Dease, and here he would find a cache under an upturned canoe and piled over with many rocks. And in this cache would be ammunition for his empty gun, fish-hooks and lines, a small net—all the utilities for the killing and snaring of food. Also, he would find flour,—not much,—a piece of bacon, and some beans.

Bill would be waiting for him there, and they would paddle away south down the Dease to the Great Bear Lake. And south across the lake they would go, ever south, till they gained the Mackenzie. And south, still south, they would go, while the winter raced vainly after them, and the ice formed in the eddies, and the days grew chill and crisp, south to some warm Hudson Bay Company post, where timber grew tall and generous and there was grub without end.

These were the thoughts of the man as he strove onward. But hard as he strove with his body, he strove equally hard with his mind, trying to think that Bill had not deserted him, that Bill would surely wait for him at the cache. He was compelled to think this thought, or else there would not be any use to strive, and he would have lain down and died. And as the dim ball of the sun sank slowly into the northwest he covered every inch—and many times—of his and Bill's flight south before the downcoming winter. And he conned the grub of the cache and the grub of the Hudson Bay Company post over and over again. He had not eaten for two days; for a far longer time he had not had all he wanted to eat. Often he stooped and picked pale muskeg berries, put them into his mouth, and chewed and swallowed them. A muskeg berry is a bit of seed enclosed in a bit of water. In the mouth the water melts away and the seed chews sharp and bitter. The man knew there was no nourishment in the berries, but he chewed them patiently with a hope greater than knowledge and defying experience.

At nine o'clock he stubbed his toe on a rocky ledge, and from sheer weariness and weakness staggered and fell. He lay for some time, without movement, on his side. Then he slipped out of the pack-straps and clumsily dragged himself into a sitting posture. It was not yet dark, and in the lingering twilight he groped about among the rocks for shreds of dry moss. When he had gathered a heap he built a fire,—a smouldering, smudgy fire,—and put a tin pot of water on to boil.

He unwrapped his pack and the first thing he did was to count his matches. There were sixty-seven. He counted them three times to make sure. He divided them into several portions, wrapping them in oil paper, disposing of one bunch in his empty tobacco pouch, of another bunch in the inside band of his battered hat, of a third bunch under his shirt on the chest. This accomplished, a panic came upon him, and he unwrapped them all and counted them again. There were still sixty-seven.

He dried his wet foot-gear by the fire. The moccasins were in soggy shreds. The blanket socks were worn through in places, and his feet were raw and bleeding. His ankle was throbbing, and he gave it an examination. It had swollen to the size of his knee. He tore a long strip from one of his two blankets and bound the ankle tightly. He tore other strips and bound them about his feet to serve for both moccasins and socks. Then he drank the pot of water, steaming hot, wound his watch, and crawled between his blankets.

He slept like a dead man. The brief darkness around midnight came and went. The sun arose in the northeast—at least the day dawned in that quarter, for the sun was hidden by gray clouds.

At six o'clock he awoke, quietly lying on his back. He gazed straight up into the gray sky and knew that he was hungry. As he rolled over on his elbow he was startled by a loud snort, and saw a bull caribou regarding him with alert curiosity. The animal was not mere than fifty feet away, and instantly into the man's mind leaped the vision and the savor of a caribou steak sizzling and frying over a fire. Mechanically he reached for the empty gun, drew a bead, and pulled the trigger. The bull snorted and leaped away, his hoofs rattling and clattering as he fled across the ledges.

The man cursed and flung the empty gun from him. He groaned aloud as he started to drag himself to his feet. It was a slow and arduous task.

His joints were like rusty hinges. They worked harshly in their sockets, with much friction, and each bending or unbending was accomplished only through a sheer exertion of will. When he finally gained his feet, another minute or so was consumed in straightening up, so that he could stand erect as a man should stand.

He crawled up a small knoll and surveyed the prospect. There were no trees, no bushes, nothing but a gray sea of moss scarcely diversified by gray rocks, gray lakelets, and gray streamlets. The sky was gray. There was no sun nor hint of sun. He had no idea of north, and he had forgotten the way he had come to this spot the night before. But he was not lost. He knew that. Soon he would come to the land of the little sticks. He felt that it lay off to the left somewhere, not far—possibly just over the next low hill.

He went back to put his pack into shape for travelling. He assured himself of the existence of his three separate parcels of matches, though he did not stop to count them. But he did linger, debating, over a squat moose-hide sack. It was not large. He could hide it under his two hands. He knew that it weighed fifteen pounds,—as much as all the rest of the pack,—and it worried him. He finally set it to one side and proceeded to roll the pack. He paused to gaze at the squat moose-hide sack. He picked it up hastily with a defiant glance about him, as though the desolation were trying to rob him of it; and when he rose to his feet to stagger on into the day, it was included in the pack on his back.

He bore away to the left, stopping now and again to eat muskeg berries. His ankle had stiffened, his limp was more pronounced, but the pain of it was as nothing compared with the pain of his stomach. The hunger pangs were sharp. They gnawed and gnawed until he could not keep his mind steady on the course he must pursue to gain the land of little sticks. The muskeg berries did not allay this gnawing, while they made his tongue and the roof of his mouth sore with their irritating bite.

He came upon a valley where rock ptarmigan rose on whirring wings from the ledges and muskegs. Ker—ker—ker was the cry they made. He threw stones at them, but could not hit them. He placed his pack on the ground and stalked them as a cat stalks a sparrow. The sharp rocks cut through his pants' legs till his knees left a trail of blood; but the hurt was lost in the hurt of his hunger. He squirmed over the wet moss, saturating his clothes and chilling his body; but he was not aware of it, so great was his fever for food. And always the ptarmigan rose, whirring, before him, till their ker—ker—ker became a mock to him, and he cursed them and cried aloud at them with their own cry.

Once he crawled upon one that must have been asleep. He did not see it till it shot up in his face from its rocky nook. He made a clutch as startled as was the rise of the ptarmigan, and there remained in his hand three tail-feathers. As he watched its flight he hated it, as though it had done him some terrible wrong. Then he returned and shouldered his pack.

As the day wore along he came into valleys or swales where game was more plentiful. A band of caribou passed by, twenty and odd animals, tantalizingly within rifle range. He felt a wild desire to run after them, a certitude that he could run them down. A black fox came toward him, carrying a ptarmigan in his mouth. The man shouted. It was a fearful cry, but the fox, leaping away in fright, did not drop the ptarmigan.

Late in the afternoon he followed a stream, milky with lime, which ran through sparse patches of rush-grass. Grasping these rushes firmly near the root, he pulled up what resembled a young onion-sprout no larger than a shingle-nail. It was tender, and his teeth sank into it with a crunch that promised deliciously of food. But its fibers were tough. It was composed of stringy filaments saturated with water, like the berries, and devoid of nourishment. He threw off his pack and went into the rush-grass on hands and knees, crunching and munching, like some bovine creature.

He was very weary and often wished to rest—to lie down and sleep; but he was continually driven on—not so much by his desire to gain the land of little sticks as by his hunger. He searched little ponds for frogs and dug up the earth with his nails for worms, though he knew in spite that neither frogs nor worms existed so far north.

He looked into every pool of water vainly, until, as the long twilight came on, he discovered a solitary fish, the size of a minnow, in such a pool. He plunged his arm in up to the shoulder, but it eluded him. He reached for it with both hands and stirred up the milky mud at the bottom. In his excitement he fell in, wetting himself to the waist. Then the water was too muddy to admit of his seeing the fish, and he was compelled to wait until the sediment had settled.

The pursuit was renewed, till the water was again muddied. But he could not wait. He unstrapped the tin bucket and began to bale the pool. He baled wildly at first, splashing himself and flinging the water so short a distance that it ran back into the pool. He worked more carefully, striving to be cool, though his heart was pounding against his chest and his hands were trembling. At the end of half an hour the pool was nearly dry. Not a cupful of water remained. And there was no fish. He found a hidden crevice among the stones through which it had escaped to the adjoining and larger pool—a pool which he could not empty in a night and a day. Had he known of the crevice, he could have closed it with a rock at the beginning and the fish would have been his.

Thus he thought, and crumpled up and sank down upon the wet earth. At first he cried softly to himself, then he cried loudly to the pitiless desolation that ringed him around; and for a long time after he was shaken by great dry sobs.

He built a fire and warmed himself by drinking quarts of hot water, and made camp on a rocky ledge in the same fashion he had the night before. The last thing he did was to see that his matches were dry and to wind his watch. The blankets were wet and clammy. His ankle pulsed with pain. But he knew only that he was hungry, and through his restless sleep he dreamed of feasts and banquets and of food served and spread in all imaginable ways.

He awoke chilled and sick. There was no sun. The gray of earth and sky had become deeper, more profound. A raw wind was blowing, and the first flurries of snow were whitening the hilltops. The air about him thickened and grew white while he made a fire and boiled more water. It was wet snow, half rain, and the flakes were large and soggy. At first they melted as soon as they came in contact with the earth, but ever more fell, covering the ground, putting out the fire, spoiling his supply of moss-fuel.

This was a signal for him to strap on his pack and stumble onward, he knew not where. He was not concerned with the land of little sticks, nor with Bill and the cache under the upturned canoe by the river Dease. He was mastered by the verb "to eat." He was hunger-mad. He took no heed of the course he pursued, so long as that course led him through the swale bottoms. He felt his way through the wet snow to the watery muskeg berries, and went by feel as he pulled up the rush-grass by the roots. But it was tasteless stuff and did not satisfy. He found a weed that tasted sour and he ate all he could find of it, which was not much, for it was a creeping growth, easily hidden under the several inches of snow.

He had no fire that night, nor hot water, and crawled under his blanket to sleep the broken hunger-sleep. The snow turned into a cold rain. He awakened many times to feel it falling on his upturned face. Day came—a gray day and no sun. It had ceased raining. The keenness of his hunger had departed. Sensibility, as far as concerned the yearning for food, had been exhausted. There was a dull, heavy ache in his stomach, but it did not bother him so much. He was more rational, and once more he was chiefly interested in the land of little sticks and the cache by the river Dease.

He ripped the remnant of one of his blankets into strips and bound his bleeding feet. Also, he recinched the injured ankle and prepared himself for a day of travel. When he came to his pack, he paused long over the squat moose-hide sack, but in the end it went with him.

The snow had melted under the rain, and only the hilltops showed white. The sun came out, and he succeeded in locating the points of the compass, though he knew now that he was lost. Perhaps, in his previous days' wanderings, he had edged away too far to the left. He now bore off to the right to counteract the possible deviation from his true course.

Though the hunger pangs were no longer so exquisite, he realized that he was weak. He was compelled to pause for frequent rests, when he attacked the muskeg berries and rush-grass patches. His tongue felt dry and large, as though covered with a fine hairy growth, and it tasted bitter in his mouth. His heart gave him a great deal of trouble. When he had travelled a few minutes it would begin a remorseless thump, thump, thump, and then leap up and away in a painful flutter of beats that choked him and made him go faint and dizzy.

In the middle of the day he found two minnows in a large pool. It was impossible to bale it, but he was calmer now and managed to catch them in his tin bucket. They were no longer than his little finger, but he was not particularly hungry. The dull ache in his stomach had been growing duller and fainter. It seemed almost that his stomach was dozing. He ate the fish raw, masticating with painstaking care, for the eating was an act of pure reason. While he had no desire to eat, he knew that he must eat to live.

In the evening he caught three more minnows, eating two and saving the third for breakfast. The sun had dried stray shreds of moss, and he was able to warm himself with hot water. He had not covered more than ten miles that day; and the next day, travelling whenever his heart permitted him, he covered no more than five miles. But his stomach did not give him the slightest uneasiness. It had gone to sleep. He was in a strange country, too, and the caribou were growing more plentiful, also the wolves. Often their yelps drifted across the desolation, and once he saw three of them slinking away before his path.

Another night; and in the morning, being more rational, he untied the leather string that fastened the squat moose-hide sack. From its open mouth poured a yellow stream of coarse gold-dust and nuggets. He roughly divided the gold in halves, caching one half on a prominent ledge, wrapped in a piece of blanket, and returning the other half to the sack. He also began to use strips of the one remaining blanket for his feet. He still clung to his gun, for there were cartridges in that cache by the river Dease.

This was a day of fog, and this day hunger awoke in him again. He was very weak and was afflicted with a giddiness which at times blinded him. It was no uncommon thing now for him to stumble and fall; and stumbling once, he fell squarely into a ptarmigan nest. There were four newly hatched chicks, a day old—little specks of pulsating life no more than a mouthful; and he ate them ravenously, thrusting them alive into his mouth and crunching them like egg-shells between his teeth. The mother ptarmigan beat about him with great outcry. He used his gun as a club with which to knock her over, but she dodged out of reach. He threw stones at her and with one chance shot broke a wing. Then she fluttered away, running, trailing the broken wing, with him in pursuit.

The little chicks had no more than whetted his appetite. He hopped and bobbed clumsily along on his injured ankle, throwing stones and screaming hoarsely at times; at other times hopping and bobbing silently along, picking himself up grimly and patiently when he fell, or rubbing his eyes with his hand when the giddiness threatened to overpower him.

The chase led him across swampy ground in the bottom of the valley, and he came upon footprints in the soggy moss. They were not his own—he could see that. They must be Bill's. But he could not stop, for the mother ptarmigan was running on. He would catch her first, then he would return and investigate.

He exhausted the mother ptarmigan; but he exhausted himself. She lay panting on her side. He lay panting on his side, a dozen feet away, unable to crawl to her.

And as he recovered she recovered, fluttering out of reach as his hungry hand went out to her. The chase was resumed. Night settled down and she escaped. He stumbled from weakness and pitched head foremost on his face, cutting his cheek, his pack upon his back. He did not move for a long while; then he rolled over on his side, wound his watch, and lay there until morning.

Another day of fog. Half of his last blanket had gone into foot-wrappings. He failed to pick up Bill's trail. It did not matter. His hunger was driving him too compellingly—only—only he wondered if Bill, too, were lost. By midday the irk of his pack became too oppressive. Again he divided the gold, this time merely spilling half of it on the ground. In the afternoon he threw the rest of it away, there remaining to him only the half-blanket, the tin bucket, and the rifle.

An hallucination began to trouble him. He felt confident that one cartridge remained to him. It was in the chamber of the rifle and he had overlooked it. On the other hand, he knew all the time that the chamber was empty. But the hallucination persisted. He fought it off for hours, then threw his rifle open and was confronted with emptiness. The disappointment was as bitter as though he had really expected to find the cartridge.

He plodded on for half an hour, when the hallucination arose again. Again he fought it, and still it persisted, till for very relief he opened his rifle to unconvince himself. At times his mind wandered farther afield, and he plodded on, a mere automaton, strange conceits and whimsicalities gnawing at his brain like worms. But these excursions out of the real were of brief duration, for ever the pangs of the hunger-bite called him back. He was jerked back abruptly once from such an excursion by a sight that caused him nearly to faint. He reeled and swayed, doddering like a drunken man to keep from falling. Before him stood a horse. A horse! He could not believe his eyes. A thick mist was in them, intershot with sparkling points of light. He rubbed his eyes savagely to clear his vision, and beheld, not a horse, but a great brown bear. The animal was studying him with bellicose curiosity.

The man had brought his gun halfway to his shoulder before he realized. He lowered it and drew his hunting-knife from its beaded sheath at his hip. Before him was meat and life. He ran his thumb along the edge of his knife. It was sharp. The point was sharp. He would fling himself upon the bear and kill it. But his heart began its warning thump, thump, thump. Then followed the wild upward leap and tattoo of flutters, the pressing as of an iron band about his forehead, the creeping of the dizziness into his brain.

His desperate courage was evicted by a great surge of fear. In his weakness, what if the animal attacked him? He drew himself up to his most imposing stature, gripping the knife and staring hard at the bear. The bear advanced clumsily a couple of steps, reared up, and gave vent to a tentative growl. If the man ran, he would run after him; but the man did not run. He was animated now with the courage of fear. He, too, growled, savagely, terribly, voicing the fear that is to life germane and that lies twisted about life's deepest roots.

The bear edged away to one side, growling menacingly, himself appalled by this mysterious creature that appeared upright and unafraid. But the man did not move.

He stood like a statue till the danger was past, when he yielded to a fit of trembling and sank down into the wet moss.

He pulled himself together and went on, afraid now in a new way. It was not the fear that he should die passively from lack of food, but that he should be destroyed violently before starvation had exhausted the last particle of the endeavor in him that made toward surviving. There were the wolves. Back and forth across the desolation drifted their howls, weaving the very air into a fabric of menace that was so tangible that he found himself, arms in the air, pressing it back from him as it might be the walls of a wind-blown tent.

Now and again the wolves, in packs of two and three, crossed his path. But they sheered clear of him. They were not in sufficient numbers, and besides they were hunting the caribou, which did not battle, while this strange creature that walked erect might scratch and bite.

In the late afternoon he came upon scattered bones where the wolves had made a kill. The debris had been a caribou calf an hour before, squawking and running and very much alive. He contemplated the bones, clean-picked and polished, pink with the cell-life in them which had not yet died. Could it possibly be that he might be that ere the day was done! Such was life, eh? A vain and fleeting thing. It was only life that pained. There was no hurt in death. To die was to sleep. It meant cessation, rest. Then why was he not content to die?

But he did not moralize long. He was squatting in the moss, a bone in his mouth, sucking at the shreds of life that still dyed it faintly pink. The sweet meaty taste, thin and elusive almost as a memory, maddened him. He closed his jaws on the bones and crunched. Sometimes it was the bone that broke, sometimes his teeth. Then he crushed the bones between rocks, pounded them to a pulp, and swallowed them. He pounded his fingers, too, in his haste, and yet found a moment in which to feel surprise at the fact that his fingers did not hurt much when caught under the descending rock.

Came frightful days of snow and rain. He did not know when he made camp, when he broke camp. He travelled in the night as much as in the day. He rested wherever he fell, crawled on whenever the dying life in him flickered up and burned less dimly. He, as a man, no longer strove. It was the life in him, unwilling to die, that drove him on. He did not suffer. His nerves had become blunted, numb, while his mind was filled with weird visions and delicious dreams.

But ever he sucked and chewed on the crushed bones of the caribou calf, the least remnants of which he had gathered up and carried with him. He crossed no more hills or divides, but automatically followed a large stream which flowed through a wide and shallow valley. He did not see this stream nor this valley. He saw nothing save visions. Soul and body walked or crawled side by side, yet apart, so slender was the thread that bound them.

He awoke in his right mind, lying on his back on a rocky ledge. The sun was shining bright and warm. Afar off he heard the squawking of caribou calves. He was aware of vague memories of rain and wind and snow, but whether he had been beaten by the storm for two days or two weeks he did not know.

For some time he lay without movement, the genial sunshine pouring upon him and saturating his miserable body with its warmth. A fine day, he thought. Perhaps he could manage to locate himself. By a painful effort he rolled over on his side. Below him flowed a wide and sluggish river. Its unfamiliarity puzzled him. Slowly he followed it with his eyes, winding in wide sweeps among the bleak, bare hills, bleaker and barer and lower-lying than any hills he had yet encountered. Slowly, deliberately, without excitement or more than the most casual interest, he followed the course of the strange stream toward the sky-line and saw it emptying into a bright and shining sea. He was still unexcited. Most unusual, he thought, a vision or a mirage—more likely a vision, a trick of his disordered mind. He was confirmed in this by sight of a ship lying at anchor in the midst of the shining sea. He closed his eyes for a while, then opened them. Strange how the vision persisted! Yet not strange. He knew there were no seas or ships in the heart of the barren lands, just as he had known there was no cartridge in the empty rifle.

He heard a snuffle behind him—a half-choking gasp or cough. Very slowly, because of his exceeding weakness and stiffness, he rolled over on his other side. He could see nothing near at hand, but he waited patiently. Again came the snuffle and cough, and outlined between two jagged rocks not a score of feet away he made out the gray head of a wolf. The sharp ears were not pricked so sharply as he had seen them on other wolves; the eyes were bleared and bloodshot, the head seemed to droop limply and forlornly. The animal blinked continually in the sunshine. It seemed sick. As he looked it snuffled and coughed again.

This, at least, was real, he thought, and turned on the other side so that he might see the reality of the world which had been veiled from him before by the vision. But the sea still shone in the distance and the ship was plainly discernible. Was it reality, after all? He closed his eyes for a long while and thought, and then it came to him. He had been making north by east, away from the Dease Divide and into the Coppermine Valley. This wide and sluggish river was the Coppermine. That shining sea was the Arctic Ocean. That ship was a whaler, strayed east, far east, from the mouth of the Mackenzie, and it was lying at anchor in Coronation Gulf. He remembered the Hudson Bay Company chart he had seen long ago, and it was all clear and reasonable to him.

He sat up and turned his attention to immediate affairs. He had worn through the blanket-wrappings, and his feet were shapeless lumps of raw meat. His last blanket was gone. Rifle and knife were both missing. He had lost his hat somewhere, with the bunch of matches in the band, but the matches against his chest were safe and dry inside the tobacco pouch and oil paper. He looked at his watch. It marked eleven o'clock and was still running. Evidently he had kept it wound.

He was calm and collected. Though extremely weak, he had no sensation of pain. He was not hungry. The thought of food was not even pleasant to him, and whatever he did was done by his reason alone. He ripped off his pants' legs to the knees and bound them about his feet. Somehow he had succeeded in retaining the tin bucket. He would have some hot water before he began what he foresaw was to be a terrible journey to the ship.

His movements were slow. He shook as with a palsy. When he started to collect dry moss, he found he could not rise to his feet. He tried again and again, then contented himself with crawling about on hands and knees. Once he crawled near to the sick wolf. The animal dragged itself reluctantly out of his way, licking its chops with a tongue which seemed hardly to have the strength to curl. The man noticed that the tongue was not the customary healthy red. It was a yellowish brown and seemed coated with a rough and half-dry mucus.

After he had drunk a quart of hot water the man found he was able to stand, and even to walk as well as a dying man might be supposed to walk. Every minute or so he was compelled to rest. His steps were feeble and uncertain, just as the wolf's that trailed him were feeble and uncertain; and that night, when the shining sea was blotted out by blackness, he knew he was nearer to it by no more than four miles.

Throughout the night he heard the cough of the sick wolf, and now and then the squawking of the caribou calves. There was life all around him, but it was strong life, very much alive and well, and he knew the sick wolf clung to the sick man's trail in the hope that the man would die first. In the morning, on opening his eyes, he beheld it regarding him with a wistful and hungry stare. It stood crouched, with tail between its legs, like a miserable and woe-begone dog. It shivered in the chill morning wind, and grinned dispiritedly when the man spoke to it in a voice that achieved no more than a hoarse whisper.

The sun rose brightly, and all morning the man tottered and fell toward the ship on the shining sea. The weather was perfect. It was the brief Indian Summer of the high latitudes. It might last a week. To-morrow or next day it might he gone.

In the afternoon the man came upon a trail. It was of another man, who did not walk, but who dragged himself on all fours. The man thought it might be Bill, but he thought in a dull, uninterested way. He had no curiosity. In fact, sensation and emotion had left him. He was no longer susceptible to pain. Stomach and nerves had gone to sleep. Yet the life that was in him drove him on. He was very weary, but it refused to die. It was because it refused to die that he still ate muskeg berries and minnows, drank his hot water, and kept a wary eye on the sick wolf.

He followed the trail of the other man who dragged himself along, and soon came to the end of it—a few fresh-picked bones where the soggy moss was marked by the foot-pads of many wolves. He saw a squat moose-hide sack, mate to his own, which had been torn by sharp teeth. He picked it up, though its weight was almost too much for his feeble fingers. Bill had carried it to the last. Ha! ha! He would have the laugh on Bill. He would survive and carry it to the ship in the shining sea. His mirth was hoarse and ghastly, like a raven's croak, and the sick wolf joined him, howling lugubriously. The man ceased suddenly. How could he have the laugh on Bill if that were Bill; if those bones, so pinky-white and clean, were Bill?

He turned away. Well, Bill had deserted him; but he would not take the gold, nor would he suck Bill's bones. Bill would have, though, had it been the other way around, he mused as he staggered on.

He came to a pool of water. Stooping over in quest of minnows, he jerked his head back as though he had been stung. He had caught sight of his reflected face. So horrible was it that sensibility awoke long enough to be shocked. There were three minnows in the pool, which was too large to drain; and after several ineffectual attempts to catch them in the tin bucket he forbore. He was afraid, because of his great weakness, that he might fall in and drown. It was for this reason that he did not trust himself to the river astride one of the many drift-logs which lined its sand-spits.

That day he decreased the distance between him and the ship by three miles; the next day by two—for he was crawling now as Bill had crawled; and the end of the fifth day found the ship still seven miles away and him unable to make even a mile a day. Still the Indian Summer held on, and he continued to crawl and faint, turn and turn about; and ever the sick wolf coughed and wheezed at his heels. His knees had become raw meat like his feet, and though he padded them with the shirt from his back it was a red track he left behind him on the moss and stones. Once, glancing back, he saw the wolf licking hungrily his bleeding trail, and he saw sharply what his own end might be—unless—unless he could get the wolf. Then began as grim a tragedy of existence as was ever played—a sick man that crawled, a sick wolf that limped, two creatures dragging their dying carcasses across the desolation and hunting each other's lives.

Had it been a well wolf, it would not have mattered so much to the man; but the thought of going to feed the maw of that loathsome and all but dead thing was repugnant to him. He was finicky. His mind had begun to wander again, and to be perplexed by hallucinations, while his lucid intervals grew rarer and shorter.

He was awakened once from a faint by a wheeze close in his ear. The wolf leaped lamely back, losing its footing and falling in its weakness. It was ludicrous, but he was not amused. Nor was he even afraid. He was too far gone for that. But his mind was for the moment clear, and he lay and considered. The ship was no more than four miles away. He could see it quite distinctly when he rubbed the mists out of his eyes, and he could see the white sail of a small boat cutting the water of the shining sea. But he could never crawl those four miles. He knew that, and was very calm in the knowledge. He knew that he could not crawl half a mile. And yet he wanted to live. It was unreasonable that he should die after all he had undergone. Fate asked too much of him. And, dying, he declined to die. It was stark madness, perhaps, but in the very grip of Death he defied Death and refused to die.

He closed his eyes and composed himself with infinite precaution. He steeled himself to keep above the suffocating languor that lapped like a rising tide through all the wells of his being. It was very like a sea, this deadly languor, that rose and rose and drowned his consciousness bit by bit. Sometimes he was all but submerged, swimming through oblivion with a faltering stroke; and again, by some strange alchemy of soul, he would find another shred of will and strike out more strongly.

Without movement he lay on his back, and he could hear, slowly drawing near and nearer, the wheezing intake and output of the sick wolf's breath. It drew closer, ever closer, through an infinitude of time, and he did not move. It was at his ear. The harsh dry tongue grated like sandpaper against his cheek. His hands shot out— or at least he willed them to shoot out. The fingers were curved like talons, but they closed on empty air. Swiftness and certitude require strength, and the man had not this strength.

The patience of the wolf was terrible. The man's patience was no less terrible. For half a day he lay motionless, fighting off unconsciousness and waiting for the thing that was to feed upon him and upon which he wished to feed. Sometimes the languid sea rose over him and he dreamed long dreams; but ever through it all, waking and dreaming, he waited for the wheezing breath and the harsh caress of the tongue.

He did not hear the breath, and he slipped slowly from some dream to the feel of the tongue along his hand. He waited. The fangs pressed softly; the pressure increased; the wolf was exerting its last strength in an effort to sink teeth in the food for which it had waited so long. But the man had waited long, and the lacerated hand closed on the jaw. Slowly, while the wolf struggled feebly and the hand clutched feebly, the other hand crept across to a grip. Five minutes later the whole weight of the man's body was on top of the wolf. The hands had not sufficient strength to choke the wolf, but the face of the man was pressed close to the throat of the wolf and the mouth of the man was full of hair. At the end of half an hour the man was aware of a warm trickle in his throat. It was not pleasant. It was like molten lead being forced into his stomach, and it was forced by his will alone. Later the man rolled over on his back and slept.

There were some members of a scientific expedition on the whale-ship *Bedford*. From the deck they remarked a strange object on the shore. It was moving down the beach toward the water. They were unable to classify it, and, being scientific men, they climbed into the whale-boat alongside and went ashore to see. And they saw something that was alive but which could hardly be called a man. It was blind, unconscious. It squirmed along the ground like some monstrous worm. Most of its efforts were ineffectual, but it was persistent, and it writhed and twisted and went ahead perhaps a score of feet an hour.

Three weeks afterward the man lay in a bunk on the whale-ship *Bedford*, and with tears streaming down his wasted cheeks told who he was and what he had undergone. He also babbled incoherently of his mother, of sunny Southern California, and a home among the orange groves and flowers.

The days were not many after that when he sat at table with the scientific men and ship's officers. He gloated over the spectacle of so much food, watching it anxiously as it went into the mouths of others. With the disappearance of each mouthful an expression of deep regret came into his eyes. He was quite sane, yet he hated those men at mealtime. He was haunted by a fear that the food would not last. He inquired of the cook, the cabin-boy, the captain, concerning the food stores. They reassured him countless times; but he could not believe them, and pried cunningly about the lazarette to see with his own eyes.

It was noticed that the man was getting fat. He grew stouter with each day. The scientific men shook their heads and theorized. They limited the man at his meals, but still his girth increased and he swelled prodigiously under his shirt.

The sailors grinned. They knew. And when the scientific men set a watch on the man, they knew too. They saw him slouch for'ard after breakfast, and, like a mendicant, with outstretched palm, accost a sailor. The sailor grinned and passed him a fragment of sea biscuit. He clutched it avariciously, looked at it as a miser looks at gold, and thrust it into his shirt bosom. Similar were the donations from other grinning sailors.

The scientific men were discreet. They let him alone. But they privily examined his bunk. It was lined with hardtack; the mattress was stuffed with hardtack; every nook and cranny was filled with hardtack. Yet he was sane. He was taking precautions against another possible famine—that was all. He would recover from it, the scientific men said; and he did, ere the *Bedford*'s anchor rumbled down in San Francisco Bay.

Hoboes That Pass in the Night

From *The Road*

In the course of my tramping I encountered hundreds of hoboes, whom I hailed or who hailed me, and with whom I waited at water-tanks, "boiled-up," cooked "mulligans," "battered" the "drag" or "privates," and beat trains, and who passed and were seen never again. On the other hand, there were hoboes who passed and re-passed with amazing frequency, and others, still, who passed like ghosts, close at hand, unseen, and never seen.

It was one of the latter that I chased clear across Canada over three thousand miles of railroad, and never once did I lay eyes on him. His "monica" was Skysail Jack. I first ran into it at Montreal. Carved with a jack-knife was the skysail-yard of a ship. It was perfectly executed. Under it was "Skysail Jack." Above was "B.W. 9-15-94." This latter conveyed the information that he had passed through Montreal bound west, on October 15, 1894. He had one day the start of me. "Sailor Jack" was my monica at that particular time, and promptly I carved it alongside of his, along with the date and the information that I, too, was bound west.

I had misfortune in getting over the next hundred miles, and eight days later I picked up Skysail Jack's trail three hundred miles west of Ottawa. There it was, carved on a water-tank, and by the date I saw that he likewise had met with delay. He was only two days ahead of me. I was a "comet" and "tramp-royal," so was Skysail Jack; and it was up to my pride and reputation to catch up with him. I "railroaded" day and night, and I passed him; then turn about he passed me. Sometimes he was a day or so ahead, and sometimes I was. From hoboes, bound east, I got word of him occasionally, when he happened to be ahead; and from them I learned that he had become interested in Sailor Jack and was making inquiries about me.

We'd have made a precious pair, I am sure, if we'd ever got together; but get together we couldn't. I kept ahead of him clear across Manitoba, but he led the way across Alberta, and early one bitter gray morning, at the end of a division just east of Kicking Horse Pass, I learned that he had been seen the night before between Kicking Horse Pass and Rogers' Pass. It was rather curious the way the information came to me. I had been riding all night in a "side-door Pullman" (box-car), and near-ly dead with cold had crawled out at the division to beg for food. A freezing fog was drifting past, and I "hit" some firemen I found in the round-house. They fixed me up with the leavings from their lunch-pails, and in addition I got out of them nearly a quart of heavenly "Java" (coffee). I heated the latter, and, as I sat down to eat, a freight pulled in from the west. I saw a side-door open and a road-kid climb out. Through the drifting fog he limped over to me. He was stiff with cold, his lips blue. I shared my Java and grub with him, learned about Skysail Jack, and then learned about him. Behold, he was from my own town, Oakland, California, and he was a member of the celebrated Boo Gang—a gang with which I had affiliated at rare intervals. We talked fast and bolted the grub in the half-hour that followed. Then my freight pulled out, and I was on it, bound west on the trail of Skysail Jack.

I was delayed between the passes, went two days without food, and walked eleven miles on the third day before I got any, and yet I succeeded in passing Skysail Jack along the Fraser River in British Columbia. I was riding "passengers" then and making time; but he must have been riding passengers, too, and with more luck or skill than I, for he got into Mission ahead of me.

Now Mission was a junction, forty miles east of Vancouver. From the junction one could proceed south through Washington and Oregon over the Northern Pacific. I wondered which way Skysail Jack would go, for I thought I was ahead of him. As for myself I was still bound west to Vancouver. I proceeded to the water-tank to leave that information, and there, freshly carved, with that day's date upon it, was Skysail Jack's monica. I hurried on into Vancouver. But he was gone. He had taken ship immediately and was still flying west on his world-adventure. Truly, Skysail Jack, you were a tramp-royal, and your mate was the "wind that tramps the world." I take off my hat to you. You were "blowed-in-the-glass" all right. A week later I, too, got my ship, and on board the steamship *Umatilla*, in the forecastle, was working my way down the coast to San Francisco. Skysail Jack and Sailor Jack—gee! if we'd ever got together.

Water-tanks are tramp directories. Not all in idle wantonness do tramps carve their monicas, dates, and courses. Often and often have I met hoboes earnestly inquiring if I had seen anywhere such and such a "stiff" or his monica. And more than once I have been able to give the monica of recent date, the water-tank, and the direction in which he was then bound. And promptly the hobo to whom I gave the information lit out after his pal. I have met hoboes who, in trying to catch a pal, had pursued clear across the continent and back again, and were still going.

"Monicas" are the nom-de-rails that hoboes assume or accept when thrust upon them by their fellows. Leary Joe, for instance, was timid, and was so named by his fellows. No self-respecting hobo would select Stew Bum for himself. Very few tramps care to remember their pasts during which they ignobly worked, so monicas based upon trades are very rare, though I remember having met the following: Moulder Blackey, Painter Red, Chi Plumber, Boiler-Maker, Sailor Boy, and Printer Bo. "Chi" (pronounced shy), by the way, is the argot for "Chicago."

A favorite device of hoboes is to base their monicas on the localities from which they hail, as: New York Tommy, Pacific Slim, Buffalo Smithy, Canton Tim, Pittsburg Jack, Syracuse Shine, Troy Mickey, K.L. Bill, and Connecticut Jimmy. Then there was "Slim Jim from Vinegar Hill, who never worked and never will." A "shine" is always a negro, so called, possibly, from the high lights on his countenance. Texas Shine or Toledo Shine convey both race and nativity.

Among those that incorporated their race, I recollect the following: Frisco Sheeny, New York Irish, Michigan French, English Jack, Cockney Kid, and Milwaukee Dutch. Others seem to take their monicas in part from the color-schemes stamped upon them at birth, such as: Chi Whitey, New Jersey Red, Boston Blackey,

Seattle Browney, and Yellow Dick and Yellow Belly—the last a Creole from Mississippi, who, I suspect, had his monica thrust upon him.

Texas Royal, Happy Joe, Bust Connors, Burley Bo, Tornado Blackey, and Touch McCall used more imagination in rechristening themselves. Others, with less fancy, carry the names of their physical peculiarities, such as: Vancouver Slim, Detroit Shorty, Ohio Fatty, Long Jack, Big Jim, Little Joe, New York Blink, Chi Nosey, and Broken-backed Ben.

By themselves come the road-kids, sporting an infinite variety of monicas. For example, the following, whom here and there I have encountered: Buck Kid, Blind Kid, Midget Kid, Holy Kid, Bat Kid, Swift Kid, Cookey Kid, Monkey Kid, Iowa Kid, Corduroy Kid, Orator Kid (who could tell how it happened), and Lippy Kid (who was insolent, depend upon it).

On the water-tank at San Marcial, New Mexico, a dozen years ago, was the following hobo bill of fare:—

(1) Main-drag fair.
(2) Bulls not hostile.
(3) Round-house good for kipping.
(4) North-bound trains no good.
(5) Privates no good.
(6) Restaurants good for cooks only.
(7) Railroad House good for night-work only.

Number one conveys the information that begging for money on the main street is fair; number two, that the police will not bother hoboes; number three, that one can sleep in the round-house. Number four, however, is ambiguous. The north-bound trains may be no good to beat, and they may be no good to beg. Number five means that the residences are not good to beggars, and number six means that only hoboes that have been cooks can get grub from the restaurants. Number seven bothers me. I cannot make out whether the Railroad House is a good place for any hobo to beg at night, or whether it is good only for hobo-cooks to beg at night, or whether any hobo, cook or non-cook, can lend a hand at night, helping the cooks of the Railroad House with their dirty work and getting something to eat in payment.

But to return to the hoboes that pass in the night. I remember one I met in California. He was a Swede, but he had lived so long in the United States that one couldn't guess his nationality. He had to tell it on himself. In fact, he had come to the United States when no more than a baby. I ran into him first at the mountain town of Truckee. "Which way, Bo?" was our greeting, and "Bound east" was the answer each of us gave. Quite a bunch of "stiffs" tried to ride out the overland that night, and I lost the Swede in the shuffle. Also, I lost the overland.

I arrived in Reno, Nevada, in a box-car that was promptly side-tracked. It was a Sunday morning, and after I threw my feet for breakfast, I wandered over to the Piute camp to watch the Indians gambling. And there stood the Swede, hugely interested. Of course we got together. He was the only acquaintance I had in that region, and I was his only acquaintance. We rushed together like a couple of dissatisfied hermits, and together we spent the day, threw our feet for dinner, and late in the afternoon tried to "nail" the same freight. But he was ditched, and I rode her out alone, to be ditched myself in the desert twenty miles beyond.

Of all desolate places, the one at which I was ditched was the limit. It was called a flag-station, and it consisted of a shanty dumped inconsequentially into the sand and sagebrush. A chill wind was blowing, night was coming on, and the solitary telegraph operator who lived in the shanty was afraid of me. I knew that neither grub nor bed could I get out of him. It was because of his manifest fear of me that I did not believe him when he told me that east-bound trains never stopped there. Besides, hadn't I been thrown off of an east-bound train right at that very spot not five minutes before? He assured me that it had stopped under orders, and that a year might go by before another was stopped under orders. He advised me that it was only a dozen or fifteen miles on to Wadsworth and that I'd better hike. I elected to wait, however, and I had the pleasure of seeing two west-bound freights go by without stopping, and one east-bound freight. I wondered if the Swede was on the latter. It was up to me to hit the ties to Wadsworth, and hit them I did, much to the telegraph operator's relief, for I neglected to burn his shanty and murder him. Telegraph operators have much to be thankful for. At the end of half a dozen miles, I had to get off the ties and let the east-bound overland go by. She was going fast, but I caught sight of a dim form on the first "blind" that looked like the Swede.

That was the last I saw of him for weary days. I hit the high places across those hundreds of miles of Nevada desert, riding the overlands at night, for speed, and in the day-time riding in box-cars and getting my sleep. It was early in the year, and it was cold in those upland pastures. Snow lay here and there on the level, all the mountains were shrouded in white, and at night the most miserable wind imaginable blew off from them. It was not a land in which to linger. And remember, gentle reader, the hobo goes through such a land, without shelter, without money, begging his way and sleeping at night without blankets. This last is something that can be realized only by experience.

In the early evening I came down to the depot at Ogden. The overland of the Union Pacific was pulling east, and I was bent on making connections. Out in the tangle of tracks ahead of the engine I encountered a figure slouching through the gloom. It was the Swede. We shook hands like long-lost brothers, and discovered that our hands were gloved. "Where'd ye glahm 'em?" I asked. "Out of an engine-cab," he answered; "and where did you?" "They belonged to a fireman," said I; "he was careless."

We caught the blind as the overland pulled out, and mighty cold we found it. The way led up a narrow gorge between snow-covered mountains, and we shivered and shook and exchanged confidences about how we had covered the ground between Reno and Ogden. I had closed my eyes for only an hour or so the previous night, and the blind was not comfortable enough to suit me for a snooze. At a stop, I went forward to the engine. We had on a "double-header" (two engines) to take us over the grade.

The pilot of the head engine, because it "punched the wind," I knew would be too cold; so I selected the pilot of the second engine, which was sheltered by the first engine. I stepped on the cowcatcher and found the pilot occupied. In the darkness I felt out the form of a young boy. He was sound asleep. By squeezing, there was room for two on the pilot, and I made the boy budge over and crawled up beside him. It was a "good" night; the "shacks" (brakemen) didn't bother us, and in no time we were asleep. Once in a while hot cinders or heavy jolts aroused me, when I snuggled closer to the boy and dozed off to the coughing of the engines and the screeching of the wheels.

The overland made Evanston, Wyoming, and went no farther. A wreck ahead blocked the line. The dead engineer had been brought in, and his body attested the peril of the way. A tramp, also, had been killed, but his body had not been brought in. I talked with the boy. He was thirteen years old. He had run away from his folks in some place in Oregon, and was heading east to his grandmother. He had a tale of cruel treatment in the home he had left that rang true; besides, there was no need for him to lie to me, a nameless hobo on the track.

And that boy was going some, too. He couldn't cover the ground fast enough. When the division superintendents decided to send the overland back over the way it had come, then up on a cross "jerk" to the Oregon Short Line, and back along that road to tap the Union Pacific the other side of the wreck, that boy climbed upon the pilot and said he was going to stay with it. This was too much for the Swede and me. It meant travelling the rest of that frigid night in order to gain no more than a dozen miles or so. We said we'd wait till the wreck was cleared away, and in the meantime get a good sleep.

Now it is no snap to strike a strange town, broke, at midnight, in cold weather, and find a place to sleep. The Swede hadn't a penny. My total assets consisted of two dimes and a nickel. From some of the town boys we learned that beer was five cents, and that the saloons kept open all night. There was our meat. Two glasses of beer would cost ten cents, there would be a stove and chairs, and we could sleep it out till morning. We headed for the lights of a saloon, walking briskly, the snow crunching under our feet, a chill little wind blowing through us.

Alas, I had misunderstood the town boys. Beer was five cents in one saloon only in the whole burg, and we didn't strike that saloon. But the one we entered was all right. A blessed stove was roaring white-hot; there were cosey, cane-bottomed armchairs, and a none-too-pleasant-looking barkeeper who glared suspiciously at us as we came in. A man cannot spend continuous days and nights in his clothes, beating trains, fighting soot and cinders, and sleeping anywhere, and maintain a good "front." Our fronts were decidedly against us; but what did we care? I had the price in my jeans.

"Two beers," said I nonchalantly to the barkeeper, and while he drew them, the Swede and I leaned against the bar and yearned secretly for the arm-chairs by the stove.

The barkeeper set the two foaming glasses before us, and with pride I deposited the ten cents. Now I was dead game. As soon as I learned my error in the price I'd have dug up another ten cents. Never mind if it did leave me only a nickel to my name, a stranger in a strange land. I'd have paid it all right. But that barkeeper never gave me a chance. As soon as his eyes spotted the dime I had laid down, he seized the two glasses, one in each hand, and dumped the beer into the sink behind the bar. At the same time, glaring at us malevolently, he said:—

"You've got scabs on your nose. You've got scabs on your nose. You've got scabs on your nose. See!"

I hadn't either, and neither had the Swede. Our noses were all right. The direct bearing of his words was beyond our comprehension, but the indirect bearing was clear as print: he didn't like our looks, and beer was evidently ten cents a glass.

I dug down and laid another dime on the bar, remarking carelessly, "Oh, I thought this was a five-cent joint."

"Your money's no good here," he answered, shoving the two dimes across the bar to me.

Sadly I dropped them back into my pocket, sadly we yearned toward the blessed stove and the arm-chairs, and sadly we went out the door into the frosty night.

But as we went out the door, the barkeeper, still glaring, called after us, "You've got scabs on your nose, see!"

I have seen much of the world since then, journeyed among strange lands and peoples, opened many books, sat in many lecture-halls; but to this day, though I have pondered long and deep, I have been unable to divine the meaning in the cryptic utterance of that barkeeper in Evanston, Wyoming. Our noses were all right.

We slept that night over the boilers in an electric-lighting plant. How we discovered that "kipping" place I can't remember. We must have just headed for it, instinctively, as horses head for water or carrier-pigeons head for the home-cote. But it was a night not pleasant to remember. A dozen hoboes were ahead of us on top the boilers, and it was too hot for all of us. To complete our misery, the engineer would not let us stand around down below. He gave us our choice of the boilers or the outside snow.

"You said you wanted to sleep, and so, damn you, sleep," said he to me, when, frantic and beaten out by the heat, I came down into the fire-room.

"Water," I gasped, wiping the sweat from my eyes, "water."

He pointed out of doors and assured me that down there somewhere in the blackness I'd find the river. I started for the river, got lost in the dark, fell into two or three drifts, gave it up, and returned half-frozen to the top of the boilers. When I had thawed out, I was thirstier than ever. Around me the hoboes were moaning, groaning, sobbing, sighing, gasping, panting, rolling and tossing and floundering heavily in their torment. We were so many lost souls toasting on a griddle in hell, and the engineer, Satan Incarnate, gave us the sole alternative of freezing in the outer cold. The Swede sat up and anathematized passionately the wanderlust in man that sent him tramping and suffering hardships such as that.

"When I get back to Chicago," he perorated, "I'm going to get a job and stick to it till hell freezes over. Then I'll go tramping again."

And, such is the irony of fate, next day, when the wreck ahead was cleared, the Swede and I pulled out of Evanston in the ice-boxes of an "orange special," a fast freight laden with fruit from sunny California. Of course, the ice-boxes were empty on account of the cold weather, but that didn't make them any warmer for us. We entered them through hatchways in the top of the car; the boxes were constructed of galvanized iron, and in that biting weather were not pleasant to the touch. We lay there, shivered and shook, and with chattering teeth held a council wherein we decided that we'd stay by the ice-boxes day and night till we got out of the inhospitable plateau region and down into the Mississippi Valley.

But we must eat, and we decided that at the next division we would throw our feet for grub and make a rush back to our ice-boxes. We arrived in the town of Green River late in the afternoon, but too early for supper. Before meal-time is the worst time for "battering" back-doors; but we put on our nerve, swung off the side-ladders as the freight pulled into the yards, and made a run for the houses. We were quickly separated; but we had agreed to meet in the ice-boxes. I had bad luck at first; but in the end, with a couple of "hand-outs" poked into my shirt, I chased for the train. It was pulling out and going fast. The particular refrigerator-car in which we were to meet had already gone by, and half a dozen cars down the train from it I swung on to the side-ladders, went up on top hurriedly, and dropped down into an ice-box.

But a shack had seen me from the caboose, and at the next stop a few miles farther on, Rock Springs, the shack stuck his head into my box and said: "Hit the grit, you son of a toad! Hit the grit!" Also he grabbed me by the heels and dragged me out. I hit the grit all right, and the orange special and the Swede rolled on without me.

Snow was beginning to fall. A cold night was coming on. After dark I hunted around in the railroad yards until I found an empty refrigerator car. In I climbed—not into the ice-boxes, but into the car itself. I swung the heavy doors shut, and their edges, covered with strips of rubber, sealed the car air-tight. The walls were thick. There was no way for the outside cold to get in. But the inside was just as cold as the outside. How to raise the temperature was the problem. But trust a "profesh" for that. Out of my pockets I dug up three or four newspapers. These I burned, one at a time, on the floor of the car. The smoke rose to the top. Not a bit of the heat could escape, and, comfortable and warm, I passed a beautiful night. I didn't wake up once.

In the morning it was still snowing. While throwing my feet for breakfast, I missed an east-bound freight. Later in the day I nailed two other freights and was ditched from both of them. All afternoon no east-bound trains went by. The snow was falling thicker than ever, but at twilight I rode out on the first blind of the overland. As I swung aboard the blind from one side, somebody swung aboard from the other. It was the boy who had run away from Oregon.

Now the first blind of a fast train in a driving snow-storm is no summer picnic. The wind goes right through one, strikes the front of the car, and comes back again. At the first stop, darkness having come on, I went forward and interviewed the fireman. I offered to "shove" coal to the end of his run, which was Rawlins, and my offer was accepted. My work was out on the tender, in the snow, breaking the lumps of coal with a sledge and shovelling it forward to him in the cab. But as I did not have to work all the time, I could come into the cab and warm up now and again.

"Say," I said to the fireman, at my first breathing spell, "there's a little kid back there on the first blind. He's pretty cold."

The cabs on the Union Pacific engines are quite spacious, and we fitted the kid into a warm nook in front of the high seat of the fireman, where the kid promptly fell asleep. We arrived at Rawlins at midnight. The snow was thicker than ever. Here the engine was to go into the round-house, being replaced by a fresh engine. As the train came to a stop, I dropped off the engine steps plump into the arms of a large man in a large overcoat. He began asking me questions, and I promptly demanded who he was. Just as promptly he informed me that he was the sheriff. I drew in my horns and listened and answered.

He began describing the kid who was still asleep in the cab. I did some quick thinking. Evidently the family was on the trail of the kid, and the sheriff had received telegraphed instructions from Oregon. Yes, I had seen the kid. I had met him first in Ogden. The date tallied with the sheriff's information. But the kid was still behind somewhere, I explained, for he had been ditched from that very overland that night when it pulled out of Rock Springs. And all the time I was praying that the kid wouldn't wake up, come down out of the cab, and put the "kibosh" on me.

The sheriff left me in order to interview the shacks, but before he left he said:—

"Bo, this town is no place for you. Understand? You ride this train out, and make no mistake about it. If I catch you after it's gone ..."

I assured him that it was not through desire that I was in his town; that the only reason I was there was that the train had stopped there; and that he wouldn't see me for smoke the way I'd get out of his darn town.

While he went to interview the shacks, I jumped back into the cab. The kid was awake and rubbing his eyes. I told him the news and advised him to ride the engine into the round-house. To cut the story short, the kid made the same overland out, riding the pilot, with instructions to make an appeal to the fireman at the first stop for permission to ride in the engine. As for myself, I got ditched. The new fireman was young and not yet lax enough to break the rules of the Company against having tramps in the engine; so he turned down my offer to shove coal. I hope the kid succeeded with him, for all night on the pilot in that blizzard would have meant death.

Strange to say, I do not at this late day remember a detail of how I was ditched at Rawlins. I remember watching the train as it was immediately swallowed up in the snow-storm, and of heading for a saloon to warm up. Here was light and warmth. Everything was in full blast and wide open. Faro, roulette, craps, and poker tables were running, and some mad cow-punchers were making the night merry. I had just succeeded in fraternizing with them and was downing my first drink at their expense, when a heavy hand descended on my shoulder. I looked around and sighed. It was the sheriff.

Without a word he led me out into the snow.

"There's an orange special down there in the yards," said he.

"It's a damn cold night," said I.

"It pulls out in ten minutes," said he.

That was all. There was no discussion. And when that orange special pulled out, I was in the ice-boxes. I thought my feet would freeze before morning, and the last twenty miles into Laramie I stood upright in the hatchway and danced up and down. The snow was too thick for the shacks to see me, and I didn't care if they did.

My quarter of a dollar bought me a hot breakfast at Laramie, and immediately afterward I was on board the blind baggage of an overland that was climbing to the pass through the backbone of the Rockies. One does not ride blind baggages in the daytime; but in this blizzard at the top of the Rocky Mountains I doubted if the shacks would have the heart to put me off. And they didn't. They made a practice of coming forward at every stop to see if I was frozen yet.

At Ames' Monument, at the summit of the Rockies,—I forget the altitude,—the shack came forward for the last time.

"Say, Bo," he said, "you see that freight side-tracked over there to let us go by?"

I saw. It was on the next track, six feet away. A few feet more in that storm and I could not have seen it.

"Well, the 'after-push' of Kelly's Army is in one of them cars. They've got two feet of straw under them, and there's so many of them that they keep the car warm."

His advice was good, and I followed it, prepared, however, if it was a "con game" the shack had given me, to take the blind as the overland pulled out. But it was straight goods. I found the car—a big refrigerator car with the leeward door wide open for ventilation. Up I climbed and in. I stepped on a man's leg, next on some other man's arm. The light was dim, and all I could make out was arms and legs and bodies inextricably confused. Never was there such a tangle of humanity. They were all lying in the straw, and over, and under, and around one another. Eighty-four husky hoboes take up a lot of room when they are stretched out. The men I stepped on were resentful. Their bodies heaved under me like the waves of the sea, and imparted an involuntary forward movement to me. I could not find any straw to step upon, so I stepped upon more men. The resentment increased, so did my forward movement. I lost my footing and sat down with sharp abruptness. Unfortunately, it was on a man's head. The next moment he had risen on his hands and knees in wrath, and I was flying through the air. What goes up must come down, and I came down on another man's head.

What happened after that is very vague in my memory. It was like going through a threshing-machine. I was bandied about from one end of the car to the other. Those eighty-four hoboes winnowed me out till what little was left of me, by some miracle, found a bit of straw to rest upon. I was initiated, and into a jolly crowd. All the rest of that day we rode through the blizzard, and to while the time away it was decided that each man was to tell a story. It was stipulated that each story must be a good one, and, furthermore, that it must be a story no one had ever heard before. The penalty for failure was the threshing-machine. Nobody failed. And I want to say right here that never in my life have I sat at so marvellous a story-telling debauch. Here were eighty-four men from all the world—I made eighty-five; and each man told a masterpiece. It had to be, for it was either masterpiece or threshing-machine.

Late in the afternoon we arrived in Cheyenne. The blizzard was at its height, and though the last meal of all of us had been breakfast, no man cared to throw his feet for supper. All night we rolled on through the storm, and next day found us down on the sweet plains of Nebraska and still rolling. We were out of the storm and the mountains. The blessed sun was shining over a smiling land, and we had eaten nothing for twenty-four hours. We found out that the freight would arrive about noon at a town, if I remember right, that was called Grand Island.

We took up a collection and sent a telegram to the authorities of that town. The text of the message was that eighty-five healthy, hungry hoboes would arrive about noon and that it would be a good idea to have dinner ready for them. The authorities of Grand Island had two courses open to them. They could feed us, or they could throw us in jail. In the latter event they'd have to feed us anyway, and they decided wisely that one meal would be the cheaper way.

When the freight rolled into Grand Island at noon, we were sitting on the tops of the cars and dangling our legs in the sunshine. All the police in the burg were on the reception committee. They marched us in squads to the various hotels and restaurants, where dinners were spread for us. We had been thirty-six hours without food, and we didn't have to be taught what to do. After that we were marched back to the railroad station. The police had thoughtfully compelled the freight to wait for us. She pulled out slowly, and the eighty-five of us, strung out along the track, swarmed up the side-ladders. We "captured" the train.

We had no supper that evening—at least the "push" didn't, but I did. Just at supper time, as the freight was pulling out of a small town, a man climbed into the car where I was playing pedro with three other stiffs. The man's shirt was bulging suspiciously. In his hand he carried a battered quart-measure from which arose steam. I smelled "Java." I turned my cards over to one of the stiffs who was looking on, and excused myself. Then, in the other end of the car, pursued by envious glances, I sat down with the man who had climbed aboard and shared his "Java" and the hand-outs that had bulged his shirt. It was the Swede.

At about ten o'clock in the evening, we arrived at Omaha.

"Let's shake the push," said the Swede to me.

"Sure," said I.

As the freight pulled into Omaha, we made ready to do so. But the people of Omaha were also ready. The Swede and I hung upon the side-ladders, ready to drop off. But the freight did not stop. Furthermore, long rows of policemen, their brass buttons and stars glittering in the electric lights, were lined up on each side of the track. The Swede and I knew what would happen to us if we ever dropped off into their arms. We stuck by the side-ladders, and the train rolled on across the Missouri River to Council Bluffs.

"General" Kelly, with an army of two thousand hoboes, lay in camp at Chautauqua Park, several miles away. The after-push we were with was General Kelly's rear-guard, and, detraining at Council Bluffs, it started to march to camp. The night had turned cold, and heavy wind-squalls, accompanied by rain, were chilling and wetting us. Many police were guarding us and herding us to the camp. The Swede and I watched our chance and made a successful get-away.

The rain began coming down in torrents, and in the darkness, unable to see our hands in front of our faces, like a pair of blind men we fumbled about for shelter. Our instinct served us, for in no time we stumbled upon a saloon—not a saloon that was open and doing business, not merely a saloon that was closed for the night, and not even a saloon with a permanent address, but a saloon propped up on big timbers, with rollers underneath, that was being moved from somewhere to somewhere. The doors were locked. A squall of wind and rain drove down upon us. We did not hesitate. Smash went the door, and in we went.

I have made some tough camps in my time, "carried the banner" in infernal metropolises, bedded in pools of water, slept in the snow under two blankets when the spirit thermometer registered seventy-four degrees below zero (which is a mere trifle of one hundred and six degrees of frost); but I want to say right here that never did I make a tougher camp, pass a more miserable night, than that night I passed with the Swede in the itinerant saloon at Council Bluffs. In the first place, the building, perched up as it was in the air, had exposed a multitude of openings in the floor through which the wind whistled. In the second place, the bar was empty; there was no bottled fire-water with which we could warm ourselves and forget our misery. We had no blankets, and in our wet clothes, wet to the skin, we tried to sleep. I rolled under the bar, and the Swede rolled under the table. The holes and crevices in the floor made it impossible, and at the end of half an hour I crawled up on top the bar. A little later the Swede crawled up on top his table.

And there we shivered and prayed for daylight. I know, for one, that I shivered until I could shiver no more, till the shivering muscles exhausted themselves and merely ached horribly. The Swede moaned and groaned, and every little while, through chattering teeth, he muttered, "Never again; never again." He muttered this phrase repeatedly, ceaselessly, a thousand times; and when he dozed, he went on muttering it in his sleep.

At the first gray of dawn we left our house of pain, and outside, found ourselves in a mist, dense and chill. We stumbled on till we came to the railroad track. I was going back to Omaha to throw my feet for breakfast; my companion was going on to Chicago. The moment for parting had come. Our palsied hands went out to each other. We were both shivering. When we tried to speak, our teeth chattered us back into silence. We stood alone, shut off from the world; all that we could see was a short length of railroad track, both ends of which were lost in the driving mist. We stared dumbly at each other, our clasped hands shaking sympathetically. The Swede's face was blue with the cold, and I know mine must have been.

"Never again what?" I managed to articulate.

Speech strove for utterance in the Swede's throat; then faint and distant, in a thin whisper from the very bottom of his frozen soul, came the words:—

"Never again a hobo."

He paused, and, as he went on again, his voice gathered strength and huskiness as it affirmed his will.

"Never again a hobo. I'm going to get a job. You'd better do the same. Nights like this make rheumatism."

He wrung my hand.

"Good-by, Bo," said he.

"Good-by, Bo," said I.

The next we were swallowed up from each other by the mist. It was our final passing. But here's to you, Mr. Swede, wherever you are. I hope you got that job.

I returned from the City about three o'clock on that May afternoon pretty well disgusted with life. I had been three months in the Old Country, and was fed up with it. If anyone had told me a year ago that I would have been feeling like that I should have laughed at him; but there was the fact. The weather made me liverish, the talk of the ordinary Englishman made me sick. I couldn't get enough exercise, and the amusements of London seemed as flat as soda-water that has been standing in the sun. 'Richard Hannay,' I kept telling myself, 'you have got into the wrong ditch, my friend, and you had better climb out.'

It made me bite my lips to think of the plans I had been building up those last years in Bulawayo. I had got my pile—not one of the big ones, but good enough for me; and I had figured out all kinds of ways of enjoying myself. My father had brought me out from Scotland at the age of six, and I had never been home since; so England was a sort of Arabian Nights to me, and I counted on stopping there for the rest of my days.

But from the first I was disappointed with it. In about a week I was tired of seeing sights, and in less than a month I had had enough of restaurants and theatres and race-meetings. I had no real pal to go about with, which probably explains things. Plenty of people invited me to their houses, but they didn't seem much interested in me. They would fling me a question or two about South Africa, and then get on their own affairs. A lot of Imperialist ladies asked me to tea to meet school-masters from New Zealand and editors from Vancouver, and that was the dismalest business of all. Here was I, thirty-seven years old, sound in wind and limb, with enough money to have a good time, yawning my head off all day. I had just about settled to clear out and get back to the veld, for I was the best bored man in the United Kingdom.

That afternoon I had been worrying my brokers about investments to give my mind something to work on, and on my way home I turned into my club—rather a pot-house, which took in Colonial members. I had a long drink, and read the evening papers. They were full of the row in the Near East, and there was an article about Karolides, the Greek Premier. I rather fancied the chap. From all accounts he seemed the one big man in the show; and he played a straight game too, which was more than could be said for most of them. I gathered that they hated him pretty blackly in Berlin and Vienna, but that we were going to stick by him, and one paper said that he was the only barrier between Europe and Armageddon. I remember wondering if I could get a job in those parts. It struck me that Albania was the sort of place that might keep a man from yawning.

About six o'clock I went home, dressed, dined at the Cafe Royal, and turned into a music-hall. It was a silly show, all capering women and monkey-faced men, and I did not stay long. The night was fine and clear as I walked back to the flat I had hired near Portland Place. The crowd surged past me on the pavements, busy and chattering, and I envied the people for having something to do. These shop-girls and clerks and dandies and policemen had some interest in life that kept them going. I gave half-a-crown to a beggar because I saw him yawn; he was a fellow-sufferer. At Oxford Circus I looked up into the spring sky and I made a vow. I would give the Old Country another day to fit me into something; if nothing happened, I would take the next boat for the Cape.

My flat was the first floor in a new block behind Langham Place. There was a common staircase, with a porter and a liftman at the entrance, but there was no restaurant or anything of that sort, and each flat was quite shut off from the others. I hate servants on the premises, so I had a fellow to look after me who came in by the day. He arrived before eight o'clock every morning and used to depart at seven, for I never dined at home.

I was just fitting my key into the door when I noticed a man at my elbow. I had not seen him approach, and the sudden appearance made me start. He was a slim man, with a short brown beard and small, gimlety blue eyes. I recognized him as the occupant of a flat on the top floor, with whom I had passed the time of day on the stairs.

'Can I speak to you?' he said. 'May I come in for a minute?' He was steadying his voice with an effort, and his hand was pawing my arm.

I got my door open and motioned him in. No sooner was he over the threshold than he made a dash for my back room, where I used to smoke and write my letters. Then he bolted back.

'Is the door locked?' he asked feverishly, and he fastened the chain with his own hand.

'I'm very sorry,' he said humbly. 'It's a mighty liberty, but you looked the kind of man who would understand. I've had you in my mind all this week when things got troublesome. Say, will you do me a good turn?'

'I'll listen to you,' I said. 'That's all I'll promise.' I was getting worried by the antics of this nervous little chap.

There was a tray of drinks on a table beside him, from which he filled himself a stiff whisky-and-soda. He drank it off in three gulps, and cracked the glass as he set it down.

'Pardon,' he said, 'I'm a bit rattled tonight. You see, I happen at this moment to be dead.'

I sat down in an armchair and lit my pipe.

'What does it feel like?' I asked. I was pretty certain that I had to deal with a madman.

A smile flickered over his drawn face. 'I'm not mad—yet. Say, Sir, I've been watching you, and I reckon you're a cool customer. I reckon, too, you're an honest man, and not afraid of playing a bold hand. I'm going to confide in you. I need help l dying, and he had only gone on a stage ahead.

There was no morning strafe, such as had been our usual fortune in the past week. I went out-of-doors and found a noiseless world under the lowering sky. The rain had stopped falling, the wind of dawn had lessened, and I feared that the storm would be delayed. I wanted it at once to help us through the next hours of tension. Was it in six hours that the French were coming? No, it must be four. It couldn't be more than four, unless somebody had made an infernal muddle. I wondered why everything was so quiet. It would be breakfast time on both sides, but there seemed no stir of man's presence in that ugly strip half a mile off. Only far back in the German hinterland I seemed to hear the rumour of traffic.

An unslept and unshaven figure stood beside me which revealed itself as Archie Roylance.

'Been up all night,' he said cheerfully, lighting a cigarette. 'No, I haven't had breakfast. The skipper thought we'd better get another anti-aircraft battery up this way, and I was superintendin' the job. He's afraid of the Hun gettin' over your lines and spying out the nakedness of the land. For, you know, we're uncommon naked, sir. Also,' and Archie's face became grave, 'the Hun's pourin' divisions down on this sector. As I judge, he's blowin' up for a thunderin' big drive on both sides of the river. Our lads yesterday said all the country back of Peronne was lousy with new troops. And he's gettin' his big guns forward, too. You haven't been troubled with them yet, but he has got the roads mended and the devil of a lot of new light railways, and any moment we'll have the five-point-nines sayin' Good-mornin' ... Pray Heaven you get relieved in time, sir. I take it there's not much risk of another push this mornin'?'

Made in the USA
Middletown, DE
06 November 2018